By Robert V. S. Redick

THE CHATHRAND VOYAGE
The Red Wolf Conspiracy
The Ruling Sea

Praise for
THE RED WOLF CONSPIRACY
by Robert V. S. Redick

"There is never a moment when Redick's masterful story-telling wobbles; even his throwaway lines deepen and open out the world he has created, moving the ever-more involving story onward. . . . The reader is dared to keep up with the never-ending stream of action and it is both a delight and a challenge that does not end until the final page."
—GAVIN J. GRANT, *Los Angeles Times*

"Vibrant, fresh and exciting . . . A living tapestry, always in danger of being rent by the conspiracy at the novel's heart. And what a conspiracy it is, portrayed by Redick with a delirious love of the genre that is nothing less than infectious."
—JEDEDIAH BERRY, *BookPage*

"What can I say about a book as exciting and fresh as *The Red Wolf Conspiracy*? I can't remember when I've been so enthralled. Maybe when I first read Philip Pullman. Wow! This was one terrific read."
—TERRY BROOKS, *New York Times* bestselling author

"Redick's debut presents a unique setting for an epic fantasy and includes memorable characters. With comparisons to George R. R. Martin and Philip Pullman, this is highly recommended for all fantasy collections."
—*Library Journal* (starred review)

"An engaging maritime fantasy adventure, set in a fully realized world . . . Will keep readers avidly turning pages—and looking forward to the next installment. A quality debut."
—*Kirkus Reviews* (starred review)

"Wonderfully inventive—Robert Redick is an extraordinary talent."
—KAREN MILLER, bestselling author of *The Innocent Mage*

"Easily the best first fantasy novel of the year."
—DON D'AMMASSA,
author of *Encyclopedia of Science Fiction*

"It's been years since I've enjoyed a fantasy novel as much as *The Red Wolf Conspiracy*. The book is wonderful in all sorts of ways: the power of the visual imagining, the intricacy of the plot, the clarity of the characterization, the sheer un-put-downableness."

—PAUL PARK, critically acclaimed author of
A Princess of Roumania

"[An] outstanding debut . . . With its colourful cast of inhabitants, which include a band of tiny, Lilliputian-style warriors, sentient rats and archetypal ancient evil the Shaggat Ness, the *Chathrand* brings to mind *The Scar*'s fantastical floating city."

—*SFX* magazine

"A strong debut . . . Redick joins the ranks of writers challenging the fantasy genre and making it exciting again."
—*The New York Review of Science Fiction*

"Firmly set in the contemporary fantasy heartland it neatly dissects Lynch and Abercrombie's work by combining both a strong protagonist narrative within the rich framework powered by the geopolitical intrigue of two warring empires—tremendously action packed. The fantasy revival continues."
—*EDGE*

"Engaging . . . This is a top-notch debut."
—Good Reading Magazine

"Insane god-kings, miniature warriors and sentient animals fight over a powerful ancient artifact in Redick's dramatic, complex debut. . . . Both adult and young adult readers will find much to enjoy in this tale of sea-faring and bloody diplomacy."

—*Publishers Weekly*

"[A] remarkable debut . . . It's a highly impressive epic fantasy replete with magic, political intrigue and breathtaking worldbuilding."
—*Romantic Times Bookreviews*

"An irresistible read."
—*Locus*

The
RED WOLF
CONSPIRACY

ROBERT V. S. REDICK

BALLANTINE BOOKS • NEW YORK

The Red Wolf Conspiracy is a work of fiction. Names, characters, places, and
incidents are the products of the author's imagination or are used fictitiously.
Any resemblance to actual events, locales, or persons, living or dead, is entirely
coincidental.

2010 Del Rey Mass Market Edition

Copyright © 2008 by Robert V. S. Redick
Excerpt from *The Ruling Sea* by Robert V. S. Redick copyright © 2010 by
Robert V. S. Redick

All rights reserved.

Published in the United States by Del Rey, an imprint of The Random House
Publishing Group, a division of Random House, Inc., New York.

DEL REY is a registered trademark and the Del Rey colophon is a trademark of
Random House, Inc.

Originally published in hardcover and trade paperback in the United Kingdom
by Gollancz, an imprint of the Orion Publishing Group Ltd., in 2008. Subse-
quently published in hardcover in the United States by Del Rey, an imprint of
The Random House Publishing Group, a division of Random House, Inc., in
2009.

This book contains an excerpt from the forthcoming book *The Ruling Sea* by
Robert V. S. Redick. This excerpt has been set for this edition only and may not
reflect the final content of the forthcoming edition.

ISBN 978-0-345-50884-3

Printed in the United States of America

www.delreybooks.com

9 8 7 6 5 4 3

For my parents

And in memory of theirs,
and Lilyan Hartley, 1915–1995

Kill one man and you are a murderer.
Kill millions and you are a conqueror.
Kill everyone and you are a god.

       —JEAN ROSTAND

Be silent, and sit down, for you are
drunk, and this is the edge of the roof.

        —RUMI

THE
MZITHRIN

Firasan
The
Jomm
Saagmundi's
(Guardian Reef)
• Surakh
BABQRI
R. Bhostal
Tsöl
Tholjassa

N. Urlanx
Ursyl
GULF
of
THOL

S. Urlanx
The
Haunted Coast
Crablands
Che

Gurishal
NELU GILA
(The Green Sea)
Mang-Mzn
Cape Cristel
Simjalla
Orme
Talt

Jitril
Simja
ISLANDS
Locostri
N

Urnsfich
CROWNLESS LANDS
Fulne
Rukn

NORTHWEST ALIFROS
941 Western Solar Year
NELU

Nurth

Serpent's
Head
Baerrids
Ullupridi Isles

Scale 700 miles
NELLURO

The Etherhorde Mariner

6th Umbrin 941

Special Notice

IMS *CHATHRAND* VANISHES AT SEA

Many fear a Tragic End for the Great Ship and her 800 souls

THE IMPERIAL MERCHANT SHIP *Chathrand* {aka "The Great Ship," "Wind-Palace," "His Supremacy's First Fancy," etc.} has disappeared on the high seas and is feared lost with all hands. HIS SUPREMACY THE EMPEROR wept at the news, calling the ship an irreplaceable TREASURE. Her owner, the Lady Lapadolma Yelig, spoke of NIGHTFALL ON TWENTY CENTURIES OF SHIPBUILDING ART.

Months of hope are drawing to a close as shore fishermen on Talturi report the discovery of the wreck of the *Chathrand*'s longboat and numerous BODIES drowned in the SURF. Of Captain NILUS ROSE, her peculiar but long-standing commander, there is no word. Rescue efforts yielded no more than spars, rigging and other floating debris.

Last harbored in Simja, *Chathrand* set sail twelve weeks ago in the mildest of summer squalls, bound for her home port of Etherhorde with a company of 600 sailors, 100 Imperial marines, 60 tarboys and sundry passengers from the lowborn to the exalted. Letters deposited at Simja describe a CALM SHIP and a VOYAGE OF SURPASSING EASE.

Yet CONFUSION PERSISTS as NO ACTUAL WRECK HAS BEEN DISCOVERED. Nor can abundant rumors quell the public clamor to know.

What Doomed This Ship of Ships?

Six centuries of war and piracy could not sink her! Six centuries of typhoonery never flooded her hold! Are we then to believe that a most survivable squall overpowered *Chathrand* and her legendary Captain? The Lord Admiral does not believe it. No more do the sailing men of Arqual, and SPECULATION OF FOUL PLAY is to be heard in every tavern of the capital.

Some few already look West for the culprit, and not infrequently pronounce a word politely shunned since the last war: REVENGE. It is beneath the *Mariner*'s dignity to fuel this fire by propagating (as other circulars do not hesitate to do) such hearsay as the presence of unusual RICHES aboard *Chathrand*, marks of VIOLENCE on the recovered BODIES, great musterings of our enemies' FLEETS, etc., but we must—in all fairness—note the lack of a competing theory . . .

-1-

Tarboy

**1 Vaqrin (first day of summer) 941
Midnight**

It began, as every disaster in his life began, with a calm. The harbor and the village slept. The wind that had roared all night lay quelled by the headland; the bosun grew too sleepy to shout. But forty feet up the ratlines, Pazel Pathkendle had never been more awake.

He was freezing, to start with—a rogue wave had struck the bow at dusk, soaking eight boys and washing the ship's dog into the hold, where it still yipped for rescue—but it wasn't the cold that worried him. It was the storm cloud. It had leaped the coastal ridge in one bound, on high winds he couldn't feel. The ship had no reason to fear it, but Pazel did. People were trying to kill him, and the only thing stopping them was the moon, that blessed bonfire moon, etching his shadow like a coal drawing on the deck of the *Eniel*.

One more mile, he thought. *Then it can pour for all I care.*

While the calm held, the *Eniel* ran quiet as a dream: her captain hated needless bellowing, calling it the poor pilot's surrogate for leadership, and merely gestured to the afterguard when the time came to tack for shore. Glancing up at the mainsails, his eyes fell on Pazel, and for a moment they regarded each other in silence: an old man stiff and wrinkled as a cypress; a boy in tattered shirt and breeches, nut-brown hair in his eyes, clinging barefoot to the tarred and salt-stiffened ropes. A boy suddenly aware that he had no permission to climb aloft.

Pazel made a show of checking the yardarm bolts, and the knots on the closest stays. The captain watched his antics, unmoved. Then, almost invisibly, he shook his head.

Pazel slid to the deck in an instant, furious with himself. *You clod, Pathkendle! Lose Nestef's love and there's no hope for you!*

Captain Nestef was the kindest of the five mariners he had served: the only one who never beat or starved him, or forced him, a boy of fifteen, to drink the black nightmare liquor *grebel* for the amusement of the crew. If Nestef had ordered him to dive into the sea, Pazel would have obeyed at once. He was a bonded servant and could be traded like a slave.

On the deck, the other servant boys—*tarboys,* they were called, for the pitch that stained their hands and feet—turned him looks of contempt. They were older and larger, with noses proudly disfigured from brawls of honor in distant ports. The eldest, Jervik, sported a hole in his right ear large enough to pass a finger through. Rumor held that a violent captain had caught him stealing a pudding, and had pinched the ear with tongs heated cherry-red in the galley stove.

The other rumor attached to Jervik was that he had stabbed a boy in the neck after losing at darts. Pazel didn't know if he believed the tale. But he knew that a gleam came to Jervik's eyes at the first sign of another's weakness, and he knew the boy carried a knife.

One of Jervik's hangers-on gestured at Pazel with his chin. "Thinks his place is on the maintop, this one," he said, grinning. "Bet you can tell him diff'rint, eh, Jervik?"

"Shut up, Nat, you ain't clever," said Jervik, his eyes locked on Pazel.

"What ho, Pazel Pathkendle, he's defendin' you," laughed another. "Ain't you goin' to thank him? You better thank him!"

Jervik turned the speaker a cold look. The laughter ceased. "I han't defended no one," said the larger boy.

" 'Course you didn't, Jervik, I just—"

"Somebody worries my mates, I defend them. Defend my good name, too. But there's no defense for a wee squealin' Ormali."

The laughter was general, now: Jervik had given permission.

Then Pazel said, "Your mates and your good name. How about your honor, Jervik, and your word?"

"Them too," snapped Jervik.

"And wet fire?"

"Eh?"

"Diving roosters? Four-legged ducks?"

Jervik stared at Pazel for a moment. Then he glided over and hit him squarely on the cheek.

"Brilliant reply, Jervik," said Pazel, standing his ground despite the fire along one side of his face.

Jervik raised a corner of his shirt. Tucked into his breeches was a skipper's knife with a fine, well-worn leather grip.

"Want another sort of reply, do you?"

His face was inches from Pazel's own. His lips were stained red by low-grade sapwort; his eyes had a yellow tinge.

"I want my knife back," said Pazel.

"Liar!" spat Jervik. "The knife's mine!"

"That knife was my father's. You're a thief, and you don't dare use it."

Jervik hit him again, harder. "Put up your fists, *Muketch*," he said.

Pazel did not raise his fists. Snickering, Jervik and the others went about their duties, leaving Pazel blinking with pain and rage.

By the Sailing Code that governed all ships, Captain Nestef would have no choice but to dismiss a tarboy caught fighting. Jervik could risk it: he was a citizen of Arqual, this great empire sprawling over a third of the known world, and could always sign with another ship. More to the point, he wore a brass ring engraved with his Citizenship Number as recorded in the Imperial Boys' Registry. Such rings cost a month's wages, but they were worth it. Without the ring, any boy caught wandering in a sea-side town could be taken for a bond-breaker or a foreigner. Few tarboys could afford the brass ring; most carried paper certifi-cates, and these were easily lost or stolen.

Pazel, however, was a bonded servant *and* a foreigner—even worse, a member of a conquered race. If his papers read *Dis-missed for Fighting,* no other ship would have him. He would be cut adrift, waiting to be snatched up like a coin from the street, claimed as the finder's property for the rest of his days.

Jervik knew this well, and seemed determined to goad Pazel into a fight. He called the younger boy *Muketch* after the mud crabs of Ormael, the home Pazel had not seen in five years. Ormael was once a great fortress-city, built on high cliffs over a blue and perfect harbor. A place of music and balconies and the smell of ripened plums, whose name meant "Womb of Morning"—but that city no longer existed. And it seemed to Pazel that nearly everyone would have preferred him to vanish along with it. His very presence on an Arquali ship was a slight disgrace, like a soup stain on the captain's dress coat. After Jervik's burst of inspiration, the other boys and even some of the sailors called him *Muketch.* But the word also conveyed a sort of wary respect: sailors thought a charm lay on those green crabs that swarmed in the Ormael marshes, and took pains not to step on them lest bad luck follow.

Superstition had not stopped Jervik and his gang from strik-ing or tripping Pazel behind the captain's back, however. And in the last week it had grown worse: they came at him in twos and threes, in lightless corners belowdecks, and with a viciousness he had never faced before. *They may really kill me* (how could you think that and keep working, eating, breathing?). *They may try tonight. Jervik may drive them to it.*

Pazel had won the last round: Jervik was indeed afraid to stab him in front of witnesses. But in the dark it was another matter: in the dark things were done in a frenzy, and later explained away.

Fortunately, Jervik was a fool. He had a nasty sort of cunning, but his delight in abusing others made him careless. It was surely just a matter of time before Nestef dismissed him. Until then the trick was to avoid getting cornered. That was one reason Pazel had risked climbing aloft. The other was to see the *Chathrand.*

For tonight he would finally see her—the *Chathrand,* mightiest ship in all the world, with a mainmast so huge that three sailors could scarce link arms around it, and stern lamps tall as men, and square sails larger than the Queen's Park in Etherhorde. She was being made ready for the open sea, some great trading voyage beyond the reach of Empire. Perhaps she would sail to Noonfirth, where men were black; or the Outer Isles that faced the Ruling Sea, or the Crownless Lands, wounded by war. Strangely, no one could tell him. But she was almost ready.

Pazel knew, for he had helped in his small way to ready her. Twice in as many nights they had sailed up to *Chathrand's* flank, here in the dark bay of Sorrophran. Both had been cloudy, moonless nights, and Pazel in any case had been kept busy in the hold until the moment of arrival. Emerging at last, he had seen only a black, bowed wall, furred with algae and snails and clams like snapped blades, and smelling of pitch and heartwood and the deep sea. Men's voices floated down from above, and following them, a great boom lowered a platform to the *Eniel's* deck. Onto this lift went sacks of rice and barley and hard winter wheat. Then boards, followed by crates of mandarins, barberries, figs, salt cod, salt venison, cokewood, coal; and finally bundled cabbages, potatoes, yams, coils of garlic, wheels of rock-hard cheese. Food in breathtaking quantities: food for six months without landfall. Wherever the Great Ship was bound, she clearly had no wish to depend on local hospitality.

When nothing more could be stacked, the lift would rise as if by magic. Some of the older boys grabbed at the ropes, laughing as they were whisked straight up, fifty feet, sixty, and swung over the distant rail. Returning on the emptied lift, they held bright pennies and sweetmeats, gifts from the unseen crew. Pazel cared nothing for these, but he was mad to see the deck of the *Chathrand.*

His life was ships, now: in the five years since Arqual swallowed his country, Pazel had spent less than two weeks ashore. The previous night, when the lift rose for the last time, caution had deserted him: he had seized a corner rope. Jervik had pried his fingers loose, sending him crashing back to the deck of the *Eniel*.

But tonight the little ship bore no cargo, just passengers: three quiet figures in seafarers' cloaks, on this passage of a single night from Besq to Sorrophran. They kept apart from the crew, and even one another. Now, as the blue gaslights of the Sorrophran Shipworks came into view, these three pressed forward, seemingly as eager as Pazel himself for a glimpse of the legendary ship.

One of the three, to Pazel's great excitement, was Dr. Ignus Chadfallow. He was a slender man with worried eyes and large, educated hands. An Imperial surgeon and scholar of note, Chadfallow had once saved the Emperor and his Horse Guard from the deadly talking fever by placing men and horses alike on a six-week diet of millet and prunes. He had also, single-handedly, saved Pazel from slavery.

The three passengers had boarded at sunset. Pazel and the other tarboys had shoved and shouldered one another at the rail, competing for the chance to lug footlockers aboard for a penny or two. Spotting Chadfallow, Pazel had leaped, waving, and nearly shouted *Ignus!* But Chadfallow shot him a dark look, and the greeting died in his throat.

As Nestef welcomed his passengers, Pazel tried in vain to catch the doctor's eye. When the cook shouted, *"Tarry!"* he sprang down the ladderway ahead of the other boys, for it was Nestef's habit to greet new passengers with a mug of blistering spiced tea. But tonight there was more to the offerings: the cook loaded the tea-tray with muskberry biscuits, red ginger candies and lukka seeds to be chewed for warmth. Balancing these delicacies with great care, Pazel returned to the topdeck and walked straight to Chadfallow, his heart thumping in his chest.

"If you please, sir," he said.

Chadfallow, his eyes on the moonwashed rocks and islets, seemed not to hear. Pazel spoke again, louder, and this time the doctor turned with a start. Pazel smiled uncertainly at his old benefactor. But Chadfallow's voice was sharp.

"Where's your breeding? You'll serve the duchess first. Go on!"

Cheeks burning, Pazel turned away. The doctor's coldness hurt him more than any blow from Jervik could. Not that it was altogether a surprise: Chadfallow often appeared frightened of being seen with Pazel, and never spoke to him at length. But he was the closest thing to family Pazel had left in the world, and he had not laid eyes on him for two years.

Two years! His hands, blast them, were trembling. He had to swallow hard before he spoke to the duchess. At least, he hoped she was the duchess, a bent and ancient woman three inches shorter than Pazel himself, who stood by the foremast mumbling and worrying the gold rings on her fingers. When Pazel spoke she raised her head and fixed him with her gaze. Her eyes were large and milky blue, and as she stared at him, her dry lips twisted into a smile.

"Ehiji!"

Her crooked hand shot out; a nail scraped his cheek. He had shed tears. The crone put her moistened finger to her lips and grinned all the wider. Then she fell upon the tea service. First she popped the three largest ginger candies into her mouth, and slid a fourth into her pocket. Next she produced an old, scorched pipe from the folds of her cloak. As Pazel watched, aghast, she tapped the half-burned plug of tobacco into the bowl of lukka seeds, stirred with a thumb and then crushed the whole mixture back into her pipe, whispering and squeaking to herself all the while. Her eyes found Pazel's again.

"Got a flint?"

"No, ma'am," said Pazel.

"That's Lady Oggosk to you! Fetch a lamp, then."

It was difficult to fetch anything while holding the tea-tray. Pazel thought his arms would break, hoisting a brass deck lamp heavy with walrus oil as Lady Oggosk struggled with her pipe.

Wafts of burning walrus, tobacco and lukka seeds flooded his nostrils, and the Lady's breath as she puffed and hiccuped was like a draft from a ginger-scented tomb. At last the pipe lit, and she cackled.

"Don't cry, my little monkey. He hasn't forgotten you—oh, not for an instant, no!"

Pazel gaped at her. She could only mean Chadfallow, but what did she know of their connection? Before he could find a way to ask, she turned from him, still chuckling to herself.

The third passenger was a merchant, well groomed and well fed. At first glance, Pazel thought him ill: he had a white scarf wrapped tight about his neck, and one hand rested there as if nursing a sore spot. He cleared his throat with a painful noise— *CHHRCK!*—nearly making Pazel spill the tea. The man had an appetite, too: four biscuits vanished into his mouth, followed by the next largest ginger candy.

"You're not very clean," he said suddenly, looking Pazel up and down. "Whose soap do you use?"

"Whose soap, sir?"

"Is that a difficult question? Who makes the soap you scrub your face with?"

"We're given potash, sir."

"You're a servant."

"Not for much longer, sir," said Pazel. "Captain Nestef has extended me his hand of friendship, for which I bless him thrice over. He says I have genuine prospects, with my flair for languages, and—"

"My own prospects are excellent, of course," the man informed him. "My name is Ket—a name worth remembering, worth jotting down. I am about to make transactions valued at sixty thousand gold cockles. And that is just one trading voyage."

"How grand for you, sir. I say, sir! Would you be sailing on the *Chathrand*?"

"You will not see sixty thousand in your lifetime—nor even six. Go now."

He placed something on the tea-tray and waved Pazel off. Pazel bowed and withdrew, then looked at the object. It was a pale green disc, stamped with the words KET SOAP.

One of those sixty thousand coins would have suited him better, but he hid the soap in his pocket nonetheless. Then he looked at the tray and his heart sank. He had nothing left for Chadfallow but a small rind of ginger and a broken biscuit.

The doctor ignored these, but pointed at the tea flask. Carefully, Pazel filled a mug. The doctor wrapped his long fingers around it, raised it to his lips and inhaled the steam, as he had told Pazel one should in cold weather, to "vivify the nostrils." He did not look at the boy, and Pazel did not know whether to stay or leave. At last, very softly, the doctor spoke.

"You're not ill?"

"No," said Pazel.

"Your mind-fits?"

"They're cured," said Pazel quickly, very glad they were alone. No one on the *Eniel* knew about his mind-fits.

"Cured?" said the doctor. "How did you manage that?"

Pazel shrugged. "I bought some medicine in Sorhn. Everyone goes to Sorhn for that kind of thing."

"*Everyone* does not live under the influence of magic spells," said Chadfallow. "And how much did they charge you for this . . . medicine?"

"They took . . . what I had," admitted Pazel, frowning. "But it was worth every penny. I'd do it again tomorrow."

Chadfallow sighed. "I dare say you would. Now what about your teeth?"

Pazel looked up, startled by the quick change of focus: his mind-fits were the doctor's favorite subject. "My teeth are just fine," he said carefully.

"That's good. But this tea is not. Taste it."

Chadfallow passed him the cup, and watched as he drank.

Pazel grimaced. "It's bitter," he said.

"More bitter for you than me. Or so you may well imagine."

"What do you mean by that?" Pazel's voice rose in confusion. "Why are you all so *odd*?"

But like the duchess and the soap man, Chadfallow merely turned to face the sea. And all through that night's crossing he showed no more interest in Pazel than in the common sailors who bustled around him.

Now, at midnight, battered and soaking and chilled to the bone, Pazel watched the Shipworks loom nearer. They were minutes from port, and still the moonlight held.

Pazel knew he'd been a fool to hope for better treatment from Chadfallow. The doctor was a changed man since the invasion of Ormael, which as the Emperor's Special Envoy he had witnessed firsthand. The violence had left him morose, and whatever spring of warmth he used to draw upon seemed to have dried up. At their last meeting, two years ago, he had pretended not to know Pazel at all.

But why was he here, on the eve of the *Chathrand*'s launch? For the doctor never appeared but when some great change was about to explode into Pazel's life. Tonight would be no different, he thought, and so he lingered by the foremast to see what Chadfallow would do.

A voice ashore hailed them: *"Bring to,* Eniel*! Bring to, there! Crowded port!"*

Captain Nestef bellowed, *"Aye, Sorrophran!"* and tugged hard at the wheel. The bosun shouted, men leaped for ropes, the white sails of the *Eniel* furled. Coasting, she passed the Sorrophran dry docks, the long files of warships with their armored bows and gunwales bristling with spikes, the shrimping fleet, the porcelain-domed Nunekkam houseboats. Then a sigh of wonder passed over the deck, breathed by officer and sailor and tarboy alike. The *Chathrand* had swung into view.

No wonder the port was full! *Chathrand* alone nearly filled it. Now that Pazel saw her plainly by moonlight, the ship seemed a thing not of men but of giants. The tip of the *Eniel*'s mainmast scarcely reached her quarterdeck, and a sailor high in her crosstrees looked no bigger than a gull. Her own masts made Pazel think of the towers of the Noonfirth Kings, soaring over the black cliffs at Pól. Beside her even the Emperor's warships seemed like toys.

"She is the last of her kind," said a voice behind him. "Do not turn around, Pazel."

Pazel froze, one hand on the mast. The voice was Chadfallow's.

"A living relic," the doctor continued. "A five-masted Segral Wind-Palace, the largest ship ever built since the days of the Amber Kings before the Worldstorm. Even the trees of which she is made are passed into legend: m'xingu for keel, tritne pine for mast and yard, rock maple for deck and wales. Mages as well as shipwrights played their part in her creation, or so the old tales claim. Such arts are lost to us now—along with so much else."

"Is it true, she crossed the Ruling Sea?"

"The Segrals braved those waters, yes: that is why they were built, in fact. But *Chathrand* is six hundred years old, boy. Her youth is a mystery. Only the elders of her Trading Family have seen the logs of her earliest journeys."

"Captain Nestef says it makes no sense to outfit *Chathrand* here, when Etherhorde is just six days away," said Pazel. "He says there are shipwrights in Etherhorde who train for years just to work on her."

"They have been brought here from the capital."

"But why? Captain Nestef says Etherhorde will be her first stop *anyway*."

"Your curiosity is in perfect health," said Chadfallow dryly.

"Thank you!" said Pazel. "And after Etherhorde? Where will they send her next?"

The doctor hesitated. "Pazel," he said at last, "how much do you remember of our lessons, back in Ormael?"

"Everything. I can name all the bones in the body, and the six kinds of bile, and the eleven organs, and the tubes in your gut—"

"Not anatomy," said Chadfallow. "Think back to what I told you of politics. You know about the Mzithrin, our great enemies in the west."

"*Your* enemies," Pazel couldn't resist saying.

The doctor's voice grew stern. "You may not be a citizen of Arqual yet, but your fortune rests in our hands. And Mzithrini tribes raided Ormael for centuries before we arrived."

"Right," said Pazel. "They tried to kill us for hundreds of years, and couldn't. You managed it in two days."

"Don't speak in ignorance, boy! If the Mzithrin had wanted to take your little country, they could have done so faster than we did. Instead they chose to bleed her quietly and deny it to the world. Now prove that you paid attention to my teaching. What *is* the Mzithrin?"

"An empire of madmen," said Pazel. "Honestly, that's how you made them sound. Crazy about sorcery and devils and ancient rites, and worshipping the pieces of a Black Casket. Dangerous, too, with their singing arrows, and dragon's-egg shot, and that guild of holy pirates, what's the word?"

"*Sfvantskor,*" said Chadfallow. "But that is not the point. The Mzithrin is a pentarchy: a land ruled by five kings. During the last war, four of those kings condemned Arqual as evil, the abode of heretics, servants of the Pits. But the fifth said no such thing. And he drowned at sea."

A horn rang out across the bay. "We're nearly there," said Pazel.

"Are you listening?" said Chadfallow. "The fifth king drowned because Arquali guns sank his ship. He never condemned us—yet him alone we killed. Doesn't that strike you as odd?"

"No," said Pazel. "You kill who you like."

"And you insist on obstinate stupidity, when in fact you are moderately wise."

Pazel shot an angry glance over his shoulder. He could tolerate most any insult except to his intelligence: sometimes it felt like the one thing he had left to be proud of.

"I ask where the *Chathrand* is going," he said, "and you talk about the Mzithrin. Were you listening to *me*?" He was getting sarcastic, but he didn't care. "Or maybe that's your answer. The ship's paying a visit to your 'great enemies,' the Mzithrin Kings."

"Why not?" said Chadfallow.

"Because that's impossible," Pazel declared.

"Is it?"

The doctor had to be teasing him. Arqual and the Mzithrin had battled for centuries, and the last war had been the bloodiest of all. It had ended forty years ago, but Arqualis still loathed and feared Mzithrinis. Some ended their morning prayers by turning west to spit.

"Impossible," mused Chadfallow, shaking his head. "There's a word we must try to forget."

At that moment the bosun's voice rang out: *"Port stations!"*

Chatter ceased; men and boys scrambled to their tasks. Pazel made to go as well—orders were orders—but Chadfallow caught him tightly by the arm.

"Your sister lives," he said.

"My sister!" cried Pazel. "You've seen Neda? Where is she? Is she safe?"

"Quietly! No, I have not seen her, but I plan to. And Suthinia as well."

It was all Pazel could do not to shout again. Suthinia was his mother. He had feared both were dead in the invasion of Ormael.

"How long have you known they were alive?"

"You must ask no more questions. For the moment they are safe—if anyone is, and that is no certainty. If you would help them, listen well. Do not go to your station. Do not, under any circumstances, go belowdecks on the *Eniel* tonight."

"But I'm to work the pumps!"

"You will not."

"But, Ignus—ah!"

Chadfallow's hand had tightened convulsively on Pazel's arm.

"*Never* use my name, tarboy!" he hissed, still not looking at Pazel but unmistakably furious. "Have I been a fool, then? For half a decade, a fool? Don't answer that! Just tell me: have you been ashore in Sorrophran?"

"Y-yes."

"Then you know that if you set foot outside the port district you're fair game for the Flikkermen, who get three gold for every boy or girl they send to the Forgotten Colonies, twenty days' march across the Slevran Steppe?"

"I know about the Flikkers, and that terrible place! But it's nothing to do with me! They're keeping me aboard tonight, and we sail at sunrise!"

Chadfallow shook his head. "Just remember, the Flikkers cannot touch you in the port. Keep away from me now, Pazel Pathkendle, and *above all stay on deck*! We will not speak again."

The doctor wrapped himself in his sea-cloak and headed aft. Pazel could sense his doom already. The first rule of survival as a tarboy is *Be quick!*—and Chadfallow was forcing him to break it. Captain Nestef hadn't noticed yet, but the common sailors, rushing about on tasks of their own, stared at him as if he were mad. What was the boy thinking? He didn't look sick, he hadn't fallen from the yardarms, he was just *standing* there.

Pazel knew what would happen next, and it did. The first mate, inspecting his topdeck men, reached Pazel and fixed him with a scandalized look.

"*Muketch!*" he bellowed. "Are ye afflicted? Get below or I'll skin yer Ormali hide!"

"Oppo, sir!"

Pazel sprinted for the main hatch, but at the top of the ladder, he stopped. He had never disobeyed Chadfallow. He looked around for another tarboy—perhaps he could trade tasks?—but they were all belowdecks, where he ought to be. Soon they would miss him, send someone looking, and he would be severely punished for breaking orders. How could he explain? He didn't understand himself.

Desperate for cover, Pazel spotted a neatly coiled hawser by the portside rail. Furtively he pushed the thick rope over, then began meticulously winding it anew. Now he would *look* busy at least. His mind reeled with Chadfallow's news. His mother and sister, alive! But where could they be? Hiding in ruined Ormael? Sold as slaves? Or had they made for the Crownless Lands, slipping free of the Empire altogether?

Then, very suddenly, Pazel felt ill. His head spun and his vision blurred. The taste of the bad tea rose in his throat. He stumbled and knocked the hawser over again.

Ignus, what did you do to me?

The next instant the feeling vanished. He was fine—but someone was snickering behind him. Pazel turned to see Jervik pointing at him triumphantly.

"I found him, sir! Skipped his station! And he's knocked over that coil on purpose, to stretch his holiday! Make *him* do it, Mr. Nicklen, sir!"

The bosun, Nicklen, slouched up behind Jervik, scowling. He was a heavy, red-faced man with eyes receded into soft pouches, like fingermarks in dough. Usually he treated Pazel well enough, taking his cue from Nestef—but the rope sprawled in an accusing heap, and when Nicklen asked if Jervik spoke the truth, Pazel clenched his teeth and nodded. Behind the officer, Jervik made a face like a grinning frog.

"Right," said the bosun. "Be off, Jervik. As for you, Mr. Pathkendle, you're in luck. You should be whipped for cutting chores. Instead all you have to do is come with me."

Forty minutes later Pazel did not feel very lucky. The rain had begun, and he stood in a half-flooded Sorrophran street with no hat (it lay in his box on the *Eniel*), listening to dim sounds of fiddle and accordion, and roars of laughter, through the stone wall of the tavern beside him. This was Nicklen's pointless punishment: to stand him here like a disgraced schoolboy while the bosun drank off his wages.

Not for the first time, Pazel cursed Jervik. He was still in the port district, and so safe from marauding Flikkermen. But if Pazel knew the older tarboy, he'd tell the first mate about the scene on deck and Pazel would *still* get a lashing.

Pazel had mentioned this suspicion to Nicklen as they marched through town. The bosun's reply was strange: he told Pazel to forget he'd ever known a fool named Jervik.

"Mr. Nicklen," Pazel had continued (the bosun was tolerating his chatter tonight), "is the *Chathrand* fast?"

"Fast!" he said. "She blary well screams along on high winds! Trouble is finding that much. Small ships can do more with a light breeze, don't ye know? That's why His Supremacy loves his wee gunboats. Loves his big ones too, mind. And middle-sized. As for *Chathrand,* she dreams of a wind that would sink yer average boat. I dare say the Nelu Peren keeps her wings clipped."

The Nelu Peren, or Quiet Sea, was the only ocean Pazel had ever sailed. It was far from quiet at times, but it was much tamer than the Nelu Rekere (or Narrow Sea) that enclosed it. Farthest of all, beyond the archipelagos of the south, lay the Nelluroq, or Ruling Sea. Legends told of great islands, perhaps whole continents, hidden in its vastness, full of strange animals, and people who had once traded and parleyed with the north. But centuries had passed, and the big ships had sunk one by one, leaving only *Chathrand,* and whatever lands there were had likewise drowned in seas of forgetting.

"Anyhow," said Nicklen, "these days she don't need to fly like a murth on the wing. She's no warship anymore."

At the mention of war, Pazel's thoughts had taken another leap.

"Were *you* in the last war, Mr. Nicklen?" he asked. "The big one, I mean."

"The Second Maritime? Aye, but just as a powder-pup. I was younger than you when it ended."

"Did we really kill one of the Mzithrin Kings?"

"Aye! The Shaggat! The Shaggat Ness, and his bastard sons, and his sorcerer, too. A famous night battle, that was. Their ship went down with all hands, not far from Ormael, as you must know. But not a trace of that ship was ever found. *Shaggat,* lad—that means 'God-King' to them mongrels."

"But was he . . . a friend to Arqual?"

At that Nicklen had turned to look at Pazel with amazement. "Is that a funny, Mr. Pathkendle?"

"No, sir!" said Pazel. "I just thought . . . I mean, I was told—"

"The Shaggat Ness was a monster," Nicklen interrupted. "A vicious, kill-crazy fiend. He weren't friend to no man alive in this world."

Pazel had never heard the bosun speak more firmly. The effort seemed to drain him: he smiled awkwardly, patted Pazel's shoulder, and when they reached the bar he bought the tarboy a leek fritter and a mug of pumpkin ale—two Sorrophran delicacies. But he wagged a finger before going in to his revels.

"Skip *this* station and I'll drown you off Hansprit," he said. "Keep your eyes peeled, eh? The captain don't approve of carousing."

Pazel nodded, but he knew the bosun was hiding something. Tarboys rarely tasted pumpkin ale. What was Nicklen up to? Not mutiny, or dealing in deathsmoke: he was too old and slow for such crimes. Nor did the customers, joking about "the little sentry" and tussling his wet hair in an annoying way, seem much like criminals.

An hour later the bosun appeared with a second fritter and an old sheepskin to keep off the rain. He was bleary-eyed and frowning; his very clothes stank of ale. "Still awake!" he said. "You're a good lad, Pathkendle. Who says Ormalis can't be trusted?"

"Not me, sir," mumbled Pazel, hiding the fritter away for breakfast.

"I never did hate 'em," said Nicklen, with a look of distress. "I wouldn't be party to such a thing—hope you know, if it were *my* choice—"

His eyes rolled, and he lurched back into the bar.

Pazel sat down on the steps, bewildered. Nicklen couldn't honestly be worried about the captain. Nestef disliked carousing, true enough. But he had better uses for his time than chasing his old bosun about in the rain.

Hours passed, drunks came and went. Pazel was half dozing under the sheepskin when he felt something warm and velvety touch his bare foot. Instantly awake, he found himself looking into the eyes of the largest cat he had ever seen: a sleek red creature, its yellow eyes gazing directly into his own. One paw lay on Pazel's toe, as if the animal were tapping him to learn if he were alive.

"Hello, sir," said Pazel.

The animal growled.

"Oh, ma'am, is it? Get along with you, whatever you are." He shrugged off the sheepskin—and the cat pounced. Not on him, but on his second fritter. Before Pazel could do more than swear, the animal had it out of his hand and was bounding for the alley. Pazel rose and gave chase (he was hungry again and quite wanted that fritter) but the lamps were dark now, and the cat vanished from sight.

"You fleabit thief!"

Even as he yelled, the sickness came rushing back. It was worse than before: he stumbled against a rubbish bin, which fell with a crash. The bitter flavor again coated his tongue, and when a voice launched insults from a window above him the words seemed pure nonsense. Then, just as suddenly, the sickness vanished and the words rang clear:

". . . out of my trash bin! Blary urchins, always up with the birds."

Fuming, Pazel walked back to the tavern. But there he stopped. It was true: the birds *were* in fact starting to sing. Dawn had arrived.

He pushed open the tavern door. The barman sprawled just beyond the threshold, looking rather drowned.

"Uch! Get on, beggar brat! The party's damn well done."

"I'm not begging," said Pazel. "Mr. Nicklen's here, sir, and I'd better wake him up."

"Are ye deaf? We drank the house dry! Nobody's here."

"Mr. Nicklen is."

"Nicklen? That putty-mug lout from the *Eniel*?"

"Eh . . . right you are, sir, that's him."

"Gone hours ago."

"What?"

"And a good riddance, too. Moaning all night. 'The doctor! The doctor paid me for a wicked deed!' Nobody could make him hush."

"What doctor? Chadfallow? What was he talking about? Where'd he run off to?"

"Softly!" groaned the barman. "How should I know what doctor? But Etherhorde, that's where! Said they were sailin' before dawn. Didn't pay for his last drink, either, the tramp—slipped out the back door. Uch!"

Pazel leaped past him. The place was utterly empty. Fooled, fooled by Nicklen! And what had the man overheard? Sailing *before* dawn?

He rushed back to the street. The rain still pelted Sorrophran, but in the east the black sky was changing to gray. Pazel flew back the way he and Nicklen had come, turned the corner, pounded down a flight of broken steps, passed the red cat devouring his fritter, knocked against more rubbish bins, turned another corner and sprinted for the wharf as if his life depended on it.

The fishermen were back from their night at sea. They whistled and laughed: *"Seen a ghost, tarry?"* He dashed through their barrels and gutting-troughs and heaped-up nets. The great hulk of the *Chathrand* loomed straight ahead, men crawling about her in the grayness like ants upon a log. But in the corner of the wharf beyond her there was no ship named *Eniel* to receive him.

He raced to the end of the fishermen's pier. He spotted her in the harbor, sails filling, picking up speed. He tore off his shirt and waved it and bellowed the captain's name. But the breeze was offshore, and the rain muffled his voice. The *Eniel* did not hear him, or did not care to. Pazel was homeless.

−2−

Clan

Twelve feet below, amidst the slosh of outflowing tide, the wet *blip-plip* of barnacles and the groans of old timbers, a woman's voice hissed in sympathy.

"*Chht,* what a sorrow! The lad's missed his boat. What will happen to him, I wonder?"

"You and your questions," answered a young man's voice. "All I want to know is, what's to happen to us?"

"Perhaps he could tell."

"What sort of nonsense is that, Diadrelu?"

"My own," said the woman. "Give us some bread."

A gull upon the water might have seen them, if it studied the shadows beneath the pier. They sat on cross-boards forming a long X just over the waterline: eight figures in a circle, and a ninth standing watch, each one about the height of a man's open hand. Copper skin, copper eyes, the women's hair short and the men's tightly braided. Within the circle, a feast: black bread, slabs of roasted seaweed, an open mussel shell with the flesh still moist and quivering, a wineskin you or I might fill with two squirts from a dropper. By every knee, a sword, thin and dark and swept back in an eyelash curve. Many also carried bows. And one figure wore a cloak of the tiniest, darkest feathers, taken from a swallow's wings, which gleamed like liquid when she moved.

This was the woman, Diadrelu, whom the others watched half consciously from the corners of their eyes.

She wiped her hands and stood. One of the men offered her wine, but she shook her head and walked out along the board to face the harbor.

"Mind your footing, m'lady," muttered the watchman.

"Oppo, sir," she replied, and her people laughed. But the young man who had spoken first shook his head and frowned.

"Arquali words. I've heard enough of them for a lifetime."

The woman made no answer. She listened to the boy above them shout, *"Captain Nestef! Captain, sir!"* until at last his voice broke into sobs. Homelessness. How could anyone who had known it feel no pity?

Sixty feet away there came a flash of light: the old fisherman was cooking his breakfast of shrimp heads and gruel on the deck of his *lunket,* a kind of patchwork boat made of hides stretched over a wooden frame. *Lunket:* that was Arquali, too. So was her favorite word in any tongue: *idrolos,* the courage to see. Her own language had no such word. And without a word to hook it, how the thought wriggles away! That old man knew *idrolos:* he had dared to see the good in her people, who mended his threadbare sails and fixed leaks in his vessel by night. And that seeing had given him a further courage: to carry them here, four clans across four fishing nights, pretending not to hear them in his hold or to notice them leaping from the stern as they docked in Sorrophran. They had never spoken, for to transport ixchel was a crime punishable by death, and only the fisherman and Diadrelu knew how she had woken him once, standing on his night-table, holding out a blue pearl larger than her own head and worth more than he would make in two years dragging nets along the coast.

"Finish your meal," she told the clan, without turning. "Dawn is come."

Her command silenced them all. They ate. Diadrelu was glad of their appetites: who knew how hungry the months ahead would prove? Good as well to find an order Taliktrum could obey without grumbling. He *was* insolent, her nephew. Already sniffing out the power he assumed would come to him. As it would, no doubt. When her group joined that of her brother Talag, the two of them would share command, and Taliktrum would be his father's first lieutenant.

She remembered the boy's birth in Ixphir Hall, twenty years ago. A hard birth, an agony for her sister-in-law, who had screamed so loudly that the Upper Watch sent a runner to warn that the mastiffs on the old admiral's porch (directly over Ixphir House) were cocking their heads. Then out he came, open-eyed like all ixchel newborns, but also gripping his umbilicus: an omen of great valor, or madness, depending on the legend you preferred. Little Taliktrum—*Triku,* they'd called him, although he soon forbade even his mother to use the nickname. Would he still obey her in his father's presence? *Yes, by Rin, he would.*

She stepped up to the watchboy, held out her hand for his spear.

"The last trawler's coming in now, m'lady," he said. "We've got a path."

She nodded. "Go and eat, Nytikyn."

"There's a crab, m'lady."

Diadrelu nodded, then detained him with a hand on his arm. "Just Dri," she said. Then she turned to face them all.

"You newcomers don't believe me," she said. "And I know that customs differ in East Arqual, where some of you were raised. But I meant what I told you last night. From here forward we are a clan of ixchel—just so. And until our next Fifthmoon Banquet or wedding, my name is Dri—just so. Or if you insist, Diadrelu. Such was always my preference in Etherhorde, in Ixphir House, and I don't mean to change it now. Discipline is one thing, servility another. Turn and look at that monster behind you. Go on."

Unwillingly, they leaned out over the water. It was a sapphire crab, wider than a human's dinner plate, clinging to the moss with its fish-egg eyes trained on them and one huge serrated claw flexed open. Such a claw, they well knew, could cut any of them in two at the midsection.

"Crabs don't say *m'lady*. Nor will that assassin, that Red River cat, if the hag Oggosk brings her aboard. Nor will the necklace-fanciers."

At the word *necklace* they shuddered, then dropped their eyes with shame.

"There will be one or two," she said. "You know this. So tell me: can I hide from *them* behind my rank? Then I won't let you hide from me behind formalities. Or from your duty to think. When all are counted we shall be four hundred and eighty. The giants will outnumber us three to one, and if we don't out-think them *at every turn* from here to Sanctuary-Beyond-the-Sea we shall all be murdered. Warriors, children, your old parents waiting in Etherhorde. By Rin, people! I'm not smart enough to do this alone! No one is. The thought you'd spare me out of meekness could be the one that saves our lives. Who doubts what I say?"

Silence. Low slap of water on wood. Far off in the village, temple bells, ringing the dawn.

"Let us board our ship, then," she said.

"Dri!" they cried, soft but earnest. All save Taliktrum. He liked ranks and titles, and would be Lord Taliktrum soon enough, when his father declared him a man.

They stood and stretched, buttoned their shirts of eelskin and sailcloth, washed their faces in a pool of rain. Then, with Diadrelu in the lead, they ran.

To see an ixchel clan set its heart on being somewhere is like watching a thought race quicksilver toward its goal. This clan of nine swarmed up the wooden piling as though mounting stairs, dashed along an upper beam that shook with the boots of fishermen inches overhead, reached a knot-hole in the boards, made a ladder of their bodies and, in a heartbeat, pulled one another up and onto the pier.

No giants saw them. A great ravenous gull did, and hopped

straight for Dri, but four needle-sharp arrows met its breast in an instant and it blundered shrieking away. This was the worst now: the open run, the wide gaps and jagged splinters in the boards, and any variety of deaths along the way. Ixchel run in formation, a fluid diamond or arrowhead, and Dri was pleased with the tight cohesion of a clan that had not existed four days ago.

It started well. The fishermen obligingly kept their toes to the harbor. A wharf-rat froze at the sight of them, hair on end and a slashed-off stump of tail twitching alarm, but it proved a wise creature and let them pass unchallenged. It even hissed a greeting: *"Fatten up, cousins!"*—which in rat terms is high courtesy.

Best of all, the wind slept. Two weeks before, Dri had lost a boy on this very dock when a sudden gust knocked him sidelong into the waves.

Mother Sky, we might not lose a soul today! thought Dri.

But halfway to land a sailor, flat on his back and reeking of pumpkin ale, came to sudden life and groped for Ensyl, the youngest of their company. Had he used his boot he might have killed her, drunk as he was. His hand, however, was bare, and Ensyl turned like a seasoned battle-dancer, her sword a blur, and cut off his forefinger at the second knuckle. The man howled, waving his mutilated hand.

"Crawlies! Muckin' sewer-sippin' whorespawned grubs! I'll kill ye!"

The evil word swept past them like fire. *Crawlies! Crawlies!* Boots shook the pier ahead and behind. A crowd of giants, two or three of them sober, pounded straight at them from the village. Others rushed to the rails of the nearest ships with lamps, squinting into the half-light. A bottle shattered, spraying them with grog.

"The barge!" cried Dri, and without hesitation flung herself from the dock. As she fell toward the water, the flaps of the swallow-suit billowed like twin sails. Diadrelu stretched out her arms, found the gauntlets sewn into the hem. The swallow's wingbones, heirlooms of her family, were fused to these gloves, and when her hands slipped inside them she became the swallow, a flying being, a woman with wings.

She barely pulled out of the fall: her feet grazed a wave. Then with four aching beats of her arms, she rose and shot to the deck of the barge, thirty feet from the pier where her people stood at bay. The barge was long and dark, and by the stillness of the lamps at the far end, she guessed its people had not yet heard the shout of *"Crawlies!"* That would change, though: in minutes every boat in Sorrophran would know of the "infestation." *Ay, Rin! The* Chathrand! *They'll search her anew!*

A thump among the fish crates beside her: Taliktrum had thrown the grapple already. Without her signal! There were two possible reasons for such a breach of protocol, neither of them good. Dri pulled her arms free of the gauntlets, dived for the hook and dragged the rope to the portside rail. In a matter of seconds the rope was tied fast: she gave two tugs, and felt it snap tight as Taliktrum bound it to the pier.

Down they slid, black beads on a string. When Taliktrum arrived seventh, his aunt could barely contain her fury.

"You might have struck *me* with that hook," she said. "And as Talag's son you should be last down the rope."

Taliktrum glared at her. "I am last," he said.

"What?" Dri counted quickly. *"Where is Nytikyn?"*

Taliktrum said nothing, but dropped his eyes.

"Oh no! No!"

"A boy did it," said Ensyl. "Some fisherman's brat."

"Nytikyn," said Diadrelu. Her eyes never stopped moving, hunting threats among the crates and timbers stacked around them—but her voice was hollow, lost.

"He saved us," said Taliktrum. "The boy was a fiend, trying to cut the rope and drown us. Who knows, Aunt? Maybe he's the same lad we heard blubbering for his ship. The one you found so charming."

Diadrelu blinked at him, then shook herself. "We run," she said.

They had no trouble on the barge, nor with the leap from her rails to the shrimper moored alongside. But once aboard the shrimper disaster nearly struck again: her crew was scrubbing the forecastle, and when the boat rocked, a wash of bilgewater struck them like a river in flood. But they locked arms, as ixchel will, and those at the end held fast to a deck cleat, and the torrent passed. Moments later they ran to the dark side of the pilot-house and scaled it to the roof.

One challenge more. A bowline from the *Chathrand* passed just above them, one of dozens of ropes tying the ship like a colossal bull to nearly every fixed object on the wharf. This line ran from the fishing pier—the very point they had been making for—looped low over the shrimper, and then rose sharply for a hundred feet or more to the *Chathrand*'s topdeck.

Leaping up to the bowline proved simple enough, but the climb was terrible. If you have ever scrambled up a wet and slippery tree, you might have some idea of their first minutes. Now imagine that the tree is not six or seven times your height but two hundred times, and branchless, and filthy with tar and algae and sharp bits of shell. Then consider that this tree lacks bark, lacks footholds of any kind, and heaves and twists with the slow rocking of the ship.

Up and up, hand over hand. When they were sixty feet from the deck the sun appeared on the horizon, peeking under rain-clouds, and Dri knew they were exposed to the sight of any giant who glanced their way. Inch after scrabbling inch, hands bleeding from the scratchy rope. All the while she waited for the shout: *Crawlies! Crawlies on the line!*

The last nightmare was the rat funnel: a broad iron cone threaded onto this and every other mooring line to keep the pests from doing exactly what they were attempting. The mouth of the funnel opened downward and spread, bell-like, farther than any of them could reach. Dri and Taliktrum had practiced for this moment on a real bell, in a temple in Etherhorde, but this was infinitely worse. The cone weighed more than all of them together.

Two of the East Arqualis climbed inside, set their shoulders to the funnel wall and pushed against the heavy rope with their feet. Gasping and sweating, they tilted the funnel to one side. Dri and Taliktrum gripped the rope with their legs as if riding a horse, and leaned the upper halves of their bodies over the lip of the funnel. "Go!" she snapped, and her people climbed over them, using their backs and shoulders like steps. Then: "Out, you!" to the pair inside the funnel, and beside her Taliktrum hissed. Dri felt it, too: the huge weight of the funnel, tearing at her ribs. The East Arqualis were crawling out past their legs, making an about-face on the rope (*Hurry, by Rin, hurry!*) and climbing, like the others, up her body and Taliktrum's. Her nephew's teeth were locked and his lips pulled back in a snarl of pain. But together they bore the weight.

"Climb, Aunty," he whispered.

Dri shook her head. "You first."

"I'm stronger—"

"Go! S'an order!" She could not manage another word. Still he disobeyed! He glanced down at her straining ribs, seemed to consider. Then, with the same acrobat's grace as his father at twenty, he loosed his grip and kicked himself past the rim of the funnel.

Something ripped inside her. She cried out. The ixchel above seized Taliktrum as he leaped, turned him in the air by his ankles, and just as Dri's grip broke his hand descended and caught her own, and dragged her past the funnel's lip.

The last thirty feet were a red agony for Diadrelu. But when they gained the ship they were safe—the rope was cleated next to a lifeboat bound under a broad tarpaulin. They slipped under this rainproof cloth with ease. Dri found her people clustered about a message scrawled with charcoal on the deck. Ixchel words, too small for giant eyes:

DOOR AT STEPRAIL, NO LATCH, 8 FT 9 IN. STARBOARD. WELCOME ABOARD, M'LADY.

Dri turned to look for the hidden door—and collapsed. The pain in her chest was like a swallowed knife. But at last it was done. Four clans brought aboard in as many days. Nine of her people killed on previous boardings, just one today. *Nytikyn.* He was to marry a girl in Etherhorde, wore her clan emblem on a chain at his wrist. Dri herself would have to tell her. And his parents. And the other parents, children, lovers of the slain.

Ten dead for this mission already. And we haven't left port.

–3–

The Master and His Lads

On a skysail mast, three hundred feet over the deck of the *Chathrand,* a bird sat in the dawn drizzle, watching the ixchel's progress up the rope with perfect indifference. He was an extraordinarily beautiful bird: a moon falcon, black above, cream-yellow below. He was smaller than a hawk but a better hunter, and quick enough to steal a fish from an eagle's claw if he took a mind to. When the she-ix flapped about in her feather suit, the falcon thought idly of killing her, out of pride more than hunger, for she was offensively ugly in flight. Not her domain. But the falcon knew his duty, and did not move as the little people staggered under the lifeboat, and a few last rats hurled themselves aboard by the gangplanks, and a toothless prisoner from the Sorrophran jail dabbed hot tar on the mast just a few yards below him, chattering foolishly: *"Lo, Jimmy Bird! Sailin' with the Great Ship, are we?"*

There were prisoners all over the ship, sanding rough planks, tarring ropes against the months of salt spray ahead, driving brass pegs into transom and mast. The falcon noted them as he would cattle in a field: inedible, useless, no threat to him. In all Sorrophran, just one thing mattered: an ornate red carriage by the Mariners' Inn, eight blocks uphill from the water. The falcon's eyes were so sharp he could count the flies on the horses' rumps, but they could not pierce the tavern door, nor see who had arrived by that carriage in the night.

" 'Ere's bread for a handsome Jim!"

The prisoner took a moldy biscuit from his pocket, snapped it in two and tossed half at the falcon. The bird did not deign to move. On the wharf, a great crowd was gathering before the *Chathrand:* street boys, staggering drunks, noncommissioned sailors with their pale wives and barefoot children, fruit-sellers, grog-sellers, Rappopolni monks in their mustard-yellow robes. All were held back from the *Chathrand*'s main gangway by a wooden fence that cut the square in two. Imperial marines, their gold helmets winking in the sun, paced just inside the fence.

At last the door of the inn swung wide. The bird tensed. Onto the porch came a heavy, muscular man, slow of step, dressed in the uniform of a merchant officer: black coat, gold trim, high collar turned up at the back. Over his chest flowed a curly, rust-red beard. The man's eyes were bright and restless. He looked suspicious of the doorway, the horses, the very air.

The carriage driver scampered down from his seat, opened the passenger door and lowered the footstool. The red-bearded man paid no attention. After a moment a servant came from the inn bearing a tray. Upon the tray, a dish, and within the dish the falcon saw four of the tiny, sky-blue eggs of milop birds. The bearded man scooped them into his hand. The servant waited, the horses stamped, the carriage driver stood in the rain, but the man had eyes only for his eggs. With great patience he lifted each one, rolled it in his palm, and then with a surprisingly delicate motion cracked it between his teeth and drank it raw. He did this four times. Then he passed the eggshells to the servant and lumbered toward the carriage.

Now the falcon saw it: the odd, toe-pointing twitch in the man's left foot. Not quite a limp, but unmistakable—his master had demonstrated. Beard, eggs, twitch. It was enough.

The carriage door closed. The driver took his seat and whipped the horses into a trot. Nearly a mile away, the falcon leaped from the mast with a warrior's cry, startling the prisoner so badly he scalded his leg with tar. The ship was already forgotten: the falcon shot like an arrow into the thunderheads, beating west and screaming defiance of the wind. Shedding rain, delighted to be under way, he climbed until land and sea vanished utterly beneath the clouds, and then higher still. At last he burst through to sunlight, and skimmed low over a wild, brooding cloudscape, a kingdom of his own.

All day the bird flew west, hardly changing the tempo of his wingbeats. Toward evening a cloud-murth on a horse like white smoke chased him, leering and waving an axe, but the falcon beat the demon to the edge of the cloudlands, and taunted it with a corkscrew dive at the setting sun. Before dark he saw a pod of whales surging east, and a ship in pursuit.

Under the moon, his name-father, the bird flew faster than ever, and at midnight with a thrill of joy he felt the wind shift behind him. *I shall be early, early!* He passed gulls, terns, cormorants as if they were standing still. Now and then a wanderstar crossed the heavens: one of the metal eyes the ancients hung over Alifros to spy on their enemies.

By the second day the wind tasted of Etherhorde. Marsh gases, city smoke, the sweet reek of farmland. At last it came: a bright coast, ships beyond counting, harbor bells and the barking of dogs, the rumbling, gabbling noise of the afternoon market, the children laughing in the slums, the fortresses, the black parade of the Emperor's Horse Guard. Etherhorde was the mightiest city in the world, and one day (so his master whispered) would be the only city where power dwelled, all others made its vassals.

Being a woken animal, the falcon lacked his wild brethren's terror of cities. Still, he could not ignore their dangers. Men fired arrows, boys threw stones. Thus the falcon took the same course always to his master's window: up the River Ool, past the cargo piers in the estuary where ships from all Alifros docked, past the marble mansions and the Queen's Park, the ironworks where cannon were made for the fleet, the home for veterans maimed by cannon fire, until at last he reached a grim stone compound at the river's edge.

Travelers on the Ool mistook the place for a prison; in fact it was an academy for girls. The unfortunate creatures trapped inside those walls knew the falcon by sight. One—the fair-haired girl who tended to sit alone by the catfish tanks—was looking up at him now. Too clever, that one. She watched him with an awareness that made the bird uncomfortable, as if she guessed his errand, or his master's name. But no matter. She was under the eye of the Sisters, and would never dare to throw a stone.

The far edge of the Academy grounds touched the wall about Mol Etheg, the sacred mountain. Etheg had long since been engulfed by the city, but the ancient pines covering its slopes were unchanged from the time of the Amber Kings, when Etherhorde was a mere collection of huts on the edge of a boundless wood. Today Etheg was under the direct protection of His Supremacy the Emperor. So dire were the punishments for harming its trees that mothers forbade their children to play with pinecones that fell outside the wall. The falcon loved this forest, devoured its rabbits and snakes, dozed in its sunny branches.

Not now, though. Up the mountain he flew, beyond exhaustion, announcing his coming with ragged shrieks. Cliffs appeared, and a lone lake, and then on the broken summit rose the huge, wet bulk of Castle Maag. The oldest structure in Etherhorde, Maag was the ancestral home of the ruling family, a darker and more private place than the five-domed seat of Empire in the city below. There the Emperor stunned his subjects with opulence: the crown of rubies, the throne cut from a single pale purple crystal. Here a pair of bejeweled concubines swatted beetles on a terrace, and an ancient gardener raked lilac petals into drifts, and the Queen Mother walked a white boar on a chain about the soggy grounds.

Above them all, in the Weather Tower, shutters flew open. Sandor Ott, Spymaster of the Imperium, held a gloved hand from the window. He was an old man, and rather short, but his body was lean and strong. Eagerly he watched the bird's approach. Below the glove the skin of his arm was a crisscrossed tangle of scars.

With a last flurry the bird alighted. The old man cooed to him and stroked his back.

"Niriviel, my champion! You'll rest, and eat from my own plate tonight! But what news, finest falcon? Tell me at once!"

Within the tower chamber, a group of younger men huddled, breathless. They were six in all: poised and muscular, with wary eyes and handsome faces. Some wore heavy silk, others the jaquina shirts of snow-white cotton made popular by a visit from the Prince of Talturi. None carried weapons (only Ott had that privilege within the castle walls) but most carried scars. One had been tending the fire when the bird arrived, and stood gaping, the poker forgotten in his hand. Indeed, no one moved a finger as Ott cocked his ear close to that savage beak. The men had spent the night shivering and sullen, not believing any bird would come; they would have laughed at the old warrior if they dared. But here it stood. Would the rest of his tale prove true? Would speech come from a wild thing, here in their very midst?

No, it would not: Niriviel's voice was only a shrill whistle, the same as any bird of prey. But Sandor Ott listened motionless, so they did as well. The bird gave a longer trill, and then a curious hop on the spymaster's arm, as if attempting a demonstration.

Ott took a deep breath. Then he walked the bird to its perch, whispering and petting him all the while. Once the falcon was settled he turned to look at them, his face wild with something, and slowly pulled off the glove. The hand that emerged flexed once, then tightened into a fist.

"Rose is found," he said.

Abruptly the room fell so quiet they could hear the bubble of sap from a pine log in the hearth. Furtively, the men sought one another's eyes. Ott noticed the glances and raised his voice nearly to a shout.

"Do you hear? Nilus Rotheby Rose is found! In Sorrophran, fresh from the Narrow Sea, and he'll be here at the helm of *Chathrand* in four days' time. Open that wine, somebody, and let us drink to good fortune. At long last the game is begun!"

The men looked at the bottle of wine and did not move. One of them picked up the corkscrew from the table, unfolded it and glanced uncertainly at his fellows. Sandor Ott walked to the center of the room.

"It's the best of news, eh, lads? The start of your golden time. Just think: a year from now His Supremacy will count you all Defenders of the Realm. And centuries hence your family names will still be praised in song. You work in secrecy today, but your grandchildren will know that they are descended from the men who saved the Empire. More than heroes, you shall— *Zirfet Salubrastin!*"

At the sound of his name a very big man, easily the strongest in the room, gave a startled jump.

"Why are you looking at the door, you straw-gutted mule?"

"I never did, sir!" blurted Zirfet. He stood rooted to the spot, his enormous frame turned slightly in the direction of the tower door. Ott crossed the room to face him. The top of the old man's head was little higher than Zirfet's elbow.

"You had a mind to slip away," said Ott, very low.

"No, sir!" exploded Zirfet.

Ott held Zirfet's gaze without moving. Then, in a smooth gesture, he unsheathed a long white knife.

"You were scheming, Zirfet," he said. "An illness, a broken leg, your dear ma dying in Hubboxum. Any story, so long as it kept you off that ship."

"You're wrong! I never—not for one minute—"

Ott slid the naked blade through Zirfet's own belt, then withdrew his hand.

"Master Ott!" Now Zirfet's great shoulders were quaking. "I don't want your knife, sir! I don't!"

"You've got the only blade in the room, lad. And I'm calling you a coward. A reeking, swill-blooded coward. You'll want to challenge me, Zirfet. It's your right."

With contemptuous slowness, the old man turned his back on the younger spy and cast a cold glance at the other five.

"Men of the Secret Fist. Which of you could stand before his father and not hang his head? By the Night Gods! I watched them leap onto burning ships. I watched them charge up ladders through the boiling pitch, into the very teeth of the Mzithrin horde. Murder in their eyes, blood to their elbows. And look at their progeny. A few years of peace and you turn into dolls. Straw dolls, scarecrows, cowards! Rin spare me, you're like old Quimby, Her Highness' pet. White flabby sows, too fond of your slops to bother with the oath you swore at the Ametrine Throne, or even to defend your own rancid, maggot-mounded, offal-heap honor! *Pelech!*"

The last word was in Old Arquali, a ritual battle-cry to be flung at an enemy, and with it the old man twisted sideways, out of the path of Zirfet's lunge. The knife missed his back by an inch, but Ott did not escape unharmed: Zirfet's huge left fist caught him squarely in the eye. The old man flung himself with the blow, rolled over the little table with the candles and the sea chart. The other men retreated to the walls. No stopping a fight the spymaster himself had provoked.

Zirfet leaped for Ott again, snarling, all hesitation gone. But Ott was quicker. His fall from the table carried back into a roll, and as he gained his feet, still spinning, he caught the table by one leg and whirled it with terrific speed. His first pass checked Zirfet's advance, his second caught the knife in mid-stab and tore it from the other's hand.

To the watching spies, the rest of the fight seemed pitifully one-sided. Zirfet rushed Ott like an elephant, Ott leaped back and let him slip on the wine. Zirfet had learned enough from his old teacher to use the fall rather than struggle against it, and sprang to his feet again with something approaching grace. But then he took another hopeless swing at Ott. The spymaster parried it easily with his knee, and at the same time broke the second wine bottle over Zirfet's head. Even as he fell, Zirfet managed to lash out with his fist. Ott merely danced backward, absorbing the blow, and seizing the big man's wrist in one hand. The blow had stretched Zirfet out, and almost at his ease the spymaster kicked him in the stomach, leaped on his back, and pressed the jagged stem of the bottle to his throat.

All was still. Sandor Ott grinned hideously, one eye blind

with blood from Zirfet's first blow. He pulled the other's head up by the hair.

"You're a coward, are you not?"

"No, sir."

"A coward, I say. A leech from a pigsty pool, like all the men of your line."

"I'll kill you, sir."

"What?"

"I swear I'll see you dead if you insult me more. I'm no coward, sir!"

A quiet sound reached the ears of the spies, and it was a moment before they recognized it as laughter. Ott's shoulders shook. He threw the bottle aside and leaped off Zirfet, who bucked himself unsteadily to his feet. Watching him, Ott laughed louder.

"If you'd answered *yes* I'd have believed it, lad. You'd be dead on this floor with your throat slit."

"Well I know it, Master," said Zirfet, wheezing.

"This knife," said Sandor Ott, tugging it from the table, "was placed in my hand by my first general, after I slew the Mzithrin Lord Tiamek on the Ega Bridge. Will you take it, Zirfet Salubrastin, as token of your honor defended?"

For the second time, Zirfet froze. Then he staggered forward, eyes wide with astonishment, and took the knife from his master's hand. Eyes met around the room; there were nods of grim approval.

The spymaster plucked the chart from the floor. Wine had ruined it: the western lands seemed to vanish in a sea of blood.

"Now hear me once and forever," said Ott. "There'll be no glancing at doors, for *there are no doors to escape by.* Not for you six, nor for me, nor even for His Supremacy. Rose will captain that ship, and we shall sail with her. The game's begun, lads. We'll play it to the last round."

-4-

Carriage

Captain Nilus Rotheby Rose felt the cat nuzzle his leg and repressed an urge to lash out. A good kick would remind the animal to keep its distance. He knew better, of course. The big red cat, Sniraga, was Lady Oggosk's darling. With luck the beast would remember his great aversion to being touched, without need of a blow that could cost him the hag's services. They had sailed together before, these three.

The carriage lumped along uphill. He sat with his big arms folded against his beard, watching the hag smoke. A new pipe. Clenched in drier lips. Lost in deeper wrinkles. But the milk-blue eyes with their predatory gaze were unchanged, and he thought: *She'll be sizing me up the same. Best note these eyes, too, you deadly old crone.*

"So," he said, "they nabbed you in Besq."

"Fah."

"Beg your pardon," said Rose. "They wooed you, perhaps? Called you *Duchess*? Handed you a card in silver writ?"

The old woman rubbed her nose vigorously. Repulsed, the captain turned to the window.

"Why are we going uphill?" he demanded. "Why aren't we making for the port?"

"Because there's a crowd like a Ballytween Fair about your vessel," muttered Oggosk. "And we've two more to pick up."

"Two? The mayor spoke of just one—that preening doctor."

Oggosk snorted. "The mayor of Sorrophran is the Emperor's bootshine-boy—nay, the rag itself. But His Supremacy doesn't own the *Chathrand*. If he hires the Great Ship, he does so at the pleasure of the Chathrand Trading Family. There will never be a crew aboard her but meets with the Family's blessing."

"Don't lecture me, Oggosk," said Rose, his voice a warning rumble. "I've commanded her. Farther and better than any man alive."

"Then you'll recall Lady Lapadolma's most irritating habit."

"Reciting that foul verse?"

"Stocking the crew!" snapped Oggosk. "Intruding on your rights as captain! Every voyage she afflicts us with one or two, her personal tattlers. No other Family presumes so much."

Rose grunted. Lady Lapadolma Yelig was the ruling grand-mother of the Trading Family that had owned and outfitted the *Chathrand* for twelve generations. She was the Emperor's own cousin, but showed no better than a formal loyalty to the Ametrine Throne. Her family had always married power, both within the Imperium and without: Lapadolma herself was the widow of the Bishwa Egalguk, monarch of the Isle of Fulne.

The Yeligs owned dozens of ships, but the *Chathrand* was their great glory. No other vessel could carry a third what she did on a trading voyage, nor earn a third the gold. And no other Family managed, under the very nose of the Emperor, to keep so much of that gold for itself. The culprit was tradition: to the Emperor's long fury, a belief held that the day *Chathrand* left port in the hands of another owner would be the day she sank. Nonsense, probably. But not even His Supremacy could risk disaster on such a monstrous scale.

Of course tradition—and nearly everything else—was about to change . . .

From her cloud of rancid smoke, the old woman chuckled.

"Nabbed!" she said. "If there's anyone nabbed it was you, Captain."

Rose shot her a dark look. The cat purred against his leg.

"You didn't want this commission," she said flatly. "You didn't want another turn behind the wheel of the *Chathrand*. Why not, when they pay you so handsomely?"

"I was bespoken."

"Only by a wish to hide. You led the Emperor on a yearlong chase, island to island, port to port. And you almost escaped—"

"Still a blary witch." Rose glared at her. "Still a trickster and a spy."

"You almost escaped," Oggosk repeated. "The Flikkermen caught you last night, with a ticket for an inland coach. Inland! Why, Captain, that'd be the first time in your life!"

"Oggosk," he growled, "be silent."

Her eyes remained fixed on him. "A secret commission, too. Sorrophran is like a hive of ants, everyone knowing the captain will be named this morning, everyone guessing wrong. Above all they wonder why *Chathrand* spent three months in this kennel of a town, and not mighty Etherhorde across the bay. Will you tell them, Captain Rose? Will you tell how certain powerful men in the capital might have grown suspicious at, say, the twelve months' provisions being laid in our hold, for a voyage of three? It would be difficult to explain—above all to the Yeligs. Suppose you gave them the truth: that His Supremacy's astrologers have convinced old Magad that this is the hour of his destiny, the moment that will see him crushed—or raised above all princes that ever were or will be. *Naya,* has it ever been different? A man will leap into a furnace if you tell him it's the way to power over others. It's a madness and a wonder that we let you rule. But the greatest wonder is the threat."

Rose's head jerked up, and Oggosk cackled.

"Ehe! The threat! What did they use on you, Captain? What drives Nilus Rotheby Rose to set sail when he hasn't the mind?"

Captain Rose's face was scarlet, but his voice when it came

was low and venomous. "You will recall, Lady Oggosk, that we shall soon be weighing anchor. And you will recall further how very few compulsions indeed this captain tolerates at sea."

The old woman dropped her eyes and shrank into her corner. For several moments they lurched along in silence. Then with a sudden *"Whoh!"* the driver pulled the horses up, bounded from his seat and flung open the door.

A black man stood framed in the doorway, clearly ready to enter the coach. He wore a dark vest over a white silk shirt, and most incongruously, a round woolen hat such as Templar monks donned for traveling. In one hand he held a parchment case, in the other a black bag with two rough wooden handles. The bag was old and worn and filled nearly to bursting. The man bowed courteously to Oggosk, then to Rose.

"Who in the nine fiery pits are you?" bellowed Rose, his nerves breaking at last.

"Bolutu, my name is Bolutu." The man had a precise voice and an unfamiliar accent. He appeared quite unaffected by Rose's outburst, which irked the captain further.

"Get along, you've no business here."

The stranger cocked his head. "No business? Perhaps that is literally true. Irrelevant, however. For although I must leave my business behind, I have orders to respect—or ignore at my peril."

"What's this Noonfirth prig raving about?" shouted Rose with a glance at his seer.

"He's no Noonfirther," said Oggosk flatly.

"He's as black as a tarboy's heel."

"I am a Slevran, Captain Rose."

Momentary confusion. Lady Oggosk dropped her pipe. It would scarcely have been more startling if the man had claimed to be a lynx. The Slevrans were savage men of the far interior, nomads of the steppe. It was they who attacked and slaughtered caravans making west to the Idhe Lands. The Emperor sent legions to exterminate them, but they merely withdrew into the hills and waited for the soldiers to grow bored and hungry, and as soon as these expeditionaries left the raids began anew. Were they even men? some asked. Did they have morals, language, souls?

"You're a liar as well as mad," said Rose. He waved impatiently at the bewildered coachman. "Drive on, you. We've a commission to respect."

"I have the same commission," said Bolutu, his hand still on the door.

"You're a barking Noonfirth dog!"

"No, Captain, I have never been to the Summer Realm. But you will be taking on a cargo of animals at Etherhorde, and I am a veterinarian. And I am ordered, by His Supremacy Magad the Fifth, to take my place as such aboard the *Chathrand*. I yet hope to soothe your anxieties about my person."

"Why do you wear a monk's hat?"

Bolutu smiled. "I was raised by the Templar brothers, and keep the journeyman's vows. Some call me Brother Bolutu, but *Mister* is quite acceptable."

"If you're not a Noonfirther, where'd you learn that tea-and-pastries talk?"

"In Yelig House."

Shocked silence again. The man was claiming to be an intimate of the Chathrand Trading Family. Rose looked at Oggosk, but the witch drew the hood of her cloak over her head, whispering and muttering. The black man climbed into the coach and sat beside her. Relieved, the driver raised the footstool and slammed the door shut.

The trip resumed. Oggosk muttered in Swalish, which the captain did not speak. Having been at sea for forty years, however, he knew a smattering of words in many tongues: *jult,* which Oggosk said many times with happy emphasis, meant "disease." At her side the black man sat motionless, eyelids half lowered. Rose thought suddenly of how he would look tumbling over the *Chathrand*'s bulwarks, head over heels into the waves. Then he recalled the Special Protection every captain of Arqual swore to provide friends of the Company. If harm befell this

Bolutu, a Company inspection would follow. Merely to be the subject of such an inspection would mark one for life.

"Is your cat a woken animal, Duchess?" asked Bolutu suddenly.

Oggosk made a rude sound in her throat: *"Glah."*

Bolutu was unperturbed. "Do you know, Captain, that the frequency of wakings is exploding? How many such animals have you heard of, in all your life? Three in twenty-eight years, for my part, and just one—a lovely bull with a taste for choral music—did I meet with face to face. But this year all bets are off! Just last month a she-wolf on Kushal pleaded for her life: sadly the hunters killed her anyway. From Bramian comes news of a stork eager to talk gold miners out of poisoning his lake. And several cats have been heard to speak in the alleys of Etherhorde itself. The *Mariner* had a report."

Sniraga purred, sliding among their legs. Rose stared out through the window. Accidents, he thought. So many kinds of accidents . . .

They had nearly reached the port: he could hear a vague roaring that could only be the muster of the crew. Then the carriage stopped again. The door opened, and before him stood Ignus Chadfallow.

This time Rose was prepared, if not pleased: the doctor was Special Envoy-at-Large to His Supremacy, dispatched throughout the world as the human seal on certain Imperial promises. Where Chadfallow sailed, Magad's word was kept. Rose should have guessed the doctor would be tossed into the bargain.

Chadfallow himself, however, looked stunned. His eyes were fixed on the captain, his face visibly paled. He made no move to enter the carriage.

"Rose," he said.

The carriage driver, holding the door once again, began to tremble. From the folds of her hood, Oggosk laughed.

"Climb in, Doctor," said Rose. And then, with a glance at Bolutu: "If you don't mind the company."

Chadfallow didn't move.

"Of course, you won't have the use of the stateroom this time," Rose added. "That goes to Isiq and his family."

"But there's some mistake," said Chadfallow. "You were in the Pellurids."

"I was," said Rose. "But that is not your concern."

"You cannot have been given the *Chathrand*."

Rose pitched forward, rage contorting his features. Oggosk touched his arm. The captain twitched in her direction, then paused and sat back. One finger stabbed out at Chadfallow.

"We're ashore, Doctor, where your tongue is your own. But tomorrow we sail. Remember that. For I *am* the captain of the Great Ship. And if you mean to board her, I warn you, envoy though you be: on the water there's no law but mine. The law of Nilus Rotheby Rose. There's a thorn in that name, and a beesting, and a blade: my kin knew what they were about when they named me Nilus—dagger. Climb in!"

"No," said Chadfallow, slowly shaking his head. "I won't sail with you, no."

Their eyes met. Rose looked caught between satisfaction and offense.

"Well," he said at last, "that is between you and your Emperor. Don't expect me to beg. Driver!"

The driver abruptly shrank three inches, his knees buckling.

"Drive on, you dumb, staring, scrofulous cur!"

Moments later the carriage was vanishing around the corner of the street. Chadfallow stood motionless, alarmed as he could not remember being in his life. When the porters reached the tavern door with his sea chest he did not know what to tell them.

-5-

A Natural Scholar

After the *Eniel* rounded the headland, Pazel spent a dismal hour on the pier. The fishermen took a brief interest in him, told him life ashore was better here than in sprawling Etherhorde, where boys were snatched in broad daylight by the Flikkermen and chained to looms in the clothing mills. One old man even offered him breakfast. Before Pazel could accept, however, a shout of *"Crawlies! Crawlies!"* had gone up around the wharf, and the men stampeded for shore. Pazel sat shivering, working old nails out of the pier and tossing them into the bay, all the while silently cursing the name of Ignus Chadfallow.

The man was a liar, and Pazel his lifelong fool. In Ormael, where Pazel had lived with his mother and sister in a stone house overlooking the city, he had thought Chadfallow magnificent and kind. His own father, a sea captain, had brought the doctor for his first visit when Pazel was but six, introducing him to the family as "our distinguished friend from Etherhorde, city of kings." After presenting his wife, Suthinia, and daughter, Neda, to the doctor, he gestured to Pazel and boomed: "That is my son, Chadfallow—a quick wit, and a natural scholar." Pazel turned scarlet from the praise, although he had something else in mind for his future than books and learning. He wanted to sail on his father's ship.

Chadfallow was one of the few Arquali to have set foot in Ormael since the end of the Second Sea War. His deep voice and elegant strange clothes left Pazel speechless with admiration. For years he pictured Arqual as a land of soft-spoken gentlemen in waistcoats.

Six months after presenting Chadfallow to his family, Captain Gregory Pathkendle sailed out of Ormael on a scouting mission and never returned. Some terrible and total accident, it was supposed. A general dismay gripped the city. Sailors' widows left gifts on the doorstep: mourning lace for his mother and sister, a black scarf for Pazel himself. Then a Rukmast merchantman brought the news that Pathkendle's boat had been spotted in the Gulf of Thól, among a flotilla of Mzithrini warships. She had been repainted, and flew the gold-and-black pennant of the Mzithrin Kings.

Chadfallow was by then the Emperor's Special Envoy to Ormael, and lived in a fine house in the city. He visited Pazel's home often during those months of fear, and always insisted that Gregory might yet be alive, imprisoned by pirates ("they spawn like eels in the Gulf") or the Mzithrinis themselves. Pazel's sister Neda asked if the doctor's great Empire couldn't send ships to rescue him. Chadfallow replied that the Mzithrin Kings ruled a territory as great as Arqual's own. If they sailed against her, he said, no one would be rescued but many more fathers would die.

Nonetheless he was a comfort to them all. Pazel's mother Suthinia often persuaded Chadfallow to stay for dinner, after which he would kiss her hand in thanks. "A meal as lovely as its authoress," he would say, making the children squirm. There was no denying Suthinia's beauty, with her dark olive skin and startling green eyes. Like Chadfallow she was a foreigner, having come down from the highlands with a troupe of merchants, dealers in cinnamon and kohl, and even long after her marriage to Captain Gregory the neighbors still treated her with unease. Beauty was one thing, but those clothes, that laugh?

Chadfallow, however, had smiled on her from the first. He

smiled at Pazel, too, in those days, praising his quick way with languages and sternly commanding him never to neglect Arquali. As months turned to years and warships of many nations were sighted offshore, Chadfallow was often called back to Arqual to consult with his Emperor. Returning to Ormael, he brought the children grammar books and dictionaries: useful gifts, if rather dull.

Then the news from the outer world darkened. Sailors brought rumors of bloodshed in distant lands, small nations devoured by larger ones, war fleets rebuilt. And it was at this moment of alarm that Pazel's father suddenly reappeared.

His old ship, still under Mzithrini flags, made a daring run past Ormael harbor at daybreak, firing shot after shot. Later it was noted that his guns hit few targets—perhaps none at all— but in the dawn confusion no one doubted that the city was under attack.

An Ormali ship immediately gave chase. Captain Gregory tacked north, almost dead into the wind, giving his pursuers many a fine opportunity to rake his sails with grapeshot. Soon Gregory's canvas was in tatters. He appeared to have trouble with his chaser-cannon, too: in any case, not a single shot was fired at his pursuers. The battle was brief: Ormael's little fighting ship emptied her guns into Gregory's, and as they neared Cape Córistel they raised a flag for his surrender. Pazel's father was heard to shout *"No!"* while waving oddly from his quarterdeck. And then the *Grygulv* rounded the cape.

She was a 120-gun Mzithrini Blodmel, or "war-angel," one of the deadliest ships afloat. In a panic, the Ormali captain ordered his men to "wear the ship"—spin her hard about and run downwind. But the *Grygulv* was already upon them, and her broadside was furious. She blasted rudder and mast from the Ormali ship, and followed up with the most feared weapon in the world—a Mzithrini dragon's-egg shot, which burst in liquid flame across the deck. When the smoke cleared the *Grygulv* was making west, alongside Gregory's ship, and thirty Ormalis lay dead.

The city, which had mourned Captain Gregory for a year after his disappearance, instantly renamed him Pathkendle the Traitor, and to many of his schoolmates Pazel became simply the Traitor's Son.

Pazel suffered terribly. Even his best friends abandoned him. Some of his teachers considered it their duty to punish the sin of bad blood: they made him sit apart and called him a lazy fool if he gave a wrong answer (which he rarely did). When his mother complained to the headmaster, the man threw up his hands: "Why blame us? You married that villain!" Suthinia flew into a rage, chased the headmaster from his office to the science hall and beat him with a stuffed marmoset. Then she pulled Pazel from school and dragged him wordlessly home. No other school would take him after the incident, however, and in three weeks she slipped the headmaster a grotesque sum to forget the whole affair.

From that day on they ate smaller meals, and burned less coal on chilly nights. And when he returned to school his classmates greeted him with a song:

> *He's Pazel Pathkendle, his daddy went bad,*
> *His mother went mad with a mar-mo-set.*

It was enough to make him hope Suthinia would never again feel the need to protect him. But her master plan for her children's safety had not even begun.

Pazel's one advantage was Chadfallow, who still dined with the Pathkendles weekly. The Special Envoy was now the most popular man in Ormael. After the *Grygulv* disaster the mayor of Ormael sent him back to his Emperor to beg for protection. The doctor returned just as a wild rumor of invasion was spreading about the city—none could say how it started—and cheers greeted him as he disembarked in Ormaelport.

"Your plea has reached the Ametrine Throne," he told the crowd. "You shall hear from the Emperor shortly."

Pazel could not have found a better champion. Everyone

knew that Arqual had fought the Mzithrin to a draw in the Second Sea War. Instead of the Traitor's Son, Pazel was now honorary nephew of the Envoy, the man who would save Ormael. The boy understood little of these matters, but he knew Chadfallow had reversed his fortunes, and loved him for it.

Just this once, moreover, Chadfallow had come with a better gift than grammar books. It was a kite in the shape of a hummingbird, which Pazel strung with fishing twine scavenged in the port and flew from the hilltops above the plum orchards. The kite was his prize toy for several months, until the day a sudden calm plunged it into the sea off Quarrel's Cliff.

Walking home that oddly still evening, Pazel remained a child, sniveling at the loss of a toy. But when he reached the stone house he found the courtyard packed with strangers. Big, sweat-soaked men. Gold helmets, shirts of metal plate, black spears crusted with gore. They were milling beneath his sister's orange tree, snatching fruit, breaking branches. On their shields was the gold fish-and-dagger symbol of Arqual. Chadfallow's brethren, come at last.

Children who have never known danger can sometimes grasp its essence in a heartbeat. Pazel stood there only an instant. Then he sprinted around the garden wall, climbed the grapevine at the corner, leaped onto the first-floor roof and slipped through his bedroom window.

The soldiers were in the kitchen downstairs, feasting and bellowing. Of his mother and Neda there was no sign. Pazel was barely eleven, but he saw clearly how everything that comprised his life would vanish into those snatching hands, that belching laughter, which were also Arqual: the real Arqual behind the doctor's finery and gifts. He took the skipper's knife his father had left him, and a thumb-sized ivory whale that had been his mother's nursery toy. Lost, he stood by his neatly made bed. He drank the water he had demanded the night before and then disdained, looking at his books and toy soldiers and model ships until the laughter reached the upstairs hall, and the doorknob turned, and Pazel fled.

From the plum orchards he saw the city burning, her great gates thrown down and the Arquali troops cheering from the wall. He saw twelve warships in port, and eight more stalled on the windless bay. The boom of cannon fire rolled up the hills, followed by the barking of dogs, hysterical and forlorn.

They caught him at dawn, quaking among the dew-damp trees. A gleeful corporal snatched the whale and the skipper's knife, then complained and kicked him because he hadn't kept the blade sharp. When he learned where Pazel lived the man kicked him again, and beat him. *Where are the women?* he screamed. *Two beautiful women! I want them!*

When Pazel made no answer the beating grew worse. He covered his head and tried not even to think of Neda or his mother. He feigned unconsciousness, but a point came when he was no longer pretending.

He awoke, bloodied, in a crowd of boys, some of whom he knew. They were all chained to the flagpole in his schoolyard, where a week before he had displayed the kite to jealous friends and boasted of his Arquali "uncle." On the roadside, Ormali captives passed by in horse carts, wearing heavy chains.

The days blurred to an aching trance. Once he woke to hear a voice shouting his name and looked up into the face of a man with mud in his hair and one eye bruised shut, who had somehow escaped his captors and rushed toward him. The apparition fell to his knees and touched Pazel's shoulder, wheezing as though about to expire: "Hold on, child, hold on!" The next instant two Arquali warriors fell on him with clubs. Only hours later did Pazel realize he had been looking at the headmaster.

That morning the soldiers marched them to the Slave Terrace at Ormaelport. The city had banned slavery in his grandfather's time; the Terrace had become a place where lovers watched the sea. But the old stockades where human beings were sold like sheep had never been dismantled, and the Arqualis saw their original purpose at a glance. In later years Pazel tried not to recall the horrors of that morning—the poking and haggling, the shrieks of pain and the sizzle of the branding iron, troublemakers beaten senseless or merely pushed into the harbor, chained. It was too awful; his mind tended to leap forward to the moment just before he himself was to be branded.

The boy just ahead of him was still screaming from the touch of the red-hot iron to the back of his neck, the slavemaster cursing as he pressed a shard of mountain ice to the welt to set the brand. Satisfied, he nodded to the men holding Pazel. But before they could chain him to the branding-post, an Arquali sergeant waded into the crowd and seized his arm.

"This one's already sold," he said.

He was an aging fighter, sighing at each step. He dragged Pazel to the far end of the Slave Terrace, then turned to look at the horrified boy.

"You've sailed?" he demanded.

Pazel opened his mouth, but no sound emerged. He had not spoken in two days.

"I asked if you've sailed."

"Sailed!" Pazel blurted. "No, sir, never. My father was Captain Gregory, but he didn't want me sailing. I'm a natural scholar, he said, and though I'm not a proud boy it's true I speak four languages, sir, and write three well enough for court, and know my complex sums, and he said I was not to be wasted on the mucking ocean when there was such a thing as school, which I rather enj—"

The sergeant slapped him with a leather-hard palm. "School's over, cub. Now listen: you sailed with your father, and you were never ill at sea. Repeat it."

"I . . . I sailed with my father, and I was never ill at sea."

The sergeant nodded gravely. "You ask the old men, the sheet-anchor men, to teach you your rigging, and your knots, and your shipboard stations, your whistles and flags. You'll be learning a new language, see? The language of a ship. Learn it fast, natural scholar, or you'll feel that iron yet."

Then he had put an envelope in Pazel's hand. It was a fine, gilt-edged envelope, sealed with wax the color of a rooster's comb and addressed in an elegant hand:

Captain Onnabik Faral
The Swan

"You'll hand this to Faral," said the sergeant. "None other. You listening, cub?"

"Yes, sir!" But Pazel could not take his eyes from the envelope. The writing looked familiar. But who would help him? Who could, with the city ablaze?

He raised his eyes—and saw the answer looking back at him. Across the Terrace, at a table outside the oystermen's pub, sat Dr. Ignus Chadfallow. In the squalid crowd he looked nobler than ever, like a prince wandered into a ragpickers' fair. Pazel would have run to him at once, but the sergeant grabbed his elbow.

Bending close to his ear, the old warrior said, not unkindly, "The sea's better than chains, lad, but it's a deadly place to be anyone's fool. Beware of smiles, eh?"

"What kind of smiles?"

"You'll know."

With that the sergeant lurched away, and Pazel sprinted to the pub. But Chadfallow was no longer at the table. Pazel rushed inside but found only soldiers and the regular boisterous girls, bouncing on Arquali instead of Ormali knees now. He fled, ran from the shipyard to the stockades and back to the pub, yet saw no trace of Chadfallow, nor ever again caught sight of him in Ormael. But on the chair where the doctor had been he found his mother's ivory whale and the skipper's knife—honed now to the sharpness of a razor.

Captain Faral took him on without question, and Pazel served more than a year on the merchant ship *Swan* as cook's aid and cabin boy. Just as the sergeant promised, the old sailors taught him his rigging, and knots, and a thousand unfamiliar words. *Capstan, spritsail, binnacle, boom:* he learned them all, and the roles they played in the great collective struggle that is sailing. Pazel was quick and good-mannered. His book-perfect Arquali made them laugh. But it puzzled them that he knew nothing of Arquali customs. Ormalis as a rule are more mystical than religious: Gregory Pathkendle had taught Pazel and Neda the sign of the Tree (the fist against the chest, opening smoothly as one raised it past the forehead), and drilled them in the first Nine of the Ninety Rules of the Rinfaith, and left it at that.

The old men of the *Swan* were indignant. "Tie him up! Leave him ashore! We'd be better off with crawlies aboard than this little savage!"

But few of them meant it. They taught him the simple but all-important prayer to Bakru, God of the winds, and were pleased when he swore to repeat it at every launch. They taught him never to laugh in the presence of a monk, never to turn his back on a temple door, never to eat at night without a glance up at the stars of the Milk Tree. They taught him his own job, too: how to fight the other tarboys for the right to freeze in a gale, swabbing rain out through the scuppers before it could leach into the hold, spreading sawdust on the quarterdeck for footing, mending ropes before anyone ordered him to do so.

They were patient, these old men. They had survived plague, scurvy, wax-eye blindness, the talking fever that killed one sailor in three during the reign of Magad IV, cholera, cyclones, war. Being old and penniless meant that they had also survived their own ambitions, and no longer blamed the world for each thwarting incident, as young men do. In his heart Pazel thanked the nameless soldier a thousand times for directing him to their care.

The *Swan* took him east, into the heart of Arqual. She had been pressed into service as a troop-carrier, but with the seizure of Ormael complete her captain returned quietly to trade, mostly in the bays of Emledri and Sorhn. Pazel supposed he would never see his mother or sister again, even if they had somehow dodged slavery and death. It was dangerous to think of them too often: when he did he became clumsy with grief, his mind filling with a bright, cold fog that frightened him. In any case there was nothing he could do.

When Captain Faral became a drunkard, Pazel found himself

transferred to another ship, the *Anju,* so abruptly he had no time
even to take leave of the old men who had taught him the ways
of the sea. This time rumor preceded him: the other tarboys
knew that some wealthy doctor had paid off the *Swan* and
arranged for Pazel to be seized like a mailbag (as indeed he
was) and flung into life aboard the *Anju.* Pazel was furious with
Chadfallow. The *Anju* was a nastier ship in every sense: a
whaler that stank of burned blubber and echoed with the laughs
of men whose lives were butchery on a giant scale. Pazel hated
it from the first. But a month after his transfer, a deckhand returned from shore leave with the news that the *Swan* had mean-
dered in a fog onto the Lava Shoals at Urnsfich, shattering her
keel and sinking in a matter of minutes. Of her ninety sailors,
just three had made it to shore.

Life on the *Anju* was a terror. She leaked badly and her bilge-
pumps clogged with whale grease. Her captain was violent and
feared his own shadow. On calm days he lowered tarboys into
the frigid seas to check for sabotage by murths or saltworms.
During lightning storms he sent them aloft to tie live chickens
to the topmasts, offerings to the demons of the sky.

None of these dangers ever touched the whaling vessel. Her
end came when the crew, their wits addled by spoiled rye, sailed
her at ludicrous speed into Pól Harbor, where she would have
rammed a Kings' clipper if the shore guns had not blown her to
bits.

The Noonfirth Kings shipped the dazed crew back to Etherhorde, where her captain was beheaded, and Pazel transferred to
a grain ship. After that, an ore-carrier, a barge on the River
Sorhn, a signal-boat guiding warships through the Paulandri
Shoals. Finally, just six months earlier, he had been assigned to
the *Eniel.* After each of these transfers, a rumor would eventually inform him that a certain nobleman, a brooding fellow with
gray temples, had made the arrangements. But Chadfallow
never sent so much as a word of greeting to Pazel himself.

In the past half year Pazel had come to love Captain Nestef.
The old navigator adored his ship and wanted a peaceable crew.

They ate well, and had music after meals, and in each port the captain bought stories or travelogues or collections of jokes from the chandleries, and read them aloud on dull nights far from land.

Of course, he was still Ormali. Jervik in particular took care that no one forgot it. He despised Ormalis—despised anyone to whom he felt superior—and just last week had stolen his skipper's knife and ivory whale, the only objects Pazel cared about in the world. They would be Jervik's forever now.

But Nestef's kindness had made it all bearable. The captain had even talked of buying Pazel his citizenship, and helping him return to school. The very thought of *reading* again filled Pazel's mind with dazzling hopes.

And now Chadfallow had blasted them. He didn't know why the doctor was interfering again, but this time he had plucked Pazel from the best ship he could ever have hoped for. And *what* had he slipped into that tea?

He stood, threw a last nail into the water and turned to face the wharf. A new life: that was what he was choosing. A life without Arquali uncles. Without their protection, or their deceit.

6

Almost Free

Niriviel, the moon falcon, shot by overhead, a cream-colored arrow. On the bench beside the splendid catfish tanks of the Lorg Academy of Obedient Daughters, the girl with blond hair felt her heart lift at the sight, and then an instant's regret at the thought that she would never see him again. An instant was all she could muster, for while she loved the falcon, she hated the Academy a thousand times more.

Behind her, a woman cleared her throat. The blond girl looked over her shoulder to see one of the Lorg Sisters frowning at her in silence. In her dark brown robe the Sister's face seemed whiter than the lilies in the tanks; whiter than the fish weaving slow paths among the stems.

"Good evening, Sister," said the girl.

"Her Grace will see you in the hatcheries," said the woman tersely.

Startled, the girl rose to her feet.

"After your meditation, child!"

The Sister turned on her heel and stalked off. The girl sat again, sidelong to hide her face from the Academy windows, and pressed her knuckles hard against the wrought-iron bench. A meeting with the Mother Prohibitor! It was a rare honor: girls did not have private audiences with the head of the Order except for the gravest of reasons. *It's a trap,* she told herself. *I knew they'd try something.*

The *Accateo,* as the Sisters liked to call it, was the most costly and exclusive school for girls in the Imperium. Also the oldest, which partly explained the Sisters' tendency to speak Old Arquali, and dress in cloaks like funeral wraps, and to serve dishes (horse-liver puddings, starling broth) that had vanished from even the most traditional Etherhorde dining rooms a century ago.

Also the loneliest, thought the girl, warming to her theme.

Also the darkest, cruelest, most ignorant heap of stone ever to disgrace the word *school.*

Her name was Thasha Isiq, and she was dropping out. It ought to have been the happiest day of the two years she had spent at the Lorg. Two years without a glimpse of father or friends, without hearing the ocean or climbing Maj Hill. Two years without laughing, except softly in corners, and at the risk of punishment.

But she could not rejoice in her coming freedom, not yet. The Sisters' power was too great. They woke you with their songs (guttural chants recounting the evil history of womankind); they studied your private journals, not just openly but with a red quill for correcting your grammar; they questioned you about your dreams; they compared you with the impossibly pure First Sisters in the time of the Amber Kings; they gave you chores in house or gardens, along with meditations to recite nonstop while doing so. Then came breakfast. And after that, the real labor: your education.

Thasha had known nothing about the Academy when Syrarys, her father's consort, announced that she was to be enrolled. When she realized Syrarys meant the walled compound with the grim towers and fanged iron gate, she refused outright. A great battle followed between daughter and consort, and Thasha lost. Or rather, surrendered: her father's illness, a brain inflammation that had lasted years, suddenly worsened, and the family doctor told her bluntly that Eberzam Isiq would not recover unless he was spared, temporarily at least, the work and worries of fatherhood.

To Thasha the diagnosis stank of trickery. Syrarys hated her, though she pretended love. And Thasha had never quite trusted Dr. Chadfallow, friend to the Emperor though he was.

The welcome letter from the Academy promised lessons in music, dance and literature, and for a while Thasha took heart, for she had dearly loved all three subjects. Today she almost hated them.

The trouble was evil. It was the great obsession of the Sisters, and with it they poisoned everything they touched. "Literature" meant poring together over the journals of former students, now wives in the richest households across the known world: journals that recorded in humiliating detail each woman's lifelong struggle against the inherent wickedness of her nature. "Dance" meant mastering the stiff waltzes and quadrilles of society balls, or the erotic performances certain families demanded of brides for twelve nights before their weddings. "Music" just meant sin. Confession of sin in whining arias. Regret for sin in madrigals that never ended. Memory of sin in low, groveling groans.

For close to a thousand years, the *Accateo* had spiritually mangled girls. They entered jittery, wide-eyed waifs; they left docile dreamers, hypnotized by the epic of their own rottenness and the lifelong struggle ahead to become slightly less so. Thasha looked over at a girl her own age, pruning the roses a few yards away: eyes heavy with lack of sleep, lips moving ceaselessly with her assigned meditation. Now and then she smiled, as if at some happy secret. A pretty girl, of course.

Thasha shuddered. It could have been her. It *would* have been her, if she had stayed much longer. When a single story about the world pursues you all day, every day, and even prowls the edges of your dreamlands, it soon becomes hard to remember that that story is just one among many. You hear no others, and if you remember them at all, it is like remembering snowflakes in the midst of a steaming jungle: silly, fantastic, almost unreal.

Of course, that was exactly the point.

But even as these thoughts came to her, Thasha felt a stab of guilt. Hadn't the Sisters themselves taught her all this about her

mind? This, and a thousand other lessons? That there was more
to love in this world than gossip and rich food and a dress from
the Apsal Street tailors? And she thanked them with hate. By
detesting them, laughing at them inwardly. By slandering them
to her father. By dropping out.

She looked down at her hands. There was an ugly scar on her
left palm that looked as though it had been made with a jagged
stick. Almost two years ago, on her fifteenth night in the Lorg,
Thasha had run to this bench in tears, guilt like she had never
dreamed of hammering in her chest: guilt for existing, for not
loving the Sisters as they loved her, for letting her father waste
his fortunes in sending her here, where she spat on every opportunity. Guilt for questioning the Sisters, guilt for trying not
to feel guilty. It was unendurable, this guilt, even before the
elder Sisters caught up with her. We warned you, they said. We
told you exactly what you would feel. A girl who chooses to be
weak may hide the truth, but her heart knows. What does it
know? That its owner is a vain and useless blight upon the earth.
A canker. A parasite. Tell us we're wrong, girl. Thasha could only
sob as they prattled on, adding up reasons for grief, and then she
reached out and snapped off a brittle rose stem and drove it
straight through her left hand.

The Sisters shrieked; one hit her on the back of the head; but
the act of mutilation saved Thasha's life. She knew it: another
minute and she would have died of self-loathing. As it was her
head cleared instantly, and she thought, *How obvious, how brilliant, to make us love them for torturing us!* And before the
Sisters marched her to the infirmary Thasha swore that however
long she stayed, she would think her own thoughts and feel her
own feelings when she sat on that bench.

Yes, she had become a woman here. By fighting them.

Thasha rose now, and with grateful fingers bid her bench goodbye. Then she turned and moved swiftly toward the fish hatcheries. She could see the Mother Prohibitor's red cloak through the
translucent glass. *Don't explode, don't attack her,* she thought.
You're almost free.

Some girls would never know freedom again. The Lorg had no graduation process. You simply stayed until you found a way of leaving, and there were not many of those. You could drop out in highest disgrace, which was Thasha's choice, even though the furious Sisters had promised to warn every other school in the city of her "spiritual deformities." You could murder a Sister, which was slightly less disgraceful. You could be recalled by your parents, as Thasha had begged her father to do in fifty-six letters, starting her first night in the Lorg. You could (this was Thasha's invention) climb Sister Ipoxia's weeping cherry until the rubbery tree bent over with your weight and dropped you over the wall; but the local constables had sharp eyes, and hauled runaways back to the Academy at once, for which they received the blessings of the Mother Prohibitor and a handful of coins.

Or you could marry. This was the one entirely legitimate way out of the Lorg. The school sponsored two Love Carnivals a year, when the Sisters dropped their teaching, gardening, wine-making and catfish cultivation to become frenetic, full time matchmakers. One of these started in just three days: by then Thasha wanted to be far from the Lorg. Her timing had enraged the Mother Prohibitor. Someone had heard her shout in the vestry: "Three hundred men seeking Love Conferences, and she renounces? What are we to tell the nine who put her at the top of their lists?"

(*Nine suitors,* girls had whispered behind Thasha's back. *And she's only sixteen.*)

As the Sister who taught Erotic Dance had told them yesterday (exhausted into something like honesty; her skills were in great demand this time of year), one needn't be rich to attend the Lorg. The school also recognized merit—that is, beauty. Thasha's classmates included a number of exceptionally lovely girls from modest households. Not a bad investment for the Lorg: what their families could not pay, their future husbands would gladly make up for in matchmaking fees.

It was a thriving enterprise. The girls nearly always consented. Marriage to a wealthy stranger felt like charity once you believed you deserved nothing more than contempt.

The Mother Prohibitor was a lanky, quick-moving old woman; in her red rector's cloak she put one in mind of a scarlet ibis looking for dinner among the tanks of newly hatched fish. When Thasha opened the door of the glass house enclosing the tanks she looked up sharply, and gestured with a dripping hand-net.

"My eyes begin to fail me," she said, in her surprisingly deep voice. "Look at their tail spines, girl. Are they yellow?"

Thasha gathered her cloak and knelt by the tank. "Most are yellow-tailed, Your Grace. But there are some with green stripes. Very pretty fish, they'll be."

"We must catch them. Those green ones. All of them, right now."

She held out the net. Thasha noted the great emerald ring on the woman's pale hand. Girls gossiped about that ring: it bore the words *DRANUL VED BRISTÓLJET DORO*—Where thou goest, I follow fast—in silver Old Arquali script about the priceless gem. Some girls thought the phrase a magic charm. Others held that it was the motto of a secret order, not the Lorg merely but some guild of crones scattered across the world and elbow-deep in the plots and schemes and stratagems that ruled it. Thasha felt the old woman watching her. She took the net from her hand.

The tank was shallow, and Thasha caught the dozen or so green-tailed hatchlings in a matter of minutes, dropping them one by one into a bucket next to the Mother Prohibitor.

"They will not be pretty fish, Thasha Isiq," said the old woman when she was done. "They will not be any sort of fish much longer. The *Accateo* now specializes in bili catfish, these yellow-tails. A more succulent meat, they have. They fetch an excellent price, and the Slugdra ghost-doctors will also pay for their intestines, which they use in love potions. There, Sister Catarh has brought your street clothes."

Thasha looked up quickly at the Sister in the doorway, who set down a bundle tied with string, bowed and withdrew.

"I will thank you not to grin like an imbecile," said the Mother Prohibitor. "Get up! So you're leaving. Did you meditate this morning on your tragically altered fortunes?"

"I did, Your Grace."

"You're lying, naturally," said the old woman, her tone matter-of-fact as she churned the water of the tank with her cane. Thasha bit her tongue. Legend held that the Mother Prohibitor felt a needle in her side whenever a girl lied in her presence. Thasha hoped for a few more opportunities.

"Failure," the Mother Prohibitor was saying, "is not an accident. Not a thug who grabs you in an alley. It is a liaison in a darkened house. It is a choice."

"Yes, Your Grace."

"Be still. The bane of that choice will pursue you. Though you flee to the ends of the earth, it will dog your heels."

Really, thought Thasha. We live just nine blocks away.

The Mother Prohibitor took a letter from her robe and studied it, as one might a fruit gone suddenly and swiftly rotten. "Failure withers the lives of those who choose it. That is why it has no place in our curriculum. Only two girls this century have left in disgrace. I praise your good father"—she raised the letter—"that he has kept you from becoming the third."

"He sent for me!" The words burst out of Thasha before she could stop herself.

"While you wear that robe you are a Lorg Daughter, and will obey me," said the Mother Prohibitor. "Yes, he sent for you. Do you know why?"

"Perhaps he misses me, Your Grace. I *know* he does."

The old woman just looked at her.

"Are you of the faith, child?" she asked. "Do you believe that there is a Tree in Heaven, the Milk Tree as we name it, and that this world of Alifros is but one of its fair fruits that in time must ripen and fall, or be picked by Rin's own hand?"

Thasha swallowed. "I don't know, Your Grace."

The old woman sighed. "The truth will find you, if you are half the young woman you seem. Go now with our blessing, and know that the voices of your sisters old and young will be raised in song, that the Angel who guides all honest pilgrims will bring you safe to distant shores."

Stunned, Thasha lowered her eyes. She had expected curses, humiliation. In the school hymnal, the canticles for dropouts read like death sentences. To invoke the Angel of Rin . . .

"Do you see that box on the workbench? Bring it here. I have two gifts ere you depart."

Thasha fetched the box, about the size of a hatbox. At the old woman's command she untied the string and lifted the lid. Inside was a buckled leather pouch, and within the pouch, a book. Thasha turned it in her hands. The book was old and very thick: four inches thick, but not heavy in the least. Its smooth black leather bore no words at all.

Thasha was struck first by the paper, which was so thin she could see her hand through a page if she lifted it alone, but sharp and white when laid against the rest.

"Dragonfly-wing leaf," said the old woman. "The thinnest paper in the world." Taking the book from Thasha, she opened it to the first page and held it up:

The Merchant's Polylex:
5,400 Pages of Wisdom
13th Edition

"You will remember the number thirteen," said the Mother Prohibitor. Then she ripped out the page. Greatly confused, Thasha watched her tear it into many pieces and drop them into the bucket with the dying catfish. "Have you seen a *Polylex* before?" the woman asked.

"Lots of them," said Thasha. "My father has—"

"The newest edition. Of course he does. Every sailing man of means owns a *Polylex,* if he owns any book at all. It is a traveler's companion—an encyclopedia, dictionary and history of the world, written and rewritten over centuries and published anew every twenty years. What are you thinking?"

Thasha blushed. "I'm sorry, Your Grace. My father says the *Merchant's Polylex* is full of rubbish and rot."

The Mother Prohibitor frowned, so that her eyebrows met like crossed knives. "This particular copy is rare. Some would call it priceless. Keep it near you—and read it now and again, girl. Decide for yourself what is rubbish, and what is gold. Now put it away, and show me that hand of yours."

Thasha knew which hand she meant. The old woman turned it palm-up and traced the old wound with her fingers. Thasha's mind was a-whirl. Why would the Mother Prohibitor make her such a gift when she had barely dodged disgrace? Why were they talking at all?

"Somewhere in the *Polylex,*" said the Mother Prohibitor, "you will find a legend from the old kingdom of Nohirin about another girl with a wounded hand. She was called Erithusmé, and she was born without fear. She laughed at earthquakes, crawled under elephants' feet, ran into burning fields to admire the flames. But on her sixteenth birthday the king of Nohirin came with his warriors and took her away to the north of that land, a place of ice-sheathed mountains, and ordered her to enter a high cave and fetch out what she found there.

"The king knew well what she would find: a magical weapon called the Nilstone, one of the great horrors of history. None knew whence it came. Out of the gullet of a dragon, said some. Fallen from the moon or a wander-star, others claimed. But all agreed that it was evil. The king's own great-grandfather had hurled it into the cave, and for a century no one who ventured within had returned alive. But fearless as ever, Erithusmé went in, braving pits and ice-weirds and darkness, and at last she found the Nilstone.

"It lay surrounded by frozen corpses—all the men the king had sent before her, slain the instant their fingers touched the cursed device. But when the girl lifted it she felt only a tiny pin-prick on her hand. And when she took it from the cave she was possessed of powers beyond any mage in Alifros. With a word she scattered the king's army; with a snap of her fingers she called up a gryphon to bear her away. For three years Erithusmé flew from land to land, working magic such as none had ever seen. Here she quelled a plague; there she made springs flow where sandstorms had raged the day before.

"But all did not go well. She stoppered a volcano, and three others exploded nearby. She drove the old king of Nohirin from power, and nine evil princes fought for his throne, begging her aid to slay one another. And she found that the stone had begun to burn her palm where she held it. Confused, Erithusmé flew to the sacred isle of Rappopolni, and entered the Dawn Temple there, and knelt before the high priestess.

"Extending her hand, she said, 'I can work miracles; why can I not heal this little burn?' The priestess replied: 'Because even you, my daughter, are not entirely free of fear. No man or woman can be. Through fear the Nilstone is poisoning you, and turning your good deeds to ruin. Your choices are but two: cast it away and become yourself again, or keep it and die.'"

The Mother Prohibitor still held Thasha's hand. Thasha waited, barely breathing.

"A legend," the old woman said at last. "And a warning, for some. You may look up the ending in your spare time. Now then, my other gift is a reminder. A Lorg Daughter is never alone. On the path you are doomed to tread, one of us at least will be near you. Remember, Thasha: in dire need you may call upon her; she cannot refuse. Now I must work. Is there anything you would ask me?"

Thasha blinked. To her amazement, she felt like crying. "My P-Promissory Tree, Your Grace. Must I kill it, with my own hand?"

Every girl entering the Lorg planted a cherry tree in the Promissory Orchard, which filled half the compound and was now in radiant bloom. Dropouts had to uproot their saplings and chop them to bits.

The Mother Prohibitor looked at her for a silent time. Then she raised her hand and made the sign of the Tree over Thasha's head.

"It has taken root, child," she said at last. "I think we must let it grow."

She turned her back without another word. Thasha left the hatchery, nearly blubbering. She loved them! Which was madness! She couldn't wait to be gone. Was it possible the old woman realized that kindness would hurt longer than cruelty as a parting gift? Or was she, Thasha, so plainly ugly inside that she saw even peace gestures as attacks?

Did they know her better than she knew herself?

Almost running, she made her way through the Great Hall. Earlier that day she had sent her belongings by coach, and made her goodbyes, which were bitter. The few friends she had told Thasha she was abandoning them. Could she deny it?

At the gatehouse the ward-sister let her into a small changing room. Alone, Thasha dried her eyes and untied her bundle of clothes. She laughed: there were the man's shirt and breeches, and even the longshoreman's cap. She had worn all these to the gate two years ago, in protest at her banishment. They were a little snug now.

When she had changed, she stepped out of the room and surrendered her school cloak.

"I'll keep it safe for you," said the ward-sister.

This was taking ceremony too far, Thasha thought. But she bowed her thanks, and the woman unlocked a small door in the fanged gate, and Thasha stepped out, free, into an exquisite summer evening and a breeze off the Ool.

She took three happy steps—and froze. A thought struck her like a boot to the shins.

She walked back to the gate. "Ward-sister!" she called. "You say you'll keep my cloak safe? What for?"

The woman looked over her shoulder. "Don't be obtuse, child. For wearing."

Thasha drew a deep breath. "Yes, Sister, for wearing. I apologize for my imprecision."

"Quite so. Good night."

"Sister, please, I meant to ask, *who* are you keeping—"

"Whom!"

"*Whom, whom,* yes," said Thasha, squeezing her eyes shut. "*Whom* are you keeping it for?"

"*For whom* is preferable, of course. Whatever is the matter, child—are you ill? We shall keep it for you."

"But I'm not coming back."

The Sister clucked impatiently. "The letter from your father's, your father's . . . from the Lady Syrarys announces quite plainly his request for your temporary removal from—"

"Temporary!" shouted Thasha.

"With the aim of improving your manners, no doubt!" snapped the ward-sister. "Three feet beyond the gate and she starts interrupting! May the Angel forgive you! A charwoman's girl would know better, but not the ambassador's daughter, no, she—"

"Ambassador!"

"Miss Thasha, you are screeching my words back at me like a circus macaw! For the last time I bid you *good night*!"

Thasha ran as she had not run since fleeing the constable, the leather pouch under her arm. All the bright life of Etherhorde—laughing boys in a fountain, old men throwing knackerballs on a close-trimmed lawn, a sourdough heat from the baker's door, Nunekkam flutes in the shadows like whistlers in a cave—all this she barely noticed despite two years of longing for it. Suddenly the evening made a horrid kind of sense. They meant to send her back! Thasha knew it had never happened before: the *Accateo* did not grant leaves of absence. It had to be her father. Only he could be influential enough to challenge seven centuries of rust-rigid practice.

Eberzam Isiq was a retired admiral, commander of not just a ship but a whole fleet that had swept down the Chereste Coast five years ago, from Ulsprit to a place called Ormael. What was it all about? Killing pirates, some said. Killing rebels, traitors to the Imperium, said others. Her father had just chuckled and said it was a matter of opinion.

But everyone seemed to agree that it had been a mighty victory, and that her father was the hero of the campaign. At banquets, fat dukes and generals pressed their wine-sour lips to Thasha's cheek. *Such an elegant girl! Eberzam has the Gods' own luck!* They said her father would make Prefect of Etherhorde one day, or perhaps governor of one of the greater Arquali territories. It made little difference to Thasha. All she knew was that her father had come back wounded—struck in the head by a fragment of cannonball—and that his illness began shortly thereafter.

He was better now, or so the letters from Syrarys claimed (Eberzam himself had written just twice, on her birthdays). But an ambassadorship? That meant sailing beyond the Empire, didn't it? And why send an old warrior across oceans to speak for Arqual?

Obeying a sudden impulse, Thasha crossed the road, climbed a low fence and dropped into Gallows Park. It was darker under the park's old oaks and conifers, but it would save her five blocks. She ran downhill, barely glancing at the famous wishing-well (some girl was always crying there, ostentatiously), or the melted iron lump that was a monument to the Heroic Blacksmiths, or the glowing webs of the torch spiders luring moths into the trees. At last she reached the Ool, flanked here by a ruined wall left over from days when bandits still dared to cross the river into Etherhorde. A few fishermen crouched among the gloomy stones. Otherwise the park looked deserted.

If it was her father who wrote to the Lorg, Thasha decided, it was Syrarys who put the pen in his hand. Every year they were together her influence over the admiral grew. And although she had never spoken of it, Thasha was all but convinced that Syrarys was behind the decision to send her away in the first place.

How long had they told the Sisters she would be gone? A month? A week?

I'll change his mind, she thought. *I have to, I—*

"Pah! Too easy!"

An arm caught her broadside across the chest. From the corner of her eye she saw a tall man step through a gap in the ruined wall. The arm that had stopped her slid to her throat and jerked her toward the gap.

No time to think. Thasha drove an elbow into the man's side, twisted out from under his arm and flung herself backward and away. Her fists were raised to strike him again. But she was off-balance, winded by his first blow. Some root or stone caught her heel, and she fell.

Instantly the man was on her. A knee pinned her legs to the ground. A dagger! In the fastest act of her life Thasha flailed at the blade as the man stabbed downward. But she was not fast enough. It was over, and she'd barely felt it. The knife was buried to the hilt in her chest.

"Dead," said the man. "Dead for a five-penny sweet."

One shock chased another: she was still breathing, she felt no pain, she appeared unharmed. Strangest of all, the face of her attacker belonged to a friend.

"Hercól! You monster!"

"You are quick," said the man, "and stronger than I recall. But carelessness trumps both speed and muscle. It is one thing to scurry through a park at night, another to do so with your mind in a fog."

"I was so anxious to get home."

The man's eyebrows rose. "If you dare make excuses to *me*."

"No excuses. I'm sorry, Hercól, I failed. May I get up now?"

The man lifted a hilt without a blade from her chest, then rose and helped her to her feet. He was a slender, elfin-eyed man in middle years, with unruly hair and somewhat threadbare clothes. Now that he was no longer attacking her he assumed a cordial air, folding his hands behind his back and smiling fondly. Thasha looked at her chest: bits of a glittering something clung to her blouse.

"Sugar knife," said Hercól. "A very popular candy. Boys across the city play with those foul things, more's the pity."

"I never thought my first fight would be with you."

"Be glad it was."

Hercól Stanapeth was her old dance instructor, from the days before the Lorg. But Thasha had learned (from certain military cousins) that he also taught fighting—that he was, in fact, from Tholjassa, where princes the world over sent for bodyguards. The cousins whispered of great deeds at arms, long ago, but Hercól would not speak of his past. He also refused to give her fighting lessons, until she began paying bullies in the street for black eyes and bloody noses. She did not fool him with this tactic, but she did convince him of her desire to learn. His price: strictest secrecy, even from her father. If there was no law against training girls to hit and kick and use knives, it was merely because such an outrage had not occurred to anyone.

"Let us be off," he said. "Even I do not linger here after dark."

They set off along the Ool. Bats skimmed low over the water, feasting on flies. In the south the countless stars that made up the Milk Tree were starting to wink above the hills.

"My letters reached you?" Thasha asked.

Hercól nodded. "I commend your decision, Thasha. The Lorg is an abomination. And of course I am happy to see you myself. What's that you're carrying?"

Thasha handed him the leather pouch, now slightly muddied. "It's just an old *Merchant's Polylex*. The Mother Prohibitor just gave it to me. She told me a strange story from it as well, about a girl called Erithusmé and her Nilstone."

"She spoke to you of the Nilstone!" said Hercól sharply. "I dare say you won't find mention of that in the *Polylex*."

"The Mother Prohibitor said I would," said Thasha. "But don't worry, I know the book can't be trusted. And this one's the thirteenth edition, so it's completely out of date."

Hercól's hand froze. "You mean of course the fourteenth edition. Or the twelfth?"

Thasha shook her head. "The thirteenth. I saw the title page, before the Mother Prohibitor tore it out. Why she did that I can't imagine—she said it was one of the most valuable books in the school."

"*The* most valuable, I should think. And the most dangerous. Put it away." He handed it back to her.

They walked on, Hercól frowning slightly. At last he spoke again.

"You're right, of course. A normal *Polylex* is a hotchpotch: the work of brilliant explorers and charlatans, geniuses and frauds, all bound together in a single volume. The newest version, for instance, declares quite seriously that Tholjassans cannot be harmed by Tholja stingrays. Trust me, we can.

"But the thirteenth *Polylex* is an entirely different matter. Each book is written by the Ocean Explorers' Guild, which is an ancient club of sailors and businessmen here in Etherhorde. His Supremacy the Emperor is their honorary president, and approves each new *Polylex* before it is sold. No one took the book seriously until a century ago, when the thirteenth *Polylex* was written. Its editor was a man named Pazel Doldur. He was the brightest historian of his time—and the first in his family ever to go to school. They were poor folk: his father and elder brother joined the army because no one starved in uniform. Both were killed in mountain campaigns. Afterward his heartbroken mother sent Doldur to the university, on 'gold the Emperor pays to widows and mothers,' she claimed. As I say, he was brilliant, and studied hard. But his mother soon grew ill and died. It was only decades later, when he was starting work on the *Polylex,* that Doldur learned she had given her body to lords and princes in the Emperor's court, night after night, in exchange for his school money. Her disease came from one of those men."

"How perfectly ghastly!"

Hercól nodded. "Doldur lost his mind with guilt. But he devised a brilliant revenge. It took many years, but he transformed the *Polylex* into an honest book: honest enough to shame all the wicked men alive, his Emperor included. It told of slave profits and deathsmoke peddlers. It revealed the existence of the Prison

Isle of Licherog—imagine, there was a time when no one knew of the place! It told how merchants buy children from the Flikkermen to work in factories and mines. It named the massacres, the burned villages and other crimes of war that kings had worked so hard to make their subjects forget.

"All this he hid, in bits and pieces, within the usual five thousand pages of flotsam. And the Emperor never noticed. Perhaps he never read a word. In any case, he quickly gave Doldur his blessing. The thirteenth *Polylex* was copied and sold.

"The scandal tore this Empire apart: others *did* read carefully, you see. Within a year, Doldur had been executed, and nearly every copy of his book tracked down and burned. Merely to speak of a thirteenth edition was dangerous. To be caught with one was punished by death."

"Death!" cried Thasha. "Hercól, why on earth would the Mother Prohibitor give such a book to *me*?"

"A fine question. Twenty years have passed since I last heard of someone caught with that book. An old witch, I believe. On Pulduraj."

"What happened to her?"

"She was tied to a dead mule and thrown into the sea."

Thasha stared at the innocent-looking pouch. "I *knew* they didn't like me," she said.

They crossed the footbridge over the old millers' canal. Hercól touched his closed fist to his forehead, as she had seen him do at the center of other bridges: a Tholjassan custom, he had told her, but what it signified he would not say.

After a few minutes the words burst out of her: "What should I do with this blary thing?"

Hercól shrugged. "Burn it. Or read it, learn from it, live with the danger of possessing it. Or take it to the authorities and condemn the Mother Prohibitor to death."

"You're a big help."

"Moral choice is not my sphere of instruction."

Thasha's face lit up suddenly. "Hercól! When can our fighting lessons start again?"

Hercól did not return her smile. "Not soon, I'm afraid. Much is happening in this city, and for good or ill I have become a part of it. The fact is I must leave you in a few minutes, and before that I have something to say. Something it were best you told your father, and soon."

He led her away from the river and into a dark stand of firs. Stopping by a large tree, he crouched low and motioned for her to do the same.

"Your family is being watched, Thasha," he whispered. "The admiral, the Lady, Nama and the other servants—now you as well. Somehow they knew you were leaving the Lorg tonight. If one good thing came of your rash plunge into this park, it is that you lost your watcher. You very nearly lost me."

"Watching us? Why?" Thasha was astounded. "Is this about what the ward-sister mentioned? An ambassadorship?"

Hercól shook his head. "Don't ask me to speculate. And the fewer people you speak to about your father's business, the better. Come now, if you tarry longer they will know you met someone in the park."

They rose and walked on, fir needles crunching underfoot. Ahead, the glow of fengas lamps pierced the trees.

"Hercól," said Thasha, "do you have *any* idea who they are?"

Hercól's voice was uncertain. "There was one, a man I thought I knew, but that is hardly possible—" He shook his head, as if dispelling a bad dream. They had reached the edge of the firs. "Tell your father," he said. "And Thasha: tell him when he's alone, will you? Quite alone?"

Without Syrarys, she supposed he meant. Thasha promised she would.

Hercól smiled. "I nearly forgot—Ramachni sends his compliments."

"Ramachni!" Thasha gripped his arm. "Ramachni's back? How is he? Where has he *been*?"

"Ask him yourself. He is waiting in your chamber."

Thasha was overjoyed. "Oh, Hercól! This is a good sign, isn't it?"

Again her teacher hesitated. "Ramachni is a friend like no other," he said, "but I would not call his visits a good sign. Let us say rather that he comes at need. Still, he was in a jolly mood tonight. He even wished to come out into the city, but I forbade it. His greeting could not have been as . . . inconspicuous as my own."

"Inconspicuous!" Thasha laughed. "You tried to kill me!"

Hercól's smile faded at the word *kill*. "Walk straight home," he said. "Or run, if you wish. But don't look back at me. I shall visit when I can."

"What's happening, Hercól?"

"That question troubles my sleep, dear one. And I have no answer. Yet."

He found her hand in the darkness and squeezed it. Then he turned and vanished among the trees.

The old sentry at her garden gate bowed with the same flourish as two years ago. Thasha would have hugged him if she hadn't known what embarrassment the man would suffer. Instead she hugged Jorl and Suzyt, the blue mastiffs who waddled down the marble stairs to greet her, whimpering with impatience at their arthritic hips. They were her oldest friends, and slobbered magnificently to remind her of it. Laughing despite herself, she finally broke away from them and faced the house again.

In the doorway above her stood the Lady Syrarys. She was beautiful, in the lush Ulluprid Isles way of beauty: dark, smoldering eyes, full lips that seemed on the point of sharing some delicious secret, a cascade of straight black hair. She was half the admiral's age, or younger.

"There, darling," she said, as those gorgeous lips formed a smile. "Out of school for one hour and you're muddier than the dogs themselves. I won't kiss you until you've washed. Come in!"

"Is he really going to be an ambassador?" said Thasha, who hadn't moved.

"My dear, he already is. He took the oath Thursday at His

Supremacy's feet. You should have seen him, Thasha. Handsome as a king himself."

"Why didn't he *tell* me? Ambassador to where?"

"To Simja—have you heard of it? Wedged between our Empire and the enemy's, imagine. They say Mzithrinis walk the streets in war-paint! We didn't tell you because the Emperor demanded strict secrecy."

"I wouldn't have told anyone!"

"But you said yourself the Sisters read your mail. Come in, come in! Nama will be calling us to table."

Thasha climbed the stairs and followed her into the big shadowy house, angry already. It was true that she'd complained of her letters arriving open and disordered. Syrarys had laughed and called her a worry-wart. But now she believed: now that those worries suited her purposes.

Thasha had no doubt what the consort's purposes amounted to. Syrarys meant to leave her behind, and wanted her to have as little time as possible to change her father's mind. *And if I hadn't been dropping out? Would they have left without saying goodbye?*

Never. She could never believe that of her father.

Watching Syrarys, she asked casually, "How soon do we sail?"

If the consort felt the least surprise, she hid it perfectly. "The *Chathrand* should be here within a week, and sail just a few days later."

Thasha stopped dead. "The *Chathrand*! They're sending him to Simja on the *Chathrand*?"

"Didn't the Sisters tell you? Yes, they're finally treating your father with the respect he's earned. Quite the expedition, it's going to be. An honor guard's been assembled for your father. And Lady Lapadolma is sending her niece along to represent the Trading Family. You remember Pacu, of course?"

Thasha winced. Pacu Lapadolma was her former schoolmate. She had escaped the Lorg ten months ago by marrying a colonel in the Strike Cavalry two decades her senior. A fortnight later she was a widow: the colonel's stallion, maddened by wasps, kicked him in the chest; he died without a sound, apparently.

"Hasn't she remarried yet?" asked Thasha.

"Oh no," Syrarys answered, laughing. "There was talk of an engagement, a Duke Somebody of Sorhn, but then came proposals from the Earl of Ballytween and the owner of the Mangel Beerworks and the animal-trader Latzlo, who was so mad for Pacu that he sent her a bouquet of five hundred white roses and fifty weeping snow-larks, all trained to cry her name. Pacu didn't care for any of them—said they all looked alike."

"Of course they did."

"The suitors, dear, not the birds. Luckily her great-aunt stepped in. By the time Pacu gets back even Latzlo may have forgotten her."

"I'm going with you," said Thasha.

Syrarys laughed again, touching her arm. "You are the *sweetest* girl."

Knowing very well that she was not, Thasha repeated: "I'm going."

"Poor Jorl and Suzyt. They'll have no one, then."

"Use any trick you like," said Thasha evenly, "but this time I'm going to win."

"Win? Trick? Oh, Thasha darling, we've no cause to start down that road. Come, I'll kiss you despite your dirt. My little *Thashula*."

It was her babytalk-name, from long ago when they were close. Thasha considered it a low tactic. Nonetheless they pecked each other's cheeks.

Thasha said, "I won't cause trouble in Simja. I have grown up."

"How delightful. Is that a promise to stop throwing your cousins into hedges?"

"I didn't throw him! He fell!"

"Who wouldn't have, dear, after the thumping you gave him? Poor young man, the lasting damage was to his pride. Knocked silly by a girl who barely reached his shoulder. Come, your father is in the summerhouse. Let's surprise him."

Thasha followed her through den and dining room, and out into the rear gardens. Syrarys had not changed. Smooth, crafty, clever-tongued. Thasha had seen her argue a duchess into tongue-tied rage, then walk off serenely to dance with her duke. In a city addicted to gossip she was an object of fascination. Everyone assumed she had a younger man, or probably several, hidden about the metropolis, for how could an old man satisfy a woman like that? "You can't kiss a medal on a wintry night, eh?" said a leering Lord Somebody, seated beside Thasha at a banquet. When he stepped away from the table she emptied a bottle of salad oil into his cushioned chair.

She had no great wish to defend Syrarys, but she would let no one cast shame on her father. He had been wounded so many times—five in battle, and once at least in love, when the wife he cherished died six days after giving birth to a daughter. Isiq's grief was so intense, his memories of his lost Clorisuela so many and sharp, that Thasha was astounded one day to hear him speak of her as "my motherless girl." Of course she had a mother—as permanently present as she was permanently lost.

Syrarys, for her part, scarcely needed defending. The consort glided among the ambushes and betrayals of high society as if born to them. Which was astounding, since she had come to Etherhorde just eight years ago in chains. Silver chains, maybe, but chains nonetheless.

Admiral Isiq had returned from the siege of Ibithraéd to find her waiting in his chambers, along with a note scrawled in His Supremacy's childish hand: *We send this woman full trained in arts of love, may she be unto you joy's elixir.*

She was a pleasure-slave. Not officially, of course: slavery had by then gone out of fashion and was restricted to the Outer Isles and newly conquered territories, where the Empire's hardest labor was done. In the inner Empire, bonded servants had taken their place—or consorts, in the case of pleasure-slaves. By law such women were one's property, but Thasha had heard of them won and lost in gambling matches, or sent back to slave territories when their looks began to fade.

She was barely eight when Syrarys arrived. Still, she would never forget how the young woman looked at her father: not cringing like other servants, but quietly intrigued, as though he were a lock she might pick with skill and patience.

Eberzam detested slavery by any name, calling it "the gangrene of empires." But to refuse a gift from the Emperor was unthinkable, so Thasha's father took the only step that occurred to him. He kept Syrarys in the house for a plausible six weeks and then declared himself in love. He petitioned the crown at once for her citizenship, but surprisingly he was rebuffed. The second note from Castle Maag read: *Wait one year one day Adml at that time if love yet flourish we shall raise this seedling to status propitiatory.* What that could mean no one knew, but the admiral obeyed, and became a reluctant slave-keeper for the first time in his life.

That year Syrarys was effectively imprisoned in the family mansion, but the sentence did not seem to trouble her. She turned her attention to Thasha, embracing the little girl half as a mother, half as older sister. She taught her Ulluprid games and songs, and persuaded the cook to make the dishes of her childhood, which Thasha agreed were more sumptuous than the best Etherhorde fare. In turn Thasha helped to perfect her Arquali, which was strong but leaned too heavily on the slave school's vocabulary of seduction.

They were best friends. The admiral couldn't have been happier. Thasha barely noticed when he stopped visiting Syrarys' bedroom and installed her in his own.

At the end of the required year he wrote again to Castle Maag, declaring his love stronger than ever, and this time it was the simple truth. Days later, admiral and slave were summoned to the Ametrine Throne, where Syrarys knelt and was named Lady Syrarys, consort to Eberzam Isiq.

The city gasped. With the stroke of a pen the Emperor had changed Isiq's slave—mere property in the eyes of the law—into a member of the aristocracy. In the long history of the Magads' rule, nothing of the kind had been done. By granting Isiq this boon, the Emperor was raising him immensely on the ladder of power. And no one knew why.

So it was that the most beautiful slave in Arqual became its most mysterious Great Lady. And ceased, from one day to the next, to be Thasha's friend.

A blue fengas lamp blazed in the summerhouse—actually just a large gazebo with a liquor cabinet. Admiral Eberzam Isiq, Prosecutor of the Liberation of Chereste and the Rescue of Ormael, among other violences, sat reading in a wicker lounger, a blanket over his legs and nearly as many moths bouncing off his bright bald head as circling the lamp above. The startling thing was that he didn't notice. As Thasha drew near she saw a big moth crawl from her father's ear to the top of his scalp. He didn't move. One hand whisked irritably at the page where his eyes were trained; that was all.

"Prahba!" she said.

It was her private nickname: *Prahba* was "the old sailor nobody could kill," a storybook hero who conquered every sea, and even outran Death, when the specter chased him against the wind. The admiral jumped, scattering the moths and slamming several in his book. He twisted to look at Thasha. He made a wordless sound of joy. Then she was hugging him, half in his lap, scratching her face on his stubbled neck and giggling as if she were not sixteen but six, and he had never banished her to a school run by hags.

"Thasha, my great girl!"

"I want to come with you."

"What? Oh, Thasha, morning star! What are you saying?"

His voice dry as coal. Two years had passed, but it might have been ten. His jaw trembled more than before, and the sideburns that were all that remained of his hair had lost their color: they were milk-white. But his arms were still strong, his beard neat, and his blue eyes, when they ceased their wandering and settled on you, were piercing.

"You can't leave me here," she said. "I'll be no trouble in Simja, I promise."

The admiral shook his head. "Simja will be the trouble, not you. A motherless girl in that cesspit. Unmarried, unprotected."

"Silly fool," she said, kissing his forehead. This was going to be easier than she thought. "You protected the whole Empire. You can protect me."

"How long?"

Thasha sat back to look at him. His eyes were forlorn.

"And the ship," he wheezed. "Those animals."

"Prahba," she said seriously, "I have to tell you something quickly. I saw Hercól on the way back from the school—"

"Eberzam!" cried Syrarys, mounting the steps. "Look who I found at the garden gate!"

The admiral had started at the mention of Hercól, but now he smiled at his daughter. "You're the living image of your mother. And that reminds me . . ." He took a small wooden box from the table and passed it to Thasha. "Open it," he said.

Thasha opened the box. Coiled inside was an exquisite silver necklace. She lifted it out: each link was a tiny ocean creature: starfish, sea horse, octopus, eel. But they were all so finely and fluidly wrought that at arm's length one saw only a silver chain.

"It's so beautiful," she whispered.

"That was hers, your mother's," said Isiq. "She loved it very much, hardly ever took it off."

Thasha looked from her father to Syrarys, barely trusting herself to speak. "But you gave it—"

"He gave it to me, years ago," said Syrarys, "because he thought he had to. As if I needed him to prove his feelings! I only accepted it as a guardian—keeping it safe until you came of age. Which, as you've just finished saying, you have." She took the necklace and put it around Thasha's neck. "Breathtaking!" she said. "Well, Eberzam, perhaps you'll consent to wear a dinner jacket tonight? Nama has lost all patience with him, Thasha. Puffing on sapwort cigars in his dressing gown. Rambling the garden in his slippers."

Isiq's eyes twinkled as he looked from one to the other. "You see how I am persecuted. In my own home."

He tossed the blanket aside and swung to his feet: an old man's imitation of military quickness. Thasha almost took his arm, but his hand waved her gently away. He leaned on no one, yet.

Thasha greeted the servants in the kitchen—Nama especially she had missed—washed her hands and ran upstairs to her old bedroom. Nothing had changed: the short, plush bed, the candle on the dresser, the table with the mariner's clock. She closed the door behind her and turned the key.

"Ramachni!"

There was no reply.

"It's me, Thasha! Come out, the door is locked!"

Silence again. Thasha rushed to the table, lifted the clock, looked behind it. Nothing.

"Blast and *damn*!"

She had spent too long in the garden, and Ramachni had left. He was a great mage; he could travel between worlds; Hercól had even seen him call up storms. He had causes and struggles everywhere. Why had she expected him to wait while she dawdled below?

"You're not going to spring out at me, are you? Like Hercól?"

Although he sometimes looked like an ordinary man, Ramachni usually visited her in the form of a mink. A jet-black mink, slightly larger than a squirrel, and he was not above nipping her if her attention wandered during their studies.

But there was no black mink in her room tonight. He was gone, and might not reappear for days, weeks, years. She could not even blame Syrarys, for the simple reason that Syrarys did not know Ramachni existed. Feeling a perfect idiot, Thasha flopped down on the bed. And froze.

Words burned on her ceiling in a pale blue fire. They were magic beyond any doubt, and her heart thrilled, for Ramachni very rarely let her see his magic. Even now she had only an instant to enjoy it, for as soon as she read a word it flickered and died. It was like blowing out candles with her mind.

Welcome out of prison, Thasha Isiq! I do not say *Welcome home,* for your notions of home are about to change, I think. Don't worry about missing me: I shall return before you know it. But Nama comes in and out of this room every minute, making sure it is ready for you, and I am tired of hiding under the dresser.

Hercól is quite correct, by the way: someone is prowling your garden. Your dogs swear to it. Jorl is so anxious he barely makes sense. When I ask about the intruder, he responds: "Little people in the earth! Little people in the earth!"

By prison you may think I mean the Lorg. Not at all! The prison you are escaping is a beautjful one: beautiful and terrible, lethal even, should you remain in it much longer. You shall miss it. Often you will long to retreat to it, to nestle in its warmth as you do now in that bed you've outgrown. Brave soul, you cannot. It is your childhood, this prison, and its door is locked behind you.

At dinner, Thasha's father spoke of his ambassadorship. In every sense an honor. Simja was a Crownless State of tremendous importance, lying as it did between Arqual and her great rival the Mzithrin. The two empires had kept an uneasy truce for forty years, since the end of the horrific Second Sea War.

But battles or not, the power-struggle continued. The Crownless Lands knew the peril surrounding them, for the last war had been fought in their waters, on their shores and streets.

"They look at us and see angels of death, as Nagan put it," said Isiq. "You remember Commander Nagan? Perhaps you were too young."

"I remember him," said Thasha. "One of the Emperor's private guards."

"Right you are," said Isiq approvingly. "But on this trip he will be protecting us. A fine man, a professional."

"He used to visit," said Syrarys. "Such a *careful* man! I feel safer knowing he'll be aboard."

Isiq waved impatiently. "The point is, the Crownless Lands fear us as much as they do the Mzithrin. And now they've gone clever on us, with this damnable Simja Pact." He bit savagely at the dinner bread. "Fine footwork, that. Don't know how they managed it in just five years."

"What is a pact?" asked Thasha.

"An agreement, darling," said Syrarys. "The Crownless Lands have sworn to keep both Arqual and the Mzithrin out of their waters. And they've promised that if one Crownless State is attacked, the rest will all come to their aid."

"But I thought Arqual had the greatest fleet on earth."

"She does!" said Isiq. "That fleet bested the Mzithrin once, and could do so again. Nor could all seven Crownless Lands defy us, should we be so cruel and stupid as to make war on them. But what if the Crownless Lands and the Sizzies fought us together?" He shook his head. "We should be hard pressed, hard pressed. And the Mzithrin Kings have the same fear: that those seven States could one day turn on them, with our own fleet alongside, and lay their empire to waste. That is what the Simja Pact guarantees: utter annihilation for either empire, should they try to seize the least barren islet of the Crownless Lands."

His hand slapped the table so hard the dishes jumped. "Obvious!" he shouted, forgetting Thasha and Syrarys entirely. "How did we not see it? Of course they'd flirt with both sides! Who wouldn't prefer a quiet wolf to one baying for your blood?"

"Prahba," said Thasha quietly, "if we're the wolves, does that make Simja the trailing elk?"

The admiral stopped chewing. Even Syrarys looked momentarily shocked. Eberzam Isiq had wanted a boy, and Thasha knew it: someone to build model ships with, to read his battle-logs to and show off his wounds. A boy to set up one day with a ship of his own. Thasha could never be an officer, nor wanted to be. Her models looked like shipwrecks, not ships.

But she had a knack for strategy that unsettled him at times.
The admiral reached unsteadily for the wine. "The wolves
and the trailing elk. I remember telling you that parable. How a
wolf pack drives and harries a herd until it identifies the slowest,
the weakest, then cuts it off from the rest and devours it. I do remember, Thasha. And I know what you're thinking: that the old
man knows how to fight wars, but not make peace. You forget
that my life did not begin when I joined the Imperial navy. And
perhaps you also forget that I have hung up my sword. When I
sail west it will be in a merchant ship, not a man-o'-war."

"Of course," said Thasha. "I've spoken foolishly. Silly ideas
come to me, sometimes."

"More than silly, in this case. Did you not hear what I said
about the Pact? If we move against any Crownless State all the
rest will turn against us, and the White Fleet of the Mzithrin will
join them."

"Eat your salad, Thasha," whispered Syrarys.

"War on that scale would make the Second Maritime look like
two brats squabbling in a bathtub," said the admiral, his voice
rising. "Do you think I would be party to such madness? I am not
a spy or a military messenger, girl! I am an ambassador!"

"I'm sorry, Father."

The admiral looked at his plate and said nothing. Thasha
found her heart pounding. She had rarely seen him so upset.

Syrarys gave a consoling sigh, and poured them each a cup of
coffee. "I know so little of the world," she said, "but it occurs
to me, Thasha darling, that such a remark—it's very clever, of
course—"

Ah, here it comes, thought Thasha.

"—but at the wrong moment, it might just . . . worry people."

"It might be a disaster!" said Eberzam.

"Surely not, dear," Syrarys countered sweetly. "When you're
careful, misunderstandings can be sorted out. Don't you think
so, Thasha?"

"Yes, I do," said Thasha tonelessly. Beneath the table her
hands made fists.

"An hour ago, for instance," Syrarys said, laying a hand on the admiral's own, "Thasha and I were recalling that summer party in Maj District. Fancy, I had the idea she had thrown her cousin into a hedge. When in fact he merely fell."

Eberzam Isiq's face clouded even further. He had been at the party, too. He took his hand from Syrarys' grasp and touched his head behind one ear, the site of the old wound. Thasha shot a glance of blazing rage at Syrarys.

"They are such an *excitable* bunch, those cousins," said the consort. "I believe there's still a rift between our households."

Another pause. The admiral cleared his throat, but did not look up. "Thasha, morning star," he said. "We live in an evil time."

"Prahba—"

"If Arqual and the Mzithrin come to blows," the admiral said, "it will not be like other wars. It will be the ruin of both. Death will stalk the nations, from Besq to Gurishal. Innocents will die alongside warriors. Cities will be sacked."

Now he raised his eyes, and the forlorn look Thasha saw in the garden was stronger than ever.

"I saw such a city. A lovely city. Bright above the sea—" His voice sounded ready to break, but he checked himself.

Syrarys laid her hand on the table. "This can wait until morning," she said firmly.

"No, it cannot," said the admiral.

"Dr. Chadfallow says you mustn't exhaust yourself."

"Chadfallow be damned!"

The consort's eyes widened, but she held her tongue.

Thasha said, "What I said was awful, Prahba, but it won't happen again. Forgive me! I've spoken to no one but the Sisters for two years. It was just a careless moment."

"Such moments can be lethal," he said.

Thasha bit her lips. She was thinking of Hercól.

"A darkness follows the death of cities," said the admiral. "A darkness of hunger and cold, and a darkness of ignorance, and a darkness of savage despair. Each darkness speeds the others, like the currents of a whirlpool. We must do everything we can to stay out of the whirlpool."

"I'm older now," Thasha said, feeling the jaws of Syrarys' trap closing on her. "I have better sense. Please—"

He held up a hand for silence: a soft gesture, but one that allowed for no contradiction. Thasha was trembling. Syrarys wore a tiny smile.

"In six days I board *Chathrand*," said the admiral. "His Supremacy has just given me the heaviest burden of my life. Believe me, Thasha: if I saw some other path I should take it. But there is none. That is why I must tell you—"

"You can't send me back to that school!"

"—that you will be sailing with us to Simja, a journey often weeks or more—"

"What!" Thasha leaped out of her chair. "Oh, thank you, thank you, my darling Prahba! You won't regret it, never, I promise!"

"And there," said the admiral, fending off her kisses, "you will be married to Prince Falmurqat Adin, Commander of the Fourth Legion of the Mzithrin Kings."

7

The Scaffold in the Square

1 Vaqrin 941
8:02 a.m.

All along the waterfront men were peering into hatches and holds. Pazel watched with indifference: the crawlies had escaped, it seemed. They were exceedingly dangerous, men claimed, and could even send a ship to the bottom of the sea. Yet Pazel had never learned to hate them like a true Arquali: he sometimes felt like an ixchel himself. A tiny, unwelcome being, hiding in the cracks and crevices of the Empire.

But what was going on beside the *Chathrand*? Two enormous gangways had been drawn up beside her, looking for all the world like a pair of siege towers beside a fortress wall. At the farther the scene was familiar: sailors and stevedores bustled up and down the zigzagging ramps, with casks and crates and other provision containers, in that state of organized frenzy that preceded the launch of any ship. But something odd was happening at the nearer ramp.

A crowd had gathered, in this first hour of dawn: a crowd of the poor and almost-poor, young men with their sweethearts, old men all bristle and bone, grandmothers in faded smocks. But most numerous were the boys: ragged, hungry boys, eyes flickering between the ship and a certain street at the back of the Plaza.

The whole crowd stood behind a newly made wooden fence,

which carved out a wide semicircle before the gangway. No one was using the ramp, but inside the fence Imperial marines stood guard with lowered spears. Next to the gangway stood a wooden scaffold upon which three sailing officers stood at attention, white uniforms gleaming, hats in hand. Despite their stillness, Pazel saw that they too were stealing glances at the street. Everyone was, in fact.

When he reached the foot of the pier, Pazel approached a group of older men standing apart.

"Your pardon, sirs. What's it all about?"

They glanced back over their shoulders, and Pazel recognized the very fishermen who had consoled him earlier that morning. Now they looked from him to one another, and their eyes twinkled with mischief. All at once they began to laugh.

"What's it all about! He he!"

One of the men raised Pazel's hand, inspecting. "Rough as hide! He's a tarboy, sure."

"Shoul' we? Shoul' we?"

"Oh, I shoul' say so. He he *he*!"

Another man—it was the old salt who had offered him breakfast—bent down and looked Pazel in the face. "You wan' we shoul' help you, then?"

"Help me?" said Pazel uneasily. "How?"

All at once the crowd stirred and a murmuring arose: *"Captain's come! The new captain!"* All eyes locked on the street, from which came a distant sound of hooves. The fishermen, still grinning, clapped their hands on Pazel's arms and pressed him forward.

"Make way, gents, ladies! Club spons'r, this one! Club spons'r!"

The fishermen had some influence, it seemed: grudgingly, the crowd let them pass. When they reached the fence they shouted to the marines.

"Here, tinshirts! Take this one! Solid tarboy, he is! Club's honor!"

Pazel started, began to struggle. "What . . . where—"

"Sss, fool!" they hissed at him. "Want a ship or don't ye?"

A marine stalked irritably toward them, pointing at Pazel. "Is he trained?" he shouted over the din.

"Trained, seasoned, sound!" The fisherman patted Pazel like a favorite dog.

"Fetch him over, then! Quick!"

Before Pazel could protest, the fishermen heaved him over the fence. He struck the ground on the far side with a thump, and the soldier pulled him instantly to his feet. As he was dragged across the square, Pazel saw the boys behind the fence glaring at him, as if he were cheating at something. And Pazel had to grin, for he knew what was happening now, and it was like a dream. This was the muster of the *Chathrand,* where gaps in the crew would be filled before the voyage out. The old men had passed him off as one of their own.

Chadfallow had wanted to strand him ashore—why, Pazel couldn't imagine—but Pazel was going to thwart his plans. He would be back on a ship before the day was out. And not just any ship!

From the other side of the fence boys poked at him, hissing: *"Not fair! Not fair!"*

At that moment a gate in the fence began to open. The soldier hauled Pazel up against the planks and ordered him to be still. As Pazel watched, a red two-horse carriage rounded the street corner. Marines walked before it, bellowing, driving a wedge through the mob. From the deck of the *Chathrand* six trumpets gave a mournful blast. As the carriage reached the fence the marines had to jab the crowd back at spear-point, and lock the gate behind them. But when the coach stopped at the scaffold, the horns and voices died as if by mutual consent. Silently the driver climbed down and opened the door.

First to emerge was an old, old woman. Pazel gaped: it was the duchess, Lady Oggosk, who had laughed at him and tasted his tears. The driver helped the old woman down, then reached into the carriage—and jerked back with a cry of pain. In the sunshine the onlookers saw bright blood on his hand. The

woman cackled. Then she herself reached in and lifted a huge
red cat from the floor of the coach. The thief! Pazel thought. For
there could be no doubt: Lady Oggosk's cat was the very animal
that had stolen his fritter. Without a glance at the crowd, Lady
Oggosk moved to the scaffold and crept laboriously up the
stairs.

Next came a black man in a smart blue vest. There were
puzzled looks. A Noonfirther? Some other, stranger race? No
one quite knew what to say. The black man too ignored them,
and ascended the scaffold behind the old woman.

Then they saw the hand. Heavy, scarred, strong, it gripped the
carriage door, and from the black sleeve and gold cufflinks they
knew that this at last was the captain of the Great Ship.

But the man who emerged stamped the crowd with the deepest silence yet. He was a large, slow-moving mariner, his red
beard neatly combed, his eyes studying the crowd from pale,
leathery sockets, the line of his mouth frozen in an expression
of anger: deferred anger, perhaps, or merely contained.

Rose.

The name broke the silence, racing through the crowd in a
frightened whisper. *Rose! Rose!* Pazel turned, bewildered. The
name was melting into a moan. Wives and husbands traded
glances; even the marines looked taken aback. By the fence, the
crowd of boys gaped at the red-bearded man, who was now
rounding the carriage with a limp.

Then the whole mob of boys turned and ran. Women
screamed, high-pitched; men bellowed at one another: *"You
said it would be Fiffengurt!" "Ay, and you guessed Frix!"* One
of the bolder men threw a melon in the direction of the carriage.
"Back to the islands, Rose! Leave our boys alone!"

But Rose, moving calmly to the scaffold, paid no attention,
and the boys were not left alone. While all eyes were on the
carriage, groups of short, thick-chested beings had taken up
positions in the streets and alleys, blocking all exits from the
square. They wore thick hoods over their heads. Their arms
seemed too long for their bodies.

"Flikkermen!" went the cry. What were they doing in the port?

The answer came soon enough. One after another the creatures ran down the fleeing boys, tore them away from their parents and friends, dragged them squealing and kicking to the scaffold. There a blond officer gave each boy a casual inspection (four limbs, two eyes, teeth), scribbled something in a ledger and tossed the Flikkerman a single gold coin.

The families in the crowd were outraged. They had already paid a fee just to enter the square, on the off-chance of finding work for their boys. Even the orphans who came alone had paid a copper whelk.

"Flikkermen! Who hired them? That rancid Company?"

"The marines shouldn't work with them bloodworms!"

"Ehe, tinshirt! Bring that Ormali cub back! Changed our minds!"

The latter shouts were from the fishermen, but the marine ignored them. He seized Pazel again and dragged him to the scaffold.

The blond officer looked him over, then scowled at the guard. "An Ormali! Are you a soldier or a junk peddler, sir?"

"Why, he's top quality!" cried the soldier. "Sponsored by the fishermen's club and all. You're a seasoned tarboy, aren't you, cub?"

Pazel hesitated only an instant. None of these screaming townsfolk knew what it was like to be an Ormali in the Empire of Arqual. However bad Rose made life on the *Chathrand,* it would be better than starving, or being sent to break stones in the Forgotten Colonies.

"I am, sir!" he cried. "I was much appreciated by Captain Nestef of the *Eniel,* who told me I knew my rigging like a true sailor, and my knots, and my flags, and my signals, to say nothing of my *dispatch* in foul weather, and he never meant to leave me ashore, I'm—"

"Buffoon!" said the blond officer to the marine. "Take that chattering monkey from my sight."

"You watch your tongue," growled the soldier. "I don't care how rich that old woman's made ye—"

"Rich enough to tire of swindlers," said the officer.

"You're addressing a member of His Supremacy's Tenth Legion!"

"Then our labors pay for your grog and boots and girlies. Now get hence."

Watching his luck slip away, Pazel took a drastic risk: he tugged at the first mate's sleeve. "Please, sir! I won't chatter, or act monkeyish, I was not known for either quality on the *Eniel,* where Captain Nestef complimented me on four occasions, twice in the presence of gentlemen, sir, and he said I was a tarboy of *distinction,* and that I was helpful on deck and below, and that my tea was fit for court, that I skinned my potatoes with great efficiency, wasting nothing but removing the rot, sir, and—"

"Mr. Uskins," said a deep voice. "Take the boy."

It was Captain Rose. Pazel looked up at the pulpit, and for an instant the big man stared back. The mouth was lost in the red beard, but the green eyes were chilling.

"My father had a chatterbox among his boys," he said. "The tailor stitched his mouth shut with twine."

Uskins tossed the marine a coin and waved irritably at Pazel. "Over there with the rest. Go on!"

Already wondering if he had made a mistake, Pazel obeyed. The boys were huddled together, whimpering. Some were mere urchins, come to work for food and shelter on the Great Ship; a few had the salt-roughened hair and strong arms of tarboys. It seemed they had passed the night on the wharf, huddled in doorways, abandoned barges, crates. But they had fled in a heartbeat at the sight of Rose.

Like all seafarers, Pazel had heard of Captain Nilus Rotheby Rose. He was the most famous commander of the *Chathrand,* and the longest serving. Famous because crafty: rumor had it that he had once smuggled a fortune in contraband silks out of Ibithraéd by sewing the priceless cloth up inside double-sails. And famous because cruel: another story had him hanging a second mate by the ankles from the bowsprit for ten leagues. The crime was yawning on watch.

Rose was also the only captain of the Great Ship ever to have been fired. Pazel had no idea why. But the Chathrand Trading Family set the highest standards in the Empire. It was a rare and shocking thing for one of their commanders to lose his ship.

And completely unheard of, a miracle almost, for him to get it back.

A few minutes more and some thirty boys had been purchased. A single glance told Pazel that he was the only Ormali. No surprise there. But it was startling how many misfits the Flikkermen had rounded up. Less than two-thirds had the black hair and broad shoulders of Arqual. The other boys were of all kinds: one had skin the color of brandy, another startling green eyes, two others sky-blue stars tattooed on their foreheads. Pazel had seen such boys over the years, but never in an Arquali crew. They would be outcasts, like Pazel himself. And that could mean—why not?—that they would be his friends.

And at the very least, Jervik was not among them.

Now the first mate, Uskins, turned to face the boys. He was smiling, suddenly. The change in his looks was so extreme he seemed almost a different man.

"Well and good, lads!" he boomed. "You've no cause for worry. Mr. Fiffengurt here will be taking you aboard. He's our quartermaster, and a Sorrophrani blood and bone, and he'll be in charge of you for the whole of your service. Any troubles you have, he'll see you through."

The still-restless townsfolk, and many of the boys, sighed their relief. The quartermaster's was an important rank in the Merchant Service, and Fiffengurt (there he was, descending the gangway) was a man they trusted. He would take care of their boys, and shield them from Rose. Pazel, however, was unconvinced, and he saw the same caution in the eyes of the older tarboys. Every voyage began with smiles and soothing noises.

Fiffengurt drew near. He was thin and strong, a boiled bone of a man with knobby joints and untidy white whiskers (a bit like shaving lather) on his cheeks and chin. He said a cordial good morning, and smiled at the boys. Or did he? Was he looking at something behind them?

Fiffengurt saw the confused turning of heads, and laughed.

"Lazy eye!" he told them, pointing to his right. "Pay no attention to this one, it's blind anyway. My left eye's the one that sees you. Listen: Mr. Uskins told you right. You tarboys are in my keeping. Do right by me and I'll do the same for you; do wrong and you'll find me a right old terror! Now let's be still and hear what the captain has to say."

Rose had indeed stepped behind the lectern. His heavy hands gripped its sides, and he looked down at the townsfolk with an inscrutable cold gaze, and waited. Again, the shouts and murmurs died away.

"You think you know me," said Rose, in a low voice that somehow rolled across the Plaza. "You do not. There was a Captain Rose who sailed the Great Ship, in all the waters from here to Serpent's Head, and who lost her ten years ago—but I am not that man. Before you stands one who has known the burden of power, and craves it no more. People of Sorrophran, I now live to serve, as once I lived to be served. At the pleasure of His Supremacy I will command *Chathrand* once more, but when this voyage ends, so too ends my career as a mariner. I will retire to the Isle of Rappopolni. I am an aspirant to the Brotherhood of Temple Roln."

The old woman jumped so violently that her cat leaped to the ground. Mr. Uskins gaped. Around the plaza there were chuckles, grunts of disbelief. Rappopolni was a sacred island in the Narrow Sea. Thousands visited its temple each year. The monks of Temple Roln embraced a life of poverty and self-sacrifice: two qualities no one would ever have attributed to Rose.

"In his kindness," Rose went on, "the Emperor has sent me a spiritual companion. On this voyage, Brother Bolutu will help me in my devotions, even as he tends, with equal compassion no doubt, to the animals in our hold."

The black man did not so much as blink. He watched Rose as

if observing a natural curiosity, such as a snake swallowing an egg twice the size of its head.

"To another matter now," said Rose. "I know that many of you fine sailors hoped to sign on this morning. It is true that we need more deckhands—three hundred more, indeed, to complete our crew. But I regret to say we will be signing crew in Etherhorde, and Etherhorde alone."

Now the people howled. "Treachery! Trickery!" A woman raised her fist and shouted: "You'll take the lads but not their fathers, will 'ee? What's it you plan to do with 'em that you can't have the fathers aboard?"

Rose lifted his broad hand. "This is a matter of Imperial law."

"Law my jaw!" cried the woman. "What law's that?"

"The Law of Royal Conveyance, madam."

This quieted the crowd: they did not know what Royal Conveyance meant, but it sounded grand, and they wanted to hear more.

"Our mission is one of trade, of course," began Rose again, "but it is also a mission of peace. In Etherhorde we will be taking aboard a passenger of the highest importance to the Imperium: none other than Eberzam Isiq, His Supremacy's retired fleet admiral and new ambassador to Simja. It is there, in neutral waters, that Isiq will meet his counterpart, a Mzithrini ambassador, to negotiate a permanent peace between the empires."

Now the silence was one of profound awe.

Rose swept on: "The Treaty of Simja, the Great Peace, will mark a turning point for this Empire, and indeed for Alifros as a whole. In transporting Eberzam Isiq and his family, we must conduct ourselves as though transporting the Imperial Person himself. There will be a full honor guard, and every luxury and comfort for the distinguished passengers. And extra pay for all you tarboys. But alas, extra precautions, too. I am therefore ordered to recruit my sailors under direct supervision of the Ametrine Throne. No one above the level of tarboy is exempt."

"What about them bleedin' guns?" shouted someone. "My son ain't signed on as a powder monkey!"

Rose glanced sharply at the speaker. He looked to be on the verge of some quick retort. But the moment passed, and he spoke in the same soothing tone as before.

"The *Chathrand* sails in peace, but she was built for war—ancient and colossal war. Those cannon are relics. Truth be told, they were better housed in a museum than a gun deck. We keep but a few in working order: enough to defend ourselves from pirates. Fear not for your sons! I tell you I shall be as a father to my crew, and they as fathers to each of your boys. And of course, every letter of the Sailing Code will be respected."

"The letters, aye," said a quiet voice at Pazel's side. "But not the words."

Pazel turned. Beside him stood the smallest tarboy he had ever seen. His head, wound in a faded red turban, barely reached Pazel's shoulder. His voice was thin and rather squeaky, but there was a quickness about his fidgeting limbs, and a sharp gleam to his eye. He looked at Pazel and gave a mocking smile.

"Lies," he said. "If he's religious I'm a blister-toad. Just wait and see."

Rose praised the Sorrophran Shipworks, invoked the long life of the Emperor and then his little speech was over. No one cheered, but neither did they hiss or throw stones: how could they, when they had just been reminded in whose name the *Chathrand* sailed? Already the crowd looked resigned, and Pazel supposed that was all the captain hoped for.

With Rose limping in the lead, the group left the scaffold and made for the gangway, while above them the trumpets resumed their cacophonous blasting. Over the noise, Fiffengurt spoke to the boys again.

"Right, lads, who's for breakfast? The captain's party is dining in the wardroom, but we've a little welcome feast of our own on the berth deck. Come, let's eat while it's hot."

With a jerk of his head he started walking toward the gangway. The boys hesitated. One or two looked as if they might make a last bolt for freedom. Fiffengurt glanced over his shoulder, checked himself and walked back to the boys.

"Now then, lads, this won't do. You're all going to board that ship. And the only ones who should be afraid are them we have to truss up like chickens and carry in a sack. Now do honor to your names and follow me."

Reluctantly, they did. The gangway was long and steep, and their footsteps boomed eerily as if they were crossing a drawbridge over some shadowy moat. Shouts and laughter rang above them on the deck. Heart racing, Pazel gazed at the *Chathrand*'s portholes (brass-fitted, beautiful), her gunports (how many per deck? He lost count at sixty), the scarlet rail sweeping away like a fence around a lord's estate, the shroud-lines joining the masts somewhere in the sky.

Up and up they marched. On the escutcheon, the ship's cast-iron nameplate, the ship's name blazed in gold letters three feet high. Beneath, in much smaller characters, ran an inscription. Pazel shielded his eyes and began to read:

Wyteralch, wadri, we: ke thandini ondrash, llemad.

Fiffengurt, climbing just ahead of him, stopped dead. The tramping boys halted in some confusion. The quartermaster stared at Pazel.

"Where'd you hear *that,* my cub?"

Only then did Pazel realize he had spoken the words aloud. He glanced from the nameplate to Fiffengurt and back again. "I—I just—"

Then it happened. The words of the inscription, which he had read effortlessly and quite without thinking, changed before his eyes. They softened like wax; they swirled, and finally snapped into a new and definite shape:

CHATHRAND
Sorcerer, sultan, storm: never my masters, these.
No banner is so broad as my purpose,
No sea so deep as my builder's dream.
Night alone can claim me when it claims the earth.

Then dry shall I sleep in the under-depths
Beside my stolen children.

Pazel was so alarmed he nearly stumbled. The ship's name was still in Arquali, but beneath it ran a new inscription—no, the very same!—but in a tongue Pazel had never seen.

It's starting, he thought. *It's starting again.*

There it was: the throbbing in the back of his head, like the purr of some waking animal. Pazel gazed at the strange letters. He did not know the name of the language—*but he could read it.* Suddenly, perfectly. And in a burst of rage he knew what Chadfallow had done.

Fiffengurt trained his good eye on Pazel. "I know *where* it's written, cleverskins," he said. "But you were speaking Arquali just now."

"Was I?"

"You blary well know you were! Fancy enough for court. Who translated the Blessing for you?"

"I . . . I must have overheard someone," Pazel said. "On my old ship, maybe."

"Name?"

"The *Eniel.*"

"Your name, lummox!"

"Pazel Pathkendle, sir!"

"Hmmph," said Fiffengurt. "Well, lads, Mr. Pathkendle has just recited the Builder's Blessing. All the old ships have 'em, some flimflam spoken by a mage or seer, or Rin knows who, before the ship ever touched the sea. Not all of them sound like blessings, as you just heard. Some are hexes, prophecies—curses, even, against those who'd do the ship harm. Nobody knows just what the *Chathrand*'s builders had in mind. But listen close: we don't speak those words aboard her. Bad luck, that is, and Captain Rose won't stand for it."

He wagged a finger at Pazel. Then he gave another of his disorienting, over-your-shoulder smiles, and resumed the climb.

—8—

The Gift

1 Vaqrin 941
9:16 a.m.

Pazel's breath came short. The animal in his mind was waking, stretching, flexing its claws. He did not know what it was, or why it lived in the cave between his ears, but he knew what it did to him. It gave him language. And took language away.

His mother Suthinia was to blame. It happened at home in Ormael, just months before the Arquali invasion. Winter was breaking up in storms, and in such weather Suthinia was at her strangest and most disagreeable. She quarreled with Chadfallow, who came to dine and found Pazel and Neda chewing last year's wrinkled potatoes: Suthinia had been too distracted to go to market. At times she seemed almost mad. In electrical storms she climbed the roof and stood with arms outstretched, although Chadfallow swore that to do so was to provoke the lightning. The night she fought with Chadfallow, Pazel had lain awake, listening, but even in their fury the adults kept their voices low, and all he heard was one exceptionally desperate cry from his mother:

"What if they were yours, Ignus? You'd do just the same! You couldn't send them away into the night as they are, friendless, lost—"

"Friendless?" came the wounded reply. "Friendless, you say?"

Moments later Pazel heard the doctor's footsteps in the garden, the sharp clang of the gate.

The next morning, Pazel's mother, surly as a bear and twice as dangerous, began cooking again. She made corn cakes with plum sauce, their father's recipe no doubt, and when they had finished she poured them each a generous mug of custard-apple pulp.

"Drink this," she told them. "For your health."

"It's sour," said Pazel, sniffing his mug.

"From special fruits, very expensive. Drink, drink!"

They choked the bad pulp down. After lunch she filled the mugs again, and the taste was even worse. Neda, who was seventeen and very wise, told him their mother was suffering "a lady's discomforts" in a tone of such gravity that Pazel felt ashamed for not liking anything she served. But as evening came they saw her in the garden, furiously squeezing custard-apple pulp through her fingers into a big stone bowl, and she had to resort to threats to bring her children to table. When they were finally seated she placed a tall pitcher of the translucent gruel before them.

"Can't we at least start with the meal?" Neda sniffed.

Suthinia filled their mugs. "This is your meal. Drink."

"Mother," said Pazel gently, "I don't care for custard apple."

"DRINK IT ALL!"

They drank. Pazel had never imagined such misery. His belly ached by the second mugful, and by the fourth he knew his mother was poisoning them, for she herself took not a drop. When the pitcher was finally empty she let them go, but they could do no more than stagger to their rooms and lie quaking, holding their stomachs. Minutes after climbing into bed, Pazel was unconscious.

That night he dreamed his mother entered his room with a cage full of songbirds. They were lovely and of many colors, and their songs took shape in the air and fell like cobwebs about the room. Each time she entered the room the birds wove another layer, until a net of solid sound hung from the walls and wardrobe and bedposts. Then his mother shouted, "Wake!" and Pazel gasped and bolted upright in bed. He was alone, and his room held nothing unusual. Yet the dream had left him with a final, ludicrous image: as he woke, gasping, it seemed that the webs of birdsong had not simply vanished but rushed into his mouth, as if he had inhaled them all on that first breath.

When he left the room he saw three startling things. The first was Neda seated at the table, head in hands, looking quite a bit skinnier than the night before. The second was his mother, in even worse shape, crying at his sister's knees, saying, "Forgive me, darling, forgive." The third was that the garden had sprouted lilies two feet tall.

Then his mother looked up, screamed with joy and ran to embrace him.

Her poison had almost succeeded: they had lain at death's door for a month. Pazel returned her embrace, and when she pressed her ivory whale into his hand and asked him to keep it always he said he would. This was the mother he knew; that other, storm-worshipping, custard-apple creature was a nomad who dropped in now and then to wreck their lives. This mother was easy to love. She guarded the house from the great world beyond, and sang him highland lullabies, and if he ran into nettles at the orchard's edge, she removed them, armed with tweezers and his father's magnifying glass.

But if he ever saw another custard apple in the house he would just run away.

Four days after rising from his coma, the purring began. It felt warm and almost pleasant. When he told his mother about it she put down the shirt she was mending and came to face him.

"Pazel," she said, lifting his chin sharply, "my name is Suthinia. I am your mother. Do you understand?"

"Of course I do, Mother."

"The geese fly east to chase the drakes."

"What geese?"

Instead of answering, she tugged him to his father's library and pulled a crumbling volume from the shelf. She pointed at the spine and told him to read. Pazel obeyed: *"Great Families of Jitril. With Sketches of Their Finest Mansions and—"*

"Ah ha ha!" she yelled in triumph.

She kissed his forehead and ran from the room, shouting for Neda. And when Pazel looked down at the book again, he realized that he had just read a language he didn't know. His father had purchased the book for its drawings, on some long-ago voyage to Jitril; neither he nor anyone they knew could read the words. *But now Pazel could.* He opened the book at random: *". . . this dread chief, scourge of the Rekere, whose noble whiskers—"*

Mother, Pazel thought. *You're a witch.*

So she was: a witch or seer or sorceress, just as the good people of Ormael had always feared. But not a very good one, it seemed. Neda did not acquire the Gift, and in fact showed no change at all except that her hair turned silver, like an old woman's. When Neda failed to read Jitrili, or to understand spoken Madingae, she gave her mother a look Pazel would remember all his life. Not one of anger, but of simple awareness: she had nearly killed her daughter for nothing.

"It may start yet, when you've grown," Suthinia said, and Neda shrugged.

Despite his body's weakness, Pazel was on fire. He ate five eggs and nine strips of bacon, then ran to the city. It was annoying how few languages were to be met with in Ormael, until he reached the port. There he heard Kushal merchants denigrating the local wine; old Backlanders who feared the rains would fail; secretive Nunekkam in their domed skiffs, twittering about the crab catch; and a red-eyed lunatic, barefoot and blistered, who screamed about a coming invasion in a language no one understood.

On that first occasion his Gift lasted three days—and ended, as it always would, in a mind-fit.

This was pure horror. Cold talons seized his head, the odor of custard apples filled his mouth and nostrils, and the purr rose to an ugly, hysterical squawking. Pazel shouted for his mother. But what came from his mouth was nonsense, a baby's blather, noise.

His mother spoke nonsense, too, and Neda. *"Gwafamogafwa-Pazel! Magwathalol! Pazelgwenaganenebarlooch!"*

He closed his eyes, plugged his ears, but the voices got through. When he looked again, Neda was pointing at him and shrieking at their mother, as if she were the one having fits. Soon his mother responded in kind. The sound was beyond belief.

"Stop! Stop!" Pazel wailed. But no one understood. When Neda began hurling onions and saucers he ran to the neighbor's house and hid under the porch.

In three hours the fit ended with a snap. He crept out: the neighbor was singing as she cooked, a normal human voice, and no sound was ever sweeter.

But at home his mother said that Neda had tied her clothes up in a bundle and left. The next week he received a letter—she was with school friends, she was looking for work, she would *never* forgive their mother.

Neda sent a boy for her things. She never visited, and did not write again. But one day Pazel found a letter in progress on his mother's dresser. *Come back for Pazel's sake, Neda,* it read. *You don't have to love me.* The letter sat there for days, unfinished: too many days, as it proved.

The magic always worked the same way: first the Gift that gave him the world, then the seizures that cut him off from everyone. A few days of wonder, a few hours of hell. The Gift was incredibly useful, of course—and he never forgot a language that he gained through it—but the fits scared him half to death. Once indeed they nearly caused his death: on board the *Anju,* the whalers sealed him in a coal sack until he fainted. He woke locked in the pigsty, and remained there till landfall. The sailors told him he was fortunate: the captain, believing him possessed by devils, had wanted to pitch him over the side.

By chance they were in Sorhn—and Pazel made straight for the famous street where witches, alchemists and Slugdra ghost-doctors plied their trades. After many inquiries they directed him to a potion-maker, who took every penny he had saved toward his citizenship and served him a thick purple oil. It bubbled, and when the bubbles burst he heard small wheezes like dying mice and smelled something putrid. He drank it in a single gulp.

The potion worked. Nearly a year passed without a mind-fit. The fact that he would learn no more languages—magically, anyway—had seemed a small price to pay. But thanks to Chadfallow, the Gift and its horrors were back. Any regrets at his decision to break ties with the doctor vanished when he remembered that smell of custard apples, that ghastly squawking. *More bitter for you than me.* How could he have done such a thing?

Let the fits come at night, he thought. *Not while I'm on duty, please!*

Shouts and Whispers

1 Vaqrin 941
9:19 a.m.

In any case (Pazel told himself, climbing the gangway), there was no need to worry for several days. He had a new ship to discover, a new life to create.

Halfway to the topdeck someone spoke his name. Pazel turned to see the small, turbaned boy walking just behind him. The boy grinned, and spoke almost in a whisper.

"Where'd you learn that language, eh? Tell the truth!"

"I *don't* know it," said Pazel, unsettled. "Like I told Fiffengurt—someone translated for me."

"Rubbish!" said the boy, and held out his hand. "I have a nose for lies, and that wasn't a very clever one. You're Pazel, you said? My name's Neeps."

"Neeps?"

The small boy's face turned serious. "A ridiculous name, of course."

"No, not at all."

"It means 'thunder' in Sollochi."

"Ah," said Pazel, although he already knew.

"Actually, it's short for Neeparvasi," said the boy, "but you can't be a Neeparvasi in the Empire of Arqual. The Emperor's favorite concubine had a son named Neeparvasi who disgraced himself somehow—used the wrong fork at dinner, maybe, or stepped on the Queen Mother's foot. His Supremacy sent him off to the Valley of the Plague, and forbade anyone to mention him, or remind him the boy had ever existed. And so the name's on a forbidden list, and I'm just Neeps Undrabust."

"Pazel Pathkendle," said Pazel. "How did you end up ashore?"

"Dismissed for fighting. What could I do? The blary lout insulted my grandmother."

Pazel wasn't eager to befriend someone who turned insults into fistfights. But he had to admit he was glad to meet another boy from the margins of the Empire.

"There's a lot of us," he whispered, looking over the crowd of boys.

Neeps caught his meaning. "Newly conquered folk? Yes, lots, and that's very strange. Arqualis don't trust anyone with an accent, or skin like yours, or one of these." He tapped his turban. "In fact they hate you a little, or a lot, until your country's been part of the Empire for a hundred years—*fully digested,* as my old captain used to say. Well, Sollochstal's not digested, I can tell you. Not by a long shot."

His voice was proud but not ill-humored, and Pazel found himself smiling.

"They think I'm just tanned, you know. About half the time."

"And then you open your mouth."

Pazel laughed, nodding. Ormali was a singsong language—and despite all his efforts its rolling cadences emerged in every tongue he spoke.

As they neared the top of the gangway the noises of the ship grew louder. Surging ahead of the boys, Mr. Fiffengurt seized a buntline and pulled himself up on the rail, giving an expansive wave.

"Aboard! Aboard! Step lively, now!"

Like goats crossing a stream, the boys leaped onto the deck. Pazel would never forget what he saw in those first moments. *A city,* he thought. *It's a city afloat!*

They were boarding amidships. Here the vessel was so wide that the *Eniel* could have sat athwart her without touching the rails. Fore and aft she seemed a broad wooden avenue, crowded with barrels, boxes, timbers, heaps of sailcloth, spools of cordage and chain. Swarming through these obstacles were hundreds upon hundreds of people—sailors, stevedores, customs officers, tearful sweethearts, efficient wives, a man selling little scraps of sandrat fur ("Nobody drowns with sandrat fur!"), monks leaving their holy thumbprints in ash on the foreheads of believers, two bald men fighting over a chicken, a tattoo artist etching a boar on a burly chest. The tarboys stood frozen, awed. They were the only stationary beings aboard.

A second headcount, and Fiffengurt led them aft, past the mainmast, the longboat, the tonnage hatch yawning like a mineshaft. Clerks and midshipmen shoved by without a glance. High on the yards the sailors looked distant indeed, and Pazel was not surprised to see Mr. Uskins inspecting their work with the aid of a telescope.

At length they reached the stern port ladderway, and Fiffengurt led them into the belly of the ship. One floor down was the main deck, every bit as crowded as the topdeck above, but quite a bit hotter and smellier. Next came the upper gun deck, where the ship's cattle were temporarily stockaded, wearing looks of bewilderment Pazel found deeply justified. Farther forward the boys caught a glimpse of the cannon themselves. They were ferocious guns, tree-trunk thick and scarred by countless years of fire and salt. "Grandfather-guns," said Fiffengurt. "Terrible weapons, to be sure. But the bow carronades throw shot like prize pumpkins. Eighty-pounders. Down we go."

On the lower gun deck a sharp smell of frying onions told them the galley was near. Through the open bulkhead Pazel glimpsed it: a steamy compartment full of pots and saucepans and hanging ladles, where a squadron of cooks busied themselves around a cast-iron stove in which one might have roasted a buffalo. "Mr. Teggatz!" shouted Fiffengurt, barely pausing. "Thirty-six for breakfast, plus the old boys! Now, if you please!"

One more descent, and they stood in darkness. Fiffengurt

strode away from them, as sure and quick as he'd been on the daylit topdeck, and Pazel wondered if he had committed the whole ship's plan to memory. A minute later they heard him striking at a flint, and then a lamp sputtered to life.

"Berth deck," said Fiffengurt. "You'll sleep right here, lads, and eat at the rear of the main mess, past the deckhands. You'll have light from the hatches in good weather, and the windscoops freshen the air a bit, once we're under way. Never mind the smell; you won't notice it in a day or two. No windows in your compartment, but if you don't act like hooligans the sailors may leave the doors open on their own berth, and you'll have a bit more light. Come on, in with you."

By the dim glow of walrus oil they explored their new home: a musty wooden cavern, its far corners lost in the gloom. Massive stanchions braced the ceiling, which was low enough for the largest boys to touch. Every beam and bulkhead wall, and even the long dining tables, were carved from the same gigantic, immeasurably ancient kind of tree. The air was heavy; it smelled like a barn sealed tight against a storm.

Fiffengurt rapped on a bulkhead. "Cloudcore oak. Strong as any wood in Alifros, but lighter by half. The gun and berth decks are almost solid cloudcore. We don't know half the secrets of the *Chathrand,* lads, but here's one we grasp well enough. Not that it does us much good: there are no more cloudcore oaks. The last fifty trees grow on Mount Etheg in a secret place. They harvest one tree a century, for essential repairs to this gray lady."

Footsteps rang on the stairs behind them. "Ah, Teggatz! Very timely!" said Fiffengurt. "My lads, be good to this man or he'll poison you: he's our head cook."

Teggatz was portly, with round red cheeks. His eyes were small and recessed nearly to the point of invisibility. He laughed, rubbing his hands together nervously. The boys waited, the laugh went on, the hands moved faster and faster. At last Teggatz spoke, in a gleeful, soft explosion:

"Shepherd's pie!"

"Shepherd's pie, is it?" said Fiffengurt. "Fancy that! Bring it on, then!"

"Fancy!" giggled Teggatz, and waved up the stairs. More footsteps, and then a second group of boys appeared, bearing plates and platters and cups. They numbered about fifteen: the senior tarboys, kept on from previous voyages. Most greeted the new boys with frank, friendly looks, but a handful gazed at them with something like hostility, as if they were sizing up the competition. Fiffengurt introduced them all by name as they set their burdens on the tables.

"These are your elder brothers," he told the new boys. "Some of them have been four years with *Chathrand*. Of course, we've all got a new captain, and new rules to learn. But until you know the ship as well as they do, see that you heed 'em. Peytr and Dastu here are your chiefs because they're the oldest—turning full sailors in a year's time, if they stay out of trouble."

Pazel studied the two older tarboys. Peytr had narrow shoulders and a pointed chin. He smiled, but there was a wariness to his look, as if he were guarding himself against some unpleasant surprise. Dastu was broad and strong, with a look of serenity to his clean-shaven face.

Fiffengurt left them as they sat down to eat. The shepherd's pie was delicious and hot, and when they finished, Peytr and Dastu led them on a tour of the *Chathrand*. This was a hasty business: the ship was set to launch at dusk and work was rising to a frenzy. Lieutenants stormed fore and aft, sweating, shouting orders nonstop. Cargo cranes rose and fell. Brigades of sailors rolled casks along the decks. The boys were shoved, stepped on, laughed at, cursed. No matter where they stood they were in someone's way.

Still, Pazel was in love. There are few things more beautiful than a full-rigged ship, and the *Chathrand* was a marvel to shame all others. Every inch of her seemed the work of mages. There were the famous glass planks: six mighty, translucent windows, built directly into the floor of the topdeck, flooding the main deck below with daylight. The main deck itself had two glass planks, and one survived in the floor of the upper gun deck. Over all of these men dragged crate and cannon without a second thought: in six hundred years they had never cracked, nor even sprung a leak. A few had been lost to great violence—cannon fire, falling masts—and had to be replaced with wood, for no record told the name of that wondrous crystal, nor how it had been made or mined.

The speaking-tubes were another marvel: slim copper pipes wrapped in leather, snaking between decks and compartments from stem to stern. They were not much good in foul weather, and useless in a fight, when the cannon deafened everyone. But on calm days the captain could address the officer at the helm without rising from his desk, or call for tea without leaving the quarterdeck.

Stranger sights abounded on the lower decks. Peytr showed them a gunport near the bows where a white, curved object the length of Pazel's forearm lay embedded in the wood. The boys gasped when they realized they were looking at a tooth. "Fang of a sea-serpent," Dastu told them. "Killed four hundred years ago by the gunners at this very window. They sealed a crack in the hull with it, as you can see: good luck, that, or so they hoped."

"And that's not the scariest thing on this ship," said Peytr.

"No, brother, it ain't," said Dastu quickly. "But some things we'll not discuss today."

Of course, not naming such "things" left the tarboys more curious than ever, and soon the rumors began. Curses; creatures in the hold; weird rites among the sailors; tarboys pickled in barrels of brine: by evening Pazel had heard them all. "There's a beam in the afterhold," a freckled boy named Durbee whispered to him, "with the names of all them what's been killed aboard since the day she launched. And even though each name's the size of a grain of rice the list stretches thirteen yards."

"Then there's the vanishing compartments," said the one called Swift. "If you ever see a door or a hatch where none should be—don't open it! Horrible things in those chambers—and one of 'em never lets you leave again if the door shuts behind you."

"And s-s-s-somewhere," put in Reyast, a kind-faced new boy whose lips quivered with his perpetual stutter, "there's a t-t-talking floorboard. It g-g-groans in the voice of a c-c-c-captain who went m-ma-maaa—"

"Nonsense, Reyast!" said Dastu, overhearing. "Rose is the only captain you should be thinking about. Fear him, if you must fear somebody, and stay out of his path. Now come along, all of you! Get those hammocks up!"

They had only just been assigned their hammocks—patched and moth-eaten, the sailors' rejects—and were scrambling to claim hanging-spots on the berth deck. The older boys showed them how to sling the hammocks from the great ceiling posts called stanchions, and how to climb the post-pegs of a lower hammock up to one's own without knocking them free and sending one's neighbor crashing down. The hammocks were hung three deep: Pazel found himself on a middle level, with Neeps above him and Reyast below.

"Footlockers to starboard," Peytr had told them, toeing a heavy box. "Lashed tight against the bulkhead except in port and between shifts. Three boys to a box. There's fresh shirts and breeches for you, but don't you touch 'em till you've been scrubbed proper—deverminated, as we say, made pretty for the home port. Like as not Mr. Fiffengurt will burn your old rags in the furnace."

At lunchtime, the new boys had to wait on the hundred sailors of the Third Watch, who gobbled their food and grog with enormous pleasure and shouted for more as the boys rushed up and down the stairs from the galley in a nonstop panic. Howling with laughter, the sailors teased them, saying that Captain Rose would make them run with a cannonball under each arm if they didn't step lively.

"And don't let yer fleas get into me sub-stunnance!"

"He he he! And some Ulluprid rum while you're at it, duckies!"

"Or better yet one o' them Ulluprid girlies. Can ye cook that up?"

As their own midday meal (beef hash with carrots and yams, this time) was ending, Fiffengurt appeared with a tattered seal-skin logbook and a blue quill. He cleared a space on the table and addressed each new boy in turn. Birthplace? Previous ship, if any? Illnesses? Schooling? Skills? Everything they told him went into his logbook.

Pazel dreaded his turn. All day long he'd heard whispers be-hind his back—guesses and speculations about his skin and ac-cent. When he named Ormael as his birthplace there were winks and muffled laughter.

Fiffengurt looked up from his book, and for the first time since their arrival looked genuinely angry. The laughter ceased. Then Fiffengurt asked for his previous ships. By the time Pazel had listed all six, the boys' faces were still and thoughtful.

"How did you learn Arquali so well?" said Fiffengurt, writing smoothly.

"I worked hard at school, sir," Pazel answered with perfect truth. His fine Arquali had nothing to do with his mother's spell.

When the interviews were done, Fiffengurt told the boys about their duties. Pazel was glad that for all the *Chathrand*'s size, the tasks that kept her sailing were like those of any ship, and he knew them well. Tarboys did not set sails, or weigh anchor, or stand watch, but they helped the sailors in all these tasks, and did a thousand more besides. If they were not mending sailcloth they might be washing uniforms, sanding anchor-chain, filing down old floor nails or hammering new ones. Then there were the running errands: coal to the galley, meals to the men, water for officers, snuff for the first-class lounge. The galley itself needed twenty boys at a shift. Each deck got a daily scrub. Every rope wore a protective skin of tar.

"How much rigging do we carry, boys?" Fiffengurt asked. "Can ye guess?"

"Leagues and leagues!"

"A mile's worth! Two miles!"

Fiffengurt laughed. "Thirty-nine miles," he said. "And there won't be a fray or a weakness in any bit 'o them, lads. Not while Nilus Rose is captain."

During the whole of that day his Gift barely made itself felt: all the boys spoke Arquali, even if a few, like Pazel himself, had a different mother tongue. Still the purring went on in the back of his head, and now and then a sailor cursed or muttered about new tarboys underfoot, and Pazel knew his Gift was translating.

Then at dusk an incident occurred that brought back his old fear of madness. The boys were on the topdeck, center aft, listening to First Mate Uskins' loud and rather sinister lecture on what he called the Five Zones. The point of his harangue seemed to be that the higher your rank, the more parts of the ship you could visit without orders or express permission. The captain was the only "Five-Zone man" aboard: he could of course go anywhere; but no one, *not even the first mate* (Uskins leaned forward and struck his own chest), might enter the captain's quarters uninvited. Think of it, boys! And he, Uskins, was a Four-Zone man!

His dramatic speech ground on toward the inevitable final comment on their own status as lowest of the low (a remark Uskins seemed to look forward to). As he boomed and huffed, Pazel realized one of the boys was whispering on his left. It was an odd whisper, not at all mindful of Uskins. Someone, thought Pazel, is making a big mistake.

When Uskins turned to gesture at the forecastle, Pazel risked a glance. There was no one on his left. He snapped his eyes forward again, perplexed. He had distinctly heard a voice.

A moment later it came again, louder this time: *"They ate well today. Shepherd's pie for breakfast."*

Definitely on his left. But before Pazel had a chance to look again a second voice answered the first. This one was low and bitterly amused.

"Of course they did. And they'll eat well until the gangway's dismantled. You can't have boys deserting before the voyage starts."

Was he dreaming? There was absolutely no one in sight: just the bare deck, and a grate covering the shot-locker hatch, the little shaft by which cannonballs could be hoisted to the forward guns. Pazel glanced quickly at Neeps. The other boy caught his eye, but there was no look of understanding. Neeps hadn't heard a thing.

"You see that posture? Chin up, hands behind the back? He's been to school, that one."

Pazel blinked. His hands were folded behind his back.

"From the Keppery Isles?" asked the first voice.

"Wrong color. That's not just sun on his skin."

Despite himself, Pazel cast a glance at his brown feet.

"Fidgets a lot. He'll stand out, Taliktrum."

"He was quite still a moment ago."

He wasn't dreaming, he was merely insane. The voices were coming from the grate. Whenever Uskins gave him the chance, Pazel squinted at it. The shaft was about two feet square. That one person might be inside it seemed absurd. That two might was simply impossible.

Then the voice said, *"Ormael."*

Pazel could not breathe. He'd had years of practice at hiding his feelings from dangerous men, but nothing had prepared him for what was happening now. They were talking about *him*!

"Ormael! That's it! Rin's eyes, a lad from the Trothe of Cher-este! He must hate them to his marrow! Give him a match and he'll burn her to the waterline!"

"That remains to be seen, Ludunte. But what's the matter with him? He's beginning to look sick."

"Just our luck if he drops dead before—"

"Quiet!"

Pazel was shaking. Fortunately Uskins took no notice: his conclusion was carrying him away: "You may not touch the ladder to the quarterdeck. You may not open a fastened hatch. You may not touch a backstay, or a forestay, or slouch against a mast, or malinger about the galley, on pain of—"

"Did you bend your voice?"

"Of course not!"

Pazel could no longer stand it. He trained his eyes directly on the grate, and the voices broke off. He could see nothing, but he had the strangest feeling that he had locked eyes with two invisible beings.

Neeps elbowed him a warning. Pazel wrenched his gaze back to Uskins, trembling. At once the two voices resumed.

"I'll be damned to the Pit! He hears!"

"He can't! He can't!"

"He does! Look at him!"

"A freak, a monster! Taliktrum, we'll have to—"

Uskins cleared his throat. He was looking straight at Pazel.

"What the devil is the matter with you?" the first mate demanded.

Now all eyes were on him.

"N-n-nothing, Mr. Uskins. Sir!"

Uskins' eyes narrowed. He squared his shoulders. "You're the Ormali," he said. "Pathkendle."

"That's right, sir."

"I do not need you to assure me I am right!" boomed Uskins, in a voice that turned heads around the topdeck.

"I'm sorry, sir."

"Tarboys do not presume to confirm an officer's statements! If the officer's word is doubted, what good can a tarboy's do? Of course it can do no good at all. Isn't that so, Pathkendle?"

"I . . . uh . . . yes, yes, sir."

"You hesitated. Why?"

"Pardon me, sir. You just told me not to confirm your statements."

"Silence! Silence! Wharf cur! You dare make sport of me? Go empty your bladder, as you so visibly need to do, and then fetch lye from the galley and scrub those heads till they gleam! And when you see your own reflection remind yourself how lucky you are not to be whipped, you miserable, clever, ruddy-skinned runt! You other boys are dismissed!"

By *heads* Uskins meant the toilets, which on sailing ships are placed as far forward as possible so that the wind, always a bit faster than the ship itself, carries the reek of them away. The *Chathrand*'s complement was two rows of eight, an astonishing number. He was still going at it with a long brush and lye when the order came to strike moorings, and sailors dashed to their stations, and the running pennants were hoisted to the topmasts. Hardly the glorious moment Pazel had dreamed of that first night on the *Eniel*. Still, he felt lucky when he thought of Uskins' error: better to be thought weak in the bladder than soft in the head. Or convulsive. Or possessed.

He was none of these, of course. Once the fright left him he had realized at once what was happening. There *had* been something in the shot-locker shaft. Two somethings, and they had watched him in fascination. Pazel had a good idea what kind of beings they were. The mystery was what they could possibly want with him.

Finally done with his smelly task, he stepped out onto the forecastle only to see Fiffengurt backing toward him, craning his neck to study the crosstrees.

"Pathkendle!" he said. "Head detail already? What's this about?"

"I . . . I don't honestly know, sir," said Pazel. "Mr. Uskins said we mustn't confirm his statements. I tried to obey him, but somehow I muddled it up."

Fiffengurt looked him over (or one eye seemed to), then nodded gravely. "Just as I feared. A born criminal."

"Sir?"

"Never mind, Mr. Pathkendle. Step this way. I have another punishment for you."

He marched Pazel across the forbidden territory of the forecastle. It occurred to the boy that if he dared tell any officer about the voices it would be Fiffengurt. He had nearly decided to do so when the quartermaster turned.

"Have you a sailor's grip, lad? Can you handle a bit of wind?"

"Certainly, sir!"

"Then scurry out the jib-stay, and be sure no snail or barnacle's

THE RED WOLF CONSPIRACY 117

defaced Her Ladyship. Work 'em free with your knife—haven't you got a knife?"

"It was stolen, sir."

"Well, take mine a spell, but don't you dare let it drop! And go easy on the girl, for pity's sake! She's old enough to be your grandmam!" He smiled and lowered his voice. "Don't rush. Some of them limpets are blary small."

"Oppo, sir! Oh, thank you, sir!"

In a flash Pazel was over the rail and easing out along the bowsprit line. He laughed aloud, thinking, *Fiffengurt's my man!* For instead of being trapped belowdecks with the rest of the boys, Pazel now swayed in the wind, one arm around the Goose-Girl figurehead, forward of every soul aboard, as the *Chathrand* slid free of the docks on the outflowing tide. The Shipworks gleamed; a black albatross skimmed low before him. Men ashore held their caps high, not waving: the dockworkers' farewell. On the deck the sailors murmured the prayer to Bakru, and Pazel did the same:

> *We go to sea, to sea, small men of soil made.*
> *Pour milk for your lions, lord of wind;*
> *Send them not hungry to the clouds,*
> *Lest they roar for our blood . . .*

Over his shoulder Pazel saw the tow-boats waiting, their men fastening lines from the *Chathrand*'s bow. Slowly the Great Ship turned in the narrow port until the Goose-Girl faced the sea. Then for the first time Pazel heard Captain Rose's thundering shout: *"Two jibs and the forecourse, Mr. Elkstem."*

"Oppo, Captain, two jibs and the fore! Spurn, Leef, Lapwing! Cast gaskets! Jump to!"

Elkstem, the sailmaster, sounded amazed to be setting sails within a stone's throw of the docks, but the men in the tow-boats grinned: Rose's haste meant their own labors would be short. Indeed, the moment the big square foresail grasped the wind the ship leaped for open water, and it was all the rowers could do to get out of her path as she gathered speed. One man laughed and pointed: "That tarboy's found him a bride!" Pazel threw a barnacle at him, laughing too.

White sail after white sail. Sorrophran vanished behind them. The light too was leaving—in half an hour it would be dark. But away west, the headland still glowed in the evening sun. And there, what a sight! Galloping to its peak was a fine black horse, and a rider in a billowing cloak.

The rider turned his steed sharply, waving. Pazel froze.

"*Kozo,* who's that nutter?" said the fore watchman, squinting up at the cliffs.

Pazel said nothing. The man was Ignus Chadfallow.

The doctor cupped his hands to his mouth and shouted: "*. . . get away, lad! Jump ship in Etherhorde!*"

"A madman!" said the sailor. "What's that language he's speaking?"

"Who knows?" said Pazel. But the tongue was Ormali, and he its only speaker aboard. As Chadfallow surely knew.

"*. . . not what I planned . . . madness . . . jump ship!*"

"Deep devils, but he looks familiar! Someone famous, maybe? You know him, tarry?"

For a moment Pazel couldn't find his voice. At last he shook his head. "No, sir. I've never seen him before in my life."

Chadfallow kept shouting as they rounded the headland. The wind shifted, and his voice began to fade.

–10–

Midnight Council

2 Vaqrin 941
12:02 a.m.

"The boy must be killed at once."

Taliktrum spoke from the fifth shelf, the highest, which was where he slept. Five feet below, on the first, Diadrelu looked up at him from the clan circle and shook her head.

"Not yet," she said.

Taliktrum sat cross-legged, sharpening a knife on the sole of his foot. Here in the bow, where the gap between the inner and outer hulls reached nearly three feet wide, they were as safe as anywhere aboard, yet his hands seemed always on his weapons. She did not like this constant fingering of blades, this stabbing at timbers and caressing of hilts. It set a bad example for the younger folk, who were busy hiding their nervousness (call it what it is: fear) behind jokes and horseplay. Survival lay in good sense, not in bravado. Yet it was easier to provoke bravado than thought.

"He must die," repeated Taliktrum. "And the sooner the better. He's a monster, a giant with ixchel ears. Already he knows enough to doom us all. We were lucky tonight that his punishment shamed him into silence. At dawn it will be another matter."

"Taliktrum," said Dri, "come down among the clan."

He obeyed with insolent slowness, climbing down the inner

hull with his knife between his teeth. Three feet above the shelf where his aunt and thirty other ixchel stood, he jumped, and landed nimble as a cat at the circle's center.

"Sheathe your knife, and act no more the fool with it," said Dri. "Listen: we do not know why the boy was silent."

"And you would wait to find out, Dri?" asked Ensyl. "What if he rises tomorrow and guesses they were ixchel voices he heard?"

"He will have guessed already," she said. "Ludunte says he looked right at our crawlway. The giants know we ride their ships. And though none can hear our natural voices—none ever, before this boy—still they know we can speak."

"They know, because some of us beg for our lives when the Arqualis catch us," said Taliktrum, looking bored and irritable. "Beg in the name of Rin and his Angel and the Milk of the One Tree. All those things the giants claim to worship. To no avail."

"Most kill us, given the chance," Dri agreed. "Not all, however. If we are to survive this mission we must not overlook those precious few."

"You believe he held his tongue for *our* sake?" said Taliktrum.

"I believe he is an Ormali as you guessed. That means he may have no love for this Empire."

"Odd crew he's chosen to ship with, in that case."

Now a few snickered openly. Dri waited until they fell silent of their own accord. Then she said, "Foreign-born youths do not serve the Empire at their pleasure. They serve to keep themselves out of gutters, or chains. And do you suppose that any of them has an inkling of the true purpose of this voyage? How could they, when after ten years of spying, we ourselves are still forced to guess?"

"I will tell you what I guess," said Ludunte. "I guess this monster-boy will speak of us to someone."

"Who will speak to someone else," said Taliktrum. "And so on, until we are the talk of the *Chathrand*. The cargo is still but half loaded. The giants can afford to tear the ship apart searching for us, and they might. No, the moment to strike is now. A fire started in a tuft of grass can be left to spread until the whole plain is burning. Or it can be snuffed out."

"Or," said Dri, "the tuft of grass can be carried to the hearth, and logs lit to keep us from freezing. Think of the ally he could make! We could speak to him in the presence of other giants. We could tell him what to ask, what to look for as he makes his rounds."

"He could get us fresh water," said someone.

"He could leave doors ajar."

"He could throw the witch's cat into the sea."

"Maybe," said Taliktrum coldly, "he will sprout wings and carry us all wrapped together in a blanket to Sanctuary-Beyond-the-Sea. Rin's name! Why do you ply us with fantasies, Dri?"

"The founder of Ixphir House was saved from death by a giant woman," said Dri. "One hundred and sixty years ago, in the gardens of the *Accateo Lorgut*. That is not fantasy. We would none of us be here without her."

"Legend," said Taliktrum. "Pretty stories for children at bedtime. Will you still take comfort in them when your gentle giants have killed us all?"

It was late when the council adjourned. Dri bid them all go to their rest on the sleeping shelves, and they went uneasily, but without grumbling. In an ixchel clan circle everyone speaks who would speak, but when the conference ends the leader must be obeyed.

She was exhausted: her ribs still ached like fire from her contortions on the rat funnel. The absurd thing was that the cursed devices never worked: the ship was boiling with rats. They slipped up gangways, burrowed into straw bales carried aboard for the manger, or merely leaped past the funnels like the ixchel themselves. And how they multiplied! A ship could set sail with just a few dozen and make landfall a few months later with thousands of starving animals in her hold.

Lying on her shelf, she could hear them in the forward hold, scurrying and chattering and chanting their songs of greed. Her people would have to guard against them as well. Rats could not be trusted. They would promise peace, and sometimes struggle to keep it for a week or two. But when food grew scarce their eyes took on a certain gleam. They would gather around the edges of ixchel bunkers, or trail menacingly behind a scouting party, or lie in wait . . .

But humans are not rats, Taliktrum, she thought, with a pleading quality she would never allow herself to voice. She could almost hear his laughing reply: *True enough, Aunt. They're worse.*

". . . be still, Ormali boy, wake and be still. You hear me, do you not? Wake; and as you value your life, be still."

In the darkness, Pazel opened his eyes. He lay in his hammock among fifty other tarboys, slung about the stuffy berth deck like hams in a smokehouse. Reyast was sleeping two feet beneath him, and Neeps two feet above. Snores and wheezes drifted about the lightless deck.

But the voice was no dream.

It came from somewhere just behind his head. It was a woman's voice, but it had the same weird, thin sound as the voices from the hatch. *The crawlies.* They had found him already. Even if he had wished to disobey, Pazel was too frightened to move.

"Good," said the voice. "Now listen well, boy. I hold a sword at your throat. If necessary I will slash your great vein and put your own knife in your hand, and in the morning the crew will bury you at sea without a death-prayer, as a suicide. Your life hangs by a thread. At any moment we choose, anywhere on this ship, we can snap that thread. And snap it we shall, instantly, if you give us the slightest cause."

Then Pazel felt it: a hand, smaller than a squirrel's paw, taking a grip on his sleep-tussled hair.

"Nod if you understand," said the woman.

Shaking with horror, Pazel nodded. The hammock ropes creaked, and he stifled a gasp. They were all over him. Legs, arms, stomach, twenty or more crawlies, tense as cats. Some infinitely pale glow from the hatches let him see their sleek movements, their limbs bristling with strength. They held swords, daggers, spears. The tip of an unseen blade scratched just below his ear—impatiently, he thought.

A tiny bare foot slapped his forehead, then another his cheek, and suddenly Pazel found an eight-inch-tall woman facing him from the center of his chest.

He could barely see her, but he knew she was their queen. Some natural dignity informed the way she stood, legs slightly apart, facing him squarely and calmly above his hammering heart.

"You will not lie," she declared, sheathing her tiny sword. "We ixchel can smell it, the change that comes over a giant when he lies. I have no wish to kill you—indeed far from it. But the path I walk allows for no turning, no mistakes. Therefore I must kill you if you lie. Tell me: have you spoken to anyone of the voices you heard on the topdeck?"

Pazel shook his head no.

"See that you do not: they will be the last words you ever speak. Now explain how it is that you can hear us, our natural voices that no human ever could, as clearly as if we were bending our speech for human ears. And tell us how you come to know our language. Speak softly, and be brief."

Nothing was more difficult for Pazel, especially when he was nervous. He opened his mouth and shut it several times.

"Speak!" the woman hissed.

"A spell!" blurted Pazel. "But it goes all wrong!"

"Are you a mage, then?"

Again Pazel shook his head. "My mother," he whispered. "It was supposed to make you better at—whatever you're good at. I'm good at languages, so the spell made me perfect. But it's awful. It works, and I can speak anything—"

"Any tongue of Alifros?"

"Anything! Then it stops, and there's terrible noises, evil bird noises, I can't—"

"We warned you not to lie, Ormali!"

It was another voice, a man's. Pazel froze. The woman looked up sharply. The voice seemed to belong to whoever was drawing the blade up and down beneath his ear.

"Any tongue in Alifros," sneered the man. "The brat thinks we're simple. And he'll be right if we go on using *our* tongues in place of swords."

"Peace, Taliktrum!" said the woman angrily. But all the ixchel were muttering and shifting now.

The man's voice went on: "You saw how they singled him out in the Plaza. They're using him like a terrier, to root us out. They taught him Ix, all right—from prisoners in their jails. They're moving him from ship to ship. Wasn't he tossed off a boat two days ago? And then this brainless fib! Very well, witch-child, answer me: *Art thou my bloodkin, lost to storm these sundering years? Shall I name thee brother?*"

Some of the crawlies sniggered. The woman whirled in a rage to face them, raising her fist in some gesture of command. But Pazel spoke first.

"Name me what you like," he said. "Brat, or bloodkin, or brother. Just don't tell me you can smell lies. My mate Neeps can do that, but clearly you can't."

The laughter had stopped at his first word. Even the woman looked stunned. "And clearly your Gift is real," she said. "Unless any here believe this lad was taught Nileskchet, dead language of our ancient bards."

She paused: no one spoke.

"I thought not," she said, and there was cold fury in her voice. "Be gone, all of you. S'an order!"

They went, silent and abashed, nearly invisible still. Pazel was left with the tiny woman standing four-square on his chest. When they were alone, she startled him by folding her hands before her face as though praying. Her voice, when next she spoke, no longer rang with power. It sounded tired and uncertain.

"My name is Dri, Pazel Pathkendle. In full, Diadrelu Tammariken ap Ixhxchr. I am the leader of my people aboard

Chathrand until my brother and co-commander joins us in Etherhorde. Trust me when I say that I regret these threats and suspicions."

"I do *not* trust you," said Pazel.

"Wise boy," she said, and laughed. "You're quite right. Don't trust. But what I say is true nonetheless. If they catch you during your mind-fit, you'll go to an asylum. Do you know what happens if they lay hold of us?"

"I know," he said, wincing at the thought. "But I'm not one of them. Arqual destroyed my home. I'm here to find my family, if they're still alive, and once I do I'll get us all out of this blary Empire forever, if I can. Honestly, I'm not like these people. I don't hate crawlies."

"Ixchel!" she said sharply. "Never use that other word. But hear me quickly, ere dawn comes. Evil is afoot, Pazel. This ship is bound for the west—to conclude a treaty of peace, they say. But in the capital some will board her with other goals, unspeakable goals, in mind. We are not even sure who they are. But they *must not succeed.*"

Far above on the main deck, the ship's bell tolled. Diadrelu started. "I must go," she said. "We will meet again, when the ship's business in Etherhorde is done. Until then our own business is survival. Pazel, do not prove me a fool before my own people. Speak to no one of us. I do not threaten you. I beg."

Above him, Neeps muttered, half waking. As if aware that she had stayed too long, the ixchel woman leaped suddenly past his head, and Pazel felt her climbing the hammock rope.

"Are you going to drown us?" he whispered, suddenly frightened of her leaving. "Will you sink the ship at night, like the stories tell?"

The woman paused. "Nonsense," she whispered. "How could a few ixchel sink the mightiest ship in Alifros?"

"And those evil goals, ma'am? What are they?"

Her voice came from farther away; she was climbing again. "We have but guesses."

"Then tell me your guesses, won't you?"

He heard no answer at first, and thought she had gone. Then her voice came once more, from somewhere across the berth deck, and faint as it was there was no mistaking the word, or her dread as she spoke it.

"War."

11

FROM THE SECRET JOURNAL OF
G. STARLING FIFFENGURT, QUARTERMASTER

Imperial Mercantile Ship Extraordinaire CHATHRAND
[Reg. 40279/Ethrhrd]
under NILUS ROSE, by Order of His Supremacy Captain
and Final Offshore Authority
In this the year 941
Being the 28th of the reign of His Supremacy Magad V

Tuesday, 4 Vaqrin. We made good speed all the first night under a jeweler's moon, & the next day had merciful clear skies. Even with the headwinds tonight I will be surprised if we are six days in reaching the capital.

The old boat has never been more fit. I so stated to the captain & 1st mate Uskins, & Capt. Rose said it was not for the quartermaster to offer casual opinions about the state of the vessel. At that the grackle-mouthed Uskins smirked & nodded. Rose spotted him & fairly blew his powder, ordering the "fatuous great fop" about his duties. I took care that my own face betrayed no satisfaction.

Of course, bad temper is no new affliction in Rose: when he commanded the *Chathrand* 12 years ago he flogged a man for hiccups. Yet something ails him, I think, & it is more than his combustible spirit. 'Tis only two days I've spent in his company, but already I sense his unease. When he came aboard with trumpets blaring, he walked up to me in front of the assembled officers & said the following, more or less:

"Mr. Fiffengurt. I know you wanted this captaincy, as you've served a good span of years on the Great Ship. But I have my commission in hand, double-signed by the ship's owners & the Emperor himself. I'm captain, and like as not you never shall be, now, for you're no spring chicken. This was probably your last chance. I advise you to chew on that unhappy fact as we cross Ellisoq Bay, and make your peace with it. And if you're not ready to serve me like any other man aboard, ship off in Etherhorde & seek another boat! Don't cross me, & don't try to curry favor with any man against me. Now give me your inventory."

With that he snatched my logbook, opened it & frowned. He said my penmanship was fussy & womanish, & gave Uskins the task of log-keeper for the voyage. I tried to look unhappy, but inside I rejoiced. Thirteen years I've kept those logs: thirteen years scribbling every cough of wind & blush of weather & blotch of ringworm in the crew. Never was I free to do as I shall henceforth: *record my private thoughts.* Here's to you, Uskins, you sow.

Of course, private notebooks are forbidden. Every word becomes the property of the Chathrand Trading Family as soon as you commit it to paper. That is why I write only in bed, like a naughty schoolboy, & hide this journal in a secret place.

How surprised Rose would be to know I never wanted his post! Indeed that I should have left the sea for good last year, & married one sweet Annabel, & joined her father's little brewery on Hoopi Street, if criminals from the thrice-damned Mangel Beerworks had not burned it to the ground. Now to help that good family recover I shall be three more years at sea. By Rin, there's no evil like profit-lust. Anni's dad brewed good ales: that was his crime. On the best of days he could not have sold a tenth as much as those scheming barons of beer.

At least I can be glad of this mission—proud of it, indeed. Bless the Emperor! Bless whatever wise men there be among the Black Rags our enemies (though Rin & his Angel are unknown to them)! This great work of peace will out-last us all, & if I have children & grandchildren with dear Anni (it is not impossible yet; not in three years, even), they shall brag a little about their daddy's part. Bless Rose, too: the Emperor named him to this task, & I must trust his reasons.

Capt. Rose still frowns when he sees me. But I do not take his abuse to heart. In every task he seems twitchy & distracted, as if thinking of some immense & immediate problem, a sea full of icebergs, plague among the crew. How strange, all this worry & anger, when only yesterday he spoke of joining the Brotherhood of Serenity.

I do hope that man Bolutu can help him; otherwise our captain will have hard sailing toward his goal. For they say monks of the Brotherhood purge themselves of all low emotions: they do not fear, or lust, or even weep at a parent's death. Above all they do not hate. In truth I cannot think of a less probable personality than *Brother* Nilus Rose.

Until yesterday I might at least have called him fearless. But this morning a thing happened that I should not have believed if any man aboard swore it by the milk of the One Tree. I had just finished the survey of our new sailors & brought the results to the wardroom for Mr. Elkstem's inspection. When I arrived Elkstem was away, but Capt. Rose stood alone at the back of the chamber, against the bulkhead, with a clutch of maps under his arm & the oddest look on his face I ever saw in a ship's commander.

"Fiffengurt," he said in a trembly voice, "come in here."

I did so. In the center of the wardroom table, the Lady Oggosk's pet, Sniraga, crouched on another map, looking sleepy & pleased with herself. She is a rascal of a cat & will bite you if you stroke her, but at that moment she was all sweet cream & purrs. Rose, however, looked at her as if at a black ship closing fast with a deck full of buccaneers. He raised his hand & pointed at the animal.

"That devil!" he said. "I didn't see it come in!"

"Yes, Captain," says I. "Cats are a race of sneaky-boots, all right. Quiet as you please."

"It's blary well not quiet now! What's it saying, Fiffengurt?"

I own I gaped at my own captain. "*Saying,* sir? That's purring, that is. Cats do that when they're glad to see you, sir."

"That damn bloodthirsty snaggle-fanged feline has no cause on earth to be glad to see me!" he roared. "Or to presume to use that tone, to threaten . . ."

His eyes had not moved from the red cat, who looked set to roll on her back & have her belly rubbed. I stood there like a mute. I knew that when the Capt. came to his senses he'd likely punish me just for witnessing him in this silly state. By Rin, it was weird! I didn't know what to say.

"Cats are curious, sir" was all I came up with.

"Get it out of here, Fiffengurt," said Rose, who still had not moved an inch.

"Oppo, sir. Shall I ask Lady Oggosk to confine the pet to her cabin?"

"Just remove it—chase it—get it out of my sight!"

I poked the animal in the ribs. She hissed at me, but shot right out of the wardroom. Then Capt. Nilus Rose shook himself & looked around as if waking from a dream, & asked what the blazes I'd come for.

Thursday, 6 Vaqrin. Not much time for you tonight, good journal! Four of the new tarboys will have to be jettisoned in Etherhorde: two brawling already over somebody's candy, one green with seasickness, the last wetting himself in his sleep like a babe, which cannot be tolerated where hammocks are slung one above the next.

So many errands in Etherhorde. We need new keys for the gate between the first-class compartments & the rest of the ship—the *Money Gate,* as my boys are already calling it. And we shall need a piano-mender: the daft steward in the first-class lounge unbolted the fixtures to wax the floor & did not think to secure them as we left port. Naturally the first big swell launched the old upright—& various tables, chairs & spittoons—across the boards like logs in a chute. The piano fetched over with a noise like Doomsday chimes. Hours I would have spent with Annabel will be lost to this foolishness, but first-class children must be free to scamper behind their gate without fear of riffraff, and first-class gents must have their dinner music.

Saturday, 8 Vaqrin. Glad I am to write these words. Etherhorde is in sight.

12

Battles with Smoke

Pazel and Neeps raced headlong across the berth deck, leaping sea chests, dodging among hammocks, crates, scores of weary sailors. They had two hours' freedom this morning, after twelve in the dark and stinking hold, and they didn't intend to waste a second. The ship had docked at midday in Etherhorde, if the word from above could be trusted. Now confused rumors were passing from sailor to sailor, deck to deck. All Pazel could glean from their shouts was that something was happening aloft.

"They'll be bringing on that ambassador, I'll bet you," huffed Neeps as they reached the midship ladderway. "That's why we finally got scrubbed—*deverminated,* I mean. That's why we're in our new clothes."

They climbed, looking much alike now that their heads were shaven, and Neeps' turban confiscated. "Have you seen the ambassador's stateroom?" Pazel asked. "Dastu says it's really four rooms in one!"

"Five!" said Neeps. "I never told you, did I? Peytr snuck us in last night. There's the main room for sitting and eating and whatnot, with big paintings in gold frames, and a windup organ that plays three hundred songs, and leather padding on the walls to keep it warm. You can barely *hear* the sea, mate! Then there's a cabin for Isiq and his Lady, and another for the girl—they say she's pretty, you know—and a washroom big enough for a bull, and a last tiny room made of glass, hanging right over the waves in the stern galleries, with a bed tucked under the window for your afternoon nap."

"Five rooms," said Pazel, shaking his head. "What on earth could he do with so much space?"

Neeps said he had an idea what the ambassador might do, but he had no chance to elaborate, for at that moment a tremendous noise rent the air. It was not the trumpet-blast they had expected; in fact it was like nothing they had ever heard: a gigantic screech, such as a tormented child might make if it were the size of an elephant. For a moment every other voice on the *Chathrand* fell silent. Pazel and Neeps gaped at each other. Then they began to climb even faster.

As they neared the topdeck the shouting of the men resumed, louder and more alarmed than before. Finally Pazel thrust his head through the No. 4 hatch into dazzling afternoon sun.

What he saw took his breath away. The ship floated just a few yards from shore, berthed in a clearing between two forests of masts that curved away endlessly north and south. This was the Royal Esplanade, the astounding deepwater channel cut right to the foot of the Emperor's Plaza of the Palmeries, from which hundreds of docks spread in long seaward-stretching fingers. Crowded tight about each of these bobbed every conceivable sort of ship: fighters, fishing-rigs, port gunners, signal-ships, lead-bellied oreships, sleek Noonfirth Javelans with their gryphon's-head bows, Opaltine merchantmen like floating teakettles, grizzled *lunkets,* porcelain-domed Nunekkamers, whalers, kelp-cutters, sloops. Farthest of all, on a blue slice of Etherhorde Bay, Pazel saw Imperial warships at anchor, served by the steady, ant-like crawling of transports.

"Get out of the way!" Neeps whispered, shoving from below. "I can't see a thing!"

The boys scrambled onto the deck—and then the sound came again, huge and furious. Spinning about, they faced a scene of horror. Above a crowd of frightened men stood a monster in chains, a slouching giant with a yellow-brown hide like that of some weird rhinoceros. It had long warty ears, jaws that might have bitten a spar in two and arms the length of a man's body ending in hands like gnarled stumps. Those arms were chained at the wrists, and the chains held by ten sailors each. Nonetheless the creature had somehow got hold of a man.

It was Mr. Frix, the bald second mate, whom everyone called Firecracker Frix because he was terrified of thunder and explosions. He looked limp with fear. The monster, overpowering scores of burly sailors, lifted Frix to its own chest and pressed him there like a bunch of roses.

"Lord Rin Himself!" shouted Neeps. "They've dragged an augrong aboard!"

"What is it?" cried Pazel.

"Frix's death, that's what it is! Strongest blary things that ever walked, or lurched. From the Griib Desert, where the Death Tribes are. Pazel, *look*!"

On shore, over another clump of frightened men, a second creature (somewhat shorter in the ears) was writhing in its chains. Its flat yellow eyes were locked on its companion. Who was in charge? Pazel looked this way and that, and finally saw Uskins and Fiffengurt upon the quarterdeck. They were arguing; Fiffengurt gestured and shook his head, as if trying desperately to talk Uskins out of his plans. But the first mate shoved him away. Leaning over the rail, he pointed down at the crew and bellowed:

"Draw pikes! Bindhammer, Fegin, Coote! Show that wretched monster he can behave or bleed!"

The pikes stood in racks near the mainmast. Sailors ran to obey Uskins' order, if only to put some distance between themselves and the augrong.

"What are they here for?" Pazel asked Neeps. "Are they slaves?"

"Nay, they're crew!" answered a voice at his shoulder. The boys turned to see Dastu, wild-eyed, standing behind them. "Anchorlifters, them two," said the elder tarboy. "Refeg and Rer—don't ask me which is which. But the old-timers say they can do the work of fifty men! Rose signed 'em on twelve years ago, when he last commanded *Chathrand*. Turns out they still live here, in a shack on the Oolmarsh. But the captain's gone to visit the Emperor, and Uskins is making a right bloody mess of things."

"Are augrongs safe?" Pazel asked.

"Not on your life!" said Dastu. "But they're placid enough, or so Mr. Fiffengurt says, if you treat 'em right. Only one thing makes 'em mean: getting separated. Word is Refeg and Rer are brothers, and the last of their tribe this side of the Griib. They're scared to death of losin' each other for good!" He lowered his voice. "Don't you two repeat this, but Uskins told Rose he was an augrong expert. And what does he do? He has 'em brought aboard one at a time!"

On the quarterdeck, Uskins screamed at his men to hurry. Then, standing well back from the rail, he pointed at the long-eared creature on the deck.

"Quick!" he cried. *"Baddy kill beast! You big fire, big fire dinner!"*

Pazel knew at once that his Gift was at work. Uskins was trying to speak to the augrongs in their own tongue and botching it terribly. Nor could the magic in Pazel's head straighten out the mess: translated nonsense is still nonsense. The augrong cast a wild, confused eye in Uskins' direction. Then it turned Mr. Frix upside down and squeezed.

The sailors returned with pikes in hand, more thoughtful than when they had run away. When they pointed them at the augrong holding Frix, its companion gave a great twisting heave, scattering men like ninepins. The first creature answered with ferocious leaps and bellows. Mr. Frix, struck dumb by his predicament until then, began to howl for his life.

Uskins waved his arms and screamed: *"Dinner or kill? Why not? You kill, kill, kill!"*

"Oh, sky!" said Pazel. "Be quiet, you fool!"

By the faces of the men he guessed that no one, least of all Uskins himself, knew what the first mate was shouting. The

augrong knew, though, and looked ready to oblige. Mr. Frix
began to wail like a man roasting on a fire.

Pazel knew what he had to do next—and before fear could
stop him, he did it. Breaking the Rule of the Five Zones, he
bounded up the ladder to the quarterdeck, darted right past
Uskins (who was still shouting *"Kill!"*), planted a foot on the
rail and, with only an instant to wonder if Frix's life was worth
losing his own for, jumped.

The height of the forecastle let him clear the heads of the
sailors with ease. But he had forgotten the augrong's chains.
Even as he leaped, the monster reared backward and the chain
about its neck drew up tight as a bowstring. Pazel met it with his
knees, spun helplessly in the air and landed with an agonizing
thump on the augrong's foot.

To the creature this was apparently the last straw. Dancing on
one foot, it tossed Frix into the bay and scooped up Pazel in one
hand, bellowing like a hundred bulls. Before Pazel knew what
was happening he found himself being squeezed in the crook of
the monster's elbow.

"Wait!" gasped Pazel. He tried to add, *Please,* but the breath
had been knocked from his lungs, and his Gift informed him in
an instant that the word did not exist in Augronga. But for an instant one word was enough: the creature hesitated, its raging red
eyes fixed on the tarboy.

"You're *both* coming aboard," Pazel managed to croak. "We
need you *both* to lift anchor!"

As soon as the words left his mouth the creature loosened its
grip. The augrong gaped at Pazel. Two hundred sailors gaped at
the augrong. And in the moment of silence that followed,
Mr. Uskins laughed aloud.

"Eat him, then, you daft dirty lizard! We need Frix, but tarboys are a penny a pound! And you'll do this ship a favor if you
can choke down that Ormali runt."

But Uskins had given up on his pseudo-Augronga, and the
creature paid no heed to his Arquali. Instead it listened to the
rest of Pazel's explanation. Then in deep-chested grunts (and

using the foulest metaphor to refer to Mr. Uskins) it relayed the message to its companion. The short-eared creature sighed like the wind.

"Anger for nothing," it said. "Battle with smoke."

Its arms fell to its sides. All about the harbor, and aboard the *Chathrand,* men echoed the sigh. The fight was over.

Pazel, however, still hung from the creature's arm. Twisting, he found himself looking sidelong at the crowded quay. It was disturbing to be watched by so many silent people. Faces leaped out at him: a one-armed veteran, a woman with a basket of melons on her head, a lean man with a fighter's muscles holding the chains of two enormous blue dogs.

From this last figure Pazel's eyes slid to a striking older man in Imperial navy uniform, leaning from a carriage window. He had a neat beard and white sideburns, and his bright blue eyes studied Pazel keenly. It was a moment before Pazel noticed that the carriage was the most elegant he had ever seen.

The old man frowned, stuck his head farther out through the window and looked up. Following his gaze, Pazel found himself looking at a girl his own age. She had climbed to the roof of the carriage for a better view. She wore a man's clothing—jaquina shirt, breeches, a broad leather belt. She was extremely pretty, with a preposterous amount of straight golden hair falling to her waist, but her arms looked strong as a tarboy's. She also looked him straight in the eye, which was something noble-born girls never did. In fact, she smiled, a bright smile full of laughter—or mockery? Startled and suddenly shy, Pazel dropped his gaze.

"No bones smashed," boomed the augrong suddenly, and set Pazel on the deck with a mighty thump. Pazel stumbled, dizzy and aching from head to toe. Neeps and Dastu caught him by the arms. But the rest of the crew backed away from him slightly, as if wondering what would next come out of his mouth.

Then Pazel saw Uskins glaring down at him from the quarterdeck.

"A meddler," said the first mate. "A clown. Do you know the captain's policy for dealing with clowns?"

There was an awful silence. Uskins crooked a finger, beckoning Pazel near.

It was at that instant that Mr. Frix, Firecracker Frix, bounded up the gangway. He had just been hauled out of the bay by sailors ashore, and seawater ran from his ears and shirt and breeches. Leaping onto the deck, he pointed at Pazel and let out a great soggy whoop.

"Saved!" he cried. "That boy saved me life! Bless him, oh bless his wee little lion's heart! Hooray!" He capered in his private puddle, wet beard flapping, and waved both hands over his head. Then he scrambled onto a rum barrel and sang out again: "Saved by the tarry, the tar-tar-tarry-boy! How's that for a wonder? Come on, boys! Three cheers for little Lionheart! Hip, hip—"

"Stand down, Mr. Frix!"

No mistaking that voice, which crashed through the hubbub like a cannonball. Even the augrongs turned their heads. Captain Rose was storming across the Plaza as quickly as his game leg allowed, face shining with wrath, a carriage stopped behind him with its door flapping still. He waved as he neared the gangway: "To your stations, you gawking gulls! Clear out! Give a man room to board his vessel! And bring that other beast up after me! What fool separated them?"

All eyes snapped to the first mate. Uskins glowered and chewed his lips, but he put on a look of humble martyrdom when Rose's own eyes found him.

"Take the augrongs below, Mr. Uskins," said Rose grimly. "I will hear your report ere we leave the capital." Then the captain raised his voice to an ear-shattering bellow: "All hands! Welcome stations! Trumpets! Pennants! Hats! First watch to the yards! Move, you port-shoddy sheep! His Excellency's waiting to board!"

Everywhere, men flew to their tasks. Then Pazel understood: the man in the elegant coach was none other than Admiral Isiq, His Supremacy's new ambassador to Simja. And that blond girl, whose smile had left him feeling such a fool? Could that be his daughter?

-13-

Turnstile

Art thou my bloodkin, lost to storm these sundering years!
Shall I name thee brother!
My soul has shed the habit of love, trust is a thing forgotten.
Come not upon me silent, brother, lest you frighten me:
Who knows what I'll do then!
Fear this blade in my hand, brother, as I have learned to fear it.

THE MAN WHO ATE GOLD, CANTO LXII
Translated from the Nileskchet by Talag Tammaruk ap Ixhxchr

9 Vaqrin 941

The old admiral had sent word: he wanted little fuss about his
boarding. This was quite unlike the Eberzam Isiq of old, who returned from battles on half-ruined warships to a thunder of guns
and a throng of well-wishers filling the Plaza of the Palmeries.
To the reporter from the *Etherhorde Mariner,* a dumpy little man
in a top hat with a bedraggled bow, it was all very suspicious.
Why were there no public announcements? he demanded,
beetling toward the ship at Isiq's elbow. Why was *Chathrand* outfitted in Sorrophran? Where were the banners, the podiums, the
Imperial orchestra?

"There are trumpets on the quarterdeck," growled Isiq. "And
more than enough sightseers."

"Not half the usual number," countered the reporter. "Why,
you might as well be stealing away in the dead of night!"

"With this morning's *Mariner* announcing it to the whole
city?"

"We barely learned of it in time! Your Excellency, a moment, I beg you. We have it reliably that a man was killed last night in your garden. Ah! Your face admits the truth! Who was he— a cutthroat? An assassin?"

Isiq plowed forward, scowling. "A common tramp. He should not have been killed, but he made blundering advances toward Lady Thasha. Our dogs brought him down, and the house guard put an arrow in his chest. That is all."

"Your house guard refused to speak to us, Excellency. Was it the Emperor himself who demanded such secrecy? There are rumors to the effect."

"Of course there are. Your readers survive on a diet of little else. Good day, sir."

Sightseers were indeed packing the waterfront, and more hurried into the Plaza by the minute. High above on the *Chathrand,* the crew stood at rigid attention. The trumpeters played an old naval song, chosen specially by Uskins because it had been popular thirty years ago in the Sugar War, when he guessed Admiral Isiq's sailing days had begun (he was quite right, but the memories the tune evoked were of scurvy and insects and boot-rotted feet).

A lizard's tongue of red carpet shot down the gangway. The admiral looked as if he would rather kick it aside. But up he tottered; and holding his arm was Syrarys, chin high, smiling ambiguously, in a sheer white dress that magnified the luster of her dark skin. From the deck Mr. Fiffengurt took one look at her and thought, *This will be a hazardous trip.*

Behind them came Thasha, with two books (a Mzithrini grammar and *The Merchant's Polylex*) in her arms and a venomous scowl on her face. Around the quay people pointed, murmuring: *"There she is, the Treaty Bride, the Emperor's gift to the savages. Getting married! Poor pretty thing! She has to marry so there'll be no more war."*

"Lady Thasha!"

It was the *Mariner* reporter. Thasha turned him an irritated glance. *I won't go through with it!* she was tempted to shout. *I'll run off with pirates before I'll marry a coffin worshipper! Print that!*

The reporter kept his voice low, one nervous eye on Eberzam Isiq. "The man in your garden, the man they killed. Who was he? What did he say to you?"

Her father would be annoyed at her for speaking, she thought. It was an incentive.

"He didn't have a chance to say much before they killed him."

So true: Jorl had closed on the wild, starved-looking man, who had risen from the ash pit in the corner of the garden and rushed at her like a sooty phantom, before he was halfway to her. It was dawn. Thasha, rising from a third sleepless night since Isiq announced her betrothal, had just stumbled into the yard, rubbing her eyes. She saw the sprinting man, his eyes fixed on her with the fire of murder or ecstatic prayer, for only an instant: the next he fell under the snarling boulder of the dog. Instead of fear, pity: Jorl had the man's whole black-bearded throat in his mouth. Thasha knew he would not kill unless the man pulled a knife—her dogs were very well trained. But so was she, in *thojmélé* fighting, bought with a thousand bruises from Hercól. She would not lose this moment, any moment, to the paralysis of surprise. She dashed forward and caught the man's hair in her hand.

"Was he a foreigner, m'lady?" asked the man from the *Mariner*.

No doubt about that. He had looked at her and squealed something in a tongue unlike any she had ever heard. He was out of his head—but with fear, not drink. There was no hint of alcohol on his breath.

"Yes, a foreigner," she said. "Now you'd better go."

"What did he tell you—before they shot him?"

She looked at the reporter, but it was that ash-covered face she saw. The same words, over and over. Her name, and—

"Mighra cror, mighra cror," she muttered aloud.

"What does that mean?" asked the reporter.

She had wondered the same thing. "Speak Arquali!" she'd

begged. Over the growls of the mastiffs (Suzyt had arrived and joined the fray), the horrified man had still managed to comply.

"Death, is death, death!" he wheezed in broken Arquali. "Yours, ours, all people together!"

"Death? Whose death? How?"

"Mighra cror—"

"What on earth is that?"

But another voice had ended it all: Syrarys, on the garden balcony, was shrieking, *"Kill him! Shoot him now!"*

And someone obeyed. The arrow lanced down from the garden wall and struck with the neatness of a tailor's button-stitch, one inch from Jorl's paw, in the man's heart. Thasha's eyes raced back along the flight path: a shadow among oak-leaves, a man leaping into the neighbor's yard. Ten minutes later the constables were rushing the body away.

Was that shadowy marksman one of these big, sweaty warriors behind her—the honor guard the Emperor had insisted on bestowing? She might never find out. Worse, she would never learn who the stranger was, a man who had thrown his life away for the chance to speak to her. She only knew that her father was wrong: the man was much more than a common tramp.

She was on the gangway, leaving the frustrated reporter hopping below. On an impulse she turned to him and said: "If it all goes wrong—if something terrible happens to us—ask the Mother Prohibitor of the Lorg School about this *'mighra cror.'*"

On deck, a grim Captain Rose bowed to the ambassador and Lady Syrarys, his red beard and blue Merchant Service ribbons fluttering in the breeze. The *Chathrand*'s senior officers stood in a file behind him, ramrod-straight. Thasha supposed they would fall like ninepins at a nudge.

After the guest of honor, the first-class passengers came aboard. They were some two dozen in all: families making west to the Crownless Lands, for pleasure or profit, men with sea-caps and tailored coats, women in summer gowns, children prancing about them like tethered imps. Lady Lapadolma's niece Pacu was there, almond-eyed and lovely, in neat, buttoned-up riding clothes ("Where's your pony, love?" called someone gaily). On her heels came a thin man with white gloves, slicked-down bangs, and a pet sloth clinging to his neck like a hairy baby. This was Latzlo, the animal-seller, who meant to continue his pursuit of Pacu alongside a few months' trade in wild creatures. Listening to his excited chatter about snowlarks and walrus hides was Mr. Ket, the soap merchant recently disembarked from a little ship called the *Eniel*. He never interrupted Latzlo, only chuckled quietly, a hand on his ragged scarf.

It fell to the officers to greet the noble-born, Captain Rose having disappeared below with Isiq and Syrarys. Mr. Uskins, always impressed by wealth and "good breeding," shook the men's arms like pump handles. The bosun, a short, heavy, hunched-over man named Swellows, grinned and minced around the ladies in a dance of servility. Mr. Teggatz offered scones.

The passengers took their time, marveling at their first glimpse of the topdeck, while six hundred sailors waited in silence. Finally the last lace parasol vanished below, and the crew relaxed their shoulders and returned to work. Now it was the servants' turn to board. These outnumbered their masters two to one, but they moved more swiftly. They did not have the strength to dawdle, for besides their own small valises they carried armloads of their masters' favorite shoes or cloaks or liquor bottles (the ones too precious to be crated), tugged their dogs, in some cases bore their swaddled infants. Among them came Hercól with Jorl and Suzyt, whining pitifully at their separation from Thasha but still inspiring the other boarders to keep a respectful distance.

Longshoremen, next. There were last supplies to be taken on: beer, salt, gunpowder, spare chain and cordage, a bone saw for Dr. Rain. All the goods the merchants hoped to sell in the west, the boots and broadcloths and calico, had to be loaded, too. And of course there were Latzlo's animals: white macaws and sable hornbills, gingham geese, six-legged proboscam bats, green

Ulluprid monkeys. Eight men hefted a Red River hog that bellowed and bashed its tusks against the cage. Stacks of smaller crates were too dark and tight for the contents to be seen.

A number of the first-class guests were moving, not traveling, and their thousand-and-one possessions were dragged up the gangway next, or raised by the cargo crane. Most important of these were the ambassador's personal effects. All the old or valuable furniture was sealed in giant crates: Eberzam Isiq's desk, Syrarys' wardrobe, Thasha's baby cradle and the huge canopy bed where the old man spent as much time as possible with his consort.

The crates were stuffed with cedar shavings, then nailed tight as coffins and the seams plastered over: fair protection against the damp, but none at all against the ixchel. Three hundred had raided the bed-crate the night before, sawn a hole with more than surgical neatness, wriggled in and glued the round plug of wood back into place so perfectly that even the fastidious butler sensed nothing amiss. Before dawn the crate was riddled with airholes smaller than fleas, and Talag Tammaruk ap Ixhxchr, mastermind of the assault on the Great Ship, lay back in the center of the ambassador's bed and fell asleep.

The crowd on the quay paid no attention as half the population of Ixphir House was lowered into the hold. Cargo bored them, unless it was obviously priceless, or kicked and snorted like Mr. Latzlo's animals. As the morning wore on, they began to drift about the square, buying fried kelp or scallops at the pushcarts, greeting friends. But they kept one eye on the *Chathrand,* and when four Trading Family officials dragged an iron turnstile to the foot of the gangway, they all rushed back to watch.

The turnstile was painted rooster-red. It had revolving arms that allowed one person at a time to pass through onto the gangway, and could be frozen at the turn of a key. When the Company officials had tested the device, they nodded at Fiffengurt, up on deck. The quartermaster hailed a sailor on the maintop. The sailor, in turn, pulled a yellow kerchief from around his head and waved it high.

Nearly a mile down the quay, hidden from the Emperor's splendid keep, squatted a large, low warehouse. Two Company men stationed at the heavy door saw the kerchief and put their shoulders to the bolt. The door swung wide. And from the black mouth of the building rushed a mob.

They were six hundred strong, laden with sacks and bundles and crates and children, some barefoot, many in little more than rags. But they ran, now and then dropping a sausage or a bag of sea biscuits, never stopping, for what good was spare food if you didn't make it aboard? These were the steerage passengers, third class. Among them were Ipulians and Uturphans, returning from seasons of labor in the Etherhorde clothing mills, often no richer, always more battered than they came. It was a diverse group. Peasants from dry East Arqual, hoping to reach Urnsfich before the tea harvest. Young couples forbidden to marry and rushing west to do just that, women whose men had disappeared. Petty criminals. Minor enemies of the crown. Refugees from the violence on Pulduraj, arrived just months ago only to find the slums of the Imperial capital more dangerous than an island at war. They had all paid in advance, and in greater numbers than the *Chathrand* could actually carry (the rest would wait days or weeks for another ship), and had spent the night on the bare warehouse floor, locked in, where the sight of them would not trouble the wealthy passengers.

The sightseers, however, had come for just this spectacle: the blind rush of whole families, like cattle driven to stampede. Gentlemen lifted well-dressed boys to their shoulders. They cheered and laughed, placed bets on which paupers would reach them first.

The mob ignored them entirely. It had been a cold, damp, miserable night, and all of them knew it was better than what awaited them aboard *Chathrand:* signs in third-class compartments read A LIGHTED MATCH IS SABOTAGE. SABOTAGE IS DEATH. Still they ran, to seize the best few square feet of floor they could in the darkness of the orlop deck. Except for a few hours a day in calm seas they would not breathe fresh air or feel the sun again for the length of their voyage.

No one noticed the exhausted reporter from the *Mariner,* jotting furiously in his notebook in the mouth of an alley past which the poor had flowed. Nor did anyone observe the four men who came upon him from behind, calmly, one with a taut wire between his hands.

At the gangway, the turnstile clicked and clicked: each click a parent, a child, a tidy sum. Waving, shouting them on (*"To the ladderway, follow my man, down you go and swiftly please!"*), Mr. Fiffengurt wondered if any of these wretches knew that they actually paid more, inch for inch, than the first-class passengers. Double, maybe, for they all but sat on each other's heads. No, it wouldn't do to speak of such things, even if he could make someone believe.

When the count reached four hundred, the Company officers locked the turnstile with a snap. A man looked back at his father, stopped behind him on the quay: *Go on,* said the old man's eyes.

14

New Orders

.

N. R. Rose, Captain
9 Vaqrin 941
Etherhorde

The Honorable Captain Theimat Rose
Northbeck Abbey, Mereldín Isle, South Quezans

Dear Sir,

Warmest greetings to you and my cherished mother. Please accept a son's apologies for not having written these many days.

You will be happy to know that I have secured a commission that will erase all debts and secure future prosperity, not just for me but for all our surviving kin. The Chathrand sails on a task of such consequence that I dare not name it here, lest our enemies seize this letter and gain a mighty advantage. But I can tell you that His Supremacy has had no choice but to agree to my demands in full. He knows that I alone may be trusted to do as he commands with the Great Ship, and so has promised me lifetime governorship of the Quezans and the title of viscount. Additionally, I am to choose three unwed or purchasable girls of any price, with another of superior beauty sent every fifth year from the Accateo Lorgut.

Many thanks for your caution regarding poison. This is a delicate moment, for I know H.S. will insert spies among my

crew—indeed, he promised no less, "for my own protection."
The aged killer Sandor Ott is among them: he poses as one
Shtel Nagan, commander of the honor guard attending Ambassador Isiq, his budding daughter and South Seas whore.
But there has been no opportunity to speak to Ott. An unfortunate incident with the augrongs kept us from meeting
ashore. Thus I have still to inform him that he must protect me
not for mere show but like the crown jewels themselves: for
should any ill befall me, the Emperor's foes will learn the
whole story of his scheming within the year.

This morning I went ashore early, crossed the Plaza of the
Palmeries and presented myself at the Keep of Five Domes.
The rumors are perfectly true: the Emperor's men take you
under the earth by a wide stair, and thence by tunnels dark
and madly circuitous, such that when I ascended at last into
a glorious salon I had no idea which of the five domes I had
entered. There they searched me like an enemy, head to toe,
and bade me sit before a little table. Scores of lackeys, soldiers, monks, doctors, astrologers and seers plied me with
questions, three hours of questions, mostly pointless, while a
slave-girl pushed chocolates under my nose and another
washed my feet. Then Prince Misoq, H.S.'s blind son, was led
in and sat beside me. He pawed at my face: to know whether
I smiled or frowned, he said.

"You will sign and swear to this cause?" he asked.

"I will sign and swear, Your Majesty, to our full agreement."

Then he snapped his fingers, and the room emptied, and a
scroll was spread before us—a scroll that could see this Empire razed to ashes, Father, were its contents known. And I
signed above my printed name.

With that we rose, the Prince clutched my arm and we left
the salon by a side door and entered a corridor, the left wall
of which let into some grander space through painted
columns. "You may gaze upon the Throne if you wish," he

said, and I saw that this hall was in fact a long balcony, looking down upon the marvel of the Chamber of Ametrine, with the great, glittering chair on its red dais standing in a pool of light. The throne was empty: candles twice a man's height burned in the stillness, and only the Imperial guard walked in their glow.

Then I heard footsteps at the end of the hall. Eight ugly brutes like armed boars marched toward me, clattering in their mail, followed by two other princes and a jester who drooled. After these came Magad himself. I dropped to my knees and kept my head bowed. Men passed around me, doors opened and boomed shut, and then His Supremacy touched my shoulder and bade me rise.

He is older than commonly thought. His body has gone to fat, he has the yellowed eyes of a deathsmoker, and some manner of disease has left red welts upon his neck. I saw a green jewel on his finger: taken by Magad I from a slain priest of the Mzithrin, so rumor tells. He studied me as you might an expensive horse. The jester held the Emperor's pipe, now and then sucking on it himself with a disagreeable slurp.

"You will dine with my sons, Captain," said Magad. "Do you like brandied quail?"

Nothing would he speak of but food and the hunt, and yet his eyes never ceased to probe me. At last he looked pointedly at the door at the end of the balcony, drew a deep breath and waved: "It is there. Go and see it." Then he departed with his entourage, and when I rose from my second bow the prince nudged me forward. I walked alone down the hallway and opened the door.

The room was about the size of my day-cabin. Torches blazed on the walls, and by their light I saw many great chests standing open. Within them—gold. Unimaginable gold. Perfect three-ounce cockles, and rods, and bricks emblazoned with the Magad seal. There were also whole chests of ivory and megrottoc horn, and four of red rubies alone—four times my weight in bloodstones, sir, I implore you to believe—and the last chest held pearls. One-third of the whole Imperial treasury is what the scroll claimed, and I doubt it not. Were I less a man than your son, my heart should have been quite faint.

"It will be taken aboard tonight," said the Prince when I returned, "and our hundred Turachs with it."

"Your Majesty," I said carefully, "the Turachs are your supreme father's most terrible warriors. Even the Imperial marines fear them. How shall I explain their presence to my crew?"

"They will be dressed and outfitted as marines—nothing more. It is not strange to arm a trade ship in those waters, Rose. Pirates swarm in Thól like flies in a stable."

"But will they obey the captain of the vessel, in an emergency? The survival of the ship could depend on it, Your Majesty."

"They will obey Drellarek. Drellarek will obey you."

"And Sandor Ott?"

"Ott commands six spies. They can hardly afford you worry, Captain, if you have nothing to hide from the crown."

I had no choice: he was a prince, and could not be reasoned with. But I saw to it that he knew better than to dream of letting those killers dispose of Nilus Rose when his usefulness was done:

"Nothing whatsoever shall I hide, Sire: neither my fears, nor my sensible precautions. In the second category are letters dispatched months ago, to certain professionals outside the Empire. In the case of my demise they will be forwarded over a span of years to the lords of the Crownless Lands, and a number of your family's internal rivals."

"Where no doubt they would be read with astonishment," laughed the blind man. He was shaken and furious and wished none to see it. Probably he could think of little besides killing me, and yet realized (as you and I did long ago) that Arqual's treason can never be revealed, nor the exact number *of those letters known, even should they extract my confession with hot iron and blades. Yet he might have threatened. He might even have had me dragged back to those tunnels and tortured for my insolence—for that I was ready. Nothing, however, prepared me for what he actually did: groping for my face again, he pulled me savagely by hair and beard, forcing his lips against my ear.*

"I know these rivals you speak of," he whispered. "Some are banished, most are dead. The sons of Maisa are dead— we have their bodies in an ice chest. The astrologers have spoken; the dead stir and the living smell death. You cannot stop us—it is the hour of Arqual, you fool."

Then he released me and smiled. We dined, the royal sons insulted one another, and I left the Keep of Five Domes just in time to avert disaster with the augrongs.

All this I tell you, sir, knowing it will gladden your heart that a Rose met the Imperial Person and set sail with a third of his wealth. Did you not swear we would one day parley with kings, and even use them for ends of our own? Perhaps you will have forgotten the occasion, but I never shall: it was a summer on Littelcatch, when you caught me dawdling with hammer and chisel, simply wasting the day, laughing among the penniless boys of the isle. I had hacked a crude figure out of driftwood. "The purpose of this, Nilus, if you please?" you asked, and I had the cheek to reply that I would learn proper sculpture, and one day carve a goddess for the figurehead of your ship. How right you were to strap me! Nonsense must be cured with clarity, and there is nothing clearer than pain.

I must post this with the Imperial Mailguard, who even now is at my door. Please do not be silent, sir, nor Mother either.

I have the honor to remain your most obedient son,

N. R. ROSE

15

Old Foes

12 Vaqrin 941

"Neeps," said Pazel, "are your parents alive?"

They were dangling from the stern of the *Chathrand,* their seat a wooden spar bound by two ropes to the taffrail, their bare feet resting on the casements of the gallery windows. Someone had the idea that Ambassador Isiq had frowned at the windows on first sight: the boys had therefore been set to polishing the brass hinges with a mixture of turpentine, tallow and cinders, until they gleamed.

Light breeze, warm sun. And biting flies attracted by the reek of tallow. To strike at them meant letting go of something: rope, window, spar. Given the sixty-foot drop to the water, they did their best to ignore the insects.

Neeps shook his head. "They died when I was three. The talking fever, you know. We had no medicines on Sollochstal."

The Great Ship was being winched away from the docks: already the Plaza lay a quarter mile behind. Small craft skated across their wake, passengers crowding the rails nearest *Chathrand,* just gazing at her. The society folk of Etherhorde were bemused, and slightly affronted: it was the fastest turnaround in living memory for the Great Ship. Barely three days in port, and no tours allowed! As for the demeanor of the Treaty Bride, and her choice of clothes—the less said the better.

"Who raised you, then?" Pazel asked.

"My father's family," said Neeps. "They have a grand house. Ten feet above the lagoon, on strong stilts."

"You lived in a stilt house!"

"Best way to live. Throw a line out through the kitchen window, snag a tasty copperfish, reel him in. Straight from cove to kettle, as my uncles used to say. Great folk, my uncles. They taught me pearl-diving. Also how to smell a lie: we had to sell our pearls to merchants from Opalt and the Quezans, and they were always trying to cheat. But no one could cheat Granny Undrabust. She ran the family business, the household, half the village. Everybody knew her because she was fearless. She used to drive off crocodiles with a bargepole. They say she killed a pirate with her fish-knife. They'd sneak into the village at night, pry jewels off the temple walls, kidnap boys. That even happened to me. *Upa!* Careful, mate!"

The platform tilted madly. Pazel, lost in Neeps' words, had nearly lost his balance, too. When they recovered he was still gaping at his friend. "You were kidnapped? By real pirates?"

"Too blary real. Their ship stank like a chamber pot. But they didn't have us long. Two months after they took us, the fools raided an Arquali fort in the Kepperies. Warships caught up with us in days, hanged the pirates and made us all into tarboys."

"And you never saw your family again?"

Neeps scrubbed vigorously at a hinge. "Oh, I saw 'em. After the Empire grabbed Sollochstal. We landed for a day and I ran off and saw Granny and my uncles. And my little sister: she was so glad to see me she dropped a whole basket of fish. But the Arqualis fetched me back that same night. Said they would have taken pearls for my freedom if I'd asked, but they couldn't reward a runaway. Granny Undrabust would have fought them, but I made her stop. And she's dead now, too. Stepped on a cobra urchin, can you believe it? A Sollochi slave told me last year. The man heard she laughed before she died: 'At least it was one of our own who finally got me. Don't be sad!' "

"What about brothers?" Pazel asked. "Do you have any?"

When Neeps did not answer, Pazel looked up. To his great surprise he saw that Neeps was furious.

"Just don't talk to me about brothers," he said.

That's a yes, Pazel thought, but he spoke not a word.

After a moment, Neeps said, "Your turn. Family."

Pazel told him about the day of the invasion, how he had never seen his mother and sister since. "But Chadfallow, that doctor I was telling you about, says they're alive. He was very fond of my mother."

"So where is she?"

"He wouldn't say. But he said he *planned to see them*. And I think he meant to help me do so, too."

Neeps squinted up at the sun. "Right. This is the same chap who put something nasty in your tea. Who paid that lout of a bosun to maroon you in Sorrophran. Who galloped along a headland shouting that you should jump ship. And who never bothered to tell your family that the Arqualis were about to invade Ormael. Have I forgotten anything?"

"He bought me out of slavery," said Pazel.

Neeps gave a judicious nod. "It all adds up, then. He's madder than a boiled owl."

"Probably," said Pazel. "But he also knows something—about my family, and the treaty with the Mzithrin, and this whole journey to Simja. There are big secrets on this ship, Neeps."

"Ooooh—"

Pazel flicked a blob of brass-cleaner at him. "*Undrabust* means 'broken toe' in Kushali, did you know that? I'm not kidding!"

"*Pathkendle* means 'smelly tarboy who dreams about rich girls.' Did you know *that*?"

They flung insults, goo and rags, never happier. The spar teetered madly, but somehow they were no longer afraid. Then a sharp voice from above made them freeze.

"What's this? A playground? You lowborn rats! Wastin' time and 'spensive re-zor-ziz!"

It was Mr. Swellows, the bosun: of all the officers save

Uskins, the one Pazel most disliked. His bloodshot eyes glared down at them: he was a heavy drinker, rumor held. He claimed special knowledge of Captain Rose's thoughts and intentions, grinning slyly but revealing very little. He had been in Rose's service twenty years.

"Hoist them two up 'ere!" he barked at the stern watchmen. "Pathkendle! Wash that smutch off your hands! The captain wants to see you."

Neeps shot Pazel a look of concern. The spar lurched upward. A moment later they were climbing over the rail.

"Captain Rose wants me?" Pazel asked, alarmed. "What for, Mr. Swellows?"

"The Red Beast."

"Sir?"

Swellows looked at him with crafty delight. He leaned closer, made a clawing motion in the air. "The Red Beast! That's what we call him! Just hope you're not his prey, he he *he*!"

"You may enter now," said Rose, cleaning his pen on a blotter.

But it was not, as he had guessed, the Imperial Mailguard. It was Uskins, and his hand gripped the arm of Pazel Pathkendle, who looked as though he had just been roughly shaken.

"Your pardon, Captain," said the first mate. "It is six bells: I report as ordered. And I found this *particularly* troublesome boy lingering in the passage."

"Bring him in. Close the door."

Uskins shoved Pazel into Rose's day-cabin, a large and elegant room beneath the quarterdeck, where the captain not only conducted his desk-duties but also bathed, shaved and dined, with invited favorites, from a silver service as old as the ship itself. The first mate closed the door and dragged Pazel with superfluous brutality across the room.

"Lest I forget, sir: the good veterinarian, Brother Bolutu"— Uskins' voice dripped with ridicule—"accosted me this morning. 'Mr. Uskins,' says he, 'I have a letter for the captain regarding certain peculiar qualities of the rats on this ship. I should like to inform you as well.' He then began to chatter about the rats' 'disciplined behavior,' if you will believe it, sir."

"I will not," said Rose. "But I have read his letter."

"Oppo, Captain. Stand straight, tarboy! You're in the commander's presence! Sir, may I congratulate you on your reception at the throne of our Emperor?"

"You may do nothing that distracts you from an account of this afternoon," said Rose. "As for this tarboy, he is here at my orders."

"Very good of you, sir: he is morbidly implicated in this affair. But even a tarboy deserves to hear the reason for his doom. Is it not so?"

"Give me your blary report!"

Uskins bowed his head, like a schoolboy preparing a recitation. His account was, to say the least, creative. He told the captain how the augrongs had suddenly run amok; how the long-eared one had rushed onto the ship, dragging twenty men with it; and how he, Uskins, managed to avert a catastrophe thanks to his grasp of the augrong language.

"Or play-language, rather," he added. "These brutes have no real speech as we know it. They are but little risen above the animals."

Rose sat back in his chair. One hand moved thoughtfully in his beard. "Dumb brutes, eh?" he said.

"I guarantee it, Captain. Great scaly apes, they are, with little more to their grasp of living than food, work and pain."

"And you employed which of these?"

"Why, pain, sir. I let them know that they would be killed, slowly, if they could not behave in a manner acceptable to civilized men. I very nearly had them tamed when this useless boy went mad and threw himself at the near one.

"I saw at once that he would be killed, and it moved my heart, sir, despite his wicked stupidity. I do not claim to have chosen wisely, but I chose to save this boy. I rushed to the quarterdeck rail and struck the augrong with a capstan bar. I repeated that he and his friend ashore would die. I saw into the brute's mind, and knew he believed me. He let the boy go. It was then, sir, that you reached the Plaza."

Pazel could only gape at Uskins' tale. Nor did the captain, nodding slowly, look very inclined to let Pazel speak. As he watched, Rose opened a ledger—the same in which Fiffengurt had recorded the tarboys' names as they were dragged before him by the marines—and flipped through the rough pages, scowling.

"What would you have us do with the boy, Uskins?"

The first mate cleared his throat. "A broken cleat must be replaced, sir, and it is no different with a tarboy. The Ormali are notoriously low and treacherous, moreover: I beg leave to remind the captain that I objected to his inclusion from the first. As it is we are lucky to have discovered his true colors in port—and in port he should remain. I suggest he be dismissed as a rioter."

"He'll never sail again."

"Nor should he, Captain. A fit of lunacy on the high seas could bring disaster."

Rose looked down at the ledger. He dipped the pen in the still-open inkwell, scratched entries by several names. After a long pause, he said, "I have your report, Uskins. You may go. Send in the clerk to deal with this lad."

Uskins could not quite suppress his smile. He bowed low. As he turned to leave, a thought seemed to strike him. "His clothes were burned, sir. Verminous. Of course, we shall wish to repossess his uniform, barely used as it is, but I'm sure some rag or other can be—"

In one violent motion Rose pushed to his feet. "We will not repossess his uniform, but supplement it with a cap and greatcoat. The boy will not be put ashore. I did not witness what occurred on deck, Uskins, but Ambassador Isiq had a clear view, and saw his actions not as madness but exceptional courage. He wishes to congratulate the boy in person, and to pay for the cap and coat himself. His Excellency's opinion of *your* conduct we will discuss another time. You are dismissed."

Abashed and fuming, Uskins left. Rose stood looking fixedly at Pazel, and Pazel stared back, wide-eyed and disbelieving. He was to meet the ambassador? What should he say? What would Rose expect of him?

The captain's steward brought in a plate of kulberries and almonds, and set it on the desk with a bow. "No tea," said Rose before the man could speak, and waved him out. Then Rose took a key from his pocket and sat down again behind his desk. Without once taking his eyes from Pazel, he unlocked a deep drawer on the right-hand side and lifted out something so horrible Pazel had to stifle a cry.

It was a cage. Very much like a birdcage, but stronger, with a small, solid padlock. Inside the cage lay what appeared to be a wound-up knot of rags, hair and dead skin. But then it moved, and groaned. Pazel felt suddenly ill. The thing was an ixchel— old, starved and indescribably dirty. His eyes were vacant, his white beard matted with grease; the arms wrapped protectively about his head were raw with open sores. A scrap of cloth at his waist, half rotted, was all he had for clothing. As Rose set the cage on his desk, the old ixchel uncurled his shaking body, groaned again most terribly and cursed them both to the Nine Pits.

Rose, of course, heard nothing. He chose a kulberry and two almonds and slid them through the bars of the cage.

"Pathkendle," he said musingly. "You're the right age, the right color. Are ye Captain Gregory's boy, then?"

Pazel nodded, still in shock. On hands and knees, the ixchel dragged himself through the filth at the bottom of his cage and fell ravenously upon the kulberry.

"Well, well," said Rose. "The traitor's son. A fine sailor, Gregory—and bold at that. Faced down Simja pirates, slipped away from warships through the Talturi reefs. Few cleverer on the quarterdeck than Gregory Pathkendle. Clever with the friends he made, too. Wasn't he tight with old Chadfallow?"

Despite himself, Pazel gave a start. Rose nodded, satisfied.

"You see? Your father was ahead of his time—playing one empire off the other. But even he made mistakes. He thought the Mzithrin would strike before we did, and so he joined them. Who knows? If he'd guessed right he might be a citizen of Arqual today. But never a sailor. His Supremacy doesn't allow traitors to sail under his flag."

"My father's no traitor, sir," said Pazel, clenching his fists behind his back.

"Lad, he's the blary definition. You're just lucky he had no one better than Ormael to betray. If Gregory had been an officer in the Imperial fleet his every son, daughter, nephew and cousin would have been crucified."

"He was taken prisoner," said Pazel, trying not to glare.

"'Course he was. And then sailed back with his captors to make war on his own countrymen."

"The Mzithrin didn't make war on my country, sir. Arqual did."

"Wrong," said Rose. "The Empire never did make war on Ormael. It devoured her at one sitting, like a lamb chop."

Pazel said nothing. At that moment he hated Rose more than Uskins, more than Swellows or Jervik or even the soldiers who had stormed his house. The old ixchel was listening intently, now, although he did not stop eating the kulberry.

"You've done well for yourself, eh?" said Rose. "Most Ormali boys are dead in the Chereste silver mines, or cutting cane in Simja, or sold to Urnsfich privateers. And you're to be received by old Isiq himself."

"Yes, sir."

"Do you see what my crawly's doing? Do you know why I keep him?"

(*"Your crawly's name is Steldak, you fat pustule,"* muttered the ixchel man.)

Pazel struggled not to look at the cage. "No, sir, I don't."

"Poison," said Rose. "Oh, I have enemies, boy, many enemies. The crawly tastes my food. A crawly's heart beats six times as fast as a man's, so his blood moves six times as fast about his body. And so does any poison, you see? What would kill me in twelve minutes will kill him in two."

(*"Your heart stopped beating long ago,"* said the ixchel.)

"Now, I don't have a crawly to spare for His Excellency," Rose went on, "but I do have tarboys. The old man's taken a shine to you. That's earned you new orders from me.

"Usually he will dine at the head of the first-class table, or here in my quarters, with me. But some meals he will take in privacy, in his rooms. You will take him those meals, Pathkendle. And you will taste every dish before you do so. In the galley, in the presence of our cook. Is that clear?"

"Yes, sir."

"Someone will be sent for you on every occasion. If his daughter or consort asks for food you will do exactly the same. It will not do for him to be killed, Pathkendle. But you: I suppose we can agree that you have been living on borrowed time?"

He glared suddenly at the cage. "Taste that almond, damn your eyes! I'm hungry!"

The ixchel looked up and drew his lips back in what looked like a grimace of pain. But then a strange, low voice came out of him—a voice any normal man could hear, and Pazel guessed this was what Diadrelu had called *bending*.

"Captain," the old man said, "I beg to tell you that my teeth have grown weak. I cannot bite into this nut, sir. If you could but crack it with a hammer . . ."

The captain snarled, but he climbed to his feet and lurched across the room. For the second time that day, Pazel knew that he had come to a moment when he must *instantly* do something dangerous, or else regret it for the rest of his life—and once again, he did it. Leaning close to the cage, he whispered: *"I'll help you, Steldak."*

Instantly, Rose stiffened.

Pazel just had time to raise his head before the captain swiveled about. His eyes were wild with suspicion as he thumped back across the room. He grabbed Pazel's hand and squeezed with agonizing force. He leaned close to Pazel's face. His breath stank of garlic and tobacco.

"You hear spirits."

"N-n-no, sir!"

"I know that you do. I saw your face. There's not many of us can hear 'em, boy. One passed through this room just now, spoke to my crawly in its own tongue. You heard it, didn't you? Tell the truth!"

"Captain, I don't—Ahh!"

Rose's hand tightened again. His furious eyes roamed the cabin walls.

"Watch out," he hissed, very low. "The world's changed 'neath our feet, when brutes like me get the hearing, pick up voices dissolved in the wind. Animals always could, then mages, spell weavers, freaks. Today, here and there, a natural man like Nilus Rose. This old unsinkable hulk, now—it's clogged with spirits. In storms they snag on the topgallants, slither down to deck, crawl in our ears. You hear 'em, too! Deny it!"

Rose was mad—but mad or not, his astonishing grip threatened to break Pazel's hand. What to say? If he gave Rose the answer he wanted, the captain would never leave Pazel alone, would expect reports on the "spirits" Pazel overheard. And what would the stowaway ixchel do to him then, when half their number already thought him a spy?

"Captain!"

The voice came from the ixchel man, bowing so low that his last remaining strands of hair dragged the floor.

"Allow me to inform Your Honor that he is but half correct. I heard a voice wish me well—a spirit-voice, certainly!—but this boy heard it not. If he looked startled it is only because I jumped suddenly to my feet."

Rose looked from the prisoner to Pazel and back again. His eyes narrowed, but slowly the pressure on Pazel's hand decreased, and he let it go. Pazel stepped backward, cradling his hand, and for just an instant his eyes met those of the ixchel prisoner. The man who had lied with such skill an instant before now gave Pazel a look full of wonder, and even—dreadful in that ruined face—hope.

Another knock. The ship's clerk was at the door, with Pazel's new coat and hat. Rose shoved the cage back into his desk, suddenly business-like. He made Pazel try on the coat, corrected his posture, even drilled him on how to address the noble family.

"*Your Excellency* is all you need say to Ambassador Isiq. For his consort, *my lady* or *Lady Syrarys* will do. And the girl is to be called *Young Mistress*—or if she should insist, *Lady Thasha*. When he compliments you for what he believes you did today, thank him. Do not chatter on. If I learn that you have been familiar or clever with His Excellency I'll make you wish I'd left you in Uskins' hands."

Pazel was barely listening. *Thasha,* he thought. *Her name is Thasha.*

Rose put the cap on his head. "These clothes are Ambassador Isiq's gift. Wear them at all times. Go and scrub your face, boy, and then report to his stateroom."

Pazel made to leave, but at the door Rose's voice stopped him cold. "A strange turn, isn't it, Pathkendle?—that of all the lords and nobles of this Empire, the one who favors you should be the conqueror of Ormael."

On the main deck, Elkstem called for topgallants. The winching was done, the miles of kedging-line were hauled slithering back into the *Chathrand.* Somewhere out on the bay a warship saluted with a cannon-shot, and all the Great Ship's poultry began to squawk. Pazel had to find Neeps. If he didn't tell someone about his morning he would simply explode. But did he dare mention Steldak? Would Diadrelu see even that as a betrayal?

He had heard Swellows order Neeps to the tailor's nook, to help with mending the reserve sails. But Neeps was not there. Pazel bent down beside Reyast, the shy tarboy with the stutter, and asked after his friend. Reyast looked up from his lapful of sailcloth and blinked.

"P-P-P-Paz-zel. You have a n-n-n-ew c-c—"

"I'll tell you about the coat later, Reyast. Where's Neeps gone off to?"

"S-s-s-s-*sickbay*."

"Sickbay! Why? What's wrong with him?"

Some minutes later, Reyast had succeeded in telling Pazel that Neeps was badly bruised. He had been pushed down a hatch by a new tarboy, brought aboard just yesterday. The new-comer was "a b-b-b-baddy," Reyast declared: older and stronger than any of them, except Peytr and Dastu perhaps, and he acted as though he were in charge of the smaller tarboys. He was enraged with Fiffengurt, who had given him no special rank, and was taking it out on the younger boys. When Neeps passed through the berth deck to retrieve his turban, the new boy had ordered him to trade shipboxes—his own had a lid that fastened poorly. Neeps laughed in his face. There were too many sailors about for a fight (which Reyast considered lucky for Neeps), but when the bigger tarboy saw the chance he had shoved Neeps from behind, sending him crashing through a hatch into the steerage compartment below—where Neeps had almost landed on a baby.

Pazel, who had seen enough cruelty for one day, found himself livid. "What's this pig's name?" he asked.

Reyast screwed up his face with effort. "*D-f-dj-d-Jervik!*"

"Jervik!" cried Pazel, aghast. "A big lout with a hole in his ear?"

Reyast nodded. Pazel questioned him no more, but ran straight for the sickbay. Jervik aboard! Had Captain Nestef finally caught him at his cruelty and sent him packing? No matter how it had occurred it was terrible news, and he hoped that somehow Reyast was mistaken. Pazel flew across the lower gun deck to the sickbay. Over the clinic's door he saw a curious sign:

SICKBAY

~~Dr. Ignus Chadfallow, ISSA, Order of the Orb~~

DR. CLAUDIUS RAIN

The first name was neatly painted in red. The second, like the line through Chadfallow's name, was a messy blue scrawl. Pazel had to steady himself on the doorjamb. Chadfallow had meant to serve on the *Chathrand*. But why had he changed his mind, and told Pazel to jump ship? *I intend to see them,* he had said of Pazel's mother and sister. Was that the reason he had planned to be aboard—or the reason he wasn't?

In the sickbay he found Neeps, slung in a hammock, with a split lip and an oilskin bag of cool water over one eye. The small boy was furious, grinding his teeth, swearing he'd teach Jervik to keep his distance.

Pazel hushed him: the new doctor, Rain, was bustling by, white eyebrows knitted. As he passed they heard him muttering to himself: "Undrabust, Neeps Undrabust, ha ha, almost broke his neck, you boys shouldn't fool about the hatches . . ."

"Let him come near me again," said Neeps when the doctor was out of earshot. "Jervik, I mean—the cowardly rat."

"But how did he end up on *Chathrand*?" said Pazel miserably.

"Said he'd just gotten rid of some tarboy he hated on his old ship," growled Neeps. "Boasted how he 'smacked 'im round fer a year, and the blary fool never hit back.' And then he helped some fat bosun strand the tarboy in Sorrophran. His captain overheard and threw a fit such as nobody'd ever seen, and chucked Jervik ashore with his own hands."

"That was *me*!" Pazel cried. "The one who got stranded!"

Neeps' unbruised eye fixed on Pazel. "I'll smash 'im," he said. "I'll knock that gold tooth down his throat. I'll wring him out like my turban."

"Neeps!" said Pazel, gripping his shoulder. "Don't fight him! Rose'll throw you to the sharks! Besides, Jervik's huge, and a dirty fighter! He'll flatten you, mate!"

"Let him try it!"

It came out *twy it,* because of Neeps' swollen lip. His tiny fists clenched at his sides.

Pazel rose slowly and set his forehead to the wall. "Everyone on this ship is insane," he said.

"Hello!" said Neeps. "Where'd you get that coat?"

And then, like a plunge into the sea, it happened. Two sailors passed the sickbay door, chatting lightly about a woman, and suddenly their voices changed—mutated, ballooned—and became a monstrous squawking.

"No!" cried Pazel, leaping up.

"Pazaaaaaaaak?" said Neeps.

Dr. Rain, turning, cried, *"Squa-qua-quaaaak?"*

There it was: the pressure on his skull. And filling the air, the smell of custard apple, worst odor in the world. His mind-fit had begun.

Leaving Neeps wide-eyed, Pazel ran from the sickbay into a horror of a ship filled with deafening, predatory bird-noises. He couldn't think where to hide—hide for four hours or more!—but hide he must, immediately. If they thought him mad he'd be tossed out with the bilgewater, or worse.

The lower gun deck was filled with newcomers, soldiers of some sort, busy, laughing, squawking. They gestured at him, wanting something. He ran. *The hold,* he thought. *Get to the hold.* Maybe the ambassador wasn't really expecting him just yet. Maybe no one would miss him.

He reached the No. 1 ladderway and began racing down the stairs. But at the berth deck Fiffengurt suddenly appeared, blocking his path. He smiled up at Pazel: *"Bachafuagaaaak!"*

Pazel made a helpless face and began climbing again, which made Fiffengurt squawk the louder. Pazel leaped out at the next deck, the upper gun deck, and fled down the long row of cannon. Men were all around him, malicious and terribly loud. *It's never been so bad,* he thought. And then he saw Jervik, dead ahead.

Both boys froze. Jervik's eyes grew wide; he squeezed the deck-mop in his hands like something that might fly away. Pazel had the sudden idea of trying to be friendly—they'd had to work together *sometimes* on the *Eniel,* after all—but how exactly was he to do that? He couldn't speak, so he tried a smile and a little wave.

Jervik threw the mop at him like a spear.

So much for friendliness. Pazel dodged the mop and tried to do the same with Jervik, but the big tarboy caught him by the shoulder.

"Gwamothpathkuandlemof!"

Jervik tore at Pazel's new coat; brass buttons popped. *Hit me, you imbecile!* thought Pazel. Fiffengurt would surely evict him if he did. But Jervik merely gushed with noise, his grip tightening. And Pazel realized that in another moment Fiffengurt would appear and catch them both. *That can't happen. They'll lock me up.*

He turned and faced Jervik. "Let go!" he cried, gesticulating madly. "I'm *Muketch,* the mud-crab sorcerer of Ormael, and I'll turn your bones to pudding if you don't!"

Of course nothing but bird-babble came from his mouth. Usually talking during a mind-fit was the worst tactic imaginable, but today it saved him. Jervik was terribly superstitious. He froze, wide-eyed. Pazel pointed at his disfigured ear and cackled. "When I'm done that'll be the handsomest part of you left! Now GO!"

Terrified, Jervik released him, stumbling backward, and slipped on one of Pazel's lost buttons. Pazel ran for his life.

Screeches, hoots, a wet stretch of floor. He smashed into one crewman after another. Grown men leaped away as if he might bite them. *This is ending badly,* he thought.

Then a hand much stronger than Jervik's seized his arm, and Pazel felt himself whirled around. For an instant he saw a man's face—gray temples, bright eyes that tapered to points—and then he was shoved bodily through a doorway, into warm smells of coffee and perfume and talc.

Little of what followed was clear to him afterward. The ambassador's face appeared in a dressing-mirror, half shaven, mouth agape. A beautiful woman swept into the room with arms outstretched, shrieking, her voice demonic. And from somewhere the golden-haired girl from the carriage appeared and looked at him with astonishment but no fear.

Then a flask was pressed to his lips, and his head forced back, and he knew no more.

16

The Uses of the Dead

12 Vaqrin 941

The men of two battle-scarred warships, anchored farther out than the rest of the Imperial fleet, were the only witnesses as *Chathrand* sailed out of Etherhorde Bay. Pennants went up their masts in salute: the green-star signal that meant nothing more complicated than "safe travel, speedy return."

A miracle if either happens, thought Sandor Ott, sealing his cabin's porthole. More likely they would be slaughtered en masse. Not he himself, perhaps, nor that lethal captain. Rose had cunning in his very pores. No doubt he had planned his own escape down to the last lie or knife-thrust or spot of blackmail. But these sailors, soldiers, boys—they could never be trusted with what they would come to know.

Eighteen million gold cockles! Four chests of bloodstone! If his own men did not betray him, surely their western partners would. *The minute that prize becomes more than a rumor, a hope in their vile hearts, we are fair game. The minute we place it in their hands, they'll wish us dead.*

Before a tall mirror, he pinned on his breast the medals that turned him into Shtel Nagan, commander of the ambassador's honor guard. He took a moment to consider his hands: brutalized, rock-steady. Then he left the cabin and climbed to the topdeck.

A fine summer's evening, the sun still whole and red above

the Emperor's mountain. He could just make out Castle Maag at the summit, and his own tower, waving a wry farewell.

In fair weather the first-class passengers could meander as they pleased about the topdeck (never the quarterdeck: that was officers' territory), and a dozen or so were at it now. Smoke Hour was past, so they chewed sapwort or sweetpine. Children galloped about, pretending to be tarboys. Men nipped whiskey from flasks.

Just one lady was on deck, but she was the only woman Sandor Ott took any interest in. Syrarys Isiq's skin glowed like polished amber in the evening light. She stood holding the arm of Eberzam Isiq, the old fool. Sandor Ott approached, but not too near; he was a bodyguard and not an equal. But when Syrarys turned her head halfway in his direction there was a gleam in her eye.

"Commander Nagan?" said a voice behind him.

Ott turned sharply. It was Bolutu, Brother Bolutu, the veterinarian. They shook hands, and Ott gave the black man a formal smile.

"You have a ravishing friend," said Bolutu.

Ott said nothing, but his heart quickened in his chest.

"I mean the bird, of course. Your moon falcon. Extraordinary."

Damn him to the Pits! thought Ott, recovering. But he said, "Ah, Niriviel! A friend indeed. He may catch us a grouse from the Dremland hills, if we pass near enough."

This one could prove a nuisance, he thought. Never a threat: no black man could be that powerful in an empire ruled by the porcelain-pale Magads. Yet Bolutu's star was rising. This very spring he had met the Queen Mother, and cured her pig of something dreadful: hiccups, maybe. He was also a longtime friend to the Trading Family. Lady Lapadolma herself had wanted him aboard the *Chathrand:* she had a soft spot for animals, if little else, and no doubt shed tears at the thought that Mr. Latzlo's cargo might suffer on the journey, before being sold for pelts and potions in the west.

Ott also needed a skilled veterinarian aboard—the best, in fact. How was it that the best was this reformed nomad, this Slevran born in some warren or wattle-house, educated by monks in an outpost temple, and seeing great Etherhorde for the first time only as a grown man? Why were there no true Arqualis fit for the job?

"Does he travel with you everywhere?" Bolutu was asking.

Ott shook his head. "The captain indulges me greatly, allowing him aboard. Have you seen him already, then?"

"I have just come from the coop. Your bird is unhappy with the darkness, but he lives in a mansion compared with the rest. He can spread his wings, and move about, and smell the chickens if not taste them. Commander, have we not met before?"

"Indeed, sir," said Ott smoothly. "As a bodyguard I have had the privilege of serving many of the Empire's finest gentlemen of trade. You I remember from the Midwinter Ball at Lord Sween's."

"And not from Castle Maag?"

"I have served in the castle, too. It is not impossible."

"Certainly it was there. Tell me, why have we taken so many soldiers aboard?"

"Only six answer to me, sir."

"Exactly," said Bolutu. "The rest are not here to guard the ambassador, as you do. And *Chathrand is* no longer a warship. What is the use of carrying a hundred soldiers on a merchant ship? Especially one on a mission of peace?"

"Mr. Bolutu," said Ott mildly—he would not be unsettled again, no matter how prying the man became—"you should direct your inquiry to their commanding officer. But I can offer a guess if you like. In a word, pirates. The Emperor's dominion stops at Ormael. The next six hundred miles are a chaos. No outright wars, but no peace, either. Sea-banditry is already common, and growing more so. The Crownless Lands do not wish our protection—"

"Curious, that." Bolutu smiled slightly.

"—and yet they cannot guard their own seas. There is no order, sir. Except the savage order of the Mzithrin, in the distant west."

"Does Simja know that His Supremacy is sending not just an ambassador and a child bride, but a vessel packed with Imperial marines? And such marines! They make the Emperor's regular forces look like milksops."

"Dear sir, you exaggerate," said Ott. "Perhaps you have not been quartered so close to His Supremacy's infantry before?"

Bolutu hesitated. "I have not. That is true."

"In any event, to leave our home waters prepared for the worst is but common sense—although I hope that will not be demonstrated."

Ott bowed to Bolutu and excused himself. Moving toward the center, or waist, of the ship, he thought: *Yes, definitely a nuisance. I do not like your tone, pig doctor.*

Two of Ott's own men watched Ambassador Isiq from a respectful distance: the old man would never be left on deck unattended. One of these was Zirfet, and when he looked at Ott his very stillness sent a message: a twitch at wrist or elbow meant *all's well,* and his men never forgot.

He nodded, giving the big fighter permission to approach. When they stood alone at the portside rail, he said, "Let's hear it, quickly."

Zirfet was trying to appear professional and bored; in fact he looked rather seasick. "Master," he whispered, "Hercól Stanapeth is aboard!"

Ott's face froze. He had served three generations of Magad Emperors, but never had he needed to hide such total surprise twice in an evening. He succeeded, of course: Zirfet had no inkling of the turmoil inside him.

"Tell me everything," said Ott.

"He came aboard with the servants," said Zirfet, "but he has a cabin—a tiny berth—next to the ambassador's own. I saw him just minutes ago, Master: I knew him at once from the Book of Faces."

Ott nodded. Anyone of the least possible interest to the crown—foreigners, nobles, rabble-rousers, soldiers who grumbled about their pay—had a portrait in the Book of Faces. His spies learned to pick them out of a crowd at a glance.

"He does not know me, of course—nor any of the others," Zirfet went on. "But you—"

"Me he knows," said Ott, nodding grimly. Hercól was his great failure: an expert fighter when Ott recruited him to join the Secret Fist. A far better fighter—admit it: his best—when the training was done. But Hercól never had the stomach for spy work. Idleness and wealth had not poisoned him, as they had these youngsters. Hercól was simply unwilling to kill. *Tholjassans revere life,* he had told Ott years ago, possibly the last time they had spoken. *So do we,* Ott had answered. *But sometimes a knife in the dark is the only way to prove it.*

He strolled aft, Zirfet at his side. He was perfectly calm now: twisting bad luck to his advantage was as familiar as putting on his shoes. "Tell me what steps you have taken, Zirfet," he said.

"I stationed Jasani at a speaking-tube. They're remarkable, Master, these hide-wrapped pipes: you can hear most anything the ambassador says from his reading chair, for instance. Last night Jasani heard Hercól say that a man whose sword is rarely sheathed will one day trip and fall upon the blade. Isiq said nothing to this, but another spoke up—an elder and a foreigner, by his voice. 'Indeed, friend,' he said. 'Many are the kingdoms reduced to dust by their own fears, and the folly fear inspires, when no power on earth could break them else. Let Arqual beware Arqual.'"

"Who is this foreigner, who speaks thus?" Ott demanded.

"The others called him Ramachni. We are making inquiries even now."

"See that you do. What is Hercól's position aboard?"

"He is Ambassador Isiq's private servant, Master. His valet, as it were. And he is the girl's . . . dance tutor."

"Thasha Isiq's tutor? Lucky girl; she'll have learned a great deal more than dance. But Hercól must never see me, lad."

"No, Master."

"And yet we cannot kill him—yet. If he should die on my watch, this ship would be flooded with talk of my incompetence as protector of the Isiq household. They might even wish to re-place me."

He fell silent, feeling the wheels within his mind, the old, flawless mechanisms of deceit.

"A fever," he said at last. "I will develop a slight fever tonight. And out of concern for others I shall keep to my cabin until we touch land in Ulsprit. There I shall disembark and make my own way west, rejoining you at Tressek Tarn. Before that time, you personally will rid us of Hercól. The task is essential. Can I trust you with it?"

"You can," said Zirfet.

Too quick, Ott decided: the lad's bravado masked fear. He raised a warning finger.

"Bloodstains will not do. Use your head before you use that knife I gave you. Consider: Hercól is not listed among the ser-vants. Isiq must have recruited him quite late. But by the Em-peror's decree every sailor, servant and marine has to meet with my approval. He is illegal, technically—a stowaway."

"Of course, sir!" whispered Zirfet. "I'll see him put off the ship!"

"Fool," said Ott. "You'll see him drowned."

As darkness fell the captain sent word to Elkstem to turn the ship south, out into the Nelu Peren. The east wind that had borne them quickly to Etherhorde now forced them to cut sharply away from the city to avoid the great peril of drifting sidelong against the shore. The lamps of a fishing village dimmed, then vanished altogether. Minutes later the coastline melted into the gray-black seam where sky and water met.

Dinner that night was a grand affair, with the captain and the ambassador joining the wealthy passengers in the first-class dining hall, which had the largest table aboard. Lamb and roast partridge, pepper vodka, mints. After drinking rather more than she was allowed at home, Lady Lapadolma's niece stood up and belted out one of her aunt's poems:

Regal traveler on the waves, over heroes' watery graves,
Peaceful palace of old wood, whither sails thy country's
      brood?
No answer gives she, yet we hear, as in a shell against the ear,
A thousand voices, living, lost, whispering their only trust:
"Over sea and under stars, noble Chathrand's *fate is ours!"*

"Drivel!" escaped from someone, but he was elbowed sharply
and drowned out by claps and cheers.

In a box-like room on the orlop deck, the steerage passengers
lined up for soup and bread. The soup had generous salt, if little
else; the bread was hard but wormless. They ate with quiet concentration and left not a crumb.

The bells rang on the half hour, the watches changed, the
cries of "Steady-on-the-fore" and "Two-points-off-the-lee" ricocheted from mast to mast. By midnight the last gentlemen in the
smoking salon departed, surrendering their pipes and matches
as they went—fire was such a danger that open flames were not
permitted outside that room—and bit by bit the *Chathrand* fell
asleep.

Only then did Sandor Ott leave his cabin. He moved silently
along the row of officers' berths (Mr. Fiffengurt snored like a
laboring cow), climbed the aft ladderway and crossed the main
deck. A moment later he knocked softly at the captain's door.

The door opened a crack, and a nervous, bloodshot eye
peered out. Swellows, the bosun. His breath stank of garlic and
rum. Ott disliked the man, Rose's most loyal bootlicker, a partner in the old rogue's career of swindling and lies. Swellows (his
spies informed him) wore a necklace of ixchel skulls: fifteen or
twenty little bird-sized bones, strung through the eye sockets on
a greasy string. Good luck, some said—but luck was a thing Ott
disdained. He put his shoulder to the door.

Swellows fell back with a whimper: "Quietly, sir, quietly!"

Rose's cabin was dark: black curtains shut out the stars. No
one sat at the desk or dining table; but along the port wall, as far
from the door as possible, figures huddled around a dim red

lamp on a smaller table. Swellows beckoned, but Ott did not wait to be led: he crossed the dark cabin in four strides and rested his hands on the back of the one empty chair.

"You're late, Commander Nagan," said Rose, looking him over.

"I think you may call me Ott here, Captain," said the spy. "Men have killed to learn my true name, others to help me hide it. But in this room it is the least of the secrets we must swear to guard."

"You're still late."

Ott smiled, offering no explanation. He took in the others at a glance: Oggosk the witch, smirking and mumbling as ever. First Mate Uskins, terrified, sweating profusely at the captain's elbow. Beside him, a savage-looking man with small, cruel eyes, his white hair pulled back in a braid. Ott knew him well: Sergeant Drellarek, "the Throatcutter" in military circles, head of the elite Turach warriors brought aboard to guard the Emperor's gold. Drellarek nodded to him: the slow nod of a pit viper coiled to strike. Ott took pleasure in the man as he would in a fine blade or hammer, any tool worn by use to smooth perfection.

There were two others: Aken and Thyne. Neat little men with the soft skin of children and the nervous twitches of a pair of squirrels. Loose paper before them on the table, quill pens in their hands. They were agents of the Trading Family.

"Put those away," said Ott, pointing at the quills. "We want no records here."

Aken, the quieter of the two, wrapped his pen hastily and hid it away. Thyne merely set his on the table, beside a jar of ink.

"We do want answers, however, Mr. Ott," he said. "Now that you've deigned to join us, perhaps we'll get a few. Won't you be seated?"

Ott remained standing, hands on the back of his chair. "We have not met, Mr. Thyne, Mr. Aken," he said. "Still, I believe you know the essence of our plan. The Mzithrinis have a rebellion on their hands, and we shall profit by it. The followers of the Mad King, the Shaggat Ness, have risen on Gurishal, where they were driven by the other Kings forty years ago, after the Shaggat died at sea.

"I say *followers,* but *worshippers* is closer to the truth, for the Shaggat took the Old Faith of the Mzithrin and hammered it into a weapon. The Five Mzithrin Kings, as you know, each guard a fragment of the Black Casket: the stone coffin wherein, ages ago, devils from the Nine Pits were burned to ashes, cleansing the people of their darkest sins. The Book of the Old Faith tells how those devils had to be lured into the Casket, and how at last the Great Devil guessed the trick and fought to escape, and the Casket broke asunder in his death-throes.

"The Kings took the shards of the Casket to their palaces and set them in high towers, to keep the remaining devils from their lands. Under their shadow the five dynasties have ruled together for a thousand years.

"But forty years ago something changed. One of the Kings went mad—or became a God, if you ask his believers. He named himself *Shaggat,* God-King, and declared that the hour had come to drive all devils from the hearts of the Mzithrini people—to make them perfect, as it were. He alone could do it, he said, for in a vision he had come upon a rope ladder dropped from heaven, and he climbed it and learned the tongues of the Gods, and many secrets, including how the Black Casket might be rebuilt."

"Nonsense! Lunacy!" hissed Thyne.

"But of course, sir," said Ott dryly.

Rose leaned back in his chair, frowning. Oggosk twisted her rings.

"And a history lecture, to boot," Thyne went on irritably. "The dead history of a lunatic cult. What of it? I find it hard to believe that we have gathered here, gentlemen, for this review of the heathen myths and squabbles of our enemies."

"But we are here," said Drellarek, glancing sidelong at Thyne. "Let him speak."

Thyne looked at the sergeant and decided to close his mouth.

Ott continued, "Lunacy or not, the Shaggat persuaded tens of

thousands to his cause. The other Kings named him Enemy of
the Faith, but he had already vowed to sweep them aside. And
now I will tell you something that does *not* appear in the history
books: Arqual owes its very survival to that madman. Do you
understand, Mr. Thyne? We were losing the Second Sea War.
The bulk of the Nelu Peren was already under the Mzithrini
flag. The whole Empire might have been conquered within the
year, and Etherhorde burned, and Magad's head hoisted on a
stake, if the Shaggat Ness had not appeared. Soon the Kings
were too busy fighting him to win the war against us. *That* is
why His Supremacy rules the greatest spread of territories on
earth. Because of one holy madman in the west."

Thyne snorted, as if he did not believe a word.

Rose stood up from the table. "I will bring wine," he said.

"The Mzithrin," Ott went on, "could not win two wars at once.
Wisely, they chose to defeat the Shaggat, but to do so they had
to pull all their forces back from the Inner Lands. We chased
them west, island by island, ship by ship. And meanwhile the
Four Faithful Kings crushed the army of the Shaggat in a terrible battle that laid waste to the Mang-Mzn and the Cities of the
Jomm. But the Shaggat escaped."

"We know all this," said Akcn, the other Company man. "He
fled the Mzithrin in a fast ship—he and his sons, and the sorcerer Arunis. The so-called Horrid Four. But their flight from
the Mzithrin brought them straight into the path of our fleet. We
cut that ship to ribbons—the *Lythra,* wasn't it?—and she sank
with all hands."

"Not all," said Sandor Ott.

Silence: the low slap of waves suddenly audible, and the oil
lamp sputtering. Thyne looked startled, even afraid; Uskins
gaped like a fish. Motionless between them, Aken looked like a
man who has just realized, very soberly, that he is seated among
ghouls and vampires.

A grin spread over Drellarek's face.

Thyne rose from his chair, steadying himself with a hand on
the table. "What are you saying?" he whispered.

"He did not drown, Mr. Thyne," said Ott. "We plucked him from the wreckage. And he awaits us on His Supremacy's prison isle of Licherog."

"Awaits us?" cried Thyne suddenly. "The Shaggat Ness, that murdering thing, that . . . creature, alive?"

"And his sons."

"But we told the world they drowned!"

"Lower your voice, Thyne," rumbled Rose, closing the wine cabinet.

Thyne did not seem to hear him. "Mr. Ott! Mr. Ott!" he cried. "The Shaggat was an animal, a beast!"

"He is that," said Ott. "And much more. In the eyes of ninety thousand rebel Mzithrini, he is a God, descended to Alifros to lead them to glory. *They* have never believed him dead. Forty years they have fought the other Kings, and prayed for his return. Exactly when they expect that miracle to occur is a great secret, and one still unknown to the Mzithrin Kings. Shall I tell you, gentlemen? Oh yes, I know their prophecy. I wrote it, you see. My spies have whispered it in Gurishal these four decades, spread it like a sweet pox of the mind. He shall return, they all now believe, *when a Mzithrin lord marries his enemy.*"

"Rin's blood!" blurted Uskins. "You arranged it! The admiral's daughter and the Sizzy prince! You set the whole thing up!"

"Very good, Mr. Uskins," said Ott. "And now you will appreciate just how vital it is that word of our plans never reaches Lady Thasha's father. For when the Mzithrin Kings grasp that young bride's place in the prophecy, they will kill her in a heartbeat. Of course, by then it will be too late. Is it not beautiful, gentlemen? Ninety thousand rebels still worship the Shaggat as a God. And we have a chance to prove them right. We shall raise him from the dead."

"This is monstrous!" said Thyne.

"It is genius," said Drellarek. He rose and bowed to Sandor Ott. "A weapon forty years in the smithing. My compliments, sir, on the tactic of a lifetime."

"Except," said Aken, "that the entire White Fleet lies between us and the Shaggat's worshippers. How do you mean to get him to Gurishal, on the far side of the Mzithrin lands?"

"Wait and see," said Ott.

"They put a new King on the Shaggat's throne, didn't they?" asked Drellarek.

"Right after the war," said Ott with a nod. "But the fanatics of Gurishal made so many attempts on his life that the Pentarchy changed the seat of that kingdom to North Urlanx. Both moves only served to deepen the hatred of the Nessarim for the rest of the Mzithrini peoples. Gurishal may be contained by the armies of the Five Kings, but it is primed to explode."

"And what of the Shaggat's mage, Arunis?" demanded Thyne. "Did he too escape the wreck of the *Lythra*? Is *he* imprisoned on Licherog?"

"No longer," said Ott. "Arunis was indeed pulled from the Gulf of Thól and imprisoned, but he met a curious fate. It appears he tried sorcery on his guards and nearly escaped the island. But one guard regained his senses and shot an arrow into the arm of the fleeing mage. It was but a scratch, but it bled, and by the spoor of blood Arunis was tracked down by dogs, recaptured—and hanged. The guard paid a high price for his valor, though. Arunis flung a curse at him with his last breath, and within weeks the guard began to lose his mind, convinced that *he* was the one dangling from a rope. He ended up in a madhouse on Opalt."

Rose limped back across the floor. Mr. Uskins, rigid with fear but with a new gleam in his eye, leaned forward. "And the gold we're carrying? What are we to do with all that gold?"

"Can't you guess?" snapped Ott. "The Shaggat is the blood enemy of the remaining Mzithrin Kings. We're sending him into battle, and battles require soldiers and horses, catapults and cannon and ships. Thanks to us he will have them. We are financing his war.

"But this war will be different. This time Arqual will be innocent, a spectator—and not a war-crippled spectator, either. As the Mzithrinis retreat, fighting themselves once again, we shall move in force to take their place—permanently. And why not? Why should men of the Crownless Lands buy their boots and coal and weapons from savages who drink one another's blood? Our boots fit. Our coal burns as hot. That business, those millions in profits, should be Arqual's—*will* be Arqual's, in due time. And naturally, ships full of valuable goods must be protected."

Drellarek looked at him sharply. "You're speaking of the Imperial navy," he said. "But would the Crownless Lands ever agree to let our ships back in their waters?"

"Dear sergeant!" said Ott. "With the Shaggat returned, and civil war to the west? They will beg us on bended knees."

"But Sizzies are Pit-fiends in a fight!" whispered Swellows, over Ott's shoulder. "Tough, and cruel, and wicked—even to their own kind."

"We need them to be wicked, fool," said Ott. "Every misery the other Kings inflict on their people makes the Shaggat that much dearer to his followers, and costly to destroy."

"What if they can't destroy him?" Swellows pressed. "Will he turn on *us*?"

A silence. "They'll destroy him," said Ott finally. "No doubt about that. But oh, gentlemen—how it will cost them! They will be Kings of rubble when it's done! In five years' time, Arqual will own the Quiet Sea."

"And in ten years?" asked Aken. "What of your further plans, Mr. Ott?"

For the briefest instant Ott looked surprised. Then he said, smoothly: "Nothing further. I am sworn to defend Arqual from the Mzithrin horde. That is enough."

Thyne gathered up his papers. "Defend it with another ship, Spymaster," he said. "You have exceeded your mandate. The Lady Lapadolma never authorized such a mission for the *Chathrand,* nor would she. We are businessfolk, not butchers."

Suddenly Oggosk laughed. The others jumped: they had all but forgotten her.

"What's the difference?" she said gleefully. "Your darling

Lady buys the bones of six thousand men and horses a year from the old Ipulia battlefields, grinds and sells them to eastern farmers to enrich their soils. She takes furs by the shipload from Idhe barons who set fire to trappers who don't catch enough mink. She buys ore mined by Ulluprid slaves, sells it to Etherhorde ironsmiths and sails back to the Ulluprids with spears and arrows for the slavemasters."

"That is different," said Thyne. "That is buying and selling, commerce among free men."

"Well then, so is our plan," said Ott. "We are buying a little room for Arqual and her manufacturers, and selling a God."

"Madness!" repeated Thyne. "There will be no profit in this for the Company, only the loss of her good reputation—"

Oggosk cackled again.

"—and this very ship, her flagship, the pride of the seas." He looked at his companion, and his voice grew shrill. "Aken, why do you just sit there? Speak up, man!"

"I can't think what to say," said Aken.

"Well, I can," said Thyne. "Take your war games elsewhere, Ott. As Company Overseer for this *trading* voyage, I hereby revoke your lease on the *Chathrand*. You all know I have that power under the Sailing Code, section nine, article four: Gross Misstatement of Mission."

As Thyne finished speaking, the spymaster turned to Drellarek and gave a small nod. Thyne saw the look and grasped its meaning instantly. "Wait, wait!" he cried, springing backward. But Drellarek's eyes had glazed over, and a knife had appeared in his hand.

Then Rose moved. With one lurch he seized Aken by the lapels, wrenched him from the chair and clubbed him brutally across the face. The small man fell like a sack of grain at Drellarek's feet.

Thyne stumbled back from the table, his mouth agape. Rose waved Drellarek off.

"Don't harm him," said the captain. "He will see reason yet. Aken here is the dangerous one, who would have betrayed us at the first chance. He sat quiet while that ninny prattled and whined. But I could hear the wheels turning in his head."

Speechless, the others watched Rose drag the unconscious man to the gallery windows. "Shutter that lamp, Uskins," he said.

Uskins closed the lamp's iron shade, plunging the cabin into darkness. The men at the table heard curtains rustle, and the squeak of a hinge. A cold finger of sea wind probed the room. Then, far away, so faint they could deny it to themselves, they heard a splash. "Leave my cabin, all of you," said Rose in the darkness. "We shall talk again in Uturphe, weather permitting."

17

Indiscretions

Was he awake or dreaming? Had the fit marooned him somewhere in between?

Pazel lay on his back at the foot of a plump, lacy bed. Still
aboard *Chathrand,* for his limbs knew her gentle rocking, and
the bed's feet were nailed down. He smelled lavender and tal-
cum powder, and thought suddenly of Neda's room, at home in
Ormael. Under his head (which still hurt and spun badly) was
the softest pillow he had ever touched. And on the edge of the
bed, looking down at him, was a small, strange animal. It was
rather like a weasel, but jet-black, with huge, dark eyes that
froze him with their gaze.

"How's this?" it said cheerfully. "A tarboy on the floor!"

"What!" croaked Pazel (his mouth was very dry).

"They are all gone away and left you," said the creature. "And
I must leave you as well. Can you really understand my words?"

"How did you . . . I mean, yes! What?"

"You do understand. Remarkable! You'll make her a very fine
tutor indeed. Tell me, was a black rat here a moment ago?"

"You're not a rat!"

"My dear boy, are you ill? Not everyone who *seeks* a rat must
be one."

The creature sprang lightly from the bed to the top of a
dresser. Pazel arched his neck: upon the dresser stood a lovely

mariner's clock, the kind rich captains kept screwed down tight on their desktops. Its round face was painted to resemble a gibbous moon. Even stranger, Pazel saw that the face—hands, numbers and all—was hinged on one side, and stood slightly ajar. Behind it, within the body of the clock, was a round darkness: somehow it felt cold and strange.

The animal nudged the clock face nearly shut, then glanced over its shoulder at Pazel.

"You won't touch this, will you?"

"W-wouldn't dream of it."

"And if I were to ask you a favor, to help me with your Gift to do a very great and dangerous thing—to prevent a war, in fact—how would you answer me?"

"What?"

"We must talk again, Mr. Pathkendle. Goodbye!"

Pazel shook himself. He was in the same place, resting on the same satin pillow. The little animal was gone; the light through the portholes had dimmed. And directly above him, sticking over the end of the mattress, were a girl's bare feet.

He turned his head to one side, and found himself nose to nose with a blue dog of terrifying dimensions. It lay with head on paws, drooling gently. *Try something,* begged its eyes. *Let me eat you.*

Overall it was better looking at the feet. In another moment, astonished, Pazel realized whose they were.

"Lady Thasha?" he whispered.

The feet jerked back, the bed creaked and the face of the ambassador's daughter appeared. Her golden hair fell almost to his nose.

"You can talk!" cried Thasha. "Hercól! He can talk!"

She leaped to the floor and pushed the dog aside. Just as when she boarded the *Chathrand,* she was dressed in a man's breeches and shirt. He was startled anew by how pretty she was, and how clean. Under his new coat and cap he remained a grimy tarboy. It had never bothered him much, until now.

"Thank the Gods!" she said. "You made such *awful* sounds! What's the matter with you, anyway?"

"I'm fine now, Mistress," said Pazel, blushing. He sat up, a little unsteadily, and tried to fasten his coat, then remembered the missing buttons and crossed his arms over his chest.

He struggled to his feet, and nearly stumbled. He put a hand on her bed, then pulled away quickly as if he'd touched something fragile. Thasha caught his arm: the strength of her grip was startling.

Don't stare, he thought. She had such pale skin. She wore a necklace beneath her shirt: ocean creatures in solid silver, astonishingly fine. The thought came to him unbidden: that necklace alone could pay off his bond debt, three or four times over.

"You were very kind to shelter me," he said.

They stood there, eye to eye, and for a moment he thought she looked as uncertain and confused as he felt himself. Then she laughed aloud.

"You don't talk like any servant I've ever met," she told him. "You don't even have an accent. You sound like my cousins from Maj District. Why, you could pass for an Arquali if I closed my eyes!"

"I could never do that," said Pazel at once, freeing his arm from her hand. "Even if I wanted to. And I don't, Lady Thasha."

"Don't be prickly," she said. "I didn't say you *should* be an Arquali. And stop this Mistress-Lady nonsense. I'm the same age as you."

Pazel just looked at her, irritated now. Age had nothing to do with it, of course. They were not equals. If she were a toddler and he a man of sixty, he would still be obliged to call her *Lady.*

"Hercól thinks you're under a curse," said Thasha. "Is he right? How often does it happen?"

"Two or three times a year, Mistress."

"You must be rather clever to survive. In the Lorg a girl with a curse like yours would be put in a barrel of icewater—to cool her evil thoughts, you know. I wonder what evil thoughts you have, Pazel Pathkendle?"

"That's not why it happens!" he said fiercely.

"Of course not. I was being ironic." She smiled, but Pazel flushed again, because now he looked like a bumpkin who took everything seriously. He longed to show her that he knew what *ironic* meant, but no words came.

Then all at once his mind took in the significance of the objects around him: bed, heaped clothes, wardrobe and mirror, writing table with stationery and quill.

"This is your cabin," he whispered. "I can't be here."

"Oh, blow!" she said. "Don't you start as well."

"You're the Treaty Bride," said Pazel. "I've got to get out of here."

"Don't call me that," said Thasha in a warning tone.

Pazel bent to look out the porthole. "What time is it, m'lady?" he asked.

"Almost dinnertime. My father's having a drink with Captain Rose."

"Who else knows I'm here? Who saw me come in?"

Impatiently she sketched the missing hours of his life. His encounter with Jervik had been loud. Thasha and her tutor Hercól had left the stateroom to investigate just as Pazel rushed into the corridor. Thasha did not seem surprised that Hercól had seized him at once, dragged him to her private room and put him to sleep with a gulp of liquor, all in a matter of seconds. Her tutor, she said, moved faster than anyone on earth.

"I saw your father," said Pazel.

Thasha nodded. "He didn't see you, fortunately. Syrarys closed the washroom door, and Prahba's a little hard of hearing. Syrarys saw you, though, and nearly had you thrown out again." Thasha put on a face of mock outrage, and a strident voice: " 'You put that boy in her *bedroom,* Hercól? What are you *thinking*? What will people *say*?' "

"She's right," said Pazel. "You're noble-born. You can't do this sort of thing."

"Rubbish," she said. "I do exactly as I please."

"Some of us don't get to live that way," he said, a bit more sharply than he intended. "And they'll gossip on the berth deck, too, m'lady. Do you know what my mates will say if they find out?"

Thasha smiled and leaned forward, intrigued—not at all the reaction he wished for. "What will they say?" she asked.

He hesitated. If she really wanted to know—

"They'll say you like *playing in the dirt.*"

Thasha's look of enthusiasm died on her face. She was shocked, but clearly didn't want him to see it. She forced out a laugh. "Tar-boys," she said.

Pazel bit his lips. *As if you knew anything about us.*

"Besides," he went on, "you're supposed to be practicing to be a Mzithrini wife, and they're not allowed to do anything."

"Rubbish!" said Thasha again. "And anyway I don't care. You're not one of those mush-dull boys who does only what he's supposed to, I hope? But of course you're not—I saw you with the augrongs. Wherever did you learn to speak Augrongi?"

"Augronga," Pazel corrected her, before he could stop himself. Then he added quickly, "I don't really speak it, of course; nobody does. But sailing here and there, you know, you hear things. And there's this book called a *Polylex,* most ships carry one."

"Not that thing," said Thasha, with an odd look. "It's all mixed up and wrong."

That was perfectly true, Pazel knew. It was even likely that Mr. Uskins had pieced together his disastrous Augronga from the "Tongues of All Alifros" chapter in the back of the book.

"Of course," said Thasha, lowering her eyes, "some versions are better than others. I have an old *Polylex* of my own. It says that drinking buffalo milk makes one smarter but also prone to 'wraths and paranoias.' And it says that long ago there were whole fleets of ships like the *Chathrand,* and they really did cross the Ruling Sea, and visited strange lands we've forgotten all about. Most of those ships were destroyed so long ago that we can't even recall their names. They were built by the Amber Kings, and one of them brought the foundation stone for the city of Etherhorde from the Court of the Archangel in the east. But over the centuries they built fewer and fewer, and the old ships began to sink. Three were destroyed in the Worldstorm, and one in a great whirlpool called the Nelluroq Vortex."

"Yes, the Vortex—"

"And do you know I've been having dreams about it, or something like it? Prahba was talking about war, and how one kind of destruction leads to another, and since then I've had this dream of a whirlpool, and a ship trapped inside it, spinning like a bit of wood, lower and lower—"

"Mistress—"

"Off the point, I know. What I mean to say is that the Vortex took *Stallion* in the year seven fifty-two, and *Urstorch* and *Bali Adro* never returned from missions across the Ruling Sea, and the last Great Ship but this one, the *Maisa*, was sunk by the Mzithrinis half a century ago. She was the sister-ship to the *Chathrand*: same size, same trim. But *Maisa* wasn't her original name. She was given that name just a few years before she sank, in honor of an Empress Maisa. My *Polylex* says she was our Emperor's stepmother."

"Yes, I knew that—"

"Did you? How strange. There was no Empress Maisa in my schoolbooks. But do you know the strangest thing about the Great Ships? The Yeligs—the *Chathrand*'s owners—are the whole reason we can't build any more! They started putting the shipwrights to death so that they couldn't sell their secrets to other Trading Families. I suppose they didn't mean to kill them *all*."

"Mistress!" Pazel broke in at last. "The Lady Syrarys knows I'm in your cabin!"

"You worry too much," said Thasha. "I can handle Syrarys. I told her I'd cut off my hair and spit sapwort at my wedding if she disturbed you. Not that there's going to be any wedding—but perhaps you'd better not tell anyone I said that. Anyway, I doubt she *could* have disturbed you after you swallowed all that Keppery gin. Do you know what's crawling around in this ship?"

"M-m-my Lady?"

"Rats!" said Thasha happily. "I saw a rat on the lower gun deck. And would you believe I heard one crawling under these very floorboards last night? It must have been a clever rat, for when I hushed my dogs it grew still, too. Are you afraid of rats?"

"No."

"Do they bite you tarboys?"

"Yes."

"What happened to your parents, then? Are they dead?"

It was most unusual for Pazel to be at a loss for words, and most uncomfortable. He had not been alone with any girl in his life save his sister, and he had rarely known anyone to talk as long and cheerfully as Thasha. He was also maddened by his own timidity before her. She was beautiful and important; did that mean she was smarter than he was? He swallowed. Then he folded his hands behind his back, schoolboy-fashion.

"Your questions, Lady Thasha," he said, "are *indiscreet.*"

Folding his hands proved a mistake: he could have used them to protect himself. Instead he found himself flat on his back again with Thasha astride him, thumping his cheeks and pouring out a whirlwind of abuse. *"Indiscreet! He runs in squawking like a . . . playing in the blary dirt . . . I'll show you who's practicing to be a wife!"*

This was how Hercól found them: red-faced and tangled, with Jorl howling at the ceiling and Suzyt doing her best to swallow Pazel's right foot. When he had separated them, and persuaded Suzyt to unlock her jaws, the tall man laughed.

"So good to find you improved, lad! But save your wrestling for other tarboys: they are far less dangerous. Come, get up, we have some things to decide. Won't you introduce us, Thasha?"

"I'm not marrying anyone!"

"In fact," said Hercól, as if no one had just bellowed at the top of her lungs, "I've heard of you already, Pathkendle. Dr. Chadfallow says you're a natural scholar. He has spoken of you for years, but I never imagined he would arrange for us all to sail on *Chathrand* together."

"*He's* a friend of Dr. Chadfallow?" demanded Thasha incredulously.

"No," said Pazel. "Not anymore."

"Do not condemn Ignus Chadfallow for the nation he was born into," said Hercól. "True friendship is not a thing given lightly, nor should it be lightly tossed away."

"Tell that to him," said Pazel.

"You have a sharp tongue," said Hercól, "but I know a little of your reasons for it. Do me a favor, now that I've rescued you from both Thasha and your shipmates: tell me exactly what's wrong with you."

Pazel looked up at the kindly but piercing gray eyes. If his evasions had not fooled Thasha, they had no chance with this man. So for the second time in ten days, he did what he had long sworn never to do: he told strangers about his Gift.

"Or curse, as you say," he added. "I always imagined—from the stories in books, and Mother's stories, too—that magic would feel like a thunderclap. In fact it's more like catching a cold. You know when a fever starts, and it feels as if some army's come in through your ears and is burning up your insides, one room at a time? Well, in my case it's a good army, at first. If I need to speak Augronga, it gives me Augronga. If I look at the *Chathrand*'s escutcheon, it tells me what I'm reading. And I never forget, even after the mind-fits."

"How many languages have you learned this way?" asked Thasha, still glowering.

"Twenty."

She gave him a skeptical smile—did she think he was joking?—and then asked him his age in Opaltik, which Lorg Daughters study as one more way to pass the years before marriage. When Pazel answered instantly, she tried something much more difficult: a nursery rhyme from the Ulluprid Isles, taught to her years ago by Syrarys. Even before it ended she knew he understood, for he looked still more flustered and uncomfortable. The rhyme was "My Darling Sailor."

"If only we could show him to Ramachni," said Thasha. She

glanced at the clock on her dresser. Then her eyes grew wide. "Hercól! It's open!"

Hercól had not noticed the clock face either. "He is aboard, then! Did you see him, Pathkendle?"

"He's a mink," added Thasha helpfully.

Pazel started. "Then I wasn't dreaming. You mean he's a woken animal? A real one? And he belongs to you?"

"One does not own a woken beast," said Hercól severely, "except as a slave-keeper."

"He's not really a mink," Thasha said. "In his own world he's a bald old man."

"Ramachni is *much* more than that," said Hercól, smiling a little now.

"Of course," said Thasha. "He's a great mage, and he's been visiting me for years by crawling through my clock."

Pazel looked from girl to man to clock, and back again.

"Have a look," said Hercól. "But touch nothing, and make no sound."

Gingerly, Thasha took hold of the clock's moon-face and opened it wide. And behind it was a tunnel.

At least, *tunnel* was the word that leaped to mind, although *pipe* might have been more accurate. Pazel looked, blinked and looked again, and found he could not tear his eyes away. He, who lived with magic in his blood, was *seeing* magic today for the first time.

And what a sight it was. Just inches wide, the tunnel ran straight through the clock and onward—forty feet onward— through wall and adjacent cabin, and the cabin beyond that. It should have ended, roughly, in the center of the first-class dining room. A cold draft flowed from its mouth, carrying a hint of cedar smoke and a few grains of dark sand that fell from the clock to scatter among Thasha's rings and bracelets.

But at the same time the tunnel was *not* there. He passed his hand behind the clock and felt nothing, looked and saw nothing but the plain cabin wall. The tunnel only existed within the clock.

And at its far end there glowed a room. It was just visible, sharp and tiny, like the view through the wrong end of a telescope: crackling firelight, a three-legged stool, a bookshelf. Just that, and the sound of a desolate wind that was not blowing around the *Chathrand*.

He straightened, gaping, and Thasha returned the clock face to its just-open position.

"Ramachni's Observatory. That's what he calls it."

"Where . . . where is it?"

"In the mountains of another world."

"His world?"

She nodded. "I've been there. In a manner of speaking." She laughed. "There's a secret way to open the clock, and they didn't think I knew it. But I'd watched Hercól do it once, pretending to be asleep, and the next night I felt like talking to Ramachni before bed, and opened the clock myself. He wasn't home, but I left the clock ajar. And that night I passed along the tunnel somehow and stepped into the Observatory. I saw wonders—a sleeping cat with smoke puffing from its nose, a bookshelf that became a wall each time I put out my hand, a great glass house full of trees and flowers, hot as anything, but built on a snowpeak.

"Suddenly Ramachni was standing among the flowers. He looked quite human. He offered me a strawberry, and when I'd eaten it he asked me to take a walk with him. We passed through the glass house and into a kind of dark toolshed, very cold—the floor was a mix of snow and sand—and then he threw open the far door and there were the peaks, huge frozen peaks all around me, and the air was thin and icy. We stepped out and I realized we were on the very edge of a cliff. So high, Pazel—I can't begin to tell you how high and terrifying it was. The wind was screaming and the ground was slick ice under my night socks, but you could see forever, and there were creatures larger than whales in the distance, gliding among the clouds. And then he asked if I knew where home lay. I was in tears, but he laughed and covered my eyes. He said the tunnel was not a plaything, and that I might be able to visit him by it just twice more in my lifetime. Then he took his hand away and I was back in my room in Etherhorde."

"Thasha has a most spectacular dream-life," said Hercól.

"It wasn't a dream," she said fiercely. "My socks were wet afterward."

"But why does he visit you?" Pazel asked. "You particularly, I mean?"

A brief silence: Thasha looked at Hercól. "They won't tell me," she said at last.

"All that I am given to tell, I tell," said Hercól. "Complain to the mage of his mysteries, once we find him. But just now, boy, I would like to test your Gift a little further."

He then asked Pazel questions in Tholjassan and Talturik and Noonfirthic, and when Pazel answered each in turn Thasha laughed in delight. Pazel smiled despite himself. She wasn't the only one with something special to her name.

"There's another thing," he said. "Sometimes I hear better than normal. Just voices—and come to think of it, just *translated* voices. If you went into the next room and whispered in Arquali, I wouldn't hear a thing, because I learned Arquali before my mother cast the spell. But I would hear perfectly if you spoke in, say, Nileskchet—"

He stopped dead.

Hercól's eyes narrowed.

Bewildered, Thasha looked from one to the other. "Nileskchet. That's a funny name for a language. I've never even heard of it. What is Nileskchet?"

"Yes," said Hercól, in a changed voice. "Can you tell us that?"

Pazel knew he had made a terrible blunder. However kind these new friends appeared, they would never forgive him for associating with crawlies. And what about the ixchel themselves? Even Diadrelu had promised to kill him if he revealed their presence.

"It's just some old language," he stammered. "I don't think anyone uses it today, except in poetry."

Hercól bent toward him, hawk-like. "Do *you,* by any chance, enjoy Nileskchet poetry?"

"I've never heard any."

"Few men have."

"Why are you so strange all of a sudden, Hercól?" said Thasha. "We should be deciding what to do about him."

Hercól kept his eyes on Pazel for another long moment. Then at last his gaze softened and he sat up. "True enough," he said. "Four hours of work you've missed. They know you're in here, of course, so we must invent a story to explain it. My suggestion is that we tell the truth: you have been entertaining us with your languages."

"Languages!" said Thasha suddenly. "Pazel, tell me this, if you can: who or what is a *mighra cror*?"

Pazel looked at her, startled anew. "Those are Mzithrini words, the first I've heard in five years. And they mean 'red wolf.' "

"Red wolf?"

He nodded. "Where did you hear such a thing?"

"From a man who hid in our garden," said Thasha. "Just before someone put an arrow in his heart."

Hercól was looking from one to the other. "You are both quite sure?" he said softly. "Of what you heard, Thasha—and you, boy, of the meaning?"

They assured him they were.

"Does it mean something to *you,* Hercól?" Thasha asked.

"It may, and it may not. I know of just one red wolf. It was a magic statue or talisman of old, fashioned by Mzithrini alchemists from enchanted iron, fused with the blood of a living man. The stories all connect this Red Wolf with some great evil that plagued the Pentarchy a thousand years ago. And yet, strangely, the Five Kings' worst fear seemed to be that it might be stolen: they carved out a mountain citadel over Babqri and placed the Wolf at its center, guarded by walls and traps and *sfvantskor* warrior-priests. Why they should keep a thing of evil at the heart of their Empire I cannot guess. The tales, in any case, are half forgotten, in this age when east and west do not speak. What *is* certain is that the citadel, for all its protections, was destroyed at the end of the last war. The fate of the Red Wolf is anyone's guess. What a peculiar thing for that man to say."

"In the middle of Etherhorde," added Thasha, shaking her head. "In *Mzithrini.*"

"Stranger still, he said it to *you,*" added Hercól. "The Treaty Bride, on the eve of her journey."

She turned back to Pazel. "If you speak Mzithrini, that means you heard someone speak it once when your Gift was working, right?"

"Yes," said Pazel. "The Mzithrin Kings had an envoy in Ormael, just like Arqual did. He had to leave when the troubles began, but in earlier days he and Dr. Chadfallow used to sit on our terrace and talk about peace—or argue about war."

"But I thought your mother cast the spell while Chadfallow was back home in Etherhorde," said Thasha.

"She did," said Pazel. "But the Mzithrini envoy . . . well, he fell in love with my mother, and spent time with us right up until the Arqualis attacked. My mother didn't particularly like him, but he kept trying. *Especially* after Dr. Chadfallow left."

"Ignus said she was a great beauty," said Hercól.

Pazel dropped his eyes. "He proposed to her," he said at last.

"Who?" asked Thasha. "The doctor or the Sizzy fellow?"

"Both," said Pazel after a moment.

"Ah!"

"She was—she *is* beautiful," Pazel went on. "And she did like Ignus. But I can't understand why she took so long to say no to the Mzithrini."

"Just imagine!" laughed Thasha. "If she'd married him, you might have gone to live in Babqri City and learned the Casket Prayers, and had your neck tattooed with the name of his tribe, and learned how to ride a war elephant!"

"And found Captain Gregory," said Hercól.

Pazel looked up at him sharply.

"Or if she'd married Chadfallow," said Thasha, "he might

have taken you to Etherhorde, and we'd have met years ago, and Hercól could have taught you *thojmélé* fighting, too. And you'd never have become a tarboy at all. You'd be Pazel Chadfallow, and you'd have been safe and sound in the doctor's house right through the Rescue of Ormael."

"Rescue?" said Pazel, turning on her in amazement. "The *Rescue of Ormael*? Do you people really call it that?"

"Well, yes," she said, taken aback. "It was a rescue, wasn't it? Otherwise you'd have been killed by the Mzithrin Kings, all of you, and had your blood mixed with milk."

"Come, Thasha, you know better," said Hercól.

Thasha was by now quite red. "Do I? Prahba says it was only a matter of time before *someone* invaded Ormael. At least we didn't kill everyone."

"You tried," said Pazel.

"Mr. Pathkendle!" said Hercól.

"You killed half the men in the invasion—that's what it was, Thasha, an *invasion*—and enslaved the rest. You sold us boys to the mining companies, and our sisters to old fat men."

"Nobody sold *you* to any mining company," said Thasha, but she could no longer meet his eye.

"You burned the city to the ground!"

"She didn't," said a voice behind them. "I did."

Admiral Eberzam Isiq stood in the doorway, heavy and grim, a pale turquoise vein standing out on his bald head. No one had heard him approach.

"Who is this boy, who calls my daughter by her given name? Why is he in her cabin?"

"Sir," said Hercól, bowing his head, "I do humbly beg your pardon. This is the tarboy you wished to congratulate, the tamer of the augrongs. I understood you were napping, and as we waited on your pleasure the boy revealed that he speaks the Mzithrini tongue." He raised a book from Thasha's table. "I thought it worth putting to the test."

"So this is Pathkendle!" boomed the ambassador. "Captain Gregory's boy! I didn't know him in that coat—but of course, it's the very coat I gave him, isn't it? Hmm! Now tell me, Pathkendle: what has happened to my doctor?"

"I . . . I've no idea, sir."

"Chadfallow has vanished," declared Isiq. "Normally he writes every week or two, but it has been almost six. His last letter said that he had booked passage on the *Eniel* to Sorrophran, where he was to board this ship. You served on the *Eniel,* I believe."

He's sharp, thought Pazel. *Who told him that?*

"Did you see him, boy? Speak to him?"

Pazel nodded.

"Well, what did he say? Out with it!"

"We spoke about the *Chathrand,* sir," said Pazel carefully. "And about the last war with the Mzithrin. Were you in that war, sir?"

"Of course. Continue."

Pazel hesitated. Chadfallow had spoken to him in great secrecy. He and Isiq were old friends, and perhaps the doctor had hoped Pazel would pass on a message—but how could he be sure?

"He . . . hinted at things, Your Excellency. That the *Chathrand* is heading for the Mzithrin lands, for instance."

"Well, so we are—to Simja, right on the border of their empire."

"Excuse me, sir: not *close to* but *into* Mzithrini waters. That's what he meant, I think."

Isiq looked sharply at Hercól, then back to Pazel. "You must have misheard."

"Not him," snarled Thasha. "Mr. Pathkendle has *very* sharp hearing."

Isiq laughed aloud. "She's fond of you. Can't you tell?" Then, abruptly, he winced and raised his hands to his temples.

Thasha rushed to his side. "Prahba," she said, clutching his arm. "Are they getting worse?"

"I'm quite all right," he grumbled. "And when we land at Tressek Tarn I shall be better still."

Pazel supposed Isiq meant to visit the famous mineral baths

of Tressek Tarn; they were said to cure all manner of diseases. What was wrong with him, though? One could tell at a glance that he suffered from more than headaches.

Isiq smiled at his daughter. "Your hand is strong," he said. "You'll represent our Empire well in this new age of peace. Now come here, Pathkendle. I have something to say."

Pazel came forward uneasily, and the admiral rested a hand on his shoulder.

"We burned your city," he said. "It was a terrible deed, and fate repays me in the same coin—I too am burning, with a brain fever that never quite subsides. But know this: my orders were far worse, not just to burn Ormael City but to flatten her, roll her founding-stone into the sea, fill her wells with corpses, plow her fields with salt. Our Emperor did not think we could hold Ormael, so far from the heart of Arqual, so close to the Mzithrin Kings. He wanted a wasteland, therefore: something no enemy could ever reclaim.

"I meant to give him his ruin. I sailed there with such purpose, believing the safety of Arqual depended on it. But when I arrived and saw proud young Ormael, beautiful as a Dlómic city out of legend, I could not."

He paused, worrying his knuckles. Thasha looked at Pazel expectantly, and Pazel felt like bolting from the room. What did they want? To be thanked?

"Imagine if I had done nothing," said Isiq at last. "Do you know what would have happened then? I should have been imprisoned, my consort given to another man, my daughter to Gods know whom. And your city would have bled all the same. Indeed, to see the job done His Supremacy would have sent one of his butchering Turach generals next. The best I could do was limit the damage and take Ormael for the Empire, alive but wounded."

"The bodies piled in Darli Square didn't look *wounded*," muttered Pazel.

"Silence!" barked Hercól, as Isiq's jaw dropped in amazement.

Thasha's tutor leaped forward to catch Pazel by the arm. "Curb your tongue, rascal! Whom do you think you're speaking to? Your Excellency, a thousand pardons! I shall remove him immediately—or after his *humblest* apologies, if that is your wish."

As Hercól fell silent, Pazel saw that the ambassador was furious: red-faced, mouth a-quiver. How long had it been since anyone dared contradict him? Backed against the wall, Thasha was staring at him, wide-eyed: for better or worse Pazel had impressed her again.

Isiq rubbed his temples with both hands. "I am more interested to know if the boy himself wishes to apologize," he said.

Pazel looked at him in silence, remembering flies and the smell of blood. Hercól gave his arm a ferocious squeeze.

Still Pazel hesitated—and then it was too late. A door crashed open in the outer stateroom, a woman gasped and Syrarys was there, lovely and furious, eyes ablaze.

"What is this? Eberzam, you're shaking! You've exhausted yourself!"

"I'm fine," said Isiq, but his voice rang suddenly weaker. "Syrarys, where have you been?"

"Making arrangements for your baths at Tressek. Sit down! Oh, Hercól, what have you done? Get that wretched boy out of here!"

"I invited him," said Thasha. "And he's no more wretched than you."

The consort turned her a scalding look. "Haven't you done enough? Will you only be satisfied when your father collapses? Hercól, take him *away*!"

Hercól bowed and tugged Pazel roughly from the cabin. Pazel had only a fleeting impression of the outer stateroom: an immense, glittering chamber, someone's greatcoat tossed casually over a blue divan, a pair of crossed swords mounted on the wall, red ribbons wound about their sheaths. As the door closed he turned and glanced back at Thasha. Her eyes were on him still.

"Splendid work," said Hercól furiously. "In ten minutes you managed to make Thasha cry, her father hate you and her tutor seem a colossal fool."

"I'm sorry," Pazel said, "but you don't know what it was like."

"Nor do you know my life's tragedies, nor hers, nor those of hundreds on this ship! Does that make your outburst any wiser? It is not a question of feelings but of self-control!"

"So I should have lied to him? Or acted grateful?"

"You should have held your tongue. Think, boy! Your father has become a Mzithrini! If anyone can help you rejoin him it will be Eberzam Isiq."

Pazel started. Rejoin his father! It had never seemed remotely possible. But if peace took hold between the empires, almost *anything* could happen. And even though his father had not wanted it, Pazel did know a bit about sailing now. Wild hopes began to swirl in his head.

They crossed the gun deck, heading forward. Sailors muttered as they passed: *"That's him, that crazy Muketch. Talks like a ghost's in his guts."*

"Will the baths help Thasha's father?" Pazel asked Hercól.

Hercól looked grave. "Who can tell? His illness is most peculiar; it is a bad time to be without Ignus Chadfallow. Now then: if anyone asks, you were helping Thasha practice her Mzithrini vows. And if you can keep out of trouble for a few days, I *might* be able to make truth of that little lie—that is, to arrange for you to be Thasha's language tutor. Of course, that would mean spending an hour or two with her every day."

Pazel stopped in his tracks.

"What is the matter?" said Hercól. "You do not wish it?"

Pazel's first thought was *Of course not!* But something made him hold his tongue. He thought again of how she'd looked at him from atop the carriage in Etherhorde, felt again her hand on his arm. *She stood up for me in front of Syrarys. Why?*

"Rose won't give me time off to be a teacher," he said.

"He might if your bond debt were paid," said Hercól.

Pazel gaped at him. "Would you do that for me? Really?"

Hercól laughed. "I would do so for every bonded servant in Arqual, if I could. Unfortunately the gold to my name would scarcely buy the two of us a good meal in Tressek Tarn. No, if you're to teach his daughter it will be the ambassador who buys your freedom. We've spoken of it already. Use your head, Pazel, and don't insult those who stand ready to help you. Hallo there, Mr. Fiffengurt! I dare say you're looking for this lad."

18

Night Village

26 Vaqrin 941
14th day from Etherhorde

My terror is the terror of the rat, but my soul is my own. My soul is my own. My soul is my own.

Say that when the panic comes. If it's true then you're safe, saved, sane. You shall prosper and escape this murdering cold water of loneliness, this whirlpool, this swill of violence and want. Find love, dry land, eyes that don't hate you when they discern you from shadow.

If it is not true—then there is no you to be saved, darling Felthrup.

So thinking, the black rat worried a path among the ghostly stores and cargo of the mercy deck. He was moving in circles: not lost, but searching in frantic haste, staring into the near-perfect blackness, straining his nocturnal eyes. What he sought was a light, the smallest, palest red light. Three times he had glimpsed it already and dashed forward with hope leaping in his heart, only to see it vanish without a trace.

Each dash was a flirtation with death. Normally he did not move two yards without a jerk of the head, a glance back over one greasy shoulder or the other. There were flickers of motion; there were drafts and tremors, and sudden anonymous sounds. Worst of all, there were smells—cloying, crowding, smothering, flooding him with fear. The smell of man was everywhere: in the greasy fingerprints left by the longshoremen, in the sweat from their backs where they had leaned against posts, in the sailors' spit and sweetpine residues, in the human breath oozing downward from the sleeping quarters.

(*My terror is the terror of the sleeper, buried alive.*)

He did not fear men, though—not at this hour. Past midnight the mercy deck belonged to others: rats, ixchel, that dark thing that lurked and snuffled, a few mice and snakes and spiders, a few million fleas. Men nicknamed it pest-deck, piss-deck, stow-away lane. To its residents it was simply Night Village.

Even at noon men worked there with lamps, for the mercy deck rode twenty feet beneath the waves. The dead of night saw no more than one man an hour trudge through its depths, blinded by his own lamp, scanning the hull for leaks.

The great danger was Sniraga. Three nights already she had come hunting, crate to crevice, an angel of death. No flood of light announced *her* visits, and no sound but the sudden, blood-freezing wail of a life cut short. Then the Red River cat would climb to a high place, a transverse beam, maybe, and devour her victim by meticulous stages. With the pitch of the ship, gall-bladders and stomachs would fall to the deck: these she did not eat.

But for the black rat there was something worse than Sniraga.

(*Mine is the terror of the drowned. When the surface is gone you can't swim for it, you can't aim for a sun without light, without warmth, the vanished laughing sun over the kelp, sun of man and glad day and woken beasts and the miracle of tears, but not your kind, darling, never your kind except from corners, cracks, burrows in filth, and just so long as your snout clears the waves. Oh, mad repellent rodent! Sweet rat of my soul! Poor scuttling susurrating slop-eating Felthrup, how long till the kelp rakes you under?*)

He was a freak: he knew it. He was a woken rat, and rats never woke. Nor did they sleep, not the warm, stupid sleep of normal creatures. Unlike any other beings he knew of, they were caught between intelligence and instinct, night and day. They lived short, snapping, bickering, miserable lives in the twilight. The ixchel term for them was best: *palluskudge*—creatures cursed by the Gods.

"Fatten up, brother!"

Felthrup shot two feet straight up in the air. Beside him a trio of rats laughed in their whispered, nasal way.

"Talking to himself!" they said. "Strange Felthrup! Wise and special Felthrup! What's he doing out here on the edge of town?"

"Water," lied Felthrup, recovering himself. "That's all. Just looking for water."

" 'Just looking for water,' " said one, in perfect mimicry. Like half of what came from rats' mouths it was said for no clear reason, but it made the others laugh. They were only slinkers: weak rats driven out of the warren by night, and allowed back in only if they could pay a tribute of food. Slinkers were the only rats most humans ever saw: the small, desperate ones, forced into mortal danger in kitchens, stables, dumps. Women saw them and shrieked amazingly, as if about to be mauled by tigers. Men traded fibs about their size.

Felthrup tried to laugh as they did, with much slurping and sniffling. "The ixchel," he said. "They're coming out of their crates now. Have you seen them?"

"Seen them," said one, and they all stared and waited. It was possible they did not understand the question.

"Yes," Felthrup tried again. "The ixchel. Crawlies. There's more of them aboard than usual—hundreds more. They're not just passengers this time. They're up to something."

"Hundreds of crawlies," muttered one of the slinkers, bored.

"Yes! They've been watching the giants, listening to them, taking risks. I tell you, it's not normal. I thought I would take a look at them for Master Mugstur."

At the mention of the Head Rat their eyes lit briefly with fear.

"Perhaps you've noticed them, brothers?" Felthrup pressed, trying not to sound too eager. "I should certainly mention your help to Master Mugstur. Back there in the manger I thought—"

"Felthrup and his stories," one broke in.

"I could tell you another story, brothers, about a monster of a man who soon will walk this ship. Niriviel the falcon spoke of him, proud as a prince. But you'd never believe me. They say this voyage is all about a wedding, a wedding to bring peace between the man-warrens. But the true purpose—"

"What's he got to *eat*?" shrilled the rat on his left, and the other two bristled with sudden alertness. Eating was the only subject of real interest to rats—besides the whereabouts of things that might eat them.

Felthrup shook his head. "Nothing, I fear."

"Always something."

"Not this time," said Felthrup. "I haven't eaten since nightfall. I'm starved."

"Why didn't you ask *us* for food, then, brother?" asked the same rat, and all three slinkers grinned.

Because you would have lied, Felthrup thought, but he knew they had caught him. All slinkers lied when they met in Night Village, and yet the practice never kept a rat—any *normal* rat—from asking. If he had pestered *them* for food, they would have suspected nothing, and let him go. Now they were closing in, sniffing at his paws and cheeks. A few more seconds and they would smell his last meal. Talk would cease instantly. They would attack.

He was more than a match for any one of them—any two, probably. But three were too many. And when he fought, he drowned, became a mean, blind brute—became truly their brother.

There was just one other choice. Felthrup shook himself, with that violent whole-body spasm peculiar to rats and weasels. The slinkers jumped back, and Felthrup spat the contents of his cheek pouches at their feet.

"Knew it!" they cried happily. "Lying, gobbling, greedy Felthrup!"

It was only a spoon's worth of soggy biscuit (dropped by a tarboy so exhausted he had fallen asleep as he chewed), but the slinkers fell on it like starved dogs, their short tongues licking at the grimy deck. Felthrup tensed and sprang—pop!—right over their heads. No point in looking back. In seconds his food would be gone. In minutes they would not remember him.

(*Mine the terror of not remembering. Who is Felthrup? Rat, freak, monster, man?*)

Now he was angry as well as tormented. That food would have bribed the door guard. To gain the daytime shelter of the warren he must seek out more, under the boys' hammocks or among the ragged, fitfully sleeping passengers in steerage. Other rats were combing the same spots; he might need hours to locate a scrap. And he had other business first.

There! A red glow, thimble-small, shedding only enough light for Felthrup to see two busy hands, and the dull glint of bronze. Felthrup dashed for it, reckless with longing. It had to be an ixchel cookstove. Humans could not smell the special coal burned in such stoves, but because ixchel could—and because a ship's cat or dog would trace the smell to its source—the little people cooked their meals on the open deck, away from the secret places where they made their homes.

When he was ten feet away the light winked out. In a panic he bounded forward.

"Cousins!" he squeaked. "Honored ixchel! Please don't go! Let me talk to you!"

He spoke in the kindest, sanest, most un-rat-like voice he could summon. But no one answered. The light was gone, and so were the ixchel.

Crushed, Felthrup scurried to the portside hull. He had spoken aloud, courted death, and for nothing! Safety, shelter! He had to find them at once. Rushing, panting, he spotted a bilge-pipe a few yards ahead. The pipe's heavy brass cap had been left unlatched, and even stood open an inch. Felthrup dashed for it. A moment later he was climbing inside.

The pipe was stoppered just two feet from its mouth (it was an emergency bilge, used only on a sinking ship) and would never do as daytime shelter. But it was dry and snug, and no Sniraga could pounce on him. Felthrup curled in a ball and began to lick the red, stinging tip of his tail. He could not manage to hate the slinkers; it was like hating cows or stones. They were one thing and he another. But if he could not hate something he would surely cry.

(*Mine is the terror of a rodent's tears. Strange spineless Felthrup, the rat who weeps in corners.*)

It was over for another night, his twenty-sixth aboard *Chathrand*. How long could he keep this up, this search for the little folk, when they so clearly had no intention of meeting him? Why was he risking his life? He had already lost a third of his tail on the Etherhorde quay, bitten off by one of the mob of wharf rats that controlled access to departing ships. Felthrup had been riding ships for eight months (seeking that place where life was good, better, less than very bad, as it were, unexcruciating) and in each port he faced the same snarling cabal of wharf rats, ferocious gatekeepers of the seas. This one had promised him safe passage aboard the Great Ship, but halfway across the Plaza he had suddenly doubled his price. Felthrup broke and ran, and the big rat and his cronies had chased him all the way to the top of the gangway, biting and snapping. His tail still hurt when it dragged in the dust.

(*You must not fall asleep here, Felthrup my boy. Dawn will come and the men will kill you.*)

Yet it had seemed worth it, all that risk, for here at last were beings like himself: careful, thoughtful, out to change things. Felthrup had not lied to the slinkers: the ixchel were up to something. He smelled them in the oddest places: under the ambassador's stateroom, at the door of the gunpowder vault, along the rudder chains. Strangest of all, three weeks ago a dozen or more had entered the berth deck and clustered about a tarboy's hammock. Felthrup had smelled the dry sweat on the hammock: a mark of human fear. Clearly the ixchel had spoken to the boy, and terrified him. *But why in all creation would they show themselves to a human?*

They have plans, Felthrup thought for the hundredth time. *And whatever those plans are—*

"Give the word, Father!"

Felthrup jumped so hard he ricocheted up and down in the pipe like a rubber ball. The voice came from the opening—where four long spears pointed straight at his heart. The ixchel! They had come to him!

They crowded around the mouth of the pipe, copper eyes gleaming. All men. Three of the four were bald and bareheaded. The last, a young man in light armor, had a smile that chilled Felthrup's blood. His spear-arm twitched impatiently.

A second voice spoke: "Let me see the creature first."

One of the spearmen fell back, and in his place appeared an older ixchel. He was clearly their leader, gray-bearded but fierce of eye, holding a broad white knife.

"C-c-cousins!" stammered Felthrup. "Bless your house and harvest!"

"It walked right into the pipe," said the young man with the smile. "We hadn't even set the bait yet."

"Bait?" said Felthrup, trying to laugh. "You need no bait to catch me, friends. I came looking for you! I wish to speak with you above all things."

"It smelled the blood of the last one," said the gray-bearded man. "That is why it entered the pipe. Rats are all secret cannibals."

"Cousins, dear ones!" said Felthrup desperately. "How sad that you should think so! Even rats do not commit that sin—or only very, very rarely! And I am not like other rats! My name is Felthrup Stargraven, and I have much to tell you."

The ixchel men glanced at one another. Rats did not have names, for they could not remember them. If one rat called to another he used whatever nickname occurred to him—whitey, wart-face, bucktooth—and forgot it as soon as the other was out of sight.

There was no time to lose: Felthrup had to prove his goodwill at once. He bowed his head and addressed their leader.

"Do you know the humans' mission, sir? I do. The moon falcon told me, and he knows—his master is the Emperor's spy. Shall I tell you? It is ghastly, abominable!"

The older man gave an irritated sigh. "Observe, Taliktrum," he said. "It will now try cunning. Odd creatures, these Sorrophran rats—"

"I'm a Noonfirther!" cried Felthrup.

"Dim-witted as any of their race, of course. But when faced with death they almost appear to possess reason, like a woken beast."

"I *am* awake! I have a mind and memory!"

"It is quite talkative," said the young man. "Diadrelu says they spout like this when rabid."

They think me mad! Felthrup raised himself up and waved his forepaws, trying to recapture their attention. He succeeded: every spear-arm tensed. With a squeak of terror he dropped and covered his eyes. Then, making a supreme effort, he lowered his voice.

"Listen, cousins, friends. I talk this way always. I talk, I reason, I think. I cannot sleep for thinking! That is why I have come looking for you. We can help one another. Trust me, believe me, sons of Ixphir House, I am more like you than I am a rat!"

The ixchel laughed softly. "Amazing!" said one of the bald spearmen. "Did you hear it, my Lord Talag?"

"I heard," said the elder. "But do not be fooled. In rats, thought is an emergency function. Many creatures have such tricks. They play dead, change color, drop their tails. This one's already used *that* maneuver!"

Felthrup hid his stubby half tail, and the ixchel laughed uproariously. He wanted to speak of his dash up the gangway, and the teeth of the wharf-rat, but the word *cannibals* still hung in the air. Furious and frightened, he began to cry.

"Please listen . . . so long . . . searching for you, for some-one—"

"To escape the shark," said the elder, "certain fish leap into the air, spread fins and glide a little distance. We call them *igri,* flying fish. But we do not call them birds."

"Drowning, always drowning," sobbed Felthrup.

Then the old man laughed, and for the first time addressed Felthrup directly. "Never fear, sir! You'll be dry enough."

In a heartbeat the ixchel were gone. Felthrup hurled himself forward, guessing what was to come. Too late. The brass lid slammed; the latch clicked shut.

-19-

Poison

9 Ilqrin 941
27th day from Etherhorde

STRICTLY PRIVATE:
SURRENDER TO THE HAND
OF EBERZAM ISIQ ONLY

His Excellency Ambassador Eberzam Isiq
IMS Chathrand

Your Excellency,
   I write in haste. Three days ahead of Chathrand *have I sailed, with no safe means to send word to you, and I must depart again before the Great Ship reaches this town. In fact I am already at the docks: the mate is calling us aboard.*
   My news is awful, my fears and guesses worse. So bad indeed that I should not dare to write them at all were it not for this good and simple man, Rom Rulf, a chemist I trained myself at the Imperial Medical School, to whose keeping I entrust this letter.
   The Lady Syrarys betrays you, Excellency. She loves another, and would kill to hide the fact. How foul the effort to write these words, how wounding that you should read them! And yet what choice do I have?
   After Chathrand *sailed with Rose at the helm I spent an*

*hour on the headland, despondent. Then I came to my senses
and jumped aboard a fast clipper to Etherhorde. We arrived
just ahead of the Great Ship. If only I had gone straight to
your door! Instead I galloped to Castle Maag. I still hoped to
change the Emperor's mind about Rose, who is one of the
vilest men ever to sully the name of Arqual.*

*The Emperor was not in his castle, but Syrarys was. She lay
among courtesans in the boudoir. The room was dim. When I
entered she mistook me for another, and called out, laughing:
"Again, love? Will you never let me sleep?" Then she saw
me and went mad. "Stop him! Shoot him! He cannot leave!"*

*She hurled a burning lamp in my direction. Had she been
dressed I should never have made it from the castle alive, for
many obeyed her once they heard her shouting. Someone
chased me all down the mountain, and sent a falcon to dive at
my face and the horse's. In the end I was thrown from the sad-
dle and thrashed blind through the trees.*

*Two days I hid in the only place one may hide from the
mighty in Etherhorde: in the hovels of the poor. It was my
good fortune to have cured many last year of the wax-eye
blindness. They remembered me, bless them, and asked no
questions. But strange men-at-arms prowled the streets, and
I am sure they were looking for me.*

*When the hunters came too near, my friends took a great
risk and smuggled me in an apple-crate to the port. I was
three days out of Etherhorde, on a ship bound for Tressek
Tarn, before the crew dared let me out. And in Tressek I find
myself little safer: the governor fears to meet with me, as do
my fellow doctors. Only this morning armed men stormed my
tavern-room—by good luck I was in Rulf's shop down the
street. Have I lost the Emperor's favor? I cannot say; I only
know that I have not fled far enough.*

*I never saw the face of the one who chased me—but I saw
Syrarys, as plain as I see this pen and ink. She is not yours,
Eberzam. Do not trust her. Do not leave Thasha in her care.*

So much for my news—more bitter than any drug I ever

made you swallow. But my fears! There is no time to explain them now. Beware the Nilstone! Did your mother never scare you with that word? It exists, and someone wants it, though to use it can only bring ruin on us all. You know the briny grave-yard where legend says it fell. Should Chathrand *near that spot, you must find a way to turn her back.*

Horrors and madness. Who would choose such a moment to unearth that weapon, that malignant hole in the weave of our world? No one but a madman, and yet—

There is the bell, damnation! I must take to my ship or be left behind. I shall write to you again when I can. Until then I ask a final favor: take care of young Pazel, Capt. Gregory's son. He is a prickly runt of no talent or significance, but I swore to his fair mother that no harm would befall him. Do not fail me in this, I beseech you.

Rulf has your medicines, sealed by my hand. Drink from no flask you do not open yourself; dispose of what Syrarys has touched. And do not despair of love, Eberzam: it surrounds you yet.

EVER THY SERVANT,
IGNUS CHADFALLOW

Syrarys dropped the letter to the floor. Then she threw back her head and laughed.

"Rom Rulf! *This good and simple man!* What was his price, a new shop window? Some other chemist driven from town?"

Reclined next to her, Sandor Ott shook his head. "Rulf does love Chadfallow. But there are those he loves more. His daughter, for one. We took the precaution of kidnapping her months ago. The good doctor has left messages with Rulf before, you see."

They lay together on a bed heaped with fine cushions and silks, sharing a little jug of wine. Through a broad window the sun was setting over the Quiet Sea. This was one of the simpler rooms of Tressek Fortress, carved out of the living rock above the city of Tressek Tarn. Centuries ago it had been a great keep; now it was a resort where rich Arqualis soaked in water piped from the boiling tarns beneath the hills. The whole place felt warm and wet.

"As for the tarboy, Pathkendle," said Ott, "the good doctor is lying. His concern stems from more than a promise to the lad's mother, even though he loved her. No, Chadfallow has some special use in mind for that one."

"Then you must get rid of him."

"The beauty of it, darling, is that your dear admiral will do it for us. They are racing toward a collision, haven't you noticed? And when they do collide, and Pathkendle is tossed ashore— well, I have arranged for his reception."

"You're a monster. Even I fear you at times."

Noises touched the room like whiffs of smoke: dogs, gulls, blacksmiths hammering steel. A closer sound—that of Eberzam Isiq, moaning strangely—came from the floor below.

"You're certain he can't hear us?" she said.

"That man hears nothing but his own sweet dreams," said Ott. "Deathsmoke is bliss—until it kills you. In a hot bath such as his, the leaves of the deathsmoke vine make the body numb, the heart beat slower and slower. The steam, meanwhile, keeps the mind in a perfect trance, even to the moment of death. We cannot risk that, of course. Isiq can be left for one hour, no more."

"An hour isn't long enough with you," she said.

Ott kissed her, but his voice was stern. "One hour. Remember that he must live through his daughter's marriage."

"And not a day longer," growled Syrarys. "How I wish I could tell the world! All those fat and fancy lords would think twice about buying young slave-brides if they knew what we were capable of."

"Tell the world you've been poisoning an admiral for years and even I won't be able to protect you," said Ott calmly. "But I must be off soon, too. Niriviel must be sent ahead, to find out what Chadfallow is up to."

She snuggled against him. "He's an insufferable pest! You should have killed him months ago."

Ott stroked her loose black hair. "In Etherhorde the man's

death would have drawn too much attention. He was to be *Chathrand*'s surgeon, after all. Besides, the Emperor adores him."

"But he saw me at the castle. In the pillow room!"

"And so signed his own death warrant. Fear not: he will never speak to the admiral again. My men will be waiting for him in Uturphe. As for our true mission, though—just look at his pitiful guesswork! The Nilstone! By Rin, it is to laugh!"

"I've never heard of the Nilstone. What is it?"

"A myth, or something as old as myth. A relic of the ancient world. Poor fool! He might as well have said we were looking for the rainbow's end."

"Chadfallow's a pest, Sandor, but he's never a fool. He cured your army of the talking fever."

"This time he's a fool," said Ott. "He was the one man I thought might deduce that the Shaggat was still alive, and in our plans. Instead he's frightened of a little sphere that darkens the sun."

Syrarys raised her head, no longer smiling. "A black sphere? The size of a plum, but heavy as a cannonball?"

"So the stories claim."

"The *gummukra*," she said. "You're talking about the *gummukra*."

Ott smiled. "There's a name for it in your tongue as well?"

"Of course. They say it's the eyeball of a murth-lord. It lets the one who holds it command the Black Bees."

"Black Bees, eh?"

"Don't laugh, you brute! We were terrified of them."

"The Rinfaithful have a different story. They say the Nilstone is like the cork on that wine jug—give it here, my sweet—plugging a tiny hole through which the Swarm of Night entered this world to lay it waste, and escaped again when the Gods rose in fury. And the Mzithrinis say the Nilstone is pure ash—the ash of all the devils burned in their Black Casket, before the Great Devil broke it asunder. That is why I laugh: each country tells a different tale. And here is Dr. Chadfallow, the scientist, joining the game."

"I wonder how the idea entered his head."

"Who knows?" said Ott. "Let us just be glad it did. Now then, about Zirfet."

Syrarys laughed, and bit his ear playfully. "Zirfet. Your enormous, handsome disciple."

"A negligent disciple," said Ott severely. "He was to have killed Hercól by now, without fail."

"But I told you, love, that was my fault. You know you ordered Zirfet to obey me in your absence."

"A kill order takes precedence, as Zirfet should have recalled." He raised his head and looked at her. "I should think you would have welcomed the Tholjassan's death."

"Eventually, of course. But Hercól is a good valet—he ran errands for me in every port. Besides, you left without a word. I had no idea that Hercól was the reason for your absence—and the dear boy didn't dare speak to me of your plans."

"Zirfet is not a boy, Syrarys. He's a member of the Secret Fist. An assassin, like me. And until he proves it I shall be forced to move with great caution about the *Chathrand*. You must keep Hercól twice as busy, until Zirfet finishes the job."

Syrarys caressed the back of Ott's neck, tracing an old knife-scar with the tip of her finger.

"He's never killed, then?" she asked softly.

Ott shook his head. "No, Zirfet has not yet killed, though he came closer than he knew with me." He rubbed two knuckles along his jaw. "Very well, I'm off."

"You think so, do you?"

She pounced on him. The wine spilled down his side, soaking the bed as she kissed his neck, eyelids, ear. All at once he was returned to his youth—but not a youth of love and caresses. His memory was of battle. He was thirteen, the army's creature already, fighting Sizzies on a cold plateau thousands of miles from the sea. His sergeant dead, his squadron decimated. He himself about to die. A Sizzy boy on top of him, a knife in his ribs, his life gushing into the sawgrass. One arm broken, the other pinned beneath his foe. Bright blue sky, like today.

Syrarys was laughing—so young, so perfectly lovely. Did she really love him? Could he ever allow himself to hope?

Gently, he rolled her aside. He placed a finger on her pouting lips.

"Go and pamper your Admiral," he said. "Isiq must never suspect you. Not once."

Minutes later he was on the fortress roof, looking down at the *Chathrand.* A sailor high on the mainmast was lowering the Emperor's flag for the night. Gold fish, gold dagger: they had loomed over his life for six decades, given meaning to his scars and his conquests, to murders and betrayals, to sweet feminine lips. *Arqual,* thought the spymaster. *My love is Arqual, till death do us part.*

He had torn that boy's throat out with his teeth. What choice did he have?

Lessons Learned

"Blar baffin mud-me," said Thasha glumly.

Pazel looked up from the grammar book, exasperated. *"Blar avfam muteti*—'My husband is my trusted guide.' There's no *d* in the sentence, m'lady."

"Stop calling me that."

Pazel lowered his voice to a whisper. "You know I can't. They'll throw me out. Honestly, Thasha, you're not even trying."

"I'm *not* getting married," she whispered, furious. "And how would you know if I was trying? All you have to do is wait for your blary Gift to translate for you."

"I told you, I learned four languages by *studying,* before Mother cast the spell. I was already good with them. If she'd cast it on you, I suppose it would have helped your fighting. Isn't that what you're best at?"

"Fighting and tactics. That's what Hercól and Prahba say, anyway."

"The point is, you have to start out good at something for it to make you better at it."

They were seated in velvet chairs in a corner of the first-class lounge. A few yards to their left, Brother Bolutu sat reading a book from the ship's library: *Venomous Pests of Alifros.* At the far end of the room, Syrarys sipped wine and chattered gaily with a crowd of women, among them Pacu Lapadolma. In the shadows behind the women stood a bucktoothed tarboy known as Sorry Suds, holding a wine jug and pulling the cord that turned the ceiling-mounted fan. Now and then a woman thrust out her cup, and the boy leaped to fill it.

Pazel's hair was so clean it felt like something he'd borrowed. Fiffengurt himself had dunked him in a tub of limewater. "You're going to tutor the Treaty Bride!" he said. "Your appearance will reflect on every boy on this ship. Imagine if a louse were to crawl from your hair onto Lady Thasha."

Jervik had called him a dandy—under his breath. He had not gotten over his terror at Pazel's unnatural fit of gibberish. But he still wouldn't return Pazel's father's knife or his mother's ivory whale—wouldn't admit to having them, in fact. "They was left on the *Eniel,* with a lot of my things," he'd told Pazel—but he smirked as he said it, and winked at his hangers-on.

"Your sister wasn't good at languages, I suppose," said Thasha, "otherwise the spell would have given her the same Gift, right? But she must have been good at something."

"Lots of things," said Pazel. "I used to think she was good at *everything,* in fact. Neda was strong, like you. She sang beautifully, and knew a thousand songs. And she understood people: that's what I remember most. I couldn't fool her, and neither could anyone else. Sometimes it made her sad. But if the spell did anything—besides nearly kill her—we didn't notice it before she ran away. I wonder sometimes if she ever forgave our mother, or if she thinks of me."

"Of course she does. Don't be daft."

"I don't even know if she's alive."

Thasha bit her lips. Pazel blinked at the page of Mzithrini script. Across the room, Pacu Lapadolma was chatting gaily about the Emperor's birthday, two weeks off but already the subject of lively anticipation. Pacu's great-aunt had presented the ship with a "party crate" to be opened on the night in question: it was certain to contain *outlandish fun.*

"Sound out the words, m'lady," said Pazel at last. " 'My husband shall never go hungry while I live.' "

"*Blur baffle*—oh, I wish they'd pipe down!" Thasha glared at Pacu. "She has a voice like a tipsy rooster. We should go to my cabin."

"That's a brilliant idea," said Pazel dryly.

A month had passed since the day of his mind-fit. Ambassador Isiq had not spoken to Pazel again: when they passed on deck he pretended not to see the tarboy. Hercól had suggested Pazel write a letter of apology. But how could he apologize for speaking the truth? In any case, the ambassador had at last given his grudging assent to these lessons. He had even come to some terms with Rose concerning Pazel's bond debt. Isiq had very little choice. Without Dr. Chadfallow, there was no Mzithrini-speaker aboard except Pazel—and at the very least, Thasha had to learn her vows.

The door opened and Hercól stepped into the lounge. He smiled at Thasha but went at once to Syrarys, bowed and handed her a small package wrapped in muslin cloth. Syrarys gave him a brief nod and hid the package away.

Only then did Hercól approach Thasha and Pazel.

"You found your buttons, Pathkendle," he said. "I'm amazed they were not stolen, after all those hours."

"I got lucky," said Pazel, raising a hand to his coat. In fact something far stranger than luck had come his way: the brass buttons had appeared in his pocket the morning after his mind-fit. He had thanked Neeps warmly, but the other tarboy had no idea what he was talking about. Neither did Reyast, in the hammock beneath him.

Pazel had decided they were teasing him, and forgotten all about it. But now, in the first-class lounge, another possibility struck him suddenly: *the ixchel.* Who else could retrieve lost buttons from cracks and crevices about the deck, and slip them unseen into his pocket?

Pazel looked with foreboding at the swordsman above him. *Does he know?* Hercól was giving him another of those raptor-like stares. But he asked no questions, and instead held out a small wooden box and flipped open the lid.

Inside was what looked like clumps of glue and orange yarn. "Spider jellies," said Hercól. "A specialty of Tressek Tarn."

Pazel thanked him, and nervously pressed one whole sticky wad into his mouth. But Thasha just sniffed at the candy.

"What did Syrarys want this time?" she asked.

Hercól's eyebrows rose. "Medicine. Drops for your father's tea. Very thoughtful of her: she wrote ahead for them, from Etherhorde."

"Every time we're in port she sends you running about."

"As valet, I am her servant as well. Thasha, has Commander Nagan been this way?"

"Who?"

"The captain of your family's honor guard, my dear. He took ill and left us in Ulsprit, but I gather he caught up with the *Chathrand* and boarded today. I wish to make his acquaintance."

"I've never seen the man. Listen to me, Hercól: you're my teacher. And there's not much time left to learn from you."

"That is so." Hercól gave her a slight smile. "One must always keep *an eye on the clock,* don't you think?"

With that he turned and left the room. Thasha looked at Pazel, suddenly breathless. "That's our code," she whispered. "Ramachni's back. Pazel, you *must* come with me now."

She rose and half dragged Pazel from the lounge. They slipped through the empty dining room, passed the Money Gate and the officers' cabins. At her door Pazel stopped.

"This is the *last* place I ought to be," he said.

"Don't worry, it's all arranged. Come in."

"Arranged?" he said. "By whom? Is your father in there?"

"No, he's not, and neither is Syrarys. Pazel, can't you trust me?"

He looked at her warily. But he followed her into the stateroom.

The red light of sunset poured in through the stern windows, glittering on the brasswork and chandeliers. There was a five-foot samovar made of porcelain and jade, a wisp of steam still rising from its spout. There was a painting of a shipwreck in a great gilded frame, and the pair of crossed swords he had spotted before. But now across the center of the floor lay a huge, tawny bearskin rug, complete with head and claws.

"Another trinket from the Tarn, I guess," he said, toeing the yellow fangs.

Thasha turned to look at him. "My grandfather killed that bear with a hunting knife, on his farm in the Westfirth. Syrarys uncrated it because her feet were cold."

Pazel pulled back his toe. Thasha gave him a wry smile as she crossed the stateroom.

The money, Pazel thought. Feelings crashed together as he followed her: he was dirty, she was pampered, he was nothing, he was better than this girl.

We had old things too, he thought, trying furiously to remember. But the few objects he could recall from his life in Ormael seemed shabby and humdrum beside this splendor. On a table by the samovar lay a piece of coffee cake no one had bothered to finish. Tarboys had fistfights over less. *What am I doing here?* he thought.

Thasha opened the door to her own cabin. With monstrous thumps, Jorl and Suzyt rolled off the bed to greet her. She glanced instantly at the clock on her dresser: as before, its hinged, moon-patterned face stood ajar. She tugged Pazel into the room.

"Ramachni," she said. "It's me. I've brought Pazel Pathkendle."

"Have you indeed?"

The voice, high and velvet-soft and utterly inhuman, seemed to emanate from Thasha's pillows. Despite himself Pazel jumped: to his chagrin he saw an amused smile on Thasha's face.

She closed the cabin door. The pillows shifted, and from among them emerged the black mink. For a moment it was almost comical, this tidy creature shaking free of the bedclothes. Then it looked at Pazel and grew still.

Pazel did not move either: the black eyes were wide, and bottomless, and fortunately very kind. *It knows me,* he thought, and trembled a bit at the oddness of the notion. Then the little creature stretched luxuriously and sprang into Thasha's arms.

She laughed as it rubbed, cat-like, against her chin. "I've missed you so much!" she said.

"And I have missed those fingernails in my fur. This ship is infested with fleas of a most bloodthirsty order."

"Where have you been hiding, Ramachni?" asked Thasha. "Hercól and I have worried ourselves sick! We only knew you'd come aboard because Pazel told us."

"I am sorry to have abandoned you," said Ramachni. "I truly had no choice. There is a murderous power loose aboard the *Chathrand:* I sensed it with my first breath. It probes, and listens, and spies on our thoughts, and it thinks no more of killing than of wiping dust from a tabletop. I was caught off-guard. I could not tell who or what it was, for it keeps its face well hidden. The best I could do was to hide myself from *it,* so that it would not know that a power to match its own had come aboard—and not threaten those who befriend me. So I waited, just inside the clock, listening as best I could, until it seemed you had all left the cabin. But I was wrong—Mr. Pathkendle remained, and saw me, and I had to place a spell of protection on him to keep that Other from reading his thoughts."

"You used magic on me?" asked Pazel sharply.

"Trust me—I had no wish to do so," said Ramachni. "This is not my world, and when I come here I must use spells the way a nomad uses the water he carries, knowing it must last him across the desert. But fear not: the spell has long since snapped. And our meeting may yet prove lucky for us both." He flashed his white fangs at Pazel. It was perhaps as close as he could come to grinning.

Thasha sighed, and dropped him on the bed. "So you've been aboard all this time?"

Ramachni nodded. "Deep in the hold, out of sight. I had to listen to the ship, and try to gain some understanding of your peril."

"And this 'Other,'" Thasha went on, "did you learn who it is?"

"Alas, no. But I did learn *what* he is. He is a mage—a magic-weaver like myself."

"But less powerful, of course," said Thasha.

"Oh no," said Ramachni. "He is mightier, for he belongs to this world. I could not, for example, pierce his veil of secrecy—and with secrecy this mage is obsessed. Yes, he is strong indeed, and that troubles me. He could be a disciple of Arunis, the Blood Mage of Gurishal, the foulest sorcerer this world ever spawned. Arunis' greed was infinite. He even plundered other worlds, my own among them, in his search for deeper powers. I fought him there a century ago, in the great Library of Imbrethothe-Under-the-Earth, and cast him from my world. He limped back to Alifros, to the Mzithrin lands, and took refuge in the court of the Shaggat Ness. And the Shaggat was his doom, it seems: Dr. Chadfallow assured me that he died shortly after the Mad King himself."

"Chadfallow assured *me* he'd be aboard, taking care of Prahba," said Thasha. "I don't trust him. But you think this sorcerer could be Arunis' pet pupil, is that it?"

"Something of the kind," said Ramachni. "Mages, like tailors and poets, have styles to their names, and in the work of this sorcerer I detect more than a little of Arunis' influence—and all of his wickedness. We must be very careful.

"The only good news is that there are so many spells and shreds of spells, so many cobwebbed centuries of magic in this ship, that a few charms of my own may pass unnoticed for a time. Oh, he will find them eventually—he will know another mage is aboard, and fighting him—but with luck that will not happen soon."

"Mr. Uskins is a bad man," said Pazel firmly. "And Captain Rose is horrible. Come to think of it, he also hears voices—*spirits,* he calls them. Could he be the one you mean?"

"Anything is possible," said Ramachni. "And Nilus Rose is a born conspirator. But there is no time to speculate. I have asked

Hercól to keep Ambassador Isiq and his Lady away for thirty minutes, and we have already talked for ten."

Ramachni looked at Pazel again. "Will you hold my paw a moment?"

Pazel hesitated only long enough to remind himself that he was not facing a wild fanged animal but a great mage, and Thasha's friend. He took the little paw in his hand.

Ramachni closed his glittering eyes. He breathed deeply. "It's true," he said. "You're a *Smythídor.*"

"I'm an Ormali," said Pazel.

"Of course. But not just any Ormali. Your mother is Suthinia Sadralin Pathkendle—a mage herself, and the daughter of mages."

"You know her name! How?"

"Elementary, boy. She signed her spell, and I have just read the signature—" Ramachni reached up to touch Pazel's lips. "—there. A formidable spell! But dissolved in some rather unsanitary fruit juice, it appears."

"Please," said Pazel, repressing a shudder, "can you switch it off? Like the potion-seller in Sorhn? It almost killed me and my sister."

Ramachni looked up at him, compassion dawning in his eyes. "Don't you understand yet, Pazel? No one can switch it off. Your mother did not just toss a spell over you like an old coat. She changed you to the last drop of blood. In a sense, she really did kill you—killed your old self so that a new self could be born. That potion-seller did not cure you. He merely slammed a lid on the boiling kettle of your Gift—a most foolish act. If Dr. Chadfallow had not slipped those antihex-salts in your tea, sooner or later you would have run mad. As I say, lad, you're a *Smythídor,* a person changed by magic forever. And I have spent half of forever looking for you."

There was a pause. Thasha looked from one to the other.

"So," she said in a constricted voice, "you've found him. And I suppose all these years you only needed my clock, needed my family and me to help you find this oh-so-special tarboy. Congratulations."

Ramachni sighed. "I will not say that you are wrong, Thasha dear."

Thasha looked as if she had hoped he would do just that. She seemed about to say more, but Ramachni spoke first:

"Mind you, I am also not saying you are right. Let me say instead that mages see but little more than normal folk of that mist-shrouded land called the future. Do you ever know *why* you make a friend, Thasha? Do you know what good or ill must come of it, in time?"

Thasha glanced shyly from mink to tarboy. Her face was crimson. "All these weeks I've been dying to talk to you. To ask you something I can ask of no one else."

Ramachni looked up at her. "Ask," he said.

"Will you help me escape this marriage? Please?"

The mink's head drooped. After a moment he said, "Yes, I will."

Thasha threw her arms around him in delight. But Ramachni raised a paw.

"I may not succeed. And if I do, the help may be as painful as what it remedies—or worse. But my heart tells me your fate will not be decided by marriage vows."

"Ha!" said Pazel. "That's for sure! *Blur baffle—*"

Thasha made a face at him. She was overjoyed.

"And now," said Ramachni, "we must concentrate on the peril at hand. This much I have learned by eavesdropping: besides the mage, who has been aboard for many weeks, another man of evil will soon be among us. Someone terrible. All the sly whispers center on him. He may be passenger or sailor or servant. He may stay aboard for weeks or hours: I do not know. But Rose and Uskins—and the mage-in-hiding, too—think of little else. And the only being of goodwill who knows this terrible man's name is a rat."

"A rat!" cried Pazel and Thasha together.

Ramachni nodded. "A *woken* rat, amazingly. You will know

him by his stumpy tail. I've tried many times to speak to him, but the rats of *Chathrand* are ruled by some awful fear and attack anyone who approaches their warren. If you find him, treat him kindly. He must be the most unhappy creature on this ship."

On that point Ramachni was wrong, Pazel thought: no one could be as miserable as Steldak, the prisoner in Rose's desk. But the little mage did not seem to know about the ixchel, and Pazel dared not speak of them. He could still hear Diadrelu: *They will be the last words you ever speak.* And she was the friendly one.

"Ramachni," he said, "why have you been looking for me?"

"To enlist your help," said the mage. "By that I mean: to ask you to accept another Gift."

A brief, astonished silence. "You're joking," said Pazel.

The mink shook his head.

Pazel fumbled behind him for the doorknob. "Absolutely not," he said.

"It would have no unpleasant effects," said the mink. "At least, not for many years."

"Fantastic—not much chance of *living* many years with this crowd. But if I do? What then? Do I sprout horns and tail, so that when I start babbling like a murth I'll look the part?"

"Oh sky!" said Thasha suddenly. "Grow up, Pazel. Ramachni's so careful with magic I didn't think he could do any for the first year I knew him. If he says it's safe, it's safe."

"But he's *not* saying that."

The mink clicked his teeth, making him appear to grin once again. "Very true, I am not."

"Pazel," said Thasha, "are you afraid?"

Idiotic question. He opened the door and fled across the stateroom—snatching up the cake as he went. Then he heard feet pounding behind him. A whirl of motion, and Thasha stood between him and the outer door.

"You can't say no to Ramachni."

"No?"

Pazel looked back at the mage, who had walked calmly into

the stateroom. "Do it to Thasha the Brave, here," he said. "One Gift was enough to ruin my life."

"It will not be enough to save your world from death," said Ramachni.

Pazel froze, the cake halfway to his mouth. Ramachni sat back on his haunches.

"Eavesdropping is difficult in the hold of a ship, but it is a thousand times more difficult from another world. For ninety years Alifros has been my chief concern, bound as it is to my own world by blood and happenstance. Dawn to dusk have I listened, and midnights, too. Now at last the moment comes. A fell power is brooding over the *Chathrand*. Greater than the evil mage already aboard her, or the horrible man who will board soon—though they perhaps seek to use it. What is it? When and how will it strike? I do not know. But I know that it cannot be ignored, for I have walked in lands where it prevailed, where men hoped it would pass them by, and were wrong. Trust me this far, Pazel Pathkendle: you do not know the meaning of *ruin*."

Pazel looked at him: a small creature on a bearskin rug, its black eyes blazing.

"What do you want?" he said.

"To listen with you. And if you should hear something . . . extraordinary, to teach you a word to know it by. Perhaps several words. It depends on what you hear."

"That's all?"

"That, Pazel, is enough to shake the foundations of this world. The words I would teach you are Master-Words: the very codes of creation, spoken in that ethereal court where will is matter, and rhymes become galaxies. Normal men cannot learn them, you see—"

"But he can," said Thasha.

"Perhaps," said Ramachni. "But Pazel's Gift is a tiny spark compared with the wildfire power of such words. Only two or three do I dare teach you—for your sake, and that of Alifros itself. And Pazel, you will only be able to speak each word once. After that it will vanish from your mind forever."

"But why don't you use them yourself?" Thasha asked.

"I am a visitor here," said Ramachni. "The Master-Words belong to this world, not mine. They would be as dust on my lips."

Still Pazel hesitated. "What am I to do with these Master-Words?"

"Fight the enemy."

"But how? You don't even know who he is!"

"In time he will show himself. And then *you* must choose the word, and the moment for its use. And you must choose wisely, for there will be no second chance."

"This is . . . absurd!" sputtered Pazel. "I don't even know who I'm supposed to fight! How can you expect me to beat him? What if he just stabs me in my sleep?"

"He will not know about you, either, nor of the power in your keeping. And years may pass before he strikes—years, or days, or mere hours. Try to understand: this is a battle in the dark, and I am as blind as any. I know only that I have found in you and Thasha my best champions—the very best in ninety years of searching. Will you refuse?"

Pazel walked slowly to the table and put down the cake. "No," he said. "I won't refuse."

"Then as soon as we can arrange a time—"

"Now."

Ramachni twitched his tail in surprise. "Are you certain? It will tire you greatly."

"I'm certain. Do it now. Before I change my mind."

Ramachni drew a deep breath. He looked at Thasha. "When this is done, Pazel will be tired, but *I* shall be exhausted. Too exhausted even to return to my world through your clock. I will go to my secret place in the hold, and sleep for some days. Can I depend on you, Thasha? Will you guard him, and guard yourself, and be strong for everyone till I awake?"

Beaming at his confidence in her, Thasha said, "I will."

"Then go to the window, *Smythidor,* and lie down."

Pazel walked to the gallery windows. The window seat was eight feet long, with red silk cushions propped in the corners.

Did they have time for this magic? Was he wrong to have insisted it happen now? He lay down, trying not to touch the cushions. Even after his bath he was still too dirty for this room.

The little mage sprang up into Thasha's arms, then twisted about to face him.

"Do not think," he said. "Thought is the task of all your life in this frail universe, but just now it is the wrong task. Instead, listen. Listen as though your life depended on it, as one day it shall."

Pazel looked at him, but the mage offered no further instructions. So Pazel crossed his arms on his chest and listened.

At first he merely heard the ship—sounds so familiar he scarcely noticed them anymore. Beneath the windows her sternpost churned the swell, and her rudder creaked as Mr. Elkstem turned the wheel. Gulls cried. Men laughed and shouted. There was nothing strange about any of it.

Then Ramachni whispered something to Thasha, and she leaned over Pazel and flung open a window. Wind filled the chamber, lifting her hair, and Ramachni slid from her arms to the window seat. Gingerly he crept onto Pazel's chest.

"Shut your eyes," he said.

Pazel obeyed, and the instant his lids closed he was gone— hurled like a leaf on a vast cyclone of sound. It was not loud, but it was deeper than the sea itself. He heard a thousand beating hearts: every one on the *Chathrand,* from the slow kettledrum hearts of the augrongs to the *bipbipbip* of newborn mice in the granary. He heard the sound of Thasha blinking. He heard Jervik laugh secretly at something, and Neeps retching at some foul chore in the galley, and the lookout sobbing a girl's name (*"Gwenny, Gwenny"*) in the privacy of the crow's nest. He heard a rat speaking, howling, about the wrath of the Angel of Rin. He heard Rose whisper, "Mother!" in his sleep.

But the sounds of the *Chathrand* were but a puff of wind in the storm. Pazel could hear all the waves in the Nelu Peren, breaking on every rock and raft and seawall in the Empire. He could hear the layers of the wind, pouring over the world like drifts of snow, mile over mile, and thinning at last to the icy flute-song of the void. He heard sea turtles hatching on a warm Bramian beach. He heard a creature many times *Chathrand*'s length devouring a whale on the floor of the Nelluroq.

Then a gentle breeze tamed the cyclone. It was Ramachni's breath, Pazel knew, and it flowed into that mad cauldron of sounds and silenced them—entirely. In seconds it was all gone, even his own heartbeat was gone. The world might have been dead, or frozen for eternity in solid diamond. And into that perfect silence Ramachni spoke three words.

He was sitting up. Dizzy, dazed. Thasha was stumbling toward an armchair. Ramachni trembled at his side.

What had happened? How much time had passed? For a moment Pazel was reminded of the time years before when he had woken to find the lilies grown tall in his mother's garden, and himself barely escaped from death. But no, not this time. Minutes had passed, not weeks, and he wasn't ill. Just full, to the very edge of madness, with remembered sounds.

"I heard the whole world breathing," he said.

Slowly, achingly, Ramachni raised his head. Pazel met his gaze.

"The words," he said. "I have them. I can *feel* them in my head! But what are they for?"

"They are the simplest of Master-Words. But when you speak them they will be spells of fabulous power. One will tame fire. Another will make stone of living flesh. And the third will blind to give new sight."

"Blind to give new sight? What does that mean?"

"You will know."

"Look at this place," said Thasha vaguely. "It's a disaster."

So it was: a whirlwind seemed to have passed through the stateroom. Pictures were crooked, chairs overturned, crumbs of cake spread everywhere. Thasha herself, with her hair bedraggled and her silver necklace twisted over one shoulder, looked as if she had just climbed down from a mast.

Ramachni touched Pazel's arm. "Remember: each word is gone forever after you speak it. Everything depends on your choices. Listen to your heart, and choose well."

He crept down from the window bench, wheezing like an old man. Thasha hurried forward and lifted him. Her face was suddenly very worried.

"Be strong, my warrior," Ramachni said to her. "Now go and find Hercól, and let him take me to my rest."

But there was no need to go looking for Hercól. Seconds later he threw open the outer door, leaped inside and slammed it behind him.

"Ramachni, you have kept them too long!" he whispered. "Hide! Her father comes! By the Night Gods, you two—straighten your clothes and sit down to your studies!"

Ramachni vanished into Thasha's cabin while Hercól began frantically putting the room in order. Snatching up Thasha's grammar book, he thrust it into Pazel's hands.

"For the love of Rin, watch that tongue of yours!"

They had just enough time to drop into studious postures before Eberzam Isiq flung open the door.

"So," he said with a glance at Hercól, "you found them."

He was furious. Pazel reflected dimly (his mind was still rather thick) that he had never apologized—but how could he apologize for speaking the truth?

Hercól cleared his throat. "I found them. Hard at the books, Your Excellency."

"But not in public chambers," said Isiq. "Did I give you the run of my cabin, Pathkendle?"

"No, sir," said Pazel, struggling to his feet. His voice sounded odd to his own ears. Thasha started to rise as well, then sat again with a thump.

"And yet you dare return," said Isiq, breathless with rage, "after your insolence a month ago."

"Don't blame him, Prahba," said Thasha, her voice equally strange. "I couldn't stand the noise in the lounge. I made him come here."

He looked at her, clearly taken aback. "You brought him? Well, then—it is not your fault, Pathkendle. But it is most improper that you two should be alone! Bring Syrarys, next time—or fetch Nama, or Hercól. Hmmph! And how is her Mzithrini, boy?"

Pazel swallowed. "She . . . amazes me, Excellency."

Isiq demanded a demonstration. Thasha cleared her throat and said, *"My husband is not always a pencil."*

"Are you laughing, boy?"

"No, sir." Pazel gave a gagging cough. Isiq took a step closer, studying him.

"Chadfallow might have adopted you," said Isiq.

Now it was Pazel's turned to be startled. "Yes, sir," he stammered. "I owe the doctor a great deal."

"You're an educated boy. Why did you risk insulting me that day?"

Pazel gripped the chair. "I have no excuse, Your Excellency."

"Just as well." Isiq forced out a chuckle. "You learned Mzithrini from their envoy, didn't you? Chadfallow called him a barbarian in silks. Perhaps a little barbarism rubbed off on you? Not a bad thing, that. A little barbarism fortifies a man."

"Yes, Excellency."

"Let us forget the past, shall we? You showed great valor with those augrongs. And when I learned that you were the son of Gregory Pathkendle I naturally wished to meet you. That coat is to your liking?"

"Yes, Excellency; I thank you."

"We shall forget the past." Isiq ruffled Pazel's hair. "A strange meeting for us both, eh? You're the first Ormali I've spoken to since the Rescue. And naturally I am the first soldier of that campaign to speak with you."

"No, Excellency. The first to speak with me was the corporal who kicked me unconscious because he wanted to rape my mother and sister, and could not find them."

After Hercól had clamped a hand over his mouth and dragged him from the stateroom (with a look that made it clear just how thoroughly Pazel had cooked his own goose), after Uskins appeared and stripped him to the waist and tied his wrists to a fife-rail, after men gathered by the score to gawk and mumble about Rose's wrath, after someone began to lash him with a knotted whip and a gleeful Uskins shouted, *"Harder, wretch, or I'll demonstrate on you,"* after Pazel heard a sob and realized Neeps had been made to deliver the punishment, after Pazel felt tears streaming down his cheeks and blood trickling to his breeches—only then did the worst result of his outburst occur to him.

He would never see Thasha again.

But that was the least of his troubles, wasn't it? He had never much bothered with girls: everyone knew they spelled disaster in a seafarer's life. *Like coral isles,* went the saying: *pretty at a distance, ringed by reefs.*

He shouldn't care. He didn't even know her, and what he did know—that she was the daughter of the man who had burned Ormael, and pampered, and rather violent, and indiscreet—he did not much like. Did he?

Fire and fumes, Pazel. You do.

It was a final, unexpected lash. She might have been a friend—after all these years, a friend!—but he would never find out now. And Neeps, his other friend: he would vanish, too, and kind Mr. Fiffengurt, and—oh, sky!—the chance of finding his parents and Neda again! If Dr. Chadfallow had really been guiding him back to them, Pazel had just thrown the chance away.

Suddenly he wished very humbly for the protection of the Imperial surgeon. What would happen to him? Who would care if he died?

Dr. Rain cleaned his wounds with eucalyptus oil and sent him back to his hammock. He could not lie in it, so he lay on his stomach on the filthy floor, hardly daring to sleep for fear that boys would tread on him in the blackness. And yet he must have slept, for sometime in that miserable night he found himself suddenly awake, possessed of a terrible awareness.

I've lost all my people.

But even as the thought crossed his mind, Neeps returned from his night shift, felt his way to Pazel and gripped his arm. Pazel sat up, wincing, and Neeps handed him a pouch.

"What's this?"

Neeps did not make a sound. Pazel untied the pouch and felt inside. Coins, six or eight of them. By the weight Pazel knew they were gold.

"Where'd you get these, mate?"

Neeps said not a word. He pressed a second object into Pazel's hand. It was a folded knife.

"Neeps! Is that my father's knife? It is, isn't it?"

Neeps was still fumbling in his pockets. At last he produced a final gift: the ivory whale.

"Did you have to fight Jervik?" Pazel whispered.

Neeps sniffed. Only then did Pazel realize that he was sobbing with rage and shame.

"By my grandmother's bones on Sollochstal," he said in his squeaky voice, "I'll see them pay for what they made me do to you."

21

FROM THE SECRET JOURNAL OF
G. STARLING FIFFENGURT, QUARTERMASTER

Saturday, 13 Ilqrin. Quiet sailing on a nervous ship. Rose is tyrannical & Uskins cruel, but both have kept to themselves these two days since the flogging of Pazel Pathkendle, as if sated by that wicked business. For Mr. P. P. of course there is no future: he shall be put ashore in Uturphe with a purse of horse-meat & the mark of shame upon his papers. Uskins that great hog tried to brand his wrists—*I* for Insolent on one, *R* for Reckless the other. He had Pathkendle in the smithy & was heating a branding iron when I arrived & intervened. Not very gently, either: I told him that iron would find new & uncomfortable quarters if he tried to use it on one of my boys. Uskins sneered at me for defending the *Muketch*—the boys' strange nickname for Pathkendle. I gather it has something to do with crabs.

Uskins did quite enough damage when he made the boy's best friend, Neeps Undrabust, dole out the lashes. Mr. Undrabust walks about looking as if he'd killed someone. He has also been fighting: Mr. Jervik Lank apparently remarked that Pathkendle was a "girly" because he'd cried under the lash—as if marines & mercenaries didn't as well!—& that Undrabust was worse, as he'd cried just because he had to whip a "daft Ormali." Undrabust went for him like a wildcat. Fortunately Peytr & Dastu were on hand & tore him away before anyone was hurt.

I looked the other way on this occasion, but I won't be able to do so again. Fighting is a plague that must be stamped out quickly, lest it escape all control.

Sunday, 14 Ilqrin. Foul dreams: Anni sick, her father forced to beg a loan from the Mangel thugs to buy medicine, a swarm of black insects over Etherhorde, a baby crying in the hold. Such visions have plagued me for weeks—since that awful night, in fact, when Mr. Aken of the Chathrand Trading Family was lost overboard, just a few leagues out of Ellisoq Bay. Only Swellows saw him fall, & though we dropped sail & put out the lantern craft, no trace of his body was found. Swellows claims he was staggering drunk, but I said nothing of this in the letter I wrote to his wife. His cabin showed no trace of liquor, & the offending bottle, if bottle there was, went with him to the deep. Rose led us in a prayer for the man's good soul—so sincerely that I could at last imagine the captain ending his days as a monk.

Currently Rose sits whole days at his desk, scribbling, leaving only for the sailmaster's report & his evening meal. Turwinnek Isle came & went, & the ruins of the ancient city of Nal-Burim on the southeast tip of Dremland. Commander Nagan's moon falcon was sent inland & returned with a fat grouse, which was served with mint at the captain's table tonight. Mr. Latzlo offered five hundred cockles for the bird, but the soldier loves his Niriviel & would not hear of it. One has to admire such gentle feelings in a fighting man.

Wednesday, 17 Ilqrin. Confusion & delays. Strong SW winds had us tacking all but back toward home from Wednesday last to yesterday morning. Since then no wind to speak of: we are reduced to a crawling two knots.

The confusion though concerns our heading. Nal-Burim is the usual signal to trim due west, for any ship bound for the Crownless Lands. But to general amazement Rose has given no such command: we are holding a south-by-southwest course, & leaving the mainland behind. Mr. Elkstem inquired at the Capt.'s door & was told to steer as instructed & blast his curiosity.

Last night Pazel Pathkendle was attacked by other boys in

the darkness—tied into his hammock & pissed upon, told that he "should have been made a slave" & not "disgraced the best ship of the best people in Alifros." His friends Undrabust and Reyast were elsewhere. No one will give me names.

For his own safety I have moved Pathkendle's hammock to the brig, where he will sleep under lock and key until expelled in Uturphe. If we ever get there.

Monday, 22 Ilqrin. Harpooned a reaper shark; Teggatz made a soup. In his gullet (the shark's) found the whole skeleton of a human hand, with a fine silver ring on one finger. Our cook presented it to me with much blinking & rubbing of hands, & minutes later managed to say: "Bad shark." I shall give the ring to Annabel one day, without the tale of its provenance.

Winds NW & freshened considerably: seven knots at the strike of the noon bell. Still bearing south.

Sunday, 28 Ilqrin. This morning Rose gave the order to bear west—finally. At a minimum we have plunged eighty leagues out of our way. To what purpose? the men demand, & I have no answer.

Here's another oddity—one I'd nearly forgotten. Back in Etherhorde, Rose spared me the quartermaster's usual task of drumming up sailors to complete our crew: I was glad, for it gave me some last precious hours with Annabel. Mr. Swellows handled the recruiting, & he is ever keen to follow Rose's orders to the letter. How, then, did he end up signing so many Plapp's Pier men? They are capable sailors, certainly. But any fool knows the Great Ship's been crewed for generations by the Burnscove Boys.* Granted, quite a few of our Burnscovers deserted in Sorrophran, perhaps (as Mr. Frix

*Plapp's Pier and Burnscove are two port districts of Etherhorde. The gangs Mr. Fiffengurt mentions control most of the dock work in the city and are bitter rivals. —EDITOR.

thinks) because they recall the first captaincy of Nilus Rose & would rather starve than serve under him again. But well over a hundred remain aboard.

I took care to sort Plapps & Burnscovers into separate watches, & to mix 'em with those who don't belong to either gang. So far there have been no brawls—yet they will come, sure as I write these words. Thasha Isiq & her prince may wed, Arqual & the Mzithrin disarm, but the holy war of Plapp vs. Burnscove will rage on so long as there are crates of fish to fight over.

Wednesday, 1 Modoli. Apparently we have a maniac aboard. Last night by the No. 3 hatch someone attacked Hercól Stanapeth, Ambassador Isiq's valet, & nearly succeeded in killing the man. He was struck a fierce blow to the head that left him briefly senseless. Next he knew, this attacker was making to hurl him over the rail. At the last instant the would-be killer groaned & stumbled, & rather than tossing Hercól far out into the waves, he managed only to roll him over the side, where the valet's ankle caught in the mizzen-chains. The maniac then drew a knife & stabbed Hercól's leg three times. But the valet, in most extraordinary fashion, kicked the knife out of the man's hand with his free foot—this while dangling upsy-downsy, bleeding from head & leg, & knocking like a landed fish against the hull.

The surprise hero of the evening is none other than Mr. Ket, Liripus Ket, the chubby merchant who has been with us since Sorrophran. This quiet seller of Opaltine soaps came out on deck while the knifing was under way, faced down the maniac with a capstan bar & so battered him that the lunatic dived back down the hatch to escape. Mr. Ket's shouts brought sailors running, but not fast enough to apprehend him. For the moment he is on the loose. Even more alarming, he was masked: neither Ket nor Hercól saw his face.

Ket is an odd bird (he clears his throat with a sound like breaking timbers & fiddles nonstop with a tattered scarf) but obviously a brave one. We made him promise not to breathe a word about this business. "I wouldn't—*CHHRCK!*—dream of it, sirs." He'd better not. The men have already begun to mutter that perhaps Aken was *helped* overboard, & there have been dark glances at Mr. Swellows. We deck officers have been all day coaxing & threatening them into silence. Terror among the passengers is the last thing we need.

Sergeant Drellarek's soldiers are even now discreetly searching the ship. But how shall we recognize the villain? Ket describes a man "of regular size," which rules out only the augrongs & Mr. Neeps. A full search of the four hundred riders in third class will start a bonfire of rumors that will never go out. And in any case those ragged souls were all locked below for the night.

Who would murder a servant? I despise Mr. Swellows but cannot believe the old toad has the courage to kill. Isiq says nothing about Hercól except that he is a grand person, well loved by all & tutor to Lady Thasha. He is Tholjassan, & they are a warrior people, but this Tholjassan is a mere servant & dancer. He cannot be rich. Why him? If the villain is after Eberzam Isiq, why attack the servant alone & apart? The crime makes no sense, & troubles me at some deep level I do not yet understand.

Mr. Hercól lost much blood before we fished him from the chains. He has not stirred these 27 hours, & I fear he may die before we reach Uturphe. The young Lady weeps at his side, & even seems a bit out of her head, calling for a certain Rawmanchy (?) although there is no one by that name aboard.

Myself, I do not pray. The Gods have better means of deciding this world's fate than by taking requests from an old quartermaster. But skies! May the man live! One senseless death on a voyage is tragic. Two could mark the beginning of a curse.

Could that be why I spared the rat?

I feel quite silly, but here is what happened: six or eight days out of Ulsprit I climbed down to the mercy deck, looking for bootblack. Just past the foremast I saw a bilge-pipe with an ill-fitting cap, & when I opened it to set it right I found myself looking into the eyes of a black rat. Of course I made to smash the creature with my crowbar. What stopped me was the sight of his little foot.

It was crushed. The beast had jammed it between pipe & lid, no doubt at the exact moment one of us slammed the lid home. The foot will never be a foot again, but it let enough air into the pipe to keep this plucky fellow alive. He was skinny & trembling—in that pipe for days, I'm sure. We gazed at each other, ratty & me, & before I could get over my shock & kill him he skedaddled away on his three good legs. I still could have slain him with the crowbar, but instead I found myself wishing him luck. What a ridiculous old softy you've become, Fiffengurt! Luckily I was quite alone.

22

Good Intentions

4 Modoli 941
52nd day from Etherhorde

Hercól lay still as death. Thasha stood in the cabin doorway, watching Dr. Rain poke and prod her tutor for the hundredth time. He looked terrible: gray blotchy skin, new wrinkles about the eyes, streaks of dark blood that had run from his leg to his chin while he dangled upside down in the chains. He had not moved since the attack four nights before.

Thasha had insisted that they bring him here, to her own chamber: it was warmer than sickbay, and the bed was a real bed, not a padded board dangling from ropes. But Rain was still the ship's only doctor. Thasha's anxiety grew the more she watched him shuffling about. He seemed a little mad. Talking to his instruments. Wiping his chin with a corner of her bedspread.

"There now, dear." Syrarys glided breezily to her side and touched her arm. "Let the doctor do his work. And lend me your necklace a moment. Your brave Mr. Ket has given me some *exquisite* silver polish."

Without a glance at the consort, Thasha removed her necklace and handed it over. They were making fast to Uturphe, supposedly. But when Thasha and her father pored over his old nautical chart (with its penciled ghosts of old war fleets, battle maneuvers, lines of attack) he showed her how far out of the way Rose had taken them. Whole days wasted, or so it seemed.

Why didn't he speak to Rose about the detour? Thasha wanted to know. The old admiral's reply was stern: "Because he is the captain."

Yet her father also declared that the winds were less favorable by the hour, and that they would be lucky to reach the city by tomorrow sunrise. Would Hercól live that long? Thasha couldn't bear to consider the question. Instead, she turned her mind to revenge.

Taking her diary and fountain pen from her room, she dropped into a grand leather chair by the fengas lamp, crossed her legs and wrote:

What I Know:
1. Someone tried to kill my best friend in the world.
2. A soap merchant named Ket prevented it.
3. The enemy is still on this ship—at least, until we land.

She paused, chewing the end of her fountain pen. Then she scribbled quickly:

4. Hercól knew there were enemies around us.
5. Hercól was afraid when Pazel Pathkendle mentioned a language—Nileskchet.
6. Everyone is talking about peace, but Prahba is afraid of war.

That meant he and Hercól were on the same side—for even though Hercól was a great warrior and served in an admiral's home, he loathed wars. So did Ramachni, of course. Once, when certain her father was not in earshot, the old mage had said: "As sure as disease grows where filth lies unburied, so every war in history sprang from someone's carelessness or neglect."

Ramachni would know what to do. But there was no chance of speaking to him with that dolt doctor running in and out of her cabin. She was on her own.

She slid down in her chair.

What I Want to Know:

1. WHO DID IT.
2. Why.
3. What's going to happen to that stupid boy, Pazel Pathkendle.
4. Where Syrarys goes after dinner—it is NOT to the first-class powder room.
5. How Hercól and Ramachni planned to get me out of this wedding.
6. Whether P. P. hates all of us or just Prahba.
7. If P. P. has ever been—

"Polished!" said Syrarys, draping the necklace around Thasha's neck. "Doesn't it shine!"

Thasha grunted.

"Is that your Mzithrini lesson, dear?" asked the consort, peering over her shoulder.

"Why, yes."

Puzzled, Syrarys drifted back to her needlepoint. Despite all her fears and worries, Thasha felt a moment's pride. She was writing in code: her own mad code, invented to outwit the Lorg Sisters. Odd words she spelled backward. Every third, fifth and seventeenth letter was a decoy, as were all the spaces and half the vowels; and of course the whole thing was read from the bottom of the page to the top. It was not the code itself she was proud of, exactly: rather it was that she could both read and write it at almost normal speed. That was the skill that had taken years.

Were codes a kind of language, too? Would Pazel be able to read her diary as plainly as she could?

And why on earth did she keep thinking of him? Hercól's attacker was the one to concentrate on. She would find him, she promised herself. And the first person to speak to was Ket. Thasha slipped into her cabin, locked her diary away in her desk, glanced once more at Hercól (he had not moved an eyelash) and left the stateroom.

The ship was chilly and dark. Sailors tipped their hats as she passed. Mr. Ket was not in the dining room, and the lounge was empty but for Latzlo the animal-seller and the veterinarian, Bolutu. They were locked in an argument about walrus-hunting. Bolutu seemed to think one could run out of walruses; Latzlo said the seas could never be emptied. The very notion appeared to irritate him.

"I know animals," he said, stroking his pet sloth with such force that its fur shed in a cloud. "Animals are my business. Do you think I would put myself out of business?"

"A grocer may run out of cabbages and not close his store," said Bolutu.

"I have no interest in vegetables!"

When Thasha finally got their attention, they told her Ket was enjoying Smoke Hour on the forecastle. Thasha set off at once, climbing to the topdeck and running in the open air. The waves were taller now, and the wind had a bite. Away to starboard the gray mountains of Uturphe looked no closer than at noon.

Smoke Hour was an arrangement for the third-class passengers, who were never permitted in the smoking salon. At dusk these poorest travelers were allowed to rent the use of a pipe on the forecastle. The fee was outrageous and the tobacco stale, but there is little an addict trapped in a cold, crowded ship will not agree to. This evening thirty men were busily puffing away: Smoke Hour in fact lasted forty minutes.

How odd to find Mr. Ket among them: *he* was certainly no third-class traveler. He wore a sea-cloak with blue silk at cuff and collar, and a gemstone on his finger flashed red in the setting sun. Instead of a blackened rental pipe he had his own, fine water pipe of burnished brass. He stood by a starboard carronade, as far from everyone else on the forecastle as he could get.

"Lady Thasha!" he said, bowing at her approach. "A very good evening to you!"

"I'm afraid it isn't," said Thasha. "My tutor's dying, and no one seems able to help."

"Poor man!" said the soap merchant, lowering his voice. "And what an ill omen for us all! Has he not woken yet?"

"No," said Thasha. "But I'm grateful to you for saving him. You're very brave, Mr. Ket."

"I had no time to be brave," he said, dropping his eyes. "I merely found myself acting."

There was, Thasha saw now, one flaw in Mr. Ket's wealthy profile: a careworn white scarf, knotted tight about his neck. Something held on to from childhood, Thasha supposed: rich men had their quirks.

"Can you tell me what happened?" she asked.

Ket shook his head. "I beg your pardon, I cannot. Mr. Fiffengurt demanded my promise not to tell anyone of this ugly event."

"I promised, too," said Thasha. "But surely he meant for us not to spread the story? Since we both know it occurred, there's no harm if we talk, is there?"

The merchant hesitated, fussing with his pipe, but it was clear Thasha would accept no refusal. After some furtive glances around the deck he spoke again, very softly.

"I honor your concern for your friend, m'lady. But I fear you would put yourself in danger for his sake. The assassin is still aboard. Any one of these men behind me could be him."

"Hercól is more than a friend," said Thasha. "He's as dear to me as an older brother. Whatever becomes of him, I must know what happened."

"Very well," Ket sighed, "but it will do you no good. For in the end, what did I see? A man I took for a sailor, crouching by an open hatch, swinging a hammer at something within. The next moment—it was very dark, you understand—I saw that man leap down onto the steps himself and return with something large and dark over his shoulder. It was Mr. Hercól, of course, but I guessed no such evil thing. The man passed out of my sight for a moment, behind the barge davit, and then I heard him cry out. I rushed forward in time to see him stumble and drop his burden—now obviously a man!—half over the rail."

"Was his voice high or low?" asked Thasha.

"Neither, especially," said Ket. "But I scarce had time to notice, for the cretin was rolling your friend over the side. Hercól was waking up from the hammer blow, but not fast enough— and it was the greatest luck that he struck the mizzen-chains. The man drew his knife, leaned over and cut your friend savagely. And then Mr. Hercól made that . . . extraordinary kick."

"Where did Hercól kick him—in the arm, or the hand?"

"The wrist," said Ket. "Why do you ask, m'lady?"

"Go on, please!" said Thasha. "What happened next?"

"The next instant—well, I seized that capstan bar and had at him."

"What made him stumble?" asked Thasha.

Ket's eyes widened. "I wish I knew," he said. "Another piece of good luck, is all I can fathom. The deck was clear enough. But without that stumble, Mr. Hercól would certainly have died."

"And he fought you, this man?"

"Indeed he did."

"Was he a trained fighter?"

Ket looked startled. "What unexpected questions," he said. "He fought well enough, I suppose. But this was the first real fight of my life—may it also be the last!—and so I am a poor judge."

"But you have answered me, you know," said Thasha. "You've told me you're not a fighter yourself, and yet you beat him."

"My dear girl, I had the capstan bar."

"But don't you see," said Thasha, struggling for patience. "A trained fighter would have run circles around you, trying to swing that heavy bar. Or just taken it away from you and broken it over your head. So he wasn't a soldier, or one of my father's guards."

"Skies above, no! Just someone crazy enough to want to kill."

"Or ordered to," said Thasha softly.

"Ordered, m'lady?"

"Never mind, Mr. Ket. Thank you again for your courage. By the way, what were you doing out on deck so late at night?"

Ket looked away, then drew a hand across his forehead. After a deep breath he said, "Confinement disturbs me. Small rooms, tight spaces . . . these trouble my soul. I cannot breathe."

"That's nothing to be ashamed of, Mr. Ket," said Thasha, for once almost liking him. "I felt the same way at school."

Dinner that evening was hosted by Mr. Uskins, whom Thasha detested, so she told her father she had no appetite, and when he and Syrarys had dressed and departed she promptly rang the bell for room service.

She frowned. Ket was something of a fool. Nothing about the attacker had made an impression: not even the amazing fact that he, Ket, a baby-faced merchant with gray hair and a paunch, had trounced the man without a scratch. Thasha, however, had learned several things. She added these to her list:

What I Know (Cont.)
7. If I should ever marry, it will not be to a soap merchant.
8. Hercól's attacker was no trained fighter.
9. That man's wrist is in agony, or broken.

Thasha knew well the force of Hercól's kicks, even on the practice floor. A kick to save his life would be simply explosive. She ought to explain this to the officers searching *Chathrand*. But how could she, without letting them know how much more than a servant Hercól was?

The tarboy who came from the galley was very short. Like most of the men aboard, he stared at her as if she were some odd and fascinating monster. "Dinner for one!" she snapped, grabbing her dogs before they could leap on him. "And no shrimp heads, please. Yesterday my dinner was like a little congregation, watching itself being eaten."

"I'm very sorry, m'lady."

"It's not *your* fault, idiot. Close the door. No, *no*—" She waved a hand. "Without leaving, yet. What's your name, any-way?"

"N-Neeps," said the small boy, shaking with relief as the dogs collapsed on the bearskin.

She cocked her head at him. "Well, N-Neeps, how many sailors are there aboard the *Chathrand*?"

"About six hundred, common and rated, Lady. And twenty midshipmen."

"And how many passengers?"

"Four hundred steerage, Mistress—and a score first-class, plus servants. And your noble family, of course."

"Half of them male . . . and a hundred marines . . . that's over nine hundred men! Well, that's simple!" She laughed aloud. "All I have to do is check nine hundred wrists before tomorrow morning! Don't ask, I won't explain! Just tell me: what have they done with Pazel Pathkendle?"

The boy jumped, but said nothing. He looked disturbed in an entirely new way.

"You know who I mean," said Thasha. "The Ormali. The one who got flogged for being rude to my father. Who flogged him, anyway—that big baboon they call Jervik? I'll bet he volun-teered."

Neeps fidgeted, glanced at the door.

"Are they going to throw him off the ship at Uturphe?"

"I can't tell you, m'lady," he said.

"Why not?" Thasha pressed. "I'm his friend, you know. Maybe his *only* friend."

Now anger sparked in Neeps' glance. "We tarboys take care of our own," he said.

"Splendid! Tell me, then: what's the punishment for insulting an ambassador?"

"Whatever the captain wants."

"What does Rose usually do?"

"Sometimes one thing, sometimes another."

"Can you"—she took a careful breath—"*at least* tell me where they're keeping him?"

"No."

They stood there, eye to eye. Jorl wheezed and flopped on his chin. Then Thasha put her hands to the back of her neck, beneath her golden hair. After a moment she frowned.

"Help me," she said curtly, turning her back and lifting the hair aside.

"M-m'lady?"

"The clasp on my necklace. It's stuck."

Neeps stared at her. She looked back steadily over her shoulder, daring him to say another word. Neeps wiped his hands on his pants, then reached into the golden hair as one might a nest of spiders. He made a face. She sighed and crossed her arms. He struggled with the clasp.

"Really, N-Neeps, it's not that— *Ouch!*"

"Augh!" screamed Neeps, as they both flinched. The necklace dropped to the floor.

"What did you *do,* imbecile?" cried Thasha, holding her neck.

Neeps scooped up the chain. "It wasn't me, Lady Thasha! It was a spark—a ferrous spark. Got me, too! Must be iron in this necklace somewhere."

"Don't be daft, it's pure silver! Let me see if it's harmed."

Neeps held out the necklace, but she made no move to take it from him. The tiny sea-creatures gleamed in the lamplight.

"Well, it's fine, anyway," she declared. "And pretty, no?"

"It's beautiful, m'lady."

"Too bad you tried to steal it."

"What?"

Neeps dropped the necklace again. Thasha caught it and draped it over a chair. "I'd taken it off to bathe, see? You slipped it into your pocket, but I noticed the bulge as you were turning to go. How do you suppose the captain punishes stealing from an ambassador's cabin?"

"You're a blary damn pigsty liar . . . m'lady!" sputtered Neeps, trembling with rage.

Thasha sighed. "Of course you *would* say that. And perhaps the officers will take your word over mine. Well, go on, back to your duties, N-Neeps. I think I'll eat in the dining room after all—now that I have something to talk about."

She was extremely proud of herself: a nicer piece of blackmail one could hardly ask for. But to her astonishment Neeps gritted his teeth and stepped toward her, only stopping when Suzyt growled.

"No, they won't believe an Outer Isles tarboy over a daisy-sweet bit of wife cargo like you. They'll clap me in jail, is what. And then make me work off twenty times that trinket's worth—and brand my arm. *That's* standard punishment for first-time thieves. Let 'em. Do your worst. But I'll not help you land Pazel any deeper in trouble. We—you've done enough to him already!"

Three steps and he was out, with a smart slam of the door. For a moment Thasha stood rooted to the spot. He was calling her bluff! Then she realized that if Neeps disappeared he would be no easier to find on the enormous ship than Pazel himself.

A moment later she was through the door, running with her boots unlaced. Neeps was thumping down the stern stairway. "Wait, wait!" she cried, tumbling after him, but he only ran faster—down and down, across the berth deck to the opposite stair and down again.

Just above the mercy deck he abruptly turned, blocking her way. It was dark: they were deeper in the ship than she had ever set foot. She smelled animals and hay.

"You really are his friend, aren't you?" she said.

"That's right," said Neeps, more winded than Thasha herself.

"I didn't know. I thought everyone hated him for being Ormali."

"Only dumb louts hate him. The rest are *afraid* of him because of what happened with the augrongs, and because a few blary idlers say they heard him speaking devil-tongue."

"Why aren't you afraid?"

Neeps just looked away. Thasha realized she already knew: this shrimp wasn't afraid of anything. *Be careful, shrimp,* she thought. *Someone may try to cut off your head.*

"What makes you so curious about Pazel?" Neeps asked.

"I don't know," she said. "Honestly I don't. But he seems special, smart maybe, also a fool like you, of course— Oh, that's not what I mean! I mean you're right. His trouble started with us, when Prahba tried to talk to him about the Rescue of Ormael. Or the"—she struggled with the word—"*invasion,* if that's what you like to call it. So at the very least I owe him some help. I want to get him out of the mess we got him into."

"Well, you can't," said Neeps. "All you can do is make things worse. There was a collection for him among the tarboys—eight gold, enough for a third-class ticket, maybe. If he's lucky he'll ship out on the next boat, get into the lawless territories of the Nelu Rekere."

"Can he sign on with another ship, out there?"

Neeps shook his head. "The Sailing Code isn't enforced in the Rekere, but most decent ships end up back in the Quiet Sea sooner or later. His name would be checked against the registry in any big port. As soon as they found out what *Chathrand* dismissed him for, he'd be charged with misleading his captain."

"Then what can he do?"

"Go out in a small fishing boat, one that doesn't stray far from its home port. Or work the docks."

Thasha couldn't believe her ears. "A docker or a fisherman? For the rest of his *life*?"

"Or a pirate. Lots of demand for pirates. Always getting killed, you see."

"This is terrible!"

" 'Course, he might try going inland from Uturphe. Folks say there's work in Torabog, cutting cane."

"You're lying!" Thasha cried. "It can't be that bad!"

"You call *me* a liar? After that little game in your cabin?"

"That was just to make you tell me where he was!"

Neeps stepped closer, and she knew he could see her tears. His voice was gentler, if only slightly. "Suppose I did tell you," he said. "What good would it do? How could you possibly help him now?"

"By hiring him," said Thasha simply.

"Hiring him? Are you cracked? What do you imagine he'd do—sew you a blary wedding dress?"

"I can't tell you what I'd hire him for. It's a secret."

"You're marrying a Sizzy prince. He'll have ten girls just handlin' your laundry. Pazel wouldn't know the word for 'sock.' "

"Yes he would!" she said, her voice rising in desperation. "Oh, sky! Can't you just take me to him?"

"I'm right here, Thasha."

Pazel stepped around the bend in the stairs and put a hand on Neeps' shoulder. "Thanks, mate," he said.

"Be careful with this one," growled Neeps. "She's a trickster. She wants to get me jailed as a thief."

"I wouldn't really have done it!"

"We can't stay here long," said Pazel. "Thasha, what's this secret you want to share? Anything you can tell me, you can tell Neeps."

"I have two," said Thasha. "But you have to swear not to betray me."

Neeps scoffed, but Pazel said: "We'll swear if you like. We're not tattlers."

After she had their promises, Thasha told them about Hercól and the mysterious attacker. As she expected, neither boy had heard of the events: Fiffengurt's rumor-control efforts had so far succeeded.

"A murderer aboard," said Neeps. "That's marvelous. He shouldn't be too hard to spot, though, if his wrist is in such bad shape. All we have to do is find out who's been let off work."

"How?" said Pazel. "Mr. Uskins keeps track of that sort of thing, and Rin knows he won't tell us. We could ask Dr. Rain who he's treated, but I doubt that whoever attacked Hercól will be looking for treatment in sickbay."

Neeps sighed. "You're right, I suppose. But you had another secret to share, Thasha. What is it?"

Thasha took a deep breath. She said, "I'm not marrying that prince. Not for Prahba or Arqual or peace or anything. Hercól was going to get me out of it, somehow. If he dies—"

Her sobs broke out in earnest. The boys looked at each other. One did not simply hug an ambassador's daughter, did one? At last, awkwardly, they gripped her by the elbows, as if propping up a rickety ladder. They could not tell if she was comforted or annoyed.

Eventually she pulled out a red handkerchief, blew her nose and continued, "If Hercól dies I'll find a way out myself. I'll have Ramachni spirit me away or turn me into a skunk. Or I'll just run off. I have enough gold to sail twice around the world."

"They'll send a *fleet* after you," said Pazel.

"Two fleets," Neeps put in. "One Sizzy, one Arquali. But who's this Ramachni?"

"Then I'll jump ship before we're anywhere near Simja," Thasha went on, ignoring Neeps. "Right here in Uturphe. With you, Pazel! And I'll buy us *both* passage to somewhere far away, in the Crownless Lands or Outer Isles. That's what I want to hire you for, see? To be my guide."

In the silence that followed they heard cows munching placidly in their stalls.

Neeps was the first one to speak. "I knew it, mate, she's cracked."

"Entirely," said Pazel. "I've never even seen the Outer Isles. And what will your father say if you disappear?"

"Whatever he likes," said Thasha with sudden anger. "He sent me to the Lorg! I blamed Syrarys for years, but it was him. He needed a daughter fit to marry a prince, and that's what the Sisters were training me for. You're right, Neeps: I'm just cargo to these people."

"One of *these people* is the Emperor," said Pazel. "Do you think he'll let you slip away?"

"Not easily. That's why I need your help."

"His help!" laughed Neeps. "I like that! Not enough that you've ended his sailing career. You want him to be a fugitive. With His Supremacy's men *and* the Black Rags combing the seas for him."

"You make everything sound so rotten," said Thasha.

"Listen, half-wit, it's rotten whatever I say. When they catch you, they'll make you marry a Sizzy. *But what do you think they'll do to Pazel?* He talks back to your dad and gets whipped like a slave. If he helps you run away—"

"They'll kill me," said Pazel quietly.

Thasha sat on a step. She covered her face with her hands, but this time she didn't cry. After a moment she looked up at them. "You're right," she said. "I have to do this alone. They'd kill Hercól, too, if he tried to help me. I'm that important, somehow. Peace is coming, and this made-up marriage is the guarantee."

"But they don't want peace," whispered Pazel. "They want war." The others looked at him, stunned.

"Who wants war?" blurted Neeps.

"Be *quiet,* you donkey!" Pazel seized his arm. "I don't know who!"

"Well where in the brimstone Pits did you get that idea?"

"I can't tell you. But it's true, Thasha: all this peacemaking is a sham. Ramachni told us there was an evil mage hidden aboard."

"Who's Ramachni?" said Neeps, stamping his foot.

"He didn't say the mage had anything to do with me," said Thasha. "Or with this Treaty Bride business."

"What else could be so important about this voyage?" Pazel went on. "And don't you see, Thasha? If someone *is* trying to start a war, breaking off the marriage will play right into their hands."

"I don't see, and I don't care," said Thasha. "Let them hand over someone else to the Sizzies!"

"Right for once," said Neeps. "I don't know the half of this— but Pazel, you're not making sense. If some fools wanted a new war with the Black Rags, they could find easier ways to start it."

No one spoke for a moment. Pazel was thinking of Chadfallow's words, ten years ago at his mother's table. *Lies, Suthinia. We are adrift without charts in a sea of lies.* And what else? *One lie can doom the world. One fearless soul can save it.*

"Thasha," he said, "who else knows you plan to run off?"

"Nobody else."

"Just think, then," said Pazel. "There's never been a marriage between Sizzies and Arqualis. But there's also been no war for forty years."

"So?"

"So what if *the marriage itself* is supposed to start the war?"

"Oh, rubbish!" said Thasha. "This whole business has been planned for decades. First the fighting stopped, then the name-calling. Then a few important men on both sides, men like Dr. Chadfallow, met and talked. Now a Mzithrini prince takes a . . . a—"

"A gift basket," said Pazel. "Tied up in bows."

She gave him a look to curdle milk. "A daughter of an enemy soldier, that's all that matters. And when I've lived seven years in Babqri City, the Mzithrin priests are supposed to pronounce me acceptable, or noncontagious, or at the very least human, and that will mean Arqual itself is no longer the enemy of the Old Faith. And then we all become friends."

"Very pretty," said Neeps.

"Foolishness and rot," said Thasha. "But it's supposed to *prevent* a war, not start one. Pazel, you're not being fair. I've told you my secrets, and you've told me nothing but your crazy guesses. If this wedding is really a sham, don't you think I have the right to know?"

"She's got a point, mate," said Neeps. "Trust and trust alike."

They waited, but Pazel just shook his head. "If I *could* explain," he said, "you'd understand why I can't."

"That's the maddest thing yet," said Neeps. "Rin help us if— oy! You there!"

The others turned. Seated primly on the stairs above them was Sniraga, Lady Oggosk's cat. The red animal looked at them serenely, like someone enjoying a bit of light theater from a balcony.

"Sniraga!" said Pazel. "Why's she always popping up?"

"That cat gives me the chills," said Thasha.

"She stole a pickle from the galley this morning," said Neeps.

"She stole my leek fritter in Sorrophran," Pazel growled. "Go on, thief, away with you!"

The cat turned Pazel an indifferent look. Then she bent her head and lifted something coiled and shiny from the deck.

"My necklace!" Thasha cried, aghast. "How did she get it? I must have left the door open!"

With the silver chain in her teeth, Sniraga stood and stretched. Then, before anyone could move, she sprang up the stairs and vanished.

"Oh, catch her, catch her!" Thasha shouted. "Prahba will murder me!"

They raced after the cat, but Sniraga was already gone from sight. At the berth deck they divided: Thasha kept climbing, muttering oaths, and the boys rushed in among the sailors. *The cat, the cat!* they begged. Had anyone seen it? No one had. But when they reached the tarboys' quarters Reyast waved them down.

"T-T-T-Teggatz is fit to k-k-kill you, Neeps!"

"Blow me down!" said Neeps. "I've been gone half an hour!"

"M-m-m-more."

"And I'm late for cow-and-pig duty," said Pazel. "Thasha will have to manage alone."

"She'll manage," said Neeps. "Stay out of trouble, mate."

Neeps rushed back to his post. Pazel returned to the manger and spent the next two hours mucking it out, and feeding the goats and cattle. Then the dairy cow needed milking, and a goat kicked over a five-gallon pail of fresh water, forcing Pazel to haul another from the deck below. When his labor was done at last, Pazel sat in the hay beside the cow and leaned into her warm flank.

He had about ten minutes before Fiffengurt locked him up in the brig for the night. He stank of manure and piss. It was the smell as much as the thought of iron bars that reminded him: *Steldak.*

His own troubles had made him forget Rose's prisoner for days. Now he felt selfish, ashamed. Someone had to help that man.

Summoning all his courage, he whispered: "Are you listening?"

The cow looked at him dreamily. Pazel waited, holding his breath. There was no sound but the slice of the ship through the waves, loud here at the waterline.

Diadrelu had said they would speak again once the *Chathrand* left Etherhorde, but she had never come. And sometime tomorrow he would be tossed ashore. If he told Neeps or Thasha about the ixchel they might be murdered in their sleep. If he didn't, Steldak would rot away in that cage until he died.

"Can you hear me?" he whispered again. "Come soon, Diadrelu. Please."

"Kit—kit—kit! Kitty—cat! Come out, you sly, stinking cheat!"
Around Thasha, sailors stifled laughs. None had seen the red cat, so sorry m'lady, and Thasha realized the chase was futile. Better to get back to the stateroom before things got any worse.

She made a quick dash across the main deck. Her door *was* ajar. Slipping inside, she kicked off her shoes and coat and ran straight to her cabin.

Hercól looked worse. Under Dr. Rain's tight bandages his leg was swollen like a fatty sausage. A low wheezing came from his throat.

Thasha fought down panic. *Hercól's dying. Ramachni's out of reach. Pazel's being thrown off the ship.* She could not remember ever feeling so trapped. Who was she, to imagine she could escape the clutches of two empires? She couldn't even escape from the Lorg.

Her misery was cut short by the sound of a key in the stateroom door. Thasha left her cabin just as her father opened the outer door.

"How is he?" Isiq asked at once.

"Not good."

Eberzam crossed the room, peered in at Hercól and shook his head. Thasha pulled her collar high around her neck, praying he wouldn't notice the missing necklace.

"Prahba," she said, "who's in charge of catching the attacker?"

"That would be Commander Nagan," said Isiq.

"Good old Nagan," she said, with less-than-perfect convic-
tion. "Where's he been lately?"

"He sailed ahead to be sure all was safe in our next port of
call. But he is back aboard now. A fine soldier, that one. By the
way, Syrarys has been asking for you."

"Oh?"

"She has grown fond of the ladies' powder room. Women can
actually talk there, she says, away from us menfolk." He smiled.
"You should join her one of these nights."

"I will," said Thasha. "Come to think of it, Prahba, I think I'll
join her now."

"Good girl," he said.

Of course Thasha's intentions were not "good" in the way her
father meant. She had already poked her head into the first-class
powder room on two previous nights and had not found Syrarys
there at all. *Once more,* she thought, *and I'll ask where she really goes after dinner—in front of Prahba, of course. And how
will you squirm out of that one, you fancy louse?*

But tonight, outrageously, Syrarys was where she claimed she
would be. "Dearest!" she cried when Thasha opened the door.
"Have you come to soak with us awhile?"

Soggy hands drew Thasha in. One of the first-class wives
(nine were stuffed in the little room) had arranged for a tub of
near-boiling water to be installed in the powder room, and they
sat around it in ecstasy, soaking their ostrich legs. "Salt water,
tut," said the wife of the Virabalm wheat merchant. "Still, it's
the *very* thing on a cold night!"

Syrarys had wrapped her hair in a towel. "Our Thasha's been
studying the enemy—oh dear, that's wrong—our *former* enemy,
of course. She knows about their history, their strange and
frightening ways. But we mustn't be frightened anymore, right,
darling? From now on we shall live and let live. And all the

more so after your marriage. Come, sit by me—and do teach us some Mzithrini."

Once again Thasha had walked right into Syrarys' trap. She could hardly accuse her of sneaking off somewhere now. "Mzithrini! Mzithrini!" the wives chirped in delight. And every minute brought them closer to Uturphe.

Thasha spoke a phrase from the back of the *Merchant's Polylex* (*"Don't touch any of my goods!"*), which was all she ever intended to say to her fiancé if the wedding somehow occurred. She told them it was a polite greeting among nobles.

Groping her way out of the steam at last, Thasha closed the door on their *"Ta-ta!"*'s and made for the topdeck. But she had not taken three steps when she saw an old soldier leaving the smoking salon, just ahead. He was short, lean, scarred, a survivor of many battles, and he wore the red beret of the honor guard.

"Good evening, Commander Nagan," she said.

Sandor Ott turned with a smile. "At your service, Lady Thasha."

"Commander, my father says you're in charge of catching—"

"Forgive the interruption," said Ott, "but if you would have me succeed, please lower your voice."

What a fool she was! She had almost blurted *catching Hercól's attacker* loud enough to carry through several cabins. It was exactly the sort of recklessness her father worried about.

"Thank you," she said, more softly. "Commander Nagan, can I tell you something that may be of help?"

"I pray you will," said Ott.

"Hercól has very strong legs, even for a dancer," said Thasha, "and Mr. Ket saw him kick the attacker in the wrist, just after he was stabbed. Whoever the man is, he'll have one blary great bruise at the wrist."

Ott looked at her with something like admiration. He folded his smoking jacket over his arm. "You're quite right, Lady Thasha. In fact, that point had not escaped my notice. And relying on your perfect discretion, I will tell you this: we have found four men aboard with such injuries. Two are common sailors, who say they were injured aloft—struck by blocks or cable-ends. The other two are steerage passengers. All four are being held and questioned, but I already have a good idea of the guilty party. His name does not matter, but his own wife admits the man is a deathsmoker, and such addicts will kill for a few cockles to buy their next pipe. Oh yes, there's deathsmoke down in steerage, m'lady, and matches, too. Of course, fire is forbidden—but what are ship's rules to one who will stab an innocent man?"

"But . . . don't third-class passengers get locked in at night?"

"Indeed they do," said Ott. "And no one recalls seeing this man return to steerage at nightfall."

"So he hid somewhere else in the ship, and waited?"

"Exactly so. And the smell of the drug was everywhere about him."

Thasha took a deep breath. A deathsmoker! Pazel's fears, and her own, began to seem far-fetched. And yet Ramachni *knew* a conspiracy was under way, an evil mage awaiting his moment to strike. And then there were Hercól's own fears, the man killed in her garden, the Red Wolf . . .

"Of course, we will take no chances," said Ott. "None of the suspects will leave our sight for a moment, from here to the port of Uturphe."

"By Uturphe, Hercól may be dead."

Ott was silent a moment. "Perhaps," he said. "But I have seen more wounds than anyone should in a single lifetime. I'm a fair judge of death's approach. Your Hercól has a warrior's toughness, m'lady. For what it's worth, I expect him to live."

Ott's words made something snap inside her. She found herself shaking. "I'm sorry," she said. "I've been terrified for him. All along. I'm not used to fear, but now I'm sick with it for his sake."

"All along?" Ott asked gently, eyebrows knitting. "Before the attack as well?"

Thasha nodded. A moment later it burst from her: "I don't trust Syrarys. I never have. I can't tell my father—he's too much in love with her to listen. I don't know what to do."

"Dear lady!" said Ott, taking her arm. "I think you know exactly what to do, for you have just done it. You have told me your fears."

"Should I have?" she asked softly. "I mean, I hardly know you."

"But I have known you all your life—from a distance. No favorite of His Supremacy is without a guardian officer like myself. When Admiral Isiq married your esteemed mother, I guarded the outer temple. When she died, I stood watch at the cemetery."

Thasha looked at him in astonishment. "You . . . were *there*?"

"When you were born," said Ott, "my guard company built the summerhouse that stands in your garden, as a token of the Emperor's affection. Your mother loved that garden. What a tragedy she enjoyed it so briefly."

A lump swelled in Thasha's throat. This old man had protected them her whole life, and never asked for a thank-you. "But why did you stop guarding us?" she said.

"I received new orders," he said. "When you get to be as old as I am, your Emperor must consider how he will replace you. I was given the honor of training a new generation of the Imperial Guard. You were but five or six. Now that training is complete, and in his generosity the Emperor has allowed me to protect his favorite admiral—and new ambassador—one last time."

"Was it you who shot that man in my garden, then?"

Ott shook his head, pursing his lips with regret. "Merely a man who works for me. The intruder should have been kept alive, and questioned. But my man feared for your safety."

How could he, Thasha wondered, with Jorl and Suzyt holding that ragged stranger in their teeth? But before she could ask, she noticed Ott glancing up and down the passage. Certain they were alone, he reached into his pocket and drew out—

"My necklace!" Thasha cried. "Commander! How in the world did you get it?"

"I'm old, Lady, but still quick." Ott grinned and raised a sleeve: there was a fresh, deep scratch on his forearm. "That Sniraga is a hell-cat, but I caught her tail and spanked her till she howled, and made her let go of this pretty thing. I knew it from your mother's neck, you see. Won't you let me fasten it anew?"

Thasha turned and lifted her hair. "I'll never let it out of my sight again," she said as Ott sealed the clasp. "Oh, Commander, thank you! My father said you were a good man, but I had no idea."

"You flatter me, Lady. But I should prefer your trust. For your father's sake, tell me all that troubles you about the Lady Syrarys. Hold nothing back, I beseech you."

So Thasha did. Once she began to speak, she realized how little she actually knew for certain. Syrarys had pretended to love Thasha as a girl, and discarded her once her place in the household was secure. She had pretended to miss Thasha when she vanished into the Lorg, pretended to be worried about her father's health (why had no doctor besides Chadfallow ever come to see him?), pretended to want nothing from life but a place at his side.

"But it's not true. She wants *much* more. And now she pretends to visit the powder room each night after dinner, but doesn't. She's going somewhere else."

"Tonight, for instance?" said Ott.

"Tonight she did go," admitted Thasha unhappily.

"Ah," said Ott.

"You think I'm a fool."

Ott shook his head. "On the contrary. I am humbled by your insight."

"Don't say that unless you mean it," she pleaded. "Commander Nagan, this isn't the babble of a jealous daughter. Promise me you'll take this seriously!"

Sandor Ott took her hand. "Forty-eight years have I served

the Ametrine Throne," he said. "I was just your age when I took the oath, at the feet of His Supremacy's grandfather. *Mind and marrow, bone and blood, to strive till my hand drop the sword and my soul leave the flesh. For Arqual, her glory and gain.* Believe me, Lady Thasha: I take nothing more seriously than that."

-23-

The Miracle of Tears

A gray dawn came, and rain soon after. Thunderheads brooded on Cape Ultu; Firecracker Frix watched them nervously through a telescope. Beyond that cape lay Uturphe, but Mr. Elkstem took no chances and steered a wide course around its rocky point. A hundred sailors sighed at his orders, but no one cursed him. Elkstem's nose for safety was legendary.

Once around the cape the rain grew stronger. Hatches were battened down; frantic tarboys swabbed rainwater off the deck. The town when it appeared was less than heartwarming: behind its green granite wall, iron towers and pointed rooftops stood like files of teeth. From his cabin window, Eberzam Isiq studied cold, closed Uturphe and thought, *No place to look for doctors.*

The town lacked a deepwater channel, so at a distance of two miles the order came to furl sails and drop anchor. Around the mainmast a handful of men in oilskin coats roared their disapproval. These were whiskey and brass merchants, desperate to buy as much as they could for resale in the west. Before the anchor struck bottom they were clustered about Mr. Fiffengurt. When might the boats be launched? How bad would the storm be? How many men could he spare for rowers? How long would they stay?

"Stand off, gentlemen!" he growled. "We've a life to save if we can."

Hercól was carried out by Isiq's honor guard. Rain battered his face, and Thasha held his cold hand, weeping: he looked dead already. For the first time, Fiffengurt thought he might like one of the noble-born youths. Most were ninnies who wailed if their soup wasn't salted or their jackets brushed. One day of tar-boy labor and galley grub would teach them to appreciate good fortune. But Lady Thasha was a different sort. She was crying, yes, but silently, and she made no complaints. The quartermaster cocked his head sideways, to see her better.

"You be brave now, Lady," he said. "Everything possible will be done for Mr. Hercól."

"That it will be," said Sandor Ott.

The boat was lowered, with Ott and Fiffengurt side by side in the bow, and the men pulled for shore. Thasha felt suddenly that she would never lay eyes on Hercól again, and not wanting her last memory of him to be that white, deathly face, she turned away. If she had not, she might have noticed that one of the honor guards did not row with his right arm, but only moved it stiffly, even painfully, in time with the oar.

Merchants were crowding, jostling to be next into a boat. One cackled beside her: "No one will eat crayfish in Uturphe tonight—no one! I bought them all. I can sell them on Rukmast for four times what I pay these beggars. A few didn't want to sell, but the duke of Uturphe persuaded them—fishermen's huts are quite flammable, you know, and the duke only asked ten percent for his services."

"Very reasonable," said another.

"Very! Oh, when will that fool let us land? I tell you I bought them *all*."

Disgusted, Thasha turned—and nearly collided with Pazel Pathkendle.

He was being hustled aft by two enormous soldiers. He had a soggy bundle in his arms and wore an old coat with a red patch at the elbow. No hat, no shoes. His brown hair was plastered flat by the rain.

He offered a weary smile. "You got your necklace back."

The soldiers appeared ready to cuff him for his familiar tone, but one look at Thasha changed their minds.

"I tried to make Prahba keep you," she said. "He just wouldn't listen."

Pazel shrugged. "I didn't listen either, did I? Where's Neeps, do you know?"

Thasha nodded. "He's working the pumps. Six hours—a punishment from Swellows. For fighting, I think."

"Tell him I said to cut that out," said Pazel, shaking his head. Then he looked at her and switched to Opaltik. "Don't forget what Ramachni said. There's an evil mage aboard, and someone else coming soon—someone even worse. Be careful, Thasha. And try to remember me, will you?"

Thasha could barely summon her school-taught Opaltik. *What's wrong with me?* she thought, blinking.

"Someone worse, yes," she muttered.

"I'm sorry about all this, Thasha," he said.

"Sorry you?" She shook her head, furious with her clumsy tongue. "Why are you feeling it? I have no ideas."

Shivering and drenched, Pazel laughed. "You have too many."

The soldiers pushed him forward. Merchants and sailors were crowding into the second boat, but one bench was empty still.

"I have to tell you something," said Pazel. "Get closer."

"I have to tell *you* something," Thasha mimicked. But she could not say it in Opaltik, and when he looked her in the eye she found she could not say it at all.

"Hold that man! I want to see him!"

The voice was Uskins'. He emerged from the wheelhouse, his blond hair flattened by the rain, and shoved his way toward the boats. Thasha followed his gaze and saw another prisoner beside the rail: a scruffy, hungry-looking man from third class. His face was sallow and bruised, and his hands were chained behind his back.

"Wrong man! Wrong man!" he shouted as Uskins neared. The first mate raised a hand for silence, then reached out and stretched one of the man's eyes wide open. He gave a satisfied nod.

"A deathsmoker, to be sure."

"Lies!" shrieked the man. "They put a gooney sack on my head! Filled it with deathsmoke!"

"Who did?" said Uskins.

"Don't know—they come at night, took me someplace dark, alone. Made me breathe that blary drug till I fainted. Now look how I shake! But I never used it before! I'm a tea picker is all!"

Uskins laughed aloud. "You should have picked a milder tea."

"I never touched that poor Mr. Hercól! I swear on the Milk of the Tree!"

Uskins slapped him. "Save your blasphemy for the court, you wretch! Load him in!"

As the man screamed and struggled, Thasha found herself beginning to doubt Nagan's story all over again. But before she could work out a way to intervene, Pazel leaned close to her and spoke very quietly through his teeth.

"There's another prisoner aboard."

"What are you talking about?" Thasha whispered back.

"You've got to find Diadrelu. Tell her Rose has him. In his right-hand desk-drawer."

"What, a key?"

"The prisoner!"

"Pazel," said Thasha, "have you lost your mind?"

"They'll kill you if you talk," he whispered. "They're ixchel, Thasha."

"Ay! Ormali dog! How dare you touch the Lady?"

He hadn't, in fact, although his lips had nearly brushed her ear. But touch or no touch, Pazel's guards were embarrassed at their oversight and struck him so hard he fell to the deck. Almost blind with pain, Pazel felt someone lifting him again. Uskins' leering face swam into view.

"Allow me," said the first mate. "Some ballast is a pleasure to drop."

He tossed Pazel into the waiting boat with a crash. Thasha shouted, *"No! No! No!"* and Uskins turned to her and said not to worry, the filthy boy would never bother her again.

Pazel found his seat beside the presumed murderer, who was still shouting, *"Wrong man!"* Pazel looked for Thasha, wondering what she had wanted to tell him, but the rail was crowded, and then his boat was lowered to the sea.

"You saw it," said Talag Tammaruk ap Ixhxchr.

"Saw what?" asked Diadrelu.

"Do not fence with me, sister," said Talag. "The boy whispered in the bridal girl's ear. And shocked her. Now do you see why we must never take chances? What good are your threats, once he is safe ashore? Taliktrum was right. You should have killed him."

The two ixchel were wedged in the solid oak of the quarterdeck, half choked with fresh sawdust, peering through drill holes no human eye could locate. Their spying ledge was scarcely big enough for them to lie side by side. It had taken their people four days' labor, burrowing like termites through the ancient wood, pausing with every lull in the wind lest their chisels and hammers be overheard. But it was worth it: they now had a splendid view of the mizzen topdeck, where boats disembarked and officers clustered, the very crossroads of the ship.

Dri pulled back from her spy-hole and looked at Talag. "Thasha was scared, true enough. But what did Pathkendle whisper? That is something we cannot presume."

"Can't we?" said Talag. "Do you mean to say the freak tarboy might possess *another* secret as awful as the fact that we're aboard?"

"There are such secrets," said Dri. "Last night we saw the ambassador's own guard torment an innocent man with deathsmoke and demand that he confess to the murder we prevented."

"You take the lot of them for *innocent men,*" said Talag derisively. "And *you* prevented that murder, not the clan. You fired the quill into the murderer's leg and made him stumble, even though that fat soap merchant might have seen you—"

"He saw *nothing*," said Diadrelu.

"—and the killer himself may find your quill later and expose us all."

"He will not find my quill, Talag. It is deep in his skin. And should he dig it out, he will find a splinter, half dissolved, and never know it for ixchel work."

"Who is presuming now?" Talag asked.

"What would you have done?" she demanded. "Let the valet die?" She knew Talag was goading her (who but a brother could do it so well?), but knowing did not make his taunts any more bearable. "I am not a fool, Talag! I presume no goodness among giants. But neither do I presume that they are all identical, mere strands in a single rope destined to be the hangman's noose for the *innocent* race of ixchel. The world is full of wickedness, yes. But none of it is simple."

"They stole us from Sanctuary-Beyond-the-Sea. They exhibited us like insects in their museums, colleges, zoos. And like insects they have killed us, ever since we escaped to infest their ships and houses. Simple, Dri. And true."

"The Abduction was five hundred years ago," said Dri. "The giants don't even remember it, and they consider our island a myth. It's *over*."

Talag looked at her with cold disdain. "It will be over when we are home," he said. "Since the wreck of the *Maisa* only one ship remains that can take us there, across the Ruling Sea. Her name is *Chathrand,* and by the sweet star of Rin, I'll see that she does."

Dri said nothing. A moment later the ship's bell rang half past eight.

"We must go," said Talag.

Moving about in the daylight was, of course, the gravest danger for the ixchel, yet there was no other way to reach the spy-ledge. Like the hollow at the center of an old tree, their tunnel bored straight down through the compartment wall, then back toward the stern by way of a two-inch gap they had found by tapping. Near the end of this crawlway Talag had drawn an X in charcoal: that marked the spot directly beneath the binnacle, or ship's compass. Talag had plans for the binnacle, but he would tell no one what they amounted to.

The crawlway ended in a tiny crack, at the ceiling of a short passageway. From there all one had to do was scurry down the rough wood to the floor, run six feet along the passage to the foot-drain and dive inside. During a storm, a bathtub or two of rain and salt spray might blow into the passage each time a sailor came in from the topdeck. The foot-drain was merely the tin pipe that let such water flow back into the sea. It had a little spring-loaded lid that swung open with the weight of water and shut again to keep out the cold ocean wind. For the ixchel it was a simple matter to cut other holes in this pipe (along its top edge, to control any telltale dripping) and use it as a corridor between the decks.

The trouble was the battalion clerk. A pale boy with the scars of recent chicken pox on his face, he crouched on a stool by the door to Sergeant Drellarek's cabin from dawn to dusk, a big weather-stained notebook on his knees. His only functions were to carry messages from Drellarek to the *Chathrand*'s officers and to keep records of the shifts and duties, the complaints and fevers and upset stomachs of the hundred soldiers under Drellarek's command.

The clerk was always there, except when running messages, and for five minutes at the change of the watch when Drellarek had him collect reports from the sergeants-at-arms and the sailmaster. Only at these times (and only if no one else was in the hall) could the ixchel come or go from their spy-ledge. Now was such a time, and Dri and Talag made haste to descend to the floor.

Even as they did so, Midryl, their replacement on watch, slipped out of the foot-drain and began climbing swiftly. When he reached the other two he paused for instructions.

"You will pay great attention to any new passengers who board today," said Talag. "And make a note of who speaks to the captain, should he appear."

"Yes, m'lord."

"The ambassador may go ashore as well," Dri added. "See that you notice who goes with him, and who returns."

"Of course, m'lady."

"The way is clear below?" Talag demanded.

"Safe and clear, Lord Talag. A rat limped by on the gun deck, nothing more. My brother Malyd is on watch."

"Go swiftly, then."

Midryl bowed his head and vanished into the crevice above. Dri and Talag reached the floor and hurried to the foot-drain. They could hear the voices of giants on the topdeck, the hiss of rain, the soggy, low-spirited gulls.

But the drain's lid would not open. Normally it swung with almost no effort at all, but though Dri and Talag pushed with all their might, it would not budge an inch.

"That fool!" Talag raged. "He's broken the hinge from the inside!"

Together they hurled themselves against the metal lid, but to no avail.

"We're trapped!" said Dri. "But what happened? How could this be an accident?"

"It was not an accident, Lady Dri," said a voice from the foot-drain.

"Who goes there, damn it—a rat?" snarled Talag in disbelief.

"No, Lord Talag," said the voice. "I am Felthrup Stargraven, and I must thank you for teaching me a great—nay, a vital—nay, an *indispensable* lesson! You see, I am not a rat. And yet I suffered so very long believing that I was. Believing, babbling, drowning in kelp—"

"Vermin!" shouted Talag. "Get your mange-rotted bodies out of our pipe!"

"I am quite alone, Lord Talag. I have jammed the door with a timber-screw."

"Remove it now," said Diadrelu quietly. "We are in danger, here."

"I regret that, m'lady," said Felthrup. "But surely you understand my own desperate circumstances? Once Lord Talag explained to me that I was not a rat, I realized it was madness—literally madness!—to go on pretending. The warren is no place of safety if you rouse the suspicion of Master Mugstur, as I have, or bear any disfigurement or sign of weakness, as I do. Are you aware of how you marked me, Lord Talag?"

Dri looked sharply at her brother. "You've spoken to this creature before!"

"Souls aflame!" shouted Talag. "It can't be that one! The same prattling, snooping rat we caught in Night Village?"

"The one who came looking for you," said the voice, "in such terrible need. Poor, frightened Felthrup, always drowning, so close to despair. But not a rat, m'lord. Have you forgotten your lecture? *Rats do not think; they only appear to think.* But I most certainly think—deep, true, tireless thoughts, machinations, meditations, bursting rockets of the mind! Therefore, despite my appearance I cannot be a rat. I think."

"You told me nothing of this," said Dri to Talag.

"Of killing a rat? Why should I? There was no bloodshed, even. We sealed him up in a bilge-pipe to suffocate."

"You see how I failed to oblige him, m'lady? I do so deeply regret it."

Dri could not tell if the voice was laughing or crying. "We have no time for this," she said. "What do you want?"

A sniffle. "You won't believe me," said the voice.

"OPEN THIS DOOR ERE WE SLAUGHTER THE WHOLE FESTERING HORDE OF YOU!" bellowed Talag.

The laughter or tears grew nearly hysterical.

Dri hissed at her brother: "Haven't you done enough? It's your cruelty drove him to this act!"

Talag opened his mouth to speak, but did not. The human voices on the deck outside grew louder.

"You there, Felthrup!" said Dri. "A giant comes! Speak now, or we both must flee. What is it you would ask of us?"

"A small thing," said the choking voice. "Your oath on the clan: not to hurt me, and to listen."

"You have my oath on the clan," said Dri.

"You cannot give your oath to a *rat,*" said Talag.

"I am *NOT A RAT*!"

"Talag!" said Diadrelu. "Stop taunting him! Where is your wisdom gone? Speak your oath, quickly, or mount to the crevice! Decide!"

Talag's fists were clenched so tight that veins stood out on his hands. "You have my oath by clan and kin," he said.

That very instant the outer door banged open and the pock-marked clerk appeared. At the same time they heard a scraping behind the foot-drain. The boy fumbled with the door in the slashing rain, still turned away from them. Talag pushed: the lid was free, and both ixchel dived into the pipe. Beside them, Felthrup let the lid snap shut. Brother and sister lay motionless where they fell, holding their breath. From inches away came the sound of the boy's heavy footfalls. He was swearing at the weather—Salvation!—for if he had just seen two crawlies he would have forgotten all about a little rain.

Quiet as shadows, the ixchel crawled down the pipe; Felthrup scurried behind them with a strange hopping sound. Only after fifty feet, where the pipe took a bend in a cable shaft far from human ears, did the odd threesome pause. They were as safe there as anywhere. Diadrelu struck a match and saw two black eyes gleaming next to her.

"But of course you're a rat," she said.

Then she winced. The beast's left forepaw was hideously mangled. That explained the hopping. Felthrup saw her look and nodded.

"The price of living," he said. "Four days I lay trapped in that pipe, m'lady. Clearing the dried blood with my teeth, so air might trickle in."

"Your name," said Diadrelu. "It sounds like a Noonfirth word."

"How wise you are, Lady!" said Felthrup in delight. "For I am a Noonfirther, and the name I chose myself. The word means 'tears.' Do you know what a miracle tears are, Lord and Lady?

Rats do not shed them: rats cannot grasp what they are for. And I was no different from any other beast in Pól Warren until the sunrise I tried to steal crumbs from a bakery. The fresh bread smelled so very tempting that morning, honeyed and butter-kissed—"

"Memories of the stomach," said Talag. "Is *that* why you risked our deaths?"

"No, Lord Talag, but it is part of why you should not wish to kill me."

"Tell your tale," said Diadrelu. "But quickly, pray."

Felthrup bowed. "It was still dark. By a broken window I leaped into the basement, then crept up the stairs and peeped into the bakery proper. There she stood! By the clay oven, her black face glowing by firelight. The first thing I saw was that she was alone. Always before her husband had worked beside her, but now he was gone. Why did I even notice? He had not taken the crumbs with him; there was plenty for me to eat. But somehow I could only stand there, watching, wondering. And the woman went into another room and returned with a painting of the two of them in wedding finery—how did I know, how?—and with a strange moan she threw the painting into the oven. Then she sat back on a stool. And cried!

"I saw her tears, cousins. And in that instant the great change occurred. I was shaken, terrified. I thought some parasite was erupting in my bowels. Yet it was not an affliction but a miracle: I had noticed tears. She was weeping for love and I understood it. And so much else, miracle after miracle! Her noise woke her little girls, they came thumping down from the loft—and suddenly, family! I grasped that, too! And names—she spoke their names, and I knew they were *permanent* names, not made up on the spot like *wart-face* and *slop-head* and other names used by rats. I sat there as the daylight grew, blind to my danger, hypnotized. She told them their father had run off with the butter-churn girl, and that they must all go to temple and pray that he quickly tired of that fat, faithless slut and came back to them. And then she pulled the picture from the oven and smothered the flames with her apron. But his head and feet were burned off already, and she cried to wake the dead. *And I understood it all!*"

Dri looked at her brother. "Are you satisfied, Talag? The rat is clearly woken. You tried to kill an innocent, thinking soul."

Talag looked away. "Next it will be fleas," he said. "And then barnacles, cabbages, scraps of wood. This ship is infested with freaks. In all history there has never been a truly woken rat. How was I to know this babbling thing possessed reason?"

"By using your own."

"We are fighting for our lives," said Talag. "That creature was a danger to our fort in Night Village. Three times he blundered about us, drawing attention, speaking aloud. And so far I've heard nothing about why."

Felthrup looked at Talag. His nose twitched.

"Oh good and gracious Lord!" he said. "How you always return me to my purpose! I bow, I sigh, I wheeze my gratitude! Will you forgive me if—just to make things simpler, marvelous Talag—I once again call myself a rat?"

"Get on with it!" spat Talag.

"Then, as a rat—as a *woken* rat—I must tell you that I am not quite alone."

"What!" cried Dri. "Do you mean that there is *another* woken rat aboard?"

"Yes, m'lady, just one. The only one I have ever met. He rules the warren, and he is thoroughly evil and depraved. His name is Master Mugstur."

"Have you spoken with this creature?"

"Yes, m'lady, but I did not let him know I was awake. He would certainly have killed me, for he wants no rivals."

"What *does* he want?" said Talag.

"He wants to eat the captain."

There was a rather long pause.

"Specifically his tongue," Felthrup continued. "The reason is simple enough. After he woke, Master Mugstur became religious, you see. He is a quite fanatical adherent to the Rinfaith—although his version of it is somewhat . . . what is the word?

Homicidal? Yes, exactly! Oh, Lady Dri, do you know how I have dreamed of such enlightened conversation? A rat would say *blary, bloody, munchy, delicious*—never *homicidal*! I am the luckiest being alive!"

"Felthrup," said Dri.

"Yes, yes! Forgive me! The point is, Captain Rose has also declared himself a believer, but he is only pretending. He takes meals with Brother Bolutu and has the man set him lessons from the Ninety Rules, but he never studies them: the old witch Oggosk answers all the questions. He says he will retire to a life of quiet prayer on Rappopolni, when in fact the Emperor has already promised him governorship of the Quezans, and many slave-wives, and a royal title. This has infuriated Master Mugstur, who will allow no one to disrespect the faith."

"Skies of Fire!" said Talag. "Rose is to govern the Quezans? He must be doing something unspeakable for the Crown!"

"We know he is," said Dri. "But what does this Mugstur imagine he can do about it?"

"Eat his tongue," said Felthrup. "It is his fate to kill Rose, he thinks. My miracle was tears; Master Mugstur's was betrayal. He watched a man selling Nunekkam emeralds to a jeweler. 'These are splendid!' said the jeweler. 'How did you come by them?' 'Oh, the Nunek gave them to me!' The other laughed. 'He needed them sent to his granddaughter in Sorhn, as a wedding gift. It's been planned for three years, that wedding. And for three years I've made it a point to be that Nunek's best friend. So when I happened to tell him I was traveling to Sorhn on business, he asked me to deliver them to the bride. Said he would trust no one else, ha ha!' "

"Very rat-like," said Talag.

"Not at all rat-like, Majestic Lord," said Felthrup. "Normal rats may lie to one another, or jump out of shadows and bite. But betray they cannot, for betrayal is not possible without trust, and rats never trust. They do not understand the word."

"He woke at that moment, as you woke in the bakery?" asked Dri.

"He did, Lady, and his waking frightened him half to death. He ran all night in the streets, and just before dawn took refuge in a temple, where the droning of the monks and the burning incense put him into a state of religious fervor, and the Angel of Rin descended from the rafters and told him his fate. He would find his way to a great mansion that moved, the Angel said, and rule its depths, while a false priest ruled above. And one day he would kill that priest and devour the part of him that lied. And in that moment a thousand eyes would open."

"Rose is the false priest, then," said Dri, "and his tongue is the lying part of him. But what of the thousand eyes?"

"I do not know. Master Mugstur only speaks of his prophecy because he thinks we are all normal rats, sleepwalkers, and will not remember it anyway. But he is determined to punish Rose for pretending to believe. No matter what it takes."

"What will he try? Sabotage?"

"My lady, he would sink the ship if the Angel wished it. Or try, in any case: I doubt he could manage anything so grand."

"He could destroy us nonetheless," said Talag. "If his mischief irritates the giants sufficiently they will gas the ship with sulphur. Every rat aboard will be killed or driven out. And every last ixchel."

"There will still be one," said Felthrup. "A prisoner by the name of Steldak."

"An ixchel prisoner!" cried Talag. "But he is not of our clan! Who is he? Where are the giants keeping him?"

"I don't know, Lord Talag. I only know that he is kept in a tiny cage and forced to taste the giants' food, in case there should be poison. He is said to be the most miserable of beings."

Talag looked at Dri, rage contorting his face. "All over, sister? All in the past? How can you be so blind? While you talk of fairness the giants keep us in cages yet, and torture us for sport. Why speak of peace with these animals?"

"Some try to build peace," said Diadrelu. "Some make it their goal in life."

"Like our good Captain Rose, and his peaceable mission to the west."

"How wry, Lord Talag!" said Felthrup, happy again. "For the *Chathrand*'s mission is black indeed. I know it all: a most, most . . . *calamitous* plan. That's the word! Shall I tell you?"

Before they could answer, noises echoed down the pipe: far-off human footfalls, a squeak of metal. A sudden breeze swept past them.

"The drain has opened!" said Dri.

"The storm must be rising!" Talag raised his head, listening. "Brace yourselves—here it comes!"

"It?" said Felthrup.

A great gush of stormwater barreled into them. Felthrup squealed piercingly—drowning of one sort or another was his deepest fear, after all—but in truth he was not in much danger. Dri, however, was knocked off her feet. She was lighter than Talag (and barely half Felthrup's weight), and the water bore her down the pipe like a twig. Her brother could not reach her, but Felthrup saw her and recovered himself. As she swept by he caught her shirt with a nimble snap of his jaws, and held fast. Ten seconds later the gush of water subsided. Diadrelu put a hand on his cheek in silent thanks.

Soaked and chilly, they descended the last length of pipe to the ixchel's escape hatch. Here Talag paused and faced the rat.

"We owe you our thanks," he said gruffly, "for your courage, and your warnings. Now we know that it will be necessary to kill this Master Mugstur."

"That may be harder than you imagine, Lord," said Felthrup.

Talag actually smiled. "We shall see about that. Come! My cooks will feed you something better than rat-scrabble. And you will share what you know of *Chathrand*'s true mission."

They pulled themselves up through the hatch and into a dim triangular chamber. This was the canvas room, in the back of the tailor's nook, a cramped compartment piled floor to ceiling with pennant silks, tarpaulins and huge bolts of white, flaxen, nearly indestructible sailcloth. They were on a wide shelf about five feet above the floor.

Somewhere in the outer compartment the tailor was humming a flat little tune beneath his swaying lamp. Diadrelu squeezed the water from her shirt.

"Felthrup," she said, "how did you learn about the ixchel prisoner?"

"And the mission of the *Chathrand,* for that matter?" put in Talag.

"The same way he learned about this tunnel of yours, crawly," said a low, rasping voice overhead. "I told him."

The two ixchel flew like arrows, dodging, rolling, drawing their swords even before they regained their feet. They were not a moment too soon. Five enormous rats pounced on the spot where they had stood a split second before, knocking Felthrup aside like a bowling pin.

"Hold that door!" snapped the voice. "Two die for every crawly who escapes!"

Out of the mounds of sailcloth they came, dozens of rats of all shapes and sizes and hues. Many squirmed about the doorway. Others appeared at both ends of the shelf and advanced toward Dri and Talag, white teeth snapping.

"Well done, Felthrup!" said the rasping voice. "I am glad of your service."

On the shelf above them appeared the largest rat Diadrelu had ever seen. He slouched forward to examine them, attended on either side by formidable guards. He was stark white with purplish eyes that bulged like overripe grapes. The hair had fallen or been worn away from his head and underside, revealing long scars and thick rolls of fat. But despite his belly dragging in the dust it was clear he was immensely strong.

Felthrup gazed at him with loathing. "I do not serve you!" he cried.

"Of course you do," said the big rat. "All rats on this ship serve Master Mugstur, just as he serves our holy Emperor in the Keep of Five Domes, and through him the Angel Most High.

I'm not surprised you kept it from these two, of course. Yes, it was *very* well done. They were so caught up with your chatter they did not even notice the missing guard."

Dri and Talag exchanged looks. It was true: an ixchel guard should have been standing by at the mouth of the escape hatch. The rats snickered, and several of the biggest licked their lips.

"Lies!" screamed Felthrup. "You told me nothing! It was the bird, the moon falcon, who told me what I know! I hate you! I would never do your bidding!"

Master Mugstur shook his head slowly. "Lying is a sin," he said.

There were now a hundred or more sleek, strong rats crowded together in the nook, all watching the ixchel.

"Lady! Lord Talag!" squeaked Felthrup. "Don't listen! Run back up the pipe!"

Master Mugstur laughed. "By all means, do! One way leads to the sea; the other to the clerk on his stool. And we shall follow close behind you."

Talag caught Dri's eye a second time. With the greatest caution he signaled her: two fingers on his sword-hilt and a lifted shoulder. Dri answered with the tiniest nod.

"Tell them the truth ere they die, Felthrup," said Master Mugstur. "They tried to kill you, brother! Why shouldn't you lead them into my trap?"

"Monster! Fiend!" Felthrup was hopping up and down on his three good legs, tearful and snarling at once. "You used me to trap them! You followed me!"

"Where is our kinsman, the one we left on guard here?" Talag demanded.

For an answer the big rat spat at one of his aides. There was a shuffling noise above and then something ragged fell onto the shelf in front of them.

It was the hand of an ixchel, nibbled almost to the bone.

"Rats of *Chathrand*," said Master Mugstur, "you heard the crawlies' words: they planned to kill me, as they tried to kill Brother Felthrup. But thanks to my agent's courage and the mercy of Rin, their wickedness ends here. Let us pray before we dine."

Mugstur raised one long-nailed paw. The rats grew still.

And the ixchel sprang.

Talag leaped straight up, grabbed the lip of the shelf above him and swung onto it. Even as he landed he beheaded the rat lurching toward him, jumped over the corpse and slit the throat of another. Dri meanwhile ran up the side of a heap of sailcloth. The mound tipped, and as it did so she leaped high into the air and landed on the shelf beside her brother.

When ixchel train together, the battle-dance they learn becomes so quick and flawless it seems almost like mind-reading, and Dri and Talag had trained as a pair from birth. Not even a glance was needed for Dri to fall to hands and knees, and then push with all her might when she felt Talag's foot upon her shoulder. In this way she helped him sail over the heads of five rats and land upon the back of one of the two great bodyguards of Mugstur himself. The beast rolled and struck, but only succeeded in helping Talag to chop off both its forepaws with one swing. When the second rat-guard snapped at his leg, Talag did not even look: he had seen Dri move from the corner of his eye. The rat died with her throwing-knife in its skull before it could tighten its jaws.

About six seconds had passed.

But there were more rats now. They came on with idiot fury, biting at Talag and Dri as Mugstur fell back, roaring. The ixchel pressed after him, spinning like lethal tops through a spray of blood and fur. Then came a great crash as something heavy, a toolbox or a pair of sail-shears, crashed from a high shelf to the ground. Twenty feet away they heard the tailor bellow, *"Ho there! What moves?"* Lamplight swung toward the room.

The ixchel were fortunate. Mugstur had ordered so many rats to guard the door that they could not all hide themselves before the tailor arrived. One rat would have startled him; dozens made him erupt in an incoherent yowl. As he stomped and cursed at the fleeing rats, Dri and Talag slid down one side of the door frame and escaped the room.

Neither had been so much as scratched. But what of Felthrup? Dri risked one backward glance: she could see no trace of him among the living or the dead.

-24-

Bad Manners

The tailor never reported the incident.

Rats in his corner of the ship could only be explained by one thing: food. No sailor was allowed to store food of any sort in his work area—and Rose, as the tailor well knew, hated hoarders above all things. A famous story involved a sailor on lookout who had once taken three apples with him to the crow's nest. Rose found out inside an hour, docked him a week's pay and forbade the crew from addressing him by any name but *hog* for the rest of the voyage. He had noticed an apple seed on the deck.

The tailor had no doubt that *someone* had brought food into the canvas room, and he delivered a blistering warning to the tarboys on the evening watch.

"Get this into your brains right now: food means crumbs. Crumbs mean rats. Rats mean nests and nibblin'. You want holes in the sails when a storm blows up, or when pirates have us in their sights?"

Among these boys was Jervik. He was angry at being assigned to what he called *girly work* and behaved with extra savagery the next morning at breakfast.

"What you know about sailing ain't worth a gull's thin spit," he told the boys at his table. "Food in the canvas room! Who did it? Speak up, you useless ninnies! You!" He pointed at Reyast.

"Always the slowest eater! I'll bet you slipped leftovers into your pockets and munched 'em on the sly."

"L-l-leftovers? N-n-n-n—"

"You calling me a liar, stutter-slug?"

Reyast looked down at his boiled beef. He nodded vigorously.

Amazed, Jervik reached out and slammed Reyast's face into his food. Neeps erupted. He leaped from the bench and hit Jervik three times before the other boy knew what was happening. When he recovered from his shock he lifted Neeps with one hand, cuffed him on both cheeks and threw him over the table. Neeps bounced to his feet and would have rushed Jervik again, but the other boys held him back. It took all their strength.

Hours later, his calm restored, Neeps put Jervik's words together with some information of his own. His day had begun with a disgusting chore. The ash dump, which carried cinders and bones and other refuse from the galley to the sea, was blocked. Mr. Teggatz had ordered Neeps, as the smallest person aboard, to crawl inside with a plunger and solve the problem. What had Neeps found but rats! Scores of dead rats! And not dead from disease or traps but from severed heads and stabbed stomachs. Weirdest of all, they were wrapped up in sailcloth. It was as if someone had crept into the galley and pushed the whole bundle down the chute on the sly.

Slaughtered rats from the canvas room: what was happening here? Could it have anything to do with those secrets Pazel hadn't wanted to share?

Pazel! thought Neeps. *Couldn't you have held your blary tongue? What's become of you now? And what will become of the rest of us?*

What became of Pazel is easily told: he had been marched to the Harbor Master's office and formally struck from the Imperial Boys' Registry. The process took about three minutes, and with that his career at sea was over. No one cared; they did not even bother to frown at him. Tarboys were thrown off ships all the time.

"Sorry about them bruises, mate," said the guards from the *Chathrand,* hustling away into the rain. "Just doing our job."

"Don't mention it," said Pazel.

He lingered in the warmth of the Harbor Office, gazing out the window at Uturphe. It was the wettest city on the Nelu Peren, sailors said. Rain fell all year, except in the dead of winter when it turned to driving sleet. There were canals and open storm drains gushing forever into the sea, and hundreds of little footbridges with loose stones and no railings. The countryside was bleak, a place of wildcats and sulphur dogs, so Uturphe grew its food in rainwater tanks: lakeweed, mud radishes, snails. Would his dinner tonight be snails?

He sighed, and stepped out into the rain. But the door had not yet closed behind him when he saw an unwelcome face: Mr. Swellows was waiting for him beneath the eaves. The bosun's breath, as always, stank of liquor.

"There you are, Pathkendle!" he said. "Time to start a new life, eh?"

"Where's Mr. Fiffengurt?" asked Pazel, ignoring the bosun's smile. He had no idea why Swellows was there, but he doubted the reason could be good.

Swellows jerked a thumb down the avenue. "Still at the hospital, with poor Mr. Hercól and Commander Nagan."

"I should catch up with them," said Pazel. "Well, goodbye, Mr. Swellows."

"Half a moment!" Swellows placed a moist hand on his shoulder. "Listen: I know I ain't treated you too candy-sweet. But I meant no harm. Started off as a tarboy myself, you see."

"Oh," said Pazel, leaning away from the bosun's hand.

"You'll need some money to keep afloat, till you find work."

"My mates took up a collection," said Pazel. "They gave me eight gold."

"Eight!" boomed Swellows, and for a moment he seemed almost outraged. Then, lowering his voice, he said, "Why not— even for an Ormali? Well, here's a bit more."

He took out his purse and counted out eight gold cockles,

hesitated a moment, then dropped them into Pazel's hand. Pazel just stared at the coins. Eight gold was a considerable sum—enough for Pazel to live comfortably for a week.

"Why, sir?" he said at last.

The bosun looked at him with no trace of a smile. At last he said, "When I was your age, somebody did for me like I'm doin' for you now. Swore I'd never forget."

He held out his hand. Still uneasy, Pazel shook it.

"Don't waste money," Swellows said. "Respect it. Guard it!"

"But I don't even know where I'm going to sleep," Pazel admitted.

"Ah, that's hard," said Swellows. "Uturphe's a city of thieves. The only honest place is the inn on Blackwell Street. That's the spot for you."

"Blackwell Street," Pazel repeated.

"Tell 'em I sent ye. Now I must get back to the ship. Remember me, will you, Pathkendle?"

"I certainly will, sir. Thank you, sir."

Swellows stalked off drunkenly into the rain, head high, as if proud of his good deed. Pazel shook his head in wonder.

But there was no time to lose now. He ran up the street Swellows had indicated. He very much wanted to catch Fiffengurt at the hospital: away from the ship, he might get a chance to tell the quartermaster about the war conspiracy—if he could somehow do so without mentioning Ramachni or the ixchel.

He crossed bridges, leaped over drains. He'd find a way. Swellows' gift had raised his spirits: if kindness could come from *him* it could come from anywhere. And with sixteen gold he could buy a third-class passage out of Uturphe. *Maybe even back to Ormael!* After all, he was closer now than ever before.

But Hercól was not at the hospital.

The nurse at the entrance told Pazel briskly that no Mr. Hercól of Tholjassa had been admitted. Indeed, no one from the *Chathrand* had visited the hospital at all.

"Is there another hospital?"

She shook her head. "Not in Uturphe."

"There's some mistake," said Pazel. "Mr. Fiffengurt and Commander Nagan were bringing him here—an old fellow with one funny eye, and a short man with scars."

"Nothing of the kind," said the nurse.

"But I came ashore with them!"

The nurse looked at him coldly, as she might at a sack of flour. "These things happen. But you're in luck, young man. The morgue is just across the street."

Pazel had never visited a morgue, and ten minutes inside Uturphe's persuaded him never to do so again. The very bricks stank of death. Men on hands and knees, scrubbing viciously at the floor, made him wonder just what kind of stains they were trying to remove. But the mortician was delighted to have a visitor. Oh yes! he said. The poor fellow from the *Chathrand*. Was Pazel here to mourn?

"Then he's dead!" cried Pazel, grief-struck.

The man blinked at him. "It's how they come, you see. Dead. I meet with few exceptions."

He led Pazel across the spotless hall and down a long spiral stair. The air grew cold. At the bottom of the steps the man unlocked a door and revealed a room that perhaps you will not wish to imagine in detail. Suffice it to say that the morgue had been built for a smaller city in a more peaceful time, and that the room's thirty or forty occupants might well have complained of overcrowding, had they been in any condition to do so.

"Turn sideways—that's it," said the mortician, sidling up to a sheeted form on a dark stone table. "Here we are. Shall I give you a moment alone with your friend?"

He pulled back the sheet, and Pazel looked into the open eyes of a corpse. The man had dried blood in his hair and an expression of terrible surprise. But he was not Hercól.

"Something wrong?" asked the mortician. "You don't know this man?"

Pazel hesitated: in fact the man *did* look slightly familiar. But—

"This is not . . . who I expected," he managed to say. "You say he came from the *Chathrand*?"

"Why, yes, early this morning."

"But he's not in a sailor's uniform."

"No indeed. I gather he was some kind of special Imperial soldier. Part of an honor guard, they said. Name of Zirfet." He read the tag on the man's earlobe. "Zirfet Salubrastin. Delivered by one Commander Nagan, of Etherhorde. Funny chap, that Nagan. After the others left he took a long knife from the belt of the deceased and held it before the lad's face. 'I gave you this in the tower,' he says, 'but we both knew it was a loan, didn't we?' Those were his final words to the lad."

One of the Isiq family guards—dead! Pazel felt a sudden acute fear for Thasha. "Can you guess how this man died?" he asked.

"Guess!" said the mortician. "I can do better than that. Look at his head: grave trauma. Listen to him gurgle!" His fist thumped the corpse's chest. "That's *water* in his lungs, not blood. This man was struck from behind, fell into the sea and drowned. A tackle block, swinging loose from the yardarm. Happens constantly. I knew it before Nagan said a word."

"But I didn't hear about any such accident," said Pazel.

"Naturally you didn't. It happened just hours ago. Shall I tell you how I know that?"

Pazel politely declined. The mortician looked disappointed.

"Guess!" he repeated. "I'll quit the day I have to guess about such a simple case. Why, there's nothing else wrong with the man, except a broken wrist. And nobody ever died from that."

By evening Pazel was near despair. He had spent too long at the morgue, and sprinted toward the docks in a panic, hoping to catch someone, anyone, from the *Chathrand* willing to bear a message: Thasha and her father had to be told of Hercól's disappearance. But his wild dash had caught the attention of a city constable, who ran him down and carried him, deaf to all protests, to the door of a windowless stone prison with the words DEBTORS & INDIGENTS carved above the threshhold.

There Pazel had at last torn one hand free of the man's bear-hug, and in perfect desperation emptied the purse of sixteen gold at his feet. The constable saw his error at once: Pazel was no debtor, he was a thief. But he withdrew this charge as well when Pazel raked half the coins into a little pile beside the man's black boot.

By the time he at last reached the docks no one from the *Chathrand* was left ashore. Even worse, no one recalled seeing a contingent from the Great Ship, bearing a wounded man. It was a horrible, helpless feeling: Hercól was simply *gone*.

Pazel had accomplished one small thing. A pair of horsemen had passed him, trotting swift and grim toward the port. Their bright eyes and lean wolfhound faces reminded him suddenly of Hercól. Sure enough, when he ran after them, he heard them speaking Tholjassan.

When he shouted in their own tongue they wheeled their horses around.

"What ho? By your face you are no Tholjassan, yet you speak like one."

"I'm an Ormali, sir, but I've lost a Tholjassan friend. He is wounded, and I fear for his life."

Their faces darkened as he told them of Hercól's disappearance. "I shall alert the Tholjassan Consul," said one. "Lad, we thank you. But we are in haste for an even more terrible reason. News came with the dawn: our coast is under siege, and children have been taken hostage. We sail this hour for Tholjassa."

"Is it war?" asked Pazel, horrified. But the rider shook his head.

"Piracy, more likely. Yet war may come of it. We Tholjassans never start a fight, but we have finished many."

And off they raced without another word. Moments later Pazel realized that any ship bound for Tholjassa would pass close to Ormael, and flew to the port. But when he located the ship her first mate said that they could not squeeze another man aboard, and would in any case be making landfall at Talturi, not Ormael. Worse still, no Ormael-bound ship was expected for at least a week. If he was to have enough money left for his passage, Pazel would have to survive in Uturphe on less than half of what he'd expected.

Over a queasy dinner (cabbage and rice in snail oil) Pazel decided to try the Blackwell Street inn. Mr. Swellows' recommendation seemed almost reason enough to avoid the place—but then again, a cheap, safe bed was what he needed. He couldn't afford any luxury.

A baker pointed the way: past Wriggle Square, around the scrap-yard, left at the knife shop on the corner. The last turn brought him to Blackwell Street—but how narrow and dark it was! Had he made a mistake? No: here was the stone archway, and the green-tinted lamplight the baker had mentioned. The door in the arch stood open. Beyond it Pazel saw a courtyard, with some kind of urn or fountain at the center.

"Hello!"

Immediately a dark form rose to block his path. The figure was slightly shorter than Pazel, but very broad, with long arms and fingers. A red lantern on a hook behind him left his face in shadow but illuminated two enormous flat ears, like wild mushrooms sprouting on either side of his head.

"Stop!" hissed the man in a dry whisper. "I do not know thee! Speak thy business or be gone!"

"Good evening!" said Pazel, quite startled. "I want a room for the night, is all. I have money, truly! Mr. Swellows of the *Chathrand* sent me, with his compliments."

The ears moved slightly, and Pazel guessed the man was smiling.

"Swellows? Ah, that is a different matter! Pass and be welcome!"

This was more to Pazel's liking. The man turned with a swish of his cloak, at the same time drawing a hood over his face, and led the way across the courtyard. How oddly he walked! Was he a hunchback? Such unfortunates often worked as night watchmen, Pazel knew, to escape the staring eyes of day.

The object in the center of the courtyard was a well, Pazel

saw now. When they reached it his guide stopped and set one of his large hands upon the rim.

"Didst thou give money to Mittlebrug Swellows?" he asked sharply.

"Is that his first name?"

"Answer! Didst thou pay him?"

"No, sir. He gave *me* money, in fact."

At that the figure gave a dry, wheezing laugh. "He would as much."

The man bent over the well and shouted one word—*"Falurk!"* And Pazel turned and ran for his life.

Swellows had sold him out. The word meant "prisoner"—in what language he could not for the moment recall. But he knew who was to be imprisoned. The man (or thing) behind him gave a croak of surprise: clearly he had never dreamed the boy would understand.

Pazel made it through the stone arch. But even as he glimpsed the brighter streets beyond the alley something grabbed him by the ankle. It was a leather cord like a bullwhip, with a little iron ball at its tip. The ball whipped round his leg, and before Pazel could begin to unwind it he was yanked off his feet and dragged backward into the courtyard.

He drew his knife and slashed at the whip. Dark forms were hopping out of the well in twos and threes. Someone was closing the gate. He screamed, but a moist hand like the underside of a frog slapped over his mouth. A flash lit the hand like burning phosphor, and Pazel felt himself go limp.

The Flikkermen had him at last.

25

Birth of a Conspiracy

The black rat was fighting for his life.

He had barely escaped the stomping heel of the tailor, and the teeth of Master Mugstur's Holy Guard, by diving back into the storm-pipe through the ixchel's door. There was no escape at the top of the pipe with the boy seated at Drellarek's door. So Felthrup had run the other way, down and aft, toward the stern transoms and the roaring of the sea. Other rats were plunging in the same direction, blind with fear. At first they ignored him. But the wind grew louder, nearer—and suddenly there was the mouth of the storm-pipe, wide open to the heaving, green-black harbor.

It was then that the rats turned on him.

"Cursed Felthrup!" they cried. "Weird, sick, Angel-maimed! He shouted at the Master! He brought the crawlies to cut off our heads! Kill him, kill before he strikes again!"

"You're wrong!" Felthrup begged. "I never meant you harm! Mugstur's the wicked one! He enslaves you!"

But they would not listen: horror was stealing what little reason they had. Felthrup saw what would happen next. The rats ahead and behind would close in, jaws snapping, making him turn at bay. He would fight them off for a while—they were cowardly enough—but when he grew tired they would bite and hold fast. Then he would be torn to shreds.

In that split second he regretted his woken state no more. His mind was fast—lightning-fast, too fast for any normal life, but perfect for now. He saw his options at a glance. Beg for mercy and die. Feign death and die. Fight back uphill against number-less rats sworn to kill him, to say nothing of the humans, and die.

Or do what he feared most: risk drowning, face the sea. That way too death was overwhelmingly likely. It was simply not guaranteed.

Five rats between him and the pipe's mouth. *Five cousins to slay. Horror of horrors, to fill one's mouth with murder.* He began.

They were expecting more tears and hysteria, not resolute killing. He went through the first two like a spear and grappled with the third in a scratching, tearing blood-blind frenzy that made it dive under him and squeal away up the pipe. The last two had backed up to the very lip, so their tails waved in the open air. They were big creatures, squared off and ready for his charge. Felthrup looked at their broad shoulders, their bared teeth. Their paws.

He leaped backward, past the bodies of the dead rats. The two at the pipe's end hissed, snapped their jaws. What was he wait-ing for?

The ship pitched downward, and then they saw: too late. Felthrup shoved the corpses at them with all his might. Slick with blood, the pipe afforded no grip. One of the rats began to scrabble over the bodies, but Felthrup pressed on mercilessly. Living rat and dead fell together to the waves.

The second rat was slipping, too. But even as it did so it gave a last lurch and clamped its jaws on Felthrup's bad leg. There it swung, teeth biting bone, as Felthrup struggled to shake it loose without falling himself. Unimaginable pain! And from behind him came the sound of still more rats, closing in.

He was oozing toward the sea. He could not reach the biting rat. From the corner of his eye he saw that he'd been right, there was a way out, two other pipes that emptied alongside this one. *Wise Felthrup, so good at everything—*

He fell.

It was a sickening plunge. The waves yawned like a pit. Mindlessly the other rat kept gnawing him in midair. They glanced off the *Chathrand*'s sternpost, barely missed being dashed to pieces on the rudder-head and vanished into the pale froth of the ship's wake. The other rat, shocked by the frigid water, released him—but when they surfaced, there it was paddling toward him, delirious with hate. With only three good legs Felthrup could barely swim. He tried in vain to put distance between them.

"Think, brother!" he squeaked. "Why fight now?"

"To hurt you more in death, Angel's foe!"

"No angel—*ECH! PHHT!*—would want such a thing!"

They were both half drowned, scrabbling up and down waves like collapsing hillsides, watching the *Chathrand* slip farther out of reach. The other rat was snapping at his toes. *It's mad, utterly mad,* Felthrup realized—but the thought gave him sudden hope.

Turning, he deliberately let the rat catch hold of the stump of his tail—a good, solid mouthful. Then he held his breath, and dived.

As he guessed, the other rat again kept its jaws locked. But it was not expecting to be pulled underwater. Nor could it fully close its mouth. It gurgled. Felthrup did not bother to strike at it—he merely writhed and shook. Instinctively the other rat bit harder. But air was bubbling through its lips, and the sea was leaking in. By the time the rat saw what was happening it had nothing to do but drown.

An eternity passed before it died. Felthrup struggled upward, still yards beneath the surface, kicking at the dead face. Then he saw his own mistake—and knew his life was over. The rat had died with locked jaws. Its lungs were flooded. It would sink like a stone, and he would go with it.

Why fight now? His own question mocked him. What was the point of it all? He could chew off the rest of his tail and bleed to death, watching the ship depart. What good was that sort of death, this sort of life, the torture of intelligence? Better to sleep, rest as he had not rested in years, let the thinking stop—

A dark shape rose beneath him. It was an animal, about the size of a hound, but blunt-faced and whiskered. A seal! A great black seal! In an instant the creature pushed him to the surface.

"Steady, Felthrup my lad! I won't let you drown."

"PHLHHHHHPT!"

"You're quite welcome."

A woken seal! Felthrup had been rescued by a being like himself!

"Don't claw me, lad. I've got to get that corpse off your tail."

Some foul crunching noises, and the skull of the dead rat broke and fell away. Then the seal turned on its back and rose, and Felthrup was lifted from the water on its chest.

He was almost in tears. "Brother, savior! Bless you, all Gods and stars and angels and whatever there may be!"

The seal might have smiled slightly, but it said no word. Its eyes were trained on the *Chathrand,* now a good hundred yards away.

"How did you find me?" Felthrup asked.

"Your voice carried. Not far, but far enough."

"Good luck! Oh great good luck, at last! Oh beloved master seal! How can I ever repay you?"

"By not calling me such nonsense. I have a name. You shall know it presently."

Felthrup forced his mouth shut. The seal was obviously wise, and did not like his chatter. He looked himself over. He was not badly hurt, for both his wounded paw and stump-tail were rather leathery and tough. The salt in his wounds burned like fire, though, and at the same time he was quaking with cold. And the ship was still moving away.

"Good sir," he said in what he hoped was a more dignified voice, "you have saved my life. It is yours, to do whatsoever you like with."

"Don't need it—got my own."

"Indisputably, sir. But I should beg the liberty of commenting on a difference between your splendid form and my own, so commonplace and ugly. Rats can swim, you see, but nowhere near so well as yourself."

The seal scratched behind an ear with a flipper.

Felthrup went on. "I can assure you—ha ha, look, they've spread more sail!—that on the best of days I could not swim ashore from here. And perhaps even you would find it difficult to bear me so far."

Silence. The *Chathrand* was now at least a quarter mile off.

"That is to say—please pardon my bluntness, sir, we rats are so ill mannered—I must board that ship, or drown."

"Quite true," said the seal.

Felthrup gave up. There was no misunderstanding. He was stranded on the chest of a taciturn seal, probably driven mad by thinking (like Mugstur, like himself), who might tire of this game at any moment, roll over and depart. But at least there was someone to talk to.

"Have you been woken long, brother?" he asked.

"All my life," said the seal.

At this Felthrup forgot himself entirely. Nearly dancing on the stomach of the seal, he cried, "You were born awake! Like a human being! Oh glory, glory, wondrous world!"

The seal glanced briefly at Felthrup. Its dark eyes softened. "In my own world there is a children's tale," it said, looking back at the ship, "about a man who woke in prison. He opened his eyes from a dream that seemed the length of his life to find himself in a pitch-black cage. It was so dark he could not see his hand before his face, so small he could not sit upright. He lay trapped in this prison for ages. He thought at times that he could hear sounds beyond the cage, but no one answered his calls. He was entirely alone.

"After a long, long time, the man found a tiny latch with one fingernail. Once he freed the latch, a door swung open and joyfully the man squeezed through. Beyond, what he found was another cage—but this one was a bit larger, and had a little light from gray windows the size of sugar cubes. In the shadows he found that he was not alone. A woman was moving about the cage, feeling the walls. They embraced, and she cried, 'Welcome, brother! You can help me look for a door!'

"Together, in time, they found a second door, and beyond it, a still larger and brighter cage. In this cage some fair green moss grew in one corner, and four people were busy searching the walls.

"Do you understand, Felthrup? True waking is not like rising from your bed, or nest, or warren. It is emerging from one cage into a larger, brighter, less lonely cage. It is a task that is never done."

The black rat's heart was pounding, but he could not speak.

"No animal, no man, no thousand-year-old mage is perfectly awake," said the seal. "In fact, merely to think so is to fall a little asleep. Fear those who tell you otherwise—help them if you can. Ah! There she is!"

Felthrup followed his gaze: in one of the stern windows of the departing *Chathrand,* a tiny light had appeared. It winked out, gleamed anew, fell dark once more. This happened three times.

"Now for it, lad," said the seal, and dived.

Once again Felthrup found himself swimming. "Help!" he cried. But the seal was gone, deep below, out of sight. "Help! Help!" There was no help. Felthrup paddled in a circle, aching everywhere, his nose barely clearing the waves. He would not last a minute.

But he did not have to. Some upwelling of water made him look down: the seal was rocketing toward him from the depths at astonishing speed. Before Felthrup could even cry out it broke the surface, catching him in its jaws as it leaped, and rose high above the water. Up and up they went. Stupefied, Felthrup watched the seal's teeth flatten and fuse into a long, sharp mass, its cheeks erupt with feathers, its small flippers stretch into wings.

It had become a bird—a great black pelican. In its ample throat, Felthrup was now riding like a rabbit in a hunter's sack. Below—dizzying sight!—he glimpsed sea and rocks and mainland, yellow lamps in Uturphe windows, a flash of lightning in the east. Then the bird croaked savagely and dived for the *Chathrand.*

They came in fast, right at the gallery windows. When they were but twenty feet away Felthrup saw that the bobbing light was a candle in a girl's upraised hand. Quickly she threw open the window and jumped aside. The pelican slowed at the last instant, fanning its wings. A final *thump,* and they were still.

Two dogs began to bark.

"Soaked!" the girl was shouting. "Look at this rug, will you? What on earth will I tell Syrarys?"

The pelican rose, wobbled and spat Felthrup onto the bearskin, along with a last gallon of seawater.

"Tell her you left a window open," it said.

Felthrup found himself looking up through a curtain of golden hair. The Treaty Bride, Thasha Isiq herself, was kneeling beside him, stroking his soggy fur. Then she turned to his rescuer and smiled.

"I like you better as a mink, Ramachni."

He was soon a mink again, but it was many minutes before Felthrup could be persuaded to stop squeaking his thanks. As Thasha hung the rug over the washbasin, he limped about the stateroom, praising everything—her kindness, Ramachni's magic, her mother's necklace, a shiny spoon. Jorl and Suzyt followed him about like twin elephants: they had taken an immediate liking to the rat.

When Thasha had mopped up as best she could, they all squeezed into her cabin. Thasha closed the door.

"Now," said Ramachni, "tell me what I dread to know, Felthrup Stargraven. For I heard you one midnight, weeks ago, addressing your kind: *I could tell you another story, brothers, about a monster of a man who soon will walk this ship. Niriviel the falcon spoke of him, proud as a prince. But you'd never believe me.* If only they had let you talk! For I never heard your voice again, until tonight."

"That is because the ixchel locked me in a pipe to die!" said Felthrup, his voice rising in pain again. "They would not listen; they assumed I was just a plain, nosy, execrable, humdrum rat. And when the fair Diadrelu rebuked her brother and took my side, what did I do? I led them to Mugstur, and for all I know he killed them."

He burst into tears again, and the mastiffs whined in solidarity.

"Hush!" said Thasha. "Diadrelu's alive—at least Pazel thought so. But he also said her people would kill anyone who talked about them."

"That is the code of the ixchel, Lady," sniffed Felthrup. "You kill *them* whenever you find them, so they try to kill you before you can reveal their presence. Rats would do the same, if they could. Master Mugstur plans to try."

"We will speak of Mugstur later," said Ramachni. "But you should thank him when next you cross paths: it was the noise of his assault that led me back to you—just in time, as it proved. But speak! Who is this evil man you told your brethren of?"

Then Felthrup told them of the falcon's boasts: about the Shaggat Ness, and the hidden gold, and the Emperor's plan to drive the Mzithrinis to war.

"The Shaggat Ness!" whispered Thasha, paling. "I read about him in the *Polylex*! It was strange—the book fell open to that page when I first looked at it, as if someone had left it open there a long time. What a monster! He became one of the Five Kings by stabbing his own uncle, and strangling his cousin. The other Kings were terrified of what he'd do next. He was completely mad, Ramachni. He declared himself a God!"

"And like a God, he will seem to conquer death," said Ramachni, shaking his head. "Ingenious."

"It all hinges on your wedding, m'lady," said Felthrup. "The prophecy of the Shaggat's return demands a union between one of their princes and a daughter of an enemy soldier."

Thasha turned away from them. She felt a sudden, physical ache at Pazel's absence. This still-unfolding horror felt infinitely harder to bear, now that he was gone. She had fought for his pardon every way she could think of. But something had come over her father, something vicious and unyielding: the same ruthlessness that had made him send her to the Lorg. Only this time Pazel had been the victim, not her. She felt an urge to weep, and with a great effort turned the feeling back into rage.

Why couldn't he just keep his mouth shut?

"Pazel was right, then," she said when she could speak again. "They do want a war. But this time Arqual will sit back and watch as the Mzithrinis kill each other."

"That is exactly the plan Niriviel boasts of," said Felthrup.

"But Ramachni," said Thasha. "If the Shaggat wasn't killed at the end of the last war, maybe his sorcerer wasn't either! What if the sorcerer on this ship really *is* the one you feared?"

"Arunis himself?" said the mage. "If that is so, then we face a worse peril than even I have dared imagine. But Dr. Chadfallow told me that Arunis was hanged, forty years ago."

"Hanged?" said Thasha. "Not drowned, like the Shaggat was supposed to be?"

"Hanged. Chadfallow was a young medical cadet, and present at the execution. You do not trust him, Thasha, and I will not advise you to ignore your suspicions. But it is difficult to lie to a mage, especially if that mage is Ramachni son of Ramadrac, Summoner of Dafvni, Ward of the Selk. Chadfallow knows better than to try."

"Well, it's not hard to lie to the rest of us," said Thasha. "These horrid people, these conspirators: who *are* they, besides Rose?"

"Loyal subjects of the crown," said Felthrup. "Drellarek the Throatcutter, for one. And Uskins and Swellows, Rose's top men. And Lady Oggosk, his seer."

"But none of these is the mastermind," said Ramachni, thoughtfully. "Nor, I think, is Rose himself. Your Emperor has often found him useful, but never trustworthy. No, there must be another conspirator in our midst—to say nothing of the sorcerer."

"And if *all* the ship's officers are involved?" asked Thasha.

"One at least is not," said Ramachni. "Mr. Fiffengurt is pure of heart. Too pure, maybe, to see the wickedness around him."

"Pazel liked him, too," said Thasha. "And, come to think of it, Firecracker Frix seems too simple to be bad."

"Do not trust appearances," said Ramachni. "Some conspirators have fair looks indeed."

"Syrarys!" said Thasha. "She's part of it, isn't she?"

"If she is, you will not easily find her out," said Ramachni gravely. "Remember that she has your father's heart in her hand. And perhaps more than his heart: he is very ill, and might not survive the shock if she has indeed betrayed him."

"Unless he's ill *because* she's betraying him," said Thasha, clenching her fists.

"Such villains!" Felthrup squeaked. "They've prepared for years—and we have just days! How can we possibly fight them?"

"Not with swords," said Ramachni. "At least not unless Hercól is returned to us."

"With tactics, then," said Thasha.

Rat, mink and mastiffs looked at her.

"You called it a conspiracy," she said. "Well, we're going to prepare a little conspiracy of our own." She rose and began to pace, frowning with concentration. "They're secretive. We'll be doubly so. They have hidden allies. We'll find our own. The ixchel, to start with."

"The ixchel look at humans and see murderers, m'lady," said Felthrup. "And they shall see the same in me after what happened in the tailor's nook."

"Such lack of trust," said Ramachni, "is more dangerous than all our enemies combined."

"Maybe the ixchel will trust us when we tell them about Rose's prisoner. Meanwhile, who else can we enlist?"

"Someone your own age, perhaps?" asked Felthrup. "That young niece of the *Chathrand*'s owner?"

"Pacu Lapadolma? Not likely! She's a fool, and mad for the glory of Arqual like her father the general. And she talks too much."

"Other passengers?" the rat persisted. "The soap man, the one who saved Hercól?"

Thasha shook her head. "He's a bit strange, that Mr. Ket. I thought *he* was a fool at first, but now I wonder if it just suits him to appear that way. No, I don't trust him."

"Commander Nagan, the head of the honor guard?" asked Ramachni.

"Yes!" said Thasha brightly. But then her face darkened. "No—not quite. I can't tell you why, Ramachni. I have more reasons to trust him than anyone aboard. He caught the man who attacked Hercól. He's guarded our family my whole life, and never asked for anything in return."

"But he certainly wants something now. He wants your trust."

"And I suppose he's earned it," said Thasha. "But I'm still uneasy about him."

"Then we must all be," said Ramachni, shaking his head. "Our list of friends is short."

"Short!" she said. "Why didn't I think of him first? Neeps! We can trust Neeps with our lives. Although he *is* a donkey."

"Hooray!" cried Felthrup, for he thought she meant that yet another woken beast was aboard. His disappointment was plain when Thasha said that she had only meant Neeps could be an imbecile.

"And if he doesn't stop fighting he'll be no help at all," she added, "because he'll be tossed off this ship."

"Your noble father must be counted our friend, of course?" Felthrup asked, sulking.

"No, he mustn't," said Thasha. "Not while Syrarys is with him. Even Hercól would have to agree, and he's been Prahba's friend almost as long as Dr. Chadfallow. That just leaves old Fiffengurt. But he's not fond of rich people. You can see it in the way he looks at first-class sons and daughters: he'd like to make them clean the pigsty. Why should he trust me?"

"Because you deserve trust," said Ramachni. "Lies and false faces grow dull over time, no matter how they are painted. But truth, goodness, a loving heart—these things only shine brighter as the darkness around them spreads. Give him a chance to trust you. He still has one good eye."

"I will speak to him," said Felthrup.

"No, Felthrup," said Thasha. "Most humans *still* don't want to believe in woken animals. I'm not sure I did until I heard you speak. Fiffengurt might just think he's losing his mind."

"I will speak to him," said the rat again, firmly. "He will remember my paw. But it may be long ere I catch him alone—Rose keeps him busier than any man aboard."

"The three of us, Neeps and Fiffengurt, and Lady Diadrelu—if we can find her," said Ramachni. "Six, against a whole shipful of murderers and rogues! Well, we must do what we can. For my part, I shall look for the ixchel."

"Be careful, Master!" said Felthrup. "They are dangerous, and silent as smoke. Turn yourself into something they will not fear—a moth, a little spider—before you enter their domain of Night Village."

"I cannot do that," said Ramachni.

They turned to him in surprise. Ramachni shook his head. "Indeed I can do no magic at all just now, save the small continuing spell I use to conceal what we say in these rooms. My world lies far beyond the sun and moon of Alifros. I brought power with me, but most I gave to Pazel in the form of Master-Words, and the rest went in lifting Felthrup from the sea."

"Do you mean you can't do magic until you return to your world?" said Thasha, aghast.

"None," said Ramachni, shaking his head. "Which is why I must retreat to it for a little while now. Alas, I fear you will need me again before I have half recovered. But if I am to fight at your side at all I must go, and regain what strength I can."

"When will that fight be?" asked Thasha.

"Soon," said Ramachni. "You must work quickly. And now listen well, Thasha: normally when I leave this world I cast a holding spell upon your clock. It has one purpose: to recognize me when I return, be it in one day or ten years, and to open the clock at that moment. Tonight I must depart without casting even that simple spell. Without it I shall be powerless to open the clock from within. Therefore you must open it for me. I believe you know how?"

"Of course," said Thasha. "I've watched Hercól do it a dozen times."

Ramachni nodded. "Wait as long as you dare. And one last request, Thasha my champion: keep thinking about trust. We are in a nest of vipers—but even a viper may wake."

Thasha looked deep into his black eyes. Then she nodded and turned to Felthrup.

"Well, rat," she said, "you and I have a conspiracy to build."

26

The Mad King

N. R. Rose, Captain
27 Modoli 941

The Honorable Captain Theimat Rose
Northbeck Abbey, Mereldin Isle, South Quezans

Dear Sir,

My thanks, dearest Father, for the gift of your counsel. You know I hold your wisdom above all others in matters of the sea. I shall take us south by the route you indicate. Your orders shall be my own.

We are now three days from Ormael City, where I shall post this letter. After that we leave Imperial waters, and I dare say this vessel will never see them again. Once His Nastiness* is delivered and the treasure discharged, and the hornet's nest is slapped and rattled into rage, my orders are to reverse course, and return to Etherhorde across the Ruling Sea—or if we are prevented, to start a fire in Chathrand's *hold, just beneath the powder room, and abandon ship. That will destroy all evidence of the ship's presence in enemy waters. It*

---

*"His Nastiness" appears in many letters and log entries by Captain Rose. Scholars debated his true identity until this letter was unearthed on Mereldín. Little doubt remains that the term refers to the Shaggat Ness. —EDITOR *will also leave us just ten minutes ere she blows like a Fifth-moon fireball.*

Of course we will not be able to return the way we came, for by that season the Nelluroq Vortex will have spread its jaws, and not even Chathrand has a prayer against that ruinous whirlpool. Nor can we sail home by the regular, crowded trade route: that would be the same as shouting what the Empire has done from every street corner in Alifros. So frightened of this possibility is old Magad that he has promised to sink Chathrand, and crucify any survivors, if we dare return by the northern route. No, we must destroy her when the job is done—a waste of this masterpiece of a ship, and some sailors, too.

The Emperor did well in choosing Sandor Ott. He is ugly and does not properly chew his food, but as a spymaster he is without equal. One of his under-assassins botched the murder of Hercól, a servant who might have known Ott by sight and revealed his true identity. When Ott found that his man had failed he took him to an empty courtyard in Uturphe and killed him with a single blow. Of course, that was his right. The lad's mistake means Hercól was never killed, for by then nosy Fiffengurt had decided to accompany him to the hospital. So Ott found another way: he paid the hospital's corrupt nurses to whisk Hercól away through the back door and off to the city poorhouse, where he will lie in filth, and surely die as his wound turns gangrenous.

Ott has solved another tricky problem for me: Eberzam Isiq. The Emperor thought him perfect: a war hero and an old fool. But he has not proved quite stupid enough. He is a true mariner and would never challenge a serving captain, but I saw him questioning the gunner and the midshipman. Later I sent for them and made them repeat his questions. To the gunner Isiq had said that the old cannon looked very clean and usable, and were they really just for show? And he asked the other why I had plotted such a long course to Uturphe.

Of course, the midshipman did not know it was because I

wished Hercól to die. Such questions lead to trouble, however, and I told Ott as much. "Leave him to me," replied the
spymaster. The next day Isiq's headaches were back, and he
has not left his cabin since. Headaches are perfect: they do
not threaten Isiq's life, but they turn him into the helpless doll
we need.

   There are other dangers. Fiffengurt is not one of us, and
must be dealt with sooner or later. And certain passengers
are nosy (Isiq's daughter, and that fancy savage Bolutu), or
merely unsettled, as if noticing some dangerous smell. Do
they detect the ghosts that clutter Chathrand? I do not think
so. One tarboy seemed to possess the gift of hearing spirits,
but he insulted Isiq and was tossed ashore. Now I wish I had
contrived to keep him. The spirits flit ever about me, pecking
at my arms like gulls. If the boy were here they might flock to
him instead and let me rest.

   But from this day forward the greatest danger is His Nastiness. What a creature, sir! He has scars on his face as if
mauled by a jungle cat. He is ancient, but muscled like Drellarek the Throatcutter, and his voice belongs to a crocodile.
Now I will tell you how he came aboard.

   His Nastiness has lain these forty years on the prison isle
of Licherog, halfway from Uturphe to the Quezans. Imperial
law bars any ship from nearing the isle unless in danger of
sinking outright, so I was forced to invent such a condition.
Swellows did it, with Uskins standing guard—sawed the portside tiller-shaft down to a nub. To make things sweeter I let
the blame fall on Fiffengurt. The old pest had the wheel at two
bells past midnight, when the wind turned of a sudden. He
gave her a sharp spin, the shaft broke and Chathrand heeled
over like a cart kicked by a mule. Twelve hundred men,
women and brats went sprawling. The men's breakfast fell off
the stove. Now Fiffengurt is less well loved than before.

   For two days we limped north. The men feared we were
lost, drifting, and cheered when the lookout cried, "Land!
Two points off the starboard!" But they shuddered and made

the sign of the Tree when that great black rock loomed out of the waves.

A cruel wall encircles Licherog, pierced only by gunnery and a solid iron gate like the door of a furnace. Birds in the thousands wheeled overhead. Miles out, the men saw sharks, big monsters gliding in our wake. Hundreds swarm those waters, and never starve: on Licherog there is no graveyard but the sea.

A skjff came out and led us through the reefs. We passed the wreck of a four-masted Blodmel, sunk half a century ago in the harbor mouth. The day was so clear I glimpsed skeletons on her deck: Sizzy men, drowned in their armor, shreds of calcified rigging in their hands.

I left Fiffengurt in charge of repairs and went ashore with Ott and Drellarek. The warden of Licherog, a gaunt old spook in a robe fashionable thirty years ago in Etherhorde, greeted us at landfall. The man is a duke from an ancient family, exiled there after selling his own niece to the Flikkermen. He knew the real purpose of our visit: I could see that in the way he sweated and squirmed. He was terribly excited at the prospect of getting rid of His Nastiness.

"Come, sirs!" he said. "You've traveled far, you'll want food and wine and a place to sit down! This port is a foul sty, but the wind is fresh up in the citadel. Follow me!"

He marched us up the bird-filthy stairs from the water. The furnace door swung open, and we entered Licherog.

We all hear ghastly tales of that prison, Father, but the reality is worse. Most of the condemned live underground, in meandering catacombs untouched by sun or rain. They have nothing. They drink from their hands, eat off the stone floor or from plates beaten together from the mud tracked in by the guards. I saw a man who had fashioned a bed from his own hair, so long had he lain in one room. The halls go on forever. Whole floors have been abandoned to anarchy: food is piled up at a master door, and bodies removed there, but no guards enter and no prisoner even dreams of escape. One level the warden calls the Faceless Floor, *comprised of those whose identities are lost or cast into doubt, or whom the Empire wishes the world to forget.*

We were a long time in reaching that fresh wind, but finally another door was unchained and we stumbled out on the top of the island itself. East to west it is perhaps six miles long, all dust and naked rock. We saw quarries where men labored under the withering sun, the gallows where some fresh trouble-maker dangled like a rag. And at the far end of the island, upon a rise, stood a fortress with an ornate little tower.

"That is your residence?" asked Drellarek.

"Oh no!" The warden laughed nervously. "That is the . . . Forbidden Place. It was built as the warden's home, but since the war—since the sinking of the Lythra*—you understand that I rarely speak of the place, or its special purpose? But soon enough I shall take you there. Come, friends, the meal is served."*

"Take us now," said Ott. "We will dine better if we know that we have not sailed all this way in vain."

"I can assure you—"

"Do no such thing," Ott interrupted. "Show us the S————."*

A little carriage was brought round. We thumped along wordlessly, guards on horseback ahead and behind. An army of near-naked prisoners gaped all around us.

The fortress was embellished with stone vultures and murths and skulls and cobras, every symbol of death one could think of. The warden pointed to a dead man sprawled on the ground and bristling with arrows. "The guards would even shoot one another, if one strayed too close without per-mission," he said proudly. "We leave the bodies in plain view until the birds tire of them. Here we are, gentlemen."

The guards here were Turachs like Drellarek (he had trained some of them in Etherhorde) with crossbows primed,

---

*In several places Rose appears to have blotted out the word *Shaggat* before sealing the envelope. —EDITOR.

and slavering hounds at their feet. When they had searched us thoroughly and taken all our weapons, the carriage was ushered in through the gate.

Inside that fortress—paradise. A green yard led to a stand of lemon trees in pungent bloom. Beyond that, frangipani and cedars, a spice garden, peacocks strutting at liberty. There was a slate terrace and a cobalt pool, where a slave girl sat bathing her feet. She fled like a doe at the sight of us, and we trailed in past a bowling court with silver pins, a glass table heaped with pomegranates, a statue of the Babqri Child. Somewhere a fiddle played. Across the yard I saw two cooks roasting a hog.

"All this . . . is for him?" I asked, disbelieving.

"Certainly not!" replied the warden. "You forget he has two sons."

We came to the tower stair, but before we could climb them the door flew open and a man of about twenty, wearing a dirty yellow robe, burst out, pointing at the warden.

"Rabbits!" he shrieked, in a voice like an old woman. "You promised, Warden!"

The warden cringed. "Your Majesty, I promised to try. My men are hunting rabbits across Licherog even now. But I fear we have eaten them all."

The man looked at us for support. "Always lying, this one! Variety! That's all I ask! How are we to put up with the same five cuts of meat, year after year? And any fool can see the island is full of rabbit holes!"

"The island is a rock, Your Majesty. And now I must change the subject. We have important guests. Would you be so very obliging as to tell your royal father—"

"Divine!"

"—that the captain of the Great Ship requests an audience?"

The man hesitated, mouth agape. Then, slow and important, he crossed his arms. "No audience," he said. "Take them away, Warden. I am not pleased with you."

"But these travelers—"

"Is not my father a God?"

The warden looked as if he had dreaded this moment from birth. He glanced at me as if hoping I knew the answer to the man's question. But then Ott leaped onto the stairs. The man screamed: Ott knocked him aside like a broom and vanished through the door. We heard him running up the inner staircase.

The tower has four levels. On the first we saw a half-eaten roast upon a table, a shattered plate, and the slave girl peering at us from beneath the tablecloth. The second was a kind of playroom, with frightfully bad paintings on easels, some knobs of stone that might have been intended for sculpture, a grand piano and a second man in yellow sitting on the floor holding his forehead, a broken fiddle beside him. Ott had needed but half a minute to tame the S———'s terrible sons.

"You see how young they are?" said the warden softly. *"That is the work of Arunis, the King's old sorcerer. When they irritated him he would cast spells to make them sleep for days, weeks, even. Once they slept for three years—then ran about like mad puppies for a month. But it is an enchanted sleep, for they age not when they slumber. They should be nearing fifty, but they are half that."*

"Is there no means of waking them?" I asked.

"Their father discovered one. He sets their clothes on fire."

"Rin's teeth!"

"That is why they refuse to wear anything but those robes. They can be thrown off in an instant."

The third floor held a library full of moldering books in Mzithrini script. We pressed on to the next floor, which was the highest. An elegant bedroom met our eyes, with large windows open to the breeze. Sandor Ott stood to our left, stock-still, fingering a sharp little piece of the broken plate, his face glowing with some unspeakable fervor. And across from him was the S———.

He stood empty-handed by the window, gazing fixedly at

the spymaster. I wrote already of his visage, his monstrous scars, but did I mention his eyes? They are red-tinted, as if he stares always through that curtain of blood he came so near to drawing over all the world. I knew he would be here, and yet I stood in awe. Those hands had strangled princes. That mouth had talked whole countries into joining his lunatic war. This prodigy of murder was now become a tool, but whose exactly? The Emperor's? Sandor Ott's? My own?

You see, Father, the S———— saw everything backward. He thought we were his.

"You are late," he rumbled, breaking the silence. "Midwinter I began to call you, bending my will across the Nelu Peren. Now at last you come, with the year half spent and the White Fleet moving again. Why do you make your lord wait?"

I have known Sandor Ott for decades, Father, but never before had I seen him afraid. He was breathing hard, and not from the exertion of the stairs. Nonetheless he stepped forward and spoke through his teeth.

"Creature!" he said. "If some part of you is untouched by madness, hear me well: in my hands you are no God. You are a maggot. And I am the fisherman who baits his hook with you! If you wriggle, you do so for my sake. If you live it is because I wish it. Displease me in the smallest matter and I shall prove your mortality by casting you into the sea!"

"Will you?" said the S————. "After forty years?"

No one answered. Ott and the S———— looked like two old wolves, each waiting for the other to spring. Then His Nastiness glanced at the rest of us for the first time, his face indifferent. We were beneath his notice.

"Warden," he said, "I choose to leave on this man's ship, for the hour foretold at the world's making is come round at last, and soon I shall possess my kingdom. But you must not think of leaving Licherog. You will stay and guard my library, and my stallions, and my goat."

The warden sniveled, like a child used to spankings. "Of

*course, Majesty! Where else would I go? What other task
could I aspire to?"*

*"Do not lie!" the S—— suddenly roared, lifting his
hands. "When I return I shall bear the Nilstone in my left
hand, Sathek's Scepter in my right! Master of all Alifros shall
I be, and whosoever lies to the Master shall know his wrath!"*

"I do not lie, Majesty—"

*"Where are my sons? You spawn of a tick! Bring them! I
swear on the Casket you shall die in the bowels of this prison,
wailing, the fires of the Nine Pits licking your mind. Your
mouth shall fill with ashes, your eyes—"*

*Ott and Drellarek moved as one. Drellarek struck His Nas-
tiness a blow to the stomach that stopped his ranting. Ott did
something with his hand, too quick for the eye to follow.
There was a splash of blood: for a moment I thought he had
murdered the fiend. Then I saw him hold up a bit of flesh between his thumb and forefinger. It was one of the S——'s
earlobes.*

*The monster-king staggered, groaning. Ott threw him a hand-
kerchief. "Stanch your wound, maggot," he said. "And never
forget this: Sandor Ott draws blood once as a warning. Once."*

*I had little appetite for dinner. That night I tried to sleep
ashore, but the spirits on Licherog outnumber the prisoners
as the dead outnumber the living, and no chains kept them
from my room, where they moaned, begged for sweets, accused me of ridiculous crimes. I went back to my ship. And
before dawn I rose and found Uskins on the forecastle as
planned. We sent the whole night watch below, and when we
stood alone Drellarek and his thugs brought His Nastiness
and sons aboard, wrapped up like babes in swaddling cloths.
They are hidden now in a deep part of the ship, as carefully
as I hid the Emperor's gold.*

*Before we cast off from Licherog the warden came to shake
my hand. "Will the Emperor let you retire now?" I asked. The
man was a simpering wretch, but he had done his job.*

"Oh!" said he. "The Emperor promised years ago that my banishment would end when those three departed Licherog. But I do not know. Every kingdom needs its jailors, and this place is not so very awful, sometimes."

"It's a swillhole! And festering with ghosts besides! Get out of here, man!"

"There's the S———'s warning to think of, Captain."

By the Pits, Father, that was the strangest moment of our landfall. This man knew the scheme: how we were throwing the S——— at our enemies as one might throw a dog at a marauding bear, not because the dog can survive, but because it can weaken and distract the bear. And yet he feared—the dog! Not the Emperor or the White Fleet, not disease, nor being strangled some night by any one of the ten thousand killers on that rock. Only his ex-prisoner: and so much so that he planned to stay on Licherog through his declining years, feeding that madman's goat.

He found time for a last loony caper, this fellow. We were on the gangway. I had just seen the S——— hidden away, and told the warden goodbye, when I saw him staring up at the Chathrand, transfixed. "I thought you had cleared the deck!" he cried.

So I had: there was no one in sight but the sailors returning to their posts, and one other: a soap merchant named Ket. The man paces many nights away on deck—says he cannot breathe in his cabin—and it was he who somehow saved that nuisance Hercól. Mr. Ket looked up, smiled and bowed to each of us in turn.

"Relax, he saw nothing," I murmured. But the warden was gone. I turned and there he was, fleeing across the quay. He did not stop running until he reached the top of the stairs and had passed through the door of his prison.

Knaves, fools, madmen: you see how I am surrounded, Father? As ever, I remain your obedient son,

N. R. ROSE

P.S. Mother is again demanding golden swamp tears. I tell her those bath crystals are hard to acquire, since they form only when lightning scalds an ancient cypress while its sap is running. Still she insists, daily now, and goes so far as to call me "an ungrateful child." Would it tax you, sir, to explain the matter gently?

27

Merchandise

The Flikkermen tied Pazel's hands and feet and threw him into the well. He plunged twenty feet into black water, certain they meant to drown him and chop his body into fish food, and blind with terror as he was, part of him felt insulted to be considered so worthless.

Seconds later he was dragged out of the water and up onto a cold stone floor. He sputtered and gagged. In the darkness ten or twelve bare-chested Flikkermen squatted around him, whispering and croaking. They soon stripped him of his gold, his knife and his mother's ivory whale. All three delighted them, and they patted his face with their round, sticky fingertips and said *"Shplegmun "*—good boy.

Pazel had learned one thing during the invasion of Ormael: when a mob lays hold of you, do not fight. Become silent, docile, do as you're told. Above all, study your captors. It was easier said than done, in that dim room. But now and then one of the creatures would flash, as if releasing energy it could no longer contain. An awful sight: the Flikkerman's whole body would light up like a glow-worm, and through its translucent flesh Pazel saw veins and roots of teeth and the six pulsing chambers of a Flikker heart.

"Swellows tricked him," one said in their tongue. "Bought his trust with coins. Does he have all his fingers?"

They worked swiftly, checking each of Pazel's joints as if to be sure his pieces were in working order, feeling his head for cracks. Then they began to argue his fate.

The Flikker who had met Pazel at the gate was for selling him to the Uturphe Bladeworks, but another felt he was too small to pour molten iron, and would not fetch a good price. Another said they should sell him to a ship bound for Bramian, where hunters needed boys to lure tigers out of their caves. Still another knew a magician who wanted to replace his last boy assistant, whom he had turned into a block of ice for a party trick and then forgotten, until the lad melted and trickled away through the floorboards.

They had many such fine ideas, and the debate wore on. At last the head Flikkerman burst into light. Since they could not agree, he declared, they would let the buyers themselves decide. The boy would go to auction.

The others grumbled: the auction was quite far away, apparently. But their chief had spoken, and they obeyed.

Soon Pazel was back in the water, this time in the bottom of a narrow boat like a cross between a decrepit fishing-dory and a gondola. With their flat feet on top of him, his captors poled down a long, dark, dripping tunnel. What it had been built for Pazel could scarcely guess, but it was clearly one of the secret ways the Flikkers moved children in and out of the city. They turned corners, ducked under low ceilings, opened moss-covered gates. Eventually they sat him up and pressed a flask to his lips. What he swallowed was sweet and briny and rushed to his head like wine.

On and on they went. At length the Flikkermen began to sing. Theirs was a cold, swift, mournful music, like that of a river approached in darkness, and it made Pazel wonder for the first time just who they were, these Flikkermen, these people who never went to sea, and lived as a race apart in the cities of humankind.

> We cut the sod where the gold wheat grows.
> We dropped the seed of the poplar groves.

Men all forget, we sing it yet:
We still recall where the deep flood goes.

We felled the trees for the conquering fleet.
We dug the ore for the blacksmith's heat.
Twilight to dawn and a century's gone:
We lay the cobbles beneath your feet.

Fearsome the wind o'er the stolen earth.
Fearsome the morning of our rebirth.
Dawn-light to day, the Flikkermen say:
We set the price of your children's worth.

Do not tarry where the schoolyard ends.
Do not linger where the alley bends.
New blossoms pale, empires fail:
We keep the coin the world expends.

Wind shall tear pennant from heartless tower.
River shall rise and wave devour.
Men all forget on what road we met:
We shall be kings in the final hour.

The last words were scarcely out of their mouths when the next song began. Pazel's head still swam with the drink. Soon he found himself drifting into miserable sleep in which the voices sang on, conjuring stories of lost tribes and swamp banquets and Flikker queens with onyx crowns and shawls of butterfly wings.

At some point he half woke, and found himself no longer underground. The boat was now gliding down a river under a brilliant moon. The banks were high, the land dew-soaked and desolate. A few stone farmhouses squatted in the distance, lamp-light blazing in their windows, and once a riderless horse pranced and nickered at them from behind a fence, but there was no one to whom he might have shouted for help.

He slept, and woke again, and it was day. The boat was surrounded by reeds and tall marsh grass; Pazel could not even see the open river. They were anchored, and the Flikkers were eating cold fish and hot peppers wrapped in some sort of leaves. When they were finished one propped him up and gave him another long drink of the salty-sweet wine. Then they checked his ropes, washed their faces with marsh water, and curled up in the boat to sleep. In a few minutes the wine did its work, and Pazel dropped forward among his captors.

He woke after nightfall, sunburned and hungry. They were back on the river. Other boats ran close beside them; other Flikkermen had joined his captors' songs. Pazel saw prisoners bound like himself, weariness and terror mingled in their looks. The countryside was open and silver by moonlight, but there was no sign of farmland or any human dwelling. After another sip of the ubiquitous wine they fed him three mouthfuls of their leaf-wrapped fish. It was sour-tasting and sharp, but he ate it eagerly, and the Flikkermen laughed: *"Shplegmun."*

A short time later he noticed that his captors were watching the shore. Lifting his head Pazel saw a pack of ghost-gray dogs racing through the underbrush, studying them with eyes that glowed red as coals. Sulphur dogs. It was said that when they killed, they ate the flesh warm and chewed the bones to daybreak, grinding them to meal. How they communicated no one knew, for they never barked or howled. For a long time Pazel lay watching the pack run in silence, keeping pace with the boats.

The next three days were much like the first—sleep by daylight, in some hollow or thicket or marsh; swift travel by night. But Pazel felt a queasy ache in the pit of his stomach. It grew hour by hour, and by the third day he was shaking and chilled.

"What's wrong with him?" the Flikkermen asked one another.

"Fever," Pazel told them. "I've got chills and a fever."

"Babbling. Delirious." They shook their heads.

"That fish would make a wharf-rat sick. Don't you have anything else?"

They wondered aloud what tongue he was speaking. And

Pazel bit his lips with rage, for he thought they were teasing him. *Your tongue, you ugly louts!* Only much later did he realize that they were right: he was delirious, and speaking Ormali, and he wondered if he might be starting to die.

Time became even more fragmented: one moment it was a hot, fly-plagued afternoon, the next a damp and chilly midnight. Through all the pain, cold sweats and dizzy spells, Pazel suffered most in his mind. Questions preyed on him like vultures, one ravenous bird after another dropping out of the sky to peck at his brain. Was Hercól alive? Who had attacked him, and who had killed that Zirfet fellow? Had the ixchel realized that Thasha knew of their presence on the *Chathrand,* and slit her throat? What would the Flikkers do if he was too weak to sell?

Clammy palms swept flies from his face. Wet cloths were pressed against his forehead, and something astringent rubbed on his chest. He was lifted in and out of boats. Warm broth was spooned into his mouth; plain water replaced the wine. Days and nights were like the violent banging of a cottage door in the wind: lamplight, darkness, lamplight again.

Then a dawn came when Pazel realized with a jolt that his illness was gone. He was thinner and weaker, but his head was so clear it was like a stiff sea-breeze driving away the clouds, revealing a cool, clean starlit night.

He was in a larger boat, with a roofed cabin. He was unbound and undressed, but wrapped in a blanket tucked snugly beneath his feet. A Flikker woman was crouching by a wood-burning stove, stirring a pot of stew and singing: *Poor little field mice, lost in a storm, only a wildcat to keep them warm.*

She was very old. Her green-brown skin was dry and wrinkled, and the joints in her great hands were swollen and stiff. She glanced at him and gave a satisfied croak.

"Awake!" she said, in the Flikkers' old-fashioned Arquali. "I knew thy heart was strong. Art thou improved, boy?"

"I'm much better," said Pazel, in her own tongue.

The old woman lit up like a firecracker, and dropped her wooden spoon. "You speak Flikker!" she cried.

"Where am I, please?" asked Pazel.

She recovered her spoon, hobbled forward and whacked him smartly with it across the cheek. "Feel that?"

"Why, yes," said Pazel, holding his cheek.

"Praise the blood of the earth! A few days ago your skin was numb—numb and cold, like a drowned man's. But look at you now! You're going to live, strange human boy."

Pazel saw his tattered clothes folded on a corner of her low wooden table. Scattered over the rest of the table, to his astonishment, were books. They were soiled, fourth-hand volumes, spines cracked and resewn, pages hanging in tatters. Nearly all were medical in nature; indeed the first book his eyes lighted upon was *Parasites: An Appreciation* by Dr. Ignus Chadfallow.

"You've been caring for me, haven't you?" he said.

"Right you are," said the old woman. "Thirteen days."

"Thirteen!"

With a kindly smile (an expression Pazel had not imagined possible on a Flikker face) she helped him out of bed and into a chair by the stove. Her name was Glindrik, she said: this was her home.

"What happened to the others? They were going to auction me off."

She cackled. "Your illness took care of that. You slept right through the auction. Old Pradjit was so angry he wanted to finish you off, boil you down to bones, and sell 'em for half a cockle to the Slugdra ghost-doctors. Luckily I got to you in time. Keep that blanket over your chest, dear. And put your feet up on the fender; they're still cold as meltwater."

She served him a bowl of hot stew, then sat across from him and began to chatter. She was plainly a most unusual Flikker, and knew it—they called her *Mad Glindrik of the Westfirth,* she observed with a certain pride. It seemed that dying humans were her hobby. For two decades she had lived alone here, just across the river from the "auction," whatever that was. And each time the Flikkermen from Uturphe arrived with a captive too sick to be sold profitably, Glindrik bought him cheaply, and set about saving a life.

When Pazel asked her why, she frowned at him. Why not? She had no children. Her husband was long dead. What else should she do with the scant years left to her?

He almost asked, *But why help humans?* Something in her eyes, however, gave him to know that the question would cause deep offense. And Pazel at once felt ashamed for assuming that no Flikker could wish him anything but harm.

Through her window he saw that the river here was enormously wide. He could make out the far shore, miles away it seemed, and scores of islands thick with dense woods, over which gulls and other shorebirds wheeled.

"We're near the sea, then, Glindrik?"

"Very near," she said. "The water's too salty even for Flikkers to drink. But there's a well on the hillside, past the apple trees."

"Are there many auctions?"

"Every fortnight. But how did you learn Flikker, boy? Were you *raised* among us?"

They talked the morning away. She wanted to know all about his Gift, and was fascinated by his mind-fits, even turning to her books in search of some other way to prevent or delay them. "Night-blooming blacksap, maybe," she said. "Chew the flowers: they dull the mind's sensitivity to spells. Worth a try, anyway."

In the afternoon he napped, and when he woke again he felt perfectly cured. He dressed, and stepped ashore by the little gangway connecting her houseboat to the bank. Over her objections he took her hatchet and split several dozen logs into pieces for her woodstove, and carried them in. Then Glindrik told him that in three or four days an elk-hunter would pass by, an "honest coot" who would take him back to Uturphe by land.

"How can I thank you?" Pazel asked her.

Glindrik smiled. "What do you want to do with your life, Pazel Pathkendle?"

Pazel looked at her, startled. "I've never been asked that before," he said. "I don't know the answer, either. Sail like my father, I always thought, but the Code will keep me from that. So perhaps I'll go back to school, one day, if I find one that takes Ormalis. But first I have to stop this blary war, and find my family, of course, and—"

He stopped abruptly. An image of Thasha's face had suddenly leaped into his mind.

Glindrik put out her spindly hand and touched his own. "Complicated!" she said. "My own dream was never so hard to tell." She smiled, rather sadly. "No, telling was easy."

"What was it, Glindrik?"

She got up with a sigh. "After I fetch the water."

"Let me," Pazel said, jumping up.

She looked at him, considering. At last she said, "Fetch it, then, dear, but whatever you do, don't be long. You'll want to lie down again soon. I want you back in ten minutes, you understand?"

"Yes, Doctor," he said, and Glindrik laughed, delighted.

The path to the well straggled up the sandy bank, through Glindrik's vegetable patch and a copse of gnarled apple trees. There were bees and grasshoppers, and rabbits growing fat on her cabbage and kale. Pazel reached the well and threw back the wooden cover.

A chill touched his spine: he thought suddenly of hands on his arms and legs. Hands like Glindrik's, lifting and hurling him down a shaft very much like this one.

Shaking off the thought, Pazel filled the buckets and set them down to rest a moment. He looked north, where the broad loops of the river vanished into the Westfirth hills. *Dry land,* he mused. To think that one could set off into it, as a ship did the open sea, and travel months or years without reaching a shore. The idea always struck him as absurd.

He looked back down the hillside. He could not make out her houseboat, but through the low pines the sea winked back at him. *Twenty years, alone,* he thought. *What was that dream of yours, Glindrik?*

Then he turned, and saw the graveyard.

It was laid out neatly beyond the apple trees: twenty or thirty graves in short rows, each one marked with river stones in the shape of the Milk Tree. Human graves, he thought: Flikkers did not worship Rin, or any god of humankind.

The scene might have been touching, but after the awful memory of his deceit in Uturphe, Pazel found himself alarmed, and suspicious. Glindrik had never spoken of those who died in her care.

Suddenly her voice rang out from below: *"Pazel! Pazel! Come back now, boy. Time to rest!"*

Pazel didn't move. Why hadn't she mentioned the graveyard, when they had talked of so much else?

Glindrik shouted again, more urgently this time. He lifted the buckets and began to pick his way down the hill. But he dragged his feet. A terrible thought came to him: had she experimented on those boys? Tried out her brews and potions on humans first, to see if they cured or killed?

Pazel stopped behind a rambling shrub. No sound but the buzzing bees: Glindrik had stopped calling his name.

This is rubbish, he thought, *she saved your life.* Yet some instinctive fear kept him where he was a moment longer. Then he took a deep breath and walked down the bank to the houseboat.

He thought she would be waiting on the shore, but she was inside.

He crossed the gangway and stepped down onto the deck. He heard her voice within the cabin.

But Glindrik was not talking to him.

"Very sick!" she was saying. "No use to you at all. And now he's gone and hobbled off into the woods. To die, I suppose."

"Didn't I tell you?" said a male Flikker, laughing.

"You told me, Pradjit. I'll never learn, old fool that I am."

Pazel froze. They were back, his captors. Silently he put the buckets on the deck.

"We should take his bones," said another Flikkerman.

"His bones are mine!" said Glindrik, almost shrieking. "I

bought him from you, remember? In any case he ran off days ago. No, friends, he's gone, *long gone!*"

"Why do you shout, woman? Are you deaf?"

Pazel knew why. Heart pounding terribly, he stepped back onto the gangway. On tiptoe he crossed the plank. Once his feet were on firm ground, however, he found it impossible not to run. Up the hillside path he sprinted, then dashed through the garden, rounded the shrub—

—and collided head-on with a Flikkerman, who croaked, dropped his armful of apples, and stunned Pazel senseless with a touch.

When he woke it was quite dark. He was facedown in one of the narrow Flikker boats: it might have been the very one that brought him from Uturphe. His hands were tied behind his back.

"The lying hag," a Flikker voice was saying. "This boy is perfectly healed; we'll get more for him tonight than we would have at last auction. Why does she lie, though? Why not sell them back to us?"

"She cheats," said a second voice. "She must have another buyer. Why else would she fight so hard to save them?"

It was all Pazel could do not to beat his head against the hull. *Idiot, flaming idiot!* Glindrik was exactly what she seemed: a friend. She had wanted him back in bed to feign sickness once more, before Pradjit and his men turned up. Now Pazel was back where he started two weeks ago. How could he have been such a fool?

Groaning with rage, he twisted around and sat up. He could just see Glindrik's houseboat by the dwindling shore, and the old woman watching sadly from the deck.

His captors no longer called him *Shplegmun.* Already their boat was nearing an island: a great river island, its sandy shores glowing by moonlight. Low trees reared up beyond the dunes.

The boat struck sand; the Flikkers leaped out and pulled it

ashore. There were other craft beached around them, and Flikker voices nearby. They pulled Pazel to his feet and nudged him onto the sand.

The voices came from a crowd at the edge of the trees: at least a dozen Flikkermen, with eight or ten captured boys. Pazel looked them over: most of these boys were tall and strong. They would sell fast enough. But one figure at the back of the crowd was very small. His captors were poking at him, grumbling: *No profit, wait and see, we'll be stuck with him at night's end.*

One yanked maliciously at the small boy's rope. The boy shouted back: "Leave off, you toad! That blary hurts!"

Pazel was thunderstruck. The high-pitched voice was unmistakable.

"Neeps!"

The small boy pushed forward through the crowd, and there he was, gaping.

"Pazel Pathkendle! I'll be blowed!"

"Neeps, you mad cat! How did they get hold of *you*?"

"Dismissed for fighting!" said Neeps.

"Not again!"

"It was that lout Jervik's fault! Him and that crook Swellows, I should have—"

"No talking!" snapped the lead Flikkerman, his body sparking with anger. "Form one line! We go to auction!"

Up the dune they marched the captive boys. Pazel felt a strange clash of emotions: joy at seeing his friend, astonishment that he should be here, dread at the thought of what lay in store for them both. Worst of all, he felt a nagging suspicion that Neeps' dismissal had something to do with him.

At the top of the dune Pazel turned and looked back the way they had come. A broad river delta spread below them in the moonlight, a fan of rippling silver and black shadow-islands. Beyond lay the open sea. Hidden among the islands, however, was a cluster of ocean ships: fifteen or sixteen little brigs and schooners bobbing at anchor.

Neeps saw them, too. "Something tells me we won't be here long," he whispered. "Belching devils, mate, I've been *such* a blary fool."

Pazel thought that Neeps couldn't possibly have outdone him in foolishness. "But how did you *get* here?" he demanded.

"Later," said Neeps. "They're watching."

After the dunes came a muddy slog through the island's brush forest, where every nightbird that ever lived whooped and whistled and trilled and honked. Now and then Pazel caught glimmers of firelight through the trees ahead. When the wind turned he caught a smell of woodsmoke and frying fish.

Harsh laughter reached his ears. The path opened suddenly into a great clearing where bonfires roared. A crowd of hundreds had gathered here—eating, wrestling, guzzling liquor, trading jibes and insults. Except for some twenty Flikkers they were all humans, but none inspired Pazel with hopes of rescue. There were many sailors—one could always spot them by their leathery skin—but when they looked at him they showed no brotherly warmth. All carried blades. Some had bones or other murth-charms knotted up in their beards. Quite a few were missing teeth or eyes or fingers. *Rin save us,* Pazel thought, *they're pirates.*

The head Flikkerman drew a line in the dirt with his bootheel, and the others arranged the boys along it by size. Was this a slave-market? Pazel wondered. Certainly it resembled what he'd seen during the rape of Ormael—except that no ownership papers were involved here, and no branding iron. And of course, the Flikkers were in charge.

They worked in pairs. One stood with his hand on the head of a captive. The other jumped onto a crate, raised his long-fingered hands over his head and sang the prisoner's qualities in a weird, half-rhyming chant: *"Strong-strong-boy, hop-a-long-boy! Clean-never-never-sick-head-thick-boy! See-how-tall-he'll-carry-all!"*

And so on. When a customer shouted out a price, the lower Flikkerman pointed in his direction and began to glow softly.

Then a higher bid would come, and the Flikkerman turned and pointed to the new customer, and glowed a little brighter, and his partner above would sing with more excitement and exaggeration: *"A perfect child! So-good-mannered-mild! Tough as a lion, wilt thou not buy 'im?"*

When someone did buy a boy, the two Flikkers cried, "Eeech!" in unison, and the glowing one went out like a snuffed candle. The whole display appeared to have a kind of hypnotic effect on the pirates, who were spending money rather freely for people who went to such lengths to obtain it.

As his captors waited their turn, however, Pazel saw that the cleverer pirates knew better than to listen to the song. They poked and prodded the boys, examined their teeth and eyes.

"Too many sellers," grumbled one of their captors. "We'll make nothing on these runts."

"These brutes don't want quality goods," whined another Flikkerman. "Any boy will do, when he's sure to be drowned or stabbed or cannon-blasted in a few months."

"So inefficient! I don't understand why humans kill one another."

"Neither do they."

Then the first speaker gave a chirp of surprise. "Ehiji, look! It's Druffle, Dollywilliams Druffle! What's *he* doing out here?"

The Mr. Druffle in question was a most unusual-looking man. He had greasy black hair that hung limply to his shoulders, a long nose and a filthy coat from which his bony hands emerged like implements for poking a fire. Over one shoulder hung something slick and rubbery. As he drew closer Pazel saw that it was an enormous eel.

Just behind Druffle came four huge men-at-arms. They had black beards trimmed to paintbrush points; their muscles bulged against iron bands around their forearms. Each carried a spear filed to razor sharpness and thick with dried gore where spearhead met shaft. As their eyes scanned the crowd, even the fiercest pirates stepped out of their way. *"Volpeks,"* men whispered. And so they were: Pazel knew them from drawings in his father's books. Now here they stood in the flesh: the dreaded mercenaries of the Narrow Sea, who would fight and kill for anyone who paid.

Behind the Volpeks shuffled a line of eight boys, chained at the wrists. Their faces and skin spoke of many homelands. One trait they had in common, however: they were all rather small.

". . . most certainly experienced!" Druffle was saying to the Flikkerman. "They won't have time to learn between here and Chereste!"

Pazel's heart skipped a beat. Chereste was home! It was the peninsula on whose tip stood Ormael City.

"But why dost thou another's bidding?" demanded the Flikker-man.

"Call it that if you will," said Druffle. "I call it gold for easy service. And gold he has, a-plenty."

"A merchant, sayest thou?"

"Aye, Froggy," said Druffle. "A gentleman bound for Ormael himself. We're to meet there in a week's time. So you see I must depart with the dawn—absolutely no later. Two more divers, just two, and I'll chance it. You!" He stopped before a skinny boy on Pazel's left. "Ever dived for pearls?"

Flabbergasted, the boy sputtered: "Yes! Oh yes, sir! Lots of times!"

"Where?"

"Where . . . where them pearls is found, sir."

"You lie. Bah, hold your breath anyway. Go ahead."

A silver pocket watch appeared in Druffle's hand. The boy took a deep breath. Druffle put his ear close to the other's face, listening for any cheating breath. Soon the boy's face began to purple.

At the end of the row, Pazel saw Neeps lean forward to look at him. Quite out loud, but in Sollochi, he said: *"Start breathing now, mate. Breathe as deep as you can—augh!"*

A Flikker cuffed him into silence. But Pazel had understood. Neeps *was* a diver—a pearl diver, in fact. Druffle would certainly buy him. And if there was any chance of them staying together, Pazel would have to pass the test as well.

The skinny boy was looking ill. Druffle slid the huge eel off his shoulder. With a wink he brought the gray-green head close to the boy's face—and then suddenly clamped its jaws tight on his nose.

"You're underwater, lad! Don't breathe, don't breathe!"

"Taauugh!"

The boy breathed. Druffle gave a snort of disgust.

Following Neeps' instruction, Pazel started gulping huge breaths. Light-headed but determined, he watched Neeps easily pass the test, and Druffle counting gold into a Flikker's hand. The man looked up and down the row.

"One more," he said.

Taking a risk, Pazel sang out in Ormali: "Try me, sir!"

The head Flikkerman raised a warning finger. Druffle, however, broke into a smile. "A Chereste boy!" he said. "Well, that makes two of us. Long since you've been home?"

"A very long time," said Pazel.

"So you'll tell me anything to get back to Ormael. Just as Froggy here will tell me anything for gold. Where did you dive?"

"Off the side of a whaler. My captain made us look for salt-worms, every fortnight."

Druffle sighed, turning away. "No long dives, then?"

"Well, sir!" said Pazel, catching his sleeve. "You wanted the truth, and the truth is I can dive like a blary seal! Pardon the adjective, sir. You'll find my lungs *capacious,* out of proportion to my size—"

"He he," laughed Druffle.

"And the murths, Mr. Druffle! I nearly forgot the sea-murths! They love whales and hate whalers, that's what our captain said. He feared they wrote hexes on the bottom of the ship, and we had to dive and look for them, sir, and erase them thoroughly, which was quite a challenge when they didn't exist—"

332   ROBERT V. S. REDICK

"Shut up! If you can hold your breath after that jib'rishing you're a diver indeed! Go on, try."

Pazel's outburst had indeed canceled out all his deep-breathing efforts, but what choice did he have? He took a last gulp of air and held it. Druffle looked at his watch. The Flikkers looked at Pazel. The Volpeks shook their massive heads.

Rather soon Pazel's own head began to feel as though it were being stepped on by a horse. "Don't breathe!" hissed Druffle, and, "Don't breathe! Don't breathe!" croaked all his captors, waving their hands and flashing like lightning bugs. The head Flikker pinched his nose.

When he had lasted twice as long as the first boy, purple spots rose before his eyes. *Don't breathe! Don't breathe!* He stamped his foot. Neeps' anxious face swam into view, but it was blotted out by Druffle's face, which seemed to be morphing into that of the eel. The purple spots became black. He was about to fall.

Goodbye, Neeps.

Suddenly Druffle lunged, knocking the Flikker's hand away. "Breathe, breathe, for the love of Rin!" he shouted. "You're mine!"

—28—

The Rescue of Steldak

25 Modoli 941
73rd day from Etherhorde

Sunset: dry wind, coppering skies. Captain Rose shut his account book (the official, laughable one, not the secret ledger of his personal gains) and set his quill on the desk. Ten feet away his steward bustled about the dining table, polishing plates, arranging the antique silver. Rose frowned. Guests at his dinner table were a formality he disliked.

At the back of the desk his crawly prisoner hunched in its filthy cage. Rose studied the creature from the corner of his eye. Something odd there: the crawly's face was too serene. It stank and shivered and attracted flies. Ghosts whirled about it, too, chattering when Rose's back was turned: he assumed that meant it was ill. But today his poison-taster was strangely calm. Rose had even caught it stretching and limbering, like an acrobat preparing for a stunt. It was suspicious behavior, and Rose decided to replace the crawly at the first opportunity. Swellows, always on the lookout for crawly skulls, would pay him something for this wretch.

"Twenty minutes, Captain," said the steward. "Do you wish to be dressed?"

"See to the table, I'll dress myself."

He put the cage in his desk-drawer and slammed it shut with

a bang. The crawly didn't even look up as Rose slid him backward into darkness.

"You witchy little grub," he said.

He stepped to the wardrobe, slid into his dinner jacket and began to comb out his beard. Mr. Teggatz came and went with little bobs and bows, carrying now the bread, now a fruit bowl, now a basin of aromatic sands into which Oggosk would spit her well-chewed sapwort. Rose's mood darkened further. She would bring the cat, naturally.

First to arrive was Sandor Ott. As Teggatz withdrew he came up behind the captain and murmured: "That's a fine guard you've placed on the Shaggat. I could not have done better myself."

"The augrongs don't care a fig who's behind that door," said Rose. "But no one else knows that."

"And His Nastiness, for all that talk of being a God, is not keen on angering those beasts. His sons are scared witless, naturally. The better to keep them all quiet, eh?"

"Nothing will keep that madman quiet for long," said Rose.

Ott smiled. " *'My wolf, my red iron wolf!'* Have you any idea what that means?"

"That he is mad."

"Of course—but long of memory, too. Operatives of the Secret Fist brought word of a certain Red Wolf of the Mzithrin. It was a thing men feared, and fought over. Why he raves of it now I should very much like to know." He shook his head. "In any case, Thasha Isiq will be married in ten days' time. And once we are on the empty sea the Shaggat can roar as he likes."

"As can I," said Rose. "Roar, and more than roar. That Bolutu will be the first to feel it."

Ott raised a finger. "You shall not kill the veterinarian, sir. He is odd, but also the Empire's best, and he must see to the health of our pigs and cattle and hens. Who knows how long we shall dine on their good flesh? 'Tis more than a century since anyone crossed the Ruling Sea. But after Thasha's marriage we may place him in chains if you like."

Rose grunted. "He can sleep where he works, among animals. And dine there. But what of the treasure, Ott? What do your men have to say?"

"What have they to say? Why, that none suspect our hiding place, of course. Fear not, Captain: it will not be stolen, or embezzled, or spilled into the sea. It will all be there when His Nastiness is ready to use it. But that day is distant yet."

The other guests began to arrive. Young Pacu Lapadolma, the musical niece, dragging a sour-faced Thasha Isiq. Bolutu himself, with his fine clothes and gentleman's smile. Thyne, the remaining Company man, who kept as far as possible from Ott and Rose. Syrarys, who made apologies for the ambassador (headaches again, poor dear).

Oggosk came last, with her cat in her arms. No sooner had the steward closed the door behind them than Sniraga gave an angry yowl and squirmed free, vanishing under the table. Pacu laughed, but Thasha Isiq scowled and put a hand on her necklace.

The dinner started badly, with Pacu reciting a bit of her great-aunt's patriotic poetry (*"In Arqual we are happy bees/but don't forget our stingers, please!"*) and Thasha choosing that moment to choke on her soup. Then Thyne made everyone stand up to toast the Great Lady back in Etherhorde, and Bolutu felt compelled to speak of Lady Lapadolma's kindness to a certain stray dog, and Pacu declared how her great-aunt had given her "everything, absolutely everything that makes me what I am today," at which Thasha raised an eyebrow as if to say, *And what would that be?*

"Three days to Ormael!" Pacu went on. "Arqual's newest territory! What do you suppose five years in the Empire has done to her? I understand her wall has been rebuilt, and the city center tidied up, the riffraff expelled, proper Arquali families installed in the better homes. Let us drink to that!"

Oggosk (who had never budged from her chair) spat noisily into her basin. "This sapwort tastes like sludge," she said.

It did not help when Ott tried to draw Lady Thasha into the

conversation: hadn't she learned rather a lot of Mzithrini by now? Thasha shook her head firmly, but Syrarys cried, "Oh, she has, I've heard her! After all, her wedding is just ten days off! Say something, dear. The sound of that language is so *primal*!"

Thasha looked at her with loathing, then suddenly growled out a few words. She told them it meant *"My enemy's enemy is my friend."* But Rose noted how Bolutu jumped, and shot her a quick glance of amazement.

Everyone was used to how little the captain spoke—and after ten weeks at sea, they did not much care. It was his cabin: they were glad enough to ignore him and devour his food. But just before the meal ended he surged to his feet with a table-jarring lurch.

"Oggosk! That thrice-damnable red cat just spoke to me!"

He pointed at his desk; all eyes turned. Sniraga was seated beside his letter box, the tip of her tail twitching slightly.

"Fah," said Oggosk.

"Captain!" cried Pacu Lapadolma. "Do you think you have a *woken* cat on your hands?"

"*I* don't have any cat at all!"

"She does cling to you, though," Bolutu observed. "What makes you her favorite, I wonder?"

Thasha Isiq's eyes narrowed. "What did she say, Captain?"

Rose hesitated, staring down at them all. "Nothing important," he said at last.

"But *surely* an animal's first words are important in themselves?" said Pacu.

"They're not her first."

"Well, then?"

Rose looked at the two girls. "Little spies," he said.

"I beg your pardon?!"

"That's what the cat said: 'Little spies.' "

No one dared to laugh. Then Oggosk wiped the grease from her fingers and glanced up.

"I've told you: Sniraga's no woken animal. She's clever in the way of cats, but no more. You're plagued by an evil visitation,

Nilus: some spirit-cat out of your childhood or family history. Don't take it out on my pet."

She spoke as if to a wearisome child. Rose dropped into his chair and began a noisy attack on an apple. Thyne and Syrarys tried to revive the conversation, but everyone was distracted by Rose, whose staring eyes followed the cat wherever it roamed about the cabin.

At last the meal was over: the guests drained their cups and left. The steward and his boy swept about the table, clearing dishes, snuffing lamps. Then they too departed, and Rose was alone.

The cabin was dim. He stood stock-still, like a nervous bull. There was no sound but the ship's churning wake.

"You're here, aren't you?" he whispered at last.

Silence. He rubbed his beard in a sudden paroxysm of nerves. "Speak! Where are you? What do you want?"

Silence, and then piano music: distantly, from the first-class lounge. *Re-mem-ber the old, old souls of Soo-li, drowned deep below.*

Rose gave a mirthless laugh, almost a sob. Then he turned and stalked out of the cabin, locking the door behind him.

For two minutes nothing stirred. Then, with the tiniest sound imaginable, something did.

In the sand basin next to Oggosk's chair, among the bits of chewed sapwort, a tiny round shape broke the surface, swiveling left and right. It was a woman's head. It studied the cabin. And then in one swift movement, five ixchel burst from the sand, backs together, hands already fitting arrows to bows.

"All clear," said Diadrelu.

"Good," Talag answered. "Out of this muck, now—down and regroup. And toss some sapwort on the floor. Make a mess."

They held breathing-tubes of hollow straw: these they minced and buried in the sand. Then they brushed one another clean, smiling but not laughing as the sand fell from their hair. Four ixchel slipped from the basin's rim to the ground, and the last kicked bits of sapwort over the basin's edge. Rats were to be blamed for this raid.

"I thought he'd found us," said Diadrelu.

"You forget Rose is a madman," said Taliktrum. "Chatting with ghosts."

His father nodded. "If he knew *crawlies* were loose on his ship there'd be no talk. He'd smoke the ship and we'd die. Ensyl! To the door frame. Fentrelu, the beams. You *must* speak to the prisoner, no matter what follows."

"I can still smell that monster, Sniraga," said Fentrelu.

"Enough of that!" snapped Talag. "If we're interrupted, lie flat in the center of the beam—you'll be out of sight from the ground. We'll return for you somehow. Have your tools? Then go."

They went, five shadows rushing over the cabin floor. There was no telling how long the captain would spend aloft before turning in for the night. They might have thirty minutes, or three.

Dri, Talag and Taliktrum made straight for Rose's desk. One leap and Dri was on his chair; another, his desktop. She looked up: there was Ensyl, already perched spider-like over the cabin door. Fentrelu she could not see; he would still be scaling the wall to the deck beams. Crouching down, she watched her brother and nephew pry at the lower drawer with the flats of their blades. The wood was old, warped. It moved a fraction of an inch and stuck fast.

"I'll help," she whispered, but Talag waved her off. He was right, of course: all five of them had precise tasks and positions. Not one was optional.

She watched the men strain, gasping. The drawer seemed hopelessly wedged. Then a voice none knew called to them— from *within* the drawer.

"Slide in through the top drawer, brothers—slide in and lift from the back!"

Dri felt her heart thrill. It was true, Great Mother! One of their kin!

"Can you open the top drawer, sister?" Talag hissed.

Dri bent and seized the handle. The drawer slid open easily.

Talag clapped his son's arm. "Up, up!"

Taliktrum went like a shot. Two leaps, a quick smile for Dri—

and into the darkness of the drawer. She heard him shoving and squirming, then a groan of effort. The lower drawer shifted in place.

Talag grabbed the brass handle and hauled with all his might. The big drawer fought him for another instant, then slid wide open.

"Get Taliktrum out of there!" Talag ordered, vaulting into the drawer.

Dri bent down and called her nephew. Out he came, smeared with pencil-dust and grime, and dropped without a word into the lower drawer, after his father.

Dimly she heard their work: assembling the crank-and-lever apparatus that would bend the bars of the prisoner's cage. If only Felthrup spoke the truth, and it was no more than a common birdcage. They could not bend hardened steel.

A thump: Fentrelu had dropped the rope from the beam above. Dri caught the end and quickly tied a pair of foot-sized loops. When she looked down again she felt a wave of relief. Talag and Taliktrum were there, helping a third man out of the drawer.

He was in bad shape—diseased, dirty—but he had not lost all his strength. If he could not quite leap to the desktop, he scrambled up the chair nimbly enough

She would not let him bow. "You honor us by your survival, brother! I am Diadrelu of Ixphir House—Dri, you must call me."

"*Formerly* of Ixphir House," said Taliktrum. "We are none of us going back."

The prisoner placed his folded hands upon his forehead—an old-fashioned gesture of thanks; Dri had not seen it since her grandmothers' day. "I am Steldak, Lady Dri. My home is Étrej in the Trothe of Chereste, but it is thirty years since I set foot in that land."

"The Trothe is gone," said Talag, "devoured by Arqual, although some giants still use the name. But I have never heard of ixchel there."

"We are there, my lord. My people had a great house in Etrela Canyon, until the giants dammed the river and flooded us out.

Many died; the rest scattered on either side of the canyon. We on the east bank made our way to sea. I do not know what happened to the western group. My wife and children were among them."

He said it simply, but Dri saw by his face that the wound still ached three decades on. Was he also a bit feverish? His eyes wandered in an unfocused manner.

"No more talk," said Talag. "Put your feet in those loops, brother. Fentrelu will haul you to safety until our work here is done."

"My lord!" said Steldak suddenly. "Rose will go mad when he finds that you've freed me. You should have waited till we were in port, and could flee inland."

"My clan does not flee," said Talag fiercely. "Up with you."

He tugged sharply on the rope, and Steldak began to rise, still looking at them oddly. The others went to work. Father and son hauled the cage forward and began strewing the filth about the drawer, simulating a struggle. Dri sprinted the length of the desktop, glided across the floor on swallow-wings and landed once more in the sand basin. There she began to dig.

The rat lay comatose, about eight inches down. It was exhausting work to drag its body to the surface, her ears pricked all the while for Ensyl's warning. At last the beast was free, and she lowered it by the tail until its whiskers brushed the floor. Then she let it drop.

When she had dragged the beast to within a few feet of the cabin door she looked at it with gratitude. It was no special rat—just one they had ambushed in Night Village for this purpose, drugged with *blanë* and carried off to the cupboard where Oggosk's sand basin was stored between meals, where it and the five of them had lain for ten hours, waiting. But it would serve their purpose, and be killed for it.

Dri sprinted back to the desk. *Blanë* meant "foolsdeath." The poison was insanely difficult to make—gold cyanide, wasp blood and octopus ink, chilled *for forty years* in lead bottles underground—and they had not a drop to spare. The results were spectacular, however: *blanë* did no harm, but mimicked death almost perfectly. Even better, it could be instantly reversed.

But the antidote that would shock a creature out of *blanë* sleep was even harder to brew. Dri pulled the coated arrow from its quiver. She would have but one shot.

It was, like all her brother's plans, brilliant. Rose's cabin had seemed impregnable: there were no crawl spaces between decks here, no empty adjoining rooms. They would have had to pass through several occupied chambers, or down the long and busy corridor, had Talag not noticed Oggosk's love of sapwort.

A *swish* and they were beside her on the desktop. "I have strewn rat-filth about the floor," said Taliktrum. "And checked for footprints. The cabin's ready."

"I will be last from this chamber," said Talag. "Sister: you will run spear-point."

Taliktrum whirled. Spear-point was the most dangerous position when ixchel ran, the spot where life-and-death decisions were made. It was the place of honor.

"You promised it to me!" he said.

"But I cannot allow it now. The prisoner is too weak, and like Fentrelu I smell something amiss in this chamber. My heart warns against it. Diadrelu will lead."

Taliktrum did not hide his fury. By leading their escape he would have completed the last rite of manhood, and could claim the title of lord.

"We *agreed*," he hissed.

"You dare to argue?" said Talag, enraged in his turn. "Look to your aunt, boy! She is overtrusting and soft of heart—but also selfless. There is no thought of herself above the clan, no distraction at this moment of peril. *That* is the mark of a leader—not your insolent whining."

Taliktrum was deeply shaken. "Father—" he began.

"Silence!" snapped Talag. "By the Pits, you shame me!"

"Fentrelu," called Diadrelu, looking up at the beam, "how is Steldak? Can he run?"

"He claims so, m'lady," came Fentrelu's voice from the darkness.

"Then he must try. Make your way to the door frame, quickly."

Then Steldak cried, "No!"

"What?" cried Talag. "How no, brother?"

"I want to stay, and kill him! Help me! Lend me a sword and the tyrant dies!"

"Are you mad? Kill Rose? You'd sign all our death warrants with the act!"

"We'll make it look like suicide, Lord Talag! Everyone knows he's cracked—"

"Not another word!" said Dri. "You will obey us and make part of our clan! Surely you owe us that much? Get to the doorway, instantly!"

"You don't understand, m'lady! He's brought the Shaggat aboard! The Shaggat! God-King of the Nessarim! Whole countries will be laid waste if Rose has his way! Arqual will seize the Crownless Lands, even the Mzithrin in time!"

"The Shaggat Ness drowned at sea," Talag said.

"A lie! Arqual's master lie! He's here, aboard—that is why we stopped at Licherog!"

Brother and sister looked at each other.

"There is no time to debate," Dri said.

"None," agreed Talag. "Hear me, Steldak. Rose will not be killed. Nor will he or the Emperor achieve their foul ends. This ship is mine. I have sworn a blood oath to see my people out of the hell of fear and misery that is Arqual—to see them returned to the isle from whence all ixchel were stolen, long ages ago. Rose alone of all men can pilot us to that place. Join us and be welcome—or by my own hand be slain! Now go!"

Steldak said no more, but Dri felt horror at his revelation. Here was the conspiracy, laid bare at last, confirming the clan's worst fears about giants and their cruelty. *And they are cruel. By the Nine Pits, the Shaggat! What would Arqual do with that butcher of a king?*

Then Ensyl cried: "Rose is come!"

No one needed commanding now. Taliktrum leaped to the dark floor; Dri bent her bow. Talag stood beside her, tense as a cheetah ready to sprint.

The door opened: Dri's arrow flew. Lamplight from the hall spilled yellow on the floor. The rat squealed to life, terrified, and bolted under the table.

"Broil and blast you!" shouted Rose, lurching after it.

Dri and Talag were already off his desk and halfway to the door, which Rose had left open for the light—as Talag knew he would. Dri saw Ensyl flit through to safety.

And then disaster. A voice overhead shouted, *"Stop!"* Brother and sister turned to see Steldak fighting on the beam with Fentrelu. The prisoner had the strength of sudden mania: even as they watched he broke free of Fentrelu and hurled himself from the beam—and onto Rose's back.

The captain was bending under the table, looking for the rat. He apparently felt something, for he half stood, hit his head on the table and roared with pain. Steldak, clinging spider-like to Rose's shirt, began moving upward.

"He has my knife!" cried Fentrelu.

The next instant Dri was in flight. It nearly broke her arms to rise airborne from a standstill, but she did it. Across the cabin she flew in a heartbeat, her own sword drawn. She would kill this poor mad Steldak, bear his body away, say a prayer for him—

A black shock of pain. Claws, fangs, falling.

Sniraga!

Dri was pierced through leg and torso. A crash: she was pinned to the floor. Her sword gone. Her swallow-wings snapped. The cat's mouth closed over her head and shoulders, its blood-scented breath filled her lungs. With her left arm she drew her knife and struck—the mouth withdrew, but a claw hooked her hand and ripped it, and then the knife was gone, too.

Rose had sensed it. *You're here, aren't you?*

The cat had been waiting all along.

Dri was ready for death. But death did not come. Instead her brother did, and Steldak himself—two blades whirling, stabbing. She saw Talag thrust his sword deep into Sniraga's neck. A deafening yowl. She was flung free.

Somewhere close, almost on top of her it seemed, Rose was bellowing: "Kill it, animal! Kill that rat and I'll almost think well of ye!"

Dri was against a table leg, bleeding fast. She forced herself to rise. Rose was staggering around the far side of the table, holding his head. *But where was Sniraga?*

Taliktrum's voice, high-pitched with fear: *"Papa!"* Years since he called Talag that.

Then Dri saw the cat. She had leaped to a dinner chair, rolling and striking at something—at Taliktrum, as the boy parried both her front paws, his sword a blinding arc. Steldak held her tail in one hand, and with the other slashed wildly with Fentrelu's knife. Talag, limp and bloodied, hung from Sniraga's mouth.

Dri sprinted for the chair. Blood was splashing from her hand but she did not feel it. *Talag! Talag!*

The chair crashed over, Taliktrum was pinned. And Sniraga, with one great bound, leaped through the open door.

Dri ran until she thought her heart would burst, no longer caring who saw her. Steldak held the cat's tail for half the length of the empty passageway. Then he too fell, gripping a handful of fur. Her neck gushing blood, Sniraga skidded around the corner and was gone.

The other ixchel escaped unseen. The prayers in the hold that night were not for Steldak—who offered suicide, and sat stonefaced, alone—but for Talag, their master, slain with no thought of self above the clan.

Running Before the Storm

2 Teala 941
80th day from Etherhorde

Druffle's ship was the *Prince Rupin,* but the only thing princely about her was her name. Pazel gasped at the sight. The vessel sagged at the waist like an old mule, her paint little more than a memory. Torn rigging dangled from her spars, and sailors aloft moved gingerly, as if expecting the footropes to snap. She had no gunports, but three rusty cannon pointed backward from the quarterdeck. Apparently she was used to being chased.

Her captain was a frowning, bushy-haired man with no love for Mr. Druffle, and, "Right hazardous, and a fool's waste of time!" was his greeting as the skiff drew up to *Prince Rupin*'s side. Druffle answered with a rude gesture involving the eel.

One by one the purchased boys climbed her ladder, followed by Druffle and his Volpek thugs. The boys huddled near the bow, ignored by the surly crew. Already men were straining at the capstan, weighing anchor. *Bakru, Wind-Sire,* they chanted, half asleep. *Do not let your lions devour us.* Soon they were drifting with the river's flow, leaving the islets behind, sliding into the sea.

Dawn was breaking, and Pazel knew from one glance at the water that it would be rough sailing. A fierce south wind battered them from portside, and yellow-black clouds like bad bruises were gathering ahead.

He wrapped the old coat about himself more tightly. The waves were ragged and confused. And yet (with Druffle at his elbow, urging him on) the captain ordered the mainsails set.

"The mains?" said Neeps, as if he couldn't believe his own ears.

Pazel looked at the wind-torn sea. "Impossible," he said.

The other boys looked at them anxiously. "What's wrong? Are you tarboys? What's impossible?"

But it was happening. Sailors aloft—leechlines freed—the big square sails flashing open—

"Hold on!" Pazel shouted.

The ship leaped forward. Timbers groaned, old sheets struggled to rip bolt from frame; on the spars above men clung to anything that seemed likely to be there a moment later. The wind was soon moaning through the stays, and the waves on the bow were like men trying to kick in a door.

Pazel and Neeps had heard all these sounds before—but never all at once, and never on such an obviously ghastly ship. But if they were frightened, the other boys were terrified. One fell seasick in the first few minutes and had to lean over the rail in the lashing spray.

Druffle, however, looked almost merry. He staggered about the deck, black coat flapping scarecrow-like, gazing up with approval at the great spread of canvas.

"He's a loon!" said Pazel. "This old hulk won't take such speed!"

Neeps shook his head. "This is bad business, mate—I can smell it. But what are we to do? It's plain they don't want our opinion."

"They don't," Pazel agreed. But he couldn't take his eyes from the sails.

"Come on," said Neeps. "Let's get out of this wind. And talk, if we can."

They took shelter behind one of the *Rupin*'s sorry-looking lifeboats. At first they could still barely hear each other. But by lying on their stomachs with their heads close together, they managed to talk almost normally. And Neeps had much to tell about the *Chathrand*. The mystery of the slaughtered rats was just the beginning. A rumor had also spread among the tarboys that the ship's carpenters and blacksmiths were at work on a secret project, deep in the ship. Whole decks were off-limits, night and day, except to sailors cleared by Rose himself.

"Reyast heard talk of an iron door and a padlock," said Neeps. "He thinks they're building an extra brig."

"But there's nobody locked up in the regular brig. What do they need two for?"

"Your guess is as good as mine," said Neeps.

"I can't guess at all," said Pazel. "But you haven't told me what happened to you."

"I'm coming to that. I told you it was Jervik's doing—blast him!—but it was also Thasha's. Honest to salt, that girl is a menace!"

It seemed Thasha and Syrarys had had a ripping fight. Thasha had caught the consort opening vials of Ambassador Isiq's headache medicine: vials sealed by Dr. Chadfallow back in Etherhorde. Syrarys claimed she was merely adding an herbal tonic to calm Isiq's nerves. "Tasteless and harmless," she told Thasha. "You could drink it by the glass." But Thasha didn't believe a word of it. She accused Syrarys of poisoning her father.

"But they're married—or close enough!" said Pazel.

"Well, mate, ain't that the question?" Neeps gave him a hard look. "Is it close enough for her to inherit his gold, if Isiq knocks off?"

"Are you saying she wants him dead?"

"Who knows? Thasha might be cracked. She thinks that old crone Oggosk is spying on her—ever since the woman's cat got hold of her necklace. And she also suspects Jervik."

"Jervik, a spy? Who would be fool enough to use *him*?"

"Nobody, but Thasha's convinced of it. We met an hour after they took you ashore. You might as well know she was crying her eyes out."

"For her father?"

348 ROBERT V. S. REDICK

"For you, you thick stump. Days running."

Pazel thought the wind had played a trick on his ears. Neeps couldn't suppress a laugh.

"Aye, Pazel, she's a wee bit fond of you! 'Money, why didn't I give him some *money*?' she kept wailing—not a bad question, either. But she's in trouble herself now. Her father took Syrarys' side in that fight. 'You may *want* what's best for me, girl,' he told her, 'but Syrarys *knows* what is.' That just about broke Thasha's heart. And it was while she was telling me all this—we were down on the mercy deck—that we heard a thump a few yards away. It was Jervik, and two other tarboys what've become his bootlicks. They were crouched behind a bulkhead, listening.

"They claimed Uskins had sent them to check on a noise in the rudder-chains. But Thasha went wild on 'em. 'Do I sound like a rudder-chain? Is that why you follow me around? Is that why you pressed that ugly ear to my door last night?' Jervik said he never did. But he said it with a wink at his mates. Oh, Pazel"—Neeps grinned from ear to ear—"he should have skipped that wink."

"What happened?"

"She whacked him silly, mate. I've never seen the like. Jervik was pinned up against the wall before he knew what hit him, protecting his tender parts. One of his mates took off running. The other one grabbed Thasha's arms from behind. I got him off—clipped him two good ones in the stomach—but he, well—"

"He beat you," said Pazel.

"Only because of his rings," said Neeps, turning scarlet. "Otherwise I'd have had him. Tubsung, that smelly hulk. Anyway, I blacked out for a moment. When my head cleared Tubsung was on the deck. So was Jervik, curled up in a ball. Thasha was standing over them, shouting, calling them worms. I mean loud, mate. Like screaming. *WOOOORMS!*"

"Oh," said Pazel. He could guess what happened next.

"A crowd came—sailors, steerage passengers, marines. Uskins was the first officer to arrive, and he had the marines whisk Thasha off to her cabin in a flash. She shouted: 'I started it! Don't blame him!' But Uskins never believed she'd done any fighting. Jervik, that filth-tongue, said *I* was the one pestering the Young Mistress. And what could I say? How could I tell 'im what we were doing on the mercy deck, when it's off-limits now? Then Jervik showed off his bruises. Said I attacked him after he caught me asking Thasha for *unseemly favors*. What do you suppose that means? First-class food?"

"It means kisses and the like, Neeps," said Pazel, smiling in his turn.

Neeps blushed brighter than before. "That scum," he said. "I'll kill him!"

"Don't even joke about that!" said Pazel, surprising himself with his own sharpness. "Besides, you can't kill all the Jerviks and Uskinses in the world."

"I'll settle for one or two."

Pazel sighed. "You still haven't explained how you ended up *here*."

"Simple enough," said Neeps. "They would have chucked me ashore at the next port of call. But about the time Uskins separated us the lookout spotted the *Lady Apsal*—the grain-carrier, you know her, don't you?"

"Of course," said Pazel. "She's an Etherhorde ship."

"She was bound back to Etherhorde, actually. We tied up to exchange mailbags. And seeing as her next stop was Uturphe, Rose asked their captain to toss us out there 'with the rest of the garbage.' How do you like that?"

"About as much as you do. What happened next?"

Neeps was working himself back into a temper. "The final touch came from Swellows—may his tongue rot out! He told me he'd sent you to an inn on Blackwell Street. Naturally I went looking for you straightaway."

"And found the Flikkermen." Pazel lay down on the deck, a hand over his eyes. "I'm sorry, brother."

"Listen, mate, never call me that."

"What, *brother*? Why not, Rin's sake? I've never had a better friend than you!"

"So call me *friend*. Not brother—not on your life."

There it was again: that seething fury in Neeps' eyes. Pazel knew better than to argue the point.

"Friend it is," he said, a bit awkwardly. Then he squinted at Neeps' collar. "Pitfire! That's a right nasty bruise on your shoulder. It's black as ink."

Neeps gaped. "Kick me, mate, I forgot! It *is* ink! It's a message for you."

"A message?" Pazel raised his head. "From whom?"

Once more Neeps grew angry. "Jervik, if you ask me. I woke up and someone had written it on my skin. Jervik knew I'd go looking for you in Uturphe. Maybe he wanted to gloat one last time. Can you believe the nerve? The oddest thing is that he used some foreign language. None of us tarboys could read it."

"But flaming fish, Neeps, *I* could have read it! And what if it wasn't Jervik?"

"Who else would do such a nasty thing?"

"The ixchel!"

"Ixchel? Ixchel?" Neeps' eyes went wide. "Are you saying *Chathrand*'s infested with *crawlies*?"

"Don't call them that."

"You mean you *knew*—and you let one use me for an ink blotter?"

"They're not as bad as we think."

"Really!" said Neeps. "And why didn't you tell anyone about your little ship-sinking friends?"

"They said they'd kill me."

"How nice. I suppose your Gift let you hear them?"

"That's how it started. But if they *want* to be heard they just strain a little—*bend their voices,* they say—and out comes words that anyone can hear."

Pazel tugged Neeps' collar back, revealing more of his shoulder, and gave a cry of dismay. "It's nearly all washed off! I can't read anything but 'Simja' and 'must.' Oh, Neeps, you offal-head! What if it was important?"

Neeps looked at him over his shoulder. Then he closed his eyes. "*Relaga Pazel Pathkendle eb Simja glijn. Ilenek ke ostrun hi Bethrin Belg.* So there. I memorized it, just in case. Pazel! What's wrong?"

Pazel had begun to shake all over. Still he dropped his eyes. "Find something to do," he whispered. "Don't make Druffle suspicious. We're going to have to escape."

"You know what it means, do you?"

"Oh, yes," said Pazel. "It's in their tongue, the ixchel's. And it's very plain: 'Tell Pazel Pathkendle he must come to Simja. They're going to murder the bridal girl.'"

Toward midday the wind ebbed slightly. Druffle again produced his eel, soot-black after hours of roasting in the galley stove, and sectioned it with an axe on the topdeck. Inside the flesh was tender and pink. Druffle tossed each boy an eel-steak large enough to choke a bear, and with bear-like ferocity they ate where they sat, forgetting their fears. Only the seasick boy lost out.

"Clean them bones!" Druffle laughed. "We need you strong for our little job on the coast!"

"What coast is that, Mr. Druffle, sir?" asked Pazel.

"Wait and see, my Chereste heart! And don't talk with your mouth full."

Pazel and Neeps leaned back against the lifeboat, chewing steadily. Escape felt more possible on a full stomach—but only just. They looked at the raucous Nelu Peren, this Anything-but-Quiet Sea. There was a dark smudge of mountains to starboard. That would be the mainland, just two or three leagues off, but it might as well have been the moon.

"We're not going anywhere while this weather lasts," said Neeps.

Pazel nodded. "And it's going to get bad again, can't you feel it?"

"I can," said Neeps. "Worse than ever, I'd guess. There's a right storm brewing, maybe."

"The other problem," Pazel went on, "is *where* to escape. All we know for certain is that *Chathrand*'s taking Thasha to Simja."

"We're heading west," said Neeps, "so I suppose those mountains could be part of Ipulia. But I thought Ipulia was a land of lakes—it's called *the Blue Kingdom,* after all."

"Maybe it has mountains, too," said Pazel. "Or maybe we're west of Ipulia already, and that ridge is part of the Trothe of Chereste. That's Ormael, Neeps. My home—or what's left of it."

"Didn't you say Ormael is just a day's journey from Simja?"

"Less," said Pazel. "But even if we land in Ormael, and somehow get away from these nutters, who's going to take us across the Simja Straits? We're not tarboys anymore. Simja may be outside the Empire, but it still uses the Sailing Code. All the Crownless Lands do."

"They won't *know* we're not tarboys in Ormael."

"Won't they? If I know Uskins, the first place he'll go is the Boys' Registry. We're probably already on the blacklist."

"That skunk!" said Neeps. "How I wish the augrong had eaten him."

The wind soon revived. They talked a little more, but the waves too were growing, and their little shelter was regularly doused with spray. The other boys were huddled as far from the sides as possible, looks of shock on their faces.

At nightfall Druffle chained them to the fife-rail. The boys themselves asked for the chain, for the sea was by this time breaking steadily over the bow, and there was a real danger of being washed overboard. Pazel and Neeps refused the chain (it carried risks of another kind), but they locked elbows with the other boys in the lee of the forecastle. Plunging, plowing, the ship kept up her hysterical westward run.

It became impossible to speak. Soaked and freezing, they watched the crew battle the storm. Pazel's teeth chattered and his feet turned a pale blue. Yet somehow he drifted into a miserable kind of sleep. He dreamed he was an eel himself, swimming at great speed around a white tower that rose from the seafloor to pierce the waves, and reached beyond them far into the sky. Around him churned fish with glowing bodies, purple gem-like eyes, dagger teeth. There were submerged windows in the tower, and even a door, still closed tight against the weight of the ocean. Then a banshee wail erupted, and Pazel woke.

The boys were leaping up—only to fall again as the *Rupin* plunged sickeningly to port.

"The topsail!" someone cried. "The topsail's split in two!"

Pazel groped for a handhold, trying to make sense of the chaos rushing his senses. Hours must have passed. The night was black, the wind furious—and something terrible lay dead ahead.

He didn't know how he knew. Around the ship all was heaving darkness. Torn canvas snapped above their heads with a sound like galloping hooves. Wind and waves and thunder drowned the cries of the men.

Lightning crackled. For an instant the world glowed madly bright and fifty sailors screamed like infants: a cliff towered over them, straight ahead and impossibly close. *Dead!* was all Pazel had time to think, and then the ship struck.

But it was no cliff: it was rain, a monstrous rain front that shattered on the bowsprit like a great glass wall. Everyone was blinded. The boys hugged the rails, the chain, one another. Somewhere the captain was screaming, "Up the fore! Up! Up!" In the next flash men could be seen already halfway to the topsail yard, axes thrust in their belts to cut away the ruined canvas. It was terrible to see them, barely supported by the rotten ropes, lashed by so much rain they seemed to be trailing icicles.

A forestay snapped like a giant bowstring. The mast tilted, a sailor screamed, and by the next bolt Pazel saw him plummeting seaward, arms flailing. Darkness took him before the sea.

Panic was spreading among the boys. Some were weeping, others screaming for Druffle to unlock them before they drowned. And they *would* drown, Pazel knew, if the bow dug under—as fast as that fallen man.

But Druffle was beyond earshot, or perhaps beyond caring. In the end Pazel did the job with a sailor's axe. Two boys were left trailing chain, but at least they were free.

"For Rin's sake, stay where you are!" Neeps shouted at them. "The rail won't give unless the ship herself breaks to pieces!"

Pazel could never afterward say how long they rolled and pitched through that storm. But a moment came at last when they swept out of it, quite as suddenly as they had entered. The rain blew past; they heard it hissing away eastward like a swarm of curses. The wind dropped; then it dropped further. Soon the only sounds were the pumps churning belowdecks, water jetting from the scuppers into the sea—and the hoarse oaths of Mr. Druffle.

"A racer, eh? A swift sea horse! That's what you called the *Rupin,* wasn't it, Captain Snaketongue? Blast you to Bramian! This ship is a disgrace!"

"Only when you drive her like a madman!" shot back the captain, miserable.

"Watch yourself, blubber-guts!"

"I've had enough!" the captain went on. "You Volpeks, there—what good's his money if we're all drowned? And how much have you seen, anyway?"

"Half," grunted one of the Volpeks, eyeing Druffle with some suspicion.

"And the rest on delivery of the goods!" snarled Druffle. "You know the rules."

"Your rules," said another Volpek. "Not ours."

"Eight feet of water in the hold!" The captain stamped his feet. "We're drinking the sea! Join with me, you fighting men! We can save this ship! And after we unload this screaming monkey we've a rendezvous with the Guild! That's right, Gregory's Guild! They'll have work for you—man's work, not sending young boys to their—"

"SILENCE!" boomed Druffle, raising his hand. The change in his voice was astonishing: it cracked like a whip across the deck. The captain stumbled backward, clutching his jaw as if reeling from a blow.

Druffle cackled. "You should know better, Captain! And you, you warty brutes"—here he turned to the Volpeks—"has

Dollywilliams Druffle ever cheated a man? What's his reputation built on, then? Gah, you insult me."

Last of all he faced the boys. "You'll be wondering at my powers, lads. How'd I make this old muskrat behave? Well, the fact is I'm a mage by family inclination. My dad was a great enchanter, what we call a *thumbaturg,* as he needed just one finger to work his spells. My uncles were sea-sorcerers in the pay of the Becturium Viceroys. And my own mother had some river-weird blood. So you see, it's best not to cross me: I'm liable to blast you to jelly whether I mean to or no."

He looked down at them happily. No one knew what to say.

But Pazel was thinking *Gregory's Guild*?

Dawn revealed a ship in ruins. From bow to stern lay a tangled mass of rigging and ribboned sails. The foremast sprawled in pieces across the deck. The main topsail yard, a thirty-foot timber, had fallen through the quarterdeck and split the captain's bed neatly in two.

But they were still moving west. A pair of trysails had survived the night, and together they just managed to keep the floating wreck in motion. It was a gentle, sunny morning. Neeps slept like a stone. But Pazel felt an odd excitement in his chest. On skinned knees and rope-burned hands he crawled to the starboard bow. And there he saw an image from his dreams.

Sandstone cliffs. Lush meadows at their heights, bold black rocks in the surf below. A pencil-thin waterfall, dissolved to spray by the wind before it touched the waves.

"Ormael!" He leaped up, forgetting his pain, forgetting everything. *"Ormael! Ormael!"*

He would have gone on shouting for the next five leagues, but a hand seized his elbow and yanked him down. It was Druffle.

"Get off there, you hullaballoonish clown! You trying to wake the whole shore?"

"But no one lives there, Mr. Druffle!"

"I know that. Ain't good for a thing, Quarrel's Cliff."

"It's good for kite-flying, Mr. Druffle! And my father says it's good for a stealthy approach to the city. Is that why *we're* sailing so close, Mr. Druffle, sir?"

"He he."

"Mr. Druffle, what is Gregory's Guild?"

"You're an Ormali. You must know about Captain Gregory Pathkendle."

Pazel's heart leaped in his chest. And in almost the same instant it occurred to him that Druffle had never once asked his name.

Before he could find his voice, one of the other boys chimed in: "Pathkendle the Traitor."

Pazel whirled, clenching his fists. Druffle raised an eyebrow.

"Now, now," he said. "That's none of our concern. Why he joined up with the Sizzies no one rightly knows. But he left 'em, see? Found himself better mates among us freebooters, and that was our lucky day. Yes indeed! To us Captain Gregory was a prince. And old Snaketongue over there is lying. Gregory never dealt with scum like him."

Freebooters meant smugglers, Pazel knew. "Are *you* part of Gregory's Guild, Mr. Druffle, sir?"

"You ask a right heap of questions."

"Thank you, sir! Is Captain Gregory still alive?"

But Druffle only wagged a finger, none too angrily, and turned away.

They crept nearer to Ormael. Pazel watched Quarrel's Cliff give way to the four named rocks (the Stovepipe, the Old Man, the Monk's Hood, the Hound). He saw goats in a high meadow where he'd picnicked once with his mother and Neda, and green bulges that he knew must be the crowns of the tallest plum trees. *My father isn't with the enemy,* he thought. *He's a smuggler. Is? Was?* Then the ship rounded the point, and he saw Ormael.

The city as he knew it was gone. Half the proud wall lay in ruins, and looking up, he could gaze—as no one at sea level should have been able to—right into neighborhoods where he had run carefree and thoughtless, five years before. They were like ash dumps. Ormael Palace itself was crumbled along one side, poorly patched with new stones and surmounted by the Arquali fish-and-dagger flag in place of the Ormali sun. Everywhere rose the black sooty skeletons of old towers, temples, shops.

Without a word, Neeps stepped up beside him.

"My house is still standing," said Pazel numbly. "See there on the ridge? It's the one with the vine-covered wall. The Orch'dury. I wonder who lives there now."

"Quite a job they did on the city," said Neeps. "On Sollochstal they just burned our shipyard. And drafted the men, of course. And fed our Queen to the crocodiles."

"I didn't know that."

"How could you? Not as if it was printed in the *Mariner.*"

"Thasha's father did this," said Pazel. "He commanded the fleet."

"And do you know what I think?" said Neeps. "It's going to happen to them. To Arqual. To Etherhorde itself, one day. Things will get out of control, and somebody, somewhere, is going to take revenge."

Pazel looked at him. For once Neeps' voice was not fierce: he took no joy in his prediction. Then Pazel's gaze slid past his shoulder. And he froze.

The *Chathrand* was anchored in the Bay of Ormael.

"Neeps—"

"I see her!"

For a moment every eye on the *Rupin* seemed to be locked on the Great Ship. As always she looked too big for her surroundings: the Ormali cargo boats streaming back and forth from shore were like ants beside a watermelon. They would need a week to unload her, Pazel thought. But he doubted she would linger so long.

"Our luck's turned at last," said Neeps. "We'll have to sail right past her to dock in Ormaelport. Close enough to shout, anyway."

"Hush a moment!" said Pazel. Neeps obeyed, mystified. For

nearly five minutes they stood in silence. Then Pazel caught his eye and led him a few paces aft.

"Those two sailors at the rail," he whispered, glancing in their direction. "They speak Kepperish to each other, and they don't think anyone else understands. I've been listening all morning with half an ear, and they finally said something useful."

"Something about us?" said Neeps softly.

Pazel nodded. " *'A lovely ship, by damn,'* said the tall one, and the short one answered him: *'Chathrand? Aye, and rich men aboard her, brother. Oh, what rich and powerful men! One gentleman's paying for this whole excursion.' 'You mean he's Mr. Druffle's boss?'* said the other. The short man said: *'Druffle calls him the Customer. He's the one who sent us after these little divers, too.'* That was all."

Neeps stared at him. "Someone on the *Chathrand* . . . bought us?"

"It sounds that way," Pazel agreed. "But who can it be? Not Rose—he had us, and didn't give a pig's whiskers. No, I'd bet my left hand it's that sorcerer Ramachni warned us about."

"And Druffle's working for him," Neeps said. "I'll bet *that's* why he's got a magic charm or two up his sleeve—something on loan from the mage. But why did they ever let us get picked up by the Flikkermen, if we're so blary important?"

"Because we're not," said Pazel. "The Flikkers didn't say a word about us coming from the *Chathrand,* and Druffle didn't ask. And he almost didn't buy me at all, remember? It's divers this sorcerer wants—any divers, not us in particular."

Neeps looked again at the *Chathrand.* "You must be right. But there's something else, mate. We're not landing at Ormael."

Pazel jumped. It was true. In the last few minutes they had passed the near approach to Ormaelport and were already drawing away. The *Rupin* was limping on.

"We should have known," said Neeps. "They can't sail into port with Volpeks aboard. I'm surprised we're passing this close."

"Neeps," Pazel whispered urgently, "could you swim as far as *Chathrand*?"

Now it was Neeps' turn to be startled. "I think so," he said. "But it's broad daylight! And the wind's so low they'd hear us jump. And besides, Druffle's got his eye on you. Don't look! Maybe he's been nice to you, since you're both Ormali, but he's not taking any chances."

"We'll have to risk it!" Pazel started unbuttoning his coat.

Neeps gripped his arm. "It's not a *risk*, it's a Volpek arrow through the shoulder blades. Slow down, mate. I know you want to go home."

"That's not why! It's for Thasha!"

"You can't help her from the bottom of the sea."

Furious, Pazel shook off his hand. But Neeps was right. Helpless, raging soundlessly, he watched his ship and city fall away.

By noon Ormael was out of sight, and the spruce-covered hills of Cape Córistel were all they could see of land. The day was bright and calm. The boys were put to work mending ropes while the sailors braced the surviving mast and spread a patchwork mainsail on its listing spars. They gained a little speed. But the captain ran frequently to the lower decks, returning each time with much anxious shaking of his head. He cast hateful glances at Druffle, and more than once was heard to mutter the word *emergency*. Pazel wondered what new disaster awaited them.

Cape Córistel was famously easy to round from east to west, and today (fortunately) proved no exception. The great surprise was what happened next. As soon as the cape's wave-battered point fell behind them, the captain shouted orders for a starboard tack. Men hauled at the makeshift sail and the *Rupin* heeled painfully around. They were going to follow the north shore. And that was simply not done.

Pazel's father had told him many stories about the Nelu Peren. One thing Pazel recalled perfectly was that *no one,* from the ancient Chereston sailors onward, turned north from Córistel. There were many perils: a maze of rocks, riptides, a pestilential swamp called the Crab Fens that choked the mainland. But one threat overshadowed them all: the Haunted Coast. Pazel wasn't sure what it was: his father would not speak of it, and the schoolyard rumors were so many and mixed he could never make sense of them. But they all agreed on one point: any ship unlucky enough to enter those waters would never escape.

Even Neeps, who had never been anywhere near Ormael, had heard of the Haunted Coast. "*That's* where we're going?" he cried, when Pazel told him. "And do you suppose *that's* where Druffle wants us to dive?"

"Not Druffle," said Pazel. "His 'Customer.'"

Neeps just looked at him.

Pazel raised his hands to his forehead. "I can almost see it," he said. "The whole game, the lie. Chadfallow was trying to tell me, back in Sorrophran. And now . . . now—"

"Give me a crack at it," said Neeps. "What did your blary doctor say?"

Pazel closed his eyes. "He hinted that *Chathrand* was heading into Mzithrini territory, even though Simja's as close as she's ever supposed to get—officially. And then he started talking about the last war, and the Five Mzithrin Kings."

"Is that all?"

"He said . . . that four of the Five Kings condemned Arqual as a land of evil. But one didn't: he was the Shaggat Ness, whose ship—"

The boys looked at each other.

"Was sunk by Arqualis," said Neeps. "I know that much."

"Somewhere north of Ormael," hissed Pazel. "Rin's teeth, mate, that's where we're going! To the wreck of the *Lythra*! Someone must have found it at last!"

"But what does this have to do with Thasha?"

"I don't know—yet. But the last war *ended* there, don't you see? With the killing of this Shaggat."

Neeps' face looked a little paler. "And something that went down with that ship—"

"Could get the next war started," said Pazel. "Stay close, mate. If the chance comes we have to be ready."

*   *   *

The chance did come—within the hour, in fact. The Rupin was but half a league from shore: a lonely shore of high dunes and small, dense oaks. The sun was hot. In the bright light the crew looked sickly and afraid.

There was food of a kind: somewhere in the depths of the Rupin a cook had boiled broth. The captain, his dignity quite gone, carried his portion about the deck; between orders he slurped from the bowl, filled his cheeks like twin balloons, considered the matter, and swallowed. Pazel watched him with pity. He was as much a ruin as his ship.

Those cheeks had just been filled once more when a deep, soft sound, like the contented grunt of a bathing elephant, rose through the planks. Every sailor froze. The sound repeated. Then the captain spat his soup all over Druffle, dropped the bowl and hurled himself down the nearest hatch.

The rest of the crew began to shout. "Pumps! Pumps!" screamed the first mate.

"What is it? What's happening?" screamed the boys.

"Not to worry, lads!" said Druffle, wiping soup from his eyes. "A leak, maybe—some little leak, he he."

But his laugh was forced. The boys let out a howl and started racing about the deck, wailing in half a dozen languages. *"Mamete! Rin-laj! Save me, sweet Angel!"*

Pazel looked at Neeps. Neeps shrugged. They walked quietly to the gunwale.

"We've struck! It's the keel!"

"It's the rudder!"

"Drop sail! Drop sail!"

Druffle was wrestling with the sickness-prone boy, who looked ready to hurl himself over the bow. Pazel and Neeps were the only calm figures on the ship. As such no one paid them the least attention.

They moved aft. Pazel dropped the old coat upon the deck. "Remember what the Flikkers said," Neeps whispered, grinning. " 'Don't breathe! Don't breathe!' "

They dived from the stern rail, wearing just their breeches, and swam as fast and far as they could. The water was cold but not icy, and the current proved gentle. Surfacing forty feet closer to shore, Pazel realized at once how visible they would be if anyone bothered to look. As the first wave lifted him he ducked underwater again. He tried to wait for the next trough, to keep a swell between him and the *Rupin*. But you couldn't make progress if you were studying the waves. He gave it up and made for shore with all possible speed, rising to breathe whenever he needed to.

No arrows flew from the *Rupin,* no shout of alarm. Off to his left, Neeps caught his eye and grinned again.

They don't really care, Pazel thought. *They still have eight boys.*

It was easy. It remained easy. Before they knew it they were halfway to shore.

Pazel risked a backward glance—and was so alarmed he swallowed seawater.

All four lifeboats were in the water, crammed with Volpeks pulling for shore with all their might. Where had so many come from? There must have been dozens hidden on the lower decks! Behind the lifeboats, the *Prince Rupin* was listing at a most unseaworthy angle. Pazel caught a glimpse of her sailors, leaping and waving, throwing themselves into the sea.

They were abandoning ship.

One lifeboat was ahead of the others, and it was coming right for them. Druffle himself was at its bow. He was pointing. He had seen them.

Where Pazel found the strength to swim faster he couldn't say. Beside him Neeps churned the sea with equal desperation. They could hear the breakers now. But the swimming was growing harder, too: an undertow was trying to snatch them down.

"I'll skewer you alive, my Chereste hearts!"

The voice was a stone's throw behind. Pazel kicked for all he was worth. There was foam on the waves, a land-taste to the water in his mouth. He spat air, breathed bubbles. A big wave lifted him, and through the shallows beneath it he saw the sea's pebbly floor.

"Nab 'em! Nab 'em or shoot 'em dead! No, NO—"

There came a sucking noise from behind, and Pazel whirled just in time to see Druffle's boat swamped by a giant roller. The Volpeks pinwheeled into the surf; Druffle was simply gone. Then the wave caught Pazel in the chest. It raised him, spun him like a cork, scraped him along the bottom, buried him in swirling grit. Then it withdrew with a hiss, leaving him flat on his stomach, ashore.

Sand was in his mouth and nose and eyes. He raised his head. The world was still spinning. He realized he had vomited into the sea.

To his left Neeps lay on his side, retching.

Pazel struggled to his feet, looking down at his friend.

"Broken bones?"

"Fah," said Neeps.

"Then get up, mate."

"I rather like it here."

Fifty yards up the beach, half a dozen Volpeks were dragging a lifeboat from the waves. Pazel yanked Neeps sharply by the arm.

"Now!"

They staggered away from shore, trying to break into a run. The dunes rose before them, and they were much taller and steeper than they had looked from the *Rupin*. Their seaward slopes, hollowed by wind, leaned over the boys.

"After them! Move, you fat farina-guts!"

The voice was Druffle's. Pazel caught a glimpse of his bony figure rising from the surf like a skinny Old Man of the Sea, but armed with a cutlass.

"Stop where you are, lads!" he shouted. "Don't make us use arrows!"

"Go kiss a squid!" Neeps yelled.

Arrows followed. Their black shafts fell around them, vanishing to their quills in the sand. The boys reached the dunes and began to scrabble up. Neeps climbed like a monkey, but Pazel found himself floundering. The sand gave way wherever he

stepped; it was like fighting the waves again. Behind him the
Volpeks laughed. Then somehow Pazel's limbs sank deep enough
for traction, and he shot up the dune in a matter of seconds.

His one thought was to hurl himself down the far slope, putting a wall between him and the archers. But when he saw what
lay ahead he froze.

The Crab Fens.

They sprawled before him, all but licking the feet of the dunes:
a gray-green morass of stunted trees and spiky brush, of moss
and vine and stagnant water, draped in white fog that oozed
about in clots. Endless they seemed, and dark. There was a great
stench of rot and brine.

"Don't stand there, you fool!"

Neeps tackled him, and together they slid down the inside of
the dune. "We've got to go in," said Neeps. "They'll never find
us if we lose 'em now."

Pazel said nothing. The Fens hummed like some vast machine,
and he realized with dread that he was hearing insect wings.

But in they plunged. There was no hint of a trail; indeed, there
was no solid ground on which a trail could run. Sand turned to
clay, and clay to black muck. The low trees closed over them
like gnarled hands.

Druffle's voice boomed from the dune-top, urging his men
down into the swamp. *Why does he care?* thought Pazel. *Why
not let two of us get away?*

It was a terrible place to be barefoot. At each step the mud
took hold like a sucking creature, and jagged sticks rose spear-
like from the depths. They could see no more than ten yards
through the brush, and as they left the dunes farther behind, the
strange clots of fog settled around them. Here and there the sun
broke through, but the bright shafts dazzled more than they illuminated. Sounds were distorted, too. Pazel could hear the
Volpeks cursing and splashing, but were they to his left or his
right? A hundred paces away or ten? Was it safe even to catch
their breath?

"... *stinking insubordinate pigfaced louts!*" came Druffle's voice, quite near. *"You'll disappoint the Customer!"*

The horrors mounted. Pazel slid into a slippery hole under the roots of a tree and nearly drowned in the mud that gushed in after him. A fat blue wasp stung Neeps' arm: he howled and smashed it dead—and the Volpeks rallied toward them. They stepped into a swarm of green *muketch* crabs, the source of Pazel's nickname, and leaped for safety with the fierce little beasts still attached to their ankles. They swam across a lagoon, scattering puffy-jawed snakes.

"Come sundown, I'll bet these 'skeeters will drink our blood dry, Pazel."

"Unless we step on a marsh ray first. They can kill you."

"Look at that blary spider."

"Look how the water boils with worms."

With such talk they managed to lower each other's spirits considerably—so much indeed that they barely noticed good fortune when it came. The Volpek voices were fading. They had shaken the pursuit.

"A leech! A stinking, bloodsucking leech!"

"Hush, Neeps! We've done it! We've lost them!"

Neeps ripped the slimy creature from his leg. "I guess we have," he said. "But all I want now is a modestly dry log, or a tree we can climb."

Pazel rubbed his eyes, turned in a circle. "There's your tree," he said, pointing across the Fens to a solitary oak. "I'll bet we could scramble up her in a pinch."

"Let's try, anyway," said Neeps.

The tree was farther than they thought, and taller than it had looked from afar. But when they reached it they found that its roots formed a kind of raised lattice over the filth and mud. They dropped, exhausted, and found it surprisingly comfortable, like a firm hammock.

For twenty minutes they lay on their backs, staring up into the vines and branches, wordless.

Then Neeps said, "We should have jumped at Ormael."

"No," said Pazel. "You were right. We didn't stand a chance."

"But what'll we do now?"

Pazel leaned his head back. "I'll tell you. We'll climb this tree and figure out where the shore is. We'll make our way back there by nightfall and walk east along the inside of the dunes. We'll be halfway to Ormael by sunrise."

"No ye won't, my Chereste heart."

Druffle leaned around from the far side of the tree, grinning. As the boys leaped to their feet he did the same, cutlass in hand. He had never looked more deranged.

"You're foxy," he said, cornering them against the trunk, "but not foxy enough for Druffle. I picked this tree out an hour ago, and watched you slog up to her. Nice of you to do that—I was wrung out, and that's the truth."

"Mr. Druffle," said Pazel, eyes on the long blade, "you're not really this sort of man, are you?"

Druffle's grin faded. He appeared deeply struck by the question. "No, I'm not," he said.

He looked at the cutlass, and heaved a great sigh. Then he plunged it into the mud and leaned on it with both hands. "I've just had such *rotten* luck. You understand, boys?"

They assured him emphatically that they did.

"I've made mistakes!" Druffle cried suddenly. "Never denied it! Dollywilliams Druffle isn't one to blame others for his faults. But all the same, rotten luck."

He shook his head, grimacing. "Ashamed, ashamed," he murmured.

"Don't be, sir," said Pazel.

Druffle gestured helplessly at the Fens. "Nobody expects to be reduced to this! Time was I could afford a decent ship, and proper mercenaries. Disgraceful! I've never seen such bad shots in my life! Why, they didn't even wound you! Still, I suppose I'd better call 'em in."

He straightened and cupped a hand to his mouth. But no shout came: instead he doubled over with a gasp. Neeps, who had guessed sooner than Pazel what Druffle was ashamed of, had dug a stone from the mud and hurled it point-blank at Druffle's side. It was a good-sized rock, and Druffle reeled, glaring like a fiend.

It was their one chance. Pazel groped for a weapon, found a fallen tree limb and swung it with all his might. The branch cracked across Druffle's back, and the wiry man staggered and cursed. He stabbed: the blade fell an inch short of Pazel's chest. Neeps, finding no further rocks, was reduced to flinging mud. Pazel swung his branch again, but Druffle dodged like a snake and clubbed him down with the hilt of his cutlass. The next instant Pazel felt the blade against his windpipe.

No one moved. Druffle wiped blood from his eye.

"I actually *liked* you two," he said. "Honest, my dears, I liked you. But orders are orders. The Customer said I was to kill any boy who raised his hand against me. As an example to the rest."

"An example?" Neeps whispered.

"You have it, lad."

"But we're all alone," whispered Pazel.

"You could just *tell* him you killed us," said Neeps.

Druffle looked gravely insulted. "Lie, you mean? For shame, lads! In business, your word is your bond! Learn that, or you'll never get anywhere."

He lifted the cutlass. But instead of bringing it down on Pazel's throat, he raised his eyes to the horizon, as if savoring a thought. Then his jaw fell open and he toppled backward into the swamp.

Neeps leaped forward and kicked away his blade. "Out cold! What happened? Is he dying?"

Pazel slapped the man's cheek. Not an eyelid flickered. He bent an ear to Druffle's mouth.

"I don't think he's breathing, Neeps."

"I'm a murderer," Neeps whispered. "I must have cracked his liver with that stone!"

At that moment came the startling sound of birds' wings. The boys jumped away from Druffle, and saw the oddest creature imaginable: a barn swallow with the face of a woman. The tiny creature swooped low past their heads, beat its wings fiercely for a moment and came to rest on Druffle's back.

"You're no murderer," she said, looking at Neeps. "And he is not dead."

On the Trail of the Sorcerer

**3 Teala 941
81st day from Etherhorde**

"Diadrelu!" cried Pazel.

For it was she, in an astounding feathered cloak that seemed to turn her arms into wings, her body into that of a dusky bird. Neeps was speechless: he had never in his life beheld an ixchel, let alone one that could fly.

"What are you doing here?" Pazel cried out.

"Saving your lives," said another voice. "Isn't it obvious?"

Pazel knew that voice: it was the younger ixchel, Taliktrum. There he was, swooping down in a suit like Diadrelu's. Pazel flinched, remembering how Taliktrum had scraped his knife back and forth behind his ear.

Diadrelu turned to Pazel. "You spoke of our presence aboard the *Chathrand*," she said severely. Then she continued more gently: "But it was only to pass word that one of our kin lay in chains, and so we pardon you."

"What's she talking about?" cried Neeps, still looking as though he expected to be bitten.

"It's a long story," said Pazel.

"Not so long," said Taliktrum with a shrug. "He gave my aunt his word. He did not keep it. Some of us died as a result, and if the girl spoke as well, before she fled the ship, Rose and his killers may be murdering our whole clan. That's the story."

"Thasha fled the *Chathrand*?"

"Yes," said Dri. "She slipped away into Ormael, and no one knows her whereabouts. The governor's men are tearing the city apart: her wedding is but five days off. But she did not reveal our presence, as you well know, Taliktrum—not even to her beloved Ramachni, the mage. It was the rat Felthrup who told him."

"They're crazy, right?" Neeps looked desperately at Pazel.

"Diadrelu," said Pazel, "what brings you out here?"

"A conspiracy," she said gravely.

"A merchant," said Taliktrum. "A fat man who sells soap."

"Soap?" said Pazel. "You mean the Opaltine fellow—Ket?"

"That is one name he uses. But come: we have miles to cover before nightfall, and the Volpeks hunt you still."

"What about Druffle? What did you do to him?"

"Something very costly, for us," Dri said. "We pricked him with an arrow soaked in *blanë*, or foolsdeath. He will soon wake: the arrow bore a minimal dose."

"Why do you carry such a strange poison?"

"That's none of your business," snapped Taliktrum. "The poison saved you from this man's blade—isn't that enough?"

"There is much to discuss," said Diadrelu. "Once we reach higher ground."

The ixchel led them north, flying from branch to branch, returning to rest on the boys' shoulders. Flying clearly was no easy matter for them, for they had landed exhausted, and Pazel wondered how on earth they had journeyed so far from the *Chathrand*.

But if the ixchel were tired, he and Neeps were wrecks. They slogged along after Dri and Taliktrum in a dumb agony of bruises, cuts and aching limbs. An hour passed, and another. The sun began to sink behind the trees.

Then all at once they were on solid earth. Pazel could hardly believe his eyes. It was a raised road of packed dirt, with two wheel-ruts carved into it and moss growing between them. Left and right it curved away through the Fens.

"By this road we entered the Fens this morning," she said,

"with Mr. Ket, and a most suspicious train of wagons. He left Ormael City in the dead of night. We were hidden in a tool chest, and could not observe what he did along the way. But three times the wagons stopped, and we heard the cries of children. When the chance came we snuck out, and saw how the wagon train entered the Fens at a place well hidden with brush and vines. My guess is that this is a smugglers' road. Ket must be far along it by now.

"You are undone," she told the boys. "Rest now; we will keep watch."

The boys made no argument, but flung themselves down. Pazel watched the ixchel fly to a branch some dozen feet above the road, where they began to pace and whisper. Taliktrum pointed at the boys and made gestures of outrage. Dri motioned for calm.

An hour later she was nudging them awake. It was now quite dark, the sun no more than a dull red glow among the trees to the west. The boys rose, groaning and stiff. The ixchel watched them with folded arms.

"Now listen well," said Dri at length. "Since your eviction, foul deeds have been done on the Great Ship. The rat-king, Master Mugstur, has declared Captain Rose a heretic and sworn to kill him. Sandor Ott   disguised as one Commander Nagan — and his lover Syrarys—"

"I knew it!" cried Neeps. "That harpy!"

"—have so weakened Thasha's father that he barely rises from his bed. We don't know what poison she employs, or how. But they will not kill him until after the marriage of Thasha and Prince Falmurqat the Younger. Nothing will be done that might prevent Thasha's wedding."

"How can you be so sure?" asked Pazel.

Diadrelu cast her eyes down. After a moment, she said, "The prisoner, Steldak, has told us a great deal. But we paid a high price for his knowledge."

"My father's death," said Taliktrum. "That was the price. Sniraga the assassin bore him away. And we are lost without him."

"Talag was also my brother," said Dri. "Yes, we are lost. But -

for his sake we must try not to be. Talag used to say that death was the moment when everything loses value but the truth. I never understood what he meant, but I think I do now. For if we remember something untrue about the dead they are doubly lost to us—in memory as well as fact. Perhaps that is how we ixchel came to the custom of writing letters to the fallen on the night they pass away—letters kept in family archives, to be read by children and grandchildren. But Talag long ago made us promise not to do so—indeed, to serve him no death-rites whatsoever until we reached—"

"Aunt Dri!" shouted Taliktrum, enraged.

Dri blinked, as if starting from a dream. "Reached the end of the struggle he lived for—that is all I meant. But there is more sad news. As we neared Ormael, the bosun Swellows murdered one of your own. You must have known him: a dark-haired tarboy with a stutter."

"Reyast!" both boys cried in anguish. In a flash Pazel recalled the gentle, often bewildered face of their friend, quick to laugh, more often laughed at.

"That monster Swellows!" he hissed. *"Why?"*

"To grasp that," said Diadrelu, "you must first know the true mission of the *Chathrand*."

Then, as the boys' flesh crawled with horror, she told them of the visit to the Prison Isle, and the Shaggat Ness, and the use the Emperor planned to make of him.

"The Shaggat's return is foretold by a prophecy," she said, "dreamed up by Sandor Ott himself and spread by spies in Gurishal: *He will return,* it declares, *when a Mzithrin prince takes an Arquali soldier's daughter for a wife.*"

"Thasha," said Pazel.

"Of course," said Taliktrum. "But the prophecy is little known outside Gurishal. Only when the marriage is sealed, and the news runs like wildfire through their lands, and the Shaggat's worshippers rise, will the Mzithrin Kings realize how they have been fooled. And kill your Thasha Isiq in a heartbeat, naturally."

"Just as Swellows killed Reyast," said Dri. "Smothered him

with a sheet, because the boy managed to befriend the augrongs—and one of them showed him what they guard: the hidden cell where the Shaggat is kept."

"Swellows made the sign of the Tree over the murdered boy," said Taliktrum. "And then he jammed a chicken bone into his throat, to make it seem the boy had choked on stolen food."

There was another silence. Pazel blinked away tears. He was cold and terrified, and had never felt so helpless in his life. But he had to act, he had to keep thinking—Thasha would be killed if he stopped.

"Just a moment," he said. "The Shaggat's followers were exiled to Gurishal. That's far in the west. The Sizzies won't let us pass through thousands of miles of their waters to drop him off."

"No indeed," said Diadrelu. "But *Chathrand* has no intention of going through them. She will go around."

"Around!" cried both boys. "Through the Ruling Sea?"

"Where none can follow her, and none shall suspect," said Dri. "That is why Rose had to be tracked down and made to pilot the Great Ship again. No other captain has braved the Nelluroq and lived."

"What happens if they succeed?" Pazel whispered.

"Civil war in the Mzithrin," said Taliktrum. "And millions dead. Cities burned, legions of soldiers slain on the battlefield or drowned with their fleets. Of course, the Shaggat will die, too—this time the Mzithrin Kings will make sure of it. But it will be a costly extermination. They will have no strength left to stop Arqual from seizing the Crownless Lands. And Magad *will* seize them—all of them, within a year or two."

"That's, that's . . . savage!" cried Neeps.

Taliktrum laughed. "But that is nothing. In time, with Arqual grown so mighty and her enemy crippled—don't you see?"

"The Mzithrin? Arqual would attack the Mzithrin itself?"

"Some madmen dream of it," said Diadrelu. "Especially the Rinfanatics, the ones who want the idols of the Old Faith broken, and their sect destroyed, and the Rinfaith forced on all the world."

"My law is Peace, and my kingdom Brotherhood," recited Taliktrum, sneering. *"Therefore dwell in my kingdom and keep my law.* Such lovely words, in the mouths of murderers and thieves. Delightful to be a giant, no? The chosen people, the lords of Alifros, squatting on a throne of skulls."

Neeps sat up, glaring. "At least we don't drill holes in ships full of women and children, and drop 'em on the seafloor!"

"You use cannon," said Taliktrum. "Life means nothing to your kind."

"What do you know, you vicious little—"

"Neeps!" cried Pazel.

"What do I know?" said Taliktrum, with a terrible edge to his voice. "Shall I tell you a bit of history, Arquali?"

"No, you shall not!" cried Diadrelu, leaping between them. "And he will not tell you that he would rather be a maggot than a son of Arqual. Fools! While we fight our enemies grow stronger! And they are strong already—stronger than you know, Taliktrum."

Her nephew looked at her, waiting for an explanation. By a sliver of moonlight Pazel saw fear in Diadrelu's eyes.

She took a deep breath. "Thasha does not suspect Sandor Ott. Her father does not suspect Syrarys. But *no one* suspects the most dangerous man aboard, the man who led us all to this place."

"You're speaking of Ket again, aren't you?" said Pazel.

"Ket is the name he goes by on *Chathrand,*" said Diadrelu, "but in the dark annals of history his name is Arunis."

Taliktrum laughed aloud.

Dri ignored him and went on. "Arunis was the Shaggat's sorcerer. His was ever the diabolical hand behind the Shaggat. Most believe that he himself invented that twisted strain of the Old Faith that justified the God-King's rise. If that madman had defeated the other kings in the last war, the true emperor of the Mzithrin would be Arunis.

"When the Shaggat and his sons were plucked from the sinking *Lythra,* so was the sorcerer. All four were hidden in

Licherog. But Arunis struggled to escape, and once nearly succeeded. It was then that Sandor Ott decided that he was too dangerous to live. Arunis was hanged on the Prison Isle, cursing his captors, the Gods, the universe entire. His body was left nine days on the gibbet, then cut to pieces and tossed into the sea—and yet he lives. Somehow, he lives."

Pazel looked from one ixchel to the other. "This Arunis . . . is aboard the *Chathrand*?"

"No," said Taliktrum bluntly.

"Yes," said Dri. "Or he was until she landed yesterday, and he began his journey here. Rose, Ott, Drellarek, Uskins—not one of those villains suspects him. Nor did we ixchel. By great efforts we discovered Ott's plan, and a monstrous discovery it was, like a pit beneath a banquet hall. Yet my heart tells me there is a pit beneath the pit."

"What do you mean?" Pazel asked. "Doesn't Arunis want the same thing as Ott and the Emperor—to start a war?"

"Oh yes," said Diadrelu. "But I think he wants a different ending."

"Arunis the sorcerer, risen from the dead," sneered Taliktrum.

"Or never dead at all," said Diadrelu.

"Diadrelu," said Pazel, "Mr. Ket saved Hercól's life. If he's such a wicked man, why would he risk his own life for a stranger?"

"We saved Hercól together," said Diadrelu with a sigh. "The arrow that made the cutthroat stumble was mine. Mr. Ket appeared moments later, and fought the man quite viciously—too viciously for a well-fed merchant. But I have asked myself the same question a hundred times since that night. Does Arunis need Hercól alive for some reason? Could they possibly be allies?"

"Absolutely not!" said Pazel. "Hercól loves Thasha like a younger sister. And he's a good man, damn it—you can just tell."

"No," said Diadrelu, "you cannot. I hope you never learn that the hard way, Mr. Pathkendle. Still, I'm inclined to agree with you about Hercól. Otherwise I should not have tried so hard to save him."

"Tried unwisely," said Taliktrum, "and failed ultimately. The valet is surely dead."

"He is a Tholjassan warrior," said Diadrelu, "and such men are hard to kill."

"Suppose you're right about Ket," said Neeps. "If he *is* a sorcerer, what's this shipwreck-raid all about? What's he trying to find?"

Diadrelu shook her head. "I thought I knew. I feared he sought the Nilstone. For once I am most glad to have been wrong, if wrong I am, for that cursed rock might indeed bring doom to this world in the hands of the Shaggat. But these men speak only of finding gold in that wreck—gold, silver and a certain iron wolf, red in color, with a forepaw raised. They are very keen on that wolf."

"A red wolf!" said Pazel. "The man in Thasha's garden said something about a red wolf, just before he was killed. Hercól said it was connected with great evil. And it vanished— Neeps! That's it! It vanished at the end of the last war!"

"If you really believe this nonsense," Taliktrum demanded, "why did you say nothing to my father—to *any* of the clan?"

"I wanted proof," Diadrelu said. "And I thought it would only be found when Arunis left the ship behind awhile, along with his disguise."

"What disguise?" roared Taliktrum. "He is a greedy merchant, not a mage! He is plundering a wreck, not making war on Alifros!"

"None will be happier than I should that be so."

"That mad wagon-ride from Ormael," said Taliktrum, his voice rising. "Daylight use of the swallow-suits, one of which you have destroyed, the pointless rescue of beggar boys—"

"Well!" said Pazel and Neeps together.

Taliktrum pointed furiously at Diadrelu. "I revered you once, Aunt. You were never my father's equal, but I admit I thought you wise. But when we return I shall ask the clan to consider your fitness to lead."

"That is your right," said Diadrelu quietly, but anger crackled behind her calm.

"You did not tell me," Taliktrum went on, "because you knew I would oppose this ludicrous excursion, and without my vote—"

"Be quiet!" said Neeps.

"Dog!" exploded Taliktrum, drawing his sword. "How dare you interfere!"

"I see torches! Quiet, fool, they'll hear you!"

Swift as mice, the ixchel scaled the boys' bodies. It was true: someone was on the Fens road, coming their way. "Off the road, off!" whispered Dri from Pazel's shoulder. "And be silent, if you value your lives!"

The boys crept back into the swamp. It was hard to be silent in that darkness of logs and vines and mudholes, but somehow they managed it. After thirty feet Dri pointed to a thicket of sedge, and there they crouched and looked back.

A horse's neigh was the first sign, and then the creak of wooden wheels.

"It is he," said Diadrelu.

There were four wagons, each pulled by a pair of sturdy mules. The men driving them were Volpeks—even from this distance Pazel could see their short beards and iron armbands. There were dozens of them, marching on either side of the wagons. Some carried spears, like Druffle's men; others bore war-hammers or cruel axes. Huge and grim as they were, they moved uneasily, casting nervous glances at the Fens.

But the light did not come from torches. Pazel felt a chill that had nothing to do with the damp: floating and bobbing before the wagons flew three blue-green orbs, like pale lanterns held by ghostly hands. Other lights of the same sort glided above the wagons themselves. All appeared to have minds of their own.

The ixchel leaped from the boys' shoulders to a low-hanging limb. "Those are bog-lamps," said Dri softly. "Trickster spirits that dwell in fens and salt marshes. They lure men to their graves in quicksand and feed on their dying souls. I did not know they could be tamed."

By the eerie light, Pazel saw that the first two wagons were heaped with work materials: rope, pulleys, saws, iron hooks. The next looked like a wooden cage on wheels, of the sort used for taking prisoners to jail. To his horror Pazel saw that it was full of young people—boys' faces, and even some girls', were peering out at the night. They looked both frightened and resigned, as if after so many shocks they lacked the strength to worry about what would come next.

The third wagon, finer than the rest, was enclosed by a hooped canopy. Pazel could see nothing of its contents except a little white dog that ran in and out of the canopy, its corkscrew tail wagging—the one eager member of the party. The final wagon was jammed with canvas sacks and other bundles.

Now and then a sharp rasping noise came from the third wagon. It reminded Pazel of a man trying to clear his throat.

"Blast me," whispered Neeps. "I've seen that dog before!"

There was no danger of being seen themselves, hunkered down in the bush. Still the boys held their breath as the strange procession passed. Some of the men carried heavy crossbows. None of them said a word.

Then the lead wagon stopped. The bog-lamps buzzed in circles, then whirled forward, and Pazel saw a good-sized tree lying across the road.

"Strange!" whispered Diadrelu. "Arunis' men have been passing this way for days. That tree must have fallen within the last hour or two."

Still wordless, the Volpeks climbed down and began trying to tug and hack at the tree, now and then glancing back fearfully at the covered wagon. Then the ixchel gave a sharp hiss of surprise.

"What is it?" Pazel whispered.

"Can you see nothing?" said Taliktrum. "Someone is in the last wagon, under the wares."

The final wagon stood momentarily abandoned, its drivers having joined the struggle with the tree. But then Pazel saw it: a figure squirming beneath the piled sacks. A slim arm worked its way free, and then the figure raised its head and looked around, bewildered.

"Thasha!" cried Pazel.

Incredibly, it was her: he would recognize that golden hair and defiant look anywhere. He felt suddenly lighter, stronger—and then appalled by the sheer madness of what he was seeing.

"The idiot!" he said. "What in Rin's name is she up to? Where is she going?"

"To her own death, if she is discovered," said Diadrelu. "Arunis will show no mercy."

"Folly!" spat Taliktrum. "Why do we waste our time with these children?"

At that moment Pazel leaped up and dashed toward the wagon. "Pazel, no!" hissed Neeps, but he paid no attention, lurching through mud and marshwater, until at last he reached the hard surface of the road.

Except for pale moonlight the wagon sat in darkness: the boglamps were at the other end of the train, hovering about the Volpeks as they worked. No one looked back along the road.

If he was stunned to see Thasha, she looked ready to faint when he emerged from the Fens. Disbelief and joy and fear mingled in her eyes. "P-Pazel? How—"

"Keep your head down!" he begged, tugging a loose sack over her golden curls. "What are you *doing* here?"

"What are *you*?"

"Get out of that wagon!" he said. "Climb down, hurry!"

Thasha shook her head firmly. "No."

"You blary fool!" he hissed, tugging at her arm. "You're in terrible danger! Climb down!"

Still Thasha refused. "Neeps was right. You're in danger when you're with *me*. And this is my last chance to get away."

"But why are you with *him*?"

"Hitching a ride, isn't it obvious? As we came into Ormael I heard Ket tell Latzlo the animal-seller that he was leaving the *Chathrand* and heading north—'to collect something very special that was left for me there.' I didn't know what he meant, and I still don't. I just knew he could get me out of the city. But he didn't go directly; first he went to a poor part of Ormael and met this wagon team. I chased 'em on foot until dark, then climbed in. Ket himself is under that canopy. Only he's not just a soap man, he's— Neeps!"

For Neeps had appeared beside them, looking mortified. "Have you both lost your minds?" he said. "They're almost finished with that blary tree!"

The boys begged, and even tried to pull her bodily from the wagon. But she shook them off.

"I tried to fight them aboard, to build a counter-conspiracy like Ramachni wanted. But they're too vicious. They killed Hercól."

"We don't know if . . . I mean, I went to the morgue—" Pazel tried to break in.

"They sold you to the Flikkers. And then poor Reyast. He came and told me he was your friend—and I put him to work looking for the Shaggat. No more! Ket keeps talking about a ship. I'll stow away, ride it as far as I can, then find another—"

"It's not a ship," said Pazel. "It's a ship*wreck*. And I blary well know he's more than a soap man! He's the evil sorcerer Ramachni was looking for, and you can bet your eyeballs he's not done with the *Chathrand*. Diadrelu's with us, and she thinks his name is Arunis—"

The moment the name left his lips, disaster struck. The little dog two wagons ahead launched itself into the air with a berserk howl. It landed running and reached them in a matter of seconds, biting and snapping at their heels. The bog-lamps whipped about and screamed toward them. Pazel just had time to shove Thasha under the tarp before they arrived, circling the boys like wasps, blinding them, singeing their arms with cold fire.

*   *   *

The sorcerer did not leave his wagon. Only his voice emerged.

"How did they escape?"

The voice was silk-smooth, and somehow all the more chilling for its gentleness. The men aiming crossbows at Pazel and Neeps glanced at each other in distress.

Finally, one said: "There's a loose slat in the roof of the pigpen, sir. But I never dreamed it was possible to escape that way! The little one's cut his shoulder. He must have squeezed through—somehow—and then pried the slat open wider for his friend."

"Nail it fast."

"Oppo, sir."

"And inform them all: henceforth you shoot to kill."

The mage cleared his throat, violently. The boys could see nothing but the glow of his pipe, which came and went under the dark canopy. Then they heard a soft chuckle.

"You wanted a little food to see you back to Ormael, eh?"

Pazel and Neeps shot each other a furtive look. They nodded.

"Idiots," said the voice. "You would not have survived the night. There are creatures in the Fens that thirst for living souls and gulp them down like wine. Stray but a little in the dark, and they have you. How lucky you are that my little dog heard your whispers. Oh, he is not a woken dog—not yet. But he is clever. He knows I do not like just anyone speaking my name. And he has *very* sharp ears."

The glowing pipe made a swift motion. "Get them back in the pigpen."

He didn't recognize us, Pazel thought, and then: *Of course! We're caked with mud!*

The door of the "pigpen" was opened and the two boys hurled inside, where the other youths backed away in fear—they at least knew quite well that Pazel and Neeps had not come from among them. A moment later the wagons began to roll.

By the light of the bog-lamps (which went on pestering them) Pazel saw some two dozen filthy, frightened captives. He and Neeps tried befriending them, asking their names, where they came from, if the Flikkermen had caught them, too. But for nearly an hour not one replied to their questions.

Finally, a girl with bright round eyes asked, "Are you ghosts?"

Then Pazel understood: this was the Haunted Coast, after all, and he and Neeps had seemingly appeared from nowhere. "Of course we're not ghosts!" he said. "I'm an Ormali, f'Rin's sake! Arun— Ah, that man, what do you call him?"

"The Customer," said a small frightened boy.

"The Devil," said the girl.

"Well, the man who bought us from the Flikkers works for him, too," said Pazel. "We gave him the slip. If he ever catches up we'll be in trouble all over again."

Eventually the others had to concede that Pazel and Neeps were human. Then everyone began to whisper at once. The prisoners were from Ormael and Étrej, and nearly half, including all the girls, came from a distant Tholjassan town famous for its sponge-divers.

"But shipwrecks are different," they said. "What do we know about wreck diving? And this is the Haunted Coast."

Pazel leaned forward and whispered, "What are we looking for?"

Twenty voices replied in unison: "The Red Wolf!"

On this matter Arunis had already addressed them. Many treasures might be found on the *Lythra,* and he would take them. But he didn't care about anything so much as a red iron statue of a wolf with its left forepaw raised. They were to seek this artifact above all things. No one would go home until it was found.

Pazel and Neeps were fools, it was agreed, to get themselves caught over a few wormy biscuits.

"We weren't after biscuits," said Neeps. "But I'm a fool anyway. Ket bought that dog off a bloke at Tressek Tarn. I watched him bring it aboard. If only I'd remembered!"

"What does he mean, not woken *yet?*" asked the girl. "Can sorcerers wake up an animal, just like that?"

"No," said Pazel firmly. "My mother used to talk about woken creatures. She said they were a great mystery. No one could force a waking, she said, and no one knew why the number of woken animals was increasing."

"And my mother talked about four-legged ducks," put in someone.

"Hush, you!" growled Neeps. "My mate's the son of a mighty conjurer. If she says it can't be done, it can't, even by a mage who's returned from the—"

"Neeps!" Pazel hissed, grabbing his arm. The others were frightened enough.

A silence. The girl trained her unreadable eyes on Pazel.

"Too bad your mother's not here," she said.

All through the night the wagons rolled. Fallen trees blocked the road several times again, making the Volpeks grumble and peer nervously into the Fens. Dazzled by the eerie lights, Pazel could see almost nothing of the Fens, but strange cries of birds and animals echoed in their depths, and often the horses started and pranced with fear. He wondered where the ixchel were now.

It was nearly impossible to sleep, for there was nowhere to lie down except on top of someone else. Still Pazel must have dozed off, and this time he dreamed of thirst—terrible thirst—as he dragged himself out of an unspeakably violent ocean upon a beach of black sand. Thasha crawled beside him, half drowned. Far along the beach huge creatures like woolly elephants were wading placidly toward them, heedless of the breakers that shattered on their flanks, and he wondered if the beasts would offer help when they arrived, or merely grind them into the sand . . .

The wagon bounced to a halt. Pazel opened his eyes. A pale dawn was beginning, and he really could hear waves. The trees had shrunk to bushes, separated by wastes of sand. Timid now, the bog-lamps hugged the wagons, as if the salt-laced breeze might blow them away.

"Stuck again!" someone was saying. "A night full of spooks and specters, and a downed tree every mile, and now these blary sinkholes! Are we cursed?"

The lead wagon had indeed fallen into a hole—a wet cavity in the sand nearly six feet deep and apparently hidden from view. Neeps and Pazel exchanged a look. This was no accident. Someone was trying to slow them down.

Arunis gave a sharp hiss. The bog-lamps, like hounds unleashed, darted back into the shadows of the Fens.

"Take the divers ahead on foot," he said. "But first let them eat a little."

Pazel gripped the bars of the wagon. Two Volpeks were moving toward the food sacks in Thasha's wagon. *Run!* he wanted to shout—but then he recalled Arunis' warning: the men would shoot to kill. It was too late, they would find her. And "Mr. Ket" could hardly fail to recognize the Mzithrin Bride-to-Be.

The men unlaced the tarp and threw it back. There was no one in the wagon. Pazel and Neeps sat back with a sigh. Thasha at least was no fool. She had slipped away in the night.

The wagon was opened, the prisoners ordered out. Biscuits were placed in their hands, and a waterskin carried from prisoner to prisoner. It was foul water, but Pazel's thirst had been more than a dream: he felt instantly better when he drank.

A quarter mile beyond the stream the brush ended in a wall of dunes. The sound of waves was quite close now. The path wriggled up the dunes through stands of yellow sea oats, and Pazel could see by a gouge in the sand that something had been dragged seaward here not long ago: something wide, smooth and massive.

The day promised to be hot. Up the dune they slogged, among the popping of sand-crickets the same bright yellow as the wild oats. Then down the far slope, and up and down again, and now the sand began to burn their feet a bit.

Neeps looked back over his shoulder. "Where do you suppose our little friends are now?" he asked softly.

"Who knows?" said Pazel. "But they'll be back. They came all this way to learn what Arunis is up to, and they won't quit now. Thasha's the one I'm worried about. She can't pass for a sponge-diver girl with three feet of golden hair."

"Maybe she's just heading north, away from Simja and her blood-drinking prince."

Pazel shook his head. "I wish she would. But she'll never leave us in such a fix."

They were nearing the top of the highest dune yet. Pazel saw that the boys ahead of them were holding still, gazing wordlessly at something below. He scrambled up the last few yards, and stopped dead himself. There at his feet lay the Haunted Coast.

He had never seen anything like it: a pale beach two miles wide, stretching south to Cape Córistel, north as far as the eye could see, and broken everywhere by dark tooth-like rocks, some no larger than carts, others tall as castles and snagged with mist. There were long, finger-like islands thick with brush, and pale sandbars winking above the foam, and a great oblong area of darkness beneath the water like a sunken forest. The patches of mist were low and extremely dense, cotton wool sliding among the rocks. Yet between them the air was clear, the sun brilliant: Pazel could see for miles. And all along that terrible coast lay shipwrecks.

They lay on dry sand, and in the breakers, and in the deeper sea. The closest was a mere skeleton, eighty feet long or so, its encrusted ribs combing each wave like a woman's hair. Farther out, an ancient merchantman lay wedged between rocks, her hull burst open at the waist by the endlessly pounding surf. Black hulks like stranded whales littered the beach in the distance. Leagues from shore, old masts tilted like gravestones.

But not every ship was a wreck. Close to shore a broad, clumsy two-master stood at anchor, very much alive. Men were busy on her deck—more Volpeks, to judge by their size. Some four miles out stood a much larger ship, a mighty brig, her double row of guns on full display.

Between these, in the center of the dark patch of water, stood the oddest vessel of all. It was something like a river barge: flat, squared off, free of guns or rigging. She was crowded with men and surrounded by smaller craft.

Mounted at one end of her deck was a massive cargo crane. And dangling from a chain beneath it, directly over the main hatch, was a gigantic brass ball. In the midday sun it dazzled their eyes. The sphere looked to be twelve or fourteen feet in diameter, and impossibly heavy. A row of porthole-like windows ran around its midline.

But there was more to the scene. At the other end of the barge from the crane, a sturdy scaffolding of iron rose from the deck. Attached to this little tower was a pair of ropes that ran taut above the waves all the way to the mainmast of the cargo ship, and from the latter right over the breaking surf to a great rock outcropping on the beach, where they entered some sort of pulley apparatus. Wagons, tents and horses clustered at the foot of the rock. Two men with telescopes kept watch at its summit.

A whisper passed among the youths. *Bathysphere.* That was what the brass ball was called; someone had heard of such things. But no one knew what they were for.

Lying still in the sea oats at the crest of a dune, Thasha watched the Volpeks march their prisoners onto the beach. She was seething with frustration. Escaping from the wagon had been easy. Tagging along in darkness had been far worse: the Fens mist shaped itself into wraiths that groped at her, trying to drag her from the road. She had fought them with her bare hands and with a Lorg Academy chant (*"My heart is sunlit, my soul is the Tree, my dance is forever: I fear not thee!"*). If she attacked them head-on they dispersed like smoke. But they always came back, and their touch was deadly cold: it turned the sweat in her hair to beads of ice. Thasha knew she could not face a whole night of them alone.

Nor could she take on fifty Volpeks and a sorcerer. And now the tarboys were crossing the wide-open sand. If Thasha followed she would be seen in an instant.

There were even more fighting men at the camp by the shore. And nowhere to turn for help. As far as she could see in any direction it was the same. Dunes, fens, rocks, ruined ships. They were in the heart of a wilderness, and she still didn't know why.

She slid down the back side of the dune. Every time Pazel got near her something terrible happened to him. *Blast those tarboys anyway! I ran off to prevent this sort of thing from happening again.*

As she lay there, raging, a flicker of movement caught her eye. She looked left—and froze in astonishment. Men were crossing the dunes. They moved in single file, crouched low, appearing to her sight for just an instant through a gap between two higher dunes. They wore black leggings and short black *tabithet* cloaks, and carried long swords strapped to their backs. Thasha caught her breath. She had never seen such men—and yet she had, a hundred times. They were the soldiers in countless "victory paintings" in the military households of Etherhorde. The dead soldiers. Mzithrinis.

It took just seconds for the figures to pass. Thasha scrambled headlong up the side of a dune to where it looked as if she might catch sight of them again—but when she reached the top she saw only a few snapped sea oats and dimples in the sand. She threw herself down the dune's far side and clawed up the next. There they were. Five men lying flat below her, raising their heads just enough to study the Volpeks and their prisoners. She could see their neck tattoos—a small symbol for their kingdom, a calligraphic letter for their tribe.

What were they doing here? How had they come? Surely they wouldn't dare to attack so many Volpeks?

If I could just talk to them. And suddenly she thought what a fool she had been, what an unforgivable fool, not to learn Mzithrini when she had the chance.

Yet she had learned a little, despite herself. She could still hear Pazel's exasperated voice, reciting: *I enjoy, you enjoyed, we would have enjoyed.*

Oh, Pazel.

She squirmed backward down the dune until she was out of sight. Then she rolled over—and found herself inches from a sword-tip.

A Mzithrini stood over her, sword in one hand and knife in another. He was gaping at her blond hair. Above the black dabs of kohl on his cheekbones his eyes were wide.

He spat out a word—nothing she was meant to answer, she thought. Then he flicked his knife sharply: *Get up.* Thasha stood. The man whistled softly, and in seconds a pair of his comrades stood beside him. All three stared at her wordlessly. Then they began to talk. She heard *"Arquali girl"* and a few other familiar words, but she could not piece them together into any sort of meaning. She tried gestures, pointing toward the shore and shaking her head: *I'm not with them.* The men paid no attention.

At last the one who had found her sheathed his sword—but not his knife—stepped forward, and took her roughly by the arm.

To a *thojmélé*-trained fighter like Thasha, his moves (sheathed weapon, casual grab) told her all she needed to know. He expected nothing from her but weakness and fear. She let him pull her a few steps. Then she whimpered, planted her feet. She gave a little tug of protest, blinking as if on the point of tears.

The other two men had not moved. The one who held her scowled and released her briefly—long enough to strike her backhanded across the face. Thasha cringed, penitent, and followed him weeping down the rest of the dune.

She could taste her own forced tears. No, that was her blood. *Wrong!* Hercól would have shouted. *That is distraction! What matters now, girl?* Her foe's impatience. The slide of his feet. The way he fingered the knife.

When a good twenty feet separated them from the men above, she blundered into him as if by accident. She floundered and cried out—still the frightened little girl. The man turned, perhaps to hit her again, but in that instant Thasha leaned back into an elbow-thrust that snapped his head sideways with the force of a wooden club.

He was enough of a fighter to stab at her even in his shock, but not enough of one to land the blow. Her right hand caught his wrist; her right knee drove up into his now-exposed belly, and as his own knees buckled her left fist smashed down against his jaw. Then she snatched the knife from his hand.

He could not even gasp. His eyes rolled, astonished. Before he fell she had the sword off his back and turned to face the others, her mouth blood-smeared and furious, a blade raised in challenge in each hand.

Plunder on the
Haunted Coast

4 Teala 941
82nd day from Etherhorde

The guards drove the prisoners on. As they neared the base camp, another facet of the operation came into view. Iron cages dangled from the ropes between the land, the cargo ship and the sea barge with its bathysphere. Shielding his eyes, Pazel saw that the ropes were threaded through a gear-and-pulley network in an enormous loop, and that the dangling cages were moving between the vessels and the shore. On the towering rock beside the shore camp, Volpeks were turning a heavy crank like a ship's capstan.

Even now a cage was making its jerky way out to sea. And inside the cage, he saw with another start, were a dozen prisoners.

"So that's how we get to the wreck," said Neeps.

"I want to go home!" sobbed the small boy. The round-eyed Tholjassan girl held him by the shoulders, then bent and whispered in his ear. The boy sniffed but cried no more.

At least twenty well-armed Volpeks were at work in the camp. Besides the gear-turners and the lookouts, a great many were clustered about a heap of what at first glance looked like no more than slimy, vaguely colorful rocks. Using picks, chisels or their bare hands, the men attacked the objects: tearing out weeds, cracking coral deposits, stripping barnacles. In most cases they

THE RED WOLF CONSPIRACY 391

found nothing but stone. In a few, however, the objects' true forms came suddenly to light: here a sea chest, there a broken amphora, elsewhere a bust of some forgotten prince. There was a birdbath fashioned from a giant clamshell, a stone eagle with a broken wing, a curling elephant's tusk banded with gold. The men pushed these treasures aside with hardly a glance. They were clearly after something quite different.

"Is it the Red Wolf they're seeking?" Pazel asked a guard.

"Of course! Now step back!"

Another cage was nearing the shore, also heaped with plunder. It passed above a tall mound of freshly dug sand.

"Hold!" shouted someone. The gears stopped; men scrambled up the mound with nets and poles. One pulled a latch and the bottom of the cage swung open like a trapdoor. Out tumbled the salvaged artifacts, into the waiting nets. A guard-captain looked around until his eyes settled on the newly arrived youths.

"Ten divers!" he shouted.

Quite at random, the Volpeks seized ten, among them Pazel and Neeps, the round-eyed girl and little boy. All were marched up the sand mound, then lifted one by one into the air.

"Grab the bars! Climb in!" roared the guards.

The young people could just reach the swinging cage. In they went, shaking with fear, and clung to the sides with hands and feet. When the last boy had entered, the men latched the trapdoor anew.

"Rest easy," they jeered. "Enjoy the ride."

Another shout and the cage began moving seaward. The prisoners gripped the salt-slimy bars, looking down as sand turned to foam beneath them. The cage moved slowly: Pazel had time to look back and see Arunis' covered wagon being carried, not rolled, over the dunes.

Then Neeps cried, "Look!" and Pazel turned in time to see the brass sphere vanish—no, *plunge*—from the arm of the crane straight down through the barge's main hatch. There came a distant *boom* and a spray of water from the hatch; then a great chain began to slither through the crane into the depths. And Pazel realized that he was not looking at a hatch at all but rather a square opening built right through the hull.

A diving portal. Of course.

"They're going to put us in that thing, aren't they?" said Neeps.

"Yes," said the girl.

"You seem to know a lot about diving," said Pazel. "Can you guess how deep it is out there?"

She frowned at the waves. "Twelve fathoms?"

"Lord Rin!" cried Neeps. Twelve fathoms was over seventy feet. How could anyone dive so far? But the girl remained calm. She had the look of someone almost irritatingly calm, Pazel thought, although the talk of ghosts had rattled her a bit.

"There's something wrong with the water," she said, pointing to their destination. "See how green it is? I think that wreck is in a kelp forest."

She was right about the water: nearly all of it near the spot where the bathysphere had plunged was shimmering green.

"But that will make finding anything *much* harder, won't it?"

The girl just nodded, her face expressionless. Her name was Marila, she told them. She had been diving for sponges in the coves around Tholjassa since she was twelve. The frightened little boy, Mintu, was her brother.

"This sorcerer's mad," she said. "Nobody ever gets away with treasure from the Haunted Coast. Everyone knows there's a curse on it. See that wreck?" She pointed at a single, tilting mast in the distance.

Pazel nodded. "What about it?"

"That's a Mzithrini Blodmel, ninety guns. Tholjassan ships turn away from land if they're close enough to see her. They say she had a captain who noticed something shiny at low tide. He dived himself and came up with a golden Star of Dremland. One little star. He tossed it up to his son, told him the seafloor was covered in jewels, and dived back for more. It was just twenty feet deep, but he vanished."

She made a little *poof* gesture with her hands.

"The ship left him and retraced its path exactly. But this time there was a reef, where there had been nothing before. It split them wide open. They abandoned ship, and a storm blew up and swamped the lifeboats, and the only one who made it out was the man who had thrown the gold star back into the water. You can't take so much as a shell from this place, everyone knows."

The Mzithrinis did what Thasha feared most. They waited.

It gave them time to think, to recover from their amazement at the defeat of their brother in a matter of seconds by an unarmed girl. She was unarmed no longer, but she was still alone.

They waited, and in seconds the remaining three fighters, those who had stayed behind to watch the Volpeks, appeared over the dune. They looked at the golden-haired apparition, the man groaning and twitching at her feet. Then all five Mzithrinis drew their swords and whirled them with easy grace, advancing.

Thasha had one skill even Hercól considered exceptional: she made choices with lightning speed. Those five spinning blades drove her next decision, and it surprised her almost as much as the Mzithrinis. She threw her own sword away.

Reason caught up with instinct a split second later. *Oh, thank the Gods.* For she knew now that to fight them was to die. The blade was strange to her, narrow at the hilt, broad and heavy near the point. She could not have prevailed against one man trained to use it, let alone five.

The men stared at her, but paused only for an instant. She still held the knife.

Thasha's next decision took longer. *Run?* Impossible. *Surrender?* Not likely—the man she'd fought could well have been taking her aside to murder her. She dropped to her knees. Seizing the wounded man by the shirt, she hauled him up against her chest and set the knife to his throat.

Now they stopped dead. The man was waking from his daze: she pressed the blade hard until he felt it. His eyes blinked open, and Thasha felt his muscles tense. For a moment nothing moved but the sea oats in the breeze.

One thing he would not do was throw himself on the knife: suicide was forbidden by the Old Faith. They were all trapped. It gave her time to think again.

Mzithrini phrases danced before her eyes. *Who shall wed? Thasha and His Highness shall wed.*

"I . . . I promise—" she stammered.

Again they were amazed. "You speak Mzithrini!" said one, apparently their leader.

"Little, little! I am friendly!"

"Friendly."

Blood trickled from the nose of the wounded man. He put a weak hand on her arm. She pressed the blade harder against his throat.

The men crept a step nearer. Could she possibly tell them she was the Treaty Bride? How could they believe her?

At last the words came back: "Hear my vow, ye many!"

It was awkward, but they understood. Thasha indicated the knife. "I give this."

"Yes," said the Mzithrini leader. "Do that."

"And you . . . you . . . don't touch any of my goods."

It was the old *Polylex* phrase. The Mzithrinis looked at one another. Then they advanced another step.

"We won't touch you, girl," said their leader. "Don't worry. We're friendly."

The man she was holding actually laughed. Only by twisting the knife even harder against him did she make them pause again. They had spread around her. She had to turn this way and that to see them all.

Suddenly the wounded man let his hand fall from Thasha's arm. He gave a low gurgle; then his body went limp. Thasha cried out. His head flopped down against her wrist.

"Oh *no*!" Thasha shook him, horrified, she had never killed, never wanted to—

He erupted beneath her. Bit her arm. Struck the knife from

her hand. The other Mzithrinis charged with a roar. Their captain raised his broad sword in an arc over her head.

And fell slain. His chest riven with arrows. The wounded man dropped beside him, a shaft piercing his neck.

Thasha leaped to her feet. Down the dune behind her rushed six or eight men, tall and gray-clothed, swords held high. They clashed with the gaping Mzithrinis with cries of *"Syr-ahdi Salabreác!"* And Thasha's heart leaped: those words she knew. They were a prayer Tholjassan warriors spoke before closing with the enemy.

The Mzithrinis begged no quarter. Their heavy blades flashed in the sun with terrible speed and rang as they met the lighter Tholjassan swords. But they were doomed: two had fallen to arrows, two more in the first moments of swordplay. The last pair rushed together and stood back to back, swords a-whirl, snarling their defiance.

"Enough!" cried a Tholjassan. *"Maro dinitre!* Fight no more, and live!"

The Tholjassans paused, giving their foes time to consider. The Mzithrinis, however, leaped once more to the attack. In a matter of seconds both lay dead at the Tholjassan's feet. But Thasha stood rooted to the spot, wondering if she had taken a blow to the head. She looked at the man who had spoken. *That voice!*

He wiped blood from his sword against his breeches. Then he turned to face her—and in broad daylight, far more clearly than the night before, Thasha saw a ghost.

Pazel winced. The iron cage was salt-corroded, the bars rusty and sharp against his skin.

They had left the surf behind and were nearly at the cargo vessel: a wide teakettle of a ship. Her captain rushed back and forth with his telescope, watching the commotion around the barge, the guns on the Volpek brig. He spared barely a glance for the prisoners in their iron cage, rumbling by on pulleys slung between his masts.

"The Customer's reached the shore!" boomed a lookout in the crosstrees. "And Druffle too, that old straggler! Looks like they're heading our way!"

"I can see the beach!" shouted the captain. "Keep your eyes on the deep water! If we're caught off-guard I'll make you sorry, by the blazin' Pits!"

The prisoners left the cargo ship behind. No one had addressed a word to them.

Neeps shook his head. "Druffle's back. Think he's missed us much?"

"I doubt it," said Pazel. But he was thinking: *Caught off-guard by whom?*

The day was brilliant and clear—except for those strange clots of mist, which seemed to prowl willfully among the offshore wrecks. Suddenly the cage picked up speed. Pazel steadied himself, then turned to look at the barge. Volpeks were straining at the capstan, two men to each bar. They were winding in the chain, winching the bathysphere up to the surface again. *That's some job,* he thought.

"Up here, lads and ladies."

Ten heads swiveled up. A Volpek crouched atop their cage, waving. He could only have come from the higher masts of the vessel behind them, but no one had heard him climb aboard. His round, bald head put Pazel in mind of a sunburned ape. He gave them a rascally grin.

"The Red Wolf!" he said. "That's your goal. Silver is sweet and gold is gravy, but we must find that red iron wolf, come storm or sunstroke. Not one of us is going home without it, see? So don't leave behind anything that might have paws. That's rule number one.

"Rule number two is stay alive. The sphere has plenty of air, but you can only take one chestful at a time down into the wreck. Search your hearts out, and when you can't hold your breath any longer, give three tugs on your rope. Then watch out! We'll haul you in faster than you can say 'drowned doggy'!

"At the end of your ropes you'll find a sack, a ring and a hook.

Little treasures go in the sack. Big stuff you wrap up tight with rope. Then clip the hook to the ring and give two tugs—just two, for merchandise—and don't forget to hold on yourself!

"You'll see the keel of the *Lythra* soon as you reach the seabed. The rest of her's spread out east of here, or maybe north. She wedged between two rocks, see, and at some point the tides just snapped her in two. Her innards have been washing about these forty years."

He paused, then gave a smile of forced good cheer. "As to the little matter of sea-murths: rubbish! Fishwife talk! There ain't been murths in the Nelu Peren for over a hundred years! Mankind's rooted 'em out. You'll do better to worry about tanglin' your line in sharp coral, or that blary weed. It's easy to get lost in a kelp forest, and this sort—ribbon kelp—is the worst of all. Greenery's worse than ghosts, mark my words."

His speech was interrupted by shouts from the barge. Men were crowding around the dive portal, waving encouragement to those working the capstan. The latter threw themselves into a final shoulder-straining heave, and with a sound like a breaching whale the bathysphere rose from the hull portal. Water gushed from it; long ribbons of weed trailed back into the sea. *To bring such a thing here!* Pazel thought. *In secret! Along with wagons, three ships, maybe a hundred men. All for an iron wolf?*

As they drew nearer, a rope ladder dropped from the bottom of the sphere. A man on deck caught the trailing end and secured it to the crane. At once a line of youths began to descend. They were shaking and slow. All looked rather ill. When they reached the deck they let themselves collapse.

Next to emerge were baskets of the kind of loot the Volpeks had been busy with ashore. These were handed up into a separate cage on the shorebound side of the pulley system. Then it was the newcomers' turn.

The bald Volpek climbed down the outside of their cage. "Stand back!" he cried, and kicked the trapdoor open with his foot. A man tossed him the end of another rope ladder. It ended in a pair of short ropes, and these he tied swiftly to the bars of the cage. Then, "Down! Down!" he cried. "Don't make me step on your fingers!"

Down they went, swaying and lurching. Pazel saw now that at the bottom of the bathysphere was a lidless hole some eight feet across. On deck the prisoners huddled together. None of those who had come from the bathysphere had yet stood up.

The Volpeks formed them into a line, toes to the edge of the dive portal. The last baskets were lowered from the sphere, and yet another ladder followed.

"Climb," they said.

Up again, into the dark mouth of the bathysphere. As Pazel stuck his head and shoulders through the hole he felt strong hands seize him by the arms. Two mighty Volpeks, wearing only loincloths and knives, pulled him up into the metallic gloom. It was clammy and cold. A bad echo distorted every sound. There were nets strung along the walls, climbing-cleats, benches high overhead. From the apex of the sphere hung an assortment of pulleys and coiled ropes.

Soon all the captives were seated inside. Each was handed a rope-end with the promised sack, ring and hook. The sacks had small holes to let the water through, drawstrings for sealing them tight. Pazel saw Marila slide a hand through her ring and push it up to her elbow. She caught his eye.

"This way . . . can't drop it," she seemed to be saying (the echo made it hard to be sure). *"Lose your rope . . . never get back . . . all that weed."*

"STOP TALKING!" bellowed their captors, who made themselves understandable by sheer volume. *"HOLD ON TO THE CLEATS!"*

The sphere gave a little jerk, like a puppet on a string. And then it plunged. The sea appeared to leap straight up. There was a deafening *boom,* and water boiled to their ankles before being checked by the stoppered air. Through the windows they saw the walls of the dive portal, then the bottom of the sea barge and a dark blue-green immensity below. It was abruptly quiet. The captives gripped the cleats in trembling fists. The water in the sphere began to rise.

"Swallow!" said Marila. "Over and over! Stretch your mouth wide or your ears will break!"

She demonstrated. Pazel copied her, and saw that Neeps and the others were doing the same. The air was indeed growing heavy, pressing in on Pazel's ears and nose and chest. The water passed their shins.

Neeps was frowning, concentrating. In fact everyone was: even Mintu had decided there was no use in tears. Pazel looked out through the windows again. Nothing but blue water—and then, like green flames all around them, the weed.

Ribbon kelp was the perfect name. The weed rose straight and thick, just inches between one flat frond and another. Pazel was surprised how delicate it looked, and how lovely. It glowed in the midday sun, but because it grew so straight the rays pierced the narrow gaps in long splinters of light. Small fish and tiny translucent shrimp darted everywhere. Yard after gentle yard spooled out before his eyes.

Sudden cold: the water had reached his waist.

"SWIM UP TO THE BENCHES!" roared the Volpeks. *"DON'T DROP YOUR BLARY ROPES!"*

When over half the sphere had filled with water, and all the youths were huddled on the benches, their descent stopped. Pazel looked down through the bathysphere's open mouth: was that sand, thirty or forty feet below?

He had little time to wonder. His captors were screaming again. *"STAY CLOSE TO YOUR MATES, BUT NOT TOO CLOSE. IF YOUR LINES CROSS EVERYBODY DROWNS."*

With those words a Volpek handed Mintu a dark stone. The boy nearly dropped it, startled by its weight, and Pazel realized it was a lead sinker. Then the Volpek grabbed Mintu's arm, yanked him from the bench and dropped him. Rope trailing, eyes fixed on his sister, he vanished below.

Marila did not wait to be yanked. She grabbed another sinker and pushed off from her bench. Seconds later she too was gone. Neeps looked Pazel in the eye.

"Right," he said, feeling above him for a sinker, "let's get this over with." And he jumped as well.

Pazel had thought himself scared all along, but now he realized his fear had scarcely begun. His heart raced. Couldn't he just sit here quietly? There were six other divers. Maybe he would be picked last. Maybe someone would find the Wolf quickly, and he'd never have to dive at all.

But Neeps and Marila and Mintu were already below. He could never face them—face Thasha—if he crouched there, hoping to be spared. He coiled the rope over his shoulder. *Do it now or the fear will stop you.* He picked up a sinker. He took a last, huge breath and jumped.

Suddenly events (or his mind, or both) sped up. The sinker dragged him straight down through the mouth of the sphere. The kelp engulfed him, the sandy bottom rushed upward. Where was the wreck? He was spinning, helpless, the rope scraping his arm. He would not even find the *Lythra,* let alone any part of her cargo, before his breath ran out.

Darkness—pitch darkness! He looked up in terror. Had he fallen into a cave? Then, just as suddenly, the light returned and he saw what had occurred. A surge of current had bent the kelp over, like prairie grass in the wind. Strand against strand, it had blotted out the sun. As soon as the surge passed it straightened, and the light flooded down.

It happened again. Darkness, light. Why hadn't anyone warned them?

Then, forty feet under the bathysphere, he saw it: a great black timber on the seabed. It was weed-wrapped and barnacle-chewed, but unmistakably a sternpost. Pazel dropped the sinker and swam for it. *There, and there!* Other divers' ropes, vanishing in the weeds. He kept his distance. His lungs were aching already. The timber pointed like a finger through an opening in the kelp, and as Pazel kicked through the gap, an awe-inspiring vision met his eyes.

The *Lythra* sprawled before him, cracked open like an eggshell. But no—it was just the stern half, snagged on a jagged rock. It was as if monstrous hands had torn the ship in two. But where had the bow section gone?

Darkness, light. He could see Neeps, swimming low beside the wreck, his eyes scanning this way and that. Pazel followed, and in a moment his fingers touched the hull. A gunport lay open before him. Inside, a crusted lump, the cannon. He was almost out of breath.

Darkness.

He put his hand through the gunport, feeling.

Something moved. Pazel let out a mouthful of bubbles. It was a leathery creature, and it shot away from him into the depths of the ruined gun deck.

Light.

Fish or shark or otherwise, it was gone—and so was Pazel's breath. He flailed for his rope. He had waited too long, couldn't possibly make it back. He gave three tugs.

All he recalled of his rescue by the Volpeks was the slap of weeds against every part of his body. When he entered the sphere, hands reached down and tore kelp in bunches away from his face.

"SPIT OUT THE WEEDS!"

He spat out the weeds. The men propped him on a bench just out of the water, where he gagged and wretched. They looked in his empty bag and frowned.

"NEXT TIME, START SWIMMING THE MINUTE YOU JUMP."

Next time? Pazel thought he'd be ready in about a week. Lying stunned on his bench, he saw Marila sitting across the sphere, watching him with those unreadable eyes. Mintu lay beside her, looking ill. The weed-darkness fell on them again, and when it passed the men had a writhing ball of kelp between them. Neeps. He blew a mouthful of water in a Volpek's face.

"Creatures!" he gagged. "Strange creatures . . . murths!"

"THERE ARE NO MURTHS IN THE QUIET SEA!"

More divers were hauled in. One had tied a whole sea chest

up in his rope. Another held up a cast-iron skillet, which a Volpek tossed angrily back into the water.

Two boys did not return at all. The men hauled in their ropes and found only weeds attached to the hook and ring. Nothing had broken. It was as if they had simply let go.

On their second dive, Pazel and Neeps kept each other in sight. They got much farther, too, for they swam for the wreck the instant they jumped. Pazel saw now that there were paths through the kelp forest: neat paths, almost like roads. In a flash of light he peered down one long avenue and thought he saw colonnades, and statues of men or animals, and moving shadows that were not cast by the kelp. But there was no time to linger. Greatly afraid, he made himself enter the wreck.

Inside was a terrifying chaos. The forces that had cracked the *Lythra* in two had also swept through her, blowing cannon through bulkheads, wrapping chains around masts, impaling skeletons on broken beams. There were skulls rolled into cabinets and wedged behind doors. There were skeletal hands in barrels, and clouds of silt, and an obscene fanged fish that lunged each time the darkness fell. Pazel struck at it desperately with his hook. How could anyone find a thing down there?

When the two boys again returned empty-handed, the Volpeks exploded. *"IF YOU DON'T FIND SOMETHING NEXT TIME, DON'T COME BACK AT ALL!"*

Neeps kicked the water into a froth. "You try it, you daft, ugly, bellyachin' baboons! Want to fight? Do you?"

Just then Marila surfaced beside them with a hideous gasp. "Mintu . . . gone . . . he's gone!"

She was in agony; she had been under twice as long as the boys. They had to hold her head above water.

"Where did he go, Marila?" Pazel squeezed her arms. "Tell us where!"

"The arch!"

"I saw it!" Neeps cried. "That coral arch? Why the blazes did he go through *there*?"

Marila gasped and sobbed. "Followed . . . couldn't find him . . . awful place—"

Her whole body began to convulse. More irritated than concerned, the Volpeks tossed her onto a bench. Pazel and Neeps looked at each other. There was nothing to say. They were not ready to dive, but they had to. No one else would even try to save Marila's brother.

Down they went for the third time. Pazel too had glimpsed an arch: an opening in a long, towering reef-wall, some distance from the *Lythra*. He couldn't imagine why Mintu would have passed through it. Had he glimpsed something beyond, a treasure he couldn't resist? Had he seen the Red Wolf?

Pazel arrived a few strokes ahead of Neeps. He saw now that the arch was actually quite deep—a tunnel, in fact, about twenty feet long. Barely a yard between the roof and the seabed. Not tempting in the least, but Neeps was poking him as if to say, *Swim, or get out of the way!* He swam.

It was worse than he feared. The tunnel floor bristled with sea urchins, black living pincushions whose spines burned like acid at the merest touch. There were also clots of translucent orange worms dangling from the roof, flexing sucker-like mouths. The only possible way through was the exact center, kicking fast lest one rise or sink, but at the same time keeping one's hands and feet very close. The orange worms writhed obscenely. The tunnel seemed to go on forever.

Yet somehow Pazel emerged unscathed. Beyond was a sandy clearing, a meadow in the kelp forest, broken here and there by red coral and towering rocks. There was no sign of Mintu.

Neeps emerged with pain in his eyes. Attached to his leg was a fat worm, already darkening with his blood. It took them several precious seconds to rip the creature loose, and a mouthful of Neeps' flesh went with it. Pazel looked at the wound, the suppressed horror in Neeps' face, the long cliff of coral stretching away left and right. This was madness. They had to go back right now, before their lungs burst and Neeps lost too much blood. Then Neeps went rigid. He grabbed Pazel's arm and spun him around.

Half a dozen sea-murths were swimming their way, faster than sharks. They were the strangest beings Pazel had ever seen. They looked like humans, girls in fact, but their limbs curved and coiled like no human limbs, and the sun struck rainbow colors where it touched their skin. Long, white hair streamed behind them, and their eyes were luminous silver. Their clothes seemed wraps of milky light.

In no time the boys were surrounded. The murth-girls had beautiful faces but very sharp teeth. Were they smiling? It appeared so, but did smiles mean friendship or menace to a sea-murth? In one sense it hardly mattered: they were out of air. They had failed Mintu, and would be lucky to escape with their lives. Pazel gestured at the tunnel: *Now.* Then a murth-girl touched his ankle, and the world changed.

A feeling of golden bliss ran up Pazel's leg. He could breathe! He knew it instantly, and without the least fear opened his mouth and filled his lungs with water. It was as effortless as breathing air. One of the creatures must have touched Neeps as well, for there he was, mouth open, grinning like a perfect fool. Their hearing had changed, too: they could hear water rushing through crevasses, the squeak of eels, the growl of a passing drumfish. Above all, like a silver music, they heard the laughter of the murth-girls.

"Look at them smile! They had even less air than the first ones!"

"I like these better. Almost grown, they are."

"Which one for a husband, Vvsttrk? He he he!"

"That one is short enough for you. But the dark one likes you better, I think."

The boys trod water, back to back, as the murth-girls flitted about them in circles. Neeps put out his hands, laughing as the last bubbles of air escaped his mouth. Then a girl stopped face to face with Pazel. She had a teasing smile, and hundreds of tiny kulri shells braided into her hair. One delicate hand touched his face, and he knew somehow (the gold was rushing through him again) that it was the same girl who had touched him before.

"Mine," she said, and her sisters laughed.

Then Pazel said, "Have you seen a small boy?"

She was gone. They were all gone. Pazel had barely caught the murth-girls' looks of terror before they vanished into the kelp.

Neeps turned to him angrily. "What did you do that for?"

"Me?"

"They just laid the sweetest magic I ever heard of on us, and you scare 'em off? What rude thing did you say?"

"Nothing! Didn't you hear me?"

"Sure," said Neeps. "I heard, *Skrreee—glik—glik—scrreeeeeeee!*"

"What?"

"Come off it, Pazel. You were speaking Murthish."

Pazel covered his ears. *Oh no.*

There it was: the purring. His Gift had started up again, and taught him their murth-tongue. But how long ago had it begun? All these days of noisy imprisonment, buzzing insects, storms. What if these were his last few hours—or even minutes?

"Neeps," he said, "you've got to listen carefully. I told you how my Gift works? How it always ends in a fit, where I can't talk or understand anyone, and those horrible noises blast me? Well, it's going to happen again."

"No worries," said Neeps, who had calmed down already. "I'll take care of you."

"Don't let the Volpeks scream in my face! Tell 'em it's something natural, like the hiccups."

"The hiccups. Have you seen yourself, mate? Not even those boneheads will— Pazel, look!"

Neeps pointed into the gloom. About sixty yards away, against a great black rock, stood the other half of the *Lythra*. Her shattered beam-ends anchored her in the sand. Her figurehead, an angel, spread her barnacled wings and gazed forlornly at the sky. A row of gaping cannon-shot wounds ran down her hull, straight as punches in a leather belt, as though she had been fired on at point-blank range.

And gazing from one of these holes was a young boy.

"Mintu!"

He waved, and his voice carried faintly to them. "Pazel! Neeps! They changed you, too?"

A murth-girl's shy, mischievous face appeared behind him.

Mintu laughed. "She's my friend!"

The boys were so delighted to find him alive that they forgot all about Pazel's impending mind-fit. Swimming toward the wreck, they heard the musical laughter again from inside the kelp forest. When the next spell of darkness came they saw the murth-girls glowing faintly in the weeds.

More laughter above. There were the other missing boys: dangling from the *Lythra*'s main topgallant, holding a slender murth by hands and feet so that she swayed between them like a hammock.

"Why are there only girls?" Neeps asked. "Not that I'm complaining, mind."

"Maybe because we're only boys," said Pazel uneasily. "We'd better be careful."

"Just *you* be careful not to insult them again."

It was no use protesting: Neeps was positively convinced Pazel had said something nasty in Murthish. They swam up to Mintu and clasped his arms. He had a girl's silver hair-clip in his own brown locks.

"She fed me clams," he said. "And she healed a cut on my foot. I don't think murths are half as bad as people say."

"Your sister nearly drowned looking for you," said Pazel. "You'd better get back to the sphere and let her know you're alive."

"Oh! Yes, I . . . I will." Mintu looked reluctantly back toward the coral arch.

"Go on," urged Pazel, "or she'll try it again. She's in no shape for that."

Mintu looked at his murth-girl playmate. She drew back into the ruined ship, eyes pouting, as if she knew their game was over.

"I'll come right back," he said.

Pazel watched Mintu swim all the way to the arch. Then he turned to see Neeps sitting cross-legged on the seabed, inches from a murth-girl in the same position.

"Hello, dream," said Neeps.

They were making faces at each other. The murth-girl laid a finger on his worm-wound—and it vanished, melting into his skin like a snowflake.

"Thank you!" laughed Neeps. "Pazel, how do you say 'thank you'?"

Pazel didn't answer. He looked up at the two boys and their friend. They had released the topgallant and were holding hands in a circle, serenely sinking. Another murth-girl, almost completely hidden in the weeds, looked out as they passed.

"They're ready, Thysstet," she told the girl as she passed.

"Almost!" laughed the other.

Ready for what? Pazel knew how to ask the question. But what if they vanished again at the sound of his voice?

The girl in the weeds leaned out farther. Pazel's heart leaped: it was her, the one who had touched him. Suddenly nothing else mattered. He swam toward her as fast as he could. Their eyes met. She was beautiful!

She was gone.

He felt stabbed in the chest. One glance and she had fled into the weeds.

And when he looked down, Neeps had vanished, too. There on the sand lay his collecting bag, hook and ring—the latter with the rope still attached.

"Neeps! Neeps!"

Pazel flew toward the sole remaining murth-girl. She saw him and cowered behind the two boys.

"Stop!" they growled at him. "What's the matter with you! She's ours!"

"It's a trap!" he cried. "They're separating us! And you've lost your ropes!"

"Who needs ropes?" laughed one boy. "Who needs them blary Volpeks and their bath-a-spear?"

"But how will you get back to land?"

"Swim! Walk! Who cares? Maybe I'll wait a week. All I know is that I'll go ashore far from Arunis! Ha! We can even say his name down here. What's he going to do about it?"

"Arunis! Arunis!" shouted the other boy.

The murth tickled him from behind. But she still watched Pazel with fear.

He begged the boys to help him find Neeps, but they called him killjoy and swam away. Pazel shouted for Neeps again. How far did his voice carry underwater? And where should he search?

Quite at random he circled the bow of the *Lythra* and the massive rock. No Neeps, no murth-girls. Only fish, a few spiny lobsters, and in the distance a red, swift shape like a flying carpet: a scarlet ray. Pazel had never seen such a huge one—it was easily twelve feet from wing tip to wing tip—and he kept his distance. Scarlet rays were not aggressive, and they had no teeth, but the stingers in their whip-like tails were notorious. In Besq, Pazel had seen a fisherman stung on the hand by a scarlet ray tangled in his net. He had passed out from sheer agony.

He set off among the rocks and weeds. Shouting for Neeps, but thinking despite himself of the girl, the girl, the girl. Of course she would be frightened to hear a human speaking Murthish. But so frightened? And what had she meant by *Mine*?

His rope went slack. He reeled it in, more alarmed by the second. Something very sharp had cut the rope, and he hadn't felt a thing. Not one of them was tethered to the bathysphere. And only he was aware of the danger.

What could he do? He rose. At thirty feet below the surface most of the reef was below him. A little farther and the kelp closed around him too. He could see nothing at all until his head broke the surface.

Where was he? The wind had risen and the waves had grown. The sun was bright as ever, but the shore seemed to have changed shape. Then he caught sight of the barge and realized he was much farther north than he had guessed. He could see the Volpeks on her deck, and in the smaller craft around her, looking anxiously at both shore and sea. Far out in the Gulf of Thól the heavily armed brig still waited, brooding. He turned to face the shore—

—and dived, just in time. A longboat was driving straight at him, making for the barge. Pazel watched as it passed a yard above his head, four pairs of oars pulling swiftly. Then he rose until his eyes just cleared the water.

Arunis was standing upright at the prow, in a dark cloak, his tattered scarf flapping in the wind. The white dog stood beside him, motionless. The sorcerer waived irritably at his men.

"Faster!" he shrieked. "Can't you see that fog bank, Druffle, you louse?"

Mr. Druffle was indeed among the rowers. Looking miserable and cold, the wiry man glanced southward. Pazel looked, too: there was indeed a broad mantle of fog upon the Gulf, two or three miles off. Like the shreds of mist he had glimpsed from the dunes, it was thick as white wool, an unnatural sight under the gleaming sun. But this fog bank stretched in an unbroken line from the southern shore deep into the Gulf. And it was creeping relentlessly their way.

Arunis screamed at the rowers again, and they increased their speed. Pazel flipped over and swam straight down. *One calamity at a time.*

Below, he found no sign of man or murth. Clownfish darted; the scarlet ray swept by near the wreck. Otherwise the sea was still.

A hunch came to him suddenly. Before he sank any farther, Pazel moved well into the ribbon kelp. Then, hand over hand, he pulled himself into the depths. If the weed could hide murths it could hide him, too.

After descending another thirty feet he held still. He could see the whole clearing, from the *Lythra* to the coral wall, but it would take a sharp eye indeed to spot him.

No one came. No silver laughter reached him. But strangely, the scarlet ray kept up its circling of the wreck. What was it up to? Not feeding: scores of fish passed right under its nose, and the giant ignored them all.

Long minutes passed. Then the ray did something odd. It stopped, pivoted its huge, flat body left and right and dived behind the wreck.

Pazel burst from the weeds. *That* was no normal behavior for a ray. He swam low, hiding behind the wreck as long as possible. When he could go no farther he shot upward, across the topdeck, and peered down along the side of the ruined hull.

The ray was hovering beside a gunport, its deadly tail writhing. Pazel heard its voice, like that of a weird overgrown bird: *"Gone-gone-gone, Lady Klyst! Come out, find your kin, land-boy loses, murth-friends win."*

The ray withdrew slightly and the girl's face appeared—his girl. Timidly she pulled herself halfway through the gunport. The golden joy coursed through Pazel again. He could not be silent.

"Klyst!"

She looked up in horror. And vanished back into the wreck. The ray, however, turned with a furious roar. *"Land-boy! Land-boy! Kill you! Kill you!"*

Pazel knew he was no match for a humiliated scarlet ray. He kicked off the broken gunwale and shot down the length of the *Lythra*'s topdeck with the beast howling behind him. He would never reach the kelp beds: the wreck itself was his only hope. Under the broken foremast he swam, dodging a skeleton snagged on the pinrail. The foreward hatch was blocked with debris. He swam on desperately. The ray's fleshy horns brushed his toes.

He jackknifed through the main hatch. The ray roared and stabbed with its tail, missing Pazel's head by an inch. Pazel seized at timbers, dragging himself farther inside as the ray tried to squeeze in after him. It succeeded, but it could not spread its wings in the cluttered wreck, and only managed to beat the algae, sand and debris into a whirlwind. Pazel choked (he was breathing it, after all) but pushed on, slamming a rotted compartment door behind him.

He passed dark cabins, broken ladderways. One of the fanged fish that had so alarmed him before rushed out of the gloom. Heedless with longing, Pazel smacked it away.

She was still there on the gun deck, her body glowing behind a mass of broken beams. She saw him and turned to flee.

"Don't go!" he cried out, and his words froze her where she stood. Amazed, Pazel swam a little closer. "Come out, Klyst, if that's your name. Why are you so afraid of me?"

She stepped out, hugging herself, literally shaking with fear.

"You could be miles away by now, if I'm so frightening. Why did you stay? Please explain all this to me!"

Her sharp teeth were chattering. She shook her head. "Can't go. Can't disobey. I love you."

"You love me! Why on earth? I mean . . . that's extremely . . . *Why?*"

"You used *ripestry*. Humans shouldn't! Humans never could!"

Pazel's Gift told him that *ripestry* was Murthish for "language." But then he started. It was also telling him the word meant "magic."

"What! Are they the same thing, to sea-murths?"

"They?" she said.

"Ripestry and *ri—"* Pazel stopped. Even his Gift couldn't provide another word. It was true: language and magic were one notion to her. *To speak was to enchant.*

"But for Rin's sake," he said, "you were the one doing love-*ripestry* to me. Weren't you?"

"Yes, yes," she said. "But when you said my name you turned it back on me. And since I'd already touched you I . . . I—"

She leaped forward and wrapped her strange arms around his legs. She pressed her face to his knees and wept—"Hoo-hoo-hoo-hoo!"

Her tears glowed luminescent as they left her eyes, in the instant before the sea diluted them.

"Why are you crying?"

"Land-boy! Land-boy! I love you!"

Her charm had backfired: he was free, she was madly in love. He tried to make her stand up.

"I'll release you," he said. "Just tell me how."

"HOO-HOO-HOO!"

"Klyst!" he said as gently as he could. "Please stop crying. We'll find a way out of this."

At once she made an effort to hold in her tears.

"That's grand," he said. "Now tell me, why did you give us water-breathing, and make us love you?"

"Can't help it," she said. "We have to drive you away."

"Well, that's a blary strange way to do it!"

She shook her head. "It always works."

"But why not just talk to us?"

"Because you're monsters," she said. "Your people, I mean. Wherever you go the *ripestry* dies. And then so do we. Starved for *ripestry,* starved to death."

Her silver eyes stared into his, beseeching, and Pazel stared back without a word. The Volpeks were right, in a sense: the murths *were* dying out in the Quiet Sea. And if he understood her, mankind was the reason. Men dispelled magic; and her people could not live without it.

"But you have *ripestry,*" she said at last, smiling. "You can stay! You can stay with me!"

Darkness. She began to kiss his hands.

"There are many men here," he said.

"Too many," she said. "They've been coming for weeks, and more all the time. Always before, for centuries, men feared the murths and ghosts and spirit-tides, and hurried off. But these men are not afraid. There is an evil *ripestry* with them that breaks our spells. My father says we must abandon these gardens, where we have lived for ten thousand years—move south, away from the monsters. But our elders are too weak for such a journey. They'll certainly die."

"You don't have to go!" Pazel said. "I know what they want. And I promise you, Klyst, they'll leave as soon as they get it. They serve a mage called Arunis. He's the one with the bad *ripestry*. But all he wants is some Red Wolf."

The light returned; he saw her look of disbelief. "*That* thing? That old iron wolf?"

"You know it!" he said.

"Of course. It went down with this ship forty years ago, when my father was a boy. But the Red Wolf is . . . ugly, bad. Why would anyone care about it?"

"I don't know. But believe me, Arunis won't leave without it. Will you take me to it, Klyst?"

"Will you marry me?"

What could he tell her? The truth? That except for a few moments under her spell he had never thought of marrying anyone, never longed in that way for anyone, except (in moments of lunacy or insight) for a land-girl named Thasha Isiq?

Feeling rather a cad, he said, "I can't breathe water forever, now, can I?"

She beamed at him. "You can if you're with me! A kiss on the hand, that's good for a whole day. You can stay as long as you like. The others will be getting air-thirst soon, of course."

"Air-thirst? What's air-thirst?"

Klyst just looked at him. Then she crossed her eyes and made desperate motions with her mouth: *gulp gulp gulp*.

"Drowning!" he cried. "They'll *drown* soon? We've got to find them! Oh, Neeps! Where are they, Klyst, *where*?"

"Different places."

"Take me! Please, hurry!"

Obedient as ever, she caught his wrist and tugged him out through the gunport. Her friend the scarlet ray was still circling the *Lythra*. Klyst gave a sharp cry and it swooped down on them like a thunderhead. As it passed overhead Klyst grabbed its wing just behind one eye, and she and Pazel were whisked away through the kelp at breakneck speed. Coral mountains whizzed by. The bathysphere flashed by like a golden apple. Then she let go of the ray and sank with Pazel toward a little trench in the seafloor.

"Too late," she said.

The pair of boys from the bathysphere were in the trench, feet pointing skyward, dead. At the bottom of the trench was a bed of clams—monstrous clams; the smallest were as broad as dinner platters. Some yawned wide, pearls like goose eggs shining in their pale flesh. Two had snapped shut on human wrists.

Klyst swam up to the nearest boy and bit him smartly on the foot. "Still warm," she said, chewing.

"Neeps!" shouted Pazel. "You've got to take me to Neeps! The other boy!"

Off they went again, flashing by a staved-in yawl, an octopus gliding among blue anemones, an anchor with a broken fluke. Suddenly the ray turned in a circle, halting.

"Blood," it said.

"Human blood," said Klyst, sniffing.

Bakru! Spare him! thought Pazel. "Where is it, Klyst?"

She swam in a circle, eyes shut and lips smacking oddly. She was tasting the sea.

"Hurry!"

Klyst stopped and looked upward. Pazel did the same. Halfway to the surface a body drifted, backlit by the sun.

"Neeps!" Pazel raced upward, dazzled by the brightness above, fighting a sob that wanted to burst from his chest. He seized the body by the arm.

It was a Volpek. Pazel turned the dead man over. The mercenary's throat had been slit. Blood still trickled from the wound.

"Others, too," said Klyst, pointing. Some yards away were three more Volpek bodies, sinking slowly. Among them, Pazel saw with a gasp, was the captain of the cargo ship. The water about him was clouded with blood.

"Your people did this?" Pazel asked.

"No!" said Klyst firmly. "We don't kill this way, with knives and mess. And we hide the bodies afterward. Humans fear most what they don't see."

Who had killed the Volpeks, then? Had someone attacked the cargo vessel? He glanced at the sunny disc of the surface overhead. *What was happening up there?*

Then he started—Neeps was still missing. "Onward!" he begged Klyst. "While he can still breathe!"

The ray bore them a little farther, to the mouth of a dark cave. Pazel caught a sickening glimpse of skulls and rib cages, and a well-fed eel. But no fresh bodies, and certainly no Neeps.

"He's not here, Klyst!"

The murth-girl looked surprised. "Vvsttrk always brings them here."

"Well, she's turned over a new leaf! Klyst, he's my best friend! Please, think! Aren't there other places you do . . . this sort of thing?"

At *best friend* her face grew hard. "Neeps." She said it the way one might say *mumps* or *hives*.

"Listen, girl," said Pazel, "if he dies I'll be *very* unhappy. With you. Forever."

The murth-girl's jaws worked. Then she called the ray back to her side, and together they shot off into the kelp.

Two minutes later they were at the stern half of the *Lythra*. She took him to the orlop deck, through a shattered door and down two levels, to what might have been the ship's brig. Old prisoners' bones (and a few not so old) lay shackled to the walls. That was all.

They checked the hold, the galley. Last of all, the captain's cabin.

"Pazel!" cried a familiar voice. Neeps was still breathing—and tied by his own rope to the foot of an ancient bed frame. "Get me out of here!" he cried. "That sea-vixen fooled me!"

Pazel was so relieved he pulled the murth-girl into a hug. She glowed like the full moon at his touch.

"You *let* her do this to you?" Pazel asked, turning back to Neeps.

Possibly the first boy ever to do so underwater, Neeps blushed. "She said she'd be right back."

"Never mind. We've got to get you back to the surface. Help us, Klyst."

The rope was no match for the murth-girl's teeth. As she chewed she stared at Neeps with unmistakable loathing.

"What's wrong with this one?" Neeps asked. "She looks like she'd rather eat me than set me free."

"She's jealous," said Pazel. "It's not her fault, exactly. Come on, your charm's wearing off."

Out through the stern windows they swam, Klyst tagging moodily behind. The bathysphere was rising: in fact it was halfway to the surface. As they sped toward it, a lone diver plunged from its dark mouth. It was Marila.

No murth-magic had been done to her: she was holding her breath, and still looked far too weak to be diving. At the sight of the boys her eyes lit up with astonishment. She didn't smile (*could* she smile?) but still she managed to look as close to happy as Pazel had seen her. Dropping her sinker, she rose with them into the sphere.

The Volpeks gaped in amazement at the boys' return. From a shelf above the waterline, Mintu laughed. "Pazel! Neeps!" he cried. "I told them you weren't dead!"

"Two of us are," said Pazel. "And Neeps almost made three. Do you hear?" He raised his voice to Volpek level. *"DON'T SEND ANYONE ELSE. I'LL BRING YOU THE WOLF."*

"YOU FOUND THE RED WOLF?!"

"JUST GIVE ME A ROPE, WILL YOU?"

Marila leaned close, whispering to fight the echo. "Hurry," she said. "They're nervous up above. Something about a mist closing in. They're afraid it's black magic."

"We shouldn't be here," said Pazel. "Humans, I mean. It's not our coast."

"Pazel," said Neeps, "you're not still under that murth-girl's charm, are you?"

"Of course not!" said Pazel. Rope in hand, he dived. Klyst emerged from the weeds and all but tackled him.

"I thought you wouldn't come back," she said, clinging to his arm. "Who was that ugly, wicked girl?"

"Nobody," said Pazel, exasperated. "Klyst, you've got to let me have that Wolf. I swear all these men will leave the Coast as soon as they get it."

"And you'll leave with them."

"I have to, Klyst."

"Then I'll follow you. I'll follow your ship."

"This is nonsense!" said Pazel. "We're trying to stop a war! A *huge* war, do you understand? And that is *much* more important than you and your silly—"

But then he saw her tears oozing into the water again. Before he could find a word of comfort she broke down completely. "HOO-HOO-HOO-HOO-HOO!"

She tore out handfuls of hair, braided shells and all. Then she dived. Pazel gave chase, but it was like a kitten chasing a mountain lion. When at last he found her she was kneeling by the coral arch, tearing the orange worms from the rock and stuffing them one after another into her mouth. Their venom burned her lips, but she kept chewing, weeping all the while.

Pazel caught her by the waist and dragged her back from the arch. "Spit them out! Out!"

She put her hands over her ears.

"You heard me!"

Reproachfully she spat out the worms. "If you go I will die! I love you!"

"Tell me how to reverse the love-*ripestry.*"

"You can't!"

"Is that true?"

She glared and glared. "You can. But it's not easy. And I'll kill myself before you do it!"

Defeated, he let her go. "Just show me the Wolf," he begged. "As soon as they have it we can sit down and talk."

"About getting married?"

"About anything you want."

She wiped her eyes and pointed into the arch. "We buried it here long ago. It attracts the worms, and other bad things."

"Right here?"

She nodded. "You can't dig it up, though. It would take you all day."

Pazel sighed. "I was afraid you'd say that. Well, I'll go and tell the others. We can dig in shifts, and maybe—"

"No," said Klyst. "No more humans."

"Why not?"

"They'll be killed," she said. "Very quickly. We start by using girls, but when that fails we have . . . other ways. Do you understand? My people won't wait much longer."

Pazel peered into the kelp forest. "Tell me what to do," he said.

Klyst paused, thoughtful. "Get ropes," she said at last. "All the ropes you have. The Wolf is *very* heavy. When you come back I will tell you more."

"What are you going to—"

"Go, land-boy. Hurry."

She glanced up at the bathysphere. He watched her for another moment: there was something she did not want to say. But he had to trust her—what choice did he have?

"Wait for me here," he said, and rose.

He met the bathysphere just below the surface. At once he shouted to the Volpeks for more ropes. Neeps, Marila and Mintu watched him with looks of dread, but none of them said a word. Suspicious, the Volpeks threw him all the rope-ends they had.

"THE CUSTOMER DIDN'T SAY IT WAS HUGE."

Not bothering to reply, Pazel dived once more, five ropes uncoiling behind him.

Was Klyst alone? For a moment Pazel thought he saw more than one figure near the coral arch. Then the darkness fell and he swam on by memory, and when he could see again there was no one beneath him but the murth-girl.

She flitted to his side and pulled him quickly down into a little rocky crevasse.

"I thought you said it was under the arch," said Pazel.

"It is. Give me the ropes."

Quickly she wound the ends of all five ropes around a coral knob. Then she backed deeper into the crevasse and beckoned him to do the same.

"Crouch down. Hold on."

There was barely room for the two of them. She smiled to be so close to him, her serpentine legs against his own. She took on a soft yellow glow.

"Klyst," he said stiffly, "we must go and get that Wolf."

"We are."

She grew very still. The sea too seemed to hold its breath. And then out of nowhere the scarlet ray shot by like a great leathery dragon, raked them with an indecipherable look, and vanished over the top of the coral wall. And in its wake came a storm of silver.

They were needlefish, thinner than broom handles and faster than arrows, and they blasted by a yard from Pazel's face in a school so tight it was like a solid body. The sound was like nothing he had ever known: a soft enormity, the pulse of a giant's vein. The school plunged right through the coral arch, blotting out all view of worms and urchins as they passed.

"What was all that for?"

"Ripestry," she said. "Don't move."

The needlefish were gone. But then Pazel felt the sea begin to change. A gentle tug at first, then a stiff current like the recoil of a wave, flowing unmistakably toward the arch. Klyst put her arms around him. The current doubled, then doubled again. It was a riptide now, gushing quietly but with immense power through the arch. Sand rose from the tunnel floor. The vile worms began peeling away.

Embracing him, Klyst began to sing. In song, her voice and

language were suddenly beautiful, and free of all fear. It was strange to hear joy in her voice, for the words were somber.

> *Mothers from out of the ancient cold,*
> *Fathers from fire descended,*
> *Bound to a destiny none foretold,*
> *Birthed us, the never-intended.*
> *Oh never, never again to be*
> *Of this mortal world, this migrant sea.*
> *Children of Isparil's morning call,*
> *Sired on Night's feral steed,*
> *Heirs to a promise that none recall,*
> *Prisoners of dawn-thwarted need.*
> *Oh never, never again to be*
> *Of this wounded world, this wastrel sea.*

The current was lifting more and more sand from the seafloor, whirling it away through the tunnel. And slowly a figure appeared.

It was encrusted with old limpets and barnacles, clams, algae, knobs of withered coral. But it was unmistakably a wolf, and its color was a dark blood-red. It stood upright, iron muzzle raised in a silent howl. Pazel felt a great menace in it, although he could not have said why.

"It's no bigger than a real wolf," he said.

"Heavy, though," said Klyst.

Even as she spoke the blasting current died away. Klyst freed the ropes from the coral and at once began trussing up the wolf. She was good with knots—Pazel tried not to imagine what she practiced on. Two ropes she looped around the Wolf's head, another two about the midsection. The last she braided through its legs.

When she had finished, Pazel gave the ropes two stiff tugs. The Volpeks responded at once. The lines tightened, shifted, tightened again. But the Wolf did not budge. This was, Pazel knew, extremely weird: five ropes and pulleys should have allowed the men to lift an iron hippopotamus. He looked up: more Volpeks were leaping through the dive portal and entering the sphere. A moment later the ropes snapped tight again.

The Wolf slid forward an inch, then another. The ropes strained tight as bowstrings. At last, like a tree wrenched from the earth, it left the seabed. First it swung out of the arch; then, revolving slowly, it rose.

Pazel heaved a great sigh. "Your people can stay," he said. "These men will be gone before you know it. They're all afraid of the Haunted Coast. They can't wait to get out of here."

With many a jerk and stutter, the Wolf climbed inexorably toward the bathysphere.

"I know you do not lie," said Klyst, taking his hand. "This is why you've come, why the Lord of the Sea gave you to us. This is why it is my fate to love you, a curse that is no curse."

Pazel was glad it was taking so long to raise the Wolf, for he had no idea how he would convince Klyst to let him break the enchantment. Simple reasoning (that he didn't eat other humans, that his *ripestry* was just a spell gone wrong) would clearly get him nowhere. He would have to tell her the worst: that he did not feel what she felt, and didn't want to.

Then he would have to command her not to do herself harm.

Silent, they watched the Red Wolf enter the sphere. Then Klyst turned and led him beneath the arch, which now bore an unfortunate resemblance to a chapel doorway. They knelt. Pazel's stomach twisted in knots. He *had* to tell her the truth. But there she was, beaming at him, pulling his hands into her hair—strange, thick hair, with those braids of tiny kulri shells. He felt as if he was holding the sea itself.

"Nine hundred shells in my hair," she said. "All perfect, white, clean. That is the rule for murth-girls: a very strict rule of purity. But one shell I keep secret. It has a rose heart. Look."

He took his hands away. And although he had not pulled or grasped at anything, there it lay on his palm. A shell like all the rest, but blood-red on the inside. She took it from him and held it for a long time, and he wondered if she was having second thoughts. Then she reached out and pressed it against his chest, just below his collarbone.

The shell vanished.

"Where did it go? Did you drop it?"

"Pinch your skin," she said.

Pazel pinched a fold of his skin, just where she had placed the shell. "It's inside me," he whispered.

She nodded. "A shell is a home that drifts. I have named you my secret home, given you my secret heart. If you want me to stop loving you, cut it from your flesh. Otherwise I am yours. Will you marry me, land-boy, and live on starfish and coral wine, and learn the songs of my grandfathers, and know the million wonders of the murth-world?"

She touched his cheek. His heart was beating so hard he thought he might faint. He no longer knew what he wanted. Images of Thasha and Neeps, of his family, of sorcerers and kings, passed before his eyes like drawings in a storybook, or a dream he was quickly forgetting. Nothing was real but her eyes.

On Klyst's face he saw the gentlest of smiles appear. He felt the beginnings of an answering smile on his own face, and a warmth where she touched him.

And at that precise moment, his mind-fit struck.

It came like a stampede of horses, thundering, trampling. Panic took him entirely. Klyst was shouting, but he heard only that dreaded noise. He knew he could not speak a word—but what was worse, silence or gibberish? Either way she would think he hated her.

"SQUALAFLAGRAPAGA! PAJ! NAG! ZELURAK!"

She was weeping and screaming. He fell back on the seafloor, covering his ears. But there was no shutting it out. And the next instant her voice was joined by others, much lower and angrier. A dozen sea-murth men were laying hands on him, biting, strangling, piercing him with their sharp nails and teeth. They must have been watching all along. Behind them Klyst wailed and pleaded.

Their argument was deafening. But Klyst won, and the

murth-men let him go. Howling with sobs, she pulled him toward the surface, the raging men just behind. Pazel found himself crying, too. But his tears did not glow, and Klyst would never know he had shed them.

The bathysphere was rising from the waves. Klyst stopped him a yard beneath it and covered his hands with kisses. She looked at him and waited. He bent to do the same to her hands, but she shook her head. She wanted him to speak.

He bit his lips. He would not subject her to that noise.

Klyst saw his look of refusal and let out a final, agonizing scream. Then, with the sound still breaking from her throat, she faded. It happened suddenly. One moment she was there, solid as he was. The next he saw the kelp through her skin. And the next (the scream snuffed out like a candle) there was no murth-girl before him at all.

Spitting hatred, the murth-men turned and fled. Pazel gasped—and choked instantly. He could no longer breathe water.

Flailing, he surfaced. He was surrounded by boats. Clouds of white mist were racing toward them over the water. Twenty feet away, the bathysphere dangled over the deck of the sea barge. All about it the Volpeks stood gaping. And directly beneath the sphere, arms raised, stood Arunis.

The Volpeks in the sphere were lowering the Red Wolf down through the hole. The sorcerer reached for it, ecstatic. When his fingers brushed it at last, he let out a bellowing noise that even through the distortion of his mind-fit Pazel knew for laughter.

What have I done?

Pazel splashed toward the barge. *Knock him into the sea, drown him, drown with him.*

Saving Klyst's people had been his only thought. But in so doing he had aided a monster.

"I'll kill you!"

Arunis glanced around, trying to locate the source of the meaningless squawk. And then—

BOOM.

A violent wave. Pazel was hurled back and down. Volpeks tumbled from the deck. Arunis lost his grip on the Wolf and plunged into the sea.

Cannon fire!

Somehow Pazel rose. No one was motionless now. Men ran, oars churned; terror showed on every face.

BOOM. BOOM.

They were under attack.

On Pazel's right a skiff was blasted to splinters. The air was full of wood, water, blood. Pazel swam toward the nearest boat, screaming for help. It was overfull: Volpeks and their young prisoners, stuffed like worms in a baitbox. And it was drawing away, much faster than he could swim.

"Help! Help!" ("Kquak! Kquak!")

He chased it, but his strength was gone. Another wave sank him, and when he struggled to the surface again he knew it was for the last time.

The drowned, like those who die of thirst, suffer visions: every sailor knows that. So Pazel was not too surprised when familiar faces appeared in the departing boat. There was Neeps, throwing punches. There was Thasha fighting like a champion. And there, dashing one Volpek after another into the sea, was Hercól of Tholjassa. A pretty dream, he thought, not believing in it for an instant.

BOOM.

The fighters ducked. Something whistled overhead. Then came pain, and darkness like sudden nightfall, and quiet at last.

—32—

A Betrayal Ended

5 Teala 941
83rd day from Etherhorde

Moonlight. No sound of a battle.

Was he sleeping on the bottom of the sea?

No, he could not breathe water anymore. If he were under the waves it meant he was dead, and that seemed likely enough. But if he had drowned his lips could not be parched, nor his scalp tickled by what felt suspiciously like a flea.

"Well," said a man's deep voice, "the last time it was you who waited on me. Now I can return the favor. Care to sit up and drink something?"

Pazel's head ached terribly. He was in a small, neat cabin without lamp or candle. And seated on the corner of the bed was Ignus Chadfallow.

"You're here!"

"And so, more surprisingly, are you. Don't jump up! You took a flying plank to the back of the head—a blow that would have split a coconut. Fortunately your skull is rather harder."

He smiled—the first smile Pazel had seen on his face in years. But Pazel found he could not return it: Chadfallow had played him one trick too many. The doctor's smile faded, and it was then that Pazel noticed how tired he looked. There were lines of care on his face that had not been there in Sorrophran, and his eyes were grim.

A memory suddenly blossomed in Pazel's head. "My father was here!" he said. "I heard him—was it just a few minutes ago? I heard him talking about me."

Chadfallow lowered his eyes. "You have been asleep for twenty hours, Pazel."

For a moment Pazel refused to believe it: the voice had been so real, so close. But of course it had been a dream; his father could not have been there. And yet—

"Where are we?"

"Two leagues from Ormael City, I should say. We'll be docking within the hour."

"Ormael! How did we get here? What ship is this?"

"The brig *Hemeddrin*. A Volpek warship, but we have found her a better flag. Rise carefully, if you can rise at all, and put these on." He handed Pazel a shirt and pair of breeches. "They are the smallest I could find. Volpeks do not keep tarboys."

Pazel got to his feet, wincing. Every muscle in his body hurt. As he dressed, Chadfallow bent over a sack at his feet and withdrew a glass bottle. Pulling the stopper, he decanted a few ounces into a mug and held it out to Pazel.

"Drink."

Pazel just looked at him. No other word could have done more to remind him of his distrust of Ignus Chadfallow. The doctor took in his expression and smiled sadly.

"It's medicine, my boy. A powerful but entirely unmagical sort, and the very thing for one in your condition. Go on, drink it down."

Pazel shut his eyes. He drank. And retched. "It tastes like something *dead*."

"Oil of grubroot," said Chadfallow. "The caviar of emetics. Here you are." He handed Pazel a brass dish.

"What's this for?"

Chadfallow said nothing; he appeared to be counting seconds. All at once Pazel doubled over, vomiting copiously into the dish. Chadfallow studied his expulsions with interest.

"No ulcranous pills!" he said. "You're lucky; but then Arunis didn't have you in his keeping long. The other divers coughed up a number of tiny pills, which were perhaps embedded in their biscuits. Awful weapons: they are coated with a lacquer that dissolves over the course of ten days. After that the beads shatter, filling the stomach with powdered glass. Death follows—slowly."

"He was going to kill us!"

"After you brought him the Wolf. He wanted no one left alive to tell tales."

"Have you given the others that grubroot stuff?"

"Of course. Now, can you walk? People are waiting to see you."

Chadfallow opened the door, and they stepped out into a small wardroom.

"Pazel!"

Thasha jumped up so fast she nearly overturned the table where she was sitting with Neeps, Marila and Mintu. She had cut her hair as short as a tarboy's—hacked it off with a knife, by the look of it. She and Neeps ran to embrace him.

"You choose the worst times to have those fits," Thasha laughed.

"There's no *good* time," said Pazel, grinning too.

"You old dog!" said Neeps. "You really fixed Arunis! Last I saw he was floundering in the water, screaming about a scarlet ray. Did your murth-girl send that ray?"

Pazel's smile faded. His murth-girl. Why had she vanished? Was that how her people died? Or could murths only be seen when you were under their spell—or when they were under yours?

He gave his chest a quick pinch. The shell was still there.

"It must have been Klyst," he said. "But what happened? Thasha, was that really you in the boat? You and—"

He whirled around. There by the masthead stood Hercól. The Tholjassan smiled warmly.

"Yes, Pazel, I too am alive—thanks to you. Had you not alerted my brethren I should have died in Uturphe, just as my old master intended."

"Your old master?"

"Sandor Ott," said Hercól.

"What?" cried Pazel.

"I couldn't believe it either," said Thasha, smiling slyly. "I knew *someone* had made a monster out of him, but—"

"Ott did not make me a warrior," said Hercól quickly, and with no hint of an answering smile. "He snatched me, rather, from a Tholjassan fighting school. Half-trained, and wholly trusting. But this is not the time to discuss my dark years with the Secret Fist."

"But you were dying in Uturphe!" said Pazel. "How in Pitfire did you get *here*?"

It had all begun with those two riders, Hercól explained. They had alerted the Tholjassan Consul, who had sprung into action when he learned of Hercól's plight, and located him the next morning in a poorhouse, his knife wound already inflamed. The Consul saw that the wound was properly cleaned and dressed. Soon Hercól woke, and begged his fellow Tholjassan to search the city for Pazel.

"He put nine men on the task," said Hercól, "and soon enough the trail led to the false inn on Blackwell Street, and to the Flikkermen. They fled my brethren down their holes and sewers, but a Tholjassan does not turn easily from his prize. Of course, you and Neeps had already been taken inland, to the flesh market. But my brethren recovered these."

Hercól held out his palm, and to Pazel's astonishment, there lay his parents' gifts, the knife and the ivory whale.

"Thank you, Hercól," he said, humbled, and pressed them to his chest.

Of course Pazel wished to know what had happened to them all. They tried to explain, but with so many tellers the tale became a patchwork of details and anecdotes, and he had to stop them time and again with simple questions. At last the picture emerged: how Hercól had subjected his wound to the lightning-fast cures of a Slugdra ghost-doctor (and survived them). How he had hunted Ott's men through the low places of Uturphe, killing three and frightening all, for these lesser spies had never crossed wits or swords with one trained to serve the Secret Fist. How he learned that Chadfallow too was marked for death, and so met his ship and persuaded him not to pass a single night in Uturphe. How together the men had boarded a Simja-bound ship full of cooks, seamstresses, masons, balladeers, dog-catchers and specialists in the elimination of wasps, all claiming some connection to Thasha's wedding. How they disembarked at Ormael to find *Chathrand* already docked and the city in an uproar, for Thasha had run away in the night.

Ott's spies were scouring Ormael City. But Hercól had turned again, as Tholjassans will in a crisis, to his kindred. As it hap-pened, several Tholjassans were preparing to ride north toward the Crab Fens, responding to an emergency letter. Apparently a Volpek brig—this very *Hemeddrin*—had been raiding the coast for a fortnight, landing men in defenseless villages and kidnap-ping boys and girls in their teens. The ship had last been spotted running straight for the Haunted Coast.

"Ott wasn't interested in Tholjassan youths," said Hercól, "but I was. And when I learned that Mr. Ket, the soap merchant with a knack for turning up at odd times, had left the *Chathrand* and was also headed north, I knew the coincidence was too great. The doctor and I set off with my countrymen on horse-back. We caught up with Arunis and his wagon-team at the edge of the Fens. But we were five men against fifty Volpeks and a mage—and we saw no sign of Thasha, hidden as she was. The best we could do was slow Arunis down."

"So it was you who blocked the road with trees," Pazel asked. Hercól nodded. "With a little help from the freebooters."

"Freebooters? You mean smugglers, men like Mr. Druffle?"

"I do," said Hercól. "But Mr. Druffle had best not show his face among the freebooters of Chereste again, after helping Arunis raid their territory. *They* are wise enough never to seek treasure among the shipwrecks of the Haunted Coast. And they appear to have made peace with the murths and spirits there. No living men know that country better."

He seemed about to say more, but then changed his mind. Pazel saw Neeps and Thasha look quickly away. Confused, Pazel glanced from face to face. No one met his eye.

Hercól cleared his throat. "Others of my kinfolk met us in the dunes. All told we were but fifteen strong. The freebooters were not many, either: another dozen at the most. They were brave, though, and they had boats hidden in a secret lodge in the North Fens. They were quite eager to help us drive the Volpeks out."

"As the Mzithrinis might have been," put in Chadfallow, "if only—"

"*Mzithrinis?*" Pazel nearly jumped from the bench. "What Mzithrinis? Where did they come from?"

"We have all been asking that question," said Chadfallow. "Perhaps they were outlaws, enemies of the Five Kings driven into exile. But it is just as likely they were spies. The Mzithrinis surely knew that something odd was brewing in the Gulf of Thól. One does not bring three ships and a hundred Volpeks that close to the Pentarchy and escape unnoticed. My guess is that they were dispatched to find out what Arunis was up to, and stumbled on Thasha quite by accident. Unfortunately—or perhaps very fortunately—they are all dead. If they were agents of the Five Kings, it would hardly do for them to turn up at Thasha's wedding and identify her."

"I wish they would," said Thasha. "If Prince Falmurqat knew what I looked like then, blood leaking down my chin and all, he'd be the one running away from this marriage."

"Hear our mistress of peace," sighed Chadfallow. "In any case, those six will make no report. But they did not walk to the Haunted Coast. Somewhere they had a boat, and few are the boats that would cross the Gulf of Thól with a crew of six. Others may have watched your fight from a dune-top, Hercól."

"What is done cannot be undone," said Hercól. "And Thasha had no better choice—indeed, she did what I would have done myself under the circumstances."

"At last a kind word," said Thasha. "Hercól cut off my hair with a knife, Pazel, and dipped me in swamp-muck, and made me go and surrender to that Druffle of yours. And Druffle actually believed I was a Tholjassan sponge-diver who'd given up trying to escape."

"You don't look a bit Tholjassan," said Marila. "Druffle must be a fool."

"He was enchanted," said Chadfallow. "Magically enslaved by Arunis, Rin knows for how long. We have never seen the real man."

"I can live without that pleasure," said Neeps. "But if only you'd caught us still ashore! If Pazel hadn't been sent underwater, and talked with the sea-murths, Arunis never would have found the Wolf at all."

There was a brief silence.

"I only wanted him to leave," said Pazel. "Klyst told me that when men disturb the Haunted Coast, it destroys the *ripestry,* the magic that keeps them alive. It's not right for men to do that. Her people have lived there for thousands of years."

"You have learned things no human ever knew," said Chadfallow quietly.

"Well, I don't want to learn another language like hers," Pazel said, so fiercely that they all looked up. "Klyst called me *land-boy*—do you want to know why? Because the word for 'human' is *striglyffn-chik,* that's why. I'll have to know that forever. But I'm not making sense. I'll be quiet. *Striglyffn-chik.* Sorry."

This time the silence was longer. The others had winced at the screeching noise: sea-murth syllables torn from a human throat. Marila and Mintu gaped like fish. "He's got the hiccups," whispered the small boy.

"Pazel," said Thasha slowly, "what will you have to know forever?"

"That word," he said. "It's the only word they have for 'human.' But it means 'the beasts who will kill us all.' That's how they see us. I wish I didn't know."

When no one resumed the tale, Pazel took a deep breath. "What I do want to know is how you beat so many Volpeks. You were outnumbered, what? Three to one?"

"Closer to four," said Dr. Chadfallow. "We owe our success to Tholjassan tactics."

"And unnaturally good luck," Hercól added. "The mist that

rolled off the Fens allowed us to move unseen, and within it sounds were deadened, too. First it blanketed Arunis' shore compound, and we fell on the Volpeks there and slew them almost in silence. Then the mist moved out to sea like a great wall, and we followed. Was it the work of Coast spirits, or the murths you befriended, Pazel? I do not know. But within that uncanny fog we stole aboard the cargo ship, and though some of our people fell we took her, too, and still Arunis suspected nothing."

"I saw your handiwork," said Pazel grimly, recalling the dead Volpek he had feared was Neeps.

"Afterward we launched her boats and sailed west into the main current, where we could fall upon the *Hemeddrin* from behind. It was vital to take her next. Her guns could have blown the sea barge to matchsticks."

"We noticed," said Neeps.

"That was the freebooters' doing," said Hercól. "A bit too eager to kill Volpeks, as it happened. We Tholjassans never planned to fire a shot. Yet there was a danger that the Volpeks would harm their captives if they learned that we had taken their fighting ship. What if they sank the sphere with captives still inside her? That is why I sent Thasha out with the last cage full of divers. And that is why four of us slipped from our boats as we passed the sea barge, and trod water in the mists and kelp, awaiting her signal that you were all safely out of the sphere."

"Only I couldn't signal," said Thasha, "because you were still missing."

"And then the freebooters fired the cannons?"

"At the sea barge," said Hercól, with a nod.

"On top of us, in other words," said Marila.

"You were very lucky, Pazel," said Neeps. "Mintu here saw you just as you were starting to sink. You were out cold."

"I owe you one, mate," said Pazel. Mintu smiled and looked at his toes.

Hercól smiled at the brother and sister. "Our countrymen will see you all safely home to your villages, once you have rested a bit in Ormael. *Fasundri,* fearless ones: that is how you shall be known."

He touched his closed fist to his forehead, the very gesture Thasha had seen him make on the bridge in Gallows Park in Etherhorde, and the Tholjassan boy and girl did the same. Pazel looked at Marila, and saw that Neeps was doing the same. They would miss her, strange cold fish that she was.

"And that is nearly the end of the story," said Chadfallow. "The Tholjassans took the ship, and paid the freebooters a tidy sum for their trouble. All the artifacts stolen from the *Lythra* they wisely returned to the sea. Many Volpeks died, along with some who fought them. But no divers perished, except the two boys killed by the sea-murths. I cannot say whether Arunis died, but at least his plans have been thwarted."

"And the Red Wolf?" said Pazel. "What became of it?"

Chadfallow and Hercól exchanged a look. The doctor closed the wardroom door.

"It is here," he said, "in the hold. Do not speak of it to anyone. When *Chathrand* sails back to Etherhorde I shall gather the best minds in the Empire: we shall try to learn why Arunis wanted it so badly."

"You should start with Ramachni," said Thasha, sullen, as if this were a point made before. Chadfallow did not even look at her.

"My great fear, Pazel, was that Arunis sought the Nilstone, a cursed thing of horrible power. It was in the keeping of the Mzithrin Kings, and vanished during the last war. The Shaggat Ness craved it to the point of madness, and one rumor placed it in his hands at the moment the *Lythra* sank. No doubt Arunis also dreams of possessing the Nilstone—and if it were here, I cannot imagine him spending his time on anything else. Still, I sense a powerful spell on this Wolf: perhaps it too is a weapon of some kind."

"Do you think he wanted it for the Shaggat Ness?" asked Pazel.

The doctor turned him a sharp look. "What do you mean, *for* him?"

Before Pazel could answer, a cry went up on the topdeck: *"Port stations! Ormael City! Clew up, boys! Furl those Volpek rags!"*

Everyone jumped to their feet.

"We can discuss this later," said Hercól. "Now we must act. Thasha, you know your part?"

A gleam appeared in Thasha's eye. "Know it? I can't *wait* for it."

"Very good," said Hercól. "Then listen well, Pazel Pathkendle, for we shall need your help as well. We have dealt with one conspirator, but two more await us."

The Imperial Governor of His Supremacy's Territories of Ormael and the Trothe of Chereste was having a bad evening. The swordfish was off. His cook had the measles. He hated this wing of Ormael Palace (the evening sun through the famous round, red window behind him slowly cooked the back of his neck), but where else could he entertain? The formal dining hall was still roofless and derelict, five years after the Rescue. The repair funds—like most of those promised for the city—had mysteriously evaporated. In truth such a theft of Imperial gold did not bother him half as much as not being invited to participate.

His subjects loathed him, an Etherhorder sent to rule Ormael in the name of a violent conqueror. And for the first time since his reign began five years ago: cannon fire along the Coast! Were they pirates, freebooters, Mzithrini? He hardly dared imagine.

It was the third straight dinner with his *Chathrand* guests, and they had long since run out of pleasantries. Uskins and Fiffengurt, two officers brought along tonight to make conversation, did nothing but glower at each other across the table. Each time Ambassador Isiq looked at him, the governor heard a silent accusation. *Why are you eating dinner? Why did you sneeze? Why aren't you out there looking for her?*

For of course nothing mattered beside the grand catastrophe hanging over him. The Isiq daughter, gone. Six hundred vessels descending on Simja for a wedding that could not occur. Day by day they were drifting toward an embarrassment that would sting for centuries. And he would be at its epicenter: the fool in Ormael who lost the Treaty Bride.

"This wine is splendid, Governor," said Syrarys.

Bless her, thought the governor. *She does try to help.*

"Jasbrea Vineyards," mumbled Captain Rose, frowning at his fish. "On Fulne."

"Right you are, Captain!" said the governor. "You're a connoisseur."

"I'm a drinker."

First Mate Uskins laughed: a sound like a sheep poked with a dagger. The governor's wife tut-tutted and made the sign of the Tree.

" 'Drink is bottled woe, I shall abandon it,' " she said. "The twenty-first Rule of Rin. Don't you find, Captain, that . . ."

Across the table, Lady Oggosk raised her milky eyes and studied the governor's wife coldly. The woman let her voice trail away.

A servant entered. By his look of nausea it was clear he bore bad news. *Keep it to yourself,* the governor thought. But he let the man whisper in his ear.

In fact the news was anything but bad. The governor jumped to his feet.

"She is found!"

"Found?" cried Eberzam Isiq. "Thasha, found? Where is she?"

"I'm right here, Prahba."

And there she was at the door! Unharmed, even tranquil. She did not run to her father but merely walked, slowly and calmly, and put a hand on his.

"My child!" he said, choking on emotion or swordfish. "Where did you—"

"Wicked girl!" shrieked Syrarys, embracing her. "I've worried myself sick! I haven't slept, do you know that?"

"I expect you pace the castle all night," said a voice at the main door.

Everyone but Thasha gasped. Dr. Ignus Chadfallow stepped into the room, followed by a bruised-looking boy.

The ambassador stood up, too. "Ignus! Pathkendle! What on earth has brought you here?"

"A Volpek ship, Your Excellency, but that is a long story. At the moment what I most recall is the horrors of their galley. Is there no hope of dinner, Governor?"

"Hello, Mr. Uskins," said Pazel quietly, looking straight at the first mate. Then he turned and smiled with great affection at Fiffengurt.

"You rascal!" said Fiffengurt, beaming.

Stuttering, the governor called for two additional plates.

"Make it four," said Chadfallow.

"You three and who else, sir?" asked Uskins.

"Hard to say, isn't it?"

The new arrivals took their seats. Thasha sat beside Syrarys, facing her father.

"Where did you go, my star?" asked Isiq bluntly.

"North," she said, "to the Haunted Coast." Then she looked at Syrarys. "I'm parched. May I taste your wine?"

Syrarys pushed it at her. "You've scared us out of our minds! We thought you were dead!"

"And that, of course, would not do at all," said Chadfallow.

"Doctor!" said Isiq furiously. "You and I are the oldest of friends, but I cannot excuse this tone! You're addressing my lady and consort!"

"It is my sad duty to inform you," said Chadfallow, "that I was addressing your poisoner."

Screams and bellows. One of the servants seemed to think Chadfallow was referring to the fish and began to cry. Syrarys wept loudly. Isiq threw down his napkin and looked ready to challenge the physician to a duel. Lady Oggosk nibbled bread.

"You're jealous!" cried Syrarys. "You never wanted Eberzam to love me!"

"On the contrary," said Chadfallow. "I wanted it a great deal. So much so that I ignored the signs of treachery until they stared me in the face."

"What the devil are you talking about, man?" shouted Isiq.

"You would know, sir, if my letters had reached you. Ah! Here's another guest for dinner."

Outside the doorway, still as death, stood Sandor Ott.

Isiq gestured sharply. "Come in, Nagan! Why do you wait?"

Ott did indeed seem reluctant to enter the room. Syrarys looked at him fixedly. At last he seemed to make up his mind, crossed the room and knelt at Thasha's side.

"Lady Thasha!" he said. "Thank all the Gods! I have hunted day and night—"

"I'll bet you have," said Pazel.

"Chadfallow," said Isiq, "are you mad? You seat this insolent boy beside my daughter, you accuse my lady of wishing me dead—"

"Oh!" cried Syrarys.

"She looks faint!" said Uskins. "Give her some wine!"

"Give her silence!" roared Isiq, and everyone obeyed.

Syrarys clung to his arm, sobbing. Then she groped for her wine and drank deeply.

"Syrarys, darling," said Thasha, "the doctor's upset you."

"He lies! He hates me!"

"You look ill," said Thasha.

"Send her away from me! Oh, Eberzam, I wish I were dead!"

Thasha reached for her hand. "You need something to calm yourself. What about a few of Prahba's special drops?"

Syrarys froze. Her wet eyes turned slowly in Thasha's direction. "If only I had them," she said. "They're in my cabin."

"No, they're not." From under the table Thasha produced a small blue vial. "I had to stop at the *Chathrand* before dinner," she said. "Really, I looked a fright. And something told me this might come in handy. *A harmless tonic to soothe the nerves*— isn't that what you called it? So I put a few drops in your wine."

Syrarys looked pale.

"There's nothing to fear," said Thasha. "Remember how you put it? *Tasteless and harmless. You could drink it by the glass.*"

"A few drops?" whispered Syrarys.

"Well, nineteen."

Syrarys' tears were gone. She sat perfectly still. Dr. Chadfallow opened his bag and withdrew a bottle of his own.

"May I acquaint you with oil of grubroot, Lady Syrarys? For your predicament there is really nothing like it."

Syrarys tensed all over. Then her face twisted into the look of rage Thasha had always known she was hiding.

"You damn doddering fool!" she screamed at Isiq. "Two more days with you and your Pit-spawn daughter! That's all we needed! Two days!" She snatched Chadfallow's bottle and ran for the kitchen.

"Do not let her escape, Governor," said Chadfallow quietly. Isiq looked as if he had been struck in the face. He gave Thasha a beseeching look. His lips trembled, as if he were about to speak, but no sound came. Thasha put her arms around his neck, and propped her chin on his hairless forehead.

"You aren't ill, Prahba. You never were."

Then Fiffengurt spoke softly: "All . . . *we* needed?"

"Quartermaster," said Captain Rose, "you will return to the ship."

Fiffengurt looked at him sharply. "Oppo, Captain. As you will."

He rose and bowed to the governor's wife, who was making the sign of the Tree over anything that moved.

"But . . . but . . . but," said the governor, looking from face to face. "It's a fair q-question, isn't it? What *did* she mean by *we*?"

"She meant herself," said Chadfallow. "And her lover, Sandor Ott." He pointed at the spymaster.

Isiq turned in his chair and cried, "No!"

Rose laughed sharply. "That old tinshirt, Sandor Ott? His Supremacy's chief assassin? Why, I wouldn't trust him to assassinate a dog."

"An excess of trust will never be *your* burden, sir," said the doctor coldly. "But you know who this is."

" 'Course I do. He's an *honor* guardsman. He's a butler with a sword."

"A butler deadly enough to kill everyone in this room and walk out unscathed," said Hercól from the doorway. "Hello, old master."

Ott leaped so fast no one saw him move. Back to the wall, he drew his sword.

"Have you lost your minds, all of you?" he said. "My name is Commander Shtel Nagan. Sandor Ott is the Emperor's spy, and no one knows what he looks like!"

"That was true once," said Chadfallow. "But your ambition has proved stronger than your wisdom in recent years. I know your face, Ott, from my time as Special Envoy in this city. You came here disguised as a merchant, but you were secretly gathering information for the Rescue of Chereste."

"*Invasion,* you mean," said Eberzam Isiq.

Pazel looked at him with amazement.

"I recognized you," Chadfallow went on, "when I returned to Etherhorde. You were always there in the shadows. At last the Emperor introduced us properly—and swore me to secrecy. But I swore another oath long before—to defend Arqual against all enemies."

"I swore the same oath," said Ott. "I have lived by it all my life."

"Not all," said Hercól, drawing closer. "Not, for instance, when you sent one of your men to knife me in the dark and cast my body to the waves. Nor when you killed him, after he failed, so that no one would see his broken wrist. Yet thanks to Pazel Pathkendle and my brethren from Tholjassa, I saw the poor lad. In the Uturphe morgue. And of course I know your face. How sad to meet this way! I once revered you so."

"Stop meddling, both of you," said Rose in a warning voice. "This man is a guest on the Great Ship."

Chadfallow smiled at him. "That, sir, is one of many reasons I am glad I did not sail with you. On the *Chathrand* you outrank us all. On dry land you outrank Fiffengurt and Uskins."

"Ambassador," said Ott, turning to Isiq, "I have watched over your family for years. Your dear first wife, your daughter, yourself."

"You have," said Isiq uncertainly. "But so has Chadfallow. And Hercól has long been my daughter's tutor."

"The doctor did not serve you on *this* voyage," said Rose. "He abandoned your family out of fear. He disobeyed the Emperor himself. And now he claims that Syrarys is this man's lover. How do you know, Doctor? Have you seen them together? Has anyone?"

No one spoke for a moment.

"Diadrelu—" began Thasha. But she caught Pazel's look of alarm and fell silent.

Slowly, Rose sat up in his chair. "What sort of name is that?"

"Never mind!" said Pazel. His voice rang in the sudden silence.

Rose turned to him, unblinking. "It sounds like a crawly name."

"How dare you!" squeaked the governor's wife. "This is the ambassador's daughter! And you imply that she talks to . . . ship maggots! For shame, for shame, Captain Rose!"

Before Rose could reply, Lady Oggosk made a sound of disgust. Leaning forward on her elbows, she gestured at Ott with a butter knife.

"I saw them together—that man and Syrarys. Of course they're lovers. I caught her with him months ago, at Castle Maag. She confessed. He was tired of being a servant, she was tired of the ambassador. Once Thasha married the Sizzy prince, and peace reigned, these two would grow rich in the new world of trade between the empires. Bribes, usury, imaginary taxes. They'd be fat as sultans. The ambassador was too sick to decide much himself, she told me. Of course, I didn't know she was poisoning him."

"You treacherous cur!" said Isiq to Ott. "You'll hang!"

The governor stood up, trembling all over. "Mr. N-Nagan," he pleaded, "or whatever your name is—will you kindly lay down your sword?"

Ott stepped forward. Hercól's eyes narrowed and his hand went to his own sword-hilt. But the spymaster merely bowed and laid his sword upon the table. A knife followed, long and white and well worn.

The governor heaved a great sigh of relief and sat down. And Ott lifted his knife again and hurled it straight at Lady Oggosk.

The next three seconds were astounding. Hercól lunged and caught the knife in midair. Oggosk screamed. Sandor Ott leaped onto the table and ran its length. Thasha plunged her dinner fork into his leg, but Ott, never slowing, dealt her a savage blow to the face. Then, reaching the table's end, he planted a foot on the governor's head, driving it facedown into his dinner, and leaped straight at the round window behind him.

But something else flew at Ott's head in that instant: a hissing red blur. Sniraga.

A horrid noise, and a downpour of colored glass. A moment later, Hercól reached the window.

"He's in the courtyard!" he shouted. "Drop the portcullis! You there! *Drop that gate!*"

Silence. Then a resounding *clang*. Hercól's shoulders slumped.

Turning back to the room, he said, "The cat is safe in the gardenias, Duchess, and her claws have marked the spymaster for life. Governor, your men have sealed the palace—"

"Victory!" cried his wife.

"—one second after Ott departed it." Hercól sighed. "You may call out your constables, your bloodhounds, the port marines. You may tear what's left of this city apart. But you won't find him."

"Do you mean to say that they had been planning this for *years*?" said the governor, as one servant picked swordfish from his beard and another lit his pipe.

"I'm certain of it," said Isiq, despondent. "Syrarys was always the one most eager to move to Simja. Now I know why."

"They subjected you to deathsmoke in Tressek Tarn," said Chadfallow quietly.

"Deathsmoke!" cried Thasha, aghast. "The monsters! Thank heaven we were only there a night."

"I will have to perform some tests," Chadfallow went on, "but I am very much afraid that the droplets you've been taking were also a deathsmoke concoction."

"But you can cure him, can't you?" demanded Thasha.

The doctor lowered his eyes.

"No," said Isiq. "He cannot. There is no permanent cure. One grows stronger with the passage of years, but a deathsmoke addict craves the drug until he dies. I have seen men die for it, too, in the navy."

"You will not die," said Chadfallow. "That much I can promise you. But you may have to fight, Excellency—like a tiger, to master yourself."

"Speaking of tigers . . . ," said Pazel.

There was a scrabble of claws, and Sniraga pulled herself in through the window. She walked primly to Lady Oggosk. Furtively, Thasha watched the old woman lift her pet. *Why did you help us?*

Oggosk seemed to feel her gaze. Her cloudy blue eyes rose to Thasha's own.

"Where thou goest, I follow fast," she whispered.

Those words. Where had Thasha heard them before? At first the memory refused to surface. Then she had it: the Mother Prohibitor's emerald ring. The words were inscribed about the emerald. Could Oggosk be a Lorg Sister? Did she have her own cherry tree in the Orchard? Had she prayed before dawn, kneeling on icy stones? Had she sat on Thasha's bench?

Dimly she recalled the Mother Prohibitor's words: *On the path you are doomed to tread one of us at least will be near you. In dire need you may call upon her; she cannot refuse.*

"If you're a friend," she whispered to Oggosk, "why did you send your cat to steal my necklace?"

Oggosk looked at the silver chain on Thasha's neck, and gave a violent sort of squirm. "Too late for all that, too late," she muttered.

"What do you mean, too late?"

But Oggosk would no longer meet her eye.

"Such lengths the villains went to!" the governor was saying. "To play with the life of His Supremacy's ambassador, to arrange a marriage across both empires—"

"Without Thasha's wedding there would be no ambassadorship," said Chadfallow, "and thus no way for Ott and Syrarys to leave Arqual. And that was the only chance they had of a life together. His Supremacy would never let Ott retire. He was too useful to be allowed to fall in love."

"Whereas I," said Isiq, "was useful *only* because I fell in love."

"Then you bring us no peace!" cried the governor's wife. "This marriage was a trick, and we must go on living with Sizzy threats and raids, and fearing a third sea war!"

"Wrong, madame," said Chadfallow.

Pazel and Thasha looked up at him, startled.

"Sandor Ott twisted events for his own purposes," Chadfallow continued, "but the wedding of Thasha and Prince Falmurqat is no trick. The Mzithrini want peace, and so does the Emperor."

"What?" cried Thasha and Pazel together.

"Hush, children—"

"The Emperor doesn't want peace!" Pazel blurted. "He wants the Sizzies fighting themselves! He wants a civil war!"

Chadfallow looked at him calmly. "Don't speak of what you don't understand, Pazel."

"Well then, how do *you* explain what happened on the Haunted Coast?"

"The two events are unconnected," said Chadfallow. "Arunis hired the Volpeks to help him raid a treasure-wreck. Had he not kidnapped Tholjassan sons and daughters—and had Thasha not found Hercól and the smugglers in good time—he might have succeeded. But one greedy conjurer hardly matters, weighed against the chance for an era of peace."

"One greedy conjurer?" said Thasha. "That's what you call Arunis?"

"Oh, Thasha," said the doctor. "You cannot think that we are speaking of *the* Arunis? That man was hanged forty years ago! This is an upstart who took the sorcerer's name, the better to frighten us with."

"Like pirates, eh?" said the governor. "There were six Billy Blacktongues."

"Just so," said the doctor. "And you see how well the tactic works? Even Thasha believed in him."

Now the young people were too afraid to shout.

"Hercól?" said Thasha quietly.

The Tholjassan was looking very hard at Chadfallow. "I am not a statesman," he said.

"But I am," said Chadfallow. "And I hope that you will trust my judgment as ever, Hercól. This so-called Arunis was a passenger on *Chathrand,* but he had nothing to do with the other criminals aboard."

"Unless you two have a . . . special source of information?" said Rose.

Pazel and Thasha looked at each other. They were trapped. To mention the ixchel would be to condemn Diadrelu and her kin to death.

"But they *were* working together," Thasha pleaded. "This is one big conspiracy!"

Chadfallow shook his head. "Two small ones, merely," he said. "And we have just dealt with both."

"You're mad!" shouted Pazel. "The Shaggat Ness is aboard the *Chathrand*!"

The adults—all of them except Hercól—laughed. Even Eberzam Isiq managed to chuckle sadly.

Thasha jumped to Pazel's defense. "It's true, Prahba! You're being fooled all over again!"

"This Ormali rat-boy's filled her head with rot," growled Uskins.

Shouting, Pazel and Thasha looked from face to face.

"There's millions in gold hidden on the ship!"

"We're not going home after Simja, we're crossing the Ruling Sea!"

"Arunis never died! He's the Shaggat's own mage!"

"Governor," said Isiq, "can you not keep order at your table?"

The governor swallowed, but he clapped his hands. "Children! Hold your tongues or . . . or depart, yes, depart!"

In the silence that followed, Isiq said, "We will sail tomorrow morning, across the Straits. There we will bow low before Prince Falmurqat and his family, and beg their pardon for this ill-considered engagement, and swear to them we mean no insult by breaking it. Pathkendle, you will stand at my side as translator."

"Your Excellency!" said Chadfallow. "You cannot believe these claims!"

"About Shaggats and sorcerers risen from the dead? Of course not."

"Then her marriage must go through!"

"An age of peace cannot begin with a plan stained by treachery," said Isiq, "nor by the sacrifice of an innocent soul. Don't argue, Doctor! Let the Emperor condemn me if he dares. But from this moment I swear before you all: Thasha Isiq's life is no one's but her own."

FROM THE SECRET JOURNAL OF
G. STARLING FIFFENGURT, QUARTERMASTER

Friday, 6 Teala. The most horrible day of my life. Is all the world gone mad? Nay, it has long been so; I just had no eyes to see it.

Fell asleep last night still jotting down all that transpired at the governor's table. Frightening enough, especially the attempt on Lady Oggosk's life, & the outlandish things Pathkendle & Lady Thasha shouted at the end. But those events were nothing.

As Mr. Hercól predicted, the remaining *five* of Ambassador Isiq's "honor guards"—all Ott's men—somehow received a signal from their master, & fled the ship before we returned. We informed the palace, & left it at that. We departed Ormael with the sunrise, making eight knots on an honest easterly.

Not a league out of Ormael port, however, a sloop came up behind us with two red pennants on her foremast: grave tidings. We heeled round, & in minutes the little ship was alongside.

Such awful news: the governor's whole palace struck down with talking fever! Fifty guards, servants, cooks, groundskeepers—& of course the governor, his wife & eight children. All babbling & foaming at the mouth. The palace was sealed tight—no one allowed in, or out. But there was worse. The Lady Syrarys, dead! Out of her mind with fever or remorse at her own evil acts, she hurled herself from her prison tower into the sea. The body is yet to be found: it seems she was in chains, & the iron bore her to the depths. Mistress Thasha & her father are still weeping, even though the woman betrayed them. Love is such a pitiless thing.

But surely the fever threatened *Chathrand,* too? After all, we dined with them night after night. Dr. Chadfallow bellowed questions to the sloop's commander, & soon believed his report: talking fever, without a doubt. Then came the only good news of the day. Turning to us, he said we had nothing to fear. "Talking fever strikes instantly, if it strikes at all," he said. "We are none of us infected."

He refused to return to Ormael, but gave strict orders for the treatment of the sick. "Millet and prunes! Nothing else for a fortnight! And send word to me in Simja of their condition!"

Rattled, we took the *Chathrand* on. We did not fall sick: thank the Gods the doctor was right. But I declare this ship is changed since Ormael. For the first time, a report of a fight between the Plapp's Pier & Burnscove Boys. Not a big fight, but as a taste of things to come it could not be worse: in Etherhorde, the two gangs never break a truce without eventually going to war.

The first-class passengers have locked themselves behind the Money Gate, afraid of the fever despite the doctor's words. And the sudden return of the ex-tarboys, Pathkendle & Undrabust, has set tongues wagging on every deck.

It is no secret that they & Lady Thasha had some adventure along the Haunted Coast & that the doctor & Mr. Hercól rescued 'em. This scares the men half to death. A mob of sailors stopped the boys on the pier & emptied their pockets, asking if they had any trinkets from the Coast. Nothing at all, they replied—but Pathkendle said this while pinching the skin of his collarbone & staring off into the distance, like a man missing his sweetheart. Of course, I knew who she must be— the somber little sponge-diver girl, Marila—but it was a weird look all the same & the men were hellish disturbed.

No one searched the rich folk, naturally, & that was how

the trouble began. Hercól came aboard this morning with
only his sword & a shoulder-bag, but the good doctor arrived
with a crate. It was no larger than a pushcart, but it took nine
strong stevedores to wrestle it up the gangplank. Was it full of
lead? Chadfallow gave no sign. "To my quarters with that!"
he ordered, directing them.

But as they set foot on deck, we all heard it: a man's voice,
far away, roaring. It seemed to come from the lower timbers
of the *Chathrand* itself. It was the voice of a madman—
wicked, murderous & joyful at once:

"GIVE IT TO ME! GIVE IT TO ME! GIVE IT TO ME!"

We all froze. All except Pazel Pathkendle, who ran up to
Chadfallow & caught his sleeve. "You can hear him! I know
you can! Please, Ignus—"

The doctor turned & shoved him so hard the boy fell to the
deck. Pathkendle jumped up & turned to us, pointing.

"You heard him! All of you heard him!"

But had we? The voice was silent now, & the sailors made
the sign of the Tree & ran about their business. And Rin forgive me, so did I. Was ever a man given a plainer choice of
bravery or skunkish fear? I chose fear, & whatever follows
now I shall blame myself.

Later in the morning I crossed paths with the boys again.
Pazel Pathkendle had a fresh black eye. "What leprous dog
gave you that?" I demanded. "Who's next off this ship?"

They hung their heads. "Rose," whispered Pathkendle at
last. "He said it was my last warning."

Then my shame grew stronger. I took a deep breath &
marched to the captain's door. I knocked. In a heartbeat Rose
threw the door open.

"What is it?" cried he. "Danger, Fiffengurt? I heard no cry.
Are we beset? Tell me, tell me, blast you!"

When I stammered out that I had come to learn the reason
for the beating of one of my tarboys (for the Code bars even
a captain from striking a boy in the absence of witnesses), he
looked at me as if I were mad.

"Pazel Pathkendle," he said, "is the most dangerous person on this ship. I shouldn't have smacked him—I should have put a knife in his gut. Look out!"

He flinched, staring wildly past my shoulder. I jumped half out of my skin & turned about: nothing. Rose slammed the door behind me.

I cleared my throat. "I won't stand for this, Captain," I shouted, not very boldly, though. He made no answer, & I turned & descended the ladderway, down & down, to the afterhold, seeking that mysterious voice. The augrongs were there, half dozing as always, & a fair number of enormous rats. But no strange men. I worked my way forward, searching for anything unusual. I was startled by how well stocked we were—enough grain & hardtack & beef chips to see us home to Etherhorde, with food to spare. Had it all been laid away in Ormael, while I was out looking for the Lady Thasha? I made a point to question Swellows.

So there I was, moving aft, when who should appear before me but that cripple-footed rat! He sat there on his haunches, waiting for me.

"Git, you!" I shouted, looking for something to throw.

And save me, Rin, the beggar answered, "No, Mr. Fiffengurt."

I nearly dropped the lamp. "You can talk!" I whispered.

Ratty just nodded, like I needn't state the obvious. Which I promptly did again.

"My name is Felthrup Stargraven," said Ratty. "You rescued me from the bilge-pipe. I am in your debt forever."

"By the buddin' branch of the blary beautiful Tree!"

"I should love to make conversation," Ratty tells me. "Nothing more so! But I am fleeing a monster. Will you kindly examine the goods stowed by the mizzenmast step?"

"You can talk!"

"Goodbye, Mr. Fiffengurt. I thank you for your *idrolos,* and for my life."

He turned & limped off into the darkness. At the edge of

my lamplight, he pulled up short & looked back at me. "By the way," he squeaks, *"everything they told you is true."*

Then he was gone. And a second later Sniraga rushed past my legs. I chased after her—what if I heard 'im plead for mercy in her mouth? But she was gone in the darkness, same as Ratty.

My Annabel likes that word, *idrolos.* The courage to see. I stood there, worried my brain had sprung a leak. Then I made my way to the mizzenmast step.

The hold of *Chathrand* is like the basement of a castle. It has rooms & shafts, catwalks & tunnels. It takes a solid week just to *count* what's stored down there. Naturally we carry enough wood for any repairs the Great Ship might require. There's spare mastwood, wales, planking, transom knees. A spare bowsprit. Even a lump of oak for carving a new Goose-Girl, should we lose Her Ladyship. But when I crept down to the foot of the mizzenmast I found timbers that had nothing to do with repairs. They were broken, smashed & filthy. Twisted bolts & snapped cleats & bits of rigging trailed from 'em. Some of the wood was even burned.

"Gods of fire!" I said. "It's parts of a wreck!"

But what wreck? It hadn't come from the Haunted Coast— these pieces were stowed *under* goods we'd taken on in Etherhorde. We'd carried this trash for months! Huge timbers, too: some of the largest I'd ever seen—except for what the *Chathrand* herself is made of. And what for pity's sake was it good for? Nothing at all, so far as I could see, except tossing over the side . . .

'Twas then I heard a rustling behind me. "Come out, whoever the blary hell you are!" I growled, spinning round. "Fiffengurt's not afraid of you!"

No one came. But now I was facing a broken beam with a copper faceplate. IMS CHATHRAND, it read. CAPTAIN'S DAY-CABIN. STRICTLY PRIVATE.

I felt a cold, murthy hand on my heart. I looked further: there was a cabin door with the Chathrand Family coat of arms. Tattered sailcloth with CHATHRAND sewn into the hem. A *Chathrand* life preserver, snapped in two.

This is wickedness, I thought. *This is evil from the Pits.*

It was our own wreck I was looking at. A simulation of it, I mean: about as much as would wash up ashore, if we wrecked nearby. Tossing over the side was *exactly* what this junk would be good for.

I had to sit down. Someone needed the world to think us wrecked. Someone meant *Chathrand* to disappear.

Ratty's voice echoed in my brain: *Everything they told you is true.* And the lad & Mistress Thasha had said we would be crossing the Nelluroq with (Rin help us) the Shaggat Ness aboard. And that his mage was alive & behind it all. And that the Emperor wanted war.

My knees were shaking. Who could I tell? Who could I trust, out of eight hundred souls? Only two tarboys, a rich girl & a rat.

Do something, Fiffengurt, I told myself. Trust someone. Form a gang. Take the ship away from Rose.

I sat down with the lamp between my feet. I let five minutes pass, then five more. And then it was too late.

"MAN ADRIFT! MAN ADRIFT! TWO POINTS OFF *THE STARBOARD BOW!"*

The voices reached me faintly. I thought, *What now, blast it, how can things get any—**

---

*At this point Mr. Fiffengurt's journal is torn in two: the remaining pages are lost. —EDITOR.

-34-

The Calm

"A man it most certainly is," said Isiq, peering through his tele-scope. "But how did he get there? He has no sail, no mast, even. There are oarlocks, but no oars. How did that boat get so far from land?"

It was a fair question. The *Chathrand* was six hours south of Ormael now, almost exactly halfway to Simja. Hundreds of men, sweating in the midday sun, gaped at the sight: a forlorn little lifeboat two miles off, with one ragged occupant, seated and barely moving, nagged by shrieking gulls. There was a fighting shield propped in the stern, and some large, lumpy shape beneath a canvas at his feet. They could see no more from this distance.

On the quarterdeck, Captain Rose was speaking to his gun-nery officer. Lady Oggosk and Sergeant Drellarek waited at his side.

Isiq and Hercól stood at the mizzen, with Pazel, Thasha and Neeps beside them. Chadfallow stood a little apart, brooding, wrapped in silence. Pazel had not spoken to him since the doctor shoved him to the deck.

"It is a Volpek lifeboat," said Hercól. "And that is a Volpek war-shield in the bow, I think. But the man is small for a merce-nary. I wish I could see his face."

Thasha took the telescope from her father, and winced a little as she raised it to her eye: Sandor Ott's fist had left a wide purple bruise on her face. The man in the boat had his back to the *Chathrand*. He was gesturing wildly, as if carrying on an excited debate. His feet rested on a black mound of some sort.

"Those hands of his," she said. "All skin and bones. I've seen them before, I—"

BOOM.

Smoke rose from a forward gunport: the *Chathrand* had fired a signal-shot. The gulls scattered briefly, but the man did not even look over his shoulder.

"He's deaf, or mad," declared Eberzam Isiq.

"May we look through your scope, Your Excellency?" Pazel asked.

Isiq nodded and Thasha handed over the instrument, and the boys passed it back and forth. Then they looked at each other and nodded.

"No doubt about it," said Neeps.

"It's Mr. Druffle," Pazel said.

And so it was. The freebooter was thinner and more ragged than ever, which Pazel would have thought impossible were he not seeing it with his own eyes. His feet were bare and sunblistered, and his black hair was snarled in dirty knots.

"How the devil did that lunkhead get out *here*?" Pazel asked.

"Not by chance, I think," said Hercól.

"What do you mean?"

Instead of answering, Hercól looked at Chadfallow. The doctor would not meet his eye.

The *Chathrand* sailed a little nearer. Captain Rose, locked in conversation with Oggosk, stole nervous glances at the lifeboat.

"There is a body beneath his feet," said a sudden voice in Pazel's ear.

Pazel reacted as if stung by a bee, making Thasha turn and stare.

"What's wrong?" she asked quietly.

The voice belonged to an ixchel man. Not Taliktrum, and yet

Pazel was certain he had heard the voice before. Whoever he was, he was hiding just a few yards away. He used his natural voice: no one but Pazel heard a thing. *"A body,"* he repeated. *"Tell them."*

And Pazel did. Once you knew what to look for it was plainly true: Druffle's feet were resting on someone's chest, draped in a black, enveloping cloak. A heavy body, it was, of a rather portly man or woman.

All at once Pazel realized where he had heard the ixchel's voice. In Rose's cabin. It was the voice of the captain's poison-taster.

"Steldak," he whispered.

"Yes, lad. Do not look for me, please."

"What about Dri, and her nephew?"

"Their Lordships never returned, Pazel Pathkendle. The council tried to warn her. It was a mad caprice, to chase a mage into the wilderness. Now the clan has lost all its princes. Their noble brother died to rescue me."

"I know," said Pazel. "She told me."

Motion on the quarterdeck: Rose appeared to have come to a sudden decision. He spoke to Uskins, who was hovering at his elbow. The first mate nodded, then turned and relayed the order:

"Due south! Full sail to Simja!"

A roar of disapproval broke from the crew. Shame, infamy! To abandon a man adrift! Isiq threw down his hat and made for the quarterdeck. Even Pazel, who somehow knew that horrible events would unfold if Druffle boarded, was appalled to think of leaving him here to die.

But there was only one captain of the *Chathrand,* and now he made his power felt. One nod to Drellarek and the sergeant was barking orders to his men. Eberzam Isiq found the quarterdeck stair blocked by crossed swords. Uskins leaned over the rail and bellowed in the face of Elkstem, who was gaping at the captain.

"Due south, Sailmaster, or is this a hangman's holiday? You want some dying, plague-breathed Ormali brought aboard, along with that wormy corpse under his toes? FULL SAIL TO SIMJA, DAMN YOUR EYES!"

With a hundred warriors breathing down their necks the sailors quickly obeyed. Elkstem spun the wheel; the port and starboard watches freed the brace-lines, and in seconds men were heaving and groaning to turn the gigantic sails into the wind.

Everyone felt the tug as the ship leaped forward. But only Pazel heard Steldak say, *"Ahh, he attends us now."*

Pazel looked out at the lifeboat. Druffle was gazing at them over his shoulder.

"We can't just leave!" said Thasha. "Chadfallow said Arunis magicked him. Perhaps Druffle's not a bad man at all!"

"Even if he is, this is wrong," said Pazel. "We're supposed to be better than Arunis."

"*We* are," said Neeps, glaring up at Rose.

"Something's happening," said another ixchel's voice. *"Look at the sails!"*

"Look at the sails!" Pazel said aloud.

On all five masts the sails were falling limp. The wind was dropping; the pennants barely fluttered. The *Chathrand*'s pace began to slow.

"Topgallants!" cried Rose, not bothering with Uskins now. "Starboard, lay aloft!"

Sailors raced up the lines like agile monkeys. High overhead, the topgallant sails were loosed and tightened. But the dying wind barely filled them, and the ship grew slower still.

"Spritsails! Moonrakers!" roared the captain. "Run out the blary studders, Mr. Frix! I want every last inch of canvas stretched!"

Studdingsail yards were hauled up from below and lashed to the tips of the spars. Four sailors crawled out past the Goose-Girl to extend the jib. No whispers about shame and infamy now: the vanishing wind was too strange, and the captain's fear too contagious. In minutes, a whole array of new sails had erupted from the ship, and the *Chathrand* looked like a great white bird spreading its wings in the sun.

For a minute, perhaps two, she gained speed: the sailors drew a nervous breath. Then the weak wind stopped blowing altogether. Thasha saw her father turn in a circle, gaping at the acres of useless sails. Even the waves flattened around them.

Suddenly Pazel noticed Jervik standing just behind them. For an instant their eyes met.

"A dead calm," whispered Jervik. "But so sudden! This ain't natural, is it?"

Pazel said nothing. It was almost more unnatural to hear Jervik address him without hate.

No one moved or spoke. The only sound was the hiss of foam on the motionless sea. And then, from more than a mile away: a laugh. Pazel and Neeps looked at each other again. The voice did not belong to Druffle.

But the freebooter was still the only figure moving. As they watched, he drew a pair of oars from beneath the black canvas. Fitting them into the oarlocks, he began to row toward the ship.

"They will be here in minutes," said Steldak.

"They?" said Pazel.

Everyone turned to look at him.

"Can't you guess, Pazel Pathkendle?"

"Gunner!" Rose bellowed. "Get your men to the lower arsenal! Run out the midship battery!"

"Which guns, sir?"

"ALL THE BLARY GUNS, MAN!"

Another scramble ensued, the men's voices strangely loud on the motionless air. Soon, enough guns to sink a warship were trained on the little rowing boat. It was then that one of the lookouts cried that a little dog had just emerged from under Druffle's seat. Pazel looked again, and saw it: a small white dog with a corkscrew tail.

Oh, fire and fumes.

He would know that dog anywhere.

Just then Pazel felt Thasha's hand on his arm. He turned: she held a finger to her lips.

"Meet me in the stateroom," she whispered. "Take the long way around, so nobody suspects. But hurry!" And she turned and made for her cabin.

Pazel knew better than to disobey. Besides, he had an inkling of what she was up to. "Cover for me, mate," he said to Neeps in Sollochi. "I'll be right back."

Neeps couldn't believe his eyes. "You're going below? What for?"

"To get help," said Pazel. With that he ran, ducking behind the crowd of transfixed sailors.

He had almost reached the No. 4 hatch when a cry broke from a hundred mouths. Pazel turned and gasped.

Halfway between the lifeboat and the ship the water was rising. A little vortex was turning, a cone of wind where none had been before. Man-high it rose, and then somewhat higher. Sudden rain dashed down upon it, and waves rose to enter it, and all at once it had arms and a face, and danced ghoulishly on the flattened sea.

"A water-weird!" cried Swellows. "He's called up a water-weird to sink us!"

A sharp command from the lifeboat, and the creature surged toward them. Rose laughed at his bosun's fear.

"Sink us—that little thing? Wash our faces, more likely! Fire!"

Three cannon gave three deafening, ear-wounding roars. Pazel looked: two shots fell wildly long of the boat. The third fell close enough to set it rocking, but no more.

Then the water-weird struck the gunports a sideways blast—and every man aboard realized what it could do. Not sink, but disarm them—for how could cannons fire if every fuse was soaked?

Suddenly Pazel remembered his rendezvous with Thasha. He spun about and rushed for the hatch—and nearly barreled into Jervik, who stood blocking his way.

"Pazel!" said the big tarboy. Still struggling to be friendly—or at least nonhostile.

"What is it?"

Jervik glanced in the direction of the lifeboat. "He's an Ormali same as you, right?"

"Druffle? That's what he told me. Listen, I really have to—"

"Then you can wish away his hex."

"What?"

"His hex. His spell on the wind. It's *muketch* magic, ain't it?"

Pazel just looked at him. The boy was perfectly serious.

"Jervik," said Pazel carefully, "the man rowing that boat isn't
doing the magic. And I don't know any spells, *muketch* or otherwise."

From the older boy's face it was clear he didn't believe a word.
Or didn't wish to. Then, to Pazel's amazement, Jervik slipped the
brass Citizenship Ring from his finger and held it up.

"Yours," he said, "if you'll just do as I'm askin'."

"But I don't know any magic."

"Come off it," said Jervik. "All those talks with that mink-
mage-thing? That Ramachni fellow? Yeah, I know about 'em!"
He looked a little sheepish, suddenly. "There's speaking-tubes
all over this ship. You can *listen* at 'em, too. Swellows made me
do it."

I'll bet you volunteered, thought Pazel. But there was no point
in denial now. "I've learned a few things from Ramachni, that's
true. And they might even help us, if you'll just—"

Jervik pawed at him. "Do it now! Wish his spell away!"

"Let me go," said Pazel, his voice hardening. "Before it's too
late."

But Jervik was too frightened to hear. His bullying instincts
returned with a vengeance: he seized Pazel by the arms and
shook him. "Wish it away! You're the only one who can!"

I'm going to have to fight this idiot, thought Pazel. And feeling the immense strength in Jervik's arms he knew he couldn't
win.

But suddenly the big tarboy screamed in pain. His leg lashed
out, and something small and black struck the open hatch-cover
with a thump, then fell senseless through the opening below.

"Bit me!" howled Jervik, releasing Pazel and clutching his ankle. "That damn blary rat!"

Felthrup!

Blood covered Jervik's hands. Pazel threw himself down the ladder, fearing the worst. There lay the short-tailed rat: barely able to raise his head. Was that Jervik's blood alone? Pazel couldn't stop to find out. He scooped up the lame creature and made a dash for Thasha's stateroom. Men stared at him: other boys were running with gunpowder and cannonballs. He was bearing a rat.

Thasha waited in her doorway. "Felthrup!" she cried. "What's happened to you?"

"M'lady—" squeaked the rat.

"Hush!" said Pazel. "Just rest! You're a hero already."

They laid Felthrup on Thasha's pillow. His breathing was shallow, and he blinked as though his eyes could not focus.

"Leave me," he said. "Do what you came to do."

As Pazel tried to make Felthrup more comfortable, Thasha turned to her clock. Around and around she spun the hands. "If he's not in his Observatory, we're done for," she said.

"Just hurry," said Pazel.

When the clock read nine minutes past seven, she stopped. "We have to wait three minutes," she said. "That's just how it works."

They were the longest three minutes Pazel had ever known. Above them, Uskins was shouting, "Fire! Fire!" But not a cannon sounded: the water-weird still lashed at the gunports. Suddenly Thasha gave his hand a fond squeeze. Pazel squeezed back, but as he did so he felt a certain unpleasant tightness in his chest.

When the minute hand moved for a third time, Thasha bent down and whispered: "Ramachni!" The clock sprang open with a snap.

There was a whirl of black fur. Almost before they saw him, Ramachni had bounded onto Thasha's bed. Gently, the mink licked the black rat's forehead. Felthrup gave a whistling sigh.

"He will sleep now," said Ramachni. "But we must make haste."

"You knew we were coming?"

"Oh no, dear girl! But I certainly hoped. Whole days have I waited at my desk. And I have certain tools for doing more than just waiting. Listen carefully, please: neither of you have ever faced a danger like the one trying to board this ship. We must work together or be swept away."

Thasha put her shawl over the clock. "It's Arunis under that canvas, isn't it?"

"Yes."

"Can you beat him?" Pazel asked.

"Not in this world, where I am but a shadow of myself," said Ramachni. "But *we* can beat him. Thasha, you will be called on to show great courage, and great self-control. Pazel, you will have but one chance to speak a Master-Word. As you know, you will forget it the instant you speak, and nevermore hear it in your lifetime. You must choose well."

Pazel looked into Ramachni's bottomless black eyes. A word that tamed fire and a word that made stone of living flesh and a word that blinded to give new sight. The simplest Master-Words of all, the least dangerous. But if he chose wrong, Arunis and the Shaggat would win, and nothing would stop the war.

"Why can't you just *tell* me which Word to use?" he begged.

"For the simplest of reasons," said Ramachni. "Because I don't know. But remember this, both of you. We are not fighting Arunis and his beast alone. We are fighting an Empire. Sandor Ott is defeated—perhaps. But many hands are yet turning the wheel he set in motion."

At that moment they heard feet running in the outer stateroom. Thasha's door flew open and Hercól stood there, breathing hard, his sword naked in his hand.

"Ramachni," he said. "The hour is come."

Dollywilliams Druffle stopped his rowing. The little dog wagged its tail. The lifeboat had come within thirty feet of the

Chathrand. Beside the motionless behemoth it was little more than a bobbing cork. A hideous smell rose from it, as of sun-rotted meat.

The water-weird still shimmered against the gunports, a moist cloud shaped like a man. Otherwise the sea lay as if dead. No wave nor puff of wind could be felt. High overhead clouds were racing, but they might have belonged to another world. Here nothing moved but the gulls.

"You there, smuggler!" cried Rose suddenly, leaning down from the rail. "Get hence with that corpse! Release this ship! You're in the Straits of Simja, no great distance from either shore. We'll lower you a mast and sailcloth, if you need them. You can sail where you like."

Druffle said nothing. His back was still to the *Chathrand.*

"Do you think that rain-fairy is going to scare us? By the Pits, I'll see those gulls glut on your entrails before I let you touch my ship!"

He stormed down the ladder and into the wheelhouse. A moment later he emerged with an immense harpoon. Raising the weapon to his shoulder, he closed one eye and rushed the rail with the force of a buffalo. The harpoon sailed straight through the water-weird and right for Druffle's neck. The freebooter never saw it coming.

But at the last second, like a dark flame, a figure leaped up from beneath the cloth, knocking Druffle sideways. For an instant it looked as if the harpoon had pierced them both. Yet there it quivered in the boat's hull, and neither man had been slain.

"It's the soap man!" blurted Uskins.

Looking steadily up at the *Chathrand,* Arunis slowly pulled his old scarf from about his neck. A small red spot stained the white cloth. He bent and wiped it on the canvas, which still appeared to be covering something rather large, and wound it about his throat once more.

"You're a good shot," he said. "But the day may come, Captain Rose, when you regret lifting your hand against me. Or even against my servant. Not that Mr. Druffle is particularly vital to my purposes. He *was,* of course—when I needed divers, he was so important that I gave him the same power over others that I have over him. You enjoyed that, didn't you, Druffle?"

Druffle gave a puppet's nod.

"But that time is past. Drop a ladder, why don't you, and let us board. We are thirsty."

"Never," said Rose.

"I shall board one way or another, you know."

Sergeant Drellarek lowered his sword to point down at the boat. "Hear me, mage or mystic, or whoever you are," he shouted. "We are on a mission consecrated by His Supremacy, Magad the Fifth. You have nothing to do with that mission, and may not interfere."

"Such discourtesy, Sergeant," said the sorcerer. "And here I stand ready to assist your cause to a degree you can scarce imagine."

"This ship is the grave of sorcerers," said Lady Oggosk suddenly. "All die who seek to use her for their wickedness. It will curse you too, Arunis. Go back!"

Arunis smiled. "The Great Ship curses those who are not great. It was built for the likes of us. But why should we argue? Our mission is the same: to return the Shaggat Ness to his worshippers on Gurishal. To urge him to war. To see the Mzithrin Kings hurled from their thrones and their power ended in this world. And I have done much for you already, Captain Rose. Each morning, as timid Mr. Ket, I wove the spell that bound the Shaggat to silence. I dare say you've missed that service since I left the *Chathrand.* And who made sure Sandor Ott caught up with your favorite witch, Captain, and persuaded her to sail with you once more? For that matter, who told Ott where *you* were hiding? You'd have missed out on the greatest command of your life without my help. I ask you again, Captain: will you let us board?"

"*We* will not let you."

Hundreds of men jumped at the unfamiliar voice. There stood Hercól, with a strange animal perched on his shoulder. It was a mink, black as midnight, white teeth bared. On Hercól's left stood Pazel, looking sick with worry; and on the man's right Lady Thasha Isiq held a sword in a manner that suggested she knew how to use it. Beside her stood her enormous dogs, Jorl and Suzyt, their eyes fixed on Arunis and low growls rumbling in their throats.

But it was the mink who was speaking. "We will not let you," it said again, "for yours is a mission of death. And your wisdom fades, Arunis, if you doubt the curse in store for you aboard the Great Ship."

For the first time, and merely for an instant, Arunis looked uncertain. Then he spread his arms and laughed.

"Ramachni Fremken! Rat-wizard of the Sunken Kingdom! Have you come all this way to fight me? Go back to your world, little trickster, and be spared! Alifros is mine!"

Ramachni answered with a soft, single word: *"Hegnos."*

And Druffle was transformed. He leaped to his feet and drew a cavernous breath, like a man pulled from the depths of the sea. Then his eyes found Arunis and swelled with hate. His hand flashed to his cutlass.

And there it stayed. Arunis raised his own hand and Druffle froze, rigid as ice, the blade half drawn from its sheath.

"Yes," said Ramachni, "I have freed his mind from your charms. And Mr. Druffle has nursed his hatred of you through months of magical slavery. He will plunge that blade into your heart the moment you tire of that holding spell."

Arunis shrugged. "Why should I tire?" And with one hand he pushed Druffle overboard.

In the unnatural stillness Druffle fell like a log. But he did not float like one, although by strange good fortune his face was the last part of him submerged. Men shouted: "Save him! Dive, somebody!" But not a sailor moved.

Hercól thrust Ramachni into Thasha's hands and leaped to the rail. But someone beat him to the jump. Neeps was over the side, dropping first onto a cannon jutting from its gunport, then dangling from its stock. He was still over forty feet above the tabletop-flat sea when he let go. Pazel thought he had never looked so small.

He struck the water some twenty feet from Druffle, van-ished for a terrible moment, then surfaced again, swimming toward the motionless smuggler. Pazel gasped with relief. Soon Neeps' arm was around Druffle's neck. Fiffengurt tossed a life preserver, and put four men on the line to haul them aboard.

Arunis did not waste a glance on Neeps or Druffle. He pulled at one oar, turning the lifeboat in a circle until the stern with the Volpek war-shield faced the *Chathrand*. Then he leaned over the black cloth, and with a sharp tug pulled it aside. The men of the *Chathrand* gasped. Not a few turned away in revulsion.

The boat was half full of body parts. Feet, fingers, whole hands. Gore-covered ribs, bloated heads. The gulls screamed: clearly this was what had drawn them, and created the terrible stench.

"Those are Volpek faces," whispered Thasha.

The dead flesh lay piled on a second cloth, spread on the floor of the boat. Arunis bent low over the stinking mass, mumbling to himself. Then he drew up the four corners of the cloth and tied them together, like some hideous picnic bundle.

"Take them!" he shrieked.

The water-weird rose, spinning like a miniature cyclone, and lifted the mass. For a moment the weight appeared too much for the creature—it was only wind and rain, after all—but then it gathered itself and gave a mighty heave. The bundle spun up-ward along the *Chathrand*'s flank. Men ducked; the bundle just cleared the rail, and with a last rush of speed burst horribly against the mainmast.

Scraps of dead men fell all about them. Pazel had never dreamed of a sight so foul. But what would it accomplish? The crew was disgusted, nothing more.

Ramachni knew, though. "Into the sea! Into the sea!" he cried. "Toss it all overboard, quickly, instantly!"

Leaping to the deck, he bit into a severed hand, and with a snap of his body flung it over the rail. Hercól joined in at once.

Thasha and the tarboys, revolted as they were, did the same. But the sailors hesitated. Were they taking orders from a weasel now?

"Do as he says, f'Rin's sake!" howled Fiffengurt, diving into the gory task. A few men followed his lead. But the Volpeks' remains were everywhere—snagged in the rigging, dangling from block and chain and cleat, kicked under tarps and equipment.

Sea-rotted flesh is ugly, but what came next was loathsome beyond words. The heads and limbs and digits began to grow, and melt, and squirm with life. Men dropped what they held, screaming. Body parts flopped about the deck like fish. Then all at once they were men. Not normal men, but full-sized Volpek corpses, bloodless and pale.

"Fleshancs!" cried Lady Oggosk. "He's turned his own dead warriors into fleshancs! *Ay Midrala,* we're doomed!"

The first monster to gain its feet rose just in front of Mr. Swellows. The bosun did not even try to run. He looked truly petrified with fear, and the fleshanc reached out rather slowly and crushed his throat with one hand. In ghastly silence, white shapes tumbled one after another from Swellows' open shirt, to bounce like walnuts on the deck: ixchel skulls, slipping from his broken necklace.

When Swellows' lifeless body followed with a *thump,* four hundred sailors fled for their lives. How many fleshancs there were none could say—perhaps thirty, perhaps twice that number—but the fear they produced was overwhelming. Sailors leaped for hatches; one threw himself into the waves. Even Drellarek's warriors looked terrified.

"Stand and fight!" bellowed Rose, hefting a boarding axe. But most of his officers had already fled, and more fleshancs had sprung to life in the rigging and were climbing down. Uskins ran to the back of the quarterdeck and crouched behind the flag locker, as if he hoped no one would notice him there. Fiffengurt stood his ground, but one swing of a Volpek fist sent him sprawling.

Then Hercól and Drellarek charged. The battle was joined in earnest, and the two warriors fought side by side, thrusting and hacking with all their might. A number of Drellarek's men rallied at his call, and some of the fiercest sailors with them. But the fleshancs were incredibly strong. A blow from their hand was like the cuff of a bear, and their grip could shatter bone and iron.

Far below in the lifeboat, Arunis stood perfectly still.

Pazel and Admiral Isiq were hauling desperately at the lifeline; the men assigned to it had let Neeps and Druffle plunge back into the sea. Chadfallow drew off the fleshancs nearest them, laying at the creatures with a heavy chain. Ramachni seemed to be everywhere at once. With mink speed he leaped from rail to rigging to monster's face, tearing out their eyes with his little claws. And when other fleshancs closed for the kill on a fallen man, Ramachni gave an earsplitting cry and gestured with one paw, and the monster flew across the deck as if struck by a cannonball. But after each such spell Ramachni looked weaker, and soon he was gasping for breath.

A few feet from Pazel, Thasha was fighting as never before. Soldiers were down, sailors down: even as she looked another was stomped lifeless beneath a fleshanc's heel. It was clear the monsters felt no pain whatsoever, and they did not bleed. You could stab them and accomplish nothing. You could even (as she managed with one particularly lucky swing) cut off an arm, and still the fleshanc would not stop. It merely seized its severed limb and used it like a club.

Her dogs fared better than she. Old they were, but battle had restored the berserk vigor of their youth. Slavering, they leaped and battered and ripped at the fleshancs, dismembering any hand that sought them. But Thasha knew their strength could not last.

The victims mounted. Those still fighting stumbled over the corpses of their friends. She saw Ramachni falter in a leap, his forepaws slippery with blood.

On her right a man gave a hideous scream: a fleshanc was crushing him against the sharp edge of a provisions crate. Leaving her own foe, Thasha hurled herself against the creature. The sailor lurched away, but Thasha fell, and the fleshanc landed atop her.

She was pinned, unable to strike. The monster put a hand on her jaw, and the reek of death was overpowering. With unspeakable disgust she recognized the face of the last Volpek she had seen on the barge, slain by Hercól before her eyes. It was about to have its revenge.

But at that instant the fleshanc fell limp. Its torpor lasted no more than two seconds, but Thasha did not hesitate: she threw the creature off and was safely away before it climbed to its feet.

Her eyes swept the deck: several other fleshancs had paused or stumbled; for a brief moment the humans had the advantage. What had happened? She looked wildly about, but no clue met her eyes. At last she ran to the rail and gazed down on Arunis.

The sorcerer was motionless, as before. But now he was sprawled on hands and knees, and glaring vaguely at his dog, as if only half aware of what he was looking at. The little creature was leaping about in excitement. It had knocked him over.

Then hope swelled in Thasha's chest, and she ran to the quarterdeck ladder. Captain Rose stood atop it, swinging his axe constantly, keeping the monsters single-handedly from gaining the deck.

"Captain! I think I know how to beat them!"

He gave her a livid glance. "Get below, you little fool!"

"Arunis is controlling their every move!"

"Rubbish! He can't even see them!"

"He doesn't need to—he sees them in his mind!"

Rose was barely listening. Thasha cursed, then turned and struggled up the mizzen ratline. When she was high enough she leaped down onto the quarterdeck and rushed to the captain's side.

"I'll hold them off! Just have a look at his face, will you?"

With that she pushed in front of the captain and slashed the nearest fleshanc almost in two. Rose lumbered toward the starboard rail.

Thirty seconds later he was back at her side. With a bellow he kicked two fleshancs backward onto the main deck. Then he gave the ladder three swift cuts with his axe and severed it from the ship. He lifted it one-handed and tossed it behind him. Then he seized Thasha by the arm.

"Can ye climb?"

"Of course!"

The next thing she knew he was lifting her bodily and hurling her back at the mizzenmast rigging. Thasha cried out, caught hold of a shroud and turned to ask what he thought he was doing. But she held her tongue. The huge old man was making the same leap himself, axe in hand. With a grunt of pain he landed in the ratlines beside her.

"Up! Follow!" he snarled, and together they climbed.

The mast was deserted. "I could give the order," he said, "but there's no more blary time! He'll have my boat in minutes, the flamin' bastard! Climb!"

Sweating and swearing, he led her to the mizzen-top, some forty feet above the deck. But they did not stop there. Through the bolt-hole they squeezed and up again. Up and up, straight at the sun, until at eighty feet they reached the mizzen topgallant yard, the massive timber to which the rearmost mainsail of the *Chathrand* was joined.

"Don't you dare look down until I say so, girl!"

Out along the footropes the captain struggled, his face so red and angry she thought it would burst. She followed, hands shaking, groping along the yard like a worm. They were headed for its outermost tip.

Or what would have been the tip, without the studdingsails. Trying to catch the last breath of wind, Rose had ordered the rigging-out of a second yard, another twenty feet of timber to which a sail could be bent. It had all been in vain, but the yard and sail were still there. Rose hefted his axe.

"The chaps first, cut 'em loose! The yard has to fall free!"

She didn't understand; she didn't know what to cut, or how to do so without plummeting to her death. She was dizzy. Rose bellowed at her. But when he pointed at specific ropes she managed to saw at them, while he chopped farther out. At last the sail slid away.

Then Rose tossed his axe into the sea. He pointed at a pair of steel clamps. "Eye bolts, top and bottom!" he shouted. "Get 'em loose!"

This was easier. She had her clamp loose faster than he managed his. And then she looked down, and knew in an instant what Rose was thinking.

The studdingsail yard jutted past the *Chathrand*'s rail. It reached, in fact, to within ten feet of the lifeboat.

"She's ready," said Rose. "But we have to help her, lass. Put that arm over the topgallant, so. Now crouch down and catch your own hand beneath." He demonstrated, and when Thasha obeyed he stripped away the second clamp.

The twenty-foot beam was loose now, resting atop the permanent spar with nothing keeping it from falling but its own great weight and the force of their arms.

"On three we slide her. Straight, straight! Like my harpoon, girl. You follow?"

She nodded. "I follow. Let's get him."

Rose counted. The spars were smooth-sanded. The tar coating them almost bubbled in the heat. When he said *"Three!"* she pushed with all her might, and Rose did the same. The spar shot forward off the end of the topgallant.

Down it pinwheeled, end over end. On deck the men fighting for their lives never saw its approach. Nor did Arunis. Only the little dog caught sight of the wooden missile. It gave a frightened *Yip!* and dashed to the boat's far end.

The yard nearly missed its mark. Half of it vanished into the sea. But the other half broke across the lifeboat's bow, standing the little craft on its nose and hurling Arunis bodily into the water.

"Now look at the deck," said Rose. "By the Gods' guts, you're a smart one."

The fleshancs had collapsed.

Ragged cheers went up from seaman and soldier alike. But their relief was short-lived.

Ramachni, running squirrel-like up the mainmast, looked down at the water and cried out: "He is coming! Throw them over the side! Obey me now or welcome death!"

This time not a man hesitated. They dragged, heaved and hurled the Volpek bodies over the opposite side, where they sank like bags of sand.

Rose and Thasha groped their way down the rigging, exhausted. Thasha looked for Arunis. He had righted the lifeboat already, and pushed his dog aboard. But the bow of the craft was ruined, and unnaturally low in the water.

The water-weird gave a last, snake-like twist and melted into the sea.

The captain and Thasha were cheered anew when they reached the deck. But Rose waved sharply for silence and pushed to the rail.

Arunis lay in the bottom of his boat, which was clearly taking on water. His breath was labored and his face downcast. Suddenly he looked quite old.

"He is drained," whispered Ramachni. "To stir the dead requires immense power. He cannot have much left."

"Will you desist?" cried Rose.

The mage raised his head. "Oh no. You will drop a ladder, and I shall board, and then we shall bring out the Red Wolf. That is what will happen next."

"You're a madman," snarled Rose.

Arunis sat up at once. "Have you written to your parents lately, Rose? I should love to have a talk with you about those extraordinary letters, sent every week to people you know to be dead."

Rose took a halting step backward. His mouth went slack and one hand groped behind him, as if searching for some wall to lean against. When he spoke, his voice was so thin it might have belonged to another man.

"They talk to me at night," he said.

"And you call me mad!" Arunis laughed, getting to his feet. "They are dead! Your mother's deathsmoke habit killed her twenty years ago. Once, true, she nearly gave up the drug, through the simple use of golden swamp tears—"

"No!" screamed Rose at the top of lungs.

"—but you couldn't be bothered to find her a regular supply, and she went back to deathsmoke."

"KILL HIM!"

"Your father, of course, never forgave you. Without a wife— or a son he could call by that name—he had nothing to live for. He drowned himself. It's all written down in the *Annals of the Quezan Islands*. But what will be written about you, I wonder, Rose? *The once-great skipper who finished his days in a madhouse, chattering with ghosts*—"

"Leave him alone, you gloating pig!" Thasha shouted. The thought of anyone, even Rose, tormented with memories of the dead was more than she could stand.

Arunis was delighted to turn his attention to Thasha. "For your sake, Lady, I will do so. After all, I owe you so much. Your marriage will give the Shaggat's worshippers the sign they are waiting for. And you are also, right now, going to make it possible for me to come aboard."

Before Thasha could reply something terrible occurred: her mother's silver necklace came to life and began to strangle her. Those nearest saw the metal move like a snake, gather itself tight around her neck and squeeze. Pazel and Neeps caught her as she fell. They clawed at the necklace but found it strong as steel.

Thasha kicked and thrashed: she could not even scream.

"He's killing her!" Pazel cried.

Isiq waved madly at Drellarek's archers. "Shoot him! Shoot him dead! I command you!"

The archers looked at Drellarek, who nodded. They rushed forward, arrows to strings.

But Ramachni cried, "No!"

"Hear the rat-mage!" said Arunis. "If I die the necklace will go on choking her, to her death and a day beyond. All my enemies die thus, as your Emperor once condemned me to perish in a noose. And if Thasha or anyone else tries to remove the necklace, she will die. As she will now, old man, if you do not see that a ladder is dropped at once."

Thasha's face had turned a hideous purple. Her eyes were glazed. Pazel saw Neeps looking at him beseechingly, almost in tears. Was this the moment? What Master-Word would save her? He looked up at Ramachni, perched again on Hercól's shoulder. *You will have but one chance.*

A sudden splash: all eyes turned forward. There stood Chadfallow, his face twisted in fury or despair. He had just rolled the boarding ladder down the *Chathrand*'s flank.

Instantly Arunis turned his craft toward the ladder. At the same time, Thasha made a ghastly sound. She was breathing! Pazel tugged at the necklace: still savagely tight. It had loosened just enough to keep her alive.

Beneath the pain on her face was a terrible rage. Voiceless, her lips formed a name: *Syrarys.*

Arunis climbed with surprising quickness, holding his dog in one arm. No one moved to stop him. He reached the deck, swung over the rail and let the dog leap down. Smiling, he put out a hand to Chadfallow. But the doctor stepped back, out of reach.

"You do not care for my friendship?" Arunis chuckled. "No matter; it is your wisdom I count on, not your love. And you have chosen wisely, Doctor. Lady Thasha deserves to live."

"SORCERER!"

The voice erupted from deep in the ship: a frightful, murderous voice.

Arunis' face took on a strange look of rapture. "My lord!" he cried. "Across world and void I come to thee! Through death's gate, by roads of darkness, wastes of years, I return!"

"GIVE IT TO ME! BRING IT FORTH NOW!"

Arunis made no reply. Instead, while the Shaggat went on howling demands, he walked calmly aft. Hundreds of men fell back at his approach, until at last he reached the little group surrounding Thasha.

"Permission to come aboard, Captain?" he said with a sneer.

Rose was deaf to his mockery. He stood apart, hands covering his eyes, trembling.

"I will take your silence for assent. Now hear me, all of you: *Chathrand* has a new master, and his name is Arunis. You thought to cancel this marriage, Isiq. That will never be. Your daughter will marry a Mzithrini, or die in torment before your eyes. And when she is wed this ship will sail for the Ruling Sea, and its rendezvous with war. Nothing can stop this from happening! If you do not trust me, trust Dr. Chadfallow."

"Trust him? Never again!" said Isiq. "I would sooner trust a crawly!"

"You are insulted, Doctor!" Arunis laughed. "But there is no time to waste. Go to the Shaggat Ness; unchain him and his sons. You will find the key on that idiot by the wheelhouse." He gestured contemptuously at Uskins. Then, barely pausing, he turned to Fiffengurt.

"In the doctor's cabin sits a crate. Bring it up. And have the blacksmith's forge hoisted to the deck as well, and a good fire built."

"What if I don't?" said Fiffengurt.

Arunis raised an eyebrow. Fiffengurt was shaking with fear. But still he managed to raise his voice defiantly, addressing the whole crew: "What if we don't, men? What if we swear to kill this cur and his Shaggat, even if he takes fifty of us with 'im, eh?"

The bravest men began to cheer, but Arunis shouted over them: "In that case I will kill Lady Thasha—and the Emperor will kill you all. Do you mean that *no one has explained*? Captain Rose?"

Rose said nothing. His back was bent, and his gaze far away.

"Well then, Sergeant Drellarek? Isn't it time you admitted what His Supremacy expects of his Turachs?"

Drellarek hesitated. Six hundred pairs of eyes were on him. "We are to keep the Shaggat alive," he said at last.

"And should any harm befall him?"

"We shall all be killed, with our families, upon return to Etherhorde. But we do not serve you, filth-mage."

"Nor do I seek your service, dog! Only recall your oath to the crown. Let no one approach His Holiness the Shaggat during the ceremony to come." He raised his voice to a shout. "You think you defeated Sandor Ott? His plan marches on! Should the Shaggat die, everyone aboard this ship will follow fast."

"But Ott thought you were dead!" said Uskins, peeping down from the quarterdeck. "You were never part of his plan!"

"That is true," said Arunis. "But I improved it—perfected it. None here can stand against me now."

Thasha, her voice a wounded rasp, said, "Ramachni can."

Arunis laughed once more. "Such faith the girl has in you, Ramachni! But I know you better. You have done too much in this world already—a healing charm I smell about you, to say nothing of your foolish freeing of Mr. Druffle. Any power left to you after that was wasted on the fleshancs. That is why I bothered with them, of course."

He stepped toward Ramachni, arms flung wide. "You, oppose me? Do it now, weasel! Save your friends!"

There it was, once more—that hint of fear in his voice. Yet Ramachni, claws tight on Hercól's shoulder, bowed his head and said nothing.

"I knew it!" said Arunis. "There's no power left in him! Stay and watch my triumph, wizard: your helplessness will make it all the sweeter. You boys!"

He pointed suddenly at Neeps and Pazel, who froze like startled deer. *He's got us,* Pazel thought. *Oh Rin! Which Master-Word?*

But Arunis showed no sign of recognizing his former captives. "Draw a circle on the deck," he commanded. "Only I, the Shaggat and those I name may enter it during the ceremony. Sergeant Drellarek, your men will kill all others on the spot."

* * *

At noon precisely "the ceremony" began.

The first-class passengers, still locked behind the Money Gate, were the first to hear the great slouching, stomping footfalls. They drew back in horror: the augrongs, Refeg and Rer, were lumbering by, turning their fist-sized yellow eyes on the speechless humans in their finery. They had only budged from their den in the forward hold to help occasionally with anchor-lifting. Now they were squeezing up the main ladderway to the topdeck, where Arunis beckoned impatiently. When they stood at last in the sun they shuffled behind him, docile as hounds.

Below, a woman screamed. While their eyes had been on the augrongs another figure had lumbered down the passage, escorted by a dozen marines. The Shaggat Ness moved like some slow, thick-bodied carnivore. His scarred face twitched like a victim of palsy, and his clouded red eyes looked at them with such hate that even those who had not quailed at the augrongs fell back in terror. Pacu Lapadolma made the sign of the Tree. Walking behind him, the Shaggat's yellow-robed sons saw her gesture and began to mutter of executions.

By Arunis' decree, the entire crew was gathered on deck. Officers and tarboys, sailors and Turach warriors stood side by side, helpless. When the Shaggat stepped out into the light they stumbled backward, like a mob of children who had woken a bear.

Arunis knelt and touched his forehead to the deck. "Master," he said. "After forty years among knaves and enemies we meet triumphant."

"Where is it?" said the Shaggat.

Arunis gestured with one hand. On the deck before the main-mast was an ash circle twenty feet across. At its center sat the forge—a mighty oven used to mend breastplates and anchors and other huge things of iron. Heaps of coal surrounded it. Six men worked the bellows that pumped air through its heart of fire. Before its open mouth the heat was so intense no one could stand it for more than a second or two.

The Shaggat stamped his foot. "There it is! Mine! Mine!"

Inside the forge, as if wading in the red-hot coals, stood the Red Wolf. A more fiendish-looking animal could scarcely be imagined. Its ruby eyes seemed fire themselves. The barnacles on its chest were exploding with heat; the lichen was in flames. It stood in a great steel crucible in the very hottest part of the fire. Already the Wolf's legs had begun to glow.

"The hour is come," said Arunis to the Shaggat. "Once you take up that which I promised you half a century ago, no horde or legion will be able to resist. And I shall walk behind you, Master of All Men—helping, teaching, guiding your hand."

Arunis cast his gaze over the crowd. "Do you see it at last, you conspirators? Ott's secret weapon will be more powerful than even he dared dream! We will not merely *hurt* the Mzithrini, we will crush them. And then we will crush Arqual. League by league we will burn both empires off the map."

"You'll need more than a Sizzy-made Wolf," said Oggosk with contempt. "A relic of the Dawn War, that's what you'll need. Find the Nilstone for your puppet-king, Arunis, if you want to rule the world."

"Puppet?" cried the Shaggat's sons. "Hang her! Hang her!"

"Soon I shall have no need of hangmen," said the Shaggat Ness.

The orange glow had spread to the Wolf's stomach. Its lower legs began to soften and bend.

Arunis turned to Lady Oggosk. "You are right, Duchess. Only one weapon will do for the next Lord of Alifros. Watch now and despair."

Pazel blinked the sweat from his eyes. The Shaggat was only an arm's length away. If he touched him and spoke the Stone-Word it would all be over—and Arunis would kill Thasha in a heartbeat.

All around them, men were murmuring prayers. *"Save us, stop him, let me live to see my wife."* Pazel looked at Ramachni.

Must I do it? he thought. *Must I let him kill her to stop the war?* Ramachni's face told him nothing.

Then Thasha caught his eye—the same direct, dazzling look she had given him from the carriage in Etherhorde so many weeks before, but sorrowful now instead of glad. It was a look of understanding, an acceptance beyond all fear.

She was giving him permission.

Pazel looked down quickly. *Let there be some other way. Any other way.*

Coal flew spade after spade into the forge, to the ceaseless huffing of the bellows. The Wolf now glowed from head to tail. If Pazel spoke the Fire-Word he might make the flame go out, and delay whatever evil thing Arunis was up to. But the mage would simply light another fire, and the Word would be gone. And if what Arunis said was true it would mean Thasha's death to use the Stone-Word against him. The cursed necklace would strangle her the instant Arunis died.

Panic seized him. He was alone—surrounded by every friend he had in the world, and still utterly alone. It was up to Pazel to stop this horror, and he had no idea what to do.

But what was this? Ormali! Someone was speaking Ormali— and although it was chanted like a prayer, the words were for him.

"Look at me! At me, my Chereste heart!"

It was Druffle. There he stood at the back of the crowd: starved, bruised and shaky. But when he looked at Pazel, the freebooter's eyes lit up with rascally mischief. Druffle's gaze slid upward—and carefully, one eye still on Arunis, Pazel looked as well.

For a moment he saw nothing but the familiar jungle of ropes and spars. Then he saw him: Taliktrum. He was hidden in the mouth of a block-pulley, ten feet overhead.

"Look away from me!" he shouted.

He used the normal voice of ixchel, the voice Pazel alone could hear. Pazel obeyed at once.

"Can you stop him?" Taliktrum went on. *"Answer in Nileskchet."*

"I could if I could touch him," Pazel said aloud. *"But I dare not."*

"No," he agreed. *"You dare not. But stay close to him, boy. We are not beaten yet."*

"He'll murder Thasha!" Pazel cried. *"And they'll kill me if I step inside that circle. How do you expect me to stay close?"*

But Taliktrum made no answer, and when Pazel risked another glance at the mainsail, he was gone.

The nearest sailors were looking at him with fear and rage: the bad-luck tarboy, speaking in witch-tongues again. But Druffle sidled up to him and clasped his arm.

"He saved me," he said wonderingly, as if he still could not believe it. "I had a Tholjassan arrowhead six inches deep in my back. He put his arm in the wound and tugged it out. A crawly. A crawly saved my life."

A sigh came from the crowd: the Wolf's legs had given way and its body now lay in a pool of molten iron, half filling the crucible.

"Taliktrum," Pazel whispered. *"You* brought him back."

Druffle nodded. "And his sister, under my clothes."

"Diadrelu!"

"Aye, Her Ladyship. After Arunis pushed me out of that little boat, they held my head above water until your friend arrived. They're the finest folk I ever met."

"Where is she?"

But Druffle made no answer. Thasha and Neeps drew near. Thasha's eyes were moist. She looked as though she was taking leave of everything.

"Pazel," said Neeps, "Arunis is destroying the Wolf!"

"Yes," said Pazel, still watching Druffle's face.

"What for? He nearly got us killed looking for the thing!"

"It's not the Wolf he wants," rasped Thasha.

The boys looked at her, speechless.

"I've been reading the *Polylex*," she whispered. "To the

Sizzies, wolves aren't evil. They're symbols of wisdom and strength. They cooperate, protect one another, care for the pack. In Mzithrini legends wolves *warn* people of danger. Don't you see? This Wolf isn't a weapon—it's a hiding place for one. Arunis wants whatever's inside."

"Thasha," said Pazel, "I'm not going to let him kill you."

To Pazel's astonishment, she hugged him tight. He tried to pull away—Arunis might punish her for anything—but she was stronger, and would not let go. Then all at once he felt movement against his chest. After Taliktrum's angry warning he knew better than to look down, but out of the corner of his eye he saw, and understood. Diadrelu was climbing from Thasha's shirt into his own.

"Hug her back, fool!" said the ixchel woman. *"The mage is watching."*

Pazel hugged her. But Dri wasn't satisfied. *"By the Pits, Arunis is staring at you! Thasha, you went to the Lorg School! Can't you feign affection?"*

"Feign?" said Pazel.

"Who's talking?" said Neeps.

Thasha kissed Pazel on the mouth.

Nothing he had ever felt was half so awkward or fascinating. But it lasted only an instant. Then came pain—a sudden, searing pain at his collarbone. Pazel gasped. His first thought was that Dri had stabbed him. But she was nowhere near the spot. No, it was Klyst: her magic shell was blazing beneath his skin, scalding him with murth-girl jealousy. He jerked his head away.

"Stop it!" he said.

Thasha dropped her arms. But now she was blazing, too. "As if it was *my* idea!" she snapped.

The pain stopped. Behind them, Arunis cackled. "Of course it wasn't!" he said. "It was your tutors'—or your father's, perhaps. Give her a tarry sweetheart—and one of the backward races, at that. Let her disgrace herself. Perhaps the Sizzies won't let one of their princes marry a tramp."

"Seal your lips, snake!" shouted Eberzam Isiq.

"Better to command your daughter thus," laughed Arunis. "But it will make no difference. She marries tomorrow."

"Thasha—" Pazel stammered.

She turned to him.

But then Dri spoke for his ears alone. *"Forget her, if you would save her. Get closer to the mage."*

"Never mind," he said. Thasha gave him a look of perfect exasperation.

Pazel squeezed through the crowd to the circle's edge, with Neeps just behind him. Inside the forge, the Wolf's body was so hot it quivered like a pudding. Its ruby eyes glowed brighter than ever.

"If you kill the mage, the voyage will go on," whispered Dri. *"Rose and Drellarek will see to that."*

"I know!" said Pazel.

"Pazel, who—" Neeps began.

"Don't talk to me!"

Pazel covered his ears. He was going mad. *Think, think, think!* Neeps fell silent, and for a time, so did everyone else. All eyes were on the Wolf, the mage, the twitching hands of the Shaggat. The heat was staggering. Then a howl tore the air—a wolf's howl, enormous and urgent—as the whole creature turned to liquid before their eyes. The howl raced down the length of the *Chathrand*, stirring the limp sails, and vanished with a last whine over the bows.

But in the pool of bubbling metal one object remained. It was a. crystal sphere about the size of a melon. The sphere glistened in the firelight—but at its heart was something impenetrably black.

Dri hissed in her throat. *"Oh no, no. Rin forbid."*

"There it is!" cried Arunis. "Take it out! Cool it with seawater! *Findre ble sondortha, Rer!*"

Dutifully Rer put his tongs into the forge and removed the sphere. Great clouds of steam rose when he plunged it into a waiting bucket. The steam drenched them all: from a distance men would have thought the *Chathrand* ablaze. Finally it subsided, and Rer lifted the sphere again and placed it in the center of the anvil. It sparkled in the sun, but the core was darker than ever. Thasha had a sudden feeling that she had seen it before.

"Now, Refeg," said Arunis.

Refeg set the tip of his chisel on the sphere.

"Arunis!" said Hercól suddenly. "Do not commit this atrocity! It will destroy you as well!"

"Break the sphere," said Arunis.

Refeg lifted his stone mallet, but before he could swing another voice thundered: *"No!"*

It was Captain Rose. He was on his feet and barreling toward the ash circle, as savagely excited as he had been numb moments before. "Don't break it! *Chabak! Chabak*, Refeg, you fool! Get it away from the fire!"

"Stop, Captain!" shouted Drellarek.

Rose did not stop. At his first step within the circle the Turachs raised their swords. But Drellarek intercepted Rose before they could pounce. He dealt Rose a blow to the head that could be heard ten yards away. Rose's body stiffened, and his eyes rolled back in his head.

"My apologies, sir," said Drellarek.

Rose staggered a last step—and fell against the mouth of the forge. There was an awful sizzling noise and a stench of burning flesh. Drellarek seized him by the shirt and pulled him backward—but not before Rose's shoulder knocked the crucible to the deck.

Screams of fear and agony. Like quicksilver, the Wolf's molten iron flashed across the deck. Everywhere, men leaped for rails and rigging—they worked barefoot, after all. The boots of the Turach soldiers burst one after another into flame; Drellarek screamed at them to hold their ground. Mr. Fiffengurt, weeping for his ship, kicked over the cask of seawater, which vaporized instantly on contact with the iron and scalded men worse than the metal itself.

Through all the chaos Arunis kept perfectly still, gripping the Shaggat's arm.

The cloud of steam lifted. Slags of iron bubbled on the deck, and Fiffengurt gave orders for them to be scooped and tossed overboard. Dr. Chadfallow ran from sailor to sailor, shouting, *"Don't walk on your burns, man!"*

Climbing down from a forestay, Pazel winced. In the frenzy a sailor had knocked him over, and his left palm had come down on a coin-sized splash of iron. With a cry he had torn it off— along with a patch of burned skin. In fact he had been lucky— the scalding steam had passed over his head—but what agony in his hand! The spot on his palm felt like hard leather, and somehow he knew it always would.

At the forge, Arunis had redrawn the circle and Drellarek's men ringed it as before. Rose lay groaning against the starboard rail, letting Oggosk wrap his burned arm in gauze. The crystal sphere had not moved from its place on the anvil. The sorcerer gestured again to Refeg.

"Break it, now."

But the augrong had flung its mallet halfway to the bow. Arunis pointed at a trembling Jervik and ordered him to fetch it. While they waited, Thasha studied the sphere. Why was it so familiar?

Then she had it: the *Polylex,* again. She had seen a drawing of just such a sphere, being rolled into a cannon's mouth.

"Oh skies," she whispered. "It's one of *those*!"

She was on the point of shouting—they were in immediate and terrible danger—when a hand closed on her shoulder, and a voice hissed: *"Shhhh."*

It was the veterinarian, Bolutu. "You're right of course, Bride-to-Be," he whispered (and his accent was very different from his normal voice—and somehow more true). "Rose guessed it also. But you must not interfere. How else will the sorcerer be defeated?"

"But we can't . . . all these people!"

Jervik had retrieved the mallet. The augrong took it and stepped up to the sphere once more.

"All these people are not a drop beside the sea of deaths he has in mind, Lady. You know I speak the truth. Let the dragon's-egg shot burst, even though we sink. Only then will Arunis—"

"Yip! Yip! Yip! Yip!"

Out of nowhere, snapping at Bolutu's heels, was the small, furious white dog. Arunis raised his hand, and Refeg paused.

"You. Black man!"

The sorcerer's arm shot out. He crooked a finger, and Bolutu stiffened and stumbled forward.

"You're keeping a secret from me," said Arunis, with a perfectly hideous smile. "Oh, there's no need to speak. You're thinking about it, that will do . . . Ah!"

His eyes grew wide with fury. He waved sharply, and Bolutu fell to his knees with a cry.

"A dragon's-egg shot! So you would let me shatter it here, where its deadly yolk would splash into the flames and explode? You knew, and said nothing? Well, since you are so fond of silence—"

What happened next gave Thasha nightmares for the rest of her life. Arunis spread his fingers. Bolutu's head jerked up, his mouth wide open. With his other hand Arunis pointed at the fire—and a coal rose and flew like a wasp of flame into Bolutu's mouth.

Bolutu gave a rending scream, then fell forward, unconscious. Beside her, Thasha saw that Ramachni *too* had crumpled, shivering in Hercól's arms.

The Shaggat Ness stepped forward and kicked Bolutu in the head. He toppled backward out of the circle. Dr. Chadfallow leaped forward and dragged him away.

Arunis watched the shivering Ramachni. "You put out the coal, Ramachni?" He laughed. "A final gasp of magical mercy? Why am I not surprised? As you will—Bolutu may live, but he will never speak again. Fiffengurt! Close the forge, let the fire die. You, Rer: drag it away."

A chain was found; Rer looped it around the iron forge and hauled the smoldering thing up the deck. Arunis watched, then gestured again at Refeg.

"Now," he said.

The augrong raised his mallet and dealt the sphere a crushing blow. The very deck of the *Chathrand* seemed to quake, but the crystal survived. Three times Refeg swung, and on the third blow the crystal shattered. From the pieces oozed a clear liquid like the white of an egg. And resting on the anvil was the oddest thing Pazel had ever seen.

It was another sphere, orange-sized or smaller, but impossible to look at directly. It seemed to be made of night. It had no surface features—no surface at all, as far as he could tell. It was merely black and cold. *And wrong.* Something in Pazel's mind and bones and blood rejected the sphere. It was a flaw, a wound in the world. Across the ship men's faces paled.

"Master," said Arunis to the Shaggat, "I keep my promises."

"No," said the Shaggat. "I take what is mine."

Suddenly his voice rose in a thunderous roar. Spittle flew from his mouth as he turned, gesturing wildly. "Bow down, sorcerer! Bow, kings, generals, all lesser princes of this world! The Shaggat is come, the Shaggat, to cleanse and claim it! Behold, I wield the Nilstone!"

Dozens of ixchel voices began to scream. *"It's true! By the hallowed names, it's true! Kill him, kill him, Pazel Pathkendle! Kill him now!"*

The little people must have been hiding everywhere. But one voice—the voice of Dri in Pazel's shirt—hissed, *"Not yet!"*

A wall of Turachs stood between Pazel and the forge, terribly nervous, ready to stab anything that moved. Even if he wanted to, Pazel doubted he could ever reach the two men.

"Bow your heads!" screamed the Shaggat Ness.

Arunis bowed. The Shaggat's sons groveled on their bellies.

Everyone else merely gaped. The Shaggat put out his hand and grasped the Nilstone. For a moment all eyes were on him.

"Now!" said Dri. *"Do it! Run!"*

Pazel burst into the circle, running full tilt, and dived beneath the legs of the nearest Turach. The man stabbed at him, but too late. Pazel crashed forward, stopping inches from the Shaggat's heels.

The mad king was raising the Nilstone to the sun. A roar of triumph came from his throat. Pazel reached up—and Arunis, catching sight of him, drew his knife. But before either could act the Shaggat's roar became a wail of pain.

The hand that gripped the Nilstone was dead. Hideously dead, the fingers rotted, the bones erupting through the skin. And death was running like flame up the Shaggat's arm.

Howling, the Shaggat whirled. "Betrayed! Betrayed! Kill the sorcerer, kill every—"

He broke off. A tarboy was looking him in the eye. And Pazel touched him and spoke the Master-Word.

It was like an earthquake beneath the sea. Pazel felt that it was not him but the entire world that had spoken, every part of it at once. The sun turned black, or else too bright for human eyes. Clouds in the distance were torn to shreds. But there was no wind, no waves—and already the Word was gone from his mind.

All about the deck, men stumbled in a daze. What had just happened? What had changed?

Pazel lowered his hand. Before him stood a statue of a king with one dead arm, raising his withered fist in the air. Within that fist lay the Nilstone, unchanged. But the Shaggat was no more.

Arunis looked at the statue and then whirled to face Pazel, his eyes bewildered and lost. It was as if he were seeing the tarboy for the first time—and seeing too his own impossible defeat.

"A child," he said, his voice deadly quiet. "A lowborn brat. What madness moves you, boy?"

Then Diadrelu spoke, for Pazel's ears alone. *"Hold your*

ground. Have no fear of him. If his knife-hand moves I shall slit his throat."

Not a man stirred on the Great Ship. But one creature did: Ramachni. Moving gingerly, the black mink walked into the circle and looked up at the mage.

"The dragonlords of old had a saying, Arunis," he said. "*No one fondles fire and escapes unburned.* How careless you have been! You raided libraries, stole many books. You knew the Nilstone could make your Shaggat invincible. But had you read further, you would have learned that every mortal man who has touched it since the time of Erithusmé has died on the spot. For what is the Nilstone, Arunis? You have spent your life craving it. Surely you know?"

"It is the greatest weapon on earth," said Arunis.

"No," said Thasha from behind them. "It's death."

No one had heard her approach. Ramachni looked at her and nodded.

"Death given form," he said. "And none who fear death in any corner of their heart may wield it. The Fell Princes drank an enchanted wine from Agaroth, the twilit land that borders death's kingdom, before they touched the Nilstone. Drinking, they knew no fear, and so they took the stone and used it for unspeakable evil. But they had only so much wine. And you have none at all."

Ramachni shook his head. "Arunis! All your will has been bent to the unleashing of violence—a war, a warlord, this evil Nilstone. You thought to control it, as you controlled the Shaggat Ness. But we are never long the masters of the violence we unleash. In the end it always masters us."

"Reverse the spell," hissed Arunis. "Make the Shaggat flesh again. Remember that Thasha Isiq is mine to kill."

"But you will not kill her," said Ramachni.

"Will I not?" screamed the mage suddenly. "How is that? Will you stop me, weasel?"

"I already have," said Ramachni. "You see, Arunis, I did not spend my power fighting the fleshancs, as you wished me to. I spent it long before. A great deal went into teaching Pazel his Master-Words. Very much worth the trouble, as it turns out."

Pazel smiled despite himself.

"Yet two problems remained," Ramachni continued. "One was the curse on Thasha's necklace, which I could not break. Tell me, did Syrarys know that she was condemning Thasha to death when she used your silver polish?"

Arunis made no answer. Pazel saw Thasha glance suddenly across the deck, to where Lady Oggosk stood beside the captain. *Pitfire,* he thought. *Was the old woman trying to save Thasha when she sent her cat to steal the necklace? What's her blary game?*

"The second problem," Ramachni went on, "was that so many people were willing to murder the innocent, should the Shaggat die. Not just you, but Sandor Ott, Drellarek, the Emperor himself. So I dared not kill the Shaggat, or even allow him to die."

"Then the spell *can* be reversed!"

"It can," said Ramachni, "but Pazel cannot do it. Nor can I, nor anyone aboard. The Shaggat will become flesh again when one soul aboard *Chathrand*—and I shall never tell you which—dies. It may be Thasha, or this boy before you. Or Rose, or Uskins, anyone at all. The minute that one dies, the Stone-Word shall be reversed."

"Is that the best you could do?" cried Arunis. "Let the Shaggat be stone, then, until we cross the Ruling Sea and meet his army of worshippers! He will be far less trouble! Once on Gurishal I shall no longer require these men. And I *shall* kill them: all six hundred, if need be. I shall find your spell-keeper!"

"And when you kill that person," said Thasha, eyes wide with understanding, "the Shaggat will turn back into flesh, and the Nilstone will kill *him*. Oh, Pazel! How did you know when to speak? You were *wonderful*!"

"And you are without friends, Arunis," said Hercól.

Rage clouded the sorcerer's eyes. He looked sharply at Thasha and raised his hand. "I do not have to *kill* her to make her suffer," he said.

Thasha's necklace gave a savage twist. She could not even scream. Her face turned crimson and tears sprang from her eyes.

Pazel's first thought was to beg the augrongs to stomp Arunis to death once and for all. But only Arunis could make the necklace stop—Ramachni had just said as much. Thasha staggered, her eyes rolling back in her head. Pazel caught her as she fell.

In the face of Eberzam Isiq, something snapped. He drew his old sword and flew at Arunis, shouting a war-cry. Just in time, Hercól leaped into his path and dragged him aside. Arunis laughed in the old man's face.

Then they all heard it: the flat sound of metal striking stone. Arunis whirled. There was Neeps, a lump of iron in his hand, smashing the toes of the Shaggat Ness.

"We don't have to kill him to make him a cripple!" he said. On his last word the Shaggat's big toe shattered to dust.

"Stop! Stop!" bellowed Arunis. "You shell-island scum! Very well, I release her—for now."

Thasha gulped air, writhing in Pazel's arms. Her throat was red and raw. Eberzam Isiq dropped heavily to his knees beside Pazel, and together they held her.

Sergeant Drellarek came forward. "Sorcerer," he said, "you speak with contempt of the Shaggat Ness. You are no believer. Why make use of him? Why did you not take the stone for yourself?"

"Keep to your own affairs, Turach," snarled Arunis.

"That's an easy one," piped up Druffle, from the edge of the crowd. "He was afraid! Didn't know what he was afraid of, exactly, but whatever the risk, he wanted somebody else to take it. The Shaggat's just your hand-puppet, ain't he, you louse?"

"The Shaggat is *everyone*'s hand-puppet!" screamed Arunis.

"Or no one's," said Ramachni.

"Idiot mage! Why do you meddle in the affairs of my world? Have men not done enough harm in your own? Look at that beast!" He stabbed a finger at the Shaggat. "Made for slaughter! A curse on any land, a plague-bearer, a despoiler of all he sees! If he ever conquers Alifros he'll find himself the emperor of ashes!"

Pazel looked up at the sorcerer. *Then why are you helping him?*

"You are wrong about humans," said Ramachni. "There is evil in them, of course. But there is also sublime beauty, and a thirst for good. It is that thirst that makes them change, and grow, and wake each day a bit more fully."

"They can no more change than His Nastiness here," said Arunis. "They are statues. Gargoyles. Souls of stone."

Ramachni shook his head. "They are fluid souls. What they can feel, and imagine, and rise to—not even they yet appreciate."

"Even the Shaggat is more than just a statue," said Hercól.

Sergeant Drellarek raised his hand. "Enough! This is a stalemate, wizard. You cannot beat them, nor they you. Leave the deck! You have already come close to sinking the Great Ship. If it is true that the Shaggat can be restored to life, then our mission will go on. I know nothing of curse-stones and magic wine, but I have my orders. The girl will marry and fulfill Ott's prophecy. We shall feign our own wreck and vanish into the Ruling Sea, and Captain Rose will see us safely across her. You, sorcerer, will have months to prove that you are smarter than three youths and a mink."

Arunis' hands clenched in rage. "You, Throatcutter—you and your kind sought to kill me forty years ago. My body hung from a noose on Licherog, but my spirit lived. Death is my servant, not my master. I *will* free the Shaggat. And Thasha will marry, or die at my feet. This I promise you."

"Then the Emperor's will be done," said Drellarek, and his warriors cheered: "His will be done! His will be done!"

"Rin help us, the idiots," Dri whispered to Pazel. *"They're cheering for their own deaths."*

Arunis looked from face to face, his eyes shining with hate. Last of all his gaze fell on Chadfallow.

"What says the good doctor?" he sneered.

Pazel and the others looked as well, hardly more friendly than Arunis. Chadfallow dropped his eyes.

"The Emperor's will be done," he said.

The Wolf-Scar Oath

6 Teala 941

The olive-green mountains of Simja rose in the west. Already the sea was festooned with sails: ten, no, eleven men-of-war, sporting flags of Arqual and Ibithraéd and Talturi, racing like the *Chathrand* toward the city between two empires. Thasha's marriage would be well attended, if it happened at all.

The Shaggat Ness was lowered through the tonnage hatch and chained to a bulkhead. Arunis screamed for the king to be put in his own cabin—but no one wanted the sorcerer left alone with the Nilstone. Drellarek set a day-and-night guard on the statue, and a more discreet watch on Arunis himself.

Farther aft, Hercól stood guard as well: just inside the closed door of the stateroom.

"You will have to shut that book at some point, Thasha," he said.

Thasha, her neck wrapped in a cotton bandage, looked up at him and smiled. She closed the *Polylex*. "I was reading about the Mzithrini diet. It says they eat beetles fried in sesame oil."

"Nonsense!" said Eberzam Isiq. "And what does it matter to you?"

"I have to go through with it, Prahba," she said quietly.

"No you don't!" shouted half a dozen voices at once.

"Shame on you, Thasha," said Neeps. "Haven't we promised to get you out of this?"

"Arunis will kill me," she said. "I'm only alive *because* he needs me to marry."

"He makes mistakes," said Pazel. "Ramachni's already fooled him once."

All eyes turned to the little mage. He was crouched beneath the dining table, beside a basket where Felthrup lay asleep, looking very frail. Ramachni did not look quite right either. Something was gone from the sheen of his fur, the glitter of those wonderful eyes. He looked up from his patient.

"Felthrup bleeds beneath his skin," he said. "I have put him in the healing-sleep, but that may only be a gentler way for him to die. I cannot tell: either he will wake, and live—or never wake at all. But there is another who needs our attention, Hercól."

He gazed over his shoulder. On the bench under the gallery windows stood Niriviel, Sandor Ott's falcon. A black hood covered his head, and his leg was tied by a leather strap to a hook on the windowsill.

Hercól and Ramachni approached him, and the Tholjassan removed the hood. Ramachni leaped to the bench.

"Will you speak to us now?" he asked.

"I will," said the bird in a voice like tearing canvas. "But what are you going to do to me?"

"Nothing whatsoever," said Ramachni. "We are not your judges."

The bird cocked an eye at Hercól, suspicious. "You hate my master," he accused.

"Never," said Hercól. "Remember that he was once mine as well. But I have outgrown him, Niriviel. Oh, not in skill at arms—that I hope will never be tested. My heart has outgrown him, outgrown the cage in which Ott prefers all hearts to dwell. The cage he cannot live without: I mean love of Arqual."

"That is no cage!" shrieked the bird suddenly, flapping his wings. "Arqual is the hope of all people! It brings safety, riches, order, peace! It is our mother and father! Arqual is the glory of this world!"

"But Arqual is not the world," said Ramachni. "Alifros is vast, and many of her people love their homelands as deeply as you do yours."

"One day they will all be Arqualis," said the falcon. "And you traitors. You shall go to Licherog and break stones."

"When I watched you from the gardens of the Lorg," said Thasha, approaching, "I used to think you were the freest soul in Alifros. But I was wrong. I don't think you know what freedom is."

"Remove this strap from my leg and I will show you what freedom is."

"That is what I hope for," said Ramachni.

He put his teeth to the leather strap, and in four bites chewed it through. Hercól, meanwhile, raised a window. Instantly the bird leaped to the windowsill. He leaned forward, wings lifting—

—and drew back. His sharp eyes darted here and there in amazement.

"You release me! Why?"

"Because we do not enslave," said Ramachni. "And you should ponder the form of slavery to which you are accustomed. Those bonds only you can break."

The bird fidgeted on the sill, one eye trained on Ramachni. "You're a mage," he said at last, "but not so very wise."

Thus speaking he dropped from the window, shrieked once and was gone.

"A child," said Ramachni, his voice heavy with sorrow. "I would hazard that he was Ott's creature long before his waking, and took the spymaster's faith and cause as his own from the first hour. A terrifying process, waking: some do not survive it with their minds intact. Others need a God or cause or enemy to anchor them, for above all they fear choice, that great abyss."

"Ramachni," said Hercól. "There is an abyss before you as well."

"I haven't forgotten *that*," laughed the mage. "Trust me, I feel it in every hair."

"Feel what?" asked Thasha.

"The need for a healing-sleep of my own," said Ramachni.

"My fight with Arunis occurred in more realms than those visible to the eye. The match was close, and it has cost me. My time here is almost spent."

"Spent?" cried Neeps. "What are you talking about? You can't go anywhere! We need you here!"

"If I do not go while I have the strength to walk away, Mr. Undrabust, I shall still depart—by burning out like a candle."

"But this is a disaster!" said Neeps. "Arunis isn't defeated yet, and Ott's still out there somewhere, *and Thasha's getting married tomorrow*! And what about Pazel? If he says the wrong word at the wrong time, maybe he'll blow Simja to the moon!"

"When will you come back, Ramachni?" asked Pazel.

"Not for a long time."

The news hung like a raincloud over the room. At last Neeps broke the silence.

"We're sunk."

"Undrabust!" said Eberzam Isiq. "In the navy you'd be flogged for throwing that word around! Here, what's that on your wrist?"

Neeps looked startled. Then he held out his arm. On his wrist was a small red scar. "Look close, it's the strangest thing," he said. "A bit of iron from the Red Wolf struck me, while it was still hot as Pitfire. But it's not just any burn. It's wolf-shaped!"

So it was: a perfect, unmistakable wolf, scarred deep into his wrist.

"And matters are stranger than you know," said Hercól. With that he lifted a corner of his shirt. Burned into the flesh just below his rib cage was the dark outline of a wolf. "They are identical. And see, a forepaw raised, exactly like the Red Wolf."

"Anyone else?" said Neeps. "I say—Pazel!"

He was holding out his left hand; the others crowded round. The burn on his palm was deeper than the other two. It had blistered, and bled a little at the edges. "It's a wolf all right," he said. "And it's as hard as leather. But I have no idea what it means."

"It means you are in the grip of a spell," said Ramachni. "But not an evil one, I think."

"Well that's just blary perfect," said Pazel. He wanted no more to do with spells, evil or benign. Then he looked at Thasha, and saw dejection on her face.

"You weren't burned by the iron, were you?"

Thasha shook her head. "Got lucky, I'm happy to say."

She sounded anything but happy. Pazel didn't know what to say, or what to think. He caught Neeps' eye; his friend looked as troubled as Pazel felt.

"Anyway," Thasha said with a forced smile, "I'll always have this."

She held up the hand she had mutilated years ago, with the rose stem at the Lorg. The others stopped what they were doing and looked at it. Or rather stared. Presently Thasha turned her palm over and looked herself.

The scar was transformed. Nothing had changed on the back of her hand, where she had stabbed herself. But the mark on her palm had become a wolf—*the* wolf, unmistakably the same.

"What's happening?" whispered Thasha. "Ramachni, did you . . . ?"

"I have not interfered. Nor would I presume to do so, without great cause, when a spell has been laid down with such care."

"Laid down by whom?" asked Pazel.

"A spirit dwelled in the Red Wolf," said Ramachni. "You heard the howl when its shape succumbed to fire. But whose spirit? I cannot tell you, but you would do well to find out."

Thasha was still looking at her scar, old and new at once. "I think I know," she said at last. "I think her name was Erithusmé."

Ramachni looked at her curiously: not quite surprised, but very intrigued. "Erithusmé," he said. "The greatest mage to draw breath since the time of the Worldstorm. How did that notion come to you, child?"

"I don't know. The Mother Prohibitor told me part of her story, and I've been searching the *Polylex* for the rest ever since. Impossible book! I still haven't found a word about her. But I'm sure she's part of this, Ramachni. As sure as if she'd walked up and told me herself."

Hercól lifted Thasha's hand and looked thoughtfully at the altered scar. "I do not know what the thirteenth edition has to say about Erithusmé," he said, "but I can tell you what I know of her. We Tholjassans live alongside the Mzithrin; we know their legends better than most. And as part of my training for the Secret Fist I took an interest in the lore of the Pentarchy. Her seers of old knew what Arunis forgot: that the Nilstone is no one's tool for long. And since it cannot be destroyed, the world must be protected from it by every possible means.

"We know that Erithusmé tried to force it upon Eplendrus the Glacier-Worm, the beast at the heart of the Tzular Mountains in the uttermost north. And we know she failed: the stone drove Eplendrus mad, so that he thrashed himself to death among the bones of his ancestors. And we know that the wizardess repented then, and came back for the Nilstone, and bore it south instead of north, into the boundless Nelluroq. Once again she tried to put it out of reach. And once again she failed.

"She made a last attempt to hide the stone. No tales reveal how, or where; this was the great secret of her life. We know now, of course: she bound it in a dragon's-egg shot, and then within the Red Wolf. The old tales always held that its redness came from the blood of a living being. Thasha is right, I believe: that blood was Erithusmé's own. And I think now that she hoped not merely to hide the Nilstone, but to ensure that anyone who tried to use it again would have a fight on their hands."

"A fight with us," said Pazel.

"As it happens," said Hercól with a nod. "For a thousand years the spirit in the Wolf kept the Nilstone safe. It inspired the Mzithrin Kings to build a citadel about it, a forbidden place of silence and forgetting. But not everyone forgot. The Shaggat laid siege to that citadel and bore the Wolf away. And perhaps it was the guardian spirit that lured his ship to its doom on the Haunted Coast, and coaxed the sea-murths to find a new hiding place for the Wolf.

"All guesses, of course. But on this last point I would stake my life: when the Red Wolf was destroyed, the spirit's last act was to mark us, that we might find one another, and join forces."

"But what if there are more of us?" said Pazel. "The iron ran everywhere. There's bits burned into planks, and stuck to rails, ropes, and people's shoes. It even spilled down the tonnage hatch. Don't we need to know who else is wearing a wolf scar?"

"Yes," said Ramachni. "There may well be more allies than we suppose. And let me warn you at once not to trust appearances."

"Never!" said Eberzam Isiq forcefully. "Or never again, I should say."

"You take but half my meaning, Excellency," said the mage. "We gave our trust to some in error, that is true. But in this fight it would be just as costly to overlook a friend, however strange or suspect he may appear. More costly, perhaps: I fear we shall need every aid imaginable before the end."

"Lady Oggosk is no friend of Arunis," said Thasha. "I still don't know if she's on our side or not, but back in Ormael she spoke a kind of password from the Lorg—or at least from the Mother Prohibitor."

"The old women of the Lorg have their hands in far more than the affairs of one school," said Hercól. "I have known some who believed they controlled the destinies of nations. But they guard their secrets like the rarest jewels, and I fear in truth they serve themselves alone."

"How are we supposed to find these allies, whoever they are?" asked Neeps. "And for that matter, how will we know we've found them all? We don't know how many people we're talking about."

They looked at one another, and no one said a word. Then Thasha turned and walked back to her book.

"Erithusmé's people were Mzithrinis, right?" she asked.

"In all but name," said Hercól. "The Nohirini, they were called, from the high country west of the Jomm."

"Well then, listen to what my *Polylex* says under *Mzithrin Kings: Superstitions*." Thasha flipped from bookmark to bookmark, scanning the diaphanous paper. At last, finding the spot, she read aloud: *"Good omens mean everything to a Mzithrini. He has dozens of holy days, scores of lucky charms and symbols. But his beliefs have room for one and only one lucky number: seven. Traditional houses have seven windows, seven lamps lit at nightfall, seven cats. Nothing important is begun except on the month's seventh day. This belief is as old as the hills, or older."*

"The book is accurate," said Isiq. "The Mzithrinis were adamant that the wedding—and the Great Peace—occur in Teala: on the seventh day of the seventh month, in fact."

"You see?" said Thasha. "I'd bet anything there are seven people aboard with wolf scars."

"And we are just four," said Hercól.

"Make that five."

Everyone jumped. Eberzam Isiq gasped aloud. Standing openly upon the bearskin rug was an ixchel woman.

"My scar is upon my breast," she said. "I will show it to Lady Thasha if you like."

The two adults were speechless. Hercól's eyes locked on the figure, and he crouched into the posture of icy stillness from which he could spring like a cat. Isiq looked around for something to throw. But Thasha and the boys rushed to her in delight, and Ramachni followed them.

"Diadrelu Tammariken," said the mage. "What an honor to meet you at last."

Even after this gesture it took the men some time to reconcile themselves to the idea that they were aboard—had been aboard for months—a ship full of "crawlies." Yet eventually they found themselves all seated together, sipping tea from the samovar. Dri sat cross-legged in Felthrup's basket, stroking his fur.

"She was the one who saved you, really," said Pazel to Hercól. "She shot Zirfet in the ankle. Otherwise you'd have gone over the edge whether Arunis liked it or not."

"In my heart I suspected it," said Hercól, whose eyes had

never left Diadrelu. "Who else but an ixchel attacks so silently? But never have I heard of your people doing a kindness to our own."

"Then you've not heard enough," said Dri.

"Who has?" said Ramachni. "Such a strange world, Alifros. Why are good deeds forgotten, and the fires of revenge stoked year after year?"

"No one ever forgets a burn," said Hercól.

"Alas, no," said Ramachni. "But you are wise enough not to live for its memory."

"You did not board *Chathrand* to fight the Shaggat conspiracy," said Hercól. "Why are you here?"

"Of that I am not permitted to speak," said Diadrelu.

"And we are merely to trust you?"

"Come, Hercól!" said Ramachni. "You are addressing the Lady Diadrelu. She is no trickster but the queen of an honorable people."

"In fact I am not," said Diadrelu heavily.

Pazel jumped again. "What do you mean, Dri?"

Diadrelu's eyes were downcast. "The clan voted to annul my title and banish me from all debates, should I reveal our presence to one human more. Well, I have done so today, for I believe as you do that this evil must be stopped. They will not kill me, perhaps, but they will not follow me either. Taliktrum must lead them now, if he can."

Her look was very grim. Then suddenly she raised her head and laughed—a lovely, musical laugh from a woman so often burdened with responsibility. "I begged them to call me Dri," she said. "Just Dri, as my brother used to. Perhaps now they will listen!"

Ramachni sighed. "At the very least I hope *you* will listen, Hercól. No better friend could you have hoped for. Just think: one word to Rose from any of us and all her people will be killed. This woman trusts you not just with her life, but with those of her whole clan. Be at least as brave."

Hercól looked taken aback: he had never been lectured by Ramachni before. He drew a deep breath, then stood and bowed stiffly to Diadrelu.

"Forgive me, lady," he said. "My burns come close to blinding me. You saved my life: I am your grateful servant."

"Be instead my comrade in arms," said Diadrelu quietly.

"I have an even better idea," said Eberzam Isiq. "You five were chosen by the Red Wolf. I was not, though of course I will fight at your side. Whatever that spirit's reasons, you must honor its choice. You're all younger than I. Heed the instinct of an old campaigner. Swear an oath."

"What would you have us swear to, Admiral?" said Diadrelu.

Isiq began to speak—then held his tongue. His gaze swung from one face to another. He put out a hand and touched the silver chain peeking innocently from beneath the bandage on Thasha's neck, then shook his head in anger.

"It is not for me to tell you," he said. "My life has gone to glorify a lie. My Emperor is exposed as a villain; my doctor and oldest friend is his accomplice. The woman to whom I swore love has tried to kill me. Arqual stands for nothing, save plunder and the sword. All my faith has been in vain."

"Not all," said Ramachni. "Indeed, your faith is all that remains to you, Excellency. Can you not see it in these faces around you?"

"I see the faces of those I have wronged," said Isiq. "You tell them what to swear to, mage. And what to swear by."

"I would merely repeat the words you have just said in your heart."

Isiq looked up, startled, and met Ramachni's motionless gaze. After a moment he took a deep breath, walked to the gallery windows and lifted a curtain. Sunlight fell on his face.

"Swear on yourselves," he said. "That's all that occurs to me. Swear that no tie of nation or blood or belief will divide you, that you renounce them all for one another. Swear on the unity we have right now, for in days ahead I fear it will be tested."

They stood still, looking at one another. *Blood?* thought

Pazel, as visions of his mother and Neda flashed before his eyes. But then he thought of Diadrelu. *Yes, blood especially.*

He stepped forward, feeling very young. He raised his scarred hand. "I'll swear to that," he said. "On my life, and yours."

As soon as he had spoken Diadrelu leaped upon the back of Isiq's reading chair. She placed her hand over her breast, and looked deliberately at Hercól as she echoed Pazel's words.

"On my life, and yours."

Thasha, Neeps and Hercól swore the same. Then Thasha went to her father and linked her arm through his. Ramachni stretched and flexed his claws.

"The Wolf will not let you forget such a promise," he said. "Indeed, you must be strong as iron yourselves, if you are to stand against Arunis and the conspirators, and the terrors of the Ruling Sea. The Nilstone cannot be destroyed—and you five cannot hope for rest until it is placed beyond the reach of evil. And now, Lady Dri, you must hide yourself."

"Why is that?" she asked, slipping behind Felthrup's basket.

"This is why," said Isiq, and swept back the curtains.

What a sight! The *Chathrand* had heeled round, and the city of Simjalla loomed to portside. The waves smashed against her seawall, so that her towers and temples and cedar groves seemed almost to rise out of the foam. Vessels of every land were ranged along her docks; in many places six or eight vessels lay side by side. Off to starboard, in deeper water, stood the greater gunships and trading vessels. Most striking of all were the Mzithrini Blodmels: sleek white warships, even their armored sides painted white, huge cannon sticking out like needles in all directions, and on their snow-white sails the red shooting stars of the Mzithrini flag.

"Eighteen ships," said Hercól with awe. "An entire squadron."

Of course even the largest was but half the size of the *Chathrand.* But so many! Pazel could not help but shudder. There came the blood-drinkers, the coffin-worshippers, the ones whose cannonballs scalded men to death. Were they, too, not to be feared?

"That first is the *Jistrolloq*," said Isiq, peering through his telescope. "Two hundred guns. 'Twas she sank *Maisa,* sister-ship to the *Chathrand*. Your expectant groom Prince Falmurqat will be aboard her, Thasha."

"Let's spare him the bad news till he's ashore," muttered Neeps.

"None of us will go ashore tonight, certainly," said Hercól, "nor will any of us sleep! For tomorrow at dawn the Templar monks will come for Thasha. She is to be drilled in her Mzithrini vows. And bathed, I think."

"Bathed?" cried Thasha. "What am I supposed to be, an infant?"

"An offering," said Hercól. "And we have only tonight to discover a means of preventing it."

"Will someone be so kind as to draw *me* a bath?" said Ramachni. "I have learned to lick many things from my fur, but Volpek blood is not among them. Besides, it is warm here, and cold where I am bound."

"There is fresh water in the washroom," said Isiq.

"I'll do it," said Pazel.

He crossed the cabin to the Isiqs' private washroom. Inside he found a small porcelain basin and held it under the spigot of the freshwater cask. *Only tonight,* he thought.

As the water splashed into the basin a curious feeling stole over him: a feeling of golden joy, as if he had just remembered the happiest dream of his lifetime. He stood amazed and shaking. His breath came short.

"Land-boy, land-boy! Love you!"

"Klyst!"

Was that her face reflected in the basin, or his own? He shouted her name again, dizzy with pleasure and fright. Then a hand touched his arm. It was Thasha.

"What's wrong?" she said. "What's that word you shouted?"

Pazel struggled to speak, and failed. Thasha stepped into the washroom, closing the door behind her. She looked at him steadily.

"Something's happening to me," she said.

Pazel looked up quickly. "What do you mean? Are you ill?"

She shook her head. "Not at all. But I'm . . . changing. When I read that book I feel—different. Older."

He stood holding the basin, knowing she had more to say.

"It's a magical book," she said at last, fearfully. "Did I tell you that I first read about the Shaggat Ness and all his crimes in my *Polylex*?"

"You mentioned it. What about them?"

"Pazel, the thirteenth edition was printed before the Shaggat was born."

Their eyes met, and Pazel suddenly understood her fright.

"And it was written long before the Mzithrinis invented dragon's-egg shots," she went on. "But I read about them, too. It's impossible, but it's happening. The book is adding entries on its own. It's writing itself."

He stared at her. "Thasha, you have to tell Ramachni."

"I did," said Thasha, "and that's the strangest thing of all. He told me not to mention it to *anyone*. Not even Hercól, nobody but—"

She broke off, unsettled, still looking him in the eye.

"I wanted to kiss you today," she said.

The water in the basin trembled.

"And I'm going to tell you the truth," said Thasha. "They don't want me to, but I will. Your father came aboard the *Hemeddrin*. After the battle with the Volpeks. It was he who led the freebooters' attack, out of the mist."

Pazel took a step toward her. "My father?"

"He didn't stay long. You were out cold. He just wanted to look at you, he said."

"I heard him," Pazel whispered. "I heard him say my name! Where did he go? Why didn't he *wait*?"

"He can't come near Ormael. He's a smuggler, Pazel. An enemy of the crown."

"But it's been nine years!" cried Pazel. "Didn't he say anything? Didn't he ask anyone to do something, tell me something?"

"I told him to write you a letter," said Thasha, her eyes bright. "He just waved me away."

"Nine years," Pazel repeated in a hollow voice.

They stood still. He looked at her bandaged neck, felt the leathery scar on his palm. Then Thasha put a hand on the back of his neck and reached for his lips with her own. And suddenly the shell in his chest was blazing, searing him with Klyst's jealousy. He turned his head away and pushed past her, avoiding her wounded gaze, slopping water onto the floor.

Ramachni splashed vigorously in the basin. He scrubbed his tail between his paws, doused his head, squirmed with delight. Even Pazel and Thasha were laughing by the time he leaped out and shook himself. But the effort exhausted him. He raised a weary paw, and Thasha gathered him into her arms.

"Now," he said, "my time is *truly* spent. Be good to one another, be fearless. And look for me when a darkness comes beyond today's imagining. Very well, Hercól."

Everyone crowded into Thasha's sleeping cabin. As she rubbed the mage dry with her towel, Hercól performed the ritual that opened the mariner's clock. There was a sharp, cold puff of air, and the sound of wind in a high place.

Then Ramachni spoke his last spell: the holding charm that would allow him to open the clock from within, one day. When he was finished, his tongue flicked once over Thasha's palm. He crawled into the dark tunnel mouth, then turned to look at them.

"Don't go," said Neeps desperately. "We can't fight them alone!"

"That is true," said Ramachni. "You cannot. But when were you ever alone? My part has not been so very great, after all. You have been saving one another since this ship left Etherhorde. You, Neeps, saved Pazel from prison in Uturphe, by your gift of eight gold. Pazel saved Hercól from dying in the poorhouse. Hercól and his countrymen saved Thasha, and Thasha saved us all from the fleshancs. And those are just a few examples. We have been struggling together since this ship left Etherhorde. Always together, and always, so far, without defeat."

"Or victory," said Diadrelu. "The Nilstone remains in that creature's hand."

Ramachni crawled farther into the darkness. When he looked back again they could see only his eyes, shining in the lamplight.

"Victory is a shadow on the horizon, and whether island or illusion you can only learn by sailing. Defeat, however—those reefs you may be certain of. They are real, they surround you. I say this not to frighten but because I cannot lie. And yet there is reason to be hopeful—even to rejoice. You are a clan now, and as Dri can tell you, a clan is a powerful thing."

"But we're losing the head of our clan," said Pazel. "And you're not just anyone. You're special."

"Not special enough," said Ramachni. "None of us are, alone."

HERE ENDS *The Red Wolf Conspiracy*,
BOOK ONE OF THE CHATHRAND VOYAGES.
THE STORY IS CONTINUED IN
The Ruling Sea,
COMING FROM DEL REY BOOKS IN 2010.

Appendix

THE *CHATHRAND*

The IMS *Chathrand* has seven decks. From high to low, they are the topdeck (open to the sky), main deck, upper gun deck, lower gun deck, berth deck, orlop deck and mercy deck. Beneath the mercy deck is the hold.

Highest of all are the forecastle (at the bow or front of the ship) and quarterdeck (at the stern or rear), both of which are reached by ladders from the topdeck. Captain Rose's cabin is beneath the quarterdeck. The Isiqs' stateroom is located two decks directly below, at the stern of the upper gun deck.

The masts of the *Chathrand,* bow to stern, are the foremast, jiggermast, mainmast, mizzenmast and spankermast.

TIME IN ALIFROS

The twelve months of the Western Solar Year are Halar, Fuinar, Sultandre (the spring months); Vaqrin, Ilqrin, Modoli (summer); Teala, Freala and Norn (autumn); and Umbrin, Ilbrin and Cadobrin (winter).

Each month has exactly thirty days. New Year's Day is the first day of spring (1 Halar). Once every seventeen years, a four day *Baalfürun* ("Carnival of Madness") precedes the New Year. These four days are not part of any month.

KEY DATES IN THE HISTORY
OF NORTHWEST ALIFROS

−1231	Old Faith born when Mäsithe of Ullum builds the Black Casket.
−501	Shattering of the Black Casket.
−500−489	The Worldstorm rages throughout Alifros; most societies collapse; the Lost Age begins.
−220	Erithusmé takes the Nilstone from the Ice Caves of Nohirin, becomes the greatest mage in Alifros.
−167	Lost Age ends with the defeat of Hurgasc the Torturer.
1	Rinfaith born when the Ninety Rules are collected in a single tome. Empire of Arqual proclaimed after Battle of Ipulia. Shards of the Black Casket recovered and placed in the Towers of the Kings; birth of the Mzithrin Pentarchy.
755	Magad I crowned Emperor of Arqual. Year of Regicides in Dremland, Westfirth, Opalt, etc.
839	The Thirteenth Edition of *The Merchant's Polylex* published in Etherhorde.
860−867	First Sea War (Arqual vs. Mzithrin).
883−887	War of the Tsördon Mountains (Arqual vs. Mzithrin).
892−901	Second Sea War (Arqual vs. Mzithrin). Rise of the Shaggat Ness and the Heresy of Gurishal; civil war cripples the Mzithrin. The Shaggat, defeated, flees east. His ship the *Lythra* sunk by Arquali navy off the Haunted Coast, ending both wars.
898−899	Sugar War in the Nelu Rekere (Arqual vs. South Isles Alliance).
913	Magad V crowned Emperor of Arqual after strange death of Magad IV.
933	Assassination of Ulmurqat, one of the Five Mzithrin Kings, nearly triggers a fourth war between the empires.

936   "Rescue" (invasion) of Ormael. Pazel Pathkendle
       made a prisoner of Arqual.

941   *Chathrand* launched from Etherhorde on 9th day
       of summer (9 Vaqrin). 7 Teala chosen as date for
       signing of the Treaty of Simja and the start of the
       Great Peace.

NEW SELECTIONS FROM
THE MERCHANT'S POLYLEX,
18TH EDITION

Dhola's Rib. A thin, curved islet between Rukmast and Talturi, abandoned by man. Possibly cursed and indisputably hard
to find (it is absent from most charts to this day), this cold rock
was once the abode of an ancient priestly order, as the ruins of
a sprawling temple attest. In the current century, talk of an orac-
ular ghost within the dark edifice has taken hold (see SIBYL OF
DHOLA'S RIB). It was here that Capt. Nilus Rose brought the
Chathrand against the wishes of His Supremacy.

Hummingbird, Jade-Breasted. A rare Dremland bird with one
curious distinction. For reasons unknown, its image (dark wings,
bright green chest) long held a secret meaning within the Arquali military. Whether displayed upon a battle standard, a mast
or a lady's brooch, the sign meant *Emergency abort—cancel
mission and withdraw.* This coded symbol was known only to
the Emperor and a handful of his confidants and was abandoned
(because of public exposure) after the Night of the Swarm.

Dr. Ignus Chadfallow is rumored to have made a gift of a
jade-breasted Dremland (or its likeness?) to Pazel Pathkendle
before the invasion of Ormael.

This hummingbird is now protected by Imperial law. Do not
kill, purchase, pluck or consume.

Indefinite Declension. An insane feature of the Opaltik language, impossible to excuse. In this tongue, verb spellings change

(drastically) according to some twenty abstract considerations, including the time of the action (day, night, after sleeping, before a meal), the probability of success, the need for cutting or chopping instruments when performing the action, the presence or absence of migrating animals in the vicinity of the action, and whether or not the action gives rise to laughter in onlookers. Thus *mar kebe,* "he speaks," is sometimes written *mar kebal, mar kebruk, mar kakebruk, mar'usal âkethet,* etc. The *Polylex* recommends gestures and prayer.

Isiq, Jandren (927–968). Grandnephew to Fleet Admiral Eberzam Isiq. Referred to as "our hidden wart" by his own kin, Jandren Isiq lurched from failure to failure: as a monk (he proved a stranger to chastity even before the temple seamstress could measure him for a cassock), as a husband (the silence of the hastily married seamstress could not be bought at any price), as an entrepreneur (a loan from his uncles, supposedly for the purchase of a shipping business, was spent instead on a notorious ball, still toasted at gatherings of divorce lawyers), and finally as an officer (Eberzam Isiq gave him a desk job in the Naval Academy. See IMPERIAL NAVY: TUITION SCANDAL). After removal from the last position, Jandren seems to have devoted what remained of his life to hard liquor. Admiral Isiq, whose sympathy for addicts is a matter of record, paid for Jandren's many life-saving stays in the Milk of Heaven Sanitorium.

No kindness goes unpunished: after doing so much to sully the name of the Fleet Admiral, Jandren Isiq roused himself from a stupor five years after Eberzam's death and filed a claim for the entire Isiq estate—mansion, grounds, gold, and the Admiral's prize collection of antique weaponry. The district judge drove him from the courtroom. Enraged, Jandren began the one serious effort of his life, petitioning everyone from the Naval Widows League to the *Chathrand* Voyage Memorial Council. He irritated many and extracted the grudging support of a few. At last, when no other heir came forward, the judge was forced to relent.

Jandren had promised to use some of Isiq's gold to erect a

statue of Eberzam, but two weeks into the project, he ordered
the sculptor to carve his own face in the white marble instead of
his uncle's. The bill he forwarded to the Admiralty, where pay-
ment was somehow, mistakenly, tendered. Jandren's delight at
this blunder was so great that he drank beyond his own notions
of excess. After midnight he staggered into the garden to admire
the statue, lost his footing in the overgrown yard, struck his head
on Isiq's toppled birdbath, and died at the foot of the marble
monument to himself. He was forty-one.

"Kites over Ormael." Any clever warning to avert a murder.
Derived from a tactic improvised by the citizens of Ormael, to
warn their beloved Duke Miatur (846–903) away from the city,
where his disloyal cousins waited with daggers drawn. Knowing
that the Duke's frigate would approach from the east, children
were dispatched to the meadow above Quarrel's Cliff, where
they flew several large kites painted with the emblems for treason and murder. The coup was averted, and a saying was born.

Layered Graves. A barbarous practice of the west. Burials in
certain families (particularly Mzithrini, though the custom
reached Chereste and beyond) were not public affairs. Even the
more distant family members were excluded from the ceremony. The reason is gruesome: buried traps set for graverobbers, often lethal in design. A popular technique used in Babqri
City involved spreading a layer of Culdendel flesh-eating moss
between two paper-thin sheets of copper, a foot or more above
the buried casket. When a spade perforated the copper, the
moss's deadly spores became airborne. The would-be thief was
usually discovered at dawn, expired in the act of clawing at his
throat. Other techniques involved pressurized beakers of acid,
wolf traps, layers of cobblestone with poisoned needles embedded on the underside, and the simple ruse of positioning the
headstone six feet left or right of the casket, with a spiked pit
hidden under a brittle clay shell in the expected location.
The ultimate threat to graverobbers was magical: cursed jade

scarabs mixed in the earth over the deceased, for example, which caused madness or blindness at a touch. Over the grave of Hurgasc the Torturer a second casket is said to rest, containing the demonically mutated soul of his chief bodyguard, eternally ready to defend his master.

Pathkendle, Captain D. Gregory. The once-notorious Traitor of Ormael, chiefly remembered today as the father of the Smythídor, Pazel Pathkendle, and the assassin Neda Ygraël. His early fame, however, grew out of his skill as a commander: to this day naval midshipmen study Pathkendle Maneuvers and trade stories of his cat-and-mouse years as a freebooter, when two imperial navies proved unable to apprehend him. Captain Gregory was a formidable man, of average height but unmistakable vigor and readiness for a fight: as a young deckhand on a fishing sloop he is said to have pried open the jaws of a reaper shark that had been hauled aboard entangled in the nets, thus saving the arm of a fellow seaman. Also to his credit are the deaths of the Brothers Strago (the Urnsfich Rapists), both of whom Gregory tracked personally to a brothel in Simjalla City and killed with a borrowed pitchfork. Indeed, Gregory's strength, courage, fighting prowess and sailing mastery—whether applied to good ends or ill—are qualities even his many enemies admit. One cannot but be startled at the absence of these qualities in his famous son.

Talking Fever. The most dreaded of modern diseases. Talking fever begins as dry mouth and labored breathing. After no more than five hours both symptoms vanish, to be replaced by a irrepressible urge to verbalize. Depending on the overall mental health of the victim, the words may be more or less coherent, but even the most rational of persons will soon run short of worthy conversation after a full day of rapid chatter—and marathons of eight or ten days have been reported. Worst of all, the very act of listening to those afflicted can cause the disease to attack the listener. Hence the instant need to quarantine the room, home, town, ship, etc. where the outbreak occurs.

After the chattering phase, the fever returns to finish the victims off. Most die still whispering through blood-flecked lips. Among the Mzithrinis a whole cult of soothsayers attends these last words, which they claim include prophecies and visions of the world to come. The great Ignus Chadfallow has affected several extraordinary cures of Talking Fever, but no other doctor has replicated his triumphs.

Ulluprid Smile. Old sailor's term: anything so sweet, fine or intoxicating (as the faces of the women of the Ulluprids) as to tempt the very soul. Frequently heard when men are recruited for dangerous service at sea. Appears in the old traveler's prayer:

> *From Ulluprid smile and panther's purr*
> *Nightshade brandy and witch's cure*
> *Sea-murth mischief and serpent's coil*
> *And all hoary fiends that below us boil*
> *Sweet Rin guide me home.*

Acknowledgments

John Jarrold and Simon Spanton, my agent and UK editor respectively, brought their great acumen and vision to this book from the start: thank you, gentlemen. My thanks as well to Gillian Redfearn, Susan Howe and the rest of the Gollancz team for their tireless help.

This American edition also benefits greatly from the keen editing of Kaitlin Heller and Betsy Mitchell at Del Rey; to both, my warmest thanks.

I thank my family, for love and support too immense to detail here; and particularly my mother, Jan A. Redick, for being the first, best reader of this novel. Stephen Klink, Tracy Winn, Tim Weed, Edmund Zavada, Jim Lowry, Hillary Nelson and Oliver Nelson also read early drafts, and shared insights for which I'm deeply grateful. Special thanks also to Katie Pugh, Veena Asher, Jim Shepard, Paul Park, Cindy Phoel, Amber Zavada, John Crowley, Karen Osborn, Corinne Demas, John Casey, Bruce Hemmer, Claire Kinney and Katheryn Sublette.

A full list of my benefactors, literary and personal, would rob this book of its svelte attractiveness. Many persons omitted here played indirect but essential roles in the birth of this novel. My debt to them is profound.

Above all, my partner Kiran Asher's love and creative brilliance kept this ship afloat. No one else could have: *gracias, amor.*

Read on for an excerpt from

The Ruling Sea

by Robert V. S. Redick

Published by Del Rey

7 Teala 941
86th day from Etherhorde
(Treaty Day)

"Eyes open, Neda."

The Father had come to her alone. He held his own cup and candle, and he smiled at the girl asleep on the granite slab under the woolen shift, who obeyed him and smiled in kind and yet did not wake or stir. Her eyes when they winked open were blue; he had seen nothing like them in any other living face. A strand of weed in her hair. Dry streaks of salt water on her neck and forehead. Like his other children she had spent the night in the sea.

She was twenty-two, the man six times her age, unbent, unwearied, his years betrayed only in the whiteness of his beard and in the voice deep and traveled and kindly and mad. The girl knew that he was mad, and knew also that the day she revealed such knowledge by glance or sigh or question would be the day she died.

She knew many secret things. Until the Father woke her she would sleep like the other aspirants, but there was a disobedient flame in her that gleamed on, thought on, insensible to his orders. She wished it out. She tried to snuff it with meditation, inner exorcisms, prayers: it danced on, full of heresies and mirth. And because the Father could peer into her mind as through a frosted window it was but a matter of time before he saw it. Perhaps he saw it now, this very minute. Perhaps he was considering her fate.

She loved him. She had never loved another thus. It was not an earthly or a simple love, but he could read its contours in her sleeper's smile as he had on his children's faces for a century.

"You dream, do you not?"

"I do," she replied.

"And yet the dream is unsteady. You are nearer to waking than I've asked you to be."

It was not a question. The girl lay watching him, asleep and not asleep. The Old Faith she had taken for her own stated that life is not a struggle against death, but rather toward that authentic death inscribed at the instant of one's birth. If he had come to kill her it meant fulfillment, the end of her work.

"You must not wake, best beloved. Turn your face to the dream. And when it surrounds you again, describe it."

The girl's eyes rolled, the lids half lowered, and watching her the Father trembled as he always did at the immensity of creation. She would see nothing more of the shrine about her—not the dawn light on the huddled sleepers nor the west arch open to the sea nor the quartz knife on his belt nor the pure white milk in his cup—but what endured were the territories within. Outside, fishermen were picking a trail through the sawgrass down to the shore, greeting one another in the happy lilt of Simja, this island unclaimed by any empire. Under the sheer wool the girl's limbs began to twitch. She was not quiet in the place of the dream.

"I am in the hills," she said.

"Your hills. Your Chereste Highlands."

"Yes, Father. I am very near my house—my old house, before I became your daughter and was yet simple Neda of Ormael. My city is burning. It is on fire and the smoke trails out to sea."

"Are you alone?"

"Not yet. In a moment Suthinia my birth-mother will kiss me and run. Then the gate will shatter and the men will arrive."

"Men of Arqual."

"Yes, Father. Soldiers of the Cannibal-King. They are outside the gate at the end of the houserow. My mother is weeping. My mother is running away."

"Did she speak no last word to you?"

The sleeping girl tensed visibly. One hand curled into a fist. "*Survive,* she said. Not how. Not for whom."

"Neda, Phoenix-Flame, you are there at the rape of Ormael, but also here, safe beside me, among your brothers and sisters in our holy place. Breathe, that's right. Now tell me what happens next."

"The gate is torn from its hinges. The men with spears and axes are surrounding my house. They're in the garden, stealing fruit from my orange tree. But the oranges are not orange, they're green, green still. They're not ripe enough to eat!"

"Gently, child."

"The men are angry. They're breaking the lower limbs."

"Why don't they see you?"

"I'm underground. There is a trapdoor hidden in the grass, overlooking the house."

"A trapdoor? Leading where?"

"Into a tunnel. My birth-father dug it with his smuggler friends. I don't know where it leads. Under the orchards, maybe, back into the hills. I thought he might be here, my birth-father, after leaving us long ago. But no one's here. I'm in the tunnel alone."

"And the men are looting your house."

"All the houses, Father. But ours they chose first—*Aya!*"

The girl's cry was little more than a whimper, but her face creased in misery.

"Tell me, Neda."

"My brother is there in the street. He's so young. He is staring at the men in the garden."

"Why do you not call to him?"

"I do. I call Pazel, Pazel—but he can't hear, and if I raise my voice they'll turn and see him. And now he's running to the garden wall."

The Father let her continue, sipping thoughtfully at his milk. Neda told how her brother pulled himself up by the thrushberry vine, crept in at his bedroom window, emerged moments later with a skipper's knife and a whale statuette. How he fled into the plum orchards. How a mob of soldiers drew near her hiding place and spoke of her mother and the girl herself in terms that made the Father put the cup down, shaking with rage. *As if they were cannibals in truth. As if souls were nothing and bodies mere cuts of meat. These men who would civilize the world.*

The dawn light grew. He pinched his candle out and beckoned the vestment-boy near to keep her face in shadow, and the lad quaked when her blue eyes fixed on him. But Neda was gone—gone to Ormael, possessed by the dream she was speaking. The soldiers' roar at the discovery of the liquor cabinet. Her girlish clothes tossed with laughter from a window, socks in the orange tree, blouses held up to armored chests. Bottles shattered, windows smashed; a ruined bleat from the neighbor's concertina. Sunset, and endless dark hours in the cave, and frost on the trapdoor at morning.

Then she cried much louder than before and he could not comfort her, for she was watching the soldiers drag her brother down the hillside, hurl him flat, and beat him with their fists and a branch of her tree.

"They hate him. They want to kill him. Father. Father. They are screaming in his face."

"Screaming what?"

"The same words over and over. I did not speak their language, then. Pazel did but he was silent."

"And you recall those words, don't you?"

She was shaking all over. She spoke in a voice not quite her own. *"'Madhu ideji? Madhu ideji?'"*

The Father closed his eyes, not trusting himself to speak. Even his own slight Arquali was enough. He could hear it, in all its snarled violence, bellowed at a child in pain: Where are the women? And the boy had held his tongue.

When he opened his eyes she was gazing right at him. He tried to be stern. "Tears, Neda? You know that is not our way. And no fury or grief or shame can best a child of the Old Faith.

And no Arquali is your equal. Stop crying. You are *sfvantskor,* best beloved."

"I wasn't then," she said.

True enough. No *sfvantskor* or anything like. A girl of seventeen at the time. Captured that very night, when thieves skulking deeper inside the tunnel chased her out at knife-point, into the hands of the Arqualis. Unable to speak to them, to plead. Brutalized, as he would not ask her to recall, before the strange Dr. Chadfallow intervened, freeing her in a shouting match with a general that came almost to blows.

The doctor was a favorite of the Arquali Emperor, who had named him Special Envoy to the city before the invasion. A friend to Neda and her family, too, it seemed, for he took the girl bleeding as she was to his Mzithrini counterpart, who was to be expelled with his household that same afternoon.

"Save her, Acheleg," he pleaded. "Take her with you as a daughter, open your heart."

But this Acheleg was a beast. He had failed to predict the invasion, and so was returning to the Mzithrin in some disgrace. He saw no reason to help his rival. Both he and Chadfallow had wished to marry Suthinia, Neda's mother, and although she had refused both and vanished none knew where Acheleg still fancied himself particularly spurned. Now fate had given him Suthinia's child. Not the great beauty her mother was, and left unclean by the enemy, but still a prize for a slouching ex-diplomat whose future conquests would be scarce. He took her to Babqri— but as a concubine, not a daughter. And only because the man was fool enough to bring her to court, when he came beetling through with his lies and flattery for the king, had the Father spotted her.

Blue eyes. He had heard of such things in the East. And when the girl saw him watching and raised those eyes the Father knew she would be *sfvantskor.* A foreign *sfvantskor*! It was a sign of catastrophe, of the old world's end. But in a hundred years of choosing he had never needed more than a glance.

Such an odd fate, Neda's. Saved from an Arquali by an Arquali, and from one Mzithrini by another. Twice taken as plunder, the third time as a warrior for the gods.

But still not a *sfvantskor,* in point of fact. None of his children
(he moved among them, speaking the dawn prayer, breaking
their sleep-trance with his fingertips) could claim the title until
he gave them up. It had always been so, and always would be:
only when they knelt before one of the Five Kings and swore
fealty were they *sfvantskors,* warrior-priests of the Mzithrin.
Until that day they were his aspirants, his children. Afterward
he would not even speak their names.

Not a *sfvantskor,* thought the girl, her dream dissolving and the
tears quite gone. Not even a normal aspirant, for she was foreign-
born. It made a difference. Even the Father could not pretend
otherwise, although he forbade the others to mention it. For two
thousand years the elders had molded youth into *sfvantskors* to
serve the Mzithrin Kings, to lead their armies and terrify their
foes. Power dwelt in them, power from the Forts of Forever, from
the shards of the Black Casket and the vault of the wind. It was
more than an honor: it was a life's destiny and a sacred trust. And
only native-born Mzithrini youths were called. That was the order
of things, until the Father brought Neda to his Citadel.

Neda Pathkendle. A row of old Masters spoke her name in the
Greeting Hall that first day, as if the very syllables displeased
them.

Neda Ygraël, said the Father. I have renamed her. Watch her;
you will understand in time.

Ygraël, Phoenix-Flame. The grandness of his gesture did not
help. The other six aspirants (four boys, two perfect girls) were
scandalized. A hazel-skinned refugee from Ormael, one of the
vassal-states of the enemy? Had they been singled out for shame?
Were they such poor candidates that the timeless customs need
not apply?

One did not question the Father—he who had sucked a black

demon from a wound in King Ahbsan's neck and spat the thing into a coal stove, where it howled and clattered for a month—but his choice tested faith. There was open hissing at the feast of Winterbane, when the new aspirants marched through Babqri City. There was the dove's carcass, burned black and left on her pillow, with the words NEVER TO RISE in ash upon the floor. There was the day she learned about Belligerent Expulsion: an ancient rule by which the other aspirants, if they declared unanimously that one of their brethren had "sought to make enemies of them all," could cast that member out.

Neda had done no such thing; she had been obedient to their whims, tolerant of their spite; and yet five of the six had voted for her removal. When the effort failed, Neda had gone quietly to the one who sided with her, a tall proud girl named Suridín. Neda knelt before her and whispered her thanks, but the girl kicked her over with a bitter laugh.

"It wasn't for *you*," she said. "I want to serve the navy, like my birth-father, and they bring witches who can smell a lie to the swearing-in. What am I going to say when they ask if I've ever given false testimony?"

Suridín's birth-father was an admiral in the White Fleet. "I understand, sister," said Neda.

"You don't understand a thing. I wish you *would* start a fight with one of us. You don't belong here, and I'd vote against you in a heartbeat if I could."

All this was horrid and prolonged. But five years later it was over, and it had ended just as the Father said it would: with Neda trained and deadly and strong in the Faith, and her six brethren embracing her (some loving, others merely obedient), and the Mzithrini common folk no longer quite sure why they had objected.

Neda, however, suffered no such confusion. They were right, her enemies. They saw what the Father did not: that she would fail, disgracing her title, if it were ever bestowed. She had fired an arrow over the River Bhosfal and struck a moving target. She had walked a rope stretched over the Devil's Gorge, and carried her own weight in water up the three hundred steps of the Citadel. But the way of the *sfvantskor* was perfection, and in one matter she was gravely imperfect. She could not forget.

For an aspirant nothing could be worse. Besides martial and religious training, a great part of the making of a warrior-priest occurred in trance. Only with those in trance could the Father share the holy mysteries; only those souls could he cleanse of fear. Neda drifted easily into the first layers of trance—sleeping and waking at his command, obeying without question, focusing her mind on whatever thought he named. But never *only* on what he named. The deepest and most sacred mode of trance was achieved when all other distractions melted away: in other words, when one forgot. *Remove the dust of Now and Before,* went the proverb, *and things eternal are yours.*

This Neda could never do. Year upon year she tried, stretched out on granite, listening to his voice. While the others shed memories like old clothes, she lay still and pretended. *Forget yesterday and today. Forget the breath before this breath.* She remembered. And when the Father told them to forget certain lessons, certain books suddenly gone from the library, certain Masters lecturing one day and the next quite vanished, Neda recalled them, too. Every word, every face. And other weaknesses of the Father, shameful for an aspirant to know.

But what damned her beyond redemption were her lies. They were skillful—flawless even—for it was never an effort to recall exactly what she should pretend *not* to know. But how long could she hide this loathing for herself?

Alone at prayer, she beat her head on the floor. In bed she cursed herself, *sfvantskor* battle-curses and sea-oaths in her father's Ormali and sibilant Highland witch-curses from her mother, whose dabbling with spells had almost killed Neda and her brother before the invasion.

And should have. For her brother, Pazel, had been carried away unconscious, to be buried with the day's thousand dead, or nursed back to health and enslaved. And Neda, spared such a fate by the Father, could not stop her mind from betraying him.

"Rise, my seven."

Quick as cats, they obeyed. All were dressed, none armed: the Simjans allowed visitors many privileges, but weaponry was not among them. The Father led them in silence through the east arch and along the marble wall, to the foot of a narrow unrailed staircase. At its top stood the Declarion: a high pedestal, topped with four pillars and a jade-green dome, on the inside of which was inscribed the Covenant of Truth in a script of flowing silver. The Father climbed, and they waited to be called.

The sun had not yet risen: its light touched only the peaks of the distant mountains of Simja, leaving the land below in darkness. Around the shrine a flock of goats had settled for the night and lingered yet, barely stirring, and not a window gleamed in the city of Simjalla across the fields. Neda listened to the waves' cotton roaring, felt the pull of them still. *I was all night in the sea. I walked from here to the surf in trance. The creatures swarmed around me, the anglerfish and skates. A witch sang spells over the water. A murth-girl was crying for a boy she loves. I'm not supposed to remember.*

She tried to empty her mind for prayer. But on the last step below the Declarion the Father abruptly turned to face them. His disciples jumped: the morning rites were not casually altered. The Father gazed at them fiercely.

"You know how long they have sought our destruction," he said. "You know the price in blood we have paid to survive. Now much is changed. Our Five Kings of the Holy Mzithrin have labored long for peace with the enemy, and when today in this very shrine our prince weds Thasha Isiq, they say the time of pain and death will be over. But I see something darker, my children. A new war: brief but terrible, as if these several centuries of war were compressed to a single year, with all the ruin but no rebirth. I see the specter of annihilation. Would you know where it resides? Look behind you, then."

As one his disciples turned. There lay Simja Harbor, thick with ships: their own white warships and Arquali dreadnoughts, the island's tiny fighting fleet, scores of vessels bearing rulers and mystics of the lesser faiths, all gathered for the wedding that would seal the peace.

Yet dwarfing them all was the Great Ship. The *Chathrand*, ancient of ancients, seemingly immortal in her seaworthiness, made by forgotten artisans in a lost age of miracles. They said six hundred men were needed just to sail her, and that twice as many could ride with ease and still leave room for grain enough to see a city through the winter, or arms enough to gird whole legions for war. She belonged to the enemy, though not to the enemy crown. By some mad twist of Arquali thinking her ownership was private: the Emperor had had to *pay* some merchant-baroness for the right to convey the Treaty Bride in such style.

"The *Chathrand*," said the Father. "Like the Plague Ships of old she comes flying the colors of peace, but in her hold the air is rife with evil. When first she weighed anchor in Etherhorde, half a world away in the bosom of the enemy, I knew she bore a threat. Each league closer I felt it grow. Wide across the Nelu Peren she sailed, and there far from land the danger grew. Then six days she lay in Ormaelport, Neda's old home, and took on some monstrous new power. And yesterday—yesterday the sun dimmed at noon, and the spell-weave of the world was stretched almost to tearing. Then nearly I saw her true intent. But the power hid itself away, and now she lies like a great docile cow, awaiting our summons.

"And we must summon her—summon the bride's party and our own Prince Falmurqat, summon all the visiting lords and nobles to this our shrine. For that is the will of the Five Kings. Who can blame them? Who does not want peace? And perhaps yesterday's burst of magic saw the evil in *Chathrand* destroyed. But my heart says otherwise. This Thasha of Etherhorde will not marry our prince, and her Empire seeks no end to war—unless our end as a people be part of it."

The Father's jaw tightened. "The Five Kings would not hear me out. 'You live in the past, Father,' they chided. 'All your long life the war has raged, and now in your waning years you can imagine only more of the same. The world has changed; the Empire of Arqual has changed, and so must we. Train your *sfvantskor*s a little longer, if you are not content to rest, but leave off statecraft.' But when have I been wrong?"

He paused deliberately. Neda dared not breathe: she alone knew when.

"They are blind," said the Father. "They see only the riches to be had through trade with the East. I see farther. But I am no king, and have no spies or soldiers to command. Yet I have the friendship of certain officers in the White Fleet. And I have you, children: *sfvantskor*s in all but final vows. You are here because of *Chathrand;* you are here to save us from the evil she brings. More than this I have told you in trance, but it is not right that you should remember yet. When the time comes the memory will return of itself. Now we must be quick: take my blessing, and confess your fears."

He stepped beneath the dome, and the first aspirant ran up the staircase and knelt. The Father spoke only briefly to each, for the sun would not hide much longer. But when Neda's turn came he set his hand upon her head, and she felt him tremble.

"Would you speak?" he asked her.

Her nails bit into her palm. "I have no fears to confess,"she said.

"You will have," he said. "Your brother is aboard that ship."

In shock Neda raised her eyes. The Father's own grew wide: aspirants were forbidden any glimpse of the dome's interior. Quickly she looked down again.

"Forgive me," she said.

"He is a servant," said the Father. "What they call a *tar-boy,* I think. And he is the special friend of Dr. Chadfallow, who is also aboard."

"Pazel," she whispered. He was alive, alive—

"You must not speak to him, Neda."

She swallowed, fighting for calm.

"Not until the wedding ends. Indeed he must not see your face. His presence here cannot be an accident. You and Ultri shall stand behind me, masked, until it is over."

"Yes, Father. But when it's over?"

He sighed. "Dear one, even I do not know what will happen then."

The Father blessed her, and she groped shaking for the stairs. The last disciple knelt before him briefly. Then the lip of the sun rose over the sea and the Father raised his arms and cried out in a voice like a roll of thunder, sending the goats bolting for their lives and larks and sparrows rising in terror across the fields. It was the *Annuncet,* the Summons, heightened by the magic of the dome, louder than Neda had ever heard it. The Father sang the ritual words again and again, seeming to need no breath at all, and he did not cease until the lamps were burning across the city, in hall and tower and anchored ship.